A SECRET OF THE UNIVERSE

A STORY OF LOVE, LOSS, AND THE DISCOVERY OF AN ETERNAL TRUTH

A NOVEL

STEPHEN L. GIBSON

Truth Driven
STRATEGIES

A Secret of the Universe: A Story of Love, Loss, and the Discovery of an Eternal Truth
Copyright © 2007 by Truth-Driven Strategies, L.L.C.

For information about this title or to order other books and/or electronic media, contact
the publisher:

Truth-Driven Strategies, L.L.C.
P.O. Box 367
Kalamazoo, Michigan, 49004-0367
www.truthdrivenstrategies.com
866-383-4624

Library of Congress Control Number: 2007901906

ISBN-13: 978-0-9793880-0-2

Printed in the United States of America

Book and cover design by 1106 Design; author photograph by Ron McLain.

Publisher's Cataloging-In-Publication Data
(Prepared by The Donohue Group, Inc.)

Gibson, Stephen L.
    A secret of the universe : a story of love, loss, and the discovery of an eternal truth : a
novel / by Stephen L. Gibson.

    p. ; cm.

    ISBN: 978-0-9793880-0-2

1. Faith—Fiction. 2. Truth—Fiction. 3. Spirituality—Fiction. 4. Christian fiction.
I. Title.

PS3607.I27 S43 2007
813/.6   2007901906

CONTENTS

PREFACE

Thank you for exploring what I hope you will agree is one of the great philosophical realizations in all of human history, even if it is one that I had failed to grasp until recently. As you will hear in Bill Vanderveen's words, "Let it be, that we listen."

While it might appear that you are holding a single book, as you read you might sense that *A Secret of the Universe* is essentially two books, synthesized into one story. One book has a non-fiction feel, and is comprised mostly of concepts and ideas about *belief* and epistemology—the fascinating study of the origins of knowledge. The other book is a coming-of-age story about love and loss, tragedy and triumph. Together, the books form a tiny microcosm of the human struggle to understand the great mysteries of our existence, and the divisions and consequences that often result from the solutions we formulate.

If you typically prefer honest, realistic fiction, I am compelled to point out that there are three chapters that convey the weightier concepts of the "non-fiction" book. I borrowed from my late mother (who herself never met a fictional tear-jerker that she didn't like) the idea of isolating some of the heavier concepts. Knowing my distaste for tomatoes, she used to make her delicious chili with large chunks of the dreadful vegetables—so as to make them clearly visible. That way, I could eat around the slimy, quivering masses, without any difficulty. It's the same here; if you don't like weighty tomatoes, you will be able to eat around them.

Conversely, if you *favor* facts and non-fiction—particularly about religion, philosophy, or big ideas—you may prefer the substance of the "tomatoes." Still, I would encourage you to read the early chapters, since these dramatic elements are relevant to understanding how and why we fail to see the *real secret.*

Each of us is the product of our experiences, genetics, environment, social interactions, egos, and education. This certainly holds true for our ideas about religion, and how we tend to make sense of life's uncertainties. I was raised Christian, in the Midwest; but what if I had been born in Saudi Arabia? Is it not much more likely that I would view the world from a Muslim perspective? Is any of us truly objective? Or if my father used bent coat hangers to find water in the yard when I was a kid, am I not more likely to believe in the "truth" of dowsing? The point is this: the human drama that encompasses much of the first half of this book is the fertile soil in which belief takes root—and it is vital to seeing the potential for unenlightened *belief* to divide humanity rather than unite it.

It is also important to point out that despite the extensive research, endnotes, and "non-fiction" elements herein, *this is a work of fiction.* Those who know me personally might be tempted to correlate real people to central characters in this story. That would be a mistake. While clearly there are many elements inspired by my own real-life struggles, and those of others, it would be a mistake to literalize this allegory. All of the central characters are fictional; they are synthesized from multiple individuals, or completely fabricated.

Non-central characters also are fictional—with a few exceptions. In Chapter 2, Mr. and Mrs. Newman—a teacher and her husband chaperoning a high school group in Madrid—are based upon my own real experiences with two real-life angels, Hugh and Ruth Moser. Additionally, Bishop John Shelby Spong, James Randi, Earl Doherty, and Bart D. Ehrman are actual scholars and authors; however, their appearances in this story are fictional. Even the "non-fiction" elements are designed more to stimulate thought than to perfectly articulate complex reality or current scholarship; so I'd encourage you to explore my citations for yourself, think independently, and draw your own estimations of "truth."

With the fictional and "non-fictional" elements combined, if I've done my job correctly you will leave this experience having been challenged—in your dogma, worldview, assumptions, or your tolerance for dissenting views. Please know, however, that it is never my intent to offend.

Lastly, in my acknowledgments at the end of this book I make an effort to recognize the many sources of revelation and knowledge that have shaped me and inspired this story. Unfortunately, a complete bibliography would be impossible, since it would include every book, TV show, podcast, conversation, and class that I've ever experienced. Despite the extensive research required to bring you this story, I stand on the shoulders of those giants whose persistence—and fascination with the world around them—has yielded such profound insights, one of which you're about to experience. For these insights, I claim no credit; I only express awe and gratitude.

Enjoy!

Chapter 1

THE EDGE OF BELIEF

Sunday, October 11th, 2009—Madison, Wisconsin

As the business jet crossed the western portion of Illinois, several hundred miles to the north of its route Bill and Christina lay beneath the covers, wrapped in the comfort of their skin-to-skin cocoon. The Madison weather was cool and rainy, which added to the intimacy of their rendezvous.

While it was warmer to the south, Madison sat just to the north of a warm front, with a strong southwest jet stream spewing warm moisture down through the low clouds and onto the streets of the city, in a continuous symphony of splats and trickles.

"That was amazing . . . you are amazing," Bill whispered to Christina. Still lying on their sides in a sustained embrace, he looked into her dark eyes and kissed her. "You have no idea how much I looked forward to being with you tonight."

She looked at him with a coy smile, kissed him back and said, "Ah, you just like having sex."

"You're terrible."

"Okay fine," Christina cooed. "If I'm forced to admit it . . . I'll confess that I looked forward to this too." A broad smile came over her face. She shifted gears slightly. "You realize we've been doing this for seven years now? I sure have enjoyed . . . uh, using you to advance my career," she joked, her more serious tone quickly reverting to playfulness.

As if protecting themselves, each of the lovers would often make their affections known, but would usually stop short of being overly explicit or emotional with any declarations. It was clear that what they had could not last forever, but it was something they had chosen not to dwell upon, as if by agreement. Each knew that something could change, and likely would change, someday.

For some reason, however, that night Bill felt compelled to assure Christina. "I try not to worry about tomorrow . . . today," he began as they were lying motionless, still basking in their naked warmth and comfort. "I know you know, but . . . I just want to make sure you know . . . that I understand there will come a time when you move on and outgrow the ability to be with me." Bill's voice conveyed a palpable touch of emotion.

For him, the relationship had been so fundamental to his ability to survive and thrive, and such a profound blessing in what had otherwise been a deeply trying, day-to-day struggle, that he would have had difficulty ever expressing it to anyone—even Christina.

Christina didn't say anything in response. She just put her face very close to his, as if studying his features. Her eyes went back to his and she kissed him again on the lips, tenderly and lovingly.

In any movie or drama, a cliché affair would have had Christina's character upset that Bill wasn't intending to leave Megan for her, but the reality of Bill and Christina was far beyond such fictional dramatics. Christina loved Bill and greatly respected him, and she understood his situation. He in turn understood hers—her career, her desire not to become mired in a traditional relationship at that point in her life. At the same time, what started as a recreational retreat from chaotic and lonely worlds had grown into something much deeper and more valuable than either had predicted.

"Hey, it's only seven-thirty you old man, let's go down and get something to eat."

"Let's do it," he replied.

Back home, Megan's depression had ebbed and flowed, though she had recently shown signs of improvement again. Still, Bill continued to see the two worlds of Christina and Megan as completely separate. That night as he and Christina got ready to head downstairs for some food, the compartments of his life were safely sealed and segregated.

The reality, however, was that he loved two women, in two very different ways. Nothing in his way of thinking would cause him to change any aspect of his situation, though he recognized, however subtly, that external forces could certainly bring change upon him. All he knew was that Christina had been a savior to him, a human companion who helped him through, second only in redeeming power to his God.

The truth was that if there was one small conduit through which ideas flowed between the two compartments of his life, it was God. Despite his profound disagreements with Ian, he had digested and affirmed in his own mind that Ian and his sources were right about the typical interpretations of Biblical statements concerning adultery and sexual ethics. To Bill, Christina was undeniably a life saver, and one who was tossed into his churning and violent sea not by a human hand, but by none other than God himself.

✛

It happened as the cockpit was quiet. Out of routine boredom, Ian reached to preset the radio with the next anticipated frequency—the one for the Chicago Center controller who would handle the succeeding segment of their flight through central Illinois. Radio tuning was in-flight housecleaning, something to do when nothing needed to be done. As his father used to say, "If you've got time to lean, you've got time to clean."

"Attention all aircraft, attention all aircraft, Chicago Center," said a low, authoritative voice. Ian and Mac snapped to attention. This was a relatively rare transmission, usually reserved on Center frequencies for a broadcast request for assistance with an aircraft that had lost communications.

The voice continued. "Attention all aircraft, all sectors. This is Chicago Center. Be advised that we are under a priority-one national emergency as of this time, 13:17 Zulu. I repeat, we are under a priority-one national emergency. We are going to need your prompt attention and cooperation in clearing all U.S. airspace for a national emergency. All aircraft will be grounded. Be advised that unlike 9/11, instrument conditions prevail through much of our Center tonight, ladies and gentlemen, so this will restrict our capacity to land you all quickly. Proceed currently AS CLEARED to your original destination, but expect holding instructions and a change of destination forthwith. Midway and O'Hare remain open now, but it is possible they could both close to inbound traffic. Break—"

The radio went silent for just a moment, long enough for Ian and Mac to look at each other with very serious expressions. Mac shook his head slightly from side to side. "Fuck," he said, under his breath.

The voice returned quickly; "Chicago Center . . . . That's it folks. Expect holds and deviations to new destinations. Please confirm instructions as briefly as possible, and hold readbacks unless you have a question. I repeat, even readbacks of holding instructions are NOT required unless you have a question; just confirm receipt of instructions with your call signs."

Ian and Mac were silent, tensed in anticipation, and the radio was silent, when a lone, unidentified voice keyed a cockpit mike and said reverently, "God bless you all, and God bless the United States of America." Silence returned.

The poignant statement moved Ian and Mac. Ian had been through a number of in-flight emergencies, and performed without undue hesitation, or even undue emotion, but suddenly he felt a surge of emotion—a mix of anger, fear, and sorrow. He felt as if his eyes were going to tear-up, but he fought the urge; to distract himself, he jumped to find approach charts for the most likely alternate airports.

There was no time to obsess about his family. He told himself that this would be an isolated event geographically, like 9/11, and that surely Sammy and the boys were safe back in Kalamazoo. The only problem was . . . it didn't help him feel much better.

Ian and Mac sat quietly for a couple of minutes, intently listening as a flurry of radio instructions began. One by one, aircraft in their sector were being diverted, routed, or directed into holding patterns. The simple reality was that the air traffic system worked fine on clear days, but any time there were instrument approaches required at big airports, delays crept into the system. The spacing between airplanes had to be kept much greater when the planes were in the clouds and could not see one another.

On 9/11, the pristine skies had allowed rapid clearing of the airspace, but this day was definitely going to be different.

"Wonder what it is?" Ian ventured, voicing the obvious question. "Almost makes you want to ask."

Mac didn't respond. He knew Ian was just venting. Neither of them would dare cause any undue delay in a packed radio frequency that was being used to deal with a national emergency. "I'll handle the radios; get on the air phone and find out what's going on," Mac instructed.

Ian was glad to hear the instruction. They didn't use the air phone very often. It wasn't that Mac didn't have the money, but in addition to its expense, they just never had call for it. This, however, was a very necessary use.

Ian thought momentarily, and then dialed Samantha. The first call didn't go through, but on the second attempt he could hear it connect. "It's ringing," he confirmed aloud.

"Hello?" Samantha answered expectantly.

"Sam it's me."

An uncharacteristically fast-paced, distraught voice was on the other end. "Oh my God, Ian! Oh my God. I'm so glad you called. I just knew you were okay. But Ian, what do we do?" There was panic in her voice.

"Honey, I need your help. I don't know anything. We're still in the air. What's happening?"

"Ian, they think . . . downtown Chicago is like . . . gone."

"Holy fuck . . . like a nuclear?—"

"Yes, Ian . . ." Samantha lamented tearfully. "Oh my God, Ian. They think it was centered right downtown."

Just then Mac raised a hand so Ian could see. A radio call was providing their amended clearance.

"Hang on for one second, sweetie. It'll be okay. Just stand by one second," Ian instructed as he put his headset back on in order to hear.

"Citation four-three-niner-mike, understand you're a lifeguard flight?"

"Affirmative, four-three-niner-mike," Mac confirmed.

"Okay, is there any reason Indianapolis wouldn't work for you, sir?" the controller asked in a rushed and stressed voice. Every other transmission had been an order and command, but the "lifeguard" status had at least garnered them one chance to reply.

Ian quickly barked to Mac through the headset, "Tell them 'No,' it's a stretcher flight with special transportation waiting in Kalamazoo."

"Negative, ATC. Sorry but we're a stretcher flight with specialized care and ambulance waiting in Kalamazoo. Flight time's the same to each so we'd request Kalamazoo please."

Ian and Mac looked at each other expectantly. Ian whispered under his breath, "Come on. Let us go home . . . let us go, it's the same frickin amount of time . . ."

"Citation four-three-niner-mike, roger, proceed direct Kalamazoo."

Ian skewed his headset and put the phone back to his ear as Mac confirmed receipt of the instruction.

"Okay Sam, it's okay. They're letting us come home to Kalamazoo. We'll be there within an hour. Now, are you okay?"

"Yes but I don't know what to do. We're just across the fricking lake from that thing, Ian, what do we do?" Sammy asked with increasing desperation.

Still talking into the phone so Sammy could hear, Ian said to Mac, "It's a nuclear explosion in Chicago; Sammy needs to know what to do in Kalamazoo."

Mac's eyes widened. Ever the military professional, he barely hesitated. "How big?" he asked.

"Don't know. Hey Samantha, what are they saying? Mac wants to know how big the explosion was?"

"I don't know. They're just saying that a bunch of buildings in the Loop have been destroyed and that sensors show it was a nuclear detonation."

Ian repeated her words to Mac, who said, "Tell her to stay inside at all times. There could be fallout headed toward her. If she has plastic and can seal any doors and windows, great. Close the chimney flue." He fired his instructions rapidly, but his final words were reassuring. "Tell her she's got time, and with any luck this southwest wind will carry any cloud north of Kalamazoo. She'll be fine. She really will."

"Sammy, Mac says you'll be fine. He knows about these things and we think a cloud, if there is one, will go north of you. I'm coming home, okay, but in the meantime you need to play it safe and do some things for me, okay?"

"Okay," Sammy replied, somewhat reassured.

"Mac says it's safe for us to come home, so don't worry. But he says you need to stay inside at all times, and seal the house up as best you can. I have some duct tape on my workbench, and just bought new plastic for moving leaves. It's on the shelves. Have the boys close the flue in the fireplace, and seal anything that is drafty, like the front bay window."

"Brooke is a wreck; is it safe for her to travel over here?" Sammy asked.

"Probably, but I'd tell her to hurry."

"Tell her to stay downstairs most of the time," Mac added.

"And Mac says to stay downstairs when you can," Ian repeated to Sammy.

"And if you have to go out, shower afterward," Mac said.

"Sam, Mac says if for any reason you do have to go outside, you should shower when you come back in." He repeated Mac's rapid-fire instructions much more slowly and with less urgency than they were received.

"And turn off the furnace blower," Mac suggested to Ian as he thought of yet another item.

"We don't have one—boiler," Ian replied to Mac.

"What did you say?" Sammy asked.

"Oh, nothing. I was talking to Mac. Okay, honey, did you get all that? It's going to be fine."

"I love you Ian, just come home. I'm okay though. The boys have been great. Just be careful and fly safely, okay?" Sammy said, now reassuring Ian.

"I will—"

"And Ian," Sammy interrupted. "I don't know who we pray to anymore, but say a prayer to the universe for John, will you?"

Ian felt a tremendous rush of emotion and could barely conclude the phone call. "I will . . . I love you . . . tell the boys how much I love them and I'll be home soon."

Chapter 2

FOREIGN NEWS

Twenty-four years earlier—Madrid, Spain, 1985

Ian Keppler stepped out into the stagnant air of the hotel hallway, mentally ready to embrace a long day, if not entirely physically ready. It had been a grueling trip; 36 hours had passed since leaving the high school parking lot in Kalamazoo for the three-hour drive to Detroit Metro. From there it was a flight to New York, a transfer across town to La Guardia, a flight to Malaga in Southern Spain, and then on to Madrid. Everyone was in good spirits upon arriving late the night before—which was Friday as Ian foggily computed. In fact, nobody even seemed bothered by the aborted takeoff from Malaga, in a Boeing 747.

How often does that happen? Fascinated by planes and aviation, Ian was intrigued by the way the pilot had taxied onto the active runway, then held the brakes as the four mighty engines were spooled to 100% takeoff power. The giant vessel stood in place as it shook, shimmied, and vibrated. The crew released the brakes to allow the mighty bird to lunge forward, and it accelerated what seemed like three-quarters of the way down the runway before the engines suddenly and without warning fell silent, only to be violently resurrected in full reverse!

Somehow, Ian, and everyone for that matter, had taken the surprise in stride, looking out the window with relative confidence that there was room to stop. Stop they did, but with little room to spare. Then, with no explanation, the crew taxied the behemoth back around via the taxiways, took the runway, spooled the engines with the same break-holding procedure, and successfully launched for the short flight up to Madrid.

Ian shook the cobwebs from his mind as he turned the corner and headed for the elevator. He was right on time despite slightly oversleeping his travel alarm clock. Luckily, he'd arranged for a 6:00 a.m. wakeup call. "Buenos Dias! Son las seis por la mañana," the voice had said in a friendly tone. How entertaining it was to be awoken by a Spanish voice.

It was hard to believe that they were finally in Spain. After studying three years of Spanish, this was the trip that "La Bruja," Mrs. Newman, masterfully orchestrated for her students every three or four years. Ian's older brother Matt had gone on the last trip, and hadn't been disappointed.

As with the previous trips, in addition to the many cultural and linguistic opportunities ten days in Spain would provide, there were special treats in store for the group, including time and freedom to roam the city. The only difference this year concerned alcohol.

The previous policy had been that responsible drinking—wine with dinner, cerveza at the disco—was perfectly acceptable. There had been an unwritten rule that so long as the students were responsible, and didn't wind up in jail—for which there could be little done on their behalf—doing as the Romans did was acceptable behavior. Overall, history had shown that these juniors and seniors could manage themselves quite well—Matt's stories of an interesting night or two not withstanding.

Unfortunately, this year some of the more pious and conservative parents had gotten to the principal with a message that was loud and clear. Poor Mrs. Newman got the same message, even louder and clearer, and there could be no complicit "looking the other way." If anyone drank or showed any signs of having been drinking, it was their expulsion, and Mrs. Newman's job if she overlooked it. In turn, the kids got the message that it would be far beyond the pale to put her in any such position.

Ian pushed the button on the elevator and watched it illuminate. To the clean-cut, brown-haired Midwesterner, the situation was surreal. He had been briefed for three years about the culture and state of both urban and rural España, yet it still seemed odd to be in Madrid, pushing a button on an elevator that functioned just the same as one in Kalamazoo or Chicago.

Ian thought back to the previous night when he had left home for the trip. *Wait,* he thought to himself. *That was two nights ago. Or was it three?* At any rate, he smiled when he recalled walking downstairs to say good-night to his parents, who had just finished an early summer evening of pulling weeds and beginning to prepare the old swimming pool for the short Michigan summer ahead. Ian had been tired from all of his own travel preparations; he'd headed to bed early with the knowledge that he had an early morning and long trip ahead.

"It's only ten o'clock," his dad had said with a smile. "Do you think you'll be able to sleep?"

"I think so," Ian had replied. "I'm pretty bushed."

"Well listen," said his dad, turning with a smile from his decades-old, brown La-z-Boy he'd inherited from Ian's grandmother, "I wanna tell you a couple things."

Ian knew how excited his dad was for his youngest son to have the opportunity to experience Spain. There had been car washes, candy sales and yes, lawn mowing, but a big part of the then-significant $1,375 cost had been volunteered by his mom and dad. Despite being of an era in which kids were arguably becoming increasingly spoiled, this was not the case with Ian. There was a mutual respect within the family—a peace, a sense of symbiosis and balance. The family was far from perfect, but it functioned, despite the new dynamic of Ian's older siblings, Matt and Lynn, both having lived away from home. Lynn was married and work-ing in Allendale, a college town outside of Grand Rapids. Matt was home for the summer, but had been away at college during the year and was scheduled to study abroad in the fall.

Ian appreciated his father's gesture deeply. He knew that while the family store placed his family half a socio-economic notch ahead of some of his classmates, the expenditure was no small sacrifice.

His father had continued, warmly, "I hope you have a GREAT time. I can't tell you how happy we are for you to be able to experience this. Enjoy it, kiddo." He opened his arms for a goodbye hug. With a slight change in tone he added, "Just be safe, and be careful, okay." Ian had embraced his father heartily, and given him a peck on the cheek.

Funny, Ian thought as his dark, sleepy eyes seemed transfixed to the swirly-black tile by the elevator entrance, *I wonder if my friends still kiss their fathers*. It almost seemed odd to him that at the age of 17 he still did; but frankly, he was okay with it.

His scattered thoughts and recollections were interrupted by the clang of the elevator bell, signaling the arrival of his elevator car. As the door opened, Ian was somewhat startled to see Mrs. Newman's husband, Norman, already in the car, despite his confidence that it had come up from the lobby, not down from the rooms.

"Good morning," Ian greeted.

Mr. Newman returned the greeting with his usual smile. "Good morning. Did you sleep okay?"

"No problem there, I was pretty tapped. I never sleep well on planes, trains or automobiles." Ian watched Mr. Newman bend slightly forward and grasp the handrail behind him with both hands. It occurred to him that Mr. Newman seemed slightly nervous, or at least anxious. Of course Ian didn't know Norman well, but he had met him on several occasions including the potluck dinner after the trip in which his brother Matt had participated.

He was a kind man, tall and lean with only a thin band of short, gray hair covering the back and sides of his head. He had retired a few years prior from his job as a scientist at the local pharmaceutical plant, yet he didn't fit the stereotype. He was always smiling, soft-spoken and polite. Perhaps being a touch jittery was just his usual demeanor? Maybe it was the mild, benign tremor that sometimes comes with age, or simply a desire to please others and be liked that had him so slightly, nearly imperceptibly, off kilter.

"You? You guys sleep okay too?" Ian asked.

"Oh yes," Norman eagerly contributed. "I was asleep as soon as my head hit the pillow."

The elevator bell clanged once again and the doors opened into the small but elegant lobby of the Hotel Convención. Mrs. Newman was standing nearby as they stepped out.

"Good morning Mrs. Newman," Ian offered in his usual congenial tone.

"Hi Ian," Mrs. Newman said in English, a concerned tone evident in her voice. Ian quickly sensed something was wrong. "We need to talk, Ian. Let's walk over there." She pointed across the lobby and beyond the check-in area as they began to walk. There was an open space in front of the restaurant, small and out of the way with clusters of club-style seating.

She continued talking as the trio walked. "I got a call from your brother at about 4:30 this morning. I'm afraid your father has had another heart attack." Ian stopped short. The gravity was tangible.

"Ohhh," he sighed softly. *Not again.* It had been five years since the very public collapse of his father after a school basketball game. As a school board president and a congenial community man who was generally well liked, Bob Keppler's collapse and near-fatal heart event on board a bus full of fans made his condition well known in the community. Yet somehow, between his mom's cancer and the healing time that had passed, heart issues had been far from Ian's mind in recent years.

"Gosh," Ian murmured, "how is he?"

"Ian. He's . . . not good," she said. The silence was brief, but meaningful. "He didn't make it . . ." After another brief pause she stoically continued, "I'm so sorry." Tears formed in her eyes as she reached to hug Ian. The three of them stood exposed between the main entrance and the reception desk; the flow of the exchange had unfolded quickly, before they could reach the privacy of the restaurant alcove.

Ian displayed every bit the mature character the Newmans had come to know, reacting with a polite, yet stunned sigh of sadness as his eyes turned downward. His mind was racing. Slowly the three resumed their steps toward the alcove, as Mrs. Newman added in her usual, in-command, soothing voice, "Let's do this. Why don't you take a few minutes for yourself up in your room, while we make a few phone calls. We're going to have to figure out how to get you headed home. In the meantime, go get it out. I think it'd do you some good to take a few minutes; then, we'll be right up and help you get a phone connection to your family."

Ian agreed and somehow still managed to thank the Newmans. His eyes were beginning to well up as his head buzzed with shock; unlike the dramatic reactions he'd seen on TV or in a movie, however, he kept his composure. At the same time, he knew he couldn't hold on forever.

Thoughts and memories flooded his mind as he headed back to the elevator and up to his room, thankful that he didn't see any of his friends or have to converse with anyone.

The door closed behind him. The tears came quickly as he looked at his suitcase and possessions, still relatively well packed. He sat and stared blankly at the items which moments before were so meaningful to him. Now they were just stuff. Dozens of thoughts raced through his head. He sat down on his twin bed and his emotions began to flow. Within seconds he felt the instinct to pray.

Tears rolling freely, he prayed quietly. "Dear Lord. Please let my father feel my love for him right now. I know he knows, but I pray that you tell him how very much I appreciate the love, more than anything . . . the amazing amounts of love, and hugs and caring that he gave me. Know that I am returning it to him a thousandfold right now, as I celebrate for him that he is in a better place. Please know that I thank you too, Lord, because I had 17 years with this wonderful human being, teaching me and loving me every step of the way. I am just so deeply thankful. My cup runneth over, truly . . . but I also pray for your support. I'm going to need your strength. And please be with Mom, Lord. She's been through so much. Nobody could go through what she has . . . so gracefully, Lord. Please comfort her with your love and let her know how many people are thinking of her now. Matt and Lynn, too. Please be with them, Lord. Amen."

The tears simply wouldn't stop. The image of his dad in his chair when they were saying goodbye was one he could see perfectly clearly. He had literally been savoring the memory just minutes before. He could feel his father's whiskers as they embraced, and when Ian pecked his cheek with a kiss. How glad Ian was to have that memory; he knew he would treasure it forever. *Who would have thought it was the last time I'd see him?*, Ian thought to himself. It was unimaginable.

Ian gained some composure but continued to stare emptily at the room. *This stuff. This room.* There was something so much greater going on. How little it mattered. He saw his camera sitting on top of the suitcase, prepared for a day of sightseeing. He picked it up and walked to the window; looking out at the small European street five stories below, he snapped two pictures. Without really knowing why, he walked to the door and turned to snap another of his hotel room, his suitcase lying open on the bed, well organized as if ready for departure already. Snap. There was a sense of peace, of preserving a poignant moment. He knew it would be one he would never forget.

✦

Kalamazoo, Michigan—Friday night

Bill tossed the last case of soda on the tall display stack with a fluid, easy movement. His seventeen-year-old frame had become that of a man. As the perennial young athlete, oh how he had tried to rush the clock to be bigger, faster and stronger. But almost like an antidote to those yearnings, actual growth and development had erased those yearnings, bit by bit, replacing them with day-to-day concerns about achievement and competence.

Gifted with good looks from birth, Bill was now past the awkward stage that had revealed itself both physically and in the way he carried himself. He had become confident, charming, and friendly—one of those all-American, blond-haired, blue-eyed guys for whom the girls simply melted, and around whom parents felt almost as comfortable and respectful as when they were around other adults. Some said Bill would be president some day. That might have been a stretch, but he was a driven young man with everything going for him, no doubt about it.

"Bill, why don't you call it a night?" shouted his store manager, Willie Groaner. Willie was a long-time fixture at their neighborhood grocery store, perhaps even a small part of the reason that hypermarket up the road hadn't swamped the little store in the ten years since it was built. Willie looked over his bifocals at the clock on the wall. "It's midnight."

"All right, Willie, let me just put the carts away and I'll punch out," Bill shouted back.

He had worked for Willie for the last two summers, and even maintained some hours during his sophomore and junior years. But as he headed into his senior year, he knew he had to pick up the pace in order to save enough for college. He knew there was no way he'd make the football team, let alone earn any athletic scholarships at a big school like the University of Michigan, despite his all-conference performances. At the same time, U of M was a well-regarded school for science and engineering, and it was going to cost money.

So that summer Bill had told Willie he was happy to work all the hours Willie could provide—forty plus. That meant closing on some nights, not just the 5:00–7:00 p.m. and 7:00–9:00 p.m. shifts he snuck in during the school year, around all sorts of practices and games.

"Okay Willie, everything under control?" Bill asked as he tossed his white apron onto the hook behind Willie's quasi office at the back of the store.

"Yup. Head out and I'm right behind you, Bill. Have a good night." Willie paused slightly and then added with a feigned look of authority, "Straight home now."

Despite being only seventeen, Bill's near perfect grades, adult demeanor and trustworthiness had earned him some generous leeway from his parents. Nevertheless, Willie knew that Bill had been known, on occasion, to stay out after closing with some friends of similar high repute, some of whom were older—say old enough to buy beer; it was a bit of an unspoken bond between Willie and Bill. Willie also knew that Bill's parents would, to say the least, disapprove of any such activity.

Bill was a good kid. His parents, Don and Cindy Vanderveen, were good people too. They were just swimming too far out in the deep end of the Jesus pool for Willie's taste, and in his opinion for Bill's healthy development.

"Not a problem tonight, Willie," Bill retorted. "Gotta help my grandma and grandpa open their pool early in the morning; then some mean old guy is making me close tomorrow night, too." Apart from Bill's early-morning family obligations, Ian was away in Spain, and Scrappy was at a wedding, so it wasn't as if he was passing up any big social opportunities.

"Good boy. Night, Bill." Willie smiled as Bill headed out with a friendly, backward wave over his head.

Bill pulled into his designated parking spot in the driveway, covering the previous oil spots from his 1976 Oldsmobile Cutlass Supreme. He couldn't help but notice that there were still lights on in the kitchen and the den. Sometimes his dad would wait up for him, reading the paper and enjoying some late-night quiet time, but usually there was at most a single light over the kitchen table, or in the den, with just the flicker of a television to add color to a relatively dark room.

Bill walked in the door to find his mom, dad and younger brother Thomas sitting at the kitchen table. "Hi guys," Bill said enthusiastically.

He set down his keys on the stand by the door. "What's up that you guys are all still awake?"

Bill's mom looked at him with her big brown eyes, now obviously puffy, as Bill got closer. "Honey," she began, then paused briefly, "Bob Keppler died tonight."

Bill couldn't believe his ears. The father of his best friend, and his parents' best friend to boot—it didn't seem remotely possible.

"Dear God say it isn't so," he said loudly as he plopped down into a chair at the table. He proceeded to hold his head in his hands before quickly asking for more information.

"What?—"

"Heart attack," his mother answered. "Went outside to pick up sticks and piles of branches. Janet got him to the hospital, but this time they just couldn't help him pull through."

Bill's mind raced. It just didn't get a lot worse than this. Mrs. K had struggled with cancer ever since Mr. K's first heart attack; she was finally in remission; against all odds everything seemed fine; Ian got to go on a trip halfway around the world, but now *this happens!* Bill felt a deep well of emotion churning inside.

Bill's own family raced through his mind. He still had all four grandparents. He vaguely remembered his great grandfather's funeral, but that was a long time ago. How was this fair, that he had never even lost a grandparent, yet Ian had no living grandparents—and now no father!

Thoughts poured through his head, bouncing between thankfulness for his own family's health and sympathy for his friend Ian. Then, the roughest thought of all popped into his mind: Mr. K in a casket, and a funeral!

It was too much. Bill bawled. He sobbed like he hadn't in years. He sobbed for Ian. He sobbed out of fear of ever facing a similar loss. He sobbed for everyone in the community because they were all losing one of those truly great guys who just didn't come along often—the ones who are the glue that holds a community of friends together. Bob was the guy who was always there—at a sporting event, or an awards ceremony. More importantly he was the guy who could firmly pat you on the shoulder, look in your eyes and ask, "How ya doin'?" And when Mr. K asked, it wasn't rhetorical. He cared. He actually cared and could sense when you needed encouragement.

There were even times when Bill's parents cracked down on him for some esoteric infraction he just didn't understand—like "sinning" by watching an episode of *Three's Company*—when Mr. K seemed to understand. Of course he wouldn't undermine Bill's parents, but Bill could tell that Mr. K understood, and that he sympathized. Mr. K had been so good to him—to all the guys in their circle of friends.

Bill's parents wrapped their arms around him, tears of their own flowing for both their son's pain, and for their own loss of a dear, dear friend. Don had known Bob Keppler since high school, and Cindy and Janet couldn't possibly have gotten along better from the first moment they met. Who'd have thought it would end so quickly?

"We just have to believe and trust that God has a plan," consoled Bill's mother through her tears. "It hurts those of us left behind, so badly, but we just have to know he's in a better place."

Bill's dad nodded, brokenly. "Can we say a few words in prayer, please."

Bill sat up suddenly while simultaneously extending one hand to each side in response to his father's suggestion. "Ian. Has anyone reached him yet?"

"They've been trying to find him in Madrid. Matt speaks Spanish so I'm sure they've reached him by now . . . But then again, it's the middle of night, their time."

The family sat at the kitchen table, hands held tight, and joined Don in prayer.

"Dear Lord, we come to you in such pain—pain for ourselves, Lord, and for Janet, Matt and Lynn Keppler, and for all those who are hurting tonight—but Lord we also come to you in celebration of a phenomenal life, a life that showed you glory and honor through love—the kind of love you taught. We pray, dear Jesus, that you comfort us in our sorrow, and that you receive Bob Keppler with open arms, and that his joy and reward in Heaven is more glorious than he ever could have imagined, which we know is true. We know we can't understand your plan, Lord, but we trust in you totally. We know you have a purpose in taking Bob now, and we love you for it, painful though it may be. Amen."

Somehow the prayer rang empty in Bill's mind as he stood to go to his room. As if reading his mind his mom added, "You should call Kim, honey. She heard the news earlier and really wanted to talk to you. She said no time was too late to call."

"Thanks Mom." Bill trudged out of the room.

✣

Madrid, Spain—early Saturday morning (6 hours ahead)

Ian had somewhat gained his composure as there was a knock at the door. It was Mrs. Newman. Ian opened the door and she greeted him with a warm hug. He felt like he was going to cry again, but fought the urge.

"Here is what I'm suggesting." Mrs. Newman took control as if to help Ian mask his self-consciousness. "Norman is going to stay with the group today. He's seen most of these sights before and is confident that he can keep the gang on track. Meanwhile, I have called the local travel office, and they suggested that you and I get down there right away so that they can help us get you on a plane. The other thing we can do is hit the phone company on the way down, so you can talk to your family. I know they're worried about you."

"Then," Mrs. Newman continued, "we'll probably have some free time for the afternoon. If you're up for it, I can even show you a couple highlights of this grand old city before you leave."

"Thank you. I'm sorry to—"

"No, I'm sorry," she interrupted. "I'm so very sorry." She looked Ian squarely in the eyes. "Please. This has to be tough, but we'll do whatever it takes to make arrangements and to get you on your way. Let's just meet downstairs in ten minutes, okay?" Ian nodded and slightly scrunched his lower lip in a polite smile that showed his appreciation. He closed the door as Mrs. Newman left.

To a large extent, in Ian's mind there was a peace settling in. Certainly there was no feeling of panic or urgency; he knew his family had one another. He knew that he had to head home, but that in fact his father was now dead. There was a peaceful slowing of time taking place. Certain things had to be done, yes, but most of the urgency in the world seemed suddenly without meaning or purpose. Ian gathered his things—a passport, his stash of traveler's checks, his camera—and headed down to meet Mrs. Newman in the lobby.

After walking only a few blocks they reached the state telephone company of Spain, and entered the large, open area at the entrance. From there he could see rows and rows of telephones, most of which were vacant at this relatively early hour. Ever the experienced pro from having lived in Madrid for three years after college, Mrs. Newman knew the drill perfectly and had Ian at a phone with his assignment ticket in a matter of a minute or two. She picked up the phone and exchanged brief pleasantries and some numbers in Spanish. The content of the short conversation flew by and Ian didn't follow most of it. She then handed him the phone and said, "It's going through. I'll be over there if you need me." She gestured to a bench along the wall of the cavernous marble-clad room.

"Hello," answered a soft voice, clearly that of his mother, Janet. The connection sounded like a tin can on string but he could hear her words without difficulty.

"Mom," he said with tension in his voice, "it's Ian."

"Oh my dear Ian, I love you so much, are you okay?" Her voice lurched from a web of emotions.

"I'm fine Mom," Ian said in a calm pace, emotion now evident. "I love you too. Are you okay?"

Janet continued stoically and reassuringly, yet with tears evident, "I want you to know that everything is okay. We are all fine. We know God has a plan and that it will be okay. We just love you and want to make sure you travel safely and that you're okay. Please know we love you."

"I will Mom, and I love you too. Mrs. Newman and I are going to make travel arrangements now and we'll keep you posted."

"Okay honey. We'll have someone pick you up in Detroit. Mr. Clark from church is going to handle funeral arrangements. We have to do some things now but we'll wait to hear from you before scheduling too much. Just please be safe and know that we're okay. I love you so much. And Ian—" there was a moment of silence— "your father couldn't have loved a son more than he loved you."

"I know, Mom." Ian choked out the words beneath the stream of tears that began anew. "I know."

"I love you," she said again.

"You too, Mom."

From the phone company, the duo proceeded to the travel agent's Madrid office to get Ian a flight to Detroit—probably by way of New York. His entire pile of traveler's checks wasn't even close to enough for a last-minute international flight, but without hesitation Mrs. Newman handed over her personal credit card, saying only, "Good thing I just raised the limit before the trip." Before long the important thing was done: Ian had a one-way ticket home, leaving Madrid at 7:53 a.m. on the following morning—Sunday.

Having the travel arrangements complete was a big load off Ian's mind. He and Mrs. Newman exited the storefront, back on to the busy Gran Vía, walking south. "Well Ian, the rest of the day is ours, and there are a couple of things you have to see. Are you up for a little whirlwind sightseeing?" Mrs. Newman asked.

The afternoon that followed became one of those bittersweet, poignant experiences that come along only a few times in a lifetime. Thanks to Mrs. Newman's knowledge of Madrid, and her tireless efforts, Ian was able to experience the Royal Palace, lunch on the Plaza Mayor, the famous flea markets, and even some of the world's greatest frescos at the world-renowned Prado art museum. While conversation occasionally turned to relevant questions—what would his mom want to do with the family business, where would the funeral be, and so forth—for the most part the day was dedicated to drinking in all the sights and sounds of Madrid.

Ever the advocate of fully understanding the Spanish culture, Mrs. Newman even pointed out a "forbidden" sangria cooler in a department store, mentioning how different it was to see free alcoholic beverages available to all ages. She then immediately, yet casually, uttered something about walking around the corner for a couple of minutes. Ian nearly laughed at the irony as she scurried out of sight. Somehow what seemed like such a huge, taboo issue in front of irate parents and the Board of Education, now seemed like such a silly, neurotic obsession. The irony was especially evident while standing among the people whose culture bore no such taboos, and after having spent the day with Mrs. Newman, as adults, dealing with reality of some of life's biggest mysteries. A sip of wine seemed so trivial. Ian couldn't help but be thankful his dad was not one of those who had raised a stink about the alcohol issue.

After uniting again with chuckles and mutual shakes of their heads at the necessity of the charade, both the clock and their feet told them it was time to rejoin the group at the hotel for dinner.

Ian stared at all the beautiful sights as they were whisked back to the Hotel Convención by taxi, marvelling to himself at the very essence of life—how it could be so incredibly kind in some ways, and so goddamned harsh in others. If his dad had said it once, he'd said it a thousand times, "Who ever said life would be fair?"

Chapter 3

THE QUEST FOR COMFORT

Kalamazoo, MI—Saturday morning (6 hours behind)

"Good morning Bill." Don Vanderveen's voice was more subdued than usual as he scooped heaping spoons of coffee into the filter. Bill stumbled sleepily across the kitchen, where his mother and father had begun preparing a breakfast. "You're up early."

"Aren't we still helping Grandma and Grandpa with chores this morning?"

"You up to it?" his dad asked. "Mom was going to go over to the house to check on Mrs. K and the kids this morning, but if you're up to helping Grandpa we can spend a few hours, and then follow Mom's lead as to what we can do for Mrs. K this afternoon. What do you think?"

"That's fine with me, Dad; I have a feeling she's got a lot going on and doesn't need a bunch of us hanging out over there at 8:00 a.m. anyway. Besides, helping Grandpa is why I set my alarm. We might as well do it." Bill rubbed his tired, red eyes. "At some point today I had planned to see Kim," he added. His dad nodded with a slight extrusion of his lower lip.

As before with other girls, Bill's father wondered in the back of his mind just how close Bill and Kim really were. They had hung out in the same peer group for several years, attended youth group together, and pretty much seemed like happy, healthy friends. Don thought quite highly of Kim, but it was clear that a romance had bloomed; and since Don Vanderveen himself had been a teenage boy, his radar was actively searching for signs that things might be getting a bit *too* serious.

"How are you this morning?" Bill's mother asked, carefully. It had been an emotional evening for everyone, but she was especially worried about Bill.

"I don't know, Mom. I guess it's still tough to believe, but I'm fine. How are you guys doing?" Bill's parents looked at each other as if they hadn't really asked themselves that question.

"I'm fine I suppose," Don volunteered quietly. "Tough stuff though. This is hard for all of us. I will say, in my morning devotions I was looking for some wisdom and clarity," he continued as he reached through the kitchen doorway to grasp the open Bible from his desk in the adjacent den. "I found Romans 8:28, 'And we know that all things work together for good to them that love God, to them who are called according to his purpose.'[1] It's some comfort to me to know this is part of a plan."

Bill didn't say anything. He headed to pour some cereal, snagging two pieces of bacon from the plate his mother was assembling on the way.

"Where's Tom?" Bill asked about his brother.

"Still sleeping," his mom replied. "But we should probably wake him if you're still going to Grandpa's house."

"How are you doing, Mom?" Bill asked, mustering the effort to reciprocate her concern.

The crackle of bacon complemented its aroma as she turned from the frying pan, glanced at Bill, then turned back to the stove. "I'm fine, Bill. Sad I guess. To be honest I'm also struggling a little with where Bob was with his faith." Bill looked puzzled as she continued. "Don't get me wrong, I know Bob is in Heaven, and that he knew in his heart that Jesus Christ was his Lord and Savior. It's just a puzzle to me."

"What do you mean, honey?" Don probed.

"Remember when Janet was so sick? How we prayed and prayed, and she got better? Well I know that doesn't always happen for believers, that there's more to God's plan than we can know, but it sure seems to me that the healer she saw played a part."

"Mom, Mrs. K didn't necessarily even believe in faith healers. She thought it was a little wacky for a United Methodist Church to entertain the guy. What are you saying?" Bill asked with mounting frustration.

"I'm only saying that between the faith healer, and Janet's faith in Christ, I believe she was healed. She had more to do here on earth. In Luke 8:50, Jesus said to Jairus, 'Don't be afraid; just believe, and she will be healed.' I just think it's sad that sometimes people aren't even given the warning they need to seek God's help."

Bill didn't like the direction of the conversation. Bob Keppler was one of the finest men he'd ever known, and one of the best Christians in his judgment—even though he wasn't dogmatic or preachy about his faith. Bill found himself resenting the fact that he felt as though he had to defend Bob at that moment. "Mom, you don't honestly believe that? You and I both know that the Bible doesn't imply that healing is something you earn by faith. Those televangelist nuts may imply it, but you and I both know it isn't there."

"I know, Bill, but my point is just that there was no warning, and to me it seems unfair. Don't misunderstand me, we're all just hurting."

Bill seemed only somewhat reassured.

"We also have to know that God works in mysterious ways, and we simply have to have faith, because ours is not to understand everything during this life," she continued.

"Well, I'm going to change," Bill said—obviously a little perturbed.

Trudging forward through the morning with his mixed and confused feelings ever near the surface, Bill was only slightly distracted by the chores. They did help pass the time, however, and eventually morning turned to afternoon. Upon returning home, Bill went to clean up as Don plopped down with a sigh in his favorite chair in the den, to watch some of the U.S. Open golf tournament. "Some" is an appropriate word, since after several long hours of work with Bill his eyes wouldn't stay open for more than a few holes. Too bad, this year was special. The U.S. Open was being held at the nearby Oakland Hills Country Club, and there was an interesting battle going between Taiwan's Tze-Chung Chen, and Andy North, a Midwesterner.

For Don it was the perfect prelude to Father's Day—help your father with chores, your son by your side, then shower and crash into the

La-z-Boy—except that this year, Ian Keppler would be without a father on Father's Day. The irony of the situation had scarcely left Don's thoughts the entire day.

"So you're going to take dinner to Janet tonight?" Don asked Cindy as she entered from the adjacent kitchen.

"Yes, and I've made extra so hope you don't mind lasagna tonight for us as well," she said.

"Sounds great . . . . Have they made funeral arrangements yet?"

"Visitation Monday from three to six, Tuesday night from six to eight, and the funeral will be Wednesday at First United Methodist downtown—eleven o'clock. That should give Ian time to get back and make the first visitation on Monday."

A blur passed between the chair and the television, headed toward the kitchen. "Okay, I'll see you guys after work," Bill said, his keys rattling as he snagged them off the little stand by the door. "I'll be at Kim's, then I'm closing tonight."

"Okay son, just be careful. And don't stay out too late. Church is going to be crowded tomorrow and I don't want to be late, okay?" Don's tone was that of a gentle reminder. Bill understood that there were certain things written in stone. He had latitude, like in regard to curfew, but come hell or high water the family was always to be up and ready for church. That's just how it was; but if the truth were told, Bill appreciated that structure and tradition. Same thing with a tie. Ties were an unspoken church rule in the Vanderveen household—there was no question about it. But again, Bill found the traditions comforting. It didn't hurt, of course, that he knew he was starting to look pretty sharp in his slacks and sport coat, and that Kim and other desirables looked pretty good in their Sunday clothes as well.

"No sweat, Dad—I love you guys!" Bill shouted as he headed out the door.

Bill navigated the few miles to Kim's house, cranking up the stereo and bouncing between thoughts of Ian, his desperate need to see and be with Kim, and a slight pang of guilt. He knew his dad wouldn't like that Kim's parents were out of town for the weekend, and that her siblings were out of the house at the moment too. Luckily, his dad hadn't asked.

Bill had always been attracted to Kim, but it wasn't until about a month prior that their long-time sparring and palling around had turned incendiary. They had been working closely on a student council fundraiser, when the tension finally broke.

They were in the close quarters of the storeroom where the candy and concession materials were kept. Kim turned around in a rush and accidentally walked directly into Bill—literally slamming into him. They had both let out a nervous chuckle as each asked if the other was okay. Bill steadied Kim beneath her elbows as she looked him in the eyes, and their lips had met in a passionate, spontaneous kiss.

Bill pulled the Cutlass into Kim's driveway, just as the Chicago song *Hard to Say I'm Sorry* was headed into the upbeat *Getaway* ending, the one radio stations always seemed to cut short. The tape deck stopped as Bill turned off the key and jumped out of the car.

As Bill approached the front step, the door swung open and Kim met him with a big hug and a kiss. "How you doing?" she asked sympathetically as they walked into the small, country-cozy ranch home.

"I'm fine . . . so glad to see you," he said, shutting the door behind them and grabbing her hand. He pulled her close for another kiss, this one slightly longer and more intense.

"Awfully forward of you Mr. Vanderveen," Kim quipped. There was a moment of quiet as she gazed at Bill, then led him to the couch to talk, still holding his hand and maintaining eye contact. "You haven't talked to Ian yet, have you?"

Kim was a sight to be seen—truly eye-catching with her prominent dark hair, dark eyes, perfect radiant smile, and yes, her appealingly tight, eighteen-year-old body. Her 5'6" build was slender and athletic, yet clearly female. Just ask her male classmates; her perfectly curvaceous chest, while not overwhelming, caught their attention regularly.

It was the way she comported herself, however, that was most appealing to Bill. She was compassionate, charming and diplomatic beyond her years. She also exuded confidence and maturity in a way that made fathers like Bill's nervous. In fact, Bill had once heard Mr. K joke that the most dangerous women were those who knew their power over men. *So true,* thought Bill at the time. And while Kim certainly did know her power, she was a responsible young woman who was not inclined to abuse it.

Bill answered her question about Ian, "No, but he had a flight leaving early this morning so he's probably well on his way. What are they, six hours ahead of us?"

"Something like that," Kim replied. "So you have to work tonight?"

"Yeah, have to close."

"Are you sure you're up to it? Can't you call in sick? You could hang with me," she cooed, eyes transmitting a message that straddled a fine line between compassion, jest, and coy flirtation. Nonetheless, she knew that Bill wouldn't do that to Willie, and it was that strength of character and mature demeanor that was so appealing to Kim.

Bill changed the subject. Looking more serious, he reflected, "Sure is a weird thing, I just can't believe Mr. K is gone . . . I feel so badly for Ian. Bob was one heck of a guy."

Kim didn't catch Bill's use of Mr. K's first name. This time it was meant nostalgically and with respect, contrary to the usual practice of using their parents' first names irreverently.

Bill never fully understood why it was so damn funny to hear his friends use their parents' first names; he just knew it was. He'd hear Ian explain why he couldn't do some activity, or had to attend a family event, "Cause Bob and Janet are having a rough day. Janet's undies are in a knot because Bob's been away too much," he would say; or, "Janet's PMS'ing." Bill didn't know if it was the humanizing picture that was painted by using first names—pulling the parents down from the superhuman realm they inhabit in kids' minds, until some certain age when the kids discover their mere mortality—or just the irreverence of the usage of the first name. Either way, he enjoyed the private little outlet of this tradition among friends.

Bill continued his thoughts with a question. "Have you ever lost anyone close to you, Kim?"

"I was pretty close to my grandma. She died about three years ago of cancer. That was pretty difficult, but losing a parent so unexpectedly is a different animal altogether." She paused, looking across the living room as if looking for the right thought, then continued, "Especially when they're not assholes—you know?"

"Sure do."

"I didn't know him like you, but Mr. K seemed like a really, really good guy." Bill nodded in agreement.

"My parents say it's 'Part of God's plan,'" Bill commented, gazing much deeper into Kim's eyes as if looking for a response.

"You know what I think, Bill?" She paused, her eyes darting between Bill's bright blue eyes and his lips. "I think I'm glad you're here," she said in a tone that would have melted the coldest of male hearts. And with that, she put a kiss on Bill that said more than words could have. It said *I'm here for you. I care about you. I don't have answers, but being in each other's arms is a safe, loving, comforting place that at its worst can't be bad, and at its best borders on the divine.*

With that they simultaneously kissed, and gracefully eased into a horizontal position, all without missing a beat. In her characteristic confidence Kim found her way on top, her tongue slowly dancing with Bill's, only breaking away long enough to allow gentle pecks on his lips before passionately returning. Bill's left hand found its way to the phenomenal curves of Kim's jeans, as his other hand caressed her back. Her breasts pushed against his chest and were perfectly distinguishable, kinesthetically, through the thin tank top she wore over her bra.

Bill's mind was a rage of electrical activity. He knew sexual desire was a sin of the heart, if not of the flesh; but another part of him said something that felt so right couldn't be wrong—especially if they didn't actually "do it." His mind went to the last time they were alone together at his house, and how far things went, just as Kim brought him back to the present by reaching between their bodies, and unbuckling Bill's belt in one continuous movement.

She looked him directly in the eyes and smiled as she yanked down his jeans and underwear in yet another confident, solitary motion. Bill was not going to argue. Kim proceeded to offer her gift of affection and consolation until he could stand it no more, and he climaxed into a heap of involuntary muscle contractions.

Bill's muscles slowly began to relax as he basked in the pleasure of the moment, his mind flashing to a discussion after their last steamy, physical interaction. Though Kim was not a virgin by a couple of counts, both she and Bill had signed an abstinence pledge the prior year, as part of a youth program at their rapidly-growing church. And despite a little fooling around, they fully intended to honor it.

The program had been quite an event. There were discussions of HPV (the newly identified virus that would later be shown to cause cervical cancer), AIDS, Herpes, other STDs, and certainly pregnancy. They had even shown close-up pictures of genital warts before Pastor Mike began a lucid discussion of religious issues and scripture relating to marriage, pre-marital sex, and homosexuality.

Among other references, he had reminded the group of the following scriptures:

> Matthew 5:27–28, "You have heard that it was said, 'You shall not commit adultery.' But, I say to you that every one who looks at a woman lustfully has already committed adultery with her in his heart."

> Exodus 22:16, "If a man seduces a virgin who is not engaged, and lies with her, he must pay a dowry for her to be his wife."

> Deuteronomy 22:28–29, "If a man finds a girl who is a virgin, who is not engaged, and seizes her and lies with her and they are discovered, then the man who lay with her shall give to the girl's father fifty shekels of silver, and she shall become his wife because he has violated her; he cannot divorce her all his days."

> Corinthians I 6:9, "Know ye not that the unrighteous shall not inherit the kingdom of God? Be not deceived: neither fornicators, nor idolaters, nor adulterers, nor effeminate, nor abusers of themselves with mankind."

> Leviticus 18:22, "You shall not lie with a male as with a woman. It is an abomination."

Leviticus 20:13, "If a man lies with a male as with a woman, both of them have committed an abomination. They shall be put to death, their blood is upon them."

The young, dynamic, good-looking Pastor Mike had wrapped-up the program only after saying that to teach them about all the other stuff—pieces and parts, birth control, anatomy, and other elements whose propriety and relevance were hotly debated—would be to miss the moral imperative of God's word. "In the end," he told them, "there is one clear path to remaining disease-free, to avoiding the trauma and pain of unwanted pregnancy, and one clear way to honor God's clear instructions." That one way was to not engage in premarital sex or sex outside the loving confines of marriage. He concluded by summarizing, "All those other things are of little importance if you do the right thing, the thing God asks of you."

Bill and Kim were both impacted. Both wanted the best for themselves, for each other, and for others. Both wanted to be good people, and good Christians.

Though Bill didn't know it, Kim had seen the consequences of pain and struggle from an unwanted pregnancy, close-up; her older sister had aborted a pregnancy two years earlier.

In short, they had signed the pledge at the end of the event. Kim was even privately instructed that by repenting and asking for forgiveness, she was a virgin again in God's eyes.

"Oh my gosh that was awesome," Bill said to Kim, reconciling the pledges and his current pleasure without difficulty. Kim still sported her seductive smile as Bill added, "Thank you."

"You're welcome. Just remember that you owe me some attention when we have more time," she said jokingly.

"I have time right now," he retorted, giving her a kiss right after.

"Not *enough* time you don't," she replied.

"Just as long as we stay within our parameters, I'm yours when you want me then," Bill volunteered with a smile.

"My philosophy remains 'anything *but*,'" said Kim. She locked eyes with Bill and added, "We'll keep you pure, but it doesn't mean we can't have fun, right up to that line." She pecked him on the lips with another energetic kiss.

They sat together on the couch as quiet settled upon them. They huddled as if watching a non-existent television in the front, not-so-formal living room of Kim's house. After a few minutes, an increasingly sleepy Bill asked, "Should I feel guilty that my best friend's dad died, he's stuck half way around the world, and I'm back here getting a phenomenal blowjob? Is that disrespectful?"

"You're not serious?" Kim said, feigning slight offence. "Clearly the two are unrelated. You're hurting too, and I just wanted to be close with you."

"I know," Bill replied. "I'm mostly joking. It's all just so weird."

The conversation soon shifted to schedules and logistics for the upcoming days; they agreed to connect at church in the morning to coordinate. "I hate to say it, but I really should get going to work," Bill groaned reluctantly.

Chapter 4

DIVINE INTERVENTION

Madrid, Spain—Sunday morning

The phone on the nightstand cut through the dark silence and startled Ian from his fitful slumber. "Buenos dias señor, son las cinco y cuarto de la mañana."

"Gracias," said Ian, sitting up despite the objections of every fiber of his body. Nonetheless, he knew he needed to be at least two hours early for his flight, so he proceeded to shower, pack his few remaining items, and head for the lobby to meet Mrs. Newman.

Upon hitting the hotel lobby, Ian found Mrs. Newman was ready and waiting to accompany him to the airport. Thirty minutes later they were in the airport, boarding pass in his hand. "I guess this is where I should say goodbye. Do you have everything you need?" Mrs. Newman asked.

"I can't thank you enough, Mrs. Newman, for everything. That was quite a tour yesterday," he said. "And we'll settle up on the ticket as soon as you get home."

"You're more than welcome, Ian," she said as she reached out to hug him, almost as if to conceal her own reddening eyes. "Please give our love to your mom, and your family. Your father was a great man, and he would be proud of you."

Ian hugged her back, and turned to head for the security checkpoint, looking back to give a final wave goodbye to a woman who had been a respected teacher, but was now a fellow participant in something a whole lot broader than that—life. He wiped a tear as he continued onward.

After breezing through security and finding his gate area to be significantly busier, Ian realized that a long day had only just begun. A wave of emotion welled up again as he found himself so very alone, with such a long trip ahead. With a two-hour wait until departure, he located a seat near the back of the waiting area and seated himself carefully so as not to bother those around him.

"Perdóneme," he said as his bag brushed the Spanish-looking businessman seated next to him.

"No hay problema," replied the casual, yet upscale appearing young man in a friendly tone. "Habla Ingles?"

"Yes, I sure do. I'm Ian Keppler. Do I look that out of place?"

"No," said the now smiling neighbor as he extended a hand, "it's just that the flight is going to New York so I figured there was a pretty good chance. I'm Daniel."

"So is New York home for you or are you going on from there?" Ian asked.

"No, actually I'm not on this flight. I'm headed back home to South Africa. I just have a long layover and had chosen this gate to rest. Looks like my quiet time is about over," he laughed. "But that's okay—I've only got about an hour left and my gate over there looks just as busy now."

"How long have you been in Spain?" Daniel asked.

"Well, about one day," Ian replied. He felt awkward but wasn't going to beat around the bush. "I'm afraid I've just received word that my father passed away suddenly."

The stranger grimaced and looked Ian in the eyes with sympathy. "My condolences," he said sincerely. "I'm very sorry."

"Thank you."

"Wow—that's really quite a blow. Was your father ill?"

"Well, he had a heart attack five years ago, but we really didn't think he was in any danger."

"Is there anything I can do for you? I travel through here quite often. I know the airport well."

"Thank you. I'm fine, but that's nice of you," Ian replied. "How about you, what do you do in South Africa?"

Daniel proceeded to chat with Ian about his luxury travel business, providing safari experiences to wealthy Spanish businesspersons. From there the conversation turned to cultural elements of South Africa, and generally light-hearted fare before each relaxed and returned to his own affairs. Ian took to his book and Daniel appeared to be tending off-and-on to business, writing intermittently on a legal pad between thoughts.

And so passed the first hour of Ian's long pilgrimage home, scattered conversation interwoven with personal activities—typical of such airport encounters where nobody wants to risk bending the other's ear relentlessly. Finally it was time, and Daniel stood and began to gather his things. "Okay my friend, I suppose I'd better go catch my flight."

Ian stood to shake Daniel's hand, but was surprised as Daniel handed him a sheet of paper from his legal pad.

"Ian, my condolences on the loss of your father. Safe journey to you," Daniel said as he handed him the piece of paper and proceeded to shake his hand warmly.

"Thank you Daniel," Ian remarked with a tinge of curiosity. And with that, Daniel turned and walked toward his own gate, disappearing quickly into the growing sea of people.

Ian sat back down with the folded note. He didn't open it immediately, but rather took a moment to reflect upon the first hour of his journey home. How ironic it was that he had met such a nice guy. He couldn't explain it, but he felt a genuine connection with Daniel—a warmth. Again he became awash in a feeling of peace. He was at peace, and the world was at peace. Time was again unfolding in slow motion. Sadness was present, but so was love, and the madness and rush of the outside world simply did not matter.

Ian unfolded the paper to reveal a handwritten note:

Dear Ian,

You have my deepest condolences for the loss of your father.

There is much we do not understand about this transition your father has made. While a few say that this is simply the end of a biological life, I suspect that is not the complete story, and I would guess that's your view as well. I do not know your particular background or religious beliefs, so I hope you don't mind if I share a few broad thoughts with you.

You see, I lost both of my parents about six years ago—to a car accident. I apologize if these concepts appear a bit morose, but thinking in these terms was a helpful part of the grief process for me.

At the time of death, there are many different beliefs and traditions on the African continent. Some cultures burn the dead to ensure that spirits do not linger— thus attracting other spirits that might do us harm. There are many traditions designed to chase away the spirits of the deceased. Some take the body deep into the jungle to keep the spirits far away. Zulus burn all of the deceased's belongings so as to keep evil spirits away that may linger near possessions. Some even grind bones and mix them with food so as to absorb the deceased. There are other traditions of course. Jews also bury immediately, then mourn for seven days, covering mirrors in the home so that mourning is not done with vanity. Christians have yet other traditions.

My point is this. While we have many different ideas about what death entails, death is by its very nature a mystery! But it is also an essential part of life. Sad it is, but this doesn't change the reality of its existence.

Since the dawn of the earth, men, women, and children have been dying every single day. We react in different ways and interpret their journey differently as well.

But there is one thing we have in common—we experienced one another! We loved together. We celebrated. We struggled. Those we've lost—touched our lives! And parents, they gave us life itself and loved and instructed us in its mysteries and wonders. Those things, my new friend, are inescapably real and true—to all faith systems.

Ian, I believe that we have to use those real experiences of love, to build upon them, and to better humankind by leveraging these memories. I sense you will be an ally in this mission. It isn't the body that matters now. It's what you do with the experiences and memories left behind.

Ian, I am so glad our paths happened to cross here. I am so convinced that the human experience and human existence is dependent most upon our ability to care for one another. Thank you for sharing this time with me. I wish you peace, love, and abundant joy. May you find comfort in your faith, and also in the arms of the others with whom you continue to share life's bounty. Treasure the great memories you have of your father. By doing so he will truly be with you always.

With sincere condolences,

Daniel

Ian slowly looked up to where Daniel had disappeared. "What a gift," he whispered aloud. Just when he needed something—some distraction or something, Daniel was right there. Ian wasn't prone to believing in miracles or angels, but could this have been a coincidence?

The feeling of peace continued over Ian as he sat thinking and watching the gathering crowd for the flight to New York. His eyes caught a beautiful young traveler, probably around his age. She was tall and of a lean build with flowing black hair, olive skin, and a natural beauty that couldn't be ignored. Ian's eyes tracked her nonchalantly.

Even at that age, Ian was conscious of the irony. Here he was having a deep and profound experience, wondering if by some slim chance he'd just been sent a divine sign of comfort, when so instinctively and involuntarily a woman could divert his attention.

Just as quickly as the girl and the ponderings had popped into Ian's mind, the dark beauty disappeared in the crowd of people. Ian's thoughts instantly bounced back to the letter he had by that time tucked into his carry-on bag.

Before he knew it he heard, "Attención pasajeros y pasajeras. Vuelo Iberia número doscientos veinte y tres—"

"Will begin boarding momentarily, he translated without difficulty. The two hours had gone mercifully quickly, with a profound and meaningful encounter to boot.

Within about ten minutes Ian found himself locating his seat in the giant 747, which was configured as usual with three seats, an aisle, five seats in the middle, another aisle, and three seats on the other side. The thing seemed so HUGE to him. With his 6'1" body, Ian had hoped for an aisle seat, but quickly figured out that he had a window seat instead. Truth be told, his fascination with the size of those massive engines, and all the other sights of airline travel, made the slight cramping of his body a reasonable trade off.

Ian was usually an easy-going, "glass is half-full" guy, but was especially so that day. His sense of suspended time was underscored by his new perspective on the fragility of life. As he watched people stress and fuss while shuffling in front of him toward the rear of the jet, he pondered the folly of sweating such little stuff.

He squeezed in by what appeared to be two members of a family of five that had spanned across an aisle. They appeared to be of Indian nationality and Ian noticed a unique smell of burnt wood. It reminded him of the bonfires he and his brother would build on those precious summer nights at the family cottage. Another pang of emotion hit him. *Damn*, he thought to himself, *I sure wish I could see these things coming.*

As he sat down and settled into his window seat, he couldn't help but wonder what would become of the family cottage. *Would Mom still want to go there without Dad? Sure, they had developed friends there over the years, but it would sure be tough.*

In a way, it was their marital retreat, and Ian knew it. Since his dad's first heart attack, and his mom's cancer, they figured they needed a refuge. His dad absolutely loved the place. It wasn't nearly as fancy, but it reminded Ian of the cottage in the movie *On Golden Pond* with Henry Fonda and Katherine Hepburn. Upon further reflection, the Keppler cottage was on more of a "pond" than that monstrous lake in the movie, and the setting not nearly as gorgeous and bug-free, but they surely still loved it.

A guilt pang struck Ian as he wondered how many nights and weekends with his father he had passed up, in favor of exercising his independence and hanging out with friends at the vacant Kalamazoo household. What experiences might he have missed? What precious few additional minutes might he have spent with this wonderful man whom he would now never be able to see or talk with again?

With the rational side of his brain, he instructed himself not to go down that road. What was done was done, and he felt profoundly lucky to have had the idyllic family and loving experiences that he did. He was blessed indeed, and any such self-flagellation would not serve any useful purpose.

After a long period of the usual controlled chaos involved with loading a 747 for transcontinental flight, the plane began to taxi for takeoff—already a bit behind schedule. After turning onto the runway for departure, this time the behemoth's engines eased up to takeoff power, and the launch was as easy and graceful as it looks in the movies.

As Ian stared out the window and watched the dry, brown land of Spain slowly fall away, it was almost as if he was trapped inside a surreal film. He had worked hard to get here. He had been so excited. Who would have thought it would end so quickly? Ian could see a hint of his own reflection in the window, and he couldn't help but think it was life imitating art. The scene felt like the end of a chapter or the close of a movie. The plane was departing with a saddened, yet peaceful young man staring out the window, suddenly older, and with a new perspective on life. Christ's words from the cross rang in Ian's head. "It is finished."[2] Indeed a chapter was closing in Ian's life.

Despite the full flight and its long duration, it seemed they were up at altitude in no time, and the hours clicked by at a reasonable pace. Ian listened to his Walkman and exchanged cordial conversation with his neighbors. They seemed very nice, actually, and through English that was difficult to understand at times, they extended their regrets after asking and learning the reasons behind Ian's solo travel.

Eventually the descent for JFK began. Apart from a clogged eustachian tube that caused an irritating inability of Ian's right ear to equalize pressure, the descent went quickly and the wheels touched down with a squeal on a sweltering runway 22-Right, at JFK airport in New York. It was just after 3:00 in the afternoon, and a record heat wave in the northeast meant the temperatures on the tarmac were well over 100 degrees, and the accompanying humidity was like that of southern Georgia. Ian bid his seatmates goodbye and endured the long deplaning of the masses, then proceeded to baggage claim to gather his luggage. Iberia did not connect to United Airlines, and his connection was going to be tight.

After retrieving his single large suitcase and figuring a way to bind together his backpack and the Lladró figurine he had managed to purchase for his mother, he quickly headed to find directions to the United desk. A grumpy airport employee begrudgingly directed him to the street, where he was forced to undertake a long hike through the stifling heat.

After about fifteen minutes, the sweat-soaked traveler entered the area of United's domestic ticketing and proceeded to the desk to obtain a boarding pass from his hand-written paper ticket.

"Ah, Mr. Keppler, checking just the one bag?" the attractive brunette ticket agent asked.

"Yes ma'am," Ian replied as she stapled something and moved some papers.

"Okay, here you are. You don't have much time so please head directly to your gate."

He thanked her and rushed through security, arriving at the gate just in time to join the boarding line. "Whew," Ian sighed under his breath. He had made it. One more leg to Detroit and then he'd be done with the longest string of travel days he'd ever imagined.

Though he didn't even know who was picking him up there, he suspected it would be his brother, Matt. His thoughts turned fondly to his siblings. Matt was a slightly darker version of his own physical person—or vice versa since Matt was older. Compared to Ian's somewhat spotty facial hair—which of course he kept closely shaven so its patchiness wasn't apparent—Matt had darker whiskers and a fuller shadow, which became visible in only a day or two without shaving. He was friendly, somewhat more reserved than Ian, and popular with a broad base of peers. He was also bright and high achieving, a tradition begun by the boys' older sister, Lynn. Some strain of perfectionism must have been in their blood, since Bob and Janet hadn't ever been the strict types who had to hound their kids to study.

"Boarding passes out and ready please," the flight attendant instructed to the line of people boarding. It didn't look as crowded, but somehow a DC-9 boarding line could never seem as sizable as that of the Boeing 747's on which he'd just traveled. There were just far fewer passengers.

Ian found his way to his seat, which this time was in the middle of three seats. The good news, however, was that a solitary young woman with cute, strawberry blond hair occupied the window seat. She seemed to force a polite smile as the two made eye contact; she sensed that Ian was going to sit next to her. She appeared about his age, with clippered short hair in the back that formed a sort of classic Dorothy Hammill look of some years earlier. Her face was pleasingly round in shape, yet perhaps most prominent were her beautiful blue eyes. From what Ian could see of her, she reminded him of a gymnast. She was an attractive, petite young woman with a friendly, yet reserved, countenance.

"Hi, my name is Ian," he volunteered as he crawled toward his seat, extending a hand.

"My name is Catalina Podor," she replied in a thick European accent that Ian couldn't place.

"Where are you headed?" Ian asked.

"To Detroit," she answered with a questioning smirk that revealed a hint of sarcasm.

Ian smiled. "I guess I should have known that, huh? Where are you from then?"

"Romania," she replied. "I'm here to visit my cousins in Detroit." She volunteered the information in a soft tone and in a somewhat guarded fashion.

"Cool. Well, welcome to the United States," Ian said sincerely as he got a good look at her sparkling blue eyes. Ian turned to organizing his Walkman and some reading material as an announcement came over the intercom.

"Thank you," she replied in her appealing Romanian accent, hitting the vowel with a much softer "a."

"Ladies and gentleman, this is Tom Burgois, your captain, speaking. I want to welcome you aboard United 653 today, with service to Detroit, and ask that you take your seats as quickly as possible as there is some weather approaching and we're going to make every effort to get in line for departure expeditiously. We should be pushing back in just a couple of minutes so your help is appreciated."

"Is this your first time to America?" Ian asked.

"Yes, and I'm not sure I like it so far," Catalina divulged somewhat curtly. Ian was surprised, and as a native felt that quick tinge of desire to attend to an unhappy customer.

"Why's that?"

"This ticket agent was so very mean to me," she replied. "He was . . . what's the word . . . shouting at me for not having my boarding pass. But when I left Bucharest, they said I was all set and had everything I needed to get all the way to Detroit." Ian could relate. In those days before e-tickets, the paperwork for international travel could be unruly at times. Combined with an inexperienced traveler, there were bound to be wrinkles.

"He just kept saying 'go back to the ticket counter,' but I knew I didn't have time. He was just so rude, as if he could talk to me like a child," she continued venting.

Despite her small stature, Ian guessed she was slightly older than he—perhaps about twenty. He could picture the impatient New York worker being less than helpful, not wholly unlike the attendant from whom he had sought directions.

Ian could see the spark of anger in her eye as she finished her sentence, and the spark quickly turned to a single tear of frustration. Catalina tried to conceal it by glancing out the window. He could sense that she was by no means a fragile young lady, which made him feel even more sympathy for her situation. Surely international travel was a new experience for her and she had probably just reached a point of fatigue and frustration when she slammed into an asshole.

Ian instinctively wanted to reassure her, squeeze her hand or something, but he didn't. Instead, he just listened sympathetically and soaked up her words as if they were flowing from the depth of her blue eyes, directly into his brown ones. "I'm sorry. That must have been incredibly frustrating," he reassured.

Catalina continued to speak, in complete control now as if talking was helping. "And then I had this four-hour layover, and people just were not friendly or helpful at all." She paused, then looked at Ian and forced a smile, saying, "I must sound like a spoiled child."

Ian laughed, "Not at all. Just hang in there because I think you'll find America is really a pretty friendly place. Sometimes there is something about a big city, especially at a busy airport, that makes it not exactly put its best foot forward."

"Best foot forward," she repeated with a smile. Her chuckle and coy expression resurrected the taste of sarcasm Ian had sensed earlier.

"Ahh, it means to not do as well as you are able to do at other times," he clarified, smiling almost as if he were conceding the point that he had broken the international rule of avoiding idioms.

A tone sounded over the airplane's speakers. "This is the captain again ladies and gentlemen, and I'm sorry to report that departures have been temporarily stopped due to a line of storms in the departure vicinity of JFK. However as you noticed we've just begun to push back from the gate so that we can get into the line for when things do clear. I do ask that you bear with us; the air-conditioning is not always very effective on the ground, so if you wish to close shades before departure you are welcome to do so. We'll keep you up to date."

Ian and Catalina looked at each other with a "what the hell" shrug of their shoulders—not at all happy with what appeared to be a lengthier delay, but also recognizing that it was out of their hands.

Little did they know that as with many of the events of Ian's last few days, there was more bittersweet reality to come. The "bitter" was to become a seemingly intolerable, four-hour delay, spent entirely in a very warm airplane, on the extremely hot taxiways of JFK, in a line of aircraft that Ian could see stretched over twenty jets in front of them, and behind them farther than he ever had occasion to count. Their first meal was served while the plane still sat motionless on the ground!

On the extreme other side of bitter, however, this would become a poignant and meaningful vignette in Ian's life—the memory of which would prompt philosophical questions and warm thoughts that would endure literally for decades.

For four hours on the ground, and then a couple more en route to Detroit, Catalina and Ian talked, perhaps in a way that only strangers—who know their paths will cross only for a limited time—can ever experience. The false pretenses were gone. The need to impress was gone. A profound air of candor and honesty sat atop the underlying layer of genuine caring. The rest of the world disappeared. This was as pure a connection between two humans as Ian had ever imagined. In fact, if he could have known the truth, its ranking as one of his most profound experiences would endure.

For six hours, they talked about family. They talked about culture, friends, and social situations at home. They talked about hopes, dreams, desires, and their individual natures and personalities. What would they look for in a mate? What baggage would they bring to parenthood? They talked about their parents, and the death of Ian's father. They laughed together, and literally cried together as Ian described his admiration for his father, and what awaited him upon arrival back home.

Indeed Ian's sense of peace and of time being completely suspended had reached its zenith. There was no outside world. There was only a relationship between two people—a closed system that seemed to transcend even time and space.

At one point later, Ian would laughingly compare the experience to half-a-dozen dates where he'd watched a movie with a woman, perhaps gotten ice cream, and headed home without really talking at all. Sure, there was attraction and passion even in some of those situations, but this was so distinctly different.

As with other big questions that grew out of those three days, and would bounce around in Ian's mind for literally decades to come, Ian would many times ponder if there were such a thing as love at first sight. His parents were master examples of moderation and judiciousness, and admonitions against over indulgence were now part of his psyche. His parents were moderate in their alcohol consumption, their expenditures, and even their religion. So while at the time it wasn't his nature to mentally jump overboard and name the emotion he was experiencing as "love," he certainly felt a deep, interpersonal connection with this woman—that transcended even seventeen-year-old, hormonal urges.

Another day he might ask himself if it was a *true* experience, or just a coincidental and convenient exchange of human interaction—bolstered to a near metaphysical level more by fantasy than reality. But at that time, such a question was dimensions away.

The descent to Detroit had begun. The suspension of time was about to end. His long journey would be complete in a few hours, and his time with Catalina in a few short minutes. He could cherish the surreal feeling of living a final scene in a movie for only a few more minutes. Catalina rested her head on his shoulder, and clasped his hand gently as they silently looked out the window at the lights of Toledo and Detroit, now visible against a stunning orange and purple sunset.

Within a few minutes the DC-9 was on a final approach through the silky-smooth, late evening air, nearly appearing stationary at times above the landscape below. Ian hardly even noticed that the decompression of his right ear at cruise altitude had ended and a clogged feeling of pressure had returned. Moments later the pilot eased the throttles back, settling the main wheels onto the runway in perfect alignment. Ian looked into Catalina's sparkling blue eyes.

"I need to write down my address for you," she said. Neither had any unrealistic expectations, which was part of the poignancy of the situation. Clearly Ian wouldn't be able to predict his schedule, even if he had time to visit before Catalina headed back. Yet they had discussed exchanging information, and each wanted the security of having done so. Catalina located something to write with and they proceeded to exchange addresses and phone numbers.

Ian knew there would never be any point in describing this experience. Any effort would be met with the appropriate voice of moderation and skepticism. "You talk like you knew her for years. You can hardly miss someone that you've known for only half a day," he could hear someone like his mother saying. Yet he knew he was going to feel a sense of missing Catalina. In fact he was somewhat embarrassed by the mere thought of anyone knowing how strongly he was feeling emotions for her. *They'd be absolutely right*, he thought to himself. At the same time it was so real.

"Ladies and gentlemen, your United Airlines crew wants to thank you for your patience today. We realize it has been a long day for everyone, including us, but we thank you and hope you'll afford us the opportunity to serve you again. Please stay seated until I turn off the seatbelt sign at the gate, and we'll see you next time," said the now too-familiar voice.

As they exited the jetway into the gate area of Detroit Metropolitan Airport, Ian saw Catalina's eyes searching, then a hand go up in the air as she spotted a large family contingent awaiting her arrival. She rushed over to them, greeting them with hugs, kisses and some words that Ian couldn't understand, but quickly she turned to introduce Ian. "I want you all to meet the man who saved me in New York—Ian," she announced in English to the joyful and friendly group.

"Hello Ian. Sounds like we owe you a thank you then," greeted the uncle as he shook Ian's hand.

After exchanging pleasantries and more greetings, and answering questions about the delays, Ian realized he hadn't seen Matt or anyone yet. He hoped they'd gotten word of the delays and adjusted appropriately. But figuring they would meet him at the baggage claim, or at least that he could find a pay phone after he got his bag, he joined the group in the walk to the claim area. The family largely surrounded Catalina, except for the uncle who walked with Ian, making polite conversation—always in a jovial tone with a thick, appealing Romanian accent.

At the baggage claim area Ian wandered from the group briefly, in search of his bag. Still no sign of a chauffeur for the three-hour drive back to Kalamazoo, but typical of his current mindset, it just didn't worry him. As more and more bags made their way around the big circle multiple times, Ian finally located his suitcase and carried it back around to the other side of the island, toward Catalina and her endearing clan. He reached Catalina and her aunt, who were in conversation. Her uncle and cousins stood ready to head out, her three bags now safely in their care.

They turned to Ian and the aunt said in a motherly tone and thick accent, "Ian, we would like to wait for you until you phone your family and see if they are here. If not, we absolutely insist that you come to our home. You can eat and spend the night and they can get you in morning."

Ian was touched. It was obvious Catalina had shared some type of information with her aunt, and in return her aunt seemed more than willing to return any favor. At the same time she was so warm and insistent that Ian suspected she'd have been as giving regardless of any extraordinary sentiments Catalina may have conveyed.

"Thank you so very much ma'am, but I'll be—"

"Ian!" interrupted a voice from nowhere that that stopped just short of a shout.

"Matt," Ian replied as if there was no surprise at all that he showed up. They embraced.

"Joseph came with me," Matt announced, just as their pastor's son Joseph Martin appeared behind him.

"Well hey Joe," Ian greeted in his usual friendly tone as Catalina and her family patiently waited. It was evident that Catalina had shared some of Ian's story with her aunt, because the site of the initial embrace of two brothers reuniting after the death of their father had created a moist appearance to her eyes. "Hey, I want you guys to meet Catalina and her family. They've been very kind," Ian said while making eye contact with them, then turning his attention to Catalina.

"I can't thank you enough," he said to her.

"It is I who thank you," she replied, embracing him with a tight, heartfelt squeeze as if they were alone again. She hugged him firmly and held on for several seconds. She then gave him a quick kiss on the neck, and moved her lips to his cheek. She held them there as she gave one final squeeze, releasing to say only a phrase in Romanian Ian couldn't understand, then whispering, "I wish you peace and joy," as she cradled his face in her hands—a hint of tears seeping from her eyes.

Ian gave one final wave goodbye to the family, and turned to follow Matt and Joe to an exit.

"How are you?" asked Matt, sensitive to some greater context of the goodbye.

"I'm fine, Matt," he assured, glancing back to watch Catalina and her family disappear from view. "It's just been quite a journey. But there's time for that later . . . . How are you? How's Mom?"

"We're fine. Obviously it's a tough time, but you know Mom. She's worried about us. I think none of us is quite sure this is real yet."

"Well it's nice of you to ride with him, Joe," Ian said to Joe Martin.

"Happy to help," Joe replied. Joe and Matt looked at each other and sort of chuckled knowingly. Ian wasn't quite sure what he was missing.

"Come on," Matt urged as they hit the bottom of the escalator, just feet from the main exit. "We're just outside the door here." Surely they hadn't left their car unattended, Ian thought to himself. They stepped out onto the curb and to a waiting van with the words "Signature Flight Support" on the side.

Fully aware that Joe had just been hired as a commuter airline pilot, Ian knew he had access to certain perks, but still he wondered what they were up to.

"What's this?" Ian asked as they rolled away.

"Just a shuttle to the car," Joe said. He and Matt exchanged another look.

"No way, did you guys fly here?" Ian asked. He had gone for a plane ride with Joe one other time, but *how cool would this be to fly out of a major airport at night?*

"No," Matt answered with a now-obvious laugh.

"Nope. Three-hour drive," echoed Joe.

"This is too cool!" Ian exclaimed as they all shared a much-needed laugh. "This is just too awesome, Joe. Thank you! I gotta tell ya that a three-hour drive didn't appeal to me much. I'm tired, I've got this plugged up ear, and I've not slept a wink."

"We'll get you up to altitude and you can probably equalize that ear. And I can ask for a slow descent for you—it's not like there are many altitude restrictions going into Kalamazoo," Joe added.

Before he knew it, the van had pulled through an access gate and delivered Ian, his brother, and their pilot friend directly to their single-engine airplane. "This looks great; what is it?" Ian asked, ever curious about anything airplane-related.

"It's a Cessna 210," Joe volunteered. "You flew with me once in a 172 I think. This is a whole lot faster—285 horse power and about 220 miles per hour, retractable landing gear, variable-pitch propeller." Ian and Matt raised their eyebrows in approval.

They climbed into the plane and Matt let Ian sit in the front with Joe. Checklists were completed expeditiously, and the large, single propeller was purring in just seconds. Switches seemed like they were everywhere, and Joe was flipping, pushing and turning things in rapid succession. He dialed a rheostat to bathe the cockpit in red light, and threw another switch to activate multi-colored exterior lights on the wings, tail, and belly.

All of the passenger seats were equipped with intercom headsets so the three could talk and communicate clearly. Joe threw more switches and then rotated several dials that changed LED numbers on the congested panel, which Ian presumed were related to radios of some type.

"Detroit clearance, Centurion 1665 X-ray, signature southeast, IFR Kalamazoo with bravo," Joe said into his headset after waiting for a gap in the chatter.

A voice immediately answered. "Centurion 1665 X-ray, cleared as filed to Kalamazoo via BOSHM-one departure, JACKO transition, maintain

3,000, ground ready to taxi," the voice instructed, but Ian could decipher only a couple words.

"Yeah—do what he said," Ian mockingly instructed for Matt's entertainment.

Joe finished jotting down some shorthand on a thick stack of documents and books, then actually repeated the whole mess back over the radio. The controller's voice answered, "Readback correct, ground point 75 to taxi, 65 X-ray. Good flight."

"This is too cool," Ian said as they taxied toward runway 27-Left, with Joe occasionally uttering radio phrases that were loaded with phonetic alphabet references.

"How you ever find your way around this place is beyond me," Ian said.

"I'd love to tell you it's easy, but Metro at night can be a real bear," Joe said.

After a number of pre-takeoff rituals and radio communications, the "big" Cessna was in line behind a DC-9, and in front of a 727. It was unique to Ian and Matt to see the huge planes so close. A second later, the DC-9 moved out on to the runway and roared off, in what seemed like seconds reducing itself to distant flashing lights.

"Centurion 1665 X-ray, you're cleared for takeoff Runway 24-Right. Maintain runway heading then JACKO departure."

"Clear for takeoff 24-Right, 65 X-ray," echoed Joe as the plane had already begun rolling onto the gigantic runway. Joe eased the power in and the acceleration pushed the trio back in their seats more than Ian had expected. They were airborne in no time.

"What a sight," Matt said.

For his part, Ian was now silent. The beauty was profound. He could see the entire airport below with nearly 360 degrees of visibility—each of the runways, taxiways, and buildings. It was the first time he could really see the layout of the intersecting runways and taxiways as they'd appeared on maps.

His thoughts returned to his father, then to Catalina. She was back there somewhere among the increasingly distant lights, headed to an adventure of her own. Now here he was, above it all and headed back to brutal reality.

What a frickin' whirlwind, he thought to himself, again reflecting on the depth of joy and despair he'd been experiencing.

It seemed clear that as tough as these days and this experience had been, they were strengthening Ian, and strengthening his faith. He thought about Daniel, and especially about Catalina. Were they figments of his imagination? *Clearly they had been real.* Uncharacteristically wistful, Ian thought to himself: perhaps they had been angels.

While his eyes remained open and transfixed on the beauty of the scene, he prayed silently. "Dear Lord, I can't begin to understand all this, I know. But I have to thank you for the experiences I've just had, and the two people who helped me along this difficult trip home. What a gift. I thank you also for Joe and this plane ride home to shorten the journey. And Lord, thank you . . . for the phenomenal experience . . . of having the father that I did."

Chapter 5

BIG QUESTIONS

Early Monday Morning

Matt pulled his mother's Toyota Camry into the driveway of the Keppler family home, as Ian observed the darkened house from the passenger seat. The trip home had been mercifully short, thanks to Joe's help, though by the time they landed, helped Joe put the plane away, and drove home from the airport, it was still well after midnight. The sizable ranch style house wore its normal middle-of-the-night appearance, but since the garage concealed the main living spaces, it was difficult to tell if Lynn and their mother were waiting up or not.

Nobody was in the main kitchen area, but down the main hall they could see a light in Lynn's bedroom. Ian dumped his luggage near the door and proceeded with Matt to greet their sister. He knocked softly, then eased the door open.

"Ian," Lynn exclaimed in a soft, sympathetic tone. "How is my baby brother?" she asked as she jumped from where she was painting her toenails to embrace Ian heartily.

The three siblings sat on her bed to catch up. Questions flew between them.

"Is Mom up?" Ian asked.

"No, but she said to wake her and give her a hug. She's so tired; still in shock. Hell, we all are. The doctor gave her something to help her get rest before the big day tomorrow, so she's out. But talk to me before you go see her," Lynn urged. Ian had never known his mom to take sleep aids, so it helped him formulate an image of her state.

"Was it a horrible trip home? You must be so exhausted," Lynn pressed. At twenty-two, Lynn was a beauty, both inside and out. She was bright, articulate, and most prominently a congenial woman whom everyone seemed to like. Warmth emanated from her to family and strangers alike. In a nutshell she was a classic overachieving first-born, with looks and brains to take those talents and compulsions far.

"It wasn't so bad, really. In a strange way it was kind of peaceful. I swear . . . that . . . I met a couple really amazing people who were just . . ." Ian couldn't find the words, and stopped trying. "It was fine. But tell me what happened with Dad."

Matt and Lynn explained the whole story. Their beloved dad had been out working in the spacious, semi-rural yard, picking up branches and sticks off the lawn when it hit. He had made it to the house and Janet got him to the hospital with Lynn. Matt had been at the wedding of an old high school friend, where he couldn't be reached.

"Mom and I got to see him while he was still alive," Lynn volunteered, now with tears beginning to flow. "They knew it wasn't good, and they let us in. He had a tube in his throat so he couldn't talk—hoses everywhere. But . . ." she paused to control her emotions and get the story out for Ian's sake. "We held his hands, and looked in his eyes. You guys, he looked scared, honestly. But he squeezed our hands so tightly, he was saying, 'I love you.' It was just so clear."

The three were in a mutual embrace, tears flowing in mourning of the man who in their eyes had been the world's greatest dad—without a doubt. Lynn pulled her head away from the others and finished by adding, "Then they asked us to leave while they continued to work on him—what a gift that they let us in that ER at all. Not five minutes later they came out and told us that he was gone."

The thought of his father having fear, and picturing the painful realization that he must have felt—knowing that he was going to die—made

Ian profoundly sad for his father. His father had been so stoic. He had been much more attentive and communicative with the family than most of Ian's friends' fathers, but still was a man's man in many ways. Indeed that must have been a moment for which there was no possible script, and in which vulnerability and discomfort must have been overwhelming. At the same time, Ian knew beyond a shadow of a doubt that his father's only thoughts while squeezing those hands, were, *"I'm sorry to do this to you. I love you. I'm so sorry to have to leave you."*

The three siblings continued to reconcile questions, share memories, cry, and even laugh. Matt and Lynn briefed Ian on all of the funeral plans, the amazing outpouring of cards, calls, food, letters, and even newspaper coverage of the "community pillar," who was taken away too soon.

After a while, Ian went to wake his mother, who awoke only briefly to again express her concern and condolences to Ian, and assure him everything would be okay. Ian understood that she was taking the only course she knew—optimism, and reassurance of others. He assured her he was fine, shared a hug, and quietly exited the room.

After grabbing a snack, Ian headed to bed. It was there in the final moments of those twenty-eight hours of intense, continuous consciousness, that another profound experience would shape his beliefs for years to come.

Ian's head was swimming as he lay in his own, dark room, with thoughts of the previous five days running through his head. Combined with the exhaustion that was now setting in, it was overwhelming. He began to pray, "Lord, thank you for returning me home safely. I try not to ask for things very often since I know how blessed I am, but tonight I need you. I need your spirit to comfort me, and surround me. I need Dad's comforting spirit as well, and to know that he's okay."

While clearly the Kepplers were good Christian believers who were raised in a church environment, they were also not overly dogmatic. They weren't the types to introduce God into a work or school conversation, and they weren't the types to emphasize or claim personal interactions with God. They were by most accounts "liberal Methodists," at least in terms of theological leanings. Apart from Lynn's brief bout with over-the-top fanaticism—the result of a strong influence from a strict pastor who preceded the Martins—they were believers in living good lives, and stressed civil behavior over theological dictums.

So it was all the more profound and meaningful when as Ian prayed, he felt the descent upon him of a physical whiteness of comfort. It felt like a cool blanket. It enveloped him totally, and peace, comfort, calm, and the presence of God was upon him at once. Finally, through that powerful religious experience, he fell into a much needed, deep sleep.

The following days were the blur that Ian had expected. Monday was consumed by preparations for the visitation, catching up with his then-awake mother, phone calls and a myriad of arrangements and details. Ian was finally able to connect with Bill by phone on Monday morning, and then see him and many other friends at the visitation that afternoon. That said, however, given the volume of attendees at the visitations and the funeral, there was little time to talk in depth with any one person.

The tribute of attendance at the funeral was extremely meaningful to Ian, as was the powerful service of tribute. Over five hundred people had signed the register book at the visitation, and the funeral itself was literally overflowing with people. Many had to strain to hear from the hallways. Others were stuck in the June heat, listening from outside the main doors of the small, traditional sanctuary, through the speakers underneath the overhang of the drop-off area. There was scarcely a dry eye in the church.

In the motorcade to the cemetery, Ian recalled looking back through the rear window of the limousine during a long stretch of unobstructed visibility, to see a string of cars that stretched well beyond what he could see. The weather was perfect at the graveside, though many in the contingent had difficulty seeing the pallbearers transition the natural wood casket to its final resting place, due to the crowd. The pallbearers were selected at Janet's request, and were largely composed of Matt and Ian's friends who had shared such a special admiration for Bob. Bill Vanderveen was among them.

Again Ian couldn't help but feel like the world had stopped—this time in tribute to his father's amazing approach to life. Like all who have experienced grief, however, he would discover that the world quickly must return to normal, and that the pomp and circumstance would be short-lived. He understood that it had to be that way, and like all optimists he strived to embrace the idea to the greatest extent possible. But like most humans who experience the loss of someone close, with whom they lived and loved, the loss would dominate his thoughts for much of the summer to come, and for years after.

Ian would be struck by the number of times he would round a corner in the basement and for a fraction of a second swear he saw his father sitting in his favorite La-z-Boy chair. Or he'd walk by the kitchen and see his dad standing by the desk, sorting bills.

Perhaps most profound, however, would be the dreams. They weren't every night, but when they did come they were vivid and disturbing. Oftentimes his father would still be alive, and would come to him to explain why he had to stage his own fictitious death and funeral. Other times he would tell Ian he was okay and happy in Heaven. In others he would discover that his father was alive, but had left the family to live a new life—without so much as a goodbye or explanation. Ian often would reflect back that he was glad he'd had the opportunity to see his father's body, so that when he awoke he could be doubly sure there was no truth to any of it.

❖

For Ian, it would paradoxically be his "summer of '69." In keeping with the evolving theme, the word "bittersweet" would echo in Ian's mind repeatedly. After the chaos of the visitation and the funeral wore to an end, Ian would spend a great deal of time with Bill and a select group of other friends. Together they cemented relationships in a special way, a way that would probably not have evolved without the surprise death of Ian's father.

For Ian it was also the first summer of adulthood, and he enjoyed a relatively unsupervised existence when he wasn't working and saving for college. Janet would frequently seek consolation and fellowship with friends at the family cottage, leaving the kids to tend to the house on weekends. Even during the week there was a sense that she needed their love and assistance every bit as much as they needed hers.

Matt worked in his field of study by researching the migration habits of waterfoul at the Kellogg Biological Station. For his part Ian left his previous year's gig at a local bakery, opting instead to continue mowing lawns and to help his mom with the family store.

The Thursday after the funeral Ian called Bill to arrange the first of the pool-side gatherings that would forever symbolize their youthful grappling with the big questions of that summer.

"Just grab Kim and head over as soon as you leave work; we'll see you tomorrow. Oh and John will have Kelly so Kim won't be the only chick," Ian added.

It didn't take much arm-twisting to launch the first of the year's "cottage parties"—as they called the gatherings. They had been so named not because they took place at the cottage, but because they had traditionally taken place when Bob and Janet were away at the cottage. Of course this would be Janet's first time staying at the cottage since Bob's death, but Cindy Vanderveen was going along to keep her company and to help ensure she indulged in a much-needed break.

The cottage parties were usually in-control and subdued. The fact was that they hadn't even been much of a secret to Bob and Janet. This was a good group of kids and much as their friends the Vanderveens let their son Bill have a generous amount of leash, so too had the Kepplers trusted their sons' judgment. Furthermore, Bob's heart attack and Janet's cancer had given them a different perspective on life. They had committed to enjoying life, which fortunately—or unfortunately in the case of Bob's death—turned out to be an excellent philosophy; they had so greatly enjoyed the weekends dedicated to rediscovering their marriage, and making such great friends.

When that Friday night rolled around, Anthony was the first to show up. It was never a mystery who was rolling in when Anthony arrived; he would arrive in his 1974 Oldsmobile 98, seemingly the largest vehicle ever known to man. Their friend John Bennett always joked that the thing had enough trunk space to fit a small rowboat. He was right. Four people could sit side-by-side in a pinch, and there was enough headroom for Kareem.

"Hola mi amigo, how's it hanging?" greeted Anthony after he emerged from the monstrosity and walked behind the house to find Ian by the pool. Anthony had been a long-time friend and schoolmate. He was Matt's age, but since he lived nearby he'd long enaged in shenanigans with whichever brother was available for fun.

"Flaco's right behind me," Anthony declared as he held his treasured bag of "BYOB" high in the air for Ian to see.

Flaco was actually Curt, though because his name didn't translate well in his Freshman Spanish class a few years ago, Curt had chosen the name Paco. One day Mrs. Newman was explaining the word for skinny, which is "flaco," and used Curt as an example. The comment irritated Curt, who prided himself on his fitness and athletic appearance. So to add insult to injury his friends made the obvious transition to calling him Flaco. The name stuck.

"Never fear, the party man is here," Flaco announced energetically as he appeared behind Anthony.

The dark, lean Flaco was probably the quintessential athlete of the group, highly competitive and smart too. He was also the life of the party and a real ladies' man, though he had no steady interest at the time. Perhaps above all he was the rowdy one—eternally poking, prodding or joking. His charm, smarts and his infectious sense of humor allowed him to get away with things the others couldn't imagine. Sometimes he approached a line that made Ian uncomfortable, but overall Ian considered Flaco a good guy, and a close friend.

Ian went behind the pump shed to "fire up" the hot tub for the evenings events, and from there he heard the commotion of new arrivals. Bill and Kim had shown up at the same time as their other best friend, John Bennett, who had his friend Kelly along. Ian could hear the girls' high-pitched chatter as they came around back to the pool.

"Hola," Ian said to his friends as he emerged.

"Hi Ian," they replied as they helped themselves to the downstairs fridge and settled in to the routine of the gathering.

"How you doin'?" Bill asked, shaking his friends' hands. Ian knew he was asking genuinely.

"Certainly not where I'd planned to be a little over a week ago as I headed to Spain, but damn glad to have you guys here with me now," Ian replied with a wry smile. "I'm fine, thanks for asking."

"To Bob," Bill said in a now-sincere use of Mr. K's first name. The group hoisted their glasses. They drank to Mr. K and proceeded to banter about in small talk while sharing intermittent memories and thoughts about him. For the most part the tone of the gathering was lighthearted; they were ready to have some fun. Before long the verbal jousting had begun, with generous use of nicknames and stereotypical slams.

"Hey Flaco, you stud puppy, where is your harem tonight?" asked Anthony.

"Don't know, Scrappy, must be that I've been riding in your boat a little too much?"

Anthony was from a good, blue-collar, Catholic family. He was a quiet guy, small in stature but smart like a fox. Having had four older brothers he was also scrappy and tough—which was how he earned his nickname "Scrappy." Certainly he wouldn't win any prizes for cleanliness or clothing style, but there was something pure in him that the friends found endearing.

He was working a factory job now; college wasn't much in his plan, which Ian respected. One thing Janet and Bob taught at an early age was that judging people based upon anything but the merits of their character, and who they were inside, was a sad mistake. Indeed the last people ever to look down on anyone were Bob and Janet Keppler. Bob himself had come from an abusive and unstable home, never spoke the King's English, yet still worked intelligently and thoughtfully to earn his position of high repute.

"Hey, that car is a chick magnet, and you know it," Anthony replied to Flaco.

"Yeah, we girls really get turned on by those giant brown, antique cars," Kelly threw into the mix. She and John had palled around in the group for years, not unlike Bill and Kim, but romance had not been a substantial part of the equation. She was a sharp girl, bright and fun. She was tall, blond and good looking in Ian's view, though was not the perfect Barbie type. She was a band geek with a slightly prominent nose, and as a fellow band geek Ian routinely noted her attractive shape during marching season. There was just something about how she could wear a pair of jeans, her hourglass figure and fit legs forming an entrancing, upside-down triangle of empty space between her upper thighs.

Was he lusting after his friend's girl? Of course not. First, she wasn't really John's girlfriend. Second, at this age—with hours and hours spent together during the school year—there wasn't a guy in any class who hadn't fully studied every girl's shape. Hell, they all thought that Eddie Murphy's comedy routine about spontaneous teenage erections was the funniest thing to ever come down the pike. When Eddie joked about being called up to do a problem on the chalkboard, and the student said, "I'll take an E for the day" to hide his embarrassment, the guys roared with sympathy. They'd all feared that situation, just sitting and minding their own business when a raging hard-on would arrive spontaneously. Indeed there was something about separating hormones from late teenagers and young college students that just couldn't be done.

At the same time, that was something that bothered Ian. In fact, the night before the funeral he had been lying in bed somewhat flagellating himself over having masturbated. How could he possibly have been horny at such a serious time? He didn't know the answer, but he had been; and it had been comforting and relaxing to accommodate himself.

Consciously he was aware that everyone did it and that it was normal; but nobody talked about it really, and even though he went to a less conservative church than Bill, Ian knew it was a sin to lust after women. It was actually "Scrappy" Anthony who had years earlier mentioned to Ian that his Catholic upbringing made clear the meaning of Matthew's words in 5:28, "But, I say to you that every one who looks at a woman lustfully has already committed adultery with her in his heart."[3]

Ian was a good kid, who like the others wanted to do right by the world, and certainly by God, but somehow there was this cognitive dissonance between knowing desire was normal, and knowing it was also sinful. In his early teens, Ian had on more than one occasion instituted something akin to a smoking cessation plan. It would be a weaning of weenie play, so to speak—a conscious reduction until he had quit. Funny, but that never happened.

The banter at the pool party focused Ian's thoughts on the present, and continued for a while to be lighthearted. As drinks and darkness settled in, however, the conversation turned more serious—even a touch philosophical.

"So Ian, how in the hell is this possible?" Bill asked casually, leaning back as if waiting for a long answer. "How is it even possible that we're sitting here and that your dad will never return home?"

Ian simply replied, "I'm with you, partner."

"It sure sucks, Ian. I sure wish there was something I could do for you," Kelly said sweetly. "I think we all do."

"Thanks. You know they say time heals all wounds. Gotta tell you though, it seems hard to believe." Ian paused momentarily. "But I suppose it's like this guy from South Africa said when we were talking in the airport on my way home, death really isn't something just invented last Friday night. We're all headed there. People have been doing it for centuries—millennia actually." Ian waxed philosophic, in some way trying to find comfort in his own words.

"I'm sure that was a reassuring message—we all die!" Scrappy joked.

"Actually, it was. He was a super nice guy—lost his own parents in a car crash. We were just talking and he was saying that the concept helped him to understand the nature of life. There is birth, there is death, and that can't be avoided. I guess we can just hope and pray—and I really believe—they are in a better place."

"Absolutely, Ian," Kim assured. "I have no doubt."

"I don't either," Bill began, slightly buzzing from the beer and apparently now irritated, "but if one more person says that this is part of God's plan, I think I'm going to puke! Are you telling me that God wanted your dad dead? Do you really believe that? God said the world is better off without Bob Keppler in it? That just makes no sense, Ian. And it's bloody unfair, my friend!"

"Hey, ours is not to question," Kim interjected. "We're not intended to understand these things."

"God is supposed to be omnipotent, right?" asked Bill. "So that means he has power over all of his creation, right?" Ian, Anthony, Kelly and Kim knew where Bill was going with his point. Flaco didn't much have a religious background, so he was just listening and drinking. John was also silent—in part because while he was raised in the church, he really wasn't one who paid much attention. It wasn't that he was intellectually sharp; religion and church just weren't parts of life that interested him much.

Then again, Ian really hadn't consciously thought much about such serious questions until now, but such events have a way of turning everyone into philosophers and theologians.

"Yes, Bill, omnipotence means He can do anything," Kim jumped in. "And I know where you are going. He is also omnibenevolent—all good and all loving; and He is omniscient, which is all knowing."

"Right," said Bill, "so how can it be both ways, this great, loving, kind, caring, fatherly figure, who has all the power to do anything He wants, but chooses to kill Mr. K?"

"Here is how I've heard it explained, Bill," Ian offered. "God can look at the earth and see past, present and future, like a timeline spread out below. And indeed He is benevolent and good. While he can see all of the possibilities of how events will unfold, and knows which ones will actually happen in the future, He has to let his creation play out. Without free will, there can be no choices. So he has to allow bad things to happen."

"Yeah but if the whole thing is planned out on the timeline, and he knows how it will end, then we aren't really making choices, are we? It's all planned out!" Bill replied.

Ian clarified, "That's not what I said. I said He can see the future, but that He isn't making the future—it's playing out on its own."

"Well, but he *can* change it if he wants to—if we pray enough. Right?" Bill challenged.

"Right, but then there isn't free will if he interferes and stops everything bad from happening," Kim retorted.

"So it's really a test? A giant Petri dish?" Bill asked. "Oh that's real kind and benevolent."

"You guys are talking in circles. Come on Kelly. Ian, is it okay if we go into the kitchen and put together some of the snacks we brought?" Kim asked.

"Go for it," Ian answered nicely, but he kept his attention focused on the topic at hand. "Bill, I don't pretend to have the answers, all I can tell you is that I believe that Dad's in a better place, and that it's beyond our ability to understand the meaning of it now," Ian summarized.

"I suppose—and you must know that if there's a Heaven, I believe Bob Keppler is there, Ian. And I do believe there is a Heaven and that he's there. I just think it sucks, and it's unfair to you, and to all of us," Bill reassured his friends. They knew that in part he was just venting; everyone understood. This was uncharted territory for the entire group.

"John. Flaco. Scrappy. Who's up for a little pool basketball?" Ian goaded.

"Not me," said John.

"Okay, Flaco and I challenge Ian and Bill to a duel," said Scrappy.

"You're going down!" Bill answered, ever the competitor.

As would often be the case that summer, philosophy was interspersed with, or truncated by, plain old immature sport. But that was the dynamic, and that was how the friendships worked. Combined with the trust that developed through the shared grief among friends, that dynamic fostered the free exchange of thoughts, fears, and questions. What was not so obvious, however, was how that dynamic would subtly influence the course of Ian and Bill's lives.

"Movie Sunday night?" Bill asked Ian as he and Kim headed out at the end of the night, the last ones to leave.

"Absolutely," Ian replied.

Chapter 6

THE SEEDS OF FALLIBILITY

Early that summer, Sunday was a night Ian dreaded. It was a night he felt most alone. It was quiet—far too quiet. Matt was often working on his research tasks, or away at the research site preparing equipment for the next day. Usually Janet had something going with one of the many friends who were working feverishly to keep her occupied, had events at church, or simply wanted the same type of quiet time everyone else did. That was all fine, but it amounted to an empty house for Ian. Everyone was always up for fun on Friday or Saturday, but somehow Sunday was different. It wasn't only that there were issues surrounding the Sabbath tradition among his friends; people just preferred to settle down on Sundays, preparing for the week ahead.

So in this way, as in others, Bill was Ian's salvation. They'd make an evening out of going to the movies—or more accurately, the movie. It was the summer of *Back to the Future* and Bill and Ian's friend Tony worked at a small cinema with only two screens, one of which was dedicated to the film for nearly the entire summer. The price was right—given that he would conveniently fail to ask them for tickets—so the options were limited. Of course this was not to detract in any way from the high regard in which they'd come to hold *Back to the Future*. Yes, sometimes they would take a break and see the feature in the other theater, but usually there was nothing better than watching Marty McFly say, "You're my density," to Lorraine at the soda fountain. In fact, the duo would eventually memorize just about every line of the film.

Clearly it wasn't the movie that mattered however. It was the car ride there, hanging out and chatting at the local McDonald's afterward, or remembering some old story. Often the stories would relate to girls.

On the Sunday of their first such outing they recalled one of their favorite tales, from seventh grade when they had ridden their bikes several miles to meet their girlfriends at a park. Ian laughed, "Remember that day we found a box on the way home from the park?"

"Oh, you mean that single greatest day of our lives?" Bill joked.

"That's the one!" Ian deadpanned, recalling the sight of the ubiquitous cardboard box lying in the tall grass by the edge of an undeveloped area of road.

"You mean the day every young man dreams of, when someone dumps a box of *Playboys* on the side of the road, unwittingly allowing two young saps to acquire its content?"

"That's the one!" Ian said again as Bill began laughing in earnest.

"The only thing that could have made that day better would have been to have had one of those carts you see people pull behind their bikes—for their kids," Bill squeaked out between gasps for air. "It was sure a double-edged sword—joy over the find—then like leaving gold bars behind because we couldn't stuff any more in our shirts."

The two friends were roaring as Ian added, "At least not and be able to balance the damn bike."

"Yeah and have any chance of not getting spotted and caught, which as you'll recall—I DID!" Bill shouted as if it were Ian's fault. "Actually, I probably got greedy. But at least it wasn't until a few very fulfilling weeks passed that it happened. You know to this day I'll never forget my father's reaction," Bill continued, now regaining his composure and assuming a slight air of seriousness. "He was so angry. He called me down to the kitchen and said, 'Sit down William,' and as I sat down he placed this heaping plate of trash in front of me and told me to eat it."

"No way! You never told me that. What'd you do?" Ian queried of his friend, somewhat still laughing.

"Yeah, well, of course I wasn't going to eat it. But he just pushed and pushed in his condescending mild tone, 'Why aren't you eating, Bill? Why aren't you eating, huh?' Then he went on to explain that if I wouldn't put garbage in my body, that there was no reason I should be putting another kind of garbage into my mind."

"Wow!" sighed Ian. "That's pretty wild."

"Yeah, well. That's life with Don and Cindy," Bill retorted, then proceeded to turn the conversation to another topic. At the same time, Ian couldn't help but again think of his dad while Bill went on with his new story. He was so glad his own father wouldn't have belittled him that way.

❖

Two weeks later the workweek was broken by the Fourth of July, and a rare opportunity to convene a Wednesday "cottage party" the night before. In addition to the regulars—Ian, Bill, Kim, John, Kelly, "Scrappy" Anthony, and "Flaco" Curt—Matt was home that night and a modest stream of friends came and went as the evening progressed. The early-evening highlight, however, was undoubtedly Flaco.

He was in rare form, regaling the group with the details of the previous evening when he and Ian had gone out looking for fun. They wound up at the mall, in the Fredrick's of Hollywood lingerie store.

Rum 'n Coke in hand he stood by the edge of the pool to entertain all who were sitting in and around the pool. "Wait, wait, wait," he said holding his free hand in the air. "The woman at the store did not have a sense of humor. I want to make that very clear. It wasn't my fault."

"It never is," Matt interjected.

"Maybe it was because you didn't look good in women's panties," John heckled as the group chuckled.

"Oh you have no idea how close you are, John," Ian shouted over the group with eyes wide open. "Just listen."

"Hey, all I was doing was trying to find a gift for my girlfriend," Flaco said in his signature lisp, which was always accompanied by effeminate hand and body motions.

"You don't have a girlfriend," Kim pointed out. Flaco stayed in character and ignored her, which only added to his act.

It was vintage Flaco humor and everyone was enjoying it as usual. "And you know, you can't just look at those tiny undies on a rack and see really *see* what they'll look like on a woman," Flaco continued.

"No way?" Kim and Kelley shouted as the scene played out in their minds, their faces already red with laughter.

"Oh yeah," Ian said with raised eyebrows, "he grabs these tiny little panties and walks over to the three-way mirror, proceeds to slide them up over his jeans, then turns around, sticks his ass way out, and literally shouts across the rack to me in his stupid lisp, 'WOW—these things make *my* butt look good, just think how good hers will look!'"

"Yeah but the clerk didn't think it was very funny," Flaco added.

"Yeah but she wasn't quite sure if you were joking or not, so she didn't throw your ass out," Ian clarified. "And of course after taking them off, he went back and forth whether to purchase them—in his best gay voice—only to decide that he'd better wait until he *sells some more night crawlers* and can afford them." The audience liked that part. They were fully capable of picturing this comedian delivering that last twist with an absolutely straight face.

"She pretty much was done with me at that point," admitted Flaco with a chuckle. "It seemed a good time to get the hell out of there."

"But wait, there's more!" Ian shouted. "We go to McDonald's and this dingbat comes out with $5 more than he went in with," he continued, now with less laughter and even a slightly accusatory tone.

"Now listen," Flaco explained, "the girl says, 'that will be $2.75.' I put down a 5-dollar bill, and the next thing I know she hands me a five, two singles, and 75 cents. I say, 'thank you,' and move on."

"That is so bogus, Flaco," Kim yelled. "That's stealing from the poor girl. She probably had to pay that out of her drawer."

"No way!" Flaco responded. "As if that place can't afford $5. After all, what does a pop cost them, all of a nickel?"

"It is true that stupid employees are a cost of doing business," Bill added, ever the economist and businessperson.

"Shut up Mr. Young Republican capitalist," chided Scrappy.

"I can't believe you said that, Bill," Kim agreed. "Are you defending him?"

"No, of course not," Bill said, backing off quickly. "I'm just saying that it's a cost of doing business."

"Yeah, you better watch it Mister," Kim scolded, flirtatiously grabbing Bill by the collar and giving him a quick peck on the neck.

For his part, Ian was not thrilled with Flaco's actions on the change mishap. As he silently pondered the situation further, he acknowledged to himself that it wasn't that unusual. Often Curt was the life of the party, fully engaged in his Flaco persona, only to teeter up to and then cross a line that detracted from the humor of the moment. Sometimes his physical humor would include bumping into things or intentionally breaking them, especially if he'd been drinking. It was funny at times—Flaco's demeanor and feigned ignorance of what he'd done as he knocked over a display rack—but Ian sometimes felt guilty for laughing and encouraging him. Just as with most humor, it was a fine line between lightening up an otherwise far too serious world on one hand, and causing someone stress, loss or harm on the other—just for laughs or to catch the attention of a new love interest.

As for Bill's quasi defense of Flaco, Ian couldn't help but wonder just where his "young Republican" friend really drew the line on the incorrect change issue. He would later hear him further rationalize such dishonesty as the vendor "paying the stupid tax" for his lack of control and training. Ian knew Bill extremely well however, and that night if there were anyone whose ethics he would trust, it would certainly have been Bill's. The quick math was done in Ian's head and the thought was discarded.

✤

That Sunday night was one of the traditional movie nights for Ian and Bill. As usual, the conversation was a cross between work and social topics, and more serious fare that would ebb and flow in and out of the conversation.

"You sure you're up for this tonight?" Ian said to his friend Bill as he entered Ian's passenger-side door. "I'm not nearly as good looking as Kim. Wouldn't you rather be spending time with her? I know your ass would be out if I had a date with this Becky chick tonight." Bill grinned as Ian pulled out of his driveway.

Becky was the strikingly beautiful young woman Ian had met at the annual Fourth of July concert in Bronson Park, just three days earlier. Bill had been working, but the fortuitous connections Ian and John had made were already crystallizing into near-legend among the group of friends.

Ian, John and Scrappy had attended the annual event partly out of boredom, partly because Ian secretly enjoyed the pomp and circumstance of the patriotic event, but mostly in the eternal hope of scoping out pretty young ladies. While the fantasy of meeting a beautiful young woman, hitting it off, and returning with her and her friend to a "cottage party" had been beyond practical hope, that's exactly what had happened.

Early in the day Ian had spotted a gorgeous young woman who turned out to be accompanied by the cousin of their friend Curt, "Flaco." Captivated by her stunning blue-pastel sundress and her chestnut hair that flowed freely in natural waves, Ian hadn't even noticed their friend's cousin standing next to her. The guys had met Cindy on previous occasions at the home of their then-absent friend Curt, including a recent graduation party for the "Flaco" guy's older brother.

Led by John's congenial confidence and his own romantic interest in Cindy, a large-chested blond bombshell herself, the three friends had settled with the two beauties to watch the concert. Scrappy, by then largely indifferent, had been merely along for the ride.

Ian had been dumbfounded by the younger Becky. While certainly it was as if her figure was made for the form-fitting cotton dress, and together they would have fit perfectly on the cover of any fashion magazine, she also exuded an unassuming, natural, girl-next-door character.

Her looks were clearly attention grabbing and had provided the initial attraction for Ian, but she had a distinctly non-sexual appeal to him as well. Her beauty was in some ways akin to a spectacular sunset or some other captivating natural phenomenon. While Ian had reached an age where love could be intertwined with sexual arousal—evidenced by the fact that his trips around the ball diamond had been to all the bases except home plate—he had privately observed that the girls he'd cared most about had often been elevated in his subconscious to a level quite above sexual fantasy.

Like all boys, Ian subconsciously maintained a "spank bank," as years later he would hear a comedian call it—a collection of women and class-mates for whom his hormones raged as his late-night fantasies played out in his mind. But ironically, his girlfriends and the girls in which he was romantically interested had to that point been conspicuously absent on that list. He had put them above such thoughts.

Was this distinction evidence of Christian underpinnings that implied sex was so bad—that it was not something with which you would denigrate someone whom you honored? Or was it a normal adolescent distinction that evolved through the teen years, destined to evaporate as the post-pubescent years went by?

As they journeyed to their movie tradition that Sunday night, all Ian knew was that he'd had a powerful interpersonal experience with Becky. While the covergirl figure and accompanying bikini had certainly not been lost on him, he had experienced a strong connection with Becky as they sat for hours in the hot tub that night. The entire experience, including the exhilaratingly passionate kiss and scheduled follow-up date, was obviously on Ian's mind when he'd asked Bill if he would rather be with Kim.

"No I'm good," Bill replied. "I got to see her some yesterday and I know I'll see her at church Tuesday afternoon. We're packing materials for a mission group that's going to Haiti."

"Cool," Ian affirmed. "It sure beats hanging out alone at home on a boring Sunday night, which would have been the case for me again tonight—nobody around. Which reminds me, I mentioned to Janet that the movie takes place in 1955, the year my mom and dad met, and sometime when she's home I told her we'd drag her along. She couldn't tonight, but sometime."

"Absolutely," said Bill. "Just count me in. Besides it saves me from going to these mission support groups at church."

"I thought you said that was Tuesday?" Ian challenged.

"That's just this week. There's an additional evening because one group is leaving for Haiti Thursday; Representative Huxley is leading that one."

"The new congressional rep? Do you know him well?" Ian asked.

"Pretty well," Bill replied. "He's a super guy. Funny. Laid back. It's really kind of wild to see him on TV all the time, then sit behind him in church. I really do think we're lucky to have him."

"So why don't you like these mission evenings?" said Ian.

"I didn't say I didn't like them, it's just that sometimes the church stuff gets to me these days. Everyone is so . . . I don't know. It's like last week; this woman I was packing boxes with lost her pencil. She couldn't find her damn pencil, yet she went on and on as she was looking for it, telling me all about how God was probably testing her patience, and that He had moved the pencil," Bill said. "It's kind of like with your dad, and those who say that God will never give you more than you can handle."

"Yeah, I love that one too," said Ian. "Just try telling my mom that one right now. Dad's heart attack, then she loses her breasts to cancer, then loses Dad!"

"Yeah, but she's handling it right?" Bill intimated. Ian shrugged in response.

"What about Kim?" Ian asked after a few moments of quiet motoring—at least as quiet as a 1975 Gremlin with a shaky muffler can muster. "How's she doing?"

"She's good," Bill said.

"You guys stuck to that pledge still?" Ian asked, half-joking and half-prodding. For as close as they were, he and Bill didn't talk about sex a lot. In fact, none of his friends did, apart from crude comments and acknowledgments about hot chicks, what they'd do with them if they could, or other such juvenile exchanges. But when it came to what actually happened, there was a reluctance to comment in too much detail. Perhaps it was the gentleman factor, not wanting to kiss and tell.

"Yes we have, thank you," Bill answered sarcastically. "Though it isn't always easy."

"I know," said Ian, "that's exactly how I felt my freshman year when I was so hot and heavy with Mary."

"Man was she hot."

"I thought so too, and I'll tell you what Bill, she was naughty—in a very good way. But I didn't give in."

"No fucking way!" Bill shouted. "You never did it with her? Oh my gosh man. Your dick must have been broken."

"Listen to your mouth Mr. pledge-man," Ian countered while laughing.

Bill sat shaking his head, "No way. I just never imagined you didn't. I actually give you a ton of credit. That must have taken some willpower."

Ian nodded, eyebrows raised in confirmation.

"Don't you ever wonder what the big deal is, Ian?" Bill continued. "Now I'm not saying we're going to break our pledge, because we are not. I know about the diseases, and about the pregnancy, but it's not like Kim and I have ever slept around. And we would use precautions. But what is it about putting it in *that* hole that is such a huge, monumental deal to God and country? I mean, it's one thing if I get oral sex, or even if we lay together naked—"

Ian interrupted abruptly in a mockingly stern tone, "Have you laid together naked?"

"Yes. Shut up. My point is what's the big deal about putting it in that hole? Why does that change the world, change your status in God's eyes, move you from one phase of your life to another, part oceans and start wars? What's the big fricking deal? It's simply putting a dick in a hole—but not just any hole, cause that's one thing and this is clearly another. It's not like being a fag or something; I mean people in the Bible did have sex, right?"

"Oh my gosh are you wacked or what?" Ian exclaimed. "You know the answers to those questions as well as I do. Not that I totally disagree, but I think our parents would tell us it's a sacred act that has consequences, and those consequences still exist today. It's a God-given gift intended for the loving confines of marriage. If people ran around committing adultery the world would be filled even more with illegitimate children that people couldn't afford to raise, right?"

"I suppose. You just asked about the mission thing, and I think I'm just tired of it all. I had to listen to people tell me your dad's death was God's loving mercy and plan, but I think some of this stuff is bullshit."

"Have you talked to Cindy and Don at all?" Ian asked.

Bill stared at Ian incredulously as the Gremlin made the final turn onto Portage Road. "Have you *met* my parents?" he sputtered. "Everything is so frickin' black and white, I swear that it's amazing they ever had me and Thomas. But then again they live in a tidy, perfect little world where that's exactly how life was *supposed* to go, so that's exactly how it went."

"I'll tell you what, you could do a lot worse," Ian remarked, trying to brighten the tone a little.

"I know, Ian. I love 'em. But you know what I mean."

"Actually, I do," Ian had to admit. Much as he thought so highly of the Vanderveens, he never fully understood them. At the same time, he wanted to do right by Bill. "Have you thought about talking to your Pastor, Mike? He sounds like a good guy. I don't think you'd be asking him anything he hasn't heard before, and he might just have some thoughts that would be insightful."

"We'll see," Bill said, thinking for a moment, then changing the topic as they pulled in the theater. "So when is your date with this Goddess?"

"Friday night," Ian replied as the Gremlin came to a stop at the familiar site. "So how about we try this *Back to the Future* flick?" he grinned. "I hear the price is right."

Chapter 7

EARTHLY ANSWERS

"Representative Huxley!" Bill exclaimed, putting his best foot forward and shaking the rep's hand, "Are you all ready for the trip?"

"Hi Bill. You bet I'm ready. You know I keep waiting for you to join us on one of these. Next time you better just plan on it. It's a heck of a reality check—an experience that'll change your life. We manage to have some pretty good laughs along the way too."

"Interesting, Representative Huxley," Bill agreed. "Tell you what—I could probably swing it either over spring break or next summer. I'll mention it to Mom and Dad."

"Bill, there's just one thing. You'd have to promise to call me Dan. This formal thing gives me the creeps. The only thing worse is 'Mr. Huxley,'" the representative scolded.

"You got it, Dan."

The packing continued until nearly 9:00 p.m., and Bill had several more exchanges with Dan Huxley that served to impress him with the man even more. By all accounts he was a rare animal for an elected official—a man of integrity, candor and morals.

As the group of volunteers thinned out, Bill helped Pastor Mike return some materials to the church offices where they belonged. As they walked, Ian's suggestion came to mind; with Kim unable to be there, it seemed like a good opportunity. Bill said, "Mike, sometime when you get a chance, I've got some questions for you—some things I just haven't been able to make sense of, I guess. Would you be willing to give me your thoughts?"

"Bill you know I'd be more than happy to chat with you. Just name the time. What are you doing right now?" the young pastor asked, always cognizant that there can be more going on in the mind of a seventeen-year-old than meets the eye. "I told Sally I'd be out all evening, so I've got time if you do."

"Sure, if you're sure you're up to it," Bill agreed.

"Let's finish cleaning up, and I've got to say goodbye to a couple of the volunteers, but why don't we meet in the office lounge in fifteen minutes," the pastor said, and then he paused as if reconsidering. "Better yet, why don't you meet me at Big Boy in twenty minutes. I'll buy the ice cream."

"Deal," Bill confirmed.

Mike seemed very approachable to Bill, and Bill was honored that the head pastor would drop everything for him. He really liked Pastor Mike. Two years ago when Mike's longtime predessor retired, the church leadership had reportedly been somewhat reluctant to hire such a young head pastor. Nevertheless, Mike swayed them all, not only with his demeanor and obvious passion for Christ and for the job, but with his scholarly wisdom and command of scripture. No one was disappointed, and this was but a small example of the dedication and energy Mike put into growing the church. He didn't hesitate to stay late for Bill, when in fact he would have enjoyed going home to see Sally for a few minutes before bed. But that was the job, and Mike was happy to be able to impact people's lives. He considered it an honor to serve God, and have a job that was so fulfilling.

Bill drove to the Big Boy and Mike was just pulling in when Bill entered the front door, so he waited before being seated. It was a Tuesday at 9:30 p.m. and there was hardly a soul in the restaurant. That was great with Bill since he wouldn't have to worry about anyone overhearing them talk.

They sat and engaged in a little small talk, before Mike joked, "Okay, I've got my patented pastor book of answers to tough questions. Fire away, Bill."

"Thanks, Mike. I suppose there are two main areas I have questions about," Bill said, feeling much more comfortable than he thought he might when Ian first suggested talking to Mike. "The first is about the death of Bob Keppler."

"Good man. I know you were close with him and his family," Mike interjected.

"Well I have to tell you I've struggled with everyone saying this is part of a plan, that we have to trust God, and that there is a higher purpose behind this," Bill said candidly as Mike nodded sympathetically.

"Go on," Mike said.

"How can we really be assured that this is what God wanted? Somehow that doesn't make a ton of sense to me," Bill finished.

"First, Bill, let me thank you for asking the question. So many people are afraid to ask questions like that. I don't know if they're worried that I'll think they're not good Christians, or what; but secondly, let me tell you that my views might not be what you would expect in this regard. I too, believe that people should be very careful about speculating about God's intent and plan. Free will is a funny thing, and can very easily be misconstrued to believe that God *caused, willed, or wanted* certain things to happen. I think we are much too quick to claim something as an action, or inaction of God."

Bill interrupted with a question, though already he felt good about where Mike was headed. "Okay, but God is supposed to be all-powerful, and able to do anything he wants, so he still lets bad things happen. I've heard you say in sermons that allowing someone to believe a lie, and not correcting them, is deceit—same as lying. Doesn't letting evil happen mean God is a willing participant in evil . . . in a way?"

"Have you ever considered going to seminary, Bill? I see a bright future for you in philosophy and religion. So many times people think of pastors as narrow-minded, unenlightened, fearful people—and don't get me wrong, a great many are just that—but what you touch upon is the very essence of my passion for Christianity. I digress, but I'm trying to say that your questions are good, and I'm excited to get you started on a road to what I believe are solid Biblical, theological, and philosophical answers. There is so much good news down the road of your inquiry, Bill. But back to your question—"

"Okay gentlemen, what can I get for you?" the server interrupted.

"Hot fudge sundae for me," the young pastor said in his typical congenial tone, "and what for you Bill? It's on me."

"Same for me please," Bill said with a nod of appreciation to Mike.
The server thanked them, grabbed the menus and scurried away.

"Back to the point, Bill. You see what you ask is a very fundamental
question. This is complex stuff, so the answer I'm about to give will be
overly simple—which is often what people want or need. But just know,
the great scholars of the Reformation, and of all of Christianity and philosophy have poured their hearts and souls, and volumes and volumes
of books out on this very question. The great minds and prophets and
Popes, and everyone else, have debated the possibilities. Just know this
is one simple answer, from one simple guy, but that great minds have
solved this apparent puzzle up to and beyond my own satisfaction, and
my belief is that you can find peace, love and God even in the death of
your friend's father, sad though it is to us who survive."

Bill pondered his words, still awaiting the second half of his answer
to why God allowing bad things to happen didn't make him complicit
in evil.

"God is indeed all the things you suggest—all powerful, all loving, all
knowing; but that doesn't mean that people don't die, right?" Pastor Mike
began. "You see, God has to allow choice. There is no freedom if there is
not latitude for us to make choices, and besides, time is not to God the
same as it is to you and me. He can see beyond the bend in the space-time
continuum, he can see the past, present, and future, but he only judiciously
uses his power of omniscience because it is vitally important that things
have the freedom to unfold as they will. And in truth, it is a mistake to
attribute every action or *inaction* to God. Sometimes bad things can just
happen. Of course sometimes God could have ulterior motives, too—like
when people unite after a senseless drunk driving accident to prevent more
deaths, or when a firefighter inspires us through his selfless bravery."

"That makes sense to me—especially the time part," Bill explained,
"because I've never really believed God was restricted to our timelines . . . since
learning about Einstein and how time isn't even what we think it is."

"Exactly, but then people will say, 'Well what about evil? What about
the man whose child is stabbed by a madman? If God created everything,

and God was only good, then where did evil come from?'" Mike leaped ahead.

"Oh, you *are* good," Bill said with a laugh, acknowledging he'd pondered this question as well.

"The answer is that once there is freedom, or *free will* as theologians call it, that allows people to choose *not* to do good. That doesn't mean that God created evil, but rather, that evil is just a lack of goodness." Pastor Mike obviously wasn't patronizing Bill. He knew Bill had the mental faculties to be introduced to some of these important issues. Actually, Mike found it irritating when other pastors would talk down to their flock, or discount their abilities. Mike felt that doing so would let the tough questions go unasked, or worse yet, unanswered.

"Not totally sure I followed that. That sounded like a trick of language," Bill said, now fully comfortable with this game of learning. He leaned back, frowning skeptically. "Evil is just a lack of goodness?"

"Well let me impress you one step further, Bill," Mike continued with a joking smirk, "because I brought one of my favorite books in anticipation of these topics, by a man who wasn't afraid to ask tough questions, and who became a Christian as a result of his inquiry. His name was C.S. Lewis, and he wrote this book, called *Mere Christianity*."[4] Mike handed Bill the small book as he continued, "It was a series of radio addresses in England during World War II, but was later combined into a book. It's easy to read, and most importantly, it brilliantly articulates the basic Christian doctrine on many of these fairly advanced concepts, in a way that the real people of the day could understand. Take it. I think you'll like it."

"Thank you very much. Man, you *are* good," Bill said again, "but are you going to answer my last question, counselor?" He was clearly enjoying the pseudo-sparring with the pastor.

"Patience my son," Mike said with a smile. "You'll find it in there, but I believe C.S. Lewis says it this way, that you can do something kind even when you don't want to. Why is that, do you think, Bill?"

"Because you know it's the right thing to do," replied Bill.

"Exactly! Perfect. Because it is right. But Lewis points out that nobody ever did anything evil or mean just because it was wrong to do so. I think he summarized, 'Goodness is, so to speak, itself: badness is only spoiled goodness.' And from there he uses the example of sexual perversion, which he says requires the perverted one to first have an understanding of normal, healthy sexuality in order to pervert it."[5]

"I think that makes sense," Bill said, his head now feeling like an over-inflated basketball.

"Sorry that I've given you such a long answer Bill, but even my long answer is, as I said, way too short and oversimplified. This is why we study this stuff for life. I'm still learning every day—still praying for wisdom and guidance, and still reading and learning from the great theologians," Mike said as they both continued to deplete their supply of ice cream.

"I can't thank you enough, Mike," Bill said politely. "I'll look forward to reading C.S. Lewis."

"Great. But you had a second question didn't you?" Pastor Mike patiently asked as he finished a bite of his sundae. "Let's see, free will . . ." he paused as if pretending to think out loud, "must be the other question is about sex and sexual urges," Mike finished with a smirk.

Bill felt awkward again, but begrudgingly said as he put his arms in the air in mock surrender, "I give up. I've been outgunned." The two exchanged a chuckle.

"You're not a kid anymore, Bill. We all have urges. I'm not going to sit here and lecture you. But I will tell you that the book you hold in your hands holds a chapter on sexual morality, and I think it's a good starting place for you to find answers and reconcile what you might find contradictory—God's word, and natural urges. I know I have to sometimes check my own mindset as I walk by the photographs of women in the checkout aisle these days," he finished.

"Good thing I'm not the only one," Bill replied. "I'll certainly get into the book right way. Thanks again for everything." The two finished up with a handshake and went their separate ways.

The very next day, Bill dug into the famous C.S. Lewis book before work, and flipped straight to the sexual morality chapter. Of course, the book was linearly constructed, and built one concept upon another, so Bill would later have to start over at the beginning. It was just that a relatively frank discussion of sexual morality, from a Christian perspective, was urgently relevant to some of his struggles.

Immediately it hit Bill that C.S. Lewis was, especially for those times, pulling no punches. There were two choices. He said it was either marriage, with complete faithfulness, or total abstinence. Okay, thought Bill, nothing too new there. Bill kept reading.

But C.S. Lewis went on to acknowledge natural urges, and to take on the apparent contradiction in God's plan head-on, saying that he thought it was the human instincts that had gone out of whack. He introduced an analogy of sex and eating. Both had biological purposes, but when taken to an extreme the difference would be clear.

> It is quite true most of us eat too much: but not terrifically too much. One man may eat enough for two, but he does not eat enough for ten. The appetite goes a little beyond its biological purpose, but not enormously. But if a healthy young man indulged his sexual appetite whenever he felt inclined, and if each act produced a baby, then in ten years he might easily populate a small village. This appetite is in ludicrous and preposterous excess of its function.
>
> —C.S. LEWIS, MERE CHRISTIANITY[6]

Bill pondered that and continued to read as C.S. Lewis expanded upon the analogy with a pretend, allegorical story to make the point. He described seeing a civilization that worshiped food with pageantry not unlike an exotic dance show. Bill was starting to get the picture of excess that was being painted. He wondered if perhaps it was akin to the moderation that Ian and he had discussed seeing in the Kepplers. Again Bill thought of the role model of Bob Keppler. Certainly you wouldn't ever see Mr. K being over-indulgent in any way, including with food. Mr. K was a fit and lean man until the day he died.

Bill had another thought; as soon as he continued to read, he found this C.S. Lewis character had obviously not just rolled out of bed with these ideas unexplored. Bill had wondered if prudish repression of normal sexuality might actually be a cause of immorality and sexual immoderation. In other words, perhaps if we were more open about the realities, there would be fewer half-naked women plastered all over the checkout lanes, teasing and titillating. But Lewis quickly shot that idea down by pointing out that the increasing liberalization and sexualization of society should be resulting in more abstinence and less perversion than in pagan times, but that was obviously *not* the case, he argued.

Bill just sat and thought, then read the final part of the analogy that said even the wackiest of food-obsessions don't result in the perversion of food. On the other hand, "Perversions of the food appetite are rare. But perversions of the sex instinct are numerous, hard to cure, and frightful," said Lewis. Bill read on as Lewis continued to say that the "mess" of sexuality is not because it was hushed, but because it has not been silenced. "If hushing it up had been the cause of the trouble, ventilation would have set it right. But it has not."

Much as Mike had anticipated his questions, it was now apparent that C.S. Lewis had done so as well. Because just as Bill was starting to form some concerns that the Christianity being painted was anti-sexual, Lewis went into a long rationale of how Christianity in fact glorifies marriage and does not consider sex bad. At the same time, "There would be everything to be ashamed of if half the world made food the main interest of their lives and spent their time looking at pictures of food and dribbling and smacking their lips," C.S. Lewis' words continued. "There are people who want to keep our sex instinct inflamed in order to make money out of us."[7]

Bill pondered this further, then continued to read about the devil's liberal use of such notions as the normalcy of desire to lure us into unhealthy, unholy activities.

Then came the key point that would resonate with Bill, and that was the concept that our natural desires must be the subject of our efforts at moderation, simply because they would have to be controlled at some point anyway. Short of ruining our lives completely through obsession and idolatry, at some point we have to step up and harness our desires and control them. In fact, he argued, even total chastity was not as impossible as many had thought.

The concept of moderation ruminated in Bill's mind again. He thought of all the time he spent pondering things of a sexual nature, and determined that a noble goal would be to keep his desires in check—for all these good reasons as well as the health and disease issues he thought of most often.

Before Bill returned to read the book from its beginning, he took limited comfort in the end of Lewis' chapter on sexual morality. After a sobering diatribe, there C.S. Lewis argued the "center of Christian morality" was *not* centered on sexuality. In fact he said that while such sins were bad, they were the "least bad of all sins." Bill thought on that notion for a long while. To his mind, sins of the flesh were the biggest of sins, and the toughest to avoid. When someone spoke of morality, he immediately thought of sexual morality. *Why was that,* he wondered.

Though in the coming years Bill would in fact "backslide" a fair amount in his behavior, and continue to grapple with guilt over sexual desires throughout his college years and beyond, the book was of significant guidance and even some comfort to him. The comfort was especially in regard to the latter point, that sins of the flesh might be lesser sins, because in fact Bill would not maintain his virginity even through his senior year of high school. He had been sold on the ideal, but would continue to fall short of his high standards in that area, more often than not returning to find comfort in the belief that just because one is unable to attain a lofty standard of conduct, that failure does not negate the merit, goodness, or moral superiority of that standard. Indeed he held high the ideal of controlled desire, or even chastity.

By the end of that "summer of '69," Bill had successfully survived the challenges to his faith brought by Bob Keppler's death, and by his struggles with sexual morality; and as a result, he was reinvigorated in his quest to grow in his faith, and in his knowledge about his Lord and Savior, Jesus Christ. It would not be until many years later that Bill would be again forced to critically examine his moral beliefs and Lewis-styled rationalizations.

❖

After a week of mowing his lawn and those of his customers, and helping Janet at the store, the night of the big date arrived and Ian anxiously found his way to the Parchment address of Leo Panerello. The directions Becky had provided were perfect and he pulled the Gremlin into the driveway a few minutes early. The home was an attractive ranch, not large but very well maintained. As he walked toward the front door a glimpse into the garage revealed the mechanical elements for the pool, and he could hear the familiar hum of a filter pump. He passed up the garage entrance in favor of the narrow sidewalk to the front of the gray-sided home.

Ian could hear activity inside the home through the open windows. He proceeded to knock gently, and almost immediately the door opened to the sweet face of the petite Mrs. Panerello.

"You must be Ian," she said in a kind, somewhat nasal-sounding voice that fit her small stature well. "Please, come in. I'm Becky's mother, Elisa," she welcomed.

"Hello Mrs. Panerello, it's nice to meet you," Ian greeted. He had just stepped into the home when a dark, unassuming man in his early forties wandered into the room.

"Ian, please meet my husband, Leonardo," Mrs. Panerello said in a jovial tone.

"Pleased to meet you, Ian," greeted Becky's father. He was also small in stature, and was a good-looking man. He had a deep suntan; a leathery appearance to his hands, face and neck; a thick six o'clock shadow; and was wearing a pair of old jeans with a white, v-neck t-shirt.

"Let me go get Becky for you," Elisa said in a soft-spoken, energetic style that calmed Ian's nerves substantially. He had been nervous about meeting the Panerellos and trying to earn their confidence, but he sensed that the parents were excited for their daughter. Ian wondered if perhaps it was her first formal date, and some nostalgic sentiments were attached for her parents.

"Sit down. Make yourself at home," Becky's dad said as he motioned Ian to follow him into the adjacent family room, where the TV was on and large, comfortable looking leather sofas were the only sign of opulence. The house was warm and had a lived-in feel. It reminded Ian in many ways of his own home, decorated with mementos, family photographs, and special touches of a clearly feminine influence. One difference was a crucifix, which reminded him of Anthony's house.

"Becky said you own a plumbing company?" Ian inquired.

"Yeah, well, it's just my nephew and me, but I've been in the trade for over a quarter century; wouldn't dream of anything else."

"Can't ask for more than that," Ian said as they sat on separate, squeaky-leather couches. The two engaged in small talk, but at no time did Mr. Panerello ever play the role of an interrogator. Quite the opposite, he seemed exceedingly genuine. What you saw was what you got, and Ian always liked that in anybody.

"Hi Ian, sorry to make you wait," Becky said as she breezed into the room. She was even more beautiful than Ian had remembered. Her long, chestnut hair had been curled and fell in beautiful long coils that accentuated her olive skin perfectly. Her fresh lip gloss and imperceptible makeup accented her natural, model-like attractiveness. Ian couldn't help but think that if it weren't for the casual, form-fitting jeans, she would be every bit presentable at the most luxurious of events. She was stunning, but in an approachable and almost naïve way.

"No problem at all, it's great to see you," Ian replied, standing to greet her.

"Daddy, did you scare Ian to death?" she asked facetiously, not the least concerned.

"Yup, but I was just about done with the fifth degree on this one, so I'm heading to find your mother and see what she wants to do for dinner." Becky's dad rose nonchalantly from the leather sofa. "Very nice to meet you Ian, hope to see you around again." Leo shook Ian's hand before leaving the room.

"You hungry?" Ian asked.

"You bet. Let's go," Becky replied enthusiastically, reaching for her purse.

They arrived at the Final Stage restaurant and Ian was greeted by the familiar host. It was a movie-themed restaurant located next to the only true multiplex in town, at a local strip mall about fifteen minutes east of Becky's home. The restaurant was dimly lit in order to accommodate the movies shown continuously on a projection screen above the second-story loft.

With the happenings of the summer, Matt, Ian, Janet and friends frequented the place. Strangely, in a series of events that later Ian couldn't quite remember, Janet had come to allow him the occasional glass of wine beginning that summer—something the staff must have either been instructed to allow, or perhaps plausibly assumed that since Ian's family and friends were often adult, that he too must have been twenty-one. In any event, Ian wouldn't have dreamt of ordering alcohol on his date with the sweet young beauty.

While Becky seemed nervous for the first few minutes, it didn't take long before they were mentally right back in the hot tub, chatting about everything from pools and summer, to Mr. Panerello's work and plans for the future. As before, Ian would intuitively note that his feelings and sensations were not the same as he experienced with Catalina, but the human connection was similarly exhilarating, refreshing and comforting.

Despite the movie after dinner, all too soon it was time to head home. They pulled back into the driveway at the house just past 10:00 p.m., and Becky turned to Ian, her sweet and stunning beauty drawing his attention. "Would you like to come in for a couple minutes?"

"Oh, I'd love to . . . but it's after 10:00, is that too late? The house looks dark," Ian replied.

"My parents said you were more than welcome to come in afterward," Becky assured confidently. Given their earlier reception, Ian agreed. Besides, he really didn't want the night to end.

The two entered the home through the garage to find Becky's parents watching TV in the family room. "Well hello you two. How was the evening?"

"Great," they each replied.

"What'd you do?" Becky's mom asked.

"We went to the Final Stage for dinner, then went and saw a movie," Becky replied, *"Back to the Future.*

"It was *really* good," Becky said sincerely. "Ian had seen it before but he thought I'd enjoy it," she continued. She looked directly at Ian as if they now had a shared secret. They did, actually, only the secret wasn't that a friend let them in free, because they had gone to the big multiplex instead. No, the secret was that Becky understood the comfort of the Sunday tradition with Bill, and she understood a great deal more about who Ian was, and where he was mentally and emotionally in that fateful summer.

"Well good, I'm glad you enjoyed it . . . . Listen, we were just headed back for the night, so the room is yours," Mrs. Panerello declared. Mr.

Panerello caught the hint and slowly grabbed his nearly empty glass of lemonade. He said good night again and the duo departed the room.

"I sure hope we didn't kick them out," Ian apologized to Becky.

"No, not at all. They always go to bed early and watch TV. Guess my older siblings trained them that the house is ours after ten," she laughed. Ian was again struck by the trust placed in him by relative strangers. Sure, in retrospect he would see that they had talked with mutual friends and discovered Mr. Keppler's respected status in the community, but Ian still appreciated the vote of confidence.

Though Becky's parents had said they could stay up until 11:30, they watched television together until just before 11:00. Ian then suggested he'd better head out.

"My parents said we could stay until 11:30," Becky offered, but Ian didn't want to overstay his welcome with them or with Becky.

The two rose to walk to the door and Ian couldn't help but arrange for another date shortly thereafter. His mind was leaping ahead to when he could see her again.

Ian stepped down to the recessed entry to the garage, and then turned to thank Becky again for the evening. He found himself eye-to-eye and face-to-face with his alluring new friend, and there was no question in either of their minds about what to do next. Their lips met in a long, deep kiss as they pressed their bodies together in a heartfelt embrace. Again the butterflies twittered in Ian's stomach as sparks of adrenaline fired throughout his body.

As the weeks went by, that evening would serve as a kind of template. Sometimes they'd break from the routine and go out with Bill and Kim when their work schedules would permit it, but most often they would go out to the Final Stage, take walks around Becky's neighborhood, or even spend time chatting with Becky's parents, who had taken a real liking to Ian.

As that pivotal "summer of '69" wound to an end, there was a final memory that would be synthesized into Ian's bittersweet recollections of love, loss, faith and hope, and Mr. Panerello would forever be incorporated into it. In the fall, Matt would be returning to school and Ian and Janet would be alone in the big old house, often running in separate directions. As a result, Janet was receptive to Ian having more reliable transportation than the old Gremlin. He knew just what he wanted; Ian had fantasized for some time about a sporty red Toyota pickup truck.

Janet even offered him a modest contribution, but it took some convincing for her when Ian suggested a brand new truck with an actual loan. Of course the truck of his dreams had been the decked-out Toyota 4x4 in *Back to the Future*, but that was not a realistic option.

A little two-wheel drive utility truck was just the ticket, and Janet agreed to co-sign for the loan. She was confident in his ability and commitment to pay the monthly installments, which were relatively small after his down payment and her modest contribution.

As with most purchases, there was an emotional payoff beyond the rationalized motive of reliable transportation and establishing credit, and that payoff wasn't only to Ian. To Janet there was something rewarding about seeing her son so thrilled after the events of that summer of '85, perhaps as if it were a parting gift, given vicariously from Bob through her. She knew she couldn't remove Ian's hurt, but it was a glimpse at new hope and excitement for both of them.

When it came time to pick it out, Mr. Panerello was a great deal of help. He'd run trucks for years in his plumbing business and had many pieces of advice for Ian, from bed liners to rustproofing.

For Ian's part it surely didn't fix anything, but he was extremely excited about the truck. The first thing he did when he pulled it off the lot was drove directly to the cemetery, where he knelt by his father's gravesite. As always in those early days, he wept as he sat looking at the name on the stone. On that day he reached down and traced the raised, bronze letters on the monument. He was excited to show his father the truck, but told him he would gladly trade it for even one more day together.

As he pulled away from the cemetery, he again felt the sense that time was suspended, and that a chapter of his life was coming to a close.

Janet had been with him at the purchase, of course, so the next stop was the Panerellos, to show Becky and Mr. Panerello the new little truck. Mr. Panerello couldn't have been nicer. He was genuinely excited for Ian and generously dispensed advice about washing, waxing, and maintenance.

As for Becky, she was proud and thrilled as well. They would share many more of their special evenings together, tooling around in the little

Toyota, her simple and unassuming countenance—her patience and kindness—fostering a friendship that Ian would long treasure.

In the scheme of things, the truck was merely the icing on the bittersweet cake that was the summer of 1985.

Ian and Becky developed a strangely adult, yet innocent relationship. In looking back, it would later become interesting to Ian that their relationship stayed decidedly non-sexual, despite their age, hormones and Becky's stunning figure. They certainly experienced passion, long evenings of holding each other, sensual kissing and surely arousal, but for whatever reason the irony that helped define that summer played out in this way as well.

Ian had found a true friend, a confidant. There were multiple occasions where a sad movie or a discussion would hit a raw nerve—the kind that only those who've suffered recent loss can fully understand and appreciate. It was a guttural pain that spared no sense of pride or self-respect when ushering tears from the eyes. And without question, Becky was there to hold Ian and be that one special person who was best able to comfort, console, and love him in the way he needed to be loved. While Becky was clearly flesh and blood, in some ways Ian secretly wondered if she was a third angel, sent to care for him during that bittersweet summer.

Time marched forward and eventually, as with all things, the summer of '85 ended. In ways Ian had wanted it to, perhaps in the way the people that age always look ahead to the next phase of life; but in other ways he wanted to remain in the gray area that summer provided—the freedom of young adulthood, without the day-to-day grind and responsibilities that he knew lay ahead. In some ways he wanted life to go on in the wake of losing his father, but in others he did not.

To the long list of ironies, it could be added that the same event that strengthened Ian's faith, had tested Bill's. By the time the summer had ended, however, the two had come to a stronger faith—but by very different paths. Bill's path was primarily philosophical, while Ian's was clearly more experiential. Nonetheless, the paths would not remain parallel or static, as the bulk of the inevitable surprises, excitement, wonder, and trauma of life remained ahead.

As for Ian and Becky, the romance would last through the fall and into the next winter, before winding down. They were different ages and had different interests, and for everything there is a season. In short, Ian was transitioning to college, while Becky rightfully had a high-school experience still owed her.

Though their time together had been deeply meaningful to Ian, he would see Becky only two additional times in his life, both within a couple years of their breakup—which was mature and amiable beyond either of their years. But thirty-two years later Ian would see an obituary in the paper. Mr. Panerello had passed away at the age of eighty-three, of a heart attack.

A smile would come to Ian's face as he remembered Mr. Panerello's kindness, and the companionship Becky provided him during that "summer of '69." Had she known what her kindness had meant to him, Ian wondered. Words would fall short, but he would then take a pen from his dress shirt and hand write a note, wishing her the same peace, companionship and love that a certain young beauty had extended to him during the summer of 1985.

Chapter 8

LOVE IN THE WINDS OF CHANGE

Seven years later—June 1992, Chicago, IL

The radio chatter between pilots and controllers was rapid-fire, a non-stop string of curt statements whose purpose was safety and efficiency before cordiality. Ian patiently awaited a step-down to a lower altitude, but he knew that the Chicago TRACON controllers were unusually busy this morning, and that being rude or impatient was not at all a good plan. Perhaps more importantly, a professional pilot demonstrated mastery of this complex system by not standing out unnecessarily. Slowly he was learning the subtle turns of a phrase or nuanced requests that could earn a pilot a brownie point or two with overstressed approach controllers. At that point Ian's primary aim was just to stick to the business of getting his passenger to Meigs Field—the executive airport on Chicago's downtown lakefront.

"United 1435 Heavy cross three-zero miles southwest of Peotone at or below one-five thousand."

"United 1435, roger, three-zero southwest Peotone at or below one-five thousand."

"American 1520 descend now to one-one, eleven thousand, traffic two o'clock, four miles will be crossing opposite direction one-zero thousand."

"American 1520, out of one-three for one-one thousand."

Ian finally heard a two-second hole in the chain of instructions and readbacks and lodged his request, quickly but clearly saying, "Three-four-bravo looking for lower when able."

Instantly a voice barked back an approval, "Centurion three-four-bravo descend now, maintain three thousand, intercept the localizer inbound 31-Center. Hold readback. Break. United 1435, descend now maintain eight thousand, contact approach 134.75."

"United 1435 down to eight and 134.75, see ya," replied the United captain in a deep, smooth voice.

"Centurion three-four-bravo, go ahead with readback," the controller barked after having dealt with the urgent handoff of United 1435.

Ian responded without hesitation. "Three-four-bravo descending to three and established now on 31-Center localizer."

Though he was a relatively low-time pilot, he'd had good fortune in his final year of college and was actually doing some real flying for hire, unlike many of his cohorts from Western Michigan University's aviation program who were either not flying, or were making $8,000 a year instructing only a handful of students at some podunk airport. Not that Ian was making much more money, but experience was everything in aviation, and single-engine, high-performance airplane hours were like gold. Though he'd taken a bit longer to graduate because of all of his supplemental flying, he viewed it much like the internship Matt was completing in medicine.

"Three-four-bravo would like to cancel the IFR and proceed to Meigs," Ian succinctly stated into his headset as he emerged from the bottom of the stratus cloud layer blanketing Chicago on that Monday morning.

"Three-four-bravo squawk 1200, frequency change approved, good day," the controller replied before immediately barking another instruction to yet another aircraft.

Ian proceeded to contact the local tower controller at Meigs, and zipped up the lakeshore for a straight-in approach to runway 36. As always, the approach to the little executive airport was a thrill. It was exciting to be able to fly beside the buildings and right along the lakeshore, with a magnificent view up the streets of Chicago.

The sole passenger of the plane was the airplane's owner, Tom Hanson, who was busy enough with his growing enterprise that he'd abandoned attempts to stay proficient with his piloting skills. This demonstrated not only prudence on his part, but dedication to his business. Also to his credit, Tom's pilot experience made him an understanding passenger when faced with landing and weather delays; Ian had heard too many stories from other pilots about walking the tightrope between safety and irate executives hell-bent on making it to a meeting.

Within moments, the Cessna T210L Centurion was on the ground, taxiing past the old firehouse and toward the municipal terminal building—still served by one small airline.

"So Ian, are you still staying here in Chicago with your friend 'til Wednesday?" Tom asked.

"Yes, if that's still good with you?" Ian replied.

"Of course—it's a win/win. Saves me a buck or two and you get spending money," Tom laughed.

One of the airport line attendants grabbed wheel chocks and fluorescent wands to direct Ian and Centurion 34B to a tiedown spot on the ramp. As soon as Ian ran the quick shutdown list, Tom jumped out, saying, "Plan on 3:00 p.m. Wednesday unless I leave you a message otherwise. Thanks, Ian. See you then." And with that, Tom strode briskly across the wind-swept tarmac and inside the terminal to catch a cab. Ian stayed to secure the airplane and perform a post-flight inspection to ensure no maintenance was needed prior to departure.

Ian couldn't help but pause and think that a full seven years had passed, almost to the week, since he had lost his father and ridden in that C210 with Joseph Martin and his brother Matt. Little did he know he'd be flying the same model plane into one of the busiest airspaces in the nation, just seven years later.

Ian presumed his father would be proud. He had worked extremely hard, especially during the previous two years. He aced several of his FAA written exams with perfect scores and had ridden in the back seat with anyone he met around the airport who would let him watch and observe. He had soaked up stories, information and real-world experience from the old salts around the airport, in addition to his studies and flight training. And after finishing his curricular certifications—Private Pilot, Instrument Pilot, Commercial Pilot, Flight Instructor, Multi-engine—he had added an Instrument Flight Instructor certificate on his own, to further add to the ways he could gain valuable flight hours and earn a better living.

The exact job goal was still unclear, but would likely include either airline duty, or work in a corporate flight department. For where he was on the career path, Ian was delighted with his progress. He walked off the tarmac still thinking of his father.

Ian entered the terminal to register and make fuel arrangements. It was a beautiful, stately building with terrazzo floors and an executive air of hustle and bustle. After registering and taking care of business, Ian headed to the pay phones to check his messages.

Ian dialed the number and punched in his codes, only to be surprised to hear he already had two messages—still before noon, Michigan time.

"Hi Ian," he heard his mother say in a tone of voice through which he immediately sensed a subdued mood. "Honey, I wondered if we could talk or have supper when you get back. I have something I need to talk with you about. I think you said you would get back Wednesday, so I know it's short notice, but if you could plan on dinner Wednesday it would sure be a help to me. I need your opinion. Call me if there is a problem; otherwise just call when you get in, or head to the house any time. Be safe, Ian. I love you . . ." his mother's voice trailed almost imperceptibly.

Ian thought to himself that Wednesday would work, even though the week was crazy between work, visiting John, getting his book for a final summer-term class he needed in order to graduate, and getting his tuxedo for Bill's big wedding on Saturday. At the same time, the message from his mother continued to puzzle Ian.

He proceeded to listen to the second message. "Ian, it's John! I'm so geeked that you're coming to stay tonight and tomorrow. It's a shame I can't ride back to the wedding with you in the plane—but it'd be a long walk home. Oh and I have to work. Hey, when you get in, I left a key for you with my doorman. Well, he's really a superintendent, but that's beside the point. He'll let you in. Make yourself at home pal. Rest up. We'll go out tonight. Can't wait to see you and catch up."

Ian laughed to himself at the concept of going out on a Monday night. But then again, he had explained that they couldn't drink on Tuesday night because he had to fly on Wednesday afternoon. But as for that night, this *was* Chicago—home of Rush Street. What choice did they have but to head out on the town?

Ian grabbed a cab and found his way to John's Lincoln Park apartment building, where he located the superintendent and before long was up in John's unit. The place was surprisingly tiny to Ian, who was used to relatively spacious Kalamazoo apartments and rental housing. The studio was composed of a little galley kitchen; one room that served as a dining area, bedroom and TV room; and a bathroom; but Ian quickly found himself romanticizing about city living, and found the urban bachelor pad held great appeal to him. After all, it was close to the amazing array of offerings the city lent to a 24-year-old: parks, beaches, bars, jobs . . . and babes.

After a little walking through the neighborhood to check things out and snag some lunch, Ian headed back to John's apartment to await his friend's arrival. He turned on the little black-and-white television. It was an old set with rotary dials, which didn't really matter anyway because John didn't have cable. Ian proceeded to turn through the channels until he happened upon an interesting TV talk show—one of those with a live audience in the studio.

There was a young Asian man standing with the host in front of a small table, on which was located an open phone book. Ian listened intently as the host dramatically introduced the man, who claimed to possess mystical powers and the ability to move things solely with his mind. He indicated that he had mastered the use of the "90% of the human brain that goes totally unused."

That phrase captivated Ian. He had long wondered about such untapped potential of the mind. As a pre-adolescent kid, when he couldn't sleep he used to ponder similar concepts and even relate them to healing and to faith. He had heard many people argue that it was a lack of faith and belief that blocked our access to hidden mental powers. That concept made a great deal of sense to Ian. There was even a time when Ian convinced himself that if he could truly believe, and trust with every fiber of his body, he could actually *walk on air.* He postulated that it was his lack of faith and

his indomitable doubt that precluded success. To Ian, this notion of faith
even explained Jesus' ability to walk on water—he could do it because
he had perfect faith.

Though he wasn't able to recite or remember the passages, Ian
had certainly heard people quote Matthew 17:20; and John 14:12–14,
respectively:

> *And Jesus said unto them, Because of your unbelief: for verily
> I say unto you, If ye have faith as a grain of mustard seed, ye shall
> say unto this mountain, 'Remove hence to yonder place'; and it
> shall remove; and nothing shall be impossible unto you.*[8]

> *And whatsoever ye shall ask in my name, that will I do, that
> the Father may be glorified in the Son.*[9]

Who was to say that these things weren't possible?

The setup for the demonstration continued with the young man painstakingly concentrating on the phone book, and holding his hands in the
air above it and to its sides. It almost appeared that he was measuring the
energy forces of the phone book. After a couple more minutes of intense
study and focus, the Asian man lowered his eyes and hands to within a
foot of the book, framing a perfect shot for the television camera. Low and
behold, Ian watched with fascination as one of the pages to which the book
was opened, actually began to quiver! It was barely perceptible, but it was
moving! Suddenly the page jumped to life and sprang with such energy that
it flopped over, exactly as advertised. This young man had turned the page
of a phone book using only the untapped mental powers of his brain!

Ian was intrigued. He sat pondering what he'd just seen, but his thought
was interrupted by a twist. The talk show host invited another guest to
join them on stage. The new guest's name was James Randi, a man who
looked familiar to Ian. He was small in stature, wore glasses, and sported
a flowing, snow-white beard that Ian knew he'd seen before. Suddenly it
hit him. Ian had seen "The Amazing Randi" on other television shows,
particularly the *Tonight Show* with Johnny Carson—both in his capacity
as a world-renowned magician and escape artist, and also as a leading
investigator of claims of paranormal abilities.

With his knowledge of magic, The Amazing Randi had become the preeminent debunker of cons, frauds, soothsayers, illegitimate faith healers, fortune-tellers and similar purveyors of "bunk." Ian previously had been intrigued by the demeanor and integrity of The Amazing Randi, and sat back as the host invited him to verify the amazing feat they had just witnessed, while it was repeated.

James Randi was polite as he methodically explained how one might test such a claim of superior abilities. To illustrate the point, Mr. Randi said that it was necessary to ensure that air was not being used to *blow* the pages over. He sought to ensure that no simple, explainable, and natural forces could be at play before anyone leapt to conclusions that were more dramatic, or awarded the Nobel Prize to the young man for his amazing new discoveries.

To ensure the veracity of the man's claims, Mr. Randi sprinkled a couple handfuls of shipping peanuts—those very light and fluffy pieces of foam—all around on the table next to the phone book.

Ian sensed that the trial was going to be entertaining; he cracked a smile as inexplicably, despite intense concentration and gyrations, the young man was completely unable to move the phonebook pages after all.

Ian had mixed sensations. His bubble had been soundly burst; after all, he had been excited to see something demonstrated that he genuinely thought possible. At the same time, he was impressed and appreciative of Mr. Randi for interrupting what he quickly saw to be his own gullibility.

Not too long after, his old pal John arrived home from work early to greet his friend. "Ian, my man!" John exclaimed as he entered the apartment. "How goes it?"

"Excellent! This place is awesome," Ian replied as they shook hands. They had remained in touch throughout their college years, so apart from catching up on details of daily life, the relationship felt no different from when they'd gathered for "cottage parties" over a half-decade before. In many ways they were like brothers, and with Matt away in Los Angeles finishing his surgical residency, Ian probably had more contact with John during college than anyone else—especially given the inherent fun of road trips to the big city.

The duo caught up over a burger and beers at a local restaurant, then headed to a Halstead area sports bar, and ultimately down to Rush near

Division—bar central. Ian couldn't help but be amazed at how many people were out, even on a Monday night. Then again, it was summer and the weather was perfect: warm but not stifling.

As they walked, Ian thought about this new phase of life. He couldn't help but think that while college had been fun, and offered its share of adventures, in many ways post-college life was looking much more promising.

As the two friends rounded the corner and headed into *Mother's*, the bar made famous by a couple of 1980s movies like *About Last Night*, Ian sensed hope and excitement in the air. The bar was jammed, but they were fortunate to find a couple of stools at one of the tall, round tables not far from the dance area. The throbbing music made it difficult to talk and hear, but the spot was ideal for people watching.

Ian spotted her almost immediately. Not entirely unlike his beloved travel companion Catalina in appearance, an adorably cute, yet totally unpretentious young woman left her group of friends from the table next to Ian and John, and navigated her way confidently through the mass on the dance floor to the DJ, and engaged her in a brief conversation. Ian's eyes remained glued to her as she then headed back across the floor to her friends. She appeared a little bit older than Ian, perhaps just due to her comportment and demeanor. Her short blond hair was indeed very similar to Catalina's, clippered in the back and naturally straight in front and on top, with a part that allowed the longer side to bounce attractively near her perfectly positioned, high cheek bones. She wore a cute, almost teenish miniskirt, black tights underneath, and what could only be described as a "bandana jacket"—a jean jacket that had the pattern and appearance of a red bandana.

Over the following several songs he would routinely glance in her direction, trying not to be too obvious. She reminded him of a character in a movie he'd seen recently. It hit him; he must have had a real attraction to blonds with short hair, because he had been intrigued by Mary Stuart Masterson's portrayal of the grunge, punk sweetheart who got the guy from Leah Thompson in *Some Kind of Wonderful*. Masterson would go on to star in *Fried Green Tomatoes*, and Ian always remained an admiring fan of her characters. In fact it was her ability to play the sensitive sweetheart, hidden beneath a jesting, tomboy character that seemed to fit Ian's impression of this young woman so perfectly.

"Ian, what have you latched onto?" John said. Answering his own question by following Ian's eyes to the table behind him, "Oh, she's a cutie. Wow, and there is more where she came from." John was referring to the table of seven young women who, similar in ages, was conveniently located just a table away.

While the young blond in black clothing had an urban appearance, and John wore a fun, dark, almost Hawaiian shirt, Ian stood out like someone from, say, Kalamazoo. He sported a white golf shirt with white tennis shoes that almost glowed beneath his boring 1980s jeans—not a particularly hip, urban outfit. Despite this, the woman made casual eye contact with Ian on a couple of occasions, glancing away almost immediately after their eyes met.

Ian's attention was clearly engaged. In addition to her obvious attractiveness, she seemed naturally at home with herself, unassuming and easy going in her interaction with her friends. Ian had to figure out some way to approach her. His chance arrived a few minutes later when she was standing with one of her friends, not far from where he was half-sitting, half-standing. As if jumping off a high-dive, he suddenly found himself standing and turning toward her without thinking.

"Has anyone ever told you that you look like Mary Stuart Masterson?" Ian ventured.

Her adorable face turned to his and Ian got his first glimpse of her green eyes. In a good-natured, sparring tone that was every bit what Ian expected, she quipped, "Literally just about a week ago a guy came up to me in a bar and told me that." She smiled sweetly as she delivered the line in such a way that Ian didn't feel rejected, but the lack of originality was made clear—even though to some degree her answer validated the resemblance between them. "Good thing I love Mary Stuart Masterson then, huh?" she added reassuringly. "I'll take it as a compliment."

"I'm Ian," he offered, extending a hand.

"I'm Samantha," she returned, just as one of her friends from the table interrupted.

"Sammy, who you talking to?" asked a more inebriated woman at the table. It was apparently a rhetorical question since the gals all laughed, made a ruckus that was audible over the music and noise of the room, and then continued talking among themselves.

"That's my friend Tammy. It's her birthday today so we're out celebrating," Sam explained.

"Looks like you've got some catching up to do," Ian joked.

"Don't think so," she replied as she took a demure sip from her bottle.

"So where are you from?" Ian asked.

"Originally from Iowa, but moved to Naperville at eleven and have lived downtown for about five years."

"No kidding? Do you know the Burlington twins, Sarah and Stephanie?" Ian asked. He intuitively sought quick connections with people. He also believed in the "six degrees of separation" theory, that any person on earth can be connected to any other through only six steps of acquaintance.

Sam looked surprised, "Oh my gosh, I do know them! How on earth do you know Sarah and Stephanie?"

"No kidding? That's a huge school! I can't believe you know them! Their parents are old high school friends of my parents," Ian explained.

"Small world," Sam said, looking Ian in the eyes with a probing stare. She was intrigued with Ian, and this thread of mutual friends lent him even greater legitimacy. They continued to discuss the uncanny connection with Sam's former classmates, before Ian explored further.

"What do you do?" Ian asked.

"I work for a marketing agency downtown," Sam said. She quickly added, "Nothing glamorous though. We help stage trade shows and expos, and I'm a project manager who helps manage the events. What about you?"

"Kalamazoo, over across Lake Michigan. I'm a pilot."

"Like for an airline?" She eyed him mischievously. "That might explain the white shirt, even in a Chicago bar."

Ian grinned, acknowledging the slam. "No, just starting out. Just finished college—well, actually I have one more class this summer. I'm freelancing for a small company that has a high–performance, single-engine airplane. Nothing glamorous," he added, echoing her. "But it's challenging and it's a good opportunity."

Amidst all the noise and the focus it took to maintain conversation, Ian didn't even notice when John left the table for the dance floor. Just as in the park so many years ago when Ian had met Becky and John connected with

Flaco's cousin, he never had to worry about John failing to fit in socially. John was clearly heading out to make some new friends.

"Don't mean to steal you away from your friends," Ian said as he motioned to the increasingly raucous group of inebriated young women, "but would you care to pull up a stool?"

"Why not," she replied.

"So can I ask you how old you are?" Ian asked.

"Twenty-seven," she replied.

Somehow the self-sufficient, unassuming aura fit a slightly older woman; Ian had glimpsed an authenticity and genuineness that he identified as scarce in girls his age, at least based upon his college dating experiences.

But there he was, looking at a woman who seemed to him to have it all. She was self-confident, yet not pretentious or arrogant. She seemed witty, was very attractive, and yet she just seemed . . . *real*. It didn't take but a few minutes and Ian was seriously interested in Samantha. He actually thought to himself, "I can see myself sharing a lifetime with a woman like this." Intuitively he felt she was the type of woman with whom he could have an authentic relationship, void of manipulative, petty or jealous interactions.

On the other hand he'd learned enough to know that often people create a fantasy of what a person is like, only to find that they entirely blame the object of their initial affection when that person behaves outside the fictional constructs of that fantasy. Ian was aware that this strong force could be in play. He also knew he ran the risk of being influenced by "beer goggles," since by that time he'd been drinking at least somewhat continuously for several hours.

As the evening progressed, however, the two talked about everything and anything. It reminded Ian of the candor that came when two people had nothing to lose, just as he had experienced on that magical flight with Catalina back in 1985. Perhaps it was an age thing now, or even a desire on both of their parts to avoid mistakes of previous relationships, but again nothing was taboo or out of bounds. They discussed old boyfriends and girlfriends, their family relationships, Bill's imminent wedding, friends, jobs and career plans, and even somewhat matter-of-factly discussed their dreams for children and family.

At the same time, the conversation was never overly emotion-laden, philosophical or political. It was just authentic and real—which of course still didn't mean both weren't experiencing the rush of powerful attraction to each other. Most certainly it was the unmistakable tingly feeling that is unique to new love.

For her part, some part of Samantha's down-to-earth demeanor was correlated with a belief that the best way to avoid disappointment was to avoid believing something *good* could also be *true*. If it was good, it was "too good to be true." In other words, if she didn't get excited, she wouldn't be disappointed. Sam was trying to be pragmatic about the butterflies in her stomach; at the same time she loved the feeling and figured she should bask in the perception of reality, even if her mental snapshots of future events were unlikely to play out.

She knew in her heart, however, that she was riveted to Ian. His eyes and face were sincere, and his almost too innocent, good-guy personality—complete with white shirt—was an overwhelmingly strong fuel for her unfolding daydream.

Sam's eyes and her plush, full lips—underscoring her elegant and striking, yet subdued and understated appearance—grew entirely too intense for Ian to resist. Compelled beyond his usual path of moderation and propriety, he leaned over and touched his lips to Samantha's, delicately at first, then more passionately in a French kiss. It didn't last long, but he felt as if it contained his soul.

While it didn't show on the outside, Sam was extremely surprised by the move. At the same time it played out even better in reality than in the self-indulgent fantasy that had been flashing through her mind.

A few minutes later, during a lull in the conversation, Sam uncharacteristically returned the favor. This time, Ian was taken by surprise. No question, he was hooked. And if there were any doubt left in Samantha's mind, the DJ jumped to the slow song she had requested, Basia's *Time and Tide*, which began with the words, "I've never felt like this before." What a prophetic request she had made, long before any connection with Ian. Coincidence? *Not a chance*, Sammy thought silently.

It was at that point that Ian's alcohol consumption most played a role in how events would unfold. Never in a million years would Ian be the slick, playboy type. He had in fact only had sexual intercourse with one woman in his life; but then again, to frame coming events in sexual terms would be an injustice. Those old lines dividing genuine caring and sexuality may have faded since the days of his youth, but all Ian knew was that a powerful voice was telling him the night should not end.

"Can we go back to your place?" Ian asked in an unheard-of leap of faith and courage, somewhat fueled by alcohol. Sam's mind raced. She characteristically reminded herself that this couldn't last; it would only be a one-night thing. She had never had a one-night stand, but this felt too right to not savor. It had the makings of a beautiful memory and experience, even if it was just a lovely vignette, or a fleeting taste of bringing fantasy into temporary reality.

She looked Ian deeply in his eyes and somewhat matter-of-factly grinned and answered, "Sure," in what was an equally daring *leap of faith* of her own.

✤

Kalamazoo, Michigan

"Hi sweetie, I'm here!" Megan shouted as she entered the quaint little ranch house. "Bill? Where are you?"

"Hey, I'm in the office," Bill answered, referring to the tiny bedroom that now contained his desk and a personal computer.

"Well, your fiancée is here—soon to be your wife." Megan wore a seductive smirk as she hustled in the room to hug and kiss her betrothed. "Can you believe it honey? After all this time I'm going to be Mrs. Vanderveen," she bubbled, giving yet another quick squeeze.

"I'm a lucky, lucky guy," Bill said. "Not only because I'll have the absolute best, hottest, sexiest wife in the world, but also because all of this wedding planning is finally over, and now we get to enjoy the fruits of our labor."

While the cliché that men don't care and don't help in planning weddings may be rooted in general truth, it was certainly not the case for Bill Vanderveen. Then again, he was marrying Megan Huxley, and this was to be a wedding fit for royalty.

Generally, Bill was not one to get nervous. This was the guy who despite being "iced" by two timeouts, hit the game-winning free throw in the

district basketball finals his senior year. But *this* was BIG! Representative
Huxley was a player in Washington D.C., and the guest list reflected it.
Some of the most important people in the world would be there. One of
the members of the powerful Ways and Means Committee of the House
of Representatives would attend, as would two other representatives from
Congress, a state senator, and another seven hundred of their "closest"
friends and family.

"How did we get so lucky to find each other?" Megan asked.

"Angel, I have no doubt about the answer to that. We were doing God's
work together, and I believe he brought us together to continue to do his
work—oh and to have great sex," Bill added as a joke, but it was obvious
there was significant anticipation surrounding the wedding *night*. This
was certainly understandable in light of their successful commitment
to abstain from intercourse throughout their courtship. Bill was to be
Megan's first.

"You are so bad, mister," Megan cooed, flashing a seductive look
back from her sparkling blue eyes to his. She was indeed a thing of
beauty—blond, blue-eyed, stunning figure, and sweetness to match. In a
way quite different from the independent-minded Sammy, Megan was still
down-to-earth and unassuming as well. There was a purity of spirit and
an overwhelming aura of kindness and peacefulness about her, stopping
just short of an aura of piety. These characteristics diminished what would
otherwise have been a stunning sensuality as well. Far from homely in
her dress and style, "conservative" was a better description.

It was during the mission trip after Bill's senior year that Megan caught
his attention. Certainly Bill had seen and met her before then, but there
really hadn't been a connection until they spent those weeks together
in Haiti. In part that disconnect was due to her relative youth—she was
a couple years younger than Bill, but there had also just been a dearth
of opportunity to spend quality time together. Bill had noticed her
around church, but by the time of their mission trip she had grown into
a lovely, classic blond beauty with whom he felt a great chemistry, and
for whom he felt quite an attraction. And while he fell for her for reasons
far beyond physical appearance, he couldn't help but regularly notice her
magnificent figure, no matter how appropriate the hot-weather apparel
that she wore.

As for the marriage, it seemed unlikely that Representative Huxley would have endorsed his daughter's marriage at such a young age were it not for the very high regard in which he held Bill. Even then, he had insisted that Megan finish her associate's degree, which she had done. She was now a licensed dental hygienist, working for a local dentist. Meanwhile Bill had finished his master's degree in electrical engineering at the University of Michigan, and had landed a great job back in Kalamazoo. The last six months had been chaotic, and had recently included the purchase of a small starter home in which the two would live after they were married.

Needless to say, life had been a blur for both of them, but especially for Bill: a home purchase, moving, graduation, wedding planning, and a new job. Luckily he had negotiated two weeks off for the wedding and honeymoon, even though they were without pay.

NALA was a large manufacturer of medical supplies and instruments. They went public back in 1987, and now in 1992 were a darling small cap of Wall Street. The sales job was a coup, but then again Bill had earned it. His long track record of high standards, extreme persistence, and mental acuity had continued during his college years at U of M. Some of his dorm mates had affectionately called him "AM," as in "Mr. All-American," due to his perfect everything—looks, grades, personality, and even piety. At the same time several of them couldn't help but be a touch jealous.

This is not to say, however, that Bill was a goody-goody. He and Megan broke up three times during the six years since they connected during the mission trip. The last one was early in his first year of grad school, and lasted only a couple months; but during those couple months he sowed some wild oats—something he'd done during the previous breakups as well. Truth be told, that final breakup was the result of his admission that he had cheated on Megan. It was an indiscretion at a beer- and pot-filled party.

Bill was crushed by his weakness and lust for a beauty who had tried to seduce him many times before. There were other exploits he never admitted to Megan, but those were fair game during their times apart. They were indulgences that while not up to his high standards of moral conduct, were at least committed with the belief that the relationship with Megan was over. But all of that was behind them now. Bill's life had come to perfectly fit the picture "Mr. All-American" had always envisioned and expected.

That Tuesday, with the rehearsal dinner looming just three days away, and the wedding Saturday, Bill and Megan were rightfully proud of their discipline. They had a deep, trusting, and spiritual connection. They would be husband and wife soon, and both were giddy with excitement.

"Did you ever hear back from Flaco?" Megan asked.

"Yeah, actually he finally returned my call at the office today. He's not coming, which I guess I expected. I guess I was just hoping anyway. All we can do is pray for him," Bill said.

"I'm sorry sweetie," Megan consoled.

"Lord knows there will be plenty of loving friends and family there for us, who also support us in our faith," Bill said, seeming to assure himself and relegate the issue to the back burner. There was too much else to worry about besides their friend's plight as a "Moonie."

Flaco's departure from the University of Illinois to take up with Reverend Sun Myung Moon's infamous Unification Church was a shock to Bill's worldview that ranked second only to the death of Ian's dad. Ever since Curt had left, at the end of his sophomore year at Illinois, the whole situation had gnawed at Bill.

Ian and Bill always knew Flaco had a great heart. In retrospect they suspected his antics and borderline callousness were all about the attention. He loved people and needed love and attention in return. In college at Illinois he had met a great many people who were different from anyone he knew back home. He also had learned about a world he hadn't known. His roommate was Iranian and had regaled him for hours with tales of the revolution under Ayatollah Khomeini. He had learned about the slaughter of innocents by U.S. forces at Mai Lai during Vietnam, and about various religions—of and about which he'd never even heard.

At least to Curt's mind, there had been a lot of expectation, a lot of sense that the world was changing and hopefully progressing. He'd felt that there was a probable sense that he could help make it better—help solve the world's problems. With a background of rather relaxed religious upbringing, Flaco had gone back and forth between ideas of atheism, where there was just plainly no God, and a sense that there was something greater out there—something special.

He had begun actively searching. It was a pretty nice time of his life thinking about those things, and he'd met somebody from the Unification Church; this young lady had introduced him, little by little, to some of the doctrines and teachings. Flaco was intrigued.

But it wasn't really until Curt had gone to the seminar, what they called a "workshop," that he was totally sold. It was a two-day, weekend program that was a very steep indoctrination and immersion into the culture and teachings, the culmination of which was a profound experience that included certain belief that Reverend Moon was the new Messiah. He was going to unite and save the world.

From then on there really had been very little to think about, very little choice in Flaco's mind. It was just a matter of tossing everything in his life, joining up and doing what the group taught. That had included mastering the process of recruiting and proselytizing, sometimes for sixteen or more hours a day. As a result, communication had been difficult for Bill in his efforts to procure Flaco's attendance at his wedding.[10]

Despite Bill's desire to see Flaco again, and a remote fantasy that he could talk some sense into his old friend if they could just sit in the same room and talk, the reality was that there was no way Flaco was going to come to the wedding. Flaco, the guy Ian and Bill had known and loved, was gone; and Curt, the "Moonie," had commitments that far exceeded the importance of attending Bill and Megan's wedding.

"So is Ian taking you out Thursday night for a 'Bachelor Party?'" Megan jibed, air-quoting the phrase with curled fingers.

"Why, are you worried?" Bill joked.

"No, I'm just trying to keep you out of trouble," Megan returned, but in truth a part of her was worried.

"Worst case scenario is that I see what I've seen at the beach before," Bill said teasingly.

"No! You are such a jerk," Megan shouted as she slapped him on his arm and laughed half-heartedly. Bill really didn't know what was planned for Thursday, but he didn't want to rule out any traditional bachelor activities. At the same time he knew where the lines were, and had no intention of getting in any trouble.

Thankfully Megan interrupted with a question. "Do you really believe that we will stay together for the rest of our lives, Bill?" she asked him. She knew the answer, but it never hurt to seek reassurance.

He looked her in the eyes and confidently, wholeheartedly replied, "You are absolutely the perfect soul mate for me. I hope you know how grateful and happy I am to have you. I do not believe that our connection was coincidental. I think there was a force greater than us that brought us together and I intend to love, honor, and cherish you so long as we both shall live." He assured her as he stood with her, holding her tight then pecking her on the lips with a gentle and loving kiss.

"I love you sweetie," she said. "It's just so overwhelming that after all this wedding work and planning we are about to commit to a forever thing. Doesn't that scare you even a bit?"

"Absolutely not, gorgeous," he said, and he kissed her again—this time much more deeply and longer. He then continued his thought as he looked her squarely in the eyes. "This really is a covenant with God you know. I know there will be tough times and things we can never predict, but I want to embrace that unknown with you, and by your side. I am going to stand up on Saturday and make that covenant with you and with God, in sickness and in health, for richer and for poorer, and pledge to be faithful and love only you, forever—until death do us part. And I will be so incredibly thankful and grateful that a sweet, beautiful, perfect woman like you is willing to have me, that I have no idea how I'll get the words out." He started to choke up at the thought.

"Shut up and kiss me good," Megan said with a tear in her eye. As always, Bill knew what she needed, and he generously gave her that, and more. And it was genuine. He loved her.

"Oh and that richer or poorer thing," he said, "is going to *richer* if I have anything to say about it."

Chapter 9

Prophetic Connections

Chicago, Illinois

Ian awoke at 6:00 a.m. to the sound of an alarm clock, and sleepily opened his eyes enough to see Sam roll over and silence the dreadful machine. She rolled back toward Ian, coming face-to-face with him. Butterflies took flight again in Ian's stomach when the reality struck him that not only was she real, but she was even more attractive than he'd remembered in the dim light of the bar and the darkness they shared upon returning to her apartment.

They'd had a beautiful night. Uncharacteristically for each of them, they'd gone straight for the futon bed, but had lain talking in the dark for at least another hour, punctuating the conversation with intermittent kisses and increasing amounts of caressing and cuddling. Ian was intoxicated by the softness of Samantha's skin, and the way their bodies fit together as they talked and loved.

Although they physically satisfied each other and thoroughly basked in each other's naked presence, ironically neither pursued intercourse despite no obvious reason not to do so. Perhaps in a way it had been a vestigial sign of that adolescent respect Ian had for true love, or a subconscious indication to Sammy that it was so much more than a one-night stand. In any event, Sammy's mind still held no hope that the loving exchange would be anything but a fantastic, fleeting memory soon afterward.

"Good morning. How you feeling, champ?" Samantha wisecracked, knowing Ian had consumed a fair amount of beer.

"I'm actually pretty good," Ian said truthfully. "But I gotta tell you that you're even more beautiful than I thought."

"You must still be drunk," she said as she rolled out of bed. "Sorry to report that I've got to go to work," she added as she knelt back down onto the floor-based futon mattress, facing Ian, "but you're more than welcome to hang, sleep as late as you want, grab some food or whatever."

"Thank you, Sammy," Ian said with sincerity as their eyes connected and he pulled her closer for a kiss, "but it's early enough that I should get back to John's so I can touch base with him before he heads to work."

They kissed once more before Sammy got up to ready herself for work in the nearby bathroom of the small apartment, which was similar in size to John's. Ian got dressed and waited for her to emerge from the shower. Wrapped in only a towel for modesty's sake, Samantha said goodbye, and Ian assured her he would call her soon. As she shut the door behind him, Sam paused, reluctantly assuring herself it was the last she would see of Ian. Nonetheless, she watched him through the peephole, her heart straining as he walked out of sight.

After the quick cab ride back to John's, Ian was thankful he still had the extra key the superintendent had given him. Nonetheless, John was still there and was up and awake when Ian tapped gently on the door and then entered the tiny apartment.

"There's the stud himself," John quipped. "You dog, I can't believe you went back to her apartment." Ian could only smile in response. He was tired but he was one happy camper, and he had a grin to prove it. "So, my friend, you *are* going to kiss and tell."

"Just hold on there, Tonto," Ian jokingly persuaded. "It wasn't like that. Well, okay, it was kind of like that—oh my, was she hot—but it wasn't really like *that*."

"No way!" John laughed. "Don't even try to tell me that it was some meaningful thing that transcended the petty fucking that the rest of us enjoy," he further ribbed Ian.

"Absolutely right, my friend," Ian said.

"You are too much."

"Hey seriously though, thanks for the nod. I really didn't mean to bail on you last night—that was not my intent at all. I really appreciate your easy-going nature, man," Ian said sincerely. "I just really clicked with this chick."

"Buddy, you know I'm happy for you—you piece of shit," John replied. "I want to know your secrets."

Ian laughed. "Yeah right. Believe me; you don't need any help . . . . What's the plan for the day though? And by the way, I'm buying dinner tonight," Ian said.

"I'm up for anything. Probably can't do lunch, I apologize, but plan on meeting back here—" He paused. "No, meet me out front of my building at 5:30. Let me give you a card with the address and we can just stay downtown. Cool with you?"

"Sure."

"What are you doin' for the day?" John asked.

"Don't know. Maybe go to the beach and run, then just hang out. I'll be good."

John put on his tie and headed out. Ian enjoyed some quiet time running on the beach boardwalk at Fullerton, then returned to the apartment for a much-needed nap. Though occasionally his mind would wander to his upcoming class, his flight planning for the trip home, the big wedding weekend ahead, or his mother's request to talk—oh and the unpleasant thought of how she would disapprove of his previous night's activities; in the end his thoughts kept returning to Sammy.

Feeling well rested and more energetic, Ian found himself arriving characteristically early outside the building where John worked. He spied a bank of telephones and figured it was worth a try.

Ian pulled the business card from his wallet and flipped it over to reveal Sammy's home phone number. It was early, but he punched in the numbers. The phone rang without an answer. He knew it wouldn't take more than six rings to reach the phone in her small apartment. He hadn't wanted to call her at work, but now was tempted. After all, if you're working past five it's probably appropriate to get a personal phone call, isn't it?

He dialed again.

"Hello, this is Samantha Hitchens," the voice said.

"Hey is it true that you love dogs?" Ian asked, referring to a portion of their conversation.

"Hi Ian, what a pleasant surprise," she said, immediately recognizing him. A rush of adrenalin filled her bloodstream.

"Do you have a quick second? I hesitated to call you at work," he said tentatively.

"Yes, absolutely. My boss is cool. Anyway, I was just packing things up to head out, what's up?" she asked, not wanting to appear too eager.

"Well I'm out with John tonight—not drinking I might add—and I have a hot date with my mother when I get back tomorrow so I didn't know if I'd have a chance to talk with you for a day or two, and I wanted you to ponder something," he said in a big, nervous mouthful of words.

"Sure. What?"

"Well you know I told you I had a wedding to go to Saturday, right?"

"Yes," she said as a tiny adrenaline aftershock hit her brain.

"Well, I have this problem. It's my best friend's wedding and I don't have a date. I wondered if you would consider coming to Kalamazoo and helping me out."

"You're not serious," she replied in her typical even-tempered tone, yet jumping up and down on the inside—abandoning briefly her rules about not getting too excited. "Well, I'd . . . love to but . . . you know I don't have a car—"

"No, no," Ian interrupted. "Kalamazoo is right on the Amtrak line and I could get you at the train station. I know you'd have to leave early to make the rehearsal, but it's okay if you could just come for the wedding on Saturday."

She smiled and bit her bottom lip in excitement, pausing momentarily to think. "Let me do this. I've been neglectful of etiquette and my safety already, and you didn't ax-murder me or anything. Let me check with my boss about getting off Friday afternoon; but yes, I will be your date."

Ian was delighted. "That is so awesome! You'll have fun, I promise. And you already know John, and my mother will be there so I won't stick you with a table of blue-haired ladies, I promise," Ian assured her, which only made Sam start to think about all the implications: meeting

Ian's mother, the wedding, not knowing anybody—at least not for longer than five days.

"Ian, are you sure about this? You really need to have your attention on your friend and your duties—this is a big formal deal isn't it? You do realize we can get together any time?" she suggested.

"One thing anyone will tell you about me, Sammy, I think things through pretty thoroughly. If you can bear with me through some obligatory formalities, I'd sure appreciate having you—not because I need a date, but because we'd have fun."

"Well then, you have yourself a date," she replied.

"Okay, I'll call you tomorrow after dinner with my mother, if it's okay if I call you a little later."

"Sure, any time. And . . ." she paused, "you're sure?"

"Absolutely," Ian said.

After they said their goodbyes and hung up, a rush of near panic set in for Samantha. Was this too fast? Was she crazy to put herself under the pressure of attending a big wedding? She was definitely outside her comfort zone. "Oh, shit," she actually exclaimed aloud. She realized that nothing in her closet was going to come even close to being appropriate. But then again what better place to find one's self during such a crisis than the Magnificent Mile? Not that she was prone to expensive clothes or shopping, but this was an emergency worth a little credit card action.

Ian noted the perfect timing. It was 5:30 exactly. He made the short walk back to the traditional old building in which John worked, and met up with him almost immediately. The two walked several blocks, looking at options for dinner.

As they walked Ian said, "You'll never guess who my date is for the wedding."

John looked perplexed for a moment, then exclaimed, "Oh my gosh. You really have gone nutty for this girl. Tell me you didn't track down the girl with the boy haircut and ask her to the wedding?"

"Sorry, can't tell you that, John," Ian said with a smirk.

"That is unbelievable. Well what the hell—good for you."

"I promised her I wouldn't stick her in a corner for the night though, so you have to help me make sure she has a good time and doesn't feel like a spare tire on an 18-wheeler, okay?"

"Absolutely," John replied.

Rounding the corner onto Walton Place, the old friends found a pub that had the right balance between atmosphere and wallet-drain, and sat down in a booth away from the bar.

"Sure you can't have just one?" John ribbed.

"Yup, I'm sure," Ian replied.

"Yeah, no wonder you waited until tonight to buy," John jabbed.

Their second evening was a great cap-off to the visit, filled with discussion of the big upcoming wedding, and punctuated by occasional digs about how quickly Ian had fallen for Samantha.

In hindsight, however, there was no way that any of the three—Ian, Samantha, or John—could possibly have known the life and death significance of that brief visit to Chicago, of Ian and Sammy's connection, or even of the location of their meeting. In some ways the poignancy would be evident immediately, but as is often the case in life, the real significance would be clear only with the passage of time.

✣

Bill and Megan arrived at the Huxley home for dinner, and for a final organizational meeting before the wedding. The home was not only magnificent, but it was located on a sprawling, divine estate on the east side of Gull Lake. While virtually any home on the lake was fetching many hundreds of thousands of dollars, even the tiniest shacks, most were in the millions. For southwest Michigan, that was real money. But even more to the point, this large inland lake had its own version of the "haves" and the "have-nots," and the old-money "upper east side" was definitely for the "haves."

The home was much like one you would expect to see in a movie about a classic, old-money home in the Hamptons, or even a majestic, southern estate. Perhaps the Huxley home wasn't quite as large, and the opulence not quite so obvious to the eye, but it was something to see nonetheless.

The babbling of the fountains escaped Bill's attention as he stepped out of the car, thanks in part to the giant oak trees that were waving noisily in the warm summer breeze. The majestic old oaks appeared as if they were taking pride in their work, blocking the sun over most of the two-and-a-half acres of perfectly manicured, soft Bentgrass.

The home was indeed worthy of a spread in *Better Homes and Gardens*. There was even a bar in the boathouse, perfect for serving small, intimate gatherings, or as a refuge for men who sought the sweet smell of cigars with their brandy and politics. Of course with all the effort put into the wedding, Mrs. Huxley had seen to it that the home was prepared for the flurry of people that would be in and out over the weekend.

"Good evening my soon-to-be-newlyweds!" greeted Mrs. Huxley as she strode out to the driveway to meet Megan and Bill. Though she had spent a significant part of the day working on the flowerbeds and gardens, she was now cleaned up, primped and ready for the final, pre-wedding dinner with her daughter and Bill.

"Hi Mom," exclaimed a jovial Megan.

"Hello my Mother-to-be" greeted Bill as the group exchanged polite, heartfelt hugs and kisses.

"Wow, do you know something I don't?" quipped the affable Mrs. Huxley. The three chuckled at Bill's unintentionally humorous line as they progressed into the spacious front entryway.

"Hey, good evening!" welcomed Dan as he emerged from his study. "How are my favorite betrothed?" The group repeated the hug and kiss greetings, which even included an embrace for Bill from Dan.

"We're great, Daddy."

"Excellent, Sir," Bill exclaimed, still feeling tension about the event, but starting to feel like the time had arrived to enjoy all their work and preparations.

"Well, Sir," Dan returned in a mocking usage meant to acknowledge the sincere, but unnecessarily formal greeting from Bill, "I'd suggest we pour some wine." The group headed to the kitchen as the chatter between Katherine Huxley and Megan began. "I have a funny feeling, Bill, that we guys may have a tough time getting a word in edgewise tonight."

The reality about Representative Huxley was that he didn't amass his political power by being a backstabbing jerk—though he had discovered there were a few in Congress who probably had. In truth, all but his most fierce political opponents revered him and considered him a man of integrity, down-to-earth and approachable.

There were many ways in which the Huxleys didn't fit the stereotypes of their grand home, their wealth, and their increasingly powerful standing—both locally and on the national stage. But again, and as Bill had seen and learned, it was Dan's integrity, approachability, and skilled diplomacy that were significant factors in his political success.

The Honorable Daniel Huxley was a man who genuinely cared about doing what he believed was right. While reasonable people would certainly disagree about what defined "the right thing," and certainly that was true of Dan's political adversaries, he had earned great respect from many people, including Bill.

Dinner proceeded after Dan offered a somewhat lengthy blessing, and the conversation was largely consumed with last-minute details about the wedding—in particular the events of the rehearsal dinner and the gathering at the Huxley home planned for Sunday. It would be a gift-opening party, and a chance for family to see one another the day after the wedding. Always the overachiever, Bill was the picture of involvement, flexibility, and earnest execution of any task thrown his way. Of course the truth was that he would have preferred to stay in bed Sunday to have more sex, but he was appreciative of the lengths to which the Huxleys had gone to throw such an extravagant event, and knew Sunday was part of the deal.

After dinner Dan suggested that the soon-to-be father-in-law have a drink with his soon-to-be son-in-law in the boathouse. The women seemed all too happy to avoid the political banter, which Bill thoroughly enjoyed. Megan grew up with all that and while not ignorant of political matters, it simply didn't interest her. It wasn't that Megan didn't care about the world around her; quite the opposite was true. At heart she was a genuine, caring, even motherly type, but her personality was simply too reserved to be suited to politics. Besides, she was more interested in making sure everyone got along than focusing on aggressive deliberation or conflict. To her, that was something that men did; and in her mind, she was happy to have it stay that way.

"So how is this Ross Perot factor going to play out?" Bill asked the moment they were away from the women, walking down the brick-paved path to the boathouse.

"Wow, I sure wish I could tell you," Representative Huxley replied. "Who would have ever thought we'd have a three-way tie going in June, right before the elections. Then again, 'right before' is an eternity in politics, so I'd say that anyone who thinks he can tell you how this will turn out is crazy."

"There is something to be said for Perot's plain talk," Bill expressed. "It really does seem to be resonating with people I talk to."

"No question about it, Bill. In a funny way, Ross Perot is *out-Republicaning* the Republicans. There is a very strong desire to 'throw the bums out.' People are mad as hell. They're mad at George Bush for going back on his pledge not to raise taxes, they're mad at the deficit, and they're mad about the overall trends in society—drugs, illegitimacy, abortion; and yes, they're even mad about family values, no matter how much crap they give Dan Quayle about Murphy Brown. Thank God the Dems just don't understand that in national elections, people vote conservatively every time."

"That's right," Bill agreed vehemently, his head nodding up and down.

"But unfortunately, so far we Republicans have failed to show them how and why our approach is better. I've been pushing awfully hard for a more aggressive and articulate George Bush, but so far Lee Atwater and others just aren't getting it."

"I saw that your fellow Democrats in the House went on the budget offensive this week," Bill commented.

"Yeah, you gotta just love that, don't you. Natcher and Fazio's little staged drama. That was the first time in 127 years that the Appropriations Committee has ever held pre-budget conversations in a public press conference. The sad part is that the little stunt will backfire because once again, they just don't get it."

"I thought the same thing," Bill jumped in. "Their solution to everything is to raise taxes and spend more. Clinton has said he wants to provide health insurance for *every* American."

"Exactly right—you have a future in politics, I'm telling you, Bill," Dan exclaimed. "You're exactly right because they cry and cry about the budget issues and the deficit, and yet their prescription will provide exactly the opposite of what they say it will. No country has ever taxed its way to prosperity."

"You know, I took economics back in high school, and essentially repeated micro and macroeconomics at U of M, and I'll tell you, I couldn't agree more. If the government's goal is to raise income, what people don't get is that the only way government gets money is if someone earns it, or money changes hands. So the way to get more money in the government's hands is to have a strong economy. You don't do that by raising taxes—even on the rich. Everything else should be secondary to encouraging more turns of dollars in the economy," Bill said.

"And you have just said succinctly what George Bush cannot seem to utter. And here we are working in Congress, as we speak, to repeal this absolutely silly luxury tax that was passed. Why?" Dan asked rhetorically, now agitated. "Because just as we knew it would, that tax cost real factory workers their jobs. It was a brilliant idea to 'tax those damn rich people when they buy airplanes and yachts and cars,' but nobody seemed to remember who builds those airplanes, yachts and luxury cars. Real people build them, and those real people have become increasingly unemployed and everybody knows it. We'll pass this repeal by the end of the month—despite the Democratic majority."

"Yeah, the Democratic majority that they say is going to grow this fall, right?" Bill added.

"Yes, right. We'll see," the representative said, pausing for a drink.

"So does Clinton have a chance?" Bill pushed.

"Well in politics anything can happen, and this Ross Perot thing is a real problem because inside polling data show that he's taking votes away from Bush. Did you see there was a piece in our local paper here by Jim Nesbitt, saying that John Silber's failed Massachusetts gubernatorial bid could be the model of Perot's downfall?"

"How's that?" Bill asked.

"Because at some point the strong leaders like Perot and Silber are so autocratic and authoritative that they're really sons-of-bitches to deal with, and the public figured that out with Silber. Voters really have to know that in addition to 'damn the torpedoes and full speed ahead,' you have to have the ability to listen to others and lead effectively."

"Good point," Bill said with a nod. "I could see that playing out."

"But then you've got the moral issues to look at. The Democrats seem to think the solution is gays in the military, more abortions, everybody smoke pot and do anything you want. The Democrats are running this draft-dodging, pot smoking Bill Clinton from Arkansas—not to underestimate his smarts however, because this guy *is* good. George Bush should own the social issues and morality, and he does, but he's sure taken heat on this Murphy Brown 'family values' thing. He's a genuine WWII hero that people always say they admire in polls; unfortunately, with the success of the Gulf War now a distant memory, he needs to take charge and remind people what he stands for."

"I see that Clinton is now happily staking the moral high ground by taking on Sister Souljah for offensive lyrics," Bill observed.

"Boy, I tell you, son, just quit that day job and come work for me," Dan said, slapping Bill on the shoulder.

As he sat chatting global politics with Representative Huxley, times were good for Bill. He was about to marry the girl of his dreams, he could talk high-level politics with a member of Congress—who was also about to be his father-in-law, and he had a high-paying job with a rapidly growing firm. Indeed the story of his life was playing out just as it should—at least so far.

Dan Huxley continued, "You're exactly right but his base isn't going to go anywhere; he can afford to grandstand for a while. In the end the Hollywood left will just take one for the team. They know he's their guy. Same thing with the minorities. Clinton has their vote."

"No question," Bill concurred.

"The wildcard is still this Perot character. I wouldn't be a bit nervous in a two-way race, but I am concerned as long as he's in it. By the way, I see he's trying to play it both ways: doesn't want anyone to be discriminated against, he says, but then says he wouldn't want the controversy of having a gay in his cabinet."

"What's with that?" Bill asked.

"That, my dear son-to-be, is called pandering. Even straight-talking Ross Perot does it. But the reality is that he knows as well as you and I know that you can say what you want, but society does not benefit from standing back and ignoring the clear fact that homosexuality is wrong . . . I mean, I don't want to sound like Jimmy Swaggart or anything, and I'm certainly not a perfect person, but right is right. But the Dems have gotten us in a position where you can't say that publicly anymore. It's just not the 'politically correct' thing to do. But that doesn't mean it isn't the gospel truth."

"Couldn't agree more," Bill echoed. He leaned back, elevating his glass in agreement. Life was good indeed.

In Bill's mind, both his success and the clear path on which he found himself—moving quickly toward his high-achieving, perfect, All-American dream—was unfolding smoothly as the direct result of his own efforts. If more people could just see the interplay of faith, hard work, and dedication, Bill was convinced that everyone could have exactly what he had—and was going to have. Nothing but blue skies lay ahead.

But if Bill could have seen that future, he surely would have admitted that rarely in life would answers ever again be so self-evident, clear and simple as they were that weekend, at the age of twenty-four.

Chapter 10

FAITH AND FATE

"That was a nice landing out of that crosswind," Tom Hanson complimented as Ian taxied the single-engine plane and performed the after-landing checklists, properly configuring the plane for ground operations. Ian dropped Tom at the executive terminal, then returned the plane to the hangar, post-flighted it, and hurriedly lowered the big hangar door. Having lost an hour due to time change, the late afternoon flight from Chicago made Ian have to hustle to reach his mother's by 6:00.

Ian made the trip home and discovered an extra car in the driveway as he arrived; he wondered whose it might be. It wasn't abnormal for extra joiners to grace the Keppler dinner table on Sundays, but the exact nature of this mid-week dinner request was still a little unclear. Ian shut his car door and entered the side door of the old ranch-style home—the only family house he'd known in his 24 years.

He heard voices upon entering the coatroom; as he rounded the corner he was shocked to see his sister and her husband, home unexpectedly from New Jersey where they had been working in the pharmaceutical industry for the previous two years.

"Ian, my sweet brother!" Lynn said as she raced to give him a hearty hug.

"Hi, Lynn! Hello, Rick!" Ian shook his brother-in-law's hand as he spoke. "Oh my gosh, what are you guys doing here?"

"Well, I talked to Mom over the weekend and she asked if we might be able to have a family dinner before the chaos of the big Vanderveen wedding got underway, and we were able to make it work," Lynn explained.

Janet Keppler came over to greet and hug Ian, saying, "I'm so very happy to have two of my three kiddos home. I'm just sorry that Matt couldn't be here."

"Wow!" Ian exclaimed as he looked around the kitchen and got a whiff of the meal Janet had prepared. "What is this, Thanksgiving?"

Janet chuckled in her usual, motherly way. She was a phenomenal cook, and for anyone who ever thought that food was love, they were right when it came to the Keppler household. Of course those days she had nobody to cook for so she especially enjoyed any excuse to feed her children and enjoy quality time together. Unfortunately the dinner was about more than just quality time.

"Oh no, it isn't Thanksgiving," Janet answered, suddenly with a stream of tears flowing from her eyes despite a forced smile and effort to fight them.

"Oh my gosh, Mom." Lynn jumped up to console her mother. She wore a puzzled look in reaction to the display of emotion.

"Oh, I'm so sorry. I didn't mean to cry. I wasn't going to cry. We were going to have a nice dinner and talk. It makes me so damn mad at myself," Janet said through her tears. She started jabbering while crying. "I *so* didn't want to spoil your weekend, but I just knew there wasn't a good time, a time when we could all be together so I could tell you in person," she continued. Lynn, Rick and Ian were now riveted by apprehension to each and every word, waiting for the other shoe to drop.

"I'll talk to Matt when he gets in Friday, but I asked you here so I could share some . . . bad news. I had my annual screenings last week, and . . . Friday I found out that . . . my cancer is back." A continuous trickle of tears spoke volumes about what was coming next. She choked out a summary. "It's not good."

A stunned Ian and Lynn wrapped their arms around their mother. They stood. They held her. They continued their comforting grasp for what seemed like minutes—the three of them embraced in a fragmented but strong vestige of what was not long ago a flourishing and complete family unit. Today it was again experiencing the inevitable cold, dark days of winter, despite the heat of the summer outside the house. A sense of disbelief again permeated the room, so soon after the family's prior struggles with death and disease.

After several minutes of love flowing wordlessly between them, Janet got her second wind. She felt a certain relief from having the disclosure behind her, and her attention shifted to her children, whom she loved so dearly. Always the caretaker, she laughed that they all had to take a timeout from their sorrow, so she could get the potatoes off the stove and mash them. It was the moment of levity that everyone needed, even though the reprieve would be short-lived.

As the dinner proceeded, questions were asked and explanations given—to the degree they were understood and available—and assurances of love and support were given abundantly by Ian, Lynn, and Rick. The fact remained, however, that the prognosis was not good. The doctors had found substantial metastasis and bone involvement from Janet's breast cancer recurrence, including tumors on two ribs, and another on her spine. The recommended treatment was a combination of aggressive chemotherapy and radiation.

"You guys really do need to know that I'm going to fight this, and that I'm going to win again," Janet said with feigned courage as they struggled to savor their turkey, potatoes, gravy and trimmings. Janet had always thought that Thanksgiving was just too good of a meal, and too much fun, to be held just once a year. And even now, her words were littered with expressions of gratitude for her life—her kids, her wonderful years with her husband, their family trips, their times around the pool, and the great fun at the cottage. In those sentiments she spoke nothing but the truth.

Her bravado, however, flowed from her innate optimism and desire above all to reassure her kids. It was fruitless in reality, but it was as strong a motherly instinct for Janet as any other. That said, she was human. She went on to share her fears and trepidation about treatment, and minutes later confessed, "I'm just not sure I want to go through all of that again."

She was not afraid to die. Her faith in God was strong. Certainly she was not one to wear that faith on her sleeve, just as Bob had not, but it was nonetheless evident through subtle words and selfless acts of service. At the same time, in the wake of comments she'd made a few times during those lonely first years after Bob died, when she and Ian would spend countless hours in the big old house, Ian sometimes wondered if her brave words weren't efforts to reassure herself as much as others. Certainly everyone has times of doubt, and Janet had pondered the very types of questions Ian and his friends had asked around the pool during their "summer of '85." Why was it that God had taken her husband so young? How was that a benevolent and useful part of his plan? Was it part of his plan at all?

But despite understandable questions uttered from the depth of loneliness, Janet's faith was real, and it ran deep—a fundamental part of who Janet was at her core. And for her, religion wasn't dogmatic; it was simply . . . faith-based. She seemed embraced by the concepts of the Bible, and genuinely felt the Spirit, yet also embraced all of the beauty and mystery that life had to offer.

Suddenly a thought occurred to Ian. He spoke slowly and sincerely. "In light of all of this I'm going to need your advice." The other three looked at Ian, puzzled. "I have invited someone to go to Bill's wedding with me," Ian offered somewhat meekly.

"Well that's great, Ian. So what's the question?" Lynn asked, trying to stay a step ahead, "You're in love, right?"

"It's not that, Lynn, but thanks for asking," he answered with a mock sneer. "You see the girl I've invited is from Chicago."

Ever the voice of moderation, his mother said, "You mean you just met someone yesterday, and you invited her to this huge event with all your family and friends?"

"I'll tell you what, Mom, I spent a fair amount of time with her while John was working over the last couple days, and you'll like her. In fact, our connection was that she went to school with the Burlington twins," Ian explained.

"In Naperville?" Janet asked, slightly reassured. "Well you're a big boy. It just seems like a big commitment to make, to have someone whom you hardly know for such a big event. But who am I to say. I'll look forward to meeting this young woman—she's more than welcome to stay here if you need space," Janet added, reverting to mother and hostess mode without realizing the silliness of her offer.

Lynn laughed aloud, "Mom, I don't think that's what a twenty-something-year-old does, has a girlfriend in town and parks her at his mother's house while he stays at his apartment." Janet laughed at herself almost instantly.

"We'll forgive you that one, Mom. It's been a long night," Ian joked. "But seriously, I wasn't worried about bringing a date into town for the wedding. I didn't think anyone would care if I fulfilled my 'and guest' invitation spot. But in light of all this, I think I should probably call her and explain why this isn't a good time—shouldn't I?"

"Absolutely not!" Janet exclaimed, laughing again at herself for her 180-degree turn. "I am not going to make this weekend about me. I simply didn't know the appropriate way to share this with you. I wanted it to be in person, and I also just needed to *have you guys near me*, and get the loving support that you have given me tonight. But that's done, for now. It's not like I'm gonna die this weekend, and this weekend is about our good friends the Vanderveens—and your friend Bill." Janet paused as Ian and Lynn glanced questioningly at each other.

Janet continued, "By the way, while we're on the topic, I haven't told Cindy Vanderveen about this news, and I'm not going to until after the wedding. I will *not* wreck this event for them, for Bill, or you, or anyone! So nobody say anything to anyone. As for your new friend, Ian, let me meet this young lady and we'll have a nice weekend."

✢

The ringing phone was piercingly loud as Ian rolled over to grab it. He looked at the red letters of his alarm clock. 3:02 a.m.! "Hello?" he answered groggily.

"Ian, this is Roger Crenshaw. I'm so sorry to bother you, but I'm calling to see if you can co-pilot again for me this morning. This is not an official

Compassion Flight, but I'm hoping you'll volunteer anyway. It's every bit as compelling a human need."

"Actually, Roger, I can do it if we'll be back by late afternoon or early evening."

"Yeah, we need to go pretty quickly if you can. It's a friend of ours from church whose son is working in Minnesota. His fiancée was killed here about two hours ago—a car accident. We need to get him home to be with family and to get him some support."

"Oh that's so incredibly sad . . . well, absolutely," Ian said sympathetically. He couldn't help but juxtapose images of Bill and Megan's happy event against this tragic news. "What time do you need me there?"

"Can you meet me at the hangar in 45 minutes—3:45?"

"I'll be there," Ian said.

"Thanks so much Ian, bye."

"Bye."

Ian jumped out of bed to take a very quick shower. He wanted to be sure that he had time to gather a thorough flight briefing from the Flight Service Station. As an instructor and commercial pilot, he knew that he shared liability for the flight, even when he was in the right seat.

His flight briefing included the myriad of usual information: flight precautions—of which there were many this morning; current synoptic discussions; current conditions; forecasts for the terminals along the route; area forecasts; winds aloft; the usual long list of technical amendments to approach procedures; and items of local interest—such as an unlighted crane two miles north of the airport. Ian had always found some of the minutiae humorous. *Believe me*, he thought to himself, *if I'm on a precision approach from the east and I have to care about an unlighted, fifty-foot crane two miles north of the airport, I have much bigger problems than that crane!*

The more pressing issues that morning were that two of the largest challenges to aviation were present along his route, and particularly at the destination—fog and thunderstorms. No matter how big the airplane, fog was a serious threat, and that was especially true at night.

Few people really understood what was involved in keeping an airplane upright and under control when flying without any visual reference to the ground. In fact, flight in the clouds or without visual reference outside an airplane was a very tricky skill to learn, and for those private pilots who didn't have these skills, it was by far the largest killer. (Some accidents over the years, like that of John F. Kennedy, Jr., would publicly illustrate the point; but for the most part, it was only pilots who really understood and conceptualized the risks.)

Pilots certified for flight under Instrument Flight Rules had extensive training, well over double the hours required to get a pilot's license in the first place. As Ian's students had often demonstrated, they initially believed they could operate in three dimensions simply by using the same sense of balance they used on the earth's surface; and when they could see, they performed well. But in reality, the semi-circular canals inside the ears didn't evolve to provide balance and positional data when working in three dimensions, especially without the visual cues of a broad horizon. With a view-limiting device, Ian could demonstrate what it was like to fly inside the clouds. The result was always disturbing, nauseating and eye-opening for the student, and mildly humorous for the instructor.

Of the "big three" threats to airplanes of any size—thunderstorms, icing, and fog—it was impossible to say which was the greatest. All Ian knew was that that night's flight was a complex and difficult one that would require good crew coordination. At the same time he felt that they could do it safely. The storms associated with the front were scattered enough that with the onboard lightning detection equipment, "Stormscope," they could probably get around the heavier cells without too much trouble.

The danger of the fog was related to fuel endurance, as well as the inability to descend and land if there were any other type of emergency. In other words, if the fog was too low to allow landing at the destination and the alternate, fuel would run out! Also, if something were to go wrong, like an engine problem, there was no way down but to fly the "roads"—extensive instrument maneuvers down to the runway—which was a delicate balancing act under the best of circumstances, and a fatally impossible one with a crippled or damaged airplane.

All that said, Ian felt the flight could be conducted safely if managed properly. Luckily, he was able to escape his small, two-bedroom apartment without waking his roommate—his old friend Scrappy-Anthony.

Ian had previously flown only two times with this particular pilot and airplane, but he felt quite comfortable because it was another Cessna 210, the same make and model of high-performance, retractable gear, six-passenger plane that he flew for Tom Hanson. As for Roger Crenshaw, Ian had some reservations, but Roger was a very nice guy and was well regarded in the community. Moreover, he had developed his chapter of Compassion Flight North America very successfully.

It amazed Ian how many times people needed specialized care that was available only in some distant city—Minnesota's Mayo Clinic, Cleveland Clinic, Mott Children's Hospital, and many other specialty centers of which he'd never heard. And in most cases the patients simply could not tolerate the rigmarole of commercial airplane travel—waiting, walking, and making connections. More importantly, they couldn't afford it. Flights with these volunteer pilot organizations were completely free of charge, charitable donations of pilots and supporters.

There were times when delivering a young child to a potentially life-saving treatment, that the outpouring of gratitude almost overcame Ian. Indeed these people were often fighting for their lives, and transportation was in many cases the Achilles' heel of the entire process.

That night as Ian drove toward the airport his thoughts were on the complexity of the flight. Clearly Roger Crenshaw had done great things for Compassion Flight. In fact he was a master of fundraising and media. His flights were routinely featured on local television stations and in area newspapers, and his church was a big supporter of his efforts, as was the broader community. And that support was vitally important to the much-needed service. The owner would provide the labor and the $150 per hour cost to operate the plane, but there were still fuel and fees to be covered.

As he drove, Ian thought about Roger and their previous flights together. Even new professional pilots like Ian could size up another pilot's skills very quickly. If she was good, it was like watching a master musician in the way she treats her instrument, even before she played it. From the subtle mastery of useful turns of a phrase on the radio, to deft taxiing skills and emergency planning, a master was a thing of beauty to see in action. Unfortunately, Ian's previous two flights with Roger had not given him reason to believe Roger was a master.

Ian pulled up to the security gate, swiped his ID card and drove to the waiting hangar. Roger had already pulled the plane out, closed the hangar door, and was standing with another man by the plane. The man looked familiar.

"Hello Ian," Roger said with a handshake and a friendly tone of voice. "Thanks so much for coming. This is Tom Reynolds." Ian had met Tom some years ago as a customer at their family store.

"Oh gosh, Tom, I'm so sorry to have to see you again under these circumstances, but it's good to see you," Ian said.

"I can't thank you enough for helping me get my son," he said. "I just talked to him on the phone—woke him up about an hour ago. Didn't want to but had to break it to him then. As a father you can't know how badly I need to be there for him. You guys are a lifesaver."

"I'm happy to help, guys," Ian said as his eyes perused the airplane.

Roger saw Ian examining the plane and said, "I've got her all pre-flighted. We're ready to go. Hop in."

"You checked the sumps and visually ensured the fuel status?" Ian asked. It was a slightly forward question to ask the owner, but Ian knew their lives depended upon such questions, so he didn't hesitate. Fuel gauges in airplanes were notoriously unreliable, and it was vital that fuel quantities were verified by a measuring stick, especially given the potential for fuel to be an issue with the fog around their destination.

"Yes sir."

It was a hazy, muggy night in Kalamazoo, with a ceiling of 2,000 feet and marginal visibility of about three miles. Ian knew as they progressed westward that the safety margin of visibility and ceiling below them would be reduced even further.

Upon entering the plane, the first thing Ian remembered was that the backrest of the co-pilot's seat was not functioning properly. It made proper posture difficult. Not a big deal, since he wouldn't be flying, but it gnawed at Ian a little. Ian began counting "strikes."

In the risk management game of aviation, there were "outs" and "strikes." These were not like baseball outs and strikes. "Outs" meant exit strategies. These were good. You typically wanted three. "Strikes," on the other hand, were little mental notes of compounding negatives.

After studying many accident cases, and even subscribing to periodicals that analyzed accidents, Ian knew that accidents were never the result of a single factor. Rather, they were the result of a chain of events. Usually there were multiple points where someone should have added up the strikes and recognized the threat, but simply didn't break out of the mental paradigm far enough to do so. While the inoperative passenger backrest adjustment was perhaps not a "strike," it was certainly worthy of a mental note.

After a short taxi into the darkness of night, Roger performed his run-up routine to check all systems, in particular the two, somewhat redundant ignition systems. One of the two magnetos exhibited a slightly higher drop than Ian would have liked, but Roger assured him it was always like that, "cold," and that on the next check it would be fine. It was a small thing, but to Ian it was another mental note—perhaps a quarter strike.

Shortly thereafter, Centurion 55BM was cleared for departure from Kalamazoo's Runway 17. The plane leaped off the runway and climbed through the murky air, eventually into the cloud layer above. Tom sat in the back seat, eyes closed and without a headset. Sometimes passengers liked to listen in, but Tom was tired and had the weight of the world on his mind.

As Roger leveled out at twelve thousand feet, there was enough light to see that the plane was between the expansive cloud layers that stretched all the way from Michigan to Minnesota. The situation actually provided a visual sense of horizon and removed some of the pressure Ian felt to monitor the autopilot and the instruments while in the clouds. Typically, Ian preferred to hand-fly in instrument conditions, in order to sharpen his skills. It was sometimes an indication of lack of skill when a pilot relied too heavily on an autopilot, but knowing the stress they would be under during the flight, the autopilot was a good strategy.

The cruise portion of the flight gave the two some time to talk. They covered little things like the quasi-bachelor party Ian was planning for that evening, what was happening in Compassion in general, and how Roger's church family continued to support him so generously. No question about it, Roger was a real people person.

As time passed, Ian raised some strategic questions about the remaining flight into Minneapolis. Roger was kind as always, and answered questions more with optimism than with a sense of planning. "I think we'll be fine—I don't see a lot of lighting on the Stormscope yet," Roger said nonchalantly. While Ian was admittedly a bit of an overachiever in his vocation, much like his friend Bill, and while he would cop to being a touch anal-retentive, what he heard come out of Roger's mouth next would intrigue him for years to come.

"Ian," Roger said, "I have a simple philosophy. God has a plan for each of us, and I believe that his word has made clear that when it's our time, it's our time. He is my copilot, and he'll look out for me; but when my number is up, my number is up."

"Okay," Ian began a polite reply, "so I have to ask, then why preflight the airplane at all?"

"Well, I don't mean you don't take reasonable steps—I won't run across a busy street without looking, but by and large I'm just saying that we don't get to choose these things."

Ian accepted the explanation, but couldn't help but believe that he now had a much better insight into what seemed like a cavalier attitude toward safety on the part of Roger Crenshaw. If nothing else, Ian figured that he was going to watch Roger even more carefully going forward. *It's my ass in this airplane too*, he thought to himself silently.

As they got within about 45 minutes of Minneapolis-St. Paul International, MSP, things started to get more interesting. For starters, the autopilot popped offline. Roger tried to re-engage it, but it refused to lock on. *A solid strike one*, Ian thought, later correcting in his mind that it was more like one and one-half. To make matters more interesting, Murphy's Law was beginning to come into play. Ian tuned in the ATIS information and heard that MSP was now reporting a 300-foot ceiling, and just one mile of visibility in rain and fog.

For even a polished pilot, this was an extremely challenging, "low" approach—very close to the absolute limit allowed. Even at an approach speed of only about 115 miles per hour, a couple hundred feet provides almost no room for error when performing the delicate balancing act of flying on instruments, barely above the treetops, in three dimensions. One tiny movement could easily result in a two-hundred-foot drop; so needless to say, Ian was a little unsure if Roger was up to the challenge.

Even more unsettling, he was now seeing lightning flashes from the cockpit. Due to the total lack of visibility of IFR flight in clouds and rain, Ian couldn't judge the distance to the strikes; certainly they were closer than he wanted them to be. Worse yet, the presence of lightning meant the presence of violent updrafts and downdrafts that were far more threatening to the plane than even a direct lightning strike. This was not good at all.

Ian keyed the mike, "Minneapolis approach, Centurion 55 bravo-mike, we appear to have an inoperative Stormscope; I realize you don't have weather radar in the TRACON but could you by chance provide us any assistance in terms of heavier areas of precipitation on the approach?"

"Roger that, 5 bravo-mike, looks like one heavier cell right between you and the field, with solid level one and scattered level two cells elsewhere. You're right on the edge of that building cell. Recommend twenty degrees left and we'll go ahead and call that a vector for the approach. 5 bravo-mike descend now and maintain three thousand, vectors for the ILS to Runway 30-Left to Minneapolis."

"5 bravo-mike, we thank you very much, descending out of five for three, twenty left vector for ILS 30-Left," Ian confirmed in a smooth, concise and professional radio voice. The inoperative Stormscope was definitely strike number two.

"That's great. Thanks, Ian," Roger said politely, not seeming to mind that Ian had taken some control. Clearly he was going to have his hands full, so Ian also performed a quick brief on the approach chart that was sitting on Roger's right leg. The chart contained all the details of the approach, such as frequencies with which to tune in the precision approach's glidepath indicator and localizer. It also told them how low they could be at the end of the approach path without having to abort, the so-called "Decision Height."

"Okay, captain, your localizer is in and verified, you call glideslope alive after established, inbound is 311, DH is 538. If we don't have solid visual of the runway by 600, abort. Missed approach is a climb to 2500 and a right turn to MSP." Ian was showing appropriate deference to the captain of the aircraft, but it was pretty clear that this was a tight situation, and Roger was actually very glad to have the help.

"Wings level! Watch your heading!" Ian instructed firmly as he glanced up from the approach chart to see that the airplane was in a steep, diving left turn. With his right hand, Ian instinctively assisted in the recovery of the two hundred feet of altitude and twenty degrees of heading that were lost. Luckily the controller didn't chastise them. Had the deviation been much farther, they would run the risk of anything from a polite inquiry, to concern, or even the possibility of a citation.

For his part, Tom Reynolds was now wide-awake and somewhat watching body language between the two pilots, but he still didn't don a headset. Now back on course, Ian said, "Is it okay if I take the radio communications?" This was not an uncommon request. Two pilot crews often split communication off to the non-flying pilot.

"Absolutely," Roger replied, without any pretense of ego. The controller then issued several heading changes back around the weather prior to directing them to intercept the precision navigation beams that Roger would follow on the several-mile final approach course. The rain pummeled the plane loudly, but the periodic bucking of moderate turbulence was largely manageable. Roger's flying, however, remained sporadic and imprecise. He was clearly in over his head.

"Centurion 55 bravo-mike, fly heading 270 until established on the localizer, maintain 3000, you're cleared for the ILS 30-Left, tower at the marker 118.30."

"5 bravo-mike, 270 'til established, 3000 and tower at the marker, 5 bravo-mike," Ian read back.

Seconds later there was another flash of lightning, and a few more continuous bumps. Part of Ian said they should get the hell out of there, but part of him was reassured that the lightning wasn't as close as he thought, at least if the controller was any guide. Then again, their radar *really wasn't* that good.

Ian wondered if the urgency of the situation was clouding his judgment. He figured that his desire to see this approach through successfully could well be strike number three, but deviation to an alternate, without a good picture of these storms, didn't seem like a good plan either.

Just as he was weighing those thoughts, the plane entered another steep turn. A sure sign of a rusty or untrained pilot is one who horses the yoke around and over-controls the plane. That's exactly what Roger was doing, and this time they wound up in a 55-degree bank from which Roger was starting to pull back, beyond a 2g-force turn. That could get dangerous in a hurry, and Ian immediately righted the plane. They were on the initial segment of the final approach and this was not the time to be doing a stall recovery.

"Sorry about that," Roger commented.

"It's fine, Roger. I'll keep an eye out, but just relax and guide the plane. You're doing fine; just don't over control. We need to really be stabilized and nail this approach if we're going to take it all the way down near minimums," Ian coached in a smooth voice. It was a darn good thing Ian was an Instrument instructor, and was competent flying instruments from the perspective of the right seat. He thought to himself that only a year or two ago, his life could have been in real danger. That's how serious this was.

"Localizer alive." Roger pointed out that the plane was now intercepting the narrow beam that was aligned with the runway. One little round instrument in the cockpit was now all-important. The 3" round navigation gauge had two needles: one vertical for the localizer, which would align the plane with the runway, and one horizontal for the glidepath, which would precisely guide the aircraft down the "banister" to the runway.

Ian watched the vertical needle move from the side of the round instrument toward the middle. "Start your turn to 310 now and we'll correct for wind in a minute," he instructed supportively and calmly.

"Okay glideslope is alive now too. We're at the outer marker," Roger said.

"Minneapolis tower, Centurion 55 bravo-mike is outer marker inbound, ILS 30-Left," Ian transmitted as they crossed the checkpoint. He then said to Roger, "Okay, landing gear down, time, throttle, talk—which I just did, flaps to approach, landing lights, landing gear checked and verified—three green." He knew Roger was in no frame of mind to run a checklist.

To Ian, Roger was like a new student who was totally overloaded just trying to keep the plane upright, walking the delicate tightrope that Ian often compared to rubbing your belly, patting your head, and playing a set of drums with your feet. Everything had to move in concert: feet on the rudder pedals, one hand on the controls, one hand on the throttle, and the brain needed to coordinate it all. In addition to written checklists, this was why Ian was always trained to commit certain "do or die" items to memory.

"Centurion 55 bravo-mike, cleared to land 30-Left, wind now 260 at 12," the voice from the tower said. The plane was then entering the critical phase of the approach. The horizontal needle and the vertical needle were now centered on the navigation guage; the plane was perfectly aligned with the end of the runway, and on the proper descent path. But from here, two things would make it increasingly difficult to stay on track. The closer the plane would get to the antennas sending the signal, the narrower the beam would become. The signals were funnel shaped, and from that point forward even a one-degree change in heading would send the vertical needle scurrying away from the bulls-eye. The same would be true for the horizontal needle if the airplane weren't perfectly trimmed and set up for the correct descent rate. It really was a tightrope, and it was getting exponentially more sensitive and delicate as they neared the runway.

"Watch the glideslope. You're low . . . You're low . . . YOU'RE LOW!" Ian said with increasing volume, as the proper correction was not made. He immediately helped Roger correct, and now put his hand on the controls with Roger. "Your airplane, but I'm on the controls for coaching," he clarified, following common crew-coordination protocol, but needing to get involved. If either needle swung all the way to the side of the instrument, they would be forced to abandon the approach, fly a missed approach procedure, and do the whole thing again. Not knowing where the lightning was for sure, Ian wasn't going to let that happen if he could help it.

"Okay, seven hundred feet to DH," Ian called out. "Watch heading. We're losing the needle. Correct 5 degrees right." Ian coached with more tension in his voice than usual when instructing, but still with an outwardly calm air of professionalism.

Finally, however, Ian knew it just wasn't going to work. "Do you mind if I take it from here, Roger?"

"Not at all."

"Okay. My airplane," Ian stated calmly—again an explicit protocol designed to avoid any confusion over who was controlling the craft. Within a few seconds he had the approach stabilized and the needles—while not perfectly centered—at least on the edge of the bull's-eye. He spoke aloud as instructors often did.

"Okay, just above glidepath which I'm okay with, just left of the doughnut and correcting 2 degrees back left on localizer. Three hundred feet to DH. Decision height is 300 feet above the ground, which is 600 MSL and absolutely nothing farther. You call the runway in sight, Roger."

The airplane continued to descend from within the clouds and fog. It was an eerie feeling for Tom, who was still sitting patiently and relatively unconcerned in the middle row of seats behind the crew. He would look at the instrument panel on occasion, but mostly stared out the side window, only able to see the extended main landing gear amidst the background of dark gray cloud.

Just a couple seconds later Tom could see ground immediately beneath him, but still nothing was visible out the front. Barely two seconds after that, at an altitude only a couple hundred feet above the abort point, Roger mercifully barked, "I've got the runway!"

"Okay, we were cleared to land, mixture rich, prop control is coming forward, landing gear is three green lights and wheels visible. Break pressure good." Seemingly emerging from the clouds just above the runway, there were but a few, final seconds that passed before Ian was easing back the nose to flare for the touchdown. It was then that he realized the serious inconvenience of his seat-back being so far reclined, but it was too late. He did his best but the landing was still solidly on the ugly side. The main wheels touched down with a firm *thunk* onto the long, rain-soaked runway, but the plane was nonetheless safely on the ground.

Roger taxied in as they both regained their mental composure. "That was a little exciting," Ian cracked, to ease tensions.

"Yeah, sorry about that. I tell you what; I didn't feel too well there. Thanks for the help. Guess I'm a little rusty, too," Roger admitted.

"That's all right. Nothing you can't sharpen back up. We'll check out the weather and regroup here," Ian said. At the same time he was thinking to himself that Roger was probably not feeling well because of the wild ride, and self-induced vertigo. It was really all about his skills.

Yes, Ian thought further, *people do get rusty,* but he couldn't help but see a clear connection between Roger's resignation to outside forces for the safety of the flight, and his flying skills. He *really did think God was his co-pilot.* Hopefully this little experience would at least be a wakeup call. Perhaps it would remind him that walking in front of traffic without looking was pretty close to what he had just done.

All of the sudden, however, as they entered the general aviation terminal and the small but luxurious waiting area, the adventures of the flight were swept away for a moment. Tom Reynolds spotted Andrew, and the two darted at each other without hesitation, embraced, and broke into a mutual sob. Tears flowed generously from both of them, and Ian felt a wave of emotion he'd not expected. He looked away, to afford them some privacy, then motioned to Roger that he would head to the briefing room. Roger began to follow, but then Tom interrupted.

"Guys, this is my son Andrew," Tom introduced.

Both men approached. Ian shook his hand firmly, squeezing Andrew's shoulder with his free hand. "I'm so sorry to have to meet you under these circumstances," Ian said. Roger then embraced Andrew, with moisture visible in his eyes as well. As the two pulled apart, Ian put a hand on Andrew's back and said, "I'm going to run and check out the storm situation to plot a new course for home, so we can get you headed home in just a couple minutes."

Ian walked to the briefing room with a flurry of thoughts bouncing in his head. He was appreciative that he'd have good access to weather radar and information here, but he was also thinking of Bill and Megan. They would be enjoying a wedding in just a couple days, but Andrew had been robbed of such a day with the love of his life. Ian also thought of Samantha. He had only spent days with her, but the thought reinforced that he couldn't imagine what it would be like to lose a fiancée. He also thought of his mother, and how he knew he was personally going to feel the deep pain of loss again soon.

But heavy on his mind, too, was Roger, and the potentially fatal consequences of fatalistic thinking. Ian resolved that after that day he would never fly with Roger again. He reasoned that if God was really Roger's co-pilot, it was quite possible that he was his mechanic as well. *Strike three!*

Chapter 11

ONE FLESH, ONE WEEKEND

After departing straight south from Minneapolis and taking a route across northern Illinois and Indiana to avoid all the convective weather, Ian, Roger, Tom and Andrew landed at Kalamazoo just before 10:00 a.m. Tom and Andrew had spent the trip in their private, back-seat cocoon, talking, grieving, and certainly at times, crying. Some years later Ian learned that Andrew had fallen in love again and married, but never did he forget his first beloved fiancée, or the love they shared. For many years after her death, she remained a constant friend and companion in Andrew's mind, to whom he would confide his deepest secrets and thoughts, and for whom he would forever yearn to spend just one more day.

But as the experience of that day drew to a close for Ian, he had little time to think. After a few short hours of sleep, Ian had errands to run: the University Bookstore, to purchase the texts for his final elective course, Basic Christian Thought; pick up his tuxedo for the wedding; buy Sammy flowers; get some food for her visit.

Late in the afternoon he called Samantha to confirm her arrival time for the following day.

"How you doin', Sam?"

"Great," she replied.

"Hey I know I had to catch you at work, so I won't keep you. I'm sorry it's been so crazy; an awful lot has happened this week."

"Is everything okay?"

"Well, yes. Well, and no. Mom's cancer has returned. It doesn't look very good. I also had a strange flight today—thought of you as I flew past Chicago, by the way. But I can explain it all later. Really everything is fine, and I can't wait to see you tomorrow. Is everything okay with you?"

"Yes, I'm fine, but Ian are you sure it's a good time for me to come?"

"Absolutely no question, and tomorrow really will be a blast. I'm looking forward to it, and to introducing you to some people."

"Okay then. If you're sure, I'll be on the train. It arrives at 5:35 I think."

"Perfect. I'll pick you up. We can run to my house, change, and be at the rehearsal at 6:30. Can't wait."

"See you then, Ian. Bye."

"Bye."

Ian glanced at the clock, hurried to clean up around the apartment while Scrappy, who had just arrived home from work, quickly showered. Together they headed out to meet Bill, his younger brother Thomas, John, and a few of their other friends. Before long the group of eight young men began the evening at the only place that made sense—their old hangout, The Final Stage.

"So Bill. No pressure tomorrow, huh?" Ian prompted as they received their first round of beer.

Bill stared back with a smirk on his face. "No, none at all . . ."

"Who would have ever thought our pretty boy—Wait! Actually, if anyone would be having members of Congress present at his marriage to a gorgeous babe, at a humungous, fancy event, it would be Bill." Scrappy loved to poke fun at "Mr. All-American," and this was the perfect evening. "But it couldn't happen to a better guy . . . to Bill!" Scrappy raised his beer mug, and the group drank in honor of their friend.

Bill jumped in, "Now since you raise the topic of what a big production this wedding has become . . . we should pay tribute to Representative Huxley—"

"To the Huxleys and the beer they provide tomorrow," Scrappy interrupted, his glass held high.

"Now having acknowledged the scope and size of the event in which I find myself embroiled, we must also properly acknowledge the importance of the event to me and my betrothed," Bill intoned with feigned theatric affectation. "Therefore, it is incumbent upon each of you to ensure that I not be 'over served' by this fine establishment, or any other, on this particular night." A chorus of boos emanated from the group.

"Actually, I'm quite serious about that part," Bill said.

"Ah, shut up and sit down."

"Have a seat."

"Give it a rest, pretty boy," John added.

Bill persisted, "Okay seriously, let me propose a toast." The guys quieted and raised their glasses to the ready position. "To a group of friends that I value tremendously. Thank you for all the laughs and for all the fun. I have been a lucky guy to count you as friends this long, and Megan and I will be lucky to count you as friends in the future. To you—the greatest friends a guy could have." The group drank yet again.

"And to Flaco," Bill added. "We love him and wish he were here—may he get his shit together." Laughter bubbled again as they tipped their glasses once more, and subsequently ordered another round.

Ian silently observed that Bill had put up a good front, but he knew Flaco's choices bothered Bill greatly. Ian was bothered as well—clearly the choices weren't healthy. But from this and other observations, Ian couldn't help feel that Bill was angered in a way that transcended his personal feelings of concern—a way that was defensive, as if Flaco had somehow attacked Bill's own beliefs. With Bill's competitive nature, he saw most things in terms of right and wrong, winners and losers, black and white.

The eight friends continued to enjoy toasting, verbal jousting, reminiscing, and plain old "bar talk" for another couple of rounds before eating some much-needed food. It was after dinner when Scrappy unabashedly yelled out, "So when do we see tits?" Peer pressure was clearly going to be leveraged, and there were no strenuous objections. Even Bill said, "Oh, you mean the *ballet* down on Covington Street?" Of course his next sentence was, "I don't know, guys, I have to be pretty careful here."

"Hey, nobody will know, Bill, and what better excuse do you have than your friends dragged you down to the nudie bar before your wedding?" John's argument was more than adequate. It didn't take any more.

"Okay, but remember your promise to me—I'm not drinking much more. One more beer, a couple of naked girls, and I'm done." The group placated him with nods, and grumbled agreement as they departed.

✙

Ian rolled over on the Friday of the rehearsal dinner, after finally getting a full night's sleep. He'd had several beers the night before, but they were over an extended period, and he awoke feeling good. As the sunlight found its way through the blinds by his bed, a memory popped into his head of one of the dancers he'd particularly enjoyed the night before. His morning erection, "EMB" as the guys jokingly referred to the infamous phenomenon, was a convenient distraction; Ian got the day off to a gratifying start.

As he headed for the shower Ian thought of his childhood guilt over such activities, and laughed at the thought, especially in light of his confident assumption that every one of the other bachelor party participants had done the same thing. In truth he was right, even about Bill, since Megan was obviously not yet staying overnight at the new home. Megan had learned to satisfy Bill—without intercourse, of course—but it really was a drop in the bucket relative to his needs, so the self-gratification wasn't uncommon. Needless to say, however, Bill was wholly looking forward to Saturday and to flying solo *far less often.*

After showering, Ian ran by the airport to check on Tom Hanson's C210. Every time a plane is flown, competent owners and operators maintain a maintenance list of items needing attention.

By afternoon he found that he had more time than he thought before Matt was to arrive around 3:00 p.m., so after lunch he was able to read the first couple chapters of his new text, *Christian Doctrine,* by ordained minister and theologian, Shirley C. Guthrie, Junior.[11]

Ian had grown up attending the local United Methodist Church, the one attended by three generations of Kepplers. Funny thing though, when Ian evaluated options for fulfilling the final credit requirement to graduate, he chose Basic Christian Thought. He had considered a comparative religion course, but figured that despite all his years of attending church, and being involved even as an adult in an interdenominational music group that exposed him to literally scores of worship services and sermons, he didn't have a good handle on the theology of his own religion. Sure, he knew the basics after all those years of Sunday school and sermons, but Biblically and theologically, Ian felt ignorant. And what better way to gain perspective, he figured, than doing it with this final credit requirement.

The book wasn't speedy reading, but Ian made it through a discussion of theology, the role of the theologian, a definition of the Reformed tradition, and a discussion of the origin and purpose of creeds and confessions. It gave Ian the sense that the book would be a thorough overview of the most fundamental Christian views, origins and rationales—how, why, and by what authority so many people had come to know the basic, true religion of Christianity, and how one could be a good student of the religion while recognizing legitimate differences of opinion within it.

Before he knew it, it was time to meet Matt. Ian hopped in his little truck, now rusted in a couple spots, thanks to all that Michigan road salt, and returned to the airport.

After standing among the other greeting committees for only a couple minutes, Ian spotted Matt. They shook hands and Ian threw his arm around Matt's shoulder.

"How are you?" Ian asked enthusiastically.

"I'm good," Matt responded.

"Are you geeked that you're almost done with your residency?"

"Absolutely," Matt replied as the duo walked toward the nearby luggage claim. "I'll just have to figure out where I'm going to wind up."

"Nearby?"

"Maybe," Matt answered. "Maybe Grand Rapids, Indy, or even here—I just don't know yet."

"Kalamazoo is nice," Ian nudged, only half-joking.

"How's Mom?" Matt asked as they waited for his suitcase. Ian was taken by surprise. There weren't secrets in the Keppler home, not like this. He didn't know what to say really. Luckily Matt said, "She called me. I know about her cancer."

"Ah, thank goodness. She said she was going to tell you today, so I didn't think it was my place. But I really didn't like the idea of hiding something like that."

"Yeah, well she called me Wednesday night after you guys left. She said she couldn't have you know and not me. I was ticked she waited several days to tell any of us," Matt continued. "So how is she?"

"I think she's fine, under the circumstances. You know Mom. She's certainly got her cheerleader's 'game face' on for the weekend—insists Vanderveens not know until after the weekend."

"Her call. She's probably right on that. I just am glad I was coming home so we can all be here for her . . . . Hey, speaking of the wedding, where's your hot date?"

"Ah, mom told you that too. Have to pick her up at 5:35 at the train station. We've got the rehearsal dinner tonight, so I'll take you home and then run. You'll meet her tomorrow though. I think you'll like her."

"Cool."

"So Matt, what's your take on Mom's situation, medically?" Ian asked.

"Well certainly I don't know, and I haven't talked with her doctors or anything, but I can tell you this: if it has metastasized into the bone, Ian, it isn't good at all." The two brothers exchanged expressions of concern.

✣

Matt and Ian caught up further on the car ride home, another bitter-sweet reunion, but they both knew the wedding would be fun and looked forward to it. By the time Ian got Matt to the Keppler home, and spent a little time with his mother, Matt, Rick, and Lynn, it was time to pick up Samantha and get to the rehearsal and dinner.

Ian parked his car not far from the classic, old-style train station in downtown Kalamazoo, and awaited the arrival of the eastbound run from Chicago. As usual there was a sign posted, saying that the train was running ten minutes late. Soon enough, however, the crossing bells started clanging wildly and the train pulled into the station. Ian's stomach jumped with anticipation. With everything else that had been happening all week, he'd been looking forward to this event continually—even more than the wedding itself.

As a trickle of passengers disembarked, he saw Samantha's short blond hair through a window, and soon she was stepping off the train. She looked just as cute has he'd remembered, if not more so. His heart rate increased as he greeted her with a polite hug and kiss on the cheek, and negotiated her bags from her through her stream of protests.

"How are you? How was your trip?" Ian asked enthusiastically as they walked toward the car.

"It was good," she said, appearing only slightly nervous and subdued.

"How you doing really? Are you up for this?"

"I think so," she replied with a smile, appreciative that he noticed her apprehension.

Ian threw her bag in his truck, stopped, and turned to Samantha. "I want you to know that I'm so glad you're here. We'll have fun; just don't hesitate to be candid with me at any time. It's going to be a little crazy, but just tell me if you get tired, need time out, or whatever, okay?"

"I'll be fine. This will be fun," she said sincerely. "Thanks though." She stepped up and gave him a peck on the lips. "You're sweet, and I'm glad to be here too." They each took a deep breath as they looked in each other's eyes. Ian winked and smiled at Samantha before they hopped in the truck to begin the weekend.

The rehearsal and the dinner that followed were beautiful, and unfolded without surprise. The stately First Church was an immaculate setting, and Ian could see that Bill and Megan were delighting in every moment of the rehearsal. It would surely be a gorgeous event. The church itself was right on Bronson Park, the lovely square in downtown where Ian had met Becky almost seven years earlier. As the recollection popped briefly into his mind, Ian smiled in fond recollection of the love and comfort she provided during that bittersweet summer of 1985. It seemed like a lifetime ago.

Sammy was delightful and beautiful, and Ian recognized he was falling for her in a big way. He beamed with pride as she politely and graciously interacted with the many people to whom she was introduced throughout the evening. There were several times while he was standing up front in the rehearsal, that he found himself catching a glimpse of Samantha sitting in a pew with one of Bill's relatives, smiling and talking politely. *God she is awesome*, Ian said to himself on multiple occasions. Occasionally their eyes would meet and they would flash each other a silly smile, while privately admiring the semi-formal attire and attractiveness of the other.

The rehearsal dinner was held at the fine Italian restaurant in the newly renovated Radisson Hotel, less than two blocks away. It was luxurious to be sure, and the Vanderveens clearly had outdone themselves; but they'd have quite an act to keep up with in the Huxleys' wedding extravagance, the following day.

Ian had a chance early on to reminisce with Cindy and Don Vanderveen, and for them to spend a few minutes with Sammy. She also got to meet Anthony, the "Scrappy" roommate he had told her about during their night in the Chicago bar. And for dinner, Sammy was seated near John and his date, a woman Ian didn't know. Sammy and John bantered like old friends, however, and together the three had a genuinely delightful time.

As Ian had immediately sensed, there was a warmth about Samantha that was difficult to explain, but it permeated her surroundings. For John, the evening provided a chance to see those prominent characteristics of Samantha's kind soul: her love of animals, her down-to-earth authenticity, and the spunky wit that percolated to the surface with only a little coaxing. Strange as it may sound, it became clear to John that evening, that he had gained a life-long friend through Ian's emerging love.

After dinner drew to a close and the departing guests extended their thanks to the Vanderveens, much of the wedding party continued on to another local haunt for a few more laughs and a nightcap. Sammy and Ian joined in, but after one more drink they decided they were done for the day. Of course, they were both looking to spend a little time alone; and in a true act of friendship, Scrappy had agreed to stay at his parents' home for the two nights, allowing both some privacy and the availability of his bed for the guest.

When the two arrived back at the small two-bedroom apartment, they plopped down on the couch in the main living area immediately upon entry.

"Wow. Are you as bushed as I am?" Ian asked Samantha.

"Pretty close, but I had fun. Thank you for inviting me, Ian." Samantha looked deeply into Ian's eyes as she leaned back on the couch and exhaled a sigh of relaxation, kicking of her shoes in the process.

"When you left my apartment last week—oh my gosh that was only Monday!" she exclaimed. "Anyway, when you left I was absolutely certain I'd never see you again."

"Why?" Ian asked. "I said I'd call you."

"I know. I just didn't want to get my hopes up, I guess. I had such a great time with you. Then I was so thrilled when you called." She paused, then continued. "Ian, I don't like making things complicated, and I don't know where this is going to go, but I'm here to see where it goes, and to do so totally without expectation or preconceptions. I like you. Just like when I thought I wouldn't see you again, that was a risk I was willing to take to be with you. But let's just promise each other something. One thing. Let's promise that we'll always be honest. I can't think of anything more important."

"I absolutely agree. You've got a deal, Samantha Hitchens," Ian said with a warm smile.

"I mean, whether it means the end of the relationship, or whatever, let's just always be honest."

"I promise," Ian said. "I totally agree."

She studied his eyes and face, and fully believed him. She also privately acknowledged to herself that she could be wrong about her feelings for him. In truth, both she and Ian were aware that they couldn't be certain the other would be the one perfect mate for forever. But they also knew they'd disclosed all of their secrets on that very first night, at a time when they had nothing to lose. Now, all they could do was live their pledge, one day at a time, encouraging the continued growth of honesty and trust by avoiding petty jealously, and by avoiding natural tendencies to react to inevitable hurt feelings with knee-jerk, emotional responses. Each was determined that the relationship be a safe place, a place of mutual respect and value where absolutely anything could be expressed, and together they could be stronger than apart.

Ian leaned over and kissed Samantha with passion, heart and love. He ignored the critical parental voice that said, "Don't fall too deeply. Don't get too serious. Moderation. You hardly know this woman." He had ignored those voices before, with terrible consequences. But somehow, age and valuable lessons learned previously had brought Ian the complete confidence that he'd felt in the bar when they'd met. He could picture spending his life with the warmth of this person.

Samantha kissed him back as they fluidly fell flat on the couch. There was an overwhelming pit of emotion in Ian's stomach. This was perfection—divinity.

"Ian," she said between his gentle, passionate kisses.

"What?"

"I want to go make love," she whispered.

✣

The majestic old church, with high stone ceilings, newly restored organ, stunning stained-glass windows, and more flowers than it had likely seen in decades, was the focal point of downtown Kalamazoo. Park Street was even closed to traffic for security and traffic-control purposes—what with several leading Congressional officials in one place. The event had also drawn television and news cameras; after all, it wasn't very often that the city saw such high-ranking VIPs.

Megan looked stunning—worthy of any bridal magazine—with her natural beauty, perfect facial features, and lovely, long blond hair that was worn up on that day.

The bridesmaids wore deep burgundy, full-length gowns and the men's tuxedos were Calvin Klein, specially ordered by the tux shop. Bill's brother, Thomas, was the best man, and Ian stood immediately behind him, followed by John, Anthony, and Bill's cousin. The maid of honor was Megan's sister, followed by a friend and three cousins. It was indeed a good-looking group of young people.

Samantha sat with Janet and Matt. Ian was able to engage and enjoy the service fully, knowing Samantha was comfortable with his mother and brother, after having spent much of the day with them. At times his mind did wander, however, as he pondered the seriousness of the event.

Like most people, Ian would occasionally think thoughts that, if ever shared, would make him appear a monster. There were times when a thought would pop into his mind that was so befuddling and out of left field that he couldn't begin to surmise its origin. As he watched Bill and Megan, and said a silent prayer to wish them well, such a thought sprang into his head.

The concept was that of statutory rape: the principle that a minor—say a sixteen-year-old girl—cannot legally consent to sexual relations with a

22-year-old man. The reasons for this were sound in Ian's mind; but similarly, he wondered if it was possible for two people to consent to fifty, sixty,
or seventy or more years together? Back in Biblical times it may have made
sense, when life expectancy was perhaps forty, but today was it really possible
to promise to God that you would remain a perfect fit for each other? For
literally scores of years? And that you would never intimately know another
human? After all, Ian thought, the divorce rate was approaching 50%.

Ian returned to the present as he stood by the altar with his friends,
who were about to take their vows. Even to Ian, however, the vows were
a surprise. Bill began:

> "Megan, I promise, with God's help, to be your faithful hus-
> band, to love and to cherish you, as Christ commands, in
> sickness and in health, for better or worse, as long as we both
> shall live, till death do us part, or until Jesus comes back."

Then it was Megan's turn:

> "William, I promise, with God's help, to be your faithful wife,
> to love and obey you as Christ commands, in sickness and in
> health, for better or for worse, as long as we both shall live,
> until death do us part, or until Jesus comes back."[12]

Ian had met Pastor Mike on several occasions over the years, but the
traditional nature of the vows caught him by surprise. To love and obey?
Then in his sermon, Mike went on to further stun the assembly.

He mentioned several verses, saying, "This is not a quaint old document,
but this is the Word of God." He then read three passages, and the faces
in the crowd increasingly bore the shock of what they were hearing:

EPHESIANS 5:22–24
Wives, submit yourselves unto your own husbands, as unto
the Lord. For the husband is the head of the wife, even as
Christ is the head of the church: and he is the savior of the
body. Therefore as the church is subject unto Christ, so let
the wives be to their own husbands in every thing.

GENESIS 3:16
Unto the woman he said, I will greatly multiply thy sorrow and thy conception; in sorrow thou shalt bring forth children; and thy desire shall be to thy husband, and he shall rule over thee.

1 CORINTHIANS 14:34–36
Let your women keep silence in the churches: for it is not permitted unto them to speak; but they are commanded to be under obedience as also saith the law. And if they will learn any thing, let them ask their husbands at home: for it is a shame for women to speak in the church.

"Now that I have your complete and full attention, I would like you to take a deep breath and relax," the pastor said with a big smile. There was a collective sigh from the attendees, and even some chuckles. Pastor Mike was masterful indeed, and Ian remained optimistic he'd pull the proverbial rabbit out of the hat at that point.

"Let's look at the larger picture, and revisit the verse that continues the Ephesians passage we heard first. Here is the continuation."

EPHESIANS 5: 25–27
Husbands, love your wives, even as Christ also loved the church, and gave himself for it; that he might sanctify and cleanse it with the washing of water by the word, that he might present it to himself a glorious church, not having spot, or wrinkle, or any such thing; but that it should be holy and without blemish.

"You see, I caution people all the time about taking scripture out of context. The point God is making is that there is a hierarchy to things. The point isn't that Bill gets to tell Megan what to do now, but rather that there are relationships in life. There's the parent-child relationship, for instance, which is quite different from a marital relationship. The point Paul is making here is about God and his children, which means you and me. He is saying that we are united, underneath God. He says in First

Corinthians, chapter 11, verse three, 'I would have you know that the head of every man is Christ; and the head of the woman is the man; and the head of Christ is God.'

"Truly I don't bring this to you today to imply Megan and Bill are not equals in this relationship. I bring it to you so that you can understand that they have come together, under God, and that this is their wish, to observe order under God—which is the context within which they selected their traditional vows.

"The Bible teaches us to obey authority, and that by doing so we honor God. At the same time we know that no instruction should be honored that is in conflict with God's laws and rules. Thus, we prevent Bill from taking advantage of the power he finds in those laws, even if he wanted to."

Ian thought to himself, *oh, I get it.* However, in reality, he did not. Though Mike continued with a much more traditional message, and commended the two on their commitment to each other, Ian continued to contemplate the pastor's point. *Either the Bible meant what it said, or it didn't. But obviously I'm no theologian.*

With that minor hiccup—at least as some saw it—the service was unparalleled in its majestic beauty, and the throngs of attendees raved about its splendor as they progressed back to the Radisson's Grand Ballroom for the "real fun." And indeed, the Huxleys did it up right. Never had Ian or Samantha seen such a spread at a wedding, not to mention the full open bar, with top-shelf liquors, Champagne, and a fantastic big–band-era dance orchestra. Certainly anyone who left the event without having fun wasn't trying very hard.

Ian and Samantha made it all the way to the end of the party, though Matt had left about 90 minutes prior, taking his mother home. Janet for her part had been a champ. She and some of the other ladies had not only made many of the elaborate decorations, but had staffed the gift tables and generally assisted the professional coordinators at the reception, diligently attending to details throughout. But with all of that done, so was Janet—her energy sapped.

Ian especially enjoyed the chance to see the official send-off of Bill and Megan. As they entered the limo for their first night together, they were all smiles. They were tired, but there was certainly a romantic element to their chastity that was now clear, and Ian was happy for them to realize the fruit of their patience.

Themselves spent, Ian and Samantha went home and crashed—of course not before making love once more.

While basking in the relaxed afterglow of their lovemaking, Ian asked, "Did you have a good time tonight?"

"I sure did. Thank you. Actually, I can't tell you how revolting the thought of reality is to me."

"Are you sure you're up for a traditional Keppler family Sunday dinner tomorrow?"

"Sure am. Did you want to go to Church?"

"Ahhh, I told Mom I'd be skipping. I think you've done enough to accommodate me for one weekend. I'm going to owe you big."

"No way. It isn't every day I go to a wedding with royalty and TV cameras—that's a touch outside my everyday experience—but then again, it's not every day I get to hang out with such a great guy and his charming family, either."

❖

Prudent as they were, Bill and Megan had kept their lodging plans for the wedding night a secret. Remaining in town for their family event the following day, they were to stay in the local honeymoon suite of an opulent corporate retreat just outside town. The lodge stood alone in the woods, but was unlike any lodge they had seen, complete with bearskin rugs, fully stocked food and drink of every kind imaginable, a giant hot tub, bathrobes, three fireplaces, roses: the whole nine yards. It was midnight as they rode the last few miles in the limo, and Bill was already doing the math. They had until 1:00 p.m. the next day before the Huxley gathering, and then it would be off to Aruba on Monday morning.

The limousine pulled into the isolated gravel driveway of the lodge, stopping right by the car Bill had dropped off earlier in the day. The beautiful log structure was romantically lighted, and even from the outside, Bill could see the flickering candles he'd requested. As the driver set the remaining bags by the door, Bill thanked the gentleman and pulled them into the immaculate entry, closing the door behind them.

The place was a remarkable sight. Red roses where scattered throughout the elegant log cabin—if you could call it that, given its expansive size and luxurious accoutrements. They took their things to the bedroom, which was also illuminated by candlelight, and the bed was sprinkled with rose pedals. As Bill flicked on the light, the ceiling caught his eye. "The ceiling is leather," he exclaimed, a feature he hadn't noticed when scouting the place a few months prior. The location for their first night together had been the one thing Bill insisted upon handling alone, as a surprise for Megan. This was the payoff, and Megan was thrilled.

"Glass of Champagne?" Bill offered.

"Sure."

"Was it everything you hoped, my sweet?" He began to remove the foil covering from the champagne, after first unbuttoning his collar.

"I don't know how anyone could ask for more. I almost feel guilty. I think of our trip to Haiti and then see this . . . . We are lucky people, Bill."

"We are. I am, actually. You have made me very happy, and I'm going to make you happy, Megan. I love you so much." Bill poured the champagne as Megan sat observing him admiringly. Bill uttered an observation or two about the big event as he poured the other glass, but Megan slowly stood and began slowly raising her dress to reveal to Bill her garter belt. She increasingly ignored his words.

"Let me help, you must be so tired of wearing that bulky dress, Mrs. Vanderveen."

"Oh, I am, Mr. Vanderveen," she cooed.

It was tough to be sexy getting out of the gown, but Bill unfastened the long row of buttons to reveal Megan's bare back, which was traversed by a small, strapless lace bra—with matching panties. As she removed the dress, Bill could see just how tiny the panties were. Her perfect body had never looked better to Bill. Her cleavage, her shape, her exquisite lingerie—Bill eased her onto the pillow-soft bed and the two embraced and kissed deeply.

Despite the obvious pressure, their first time together was poetic. Just as Megan had learned to satisfy Bill previously, he too knew how to please Megan. It had taken patience, but she had finally learned to achieve orgasm in the months prior to the wedding, so the interactions weren't a total mystery. The newlyweds collapsed together and cuddled for some time, wrapped in a sense of joy, achievement, love and exhaustion.

Nonetheless, Megan hopped back out of bed unexpectedly. "Where you going, sweetie?" Bill asked.

"I'm gonna take a quick shower," Megan answered. "I feel kind of gross after sweating and hugging people all day.

"Okay, I'll join you," Bill said, delighted to have all legal restrictions removed.

❖

The following morning was a great pleasure to Ian and Samantha. They slowly began to awaken late, about 10:15 a.m., and felt the joy of not having to be anywhere but with each other. It was like a mini-vacation of their own. Ian rolled to look at the awakening Samantha. He quietly studied her profile, thinking about how good-hearted she seemed. While it was difficult to put a finger on, there was a safety, a peace, a genuine nature about her that was just self-evident. He recalled Samantha sharing a vision of her fantasy life, a simple life in the mountain west with just a Jeep, a dog, and the beauty of their surroundings to fill their days. In words that would echo through his head perpetually, he thought to himself that she was simply a *good soul*. That was it. That summed it up in Ian's mind. Samantha was a good soul.

Ian's next thought was more pragmatic. He facetiously wondered if his brain was excreting too much dopamine due to his infatuation. He smiled at the self-analytical thought. Perhaps he would discover she was a raving lunatic once he got to know her better. Or perhaps they would develop different interests and not remain a good fit in the long run. But again, it was the even temperament and caring heart that—even at this stage—separated her from any other woman he'd known. Of course in some twisted way he had loved the passion and hot sex of some of his previous, dysfunctional relationships, but he now fully realized it wasn't worth it. Yes, part of it was the maturity and age of Samantha. But more and more, he reiterated to himself, *she's such a good soul*.

Ian snuggled in closer. Samantha opened her eyes more fully, and stared back into his. They sat for a minute or two just absorbing each other, fully aware that after the Keppler family's Sunday dinner, they'd be apart again. Ian studied Samantha's face.

"What?" she asked.

"Nothing. I'm just looking."

"Well . . . don't," Samantha replied in the refreshing spunky tone Ian so enjoyed. "My breath stinks."

"Uh-oh," Ian said smiling and rolling onto her. "Now I've figured out what's wrong with you. You're one of them aren't you?"

"What the hell?"

"You're one of those people whose mouths, you know, don't grow Scope overnight, aren't you? Your breath stinks in the morning doesn't it?" Ian continued mockingly. "I knew there'd be something wrong with you after all. But that . . . stinky breath, I think I'm going to have to ask you to leave," he finished with a laugh.

"Screw you!" Sammy jabbed, wrestling him away.

"Come here," Ian replied as he rolled her back toward him and offered a sincere and tender good-morning kiss. "By the way, your breath isn't bad," he laughed. She smiled, and kissed him again. The two melted into one as they basked in their time together.

Finally, just after 11:00 a.m. they arose to get on with the day—shower, pack Samantha's things—and head to Janet's for dinner.

Once again Janet had prepared a classic family meal, this time steaks on the grill. Also once again, it was a bittersweet gathering. Having everyone together was such a treat for Janet, but of course the cloud of her cancer cast a shadow on the day, as did the shared realization that everyone would be gone again so quickly. Nonetheless, Janet was grateful and she maintained her characteristic "stiff upper lip" throughout most of the day.

The most notable development of that afternoon, however, was the relationship forged between Samantha Hitchens and Janet. Janet prided herself on not being judgmental, and in truth for the conservative community in which she and Bob had lived, she was somewhat liberal. She saw the good in anyone and everyone, and was ardently aware of various forms of prejudice and discrimination in the world around her, and simply never understood it.

But Janet was also a master of women's intuition when it came to the character of an individual. As she had with some of Ian and Matt's less wholesome girlfriends, she could pretty accurately size up an individual in just a matter of minutes. Whether or not women's intuition was real, Ian was pretty sure that it was, and that Janet had it. And given the mild skepticism Ian had detected when initially discussing with Janet the prospect of a Chicago liaison attending the big wedding, it was all the more affirming of Ian's own intuition when Janet fell in motherly love with Samantha in that single afternoon. In fact, Janet would whisper to Lynn later that day, "I just absolutely adore that Samantha."

Of course, these were not usual meeting circumstances for a son's girlfriend and his mother. As the day had gone on, they shared some intense emotions and feelings, and in many ways it was Sam's compassion, sympathy, and her willingness to listen and care that touched Janet the most.

Certainly the feeling was mutual, and Sammy was overwhelmed that Ian, and now his entire family, were evolving from a fictional fantasy in her mind—one that could never work out—to a warm *reality*. In turn, they saw in Sammy the good soul that she worked so hard to convince herself either didn't exist, or would remain invisible to others forever.

It was another of those days of which the memories didn't fade over time, the way most memories did. It was poignant for its bittersweet nature, and also because the world again seemed to stand still that afternoon. The family didn't fuss over dishes or little details of daily life. They sat at the dinner table, or in the living room, and they talked. They shared fears. They laughed a bit and cried a bit, fully aware of the unspoken reality that Janet, the ultimate mother in their eyes, was very likely not going to be with them much longer. At the same time Ian found himself choked up repeatedly during that slow-motion afternoon, consumed by the thought of the world's greatest mother being reunited with the world's greatest father.

Eventually however, time did march forward that afternoon and the remaining Keppler family members said their goodbyes as they began to scatter to their respective parts of the country. The difference now was that communication would be frequent. As it turned out, this was true not only with the Keppler kids, but with Samantha as well.

Beginning with a simple thank-you note from Samantha, and then a phone call or two, Samantha and Janet formed a regular chain of communication, and ultimately a bond of mutual trust and sharing that would be very strong indeed. In truth, and although their time together would be short, Samantha would later know those treasured hours on the phone with Janet as her own version of *Tuesdays With Morrie*[13]—full of love, depth, and lessons, the likes of which she never would experience again, with a single exception.

Sam and the Keppler kids were committed to do everything they could to help Janet, and certainly to keep her comfortable, regardless of treatment options selected—if any.

As for Ian and Samantha, it would take a few more months before they would know it for certain, but in each other they had indeed found life partners. It was the antithesis of the types of relationships people simply endured; despite the ebb and flow of romantic love and mutual interests, it would never waver in its sincerity, conviction, genuineness, and absolute love and respect. It was one of the purest things Ian would know in his life, right up there with the unwavering love for one's parents, and the love of a parent for a child. While life's unexpected turns would shake them to their cores, this purity would remain. Ian had fallen in love with Samantha, and Samantha had fallen in love with him.

Chapter 12

THE BREATH OF LIFE

September, 1992—three months later

The ringing phone pierced the quiet of the old Keppler home.

"Hello?"

"Janet, I desperately need to talk with you." Positive excitement was apparent in the voice on the other end of the phone.

"Well hello, Marcia . . . it's so good to hear from you," Janet replied, a little taken aback by the apparent excitement. With a slight chuckle of curiosity she asked, "What on earth are you up to?"

"I'm sorry to disturb you, but I have to talk to you, in person, about a treatment option. I've been doing a lot of research since we spoke last week, and I simply have to share what I've discovered! I think it could hold some real promise!" Marcia energetically exclaimed. "How are you feeling today? Would it be possible for me to come see you?"

Janet pondered the request. She didn't feel very well at all, and she was always somewhat skeptical in light of all the sham cures she'd seen in her first bout with breast cancer. On the other hand, Marcia had been a good friend for many years, and she wasn't the type to go off the deep end without doing her research. "Sure, Marcia, we can talk."

"I'll be there in a half hour then. Thank you! I'm just so hopeful about this. Bye."

"Bye," Janet replied, eyebrows raised as she hung up the phone.

Sure enough, the doorbell rang about twenty minutes later, and Marcia appeared with a binder full of materials and a paperback book.

"Hello my dear," Janet greeted. As she'd waited, Janet had reflected on the devotion her friend Marcia had shown her in the months since her diagnosis. Marcia Hoffman and Cindy Vanderveen had been saints. They had taken turns driving Janet to chemo, making meals, and mostly just hanging out and being good friends. Sometimes when she really didn't feel well, Janet almost wished she were alone more; but by and large, she was not only appreciative of the company, she valued the love and care being so thoughtfully dispensed by her friends.

"Hi you poor thing. Pretty rough day is it?" Marcia asked in a sympathetic whine, clearly able to see the frailty in Janet's locomotion.

"I've certainly had better," Janet replied as she gave her friend a gentle hug.

As they settled into the kitchen, Janet offered tea—ever the hostess. "Oh, goodness no, you're not going to wait on me, but can I get *you* some tea? Anything?" offered Marcia.

"No, I'm just waiting to hear what has you so excited."

"Okay, as I understand it, you have recurrent breast cancer that is fed by your hormones. They say that you are estrogen–receptor positive, so you are currently on tamoxifen to slow or stop your breast cancer growth." Janet listened silently. "To complicate things, you also have myeloid leukemia, which, as you know, probably came from your first rounds of chemotherapy years ago. So although cancer is named after its place of origin, in your case breast cancer, nonetheless you essentially have two types of cancer at this point—not just one. Do I have all that right?"

"I think so," Janet replied, impressed by Marcia's grasp of the situation, and also by her genuine, caring interest. "Go on."

"Well as they readily admit, the chemotherapy is wholly toxic, and is actually part of the cause of your new illness. This stuff is not good for you, Janet, I'm convinced. But let me back up."

Marcia continued, with energy. "It began last week when you were talk-ing about your prognosis. I remembered a good friend of mine, Margaret Lancaster. Did I ever mention her to you?"

"No. I don't think so," Janet replied.

"She lives in Indianapolis and I've know her for years. I remembered that her sister had breast cancer, and a recurrence, so I called Margaret to get her number, then called and talked directly with her sister, Jane. It turns out that she had exactly the same situation you do!" Janet was now listening attentively, though still didn't quite know where this was going.

Marcia went on to say, "I know you'll think this is crazy, but you have to hear me out. Janet, she is now fully in remission, and she told me stories of many other women with similar outcomes. She said there is plenty of research to support this cutting-edge approach, so I called the clinic she recommended and had them Fed-Ex me these materials and this book."

"Where is the clinic?" Janet asked.

"Mexico, Janet, but don't let that scare you. Jane said the place is state-of-the-art."

"Well if so, why isn't it here in the U.S.?"

"It's all in here, Janet," Marcia said pointing to the stack of information. "The fact is that the FDA is impossibly bureaucratic, and it would have cost this Doctor Marquesso millions and millions of dollars, and even then his work would have taken decades before it could be used to help people. Actually, he has funded a U.S. lobbying group that is leading a campaign against both the FDA and the FTC for what he says is a viola-tion of his free speech rights to advertise and promote the facts about his medicines and therapies." Marcia spread out the book and the binder of materials on the table.

"I've pored over all these materials, and this really is amazing, Janet. I just want to leave them and have you consider it. It makes so much sense that these poisons they give people to cure these cancers are tantamount to the primitive 'bleeding' they used to do when people were sick," Marcia pushed.

"But what do they have instead?"

"That's just it. They have something almost too good to be true, but it appears it *is* true. They say that this narrow range of natural, Brazilian-found compounds is based on a discovery made in 1954, in the rainforest. I know it sounds conspiratorial, but it really sounds like there is a governmental and pharmaceutical establishment that just chooses to ignore the weight of these data—for whatever reasons. Maybe it is out of ignorance and bureaucracy on one extreme; or, maybe it is out of greed on another. But the research in this binder is amazing; it says that variations of this compound are over 87 to 93% effective on most breast cancers, *and also on myeloid leukemia*! Isn't that amazing?"

Janet browsed the materials in the binder, and the book by Dr. Marquesso, *Redefining Cancer Treatment: How to Beat 'Big Medicine' in Your Fight Against Disease.*

"So you talked to this Jane and she saw other success stories in addition to her own?"

"Absolutely. And she was happy to talk with you if you want to call her. I put her number on the inside of the binder."

"Well, I have to tell you it sounds too good to be true, Marcia. But on the other hand what if it were true?"

"Exactly! But there is one other thing. It isn't cheap. A course of treatment is three weeks, and the cost is $87,000. That doesn't include travel expenses, but usually one course of treatment is adequate according to the studies," Marcia added.

"Holy macinolli, Marcia, you've got to be kidding me!"

"I know, Janet, but if I really thought this would work for you, we'd find you the money."

"Oh, don't be silly. I may not be rich, but I'd never let anyone else pay for such a thing. If it's worth doing, if it would work, I'd certainly pay it myself." Janet continued to thumb through the materials.

"I know you don't feel well, and I'm sorry to barge in and dump this on you. I feel like I'm here trying to sell you on this, but I must say I just got so excited in talking with Jane, that I just had to get you this information as soon as possible," Marcia explained. "I just know that . . . time isn't on our side."

The two friends shared a look into each other's eyes, and squeezed each other's hands. Janet couldn't help but feel this was worth exploring further. "Thank you so much for doing all this and caring so much. I'll talk to the kids about it."

✦

"Megan, the house looks so nice," Sammy commented. She and Ian took off their jackets and handed the Vanderveens a bottle of wine as they entered Bill and Megan's quaint little starter home. It was beautifully decorated in a country motif: clearly the feminine touch of Megan.

"Oh, thank you, Samantha. It's just so good to see you! Hi there, Ian!" The four greeted one another with hugs for the women, and appropriately macho handshake-hugs between the men.

"What time did you get in, Samantha?"

"Ian just picked me up from the train station."

"I bet you guys are getting that routine down pretty well by now?" Bill asked.

"Yeah. It's not too bad though. Ian's been good about driving to Chicago too, so we keep things mixed up enough that I don't mind the train too much," Sammy added. "At least not so much coming here. I must say that the late-night trips back on Sunday are not my favorite."

"Speaking of that, have you guys seen John?" Bill asked.

Ian replied, "Yeah, that's one of the other benefits of my going there. We just saw him last weekend. He's doing great with his job and seems to absolutely love living in Chicago."

"Well, I sure hope you guys don't have your hopes too high for dinner; cooking is not my strong suit, but we just thought it'd be fun to get together," Megan commented as she continued to race around the kitchen as she talked.

Sammy assured, "Heck, you should see what I eat on a daily basis, Megan. I'm sure anything you make will beat my Captain Crunch."

"Bill, why don't you show Ian and Samantha around the house while I check the chicken," Megan suggested.

As Bill conducted the mini tour, mostly for Samantha's benefit, Megan nervously hustled around the kitchen, tending to the mixed vegetables and finishing a quick tossed salad. She had been working on the meal virtually since she arrived home from work. At the conclusion of the tour there was pouring of wine, followed by more chatter—the two women on their own topics as the men talked about work.

Before long, they sat down to dinner as Megan loaded the table with food that, as it turned out, appeared far more palatable than it tasted. Ian held an expressionless poker face as he bit into the horrifically tough and leathery chicken. He could read Samantha's complete lack of reaction, followed by her polite comment of a nebulous nature, and he knew that she too, was wondering how on earth she could consume the impossibly tough chicken. It wasn't just rubbery and chewy, it was world-record tough, as if it had been marinated in Elmer's glue and then sun-dried.

The newlywed husband also said nothing. It wasn't until Megan herself started her second bite of the chicken that the elephant in the room was fair game. "Oh my gosh! That chicken is horrible!" she exclaimed in horror as the other three looked at her then looked at each other.

Almost as if rehearsed for a TV sitcom, the other three dropped any attempt at lying about the chicken. It was *that* bad. They each laughed as they simultaneously let it fly.

"Horrible."

"Can't make that shit up!"

"Stuff could gum up the intestines of a bull."

"Poor Megan," Samantha said with sincere sympathy. They were not laughing at her, but were facing the excruciatingly obvious reality head-on, in hopes Megan would also be able to laugh. But understandably, she was steamed. A sudden wave of uncharacteristic frustration was apparent. There was silence.

"Unbelievable!" she exclaimed with emotion boiling to the surface over her failed first effort at entertaining in the home. After another second, she blankly stared at the table and looked like she was about to cry.

But with perfect timing after the brief, awkward silence, Ian provided the needed levity, rather than sympathy. "What'd you do, soak that stuff in Liquid Nails?"

Megan smacked Ian on the arm in jest, blowing off steam and laughing her way through the tear she had shed.

"I'm so pissed," she exclaimed as she stood and removed the chicken from the table, with everyone now laughing. Bill jumped up and hugged her. "Believe me," he said, "there is no way on earth that this is your fault. That is some seriously defective chicken there."

"He's right, Megan. It's like they injected that sucker with resin instead of a growth hormone," Ian added.

"So what are we going to eat now?" Megan whined.

Again the three looked at one another as if in their sitcom roles. "Final Stage," they blurted in unison as they pushed back from the table. "Get your jackets."

Of course by the time they cleaned up and headed out for the Final Stage, any anxiety or embarrassment on Megan's part was gone, thanks in large part to Sammy's warm countenance. Sammy had helped Megan clean up, and at one point shared a very similar story of a culinary mishap of her own. Soon they'd had such good laughs over the soon-to-be infamous first dinner at the Vanderveen house, that Megan was again having fun and enjoying the warmth and humor that enveloped the four friends.

The four rode in Bill's late-model Oldsmobile as they made the trip to the nearby restaurant. It was a dark, moonless Friday evening in late September. They were on Sprinkle Road, which was a major artery that would get them to the cross street where all the businesses and restaurants were located. It was five lanes wide to accommodate the brisk, 50-mile-per-hour traffic, but traffic was nonetheless sparse at most times of the day. That night, there were not even any headlights in sight as the mile-long, sweeping curve stretched ahead of them. It was there that it happened.

Wham! It was extremely loud. The staccato crunch of metal echoed startlingly, and came without warning. There was a loud impact into the passenger side of the car where Ian was sitting—a deer had come from the shoulder of the road and run full-speed into the car.

"Shit," was the first thing Bill could utter. The window by Ian had cracked and the noise and impact had taken the four of them completely by surprise. Bill pulled the car to the shoulder of the road. Nobody had been hurt, but everyone was visibly shaken; everything had happened so quickly.

Bill grabbed a flashlight, and the other three went with him to survey the damage. Immediately they could see the deer on the shoulder of the road behind them, still alive with motion. Another car rounded the corner and came to a stop behind the deer. The driver hopped out and walked toward the deer, and the five of them converged upon the struggling animal, which was still writhing in a grotesque display of survival instinct.

"I called the police on my cellular phone. You guys okay?" the stranger said. "Be careful there. You don't want him to get you with those antlers; that's one strong animal."

It was quickly obvious, however, that the deer's injuries were severe enough that he wasn't a threat. In fact the hoof motions and writhing had quickly abated, but the once majestic animal was still alive. There was blood coming from his mouth, and Sam could see his labored breath in the cold night air. The deer's big, brown eyes remained open and moving, almost as if tracking Samantha.

Ian knew Bill was a hunter and he'd seen such sights before. Ian's brother Matt was a hunter too, and Ian had even helped clean a carcass with Matt once before. But somehow, he saw this situation very differently.

Samantha felt a strong pang of sympathy for the deer, yet she was helpless to relieve its suffering. Ian moved behind Samantha, but she remained intently focused on the deer. She slowly and carefully knelt down from about ten feet away, drawn to the suffering of the animal. "Man, don't get too close," Ian said, but Samantha was transfixed. She could actually hear the slow, raspy intake of air, before seeing the white cloud of mist expelled from the feeble respiration.

"I'll bet his back is broke," the stranger said from behind.

Samantha remained focused on the deer, hearing only muffled sounds as Bill exchanged words with the man in the background. Strange as it may sound, she couldn't help but think of the story Ian had told her about his father, lying there in the hospital with Lynn and his mom at his side, and how they said he had squeezed their hands as he knew he was going. Samantha wondered if the deer had thoughts of life and death, or if he was scared. Suddenly she wished she could console the animal as it transitioned out of life.

With some trepidation Samantha reached down and put a hand on its neck, feeling the softness of his coat as she gently stroked with the grain of the short, brown bristles. The deer didn't seem to respond except with a minute eye movement. Sammy looked into the large brown eyes.

Ian glanced down to look at the now less-frequent breath coming from the deer's blood-filled mouth, and remembered a discussion from his religion class, about the doctrinal belief of the magic spirit that entered the soul through respiration. It was the *pneuma*—the magical "breath of life"—and it was slipping out of this animal rapidly.

Sam watched calmly as one final wisp of moisture was exhaled. The gurgling stopped.

"The poor thing," Megan said softly from behind Ian. Samantha remained transfixed for a few more seconds before she snapped out of her contemplative sympathy and stood up with the others, wiping a tear from her right cheek.

"Well at least he's out of pain now," Samantha said, returning to a more conventional demeanor.

"I had a friend once who had to watch a deer without rear legs struggle around for 30 minutes before the sheriff arrived and could shoot him," Ian wryly observed.

As if prompted by Ian's statement, the flashing lights of a deputy illuminated behind them. A police report was made out, the stranger thanked, and before long the four were getting back into the damaged sedan. Apart from the cracked passenger window, two dented doors and a dented quarter panel, the car could still be driven without any problem.

"Wow. Anybody else work up an appetite?" Bill quipped as he started the car.

"Man! What a night! Bet you're glad you rushed to Kalamazoo for this one, Samantha," Megan added.

"I'm sorry for your car," Ian sighed sympathetically.

"I'm sorry for the deer," Samantha retorted.

"It'll be a hassle, but that's what insurance is for," Bill said. "Let's eat. The night's not over yet, darn it. We're bound and determined to get a meal in and have some fun. It's only eight-fifteen." They all laughed in disbelief at the strange events of their evening.

They four finally settled in at the restaurant and had their dinner. After a couple of drinks and food, they had already put the evening into its legendary perspective—memorable as it no doubt would be—and moved on to the intended opportunity to catch up with one another.

"So how's married life?" Sammy asked.

"It's great," said Bill.

"Yeah," agreed Megan, adding, "I mean it's still pretty new—having someone in bed with you every night and all, but it's wonderful. It really is."

"No fights over the toothpaste cap yet?" Ian joked.

"No. Not so far. He's actually pretty neat." Megan was clearly happy. She loved Bill, and Bill loved her. Together they were settling into daily life and acclimating to the delicate balance that is marriage. When the ladies excused themselves, however, Bill made a comment that revealed one area in which he was struggling a little.

Half in jest, Ian asked, "So how's the sex? Twice a day?"

Bill replied with a slightly disappointed look, "Not exactly."

Ian couldn't help but feel as though he'd stepped in it a bit. He tried to recover. "Yeah, it probably takes a little while to get into the swing of things, get used to new living habits, etcetera. But as they say, at least it's one area where practice isn't a bad thing." They smirked.

"Don't get me wrong, everything really is great. I love her to death. I just feel like we waited so long, and now I'm wanting some of the payoff and it just seems she's not as into it as I am."

"Yeah, well, I hear that's not uncommon at any point in marriage," Ian laughed. "But you're in your prime, my man." Bill grinned.

"With that very minor exception, it really is awesome to finally be sleeping together at night . . . waking up together. I absolutely love it.

"Good man. I'm happy for you," Ian said.

After a short discussion of the fascinating mystical force that make women have to go to the bathroom at the same time, the ladies returned. As Samantha sat she said, "Hey, did Ian tell you he's got an interview for a new job?"

"No, what's the deal?" Megan asked with her characteristicly sweet smile and genuine interest.

"It's just an interview, but I'd sure love the opportunity. I'll tell you what; I can't begin to survive on the peanuts I'm getting freelancing for $25 per hour here and there. But the interview is with Michael Alan Conklin—"

"The mega-rich Wall Street tycoon?" Bill interrupted with excitement.

"Yes sir. The one and only," Ian replied.

"Do you know him?" Samantha asked.

"Don't know him personally," Bill clarified, "but everyone locally knows of Mike Conklin. He's been in the paper a lot. Most people in big business know of him too. He was a fighter pilot in Vietnam—a local hero and all-American success story, but when he returned from the war he attended Yale and then went straight to Wall Street. Made an absolute killing in the 1980s. I think he's ranked like around 200 on the list of richest people in the U.S. But apparently he's cashed in his chips and is moving back home to Kalamazoo to retire and start—" Bill motioned to Ian to deliver the punch line.

"A charter airline service . . . . Apparently flying is still his real love, and between taking care of his elderly father and managing his own affairs, he's starting what they call a Part 135 operation. That's what the FAA calls air taxi and commuter airlines. It's named after the section of the regulations they operate under. Apparently he's quite a way through the mountain of red tape; the only problem is that he'll have every starving flight instructor and commercial pilot around here vying for the co-pilot seat. It seems like a bit of a long-shot for me."

"Hey, he'd be a fool not to get a quality guy like you," Bill encouraged.

"Well I don't know, but we'll see. Luckily some of my friends at the airport were able to mention my name to him, so I dropped him a résumé. His administrative person called the next day to set up an interview!"

"That's awesome, Ian. Good luck with that."

"Hey, I'm sorry too, that with all the chaos of our night I didn't ask how your mom was doing."

Ian paused to find an honest, candid answer. In everyday life he was used to offering a canned reply to that question, but these were dear friends who wanted to know what was happening. "She's strong. I guess she's doing okay, but I know it's not easy. She really doesn't feel well at all. I got her out for dinner on Tuesday though, so she's still able to be out and about on some days."

"We've all been praying for her, and she's on our prayer list at church. She's probably on your church's list too, so I'll bet God's probably getting a ton of mail on this topic," Bill said in a mixed metaphor of God and politics.

"Yeah, I guess she's been talking with Matt and Lynn about some new treatment Marcia Hoffman suggested to her. It's one of those Mexico things. My brother and sister aren't real happy. It's a good thing Matt is moving back here to Kalamazoo where he'll be better able to help with this kind of medical stuff."

"When does he come back for good?" Bill asked.

"This is the final trip. He's driving now and due home this weekend sometime."

"Awesome," Bill said as he leaned back. "Tell him we said hello and that we'll look forward to seeing him."

"You know, the whole thing with your mom sure doesn't seem fair. I know how we used to talk, after your dad died, about Job, and how it irritated you when people said that God would never give you more than you can handle, or that it was part of his plan." Bill paused, and had a more serious look on his face. "But I've sure been thinking about your mom and your dad, and I really do believe that they have done so much good, and planted so many seeds here that it is *possible* that a well-deserved, glorious reunion is exactly what God says they deserve. I absolutely loved your dad, and I love your mom too. Wonderful people, my friend."

"Thanks, Bill. They obviously had nothing but respect for you too. And you may well be right, and I will take *great* comfort in the thought of them seeing each other again when that time comes. You know though, in the class I took this summer, I pondered our conversations about the pencil—several times."

"The pencil?" Samantha asked.

"Yeah, Bill was telling me about this woman at their church who every time anything would happen, would assume it was some divine interaction by God. If she lost her pencil, it was God testing her patience. Essentially she leaped to a supernatural explanation—a leap of *faith* that there just couldn't have been a natural, worldly explanation."   .

"In fairness, I have to say that while I still think she was overdoing it, I was struggling with my faith at the time. I really do believe that God works in mysterious ways," Bill clarified.

"I understand. I guess that the point I was going to make in regard to Mom and Dad is that sometimes things just happen. One of my dad's favorite sayings was 'Life isn't fair,' and I think he was totally right. Take for instance that deer tonight. It's a tough life. If starvation or hunters don't get you, a car does. Was that God's plan for the deer tonight, or was it just chance? I personally think it was a random accident."

"Actually, it was pretty poor street-crossing skills on the part of the deer," Bill said wryly. The other three grimaced, satisfying him that it was funny enough. "Seriously, no question about it Ian, there is free will in the world, and with that freedom comes the reality that things can just happen; but there are many miracles every year that are certified by the Catholic Church. Our church doesn't certify miracles, but don't think for a minute that they don't happen. Don't think that God can't work in mysterious ways, or work miracles. I'm hoping he'll do exactly that for your mother." Bill was becoming slightly impassioned.

"I guess all I'm saying is that for me, personally, I think God must be a little busy to hear every prayer for every sick person, or every prayer asking to win a basketball game. Perhaps what happens on earth is most often just a result of . . . *what happens on earth.*"

"Let me ask you this, Ian," Bill coaxed. "Do you believe that you and Samantha were destined to be together? Or was it just chance?" It was an interesting question for which Ian was unprepared.

Ian looked at Samantha and paused. Samantha was not an overly religious person. In fact, she had rarely ever been to church as a child. Suddenly, Ian was reminded that religious beliefs were something about which they really hadn't talked. He had told her of his church activities and the music group to which he belonged, so obviously she wasn't turned off by any of that. Ian almost felt guilty again, as he had when he'd recently realized that he didn't even know if she believed in God. He felt badly that this matter, which should be so important, had been so low on his radar.

Ian and Samantha never walked on eggshells around each other, so he knew he would be honest in responding to Bill. First, he wondered how Samantha would answer. "What do you think, Sammy? Were we meant to be together, or was it chance?" He provided no indication of his own leaning.

"I don't know . . . . The truth, I guess, is that a lot of times I've thought of you and your relationship with your father. I have to say, I've often felt that with our mutual friends—and that out of all those people in the bar, we sat next to each other that night—I've sensed something brought us together. I don't know that I would call it God, but I certainly felt that something was there."

Ian was touched by the sentiments. He leaned over and gave Sammy a kiss on the cheek.

"Thank you," Ian whispered softly to her.

Bill interjected. "I rest my case."

Chapter 13

WHERE ONE DOOR CLOSES

Saturday was to be their mini "vacation day" of the weekend, and Sammy and Ian treasured those days alone. At least they were mostly alone, since Scrappy didn't spend much time in the apartment, between work and a new love interest. With Scrappy mostly away at his girlfriend's place, Ian and Sammy could generally spend their day however they wished. They would long treasure and remember those weekends devoted solely to each other.

Sometimes they would stay in bed and watch TV, or enjoy a couple of rented movies. They would talk, share, sleep, and of course enjoy making love whenever the urge struck. On that particular Saturday they decided to go out and see one of the new scary movies.

It never ceased to amaze Ian how tense he could become while watching such movies. This was especially true for the films that involved the spiritual realm. It was one thing to watch a deranged person there on earth, slinking around the Bates Motel or the great resort in *The Shining*, butchering people to death; but to Ian, it was yet another level of scariness when mystical, spiritual, or supernatural forces were involved, as in *The Omen*, *The Fog*, *The Amityville Horror*, or *The Exorcist*.

"So were you scared? Ian asked.

"Yeah, I'd say there were a couple scenes that had me on edge." Samantha huddled close while they walked, as if scared. She had actually covered her eyes during some of the scenes.

"I was thinking in there. Do you know what made that movie so scary to me?"

"What?"

"It's that it really could happen! It could have been real! What's scary is this notion that there are ghosts around us—that there are spirits around us—and especially that some could want to hurt us."

Ian continued as they walked. "I've gotta say, do you have any idea, in the summer after my father died, how many times I saw him in our house? I mean, I don't really think I saw him," he clarified quickly, "but I can tell you that many times I would round a corner and see him in his chair, watching TV, or I'd see him standing by his workbench when I'd pass by the open door to the workroom downstairs. And as quickly as I'd do a double take, he'd be gone."

"Do you think that you really saw something?" Samantha inquired.

Ian thought. "No, I think it's just the flawed way the mind works. I think it's unable to reconcile that a permanent and frequent part of the landscape is suddenly and permanently absent. A part of the picture the mind expects to see is missing, and it just reconstructs the image using old memories . . . . But let me ask you, do you think there are spirits out there? Capable of killing us?"

"You're asking me if I believe in ghosts; and that *is* the appropriate first question to ask. Whether there are good ghosts or bad ghosts, or if they can interact with us, those are later questions, right?" Sammy had a knack for framing issues clearly. "I guess I never really thought of it that way. I wonder what most people would say?"

"I think most people would say that they *do* believe in ghosts," Ian postulated.

"I don't know about that. Most people tell their kids there is no such thing as ghosts."

"Oh, but do they? I couldn't disagree more. Not only do I believe many times that my dad was looking down or even was beside me, like at my graduation, but I think we routinely teach kids about the Holy Spirit,

God moving pencils, or that deceased loved ones are among them. You said last night that you thought my dad might have brought us together. We really do preach that the spirit world is alive and well! Hell, if you think about it, we think it's thriving with all sorts of ghosts, goblins and demons among us."

"So are you telling me you don't believe in any of those things?" Samantha asked.

"Well, I guess I'm actually saying the opposite. I *must* believe in at least some of those things . . . clearly I do," he repeated upon further reflection. "And I think it's *because* of that belief that those dang movies always freak me out more than your basic slasher movie."

The following morning Ian sat in church with Samantha, his mother, and Matt. Janet had suggested she'd cook a "good Sunday dinner" in celebration of Matt's return to town, but it was Samantha, during one of her telephone conversations with Janet during the previous week, who had offered to get up on Sunday and drive Ian's mother to church.

Ian looked to his right. He had never experienced someone so willing to give of herself, when it was clear that there was nothing expected in return, and no ulterior motive. She wasn't even brown-nosing. It was just who she was. She was authentic.

The congregation rose and recited the words of the Apostles' Creed:

> I believe in God the Father Almighty, Creator of Heaven and earth
>
> And in Jesus Christ, His only Son, our Lord;
>
> Who was conceived by the Holy Ghost, born of the Virgin Mary,
>
> Suffered under Pontius Pilate, was crucified, dead, and buried;
>
> He descended into hell; the third day He rose again from the dead;
>
> He ascended into Heaven, sitteth at the right hand of God the Father Almighty;

From thence He shall come to judge the living and the
dead.

I believe in the Holy Ghost,

The Holy Catholic Church, the communion of saints,

The forgiveness of sins,

The resurrection of the body, and life everlasting.

It was a fleeting thought, but Ian considered that the chanting of the
words in unison was eerily similar to the devil-worshiping, mind-control
wackiness of cults like the one he and Sammy had seen in the movie the
day before. His recent class had covered the various creeds at an elementary level, but watching everyone chant together made him curious about
the deeper, symbolic meaning and origins.

However, as Ian sat in church that morning, he was newly energized
spiritually by his summer course on the basics of Christian theology.
Though he had been somewhat surprised by his own naïveté—for instance
in learning that other religions had miracles, healings, crucifixions and
resurrections—he had also come to better understand what he believed
to be Christianity's unique fulfillment of prophesy, and its unique concept
of the trinity.

Most of all, however, Ian loved the chance to sit and to be still, alone
with his private thoughts. It wasn't something he did often—*nothing*. In
reality, however, doing nothing was a chance to be spiritual, and to be
appreciative. One thing Bob Keppler had religiously driven home with his
kids was an understanding that they were not to take anything for granted.
Indeed, Ian always felt a deep sense of appreciation for his many blessings,
and that time in church was a wonderful time to count them.

This day, he was grateful for Sammy. He was grateful that Matt was
back in town. He was grateful that Janet was able to be out and about,
and that despite her grave situation she was enjoying the morning and
experiencing at least a modest level of energy.

As the closing hymn rang out and the majestic old church organ was
fully uncorked for the fourth stanza, Ian was grateful that if all else failed
he would be certain of his mother's warm embrace in Heaven, by a God

who loved her and a husband whose warm smile would be a thousand times worth the pain of any final struggle on earth. In his private, quiet world in that pew, Ian let the voluminous sound of the organ wash over him, his wave of emotion broken only by the need to prevent those around him from seeing his watery eyes.

It was one of many such moments that the end of a worship service would provide for him, particularly fueled by the timeless hymns he so long adored.

After the service, the group headed home for another of Janet's bountiful feasts. As his father used to say, it was fit for a king. The amazing thing to Ian, Samantha, and Matt was that she had the energy to prepare a traditional Sunday meal. But prepare a meal she did, and the four of them celebrated Matt's return and basked in the quality time with Janet.

As one might expect, however, at some point the conversation unavoidably turned to the treatment option in Mexico. "Okay, let me go ahead and tell you where I am with all this," Janet began. "I've heard the same speeches this time as I did when I first learned of my cancer. I told you that last month Cindy Vanderveen tried to arrange my cross-country travel to the healer—the one who I saw at church before my last remission . . . I don't know, maybe I should have gone?" The two brothers and Sam showed no response, only an intention to hear her out. "But that's neither here nor there since I'm not going to do it. But I've also had vitamin miracle cures brought to me by two different people, and I spent several hours with them being polite but rejecting their suggestions. The point is that I'm no fool. I know those things won't work."

Matt chimed in. "It just grinds me that when you're so sick, people browbeat you with these 'miracle cures.' I mean, if I had the flu and someone wanted to spend the morning telling me about a flu remedy, I'd kill them."

"I know, Matt, but understand. These people care about me, and they are absolutely certain that their solution will work—even if their solution is just to pray harder that I'll be healed. And once again, maybe they're right."

"Mom, you and I both know that's not how it works," Ian said.

"I know, but I'm getting off the point. I really think that this Dr. Marquesso *might really be on to something!*"

"But Mom—," Matt interrupted, only to be cut off himself.

"Let me finish. I realize you'll probably give the reasons this won't work, and I want to hear those and be realistic, Matt. I just want to tell you about the phone calls I made."

"Sorry Mom. Go ahead," Matt said with newfound patience.

"I not only called Marcia's friend's sister, Jane, but after hearing her—and you really would be moved if you could hear her tell about how this saved her life—she told me about another woman *she* had talked with before she went to the clinic. It was a very similar story!"

Matt was having a hard time being patient now. "And I'll bet you dollars to doughnuts that she's not alive today if you tried to track her down. And even if she was—"

"She *is* still alive Matt, because I've talked with her!"

Matt could be silent no more. "Okay Mom, I have to chime in here."

"Okay, go ahead," Janet said with some level of irritation. She leaned back, ready to listen, "but know that I know what you're going to say . . . and that you're probably right. It's just . . . the excitement and hope that I started to feel . . . it was amazing!" Janet began to cry. Samantha was first to go comfort her, joined by the boys in providing much-needed hugs of support.

Moments later, Matt began again. "I understand Mom, and please know that I certainly don't want to talk you out of hope. This is a difficult situation for me too, because I have a choice between not giving you the other side of this book and these so-called studies you've read, or stomping on hope. I don't like this choice." He paused. "But I think I have to give you a medical perspective on this."

Janet now chuckled and kicked in to her motherly mode. "Shut up and get on with it. Besides, I've talked with Lynn and she's told me all about studies and double-blindness and all that jazz, so go for it." She appeared to be chuckling at herself at that point. Intuitively she knew Matt was going to be correct in what he was about to say.

"Okay, so she told you that these studies are not legitimate science. There are protocols in real science. You see, people just don't really understand scientific methodologies. Scientists are not machines, they are people. They're prone to the same errors in thinking that we all are. There have been *so many cases* where the results of a scientific study confirm what the scientist expected, in fact *hoped* to see. It's called the 'expectation bias.' It's one of many ways the mind is tricked—like an optical illusion, but of the brain rather than the eyes. The mind is a funny thing, and it can guide our behaviors in very subtle, unrecognizable ways so that we see what we expect to see."

Ian chimed in. "Do you guys remember the backward masking craze when we were kids? We would play *Stairway to Heaven* backwards on Matt's turntable, and hear all these devil-worship quotes. But Mr. Strauss, our science teacher showed us how he could play virtually anything backwards, like Pat Boone or a reading from the Bible, and we'd hear nothing but gibberish. But then he'd tell us the secret phrases he'd heard, and suddenly we'd hear them plain as day." Matt and Ian laughed at the humor of some of the phrases.

"So it's kind of like when we were kids and we used to lie on the grass and try to make animals out of the puffy clouds?" Samantha asked.

"Absolutely. That's a good one. Once someone pointed it out, all of the sudden you could see things clearly. And that's exactly what happens in these studies. I'm not saying they fake things necessarily, but they're *not* legitimate because they're not properly controlled to prevent bias, and they aren't subject to the scrutiny of other scientists. That's how real science works; the thing this Dr. Quack calls 'institutional bureaucracy' is actually called 'peer review,' and that means you publicly disclose your methods and findings for other scientists to poke holes in. These guys haven't done that."

"Interesting," Ian agreed.

Matt was on a roll. "They aren't published in mainstream medical journals, because *they aren't real studies!* Their methods are so screwy that there's no point in other scientists' reviews. They'd laugh. It's pseudoscience. Besides, if they had anything legitimate about the results they claim, this doctor would be up for Nobel Prize and would win fame, fortune and one million dollars."

One of the great things about Janet was her eternal optimism. She was hearing what she didn't want to hear, but knew was true, yet she faced it with the same determination and positive attitude with which she faced everything. Unbelievable as it may sound, that's the way she was. She was emotion-driven and would run with what she wanted to be true, but only to a certain extent. Somehow she always kept one foot firmly planted in reality. In this case, she intuitively knew the claims were too good to be true; she had just so very desperately wanted them to be true.

She actually began to chuckle at herself. "Ahh, you just don't want me to spend your inheritance," she quipped.

"You are terrible," laughed her admirer Samantha, in mocked admonishment. Ian remained silent. He couldn't help but ponder the many people who forked over the cash and invested emotionally in the cure, perhaps to the exclusion of earlthy relationships—and precious time with family and friends.

Matt laughed but turned serious again. Just as they had all experienced after Bob's death, you could never predict when waves of thought would sweep you into an emotional state. Matt's eyes welled up in what was an atypical display. He choked out his thought: "I so very much wish . . . there were something more I could do for you. You do know . . . that we'll be fine. You could spend every penny of your money and we'd understand and love you and not care a bit, if it made you happy."

Matt's tears and obvious pain moved everyone else to tears, and especially touched Janet. She rose and walked to his chair to console him. In what was a harbinger of things to come, Matt had shifted into the parental role, worried that she knew the only thing that mattered to him was *her* comfort and well-being. He wanted to reassure her that her children were safe, and that they were stabilizing themselves in good careers. In essence, she had done her job and could now at least rest in the comfort of that knowledge.

In the coming weeks it would be time for the children of Janet Marie Keppler to live out this transformation of roles, and with Matt's guidance, they did just that. Indeed with the help of Janet's sister, and visits from Lynn, Janet would make it to the end without a single night in the hospital.

It was just after midnight on a dark, rainy night in October, when Janet Keppler drew her last breath. Ian and Matt had been there throughout a long evening; Lynn was to arrive the following morning. Matt's medical experience told him that her deep coma and "death rattle" meant that her joyous days of spreading laughter and love were eminently drawing to a close. Their primary worry was that she be comfortable.

Though she was largely comatose that evening, she had been somewhat conscious in the afternoon—even asking for assistance to go to the bathroom. To others it might seem indignant or unwelcome, but in a strange way the reversal of caretaking roles was an honor for the two sons. There was no one else they would have wanted to care for their mom in her final hours, and there was no one Janet would have preferred do so than her children.

As if in a final gesture of love and appreciation for all the caretaking she had provided, and all the love and incalculable sacrifice, the two sons gently and tenderly cleansed their sweat-soaked mother. They changed her gown and bedding, and proceeded to sit quietly through the late-night hours. There was no fear. There was just a sense of love, gratitude and deep appreciation.

Ian sat on the open side of the king-sized bed that seemed only yesterday was where his father had lain. Matt knelt on the floor at his mother's other side. As her body's relentless struggle to breathe drew to a close, the pauses between strained breaths grew longer. Ian could clearly see the rising and falling of her abdomen with each labored breath. Each son quietly and gently grasped one of their mother's hands for the last several minutes, until there was a final, ever-so-slight exhalation—then silence. Janet Keppler passed away peacefully in her home, surrounded by the pure light of love.

Where an earthly door had closed, Ian took solace in believing that a perfect, heavenly gate had just opened.

◆❖◆

Chapter 14

TESTING AUTHORITY

Four Years Later, Washington, D. C.—November, 1996

Ian sat in the public gallery of the House of Representatives, looking down at the Congressional proceedings below. While the experience was always fascinating, between the history of the room, the rich décor, and the palpable sense of global power beneath his feet, this time was unique. He was watching his best friend's father-in-law, Representative Huxley, speaking from the floor. While Dan Huxley had made tickets to the gallery available for Ian on other occasions when he was in Washington, never had Ian actually seen Dan addressing the House while it was in session.

The House was debating a Republican-proposed amendment to strike down President Clinton's Executive Order that ended discrimination in federal agencies based upon sexual orientation. The order had expanded upon President Nixon's similar action, which precluded discrimination based upon race, ethnic origin, or age.

As Ian watched, the Honorable Daniel Huxley concluded his remarks. "I am concerned that the party to which I belong—the party of Lincoln, the party that ended slavery, and the party that opposes abortion—would be sadly forsaking its long tradition of doing the right and moral thing, should it abdicate its responsibility and fail to pass this amendment to dispatch with the president's overzealous Executive Order."

Upon hearing those words, the excitement of the moment was somehow diminished for Ian; however, while there were times he found himself questioning some of Huxley's politics, he respected and liked the man a great deal. They saw each other on occasion at parties or special events, like four months earlier in July when Megan and Bill had celebrated their son Zachary's second birthday. The representative had even once hosted Ian for lunch in the official House commissary. And as Ian pondered Huxley's opposition to the Executive Order that day, he recalled that in a matter of days he would return to the luxurious Huxley home on Gull Lake, this time for a Sunday party following the baptism of Bill and Megan's beautiful new daughter, Hanna.

The sweet little fair-haired, blue-eyed amalgam of Megan and Bill was clearly evidence of her quality parental DNA. Even at this young age it was evident that she was going to be graced with the all-American, dashing good looks of both her parents.

As Ian peered over the gallery rail, he thought how time seemed to have flown. Bill and Megan had been married four years already, and he and Samantha three; and oh how life had changed in such a short period of time. With two little boys at home life was crazy, but a type of crazy that he knew he had to enjoy while it lasted.

Ian's son Andrew was already ten months old, and his big brother Brandon was about to turn two. He and Samantha loved them dearly, but he couldn't help but think that there was too little "down time" around the house those days. Sometimes he felt guilty for having free time during his overnights away from home while Sam was home with the kids, changing diapers, giving baths, and doing all the work. Though it was a stretch, at least they had been making it work financially with only Ian earning an income.

Checking his watch, Ian realized he needed to catch a cab and get back to National Airport. It was his job to pay the landing fees with the Mac-Aero credit card, and prepare the plane for departure. The passengers' meeting with the FDA was probably winding to a close, and Ian knew his boss, Michael Alan Conklin, was going to be arriving from a private meeting of his own with little time to spare. And one thing Ian knew about flying out of National was that he didn't want to be late. It was one of the few overcrowded airports in the country that used an FAA-controlled reservation system to assign departure and arrival slots; having reserved their departure slot days in advance, and with only a one-hour window in which to use it, he did not want to risk a highly embarrassing, unplanned overnight with passengers.

But these were the things Ian loved about his job, and he was grateful for it. It would have been a terrible time to search for employment as a pilot; many of his fellow graduates from major aviation programs had left flying altogether. They had invested countless hours of airport grunt-work in the early nineties, then worked long years as underpaid flight instructors, only to find that the promise of an airline hiring boom never materialized. By that time in 1996 the forecasted hiring boom to replace retiring Vietnam "boomers" had been pushed all the way into the early days of the new millennium.

As for Michael Alan Conklin, Ian had come to know him better and he respected him greatly. Of course it wasn't always easy. Mike Conklin was a complex person, and the development of trust and friendship between them had taken some time.

Within the previous year or so, the two had begun playing golf when waylaid in far-off places. Unlike in the big cities where Mike would tend to run off to undisclosed meetings, he had no other business to conduct when clients or Compassion missions took them to places like Athens, Georgia, or Springfield, Missouri. Those opportunities for casual time together had provided an environment conducive to sharing and disclosure; through those times, Mike had begun to see hints of Ian's emergent interest in the origin of his own beliefs and worldview, as well as those of others.

But that day in D.C., as Ian warmed himself in the cab and peered out the window to see the Jefferson Memorial and the Potomac pass by, thoughts of his interview with Mike popped into his mind from four years earlier. It wasn't that Mike had been rude at all. He had not. It was more that he struck Ian as a professional who intentionally maintained some distance from his staff. He had been polite and friendly, but in a formal way that simultaneously garnered respect and attention. Ian would later see the clear connection between his mannerisms, and his military training and service in Vietnam.

In fact, during that first interview, after having asked all of the aviation-specific questions he was going to ask, Michael Alan Conklin had made a concerted effort to address some interesting interpersonal concerns. With somewhat militaristic precision of language, he had said, "Ian, as one of my first hires, if we reach an agreement on terms, you and I will be working closely together. Therefore, there are some things you should know. First, you should know that I'm convinced you are the best applicant for the job. You've been flying real passengers on cross-country trips, in low-level, dense terminal operations, with poor weather-avoidance equipment and anti-icing capabilities, and in the tough weather environment leeward of the Great Lakes. Seeing as you haven't killed anyone or bent any metal, and based on what I hear about you, these are good things."

"Thank you, sir," Ian said.

"Thank you for the title, but I've not been knighted by the queen and we're not in the military so you can just call me Mac. My point is that you are hired as a pilot and a vital crewmember, and that is of utmost importance. I'm out to ensure the safety of our passengers, our equipment, and myself."

"I understand. Thank you, sir—I mean Mac." Nearly everyone called him Mac because of his initials, which also formed the foundation of his company's name, Mac-Aero, L.L.C.

"On the other hand you should know that I have created this operation, and purchased the initial three aircraft, for three reasons. First, because I love aviation. Second, although I have plenty of money I'm also an idealist, and I would like the planes to be fully utilized and even earn some money to offset their operating costs. Third, and this is my central point to you, the aircraft enable me to travel in pursuit of my passions, which relate to the study of history, philosophy, and religion." Mac spoke while pacing the floor slowly as if giving a military briefing.

"The reason I share this with you is that I hold some, shall we say 'nontraditional views' for this part of the country, and you will be in contact with some controversial people in the course of our travels. I want to be crystal clear that I don't know your worldview, values, and morals. And frankly, I don't care. I only care that you can be the best possible pilot by my side, and that my open inquiry and study of controversial matters will not be objectionable to you, or affect your ability to perform your pilot functions to the best of your ability."

At the time Ian hadn't been quite sure who they would carry or what to make of these "controversial views" of the tall, dark, somewhat leather-skinned Conklin, but he wasn't worried. Time would bear that out. All he knew was that Mac was not only extremely wealthy, but was highly regarded and respected by many. And whether it was the business world or the aviation community, reputation usually told a lot. Ian would never sell himself out, even for an opportunity like this one, but he was more than comfortable with working for the legendary Mike Conklin.

As a result, Ian had confidently responded, "I understand, Mac. And without full knowledge of the types of work and interests you speak of, I can simply assure you of this; so long as it isn't illegal, doesn't jeopardize my safety, and doesn't involve the ritual blood sacrifice of animals or little children, I think we've got a deal."

In the taxicab, Ian smiled to himself at the recollection of Mac's face in response to his confident answer. In retrospect, it had been another one of those small, but pivotal turning points in life. Little did Ian know what a profound effect it would ultimately have on him and his family. No, on that day in the Washington D.C. cab he simply knew that Mac had liked his answer; the rest was history. Ian thought to himself, *who knows where I'd be if it weren't for Mac.* Perhaps like many of his friends, he'd have been out of aviation entirely.

But thanks to Mac, and with credit due to Ian's hard work and then-outstanding proficiency, he was helping manage and fly three great air-craft: a Citation Jet II, state-of-the-art corporate jet; a Beach Baron, which was a high-performance, twin engine "sports-car;" and still a beloved Cessna Centurion T210L, the six-place single that was the same model he had flown for Tom Hanson four years prior. In fact, he had since talked Tom into selling his aircraft and becoming a charter client of Mac-Aero, a sign of dedication that had greatly impressed Mac. And while the Citation remained his favorite of the three planes, he still enjoyed the unique chal-lenges posed by flying the two piston-powered planes.

Soon after Ian's pre-flight of the jet on the wind-swept, cold concrete of the general aviation ramp at Washington National, Mac arrived from his meeting. Conveniently, the client-passengers also arrived shortly thereafter, and all systems were go for an on-time departure. After the winding taxi out through the airline gates, and after all the preflight checks and clearances were handled and confirmed, the controller snapped out the clearance. "Citation four-three-niner-mike, cleared for takeoff runway one."

"Clear to go runway one, three-niner-mike," Ian responded just as Mac began easing the throttles forward. The acceleration was a feeling that Ian still relished, and as the airplane leaped into the air and began a slight left turn, he glanced down at the Pentagon. For a flash of a second he again noted just how close it was to the runways, something he'd observed on prior flights.

From the Pentagon on the left, Ian turned to his right and glanced directly down the Capitol Mall, his mental attention still focused on the radio chatter of the busy D.C. airspace.

There was a concept that the airlines developed years earlier called the "sterile cockpit," which was procedurally in place in Mac-Aero's charter operations as well. Like most safety procedures it had its foundation in prior accidents, in this case those into which cockpit chatter or banter between crew had been a contributing factor. As a result, a sterile cockpit meant non-essential talk between crew was forbidden below 10,000 feet. Especially now that they had become more talkative with each other, Ian and Mac were ever more vigilant not to break the sterile cockpit rule. That day was no different, as the jet climbed out through the busy northeast corridor.

Above 10,000 feet an increase in personal conversation had come as Ian and Mac started to discover that they were on parallel paths in many ways. Mac was continuing his quest to better understand and synthesize his own worldly experiences with a better understanding of history and religion. Initially unbeknownst to Mac, Ian's own life experiences had placed him on a similar path of inquiry. Ian was becoming overwhelmingly fascinated with human nature, and human beliefs—including deeper questions about fate and free will, ghosts and spirits, faith and reason.

He later learned the fancy word for his area of inquiry, "epistemology," which defined the study of the origin and nature of knowledge and belief. For the time being, however, he simply knew he'd begun the process of realizing that so many things he had believed, or wanted to believe, were more at odds with his increasing knowledge of how the world really worked, than he ever imagined.

Perhaps his quest was just the beginning of maturity, of getting past that late-teen, early-twenties stage when every overachiever thought he had all the answers. Time would certainly tell, but one thing was for sure: there were several other parallels between Mac and Ian's ways of thinking.

For starters, Mac's horrendous experiences in Vietnam had shaped his worldview in a dramatic way, such that it was clearly not mainstream or ordinary. He had witnessed horrific acts and seen the results of indescribable carnage. He had never shared many of the things he had seen; he could simply see no value in allowing those memories any further exposure to the world.

But as time moved on after he had arrived back stateside and finished school at Yale, and especially after the years on Wall Street began ticking by, he had become less and less satisfied with his life. He had become fully aware that *his days*, too, were limited; and he had become convinced that he needed to change how he spent them.

It's worth noting that Mac's conclusions had come despite being one of the richest, most "successful" individuals in the U.S., and even in the world. But in the life he had built for himself on Wall Street—fast cars, fast women, jets and eighteen-hour days—there was little to life but making money, grooming protégés, watching markets, and making more money.

Much more importantly, he just couldn't get over how seriously he had taken himself—his life, his money, and his career—and how seriously the young Turks that he worked with were taking themselves, as well.

He'd made it through the eighties okay, but somehow by the late eighties and early nineties something had changed. He didn't know if it was he that changed, or his attitudes and approach in regard to business, but he knew it was time to quit when he felt like every young kid was talking in military metaphors around the office, "as if it were a life-and-death battle being waged in the fricking workplace."

It wasn't the vocabulary that bothered Mac, it was that they thought what they were doing was tantamount to warfare. They stayed up all night drinking caffeinated beverages. They plotted. They talked of destroying their enemies. They harbored anger, twisted and hidden in pride and ego.

There were times when Mac thought he was actually going to snap, grab one of the boastful, aggressive, snot-nosed warrior kids by the ear and scream, *"Do you have any idea what the hell you're saying? You're talking about killing people, and defending your turf, and maneuvering to wipe out the enemy. You have no idea what life is about. I've seen real people die horrible deaths. I've seen real matters of life and death. I've seen my buddies guts splattered on the ground in front of me, and had their brains sprinkle my face as their heads exploded. You think this fucking shit matters. You think this job and this money are so fucking important. They aren't! It just doesn't matter!"*

Of course Mac never did say such things, and consciously he knew it wasn't their fault. They were just working hard and living the dream of a generation that grew up with video games and not a care in the world—"young, dumb, and full of cum" as the saying went. But Mac knew that it was time for him to get out, and get out is exactly what Mac did.

From Ian's perspective, there were similar questions about life, and his worldview certainly contained the reality that life had the potential to be short—or to paraphrase Hobbes, be nasty, brutish, and short. The irony in his mind was that he felt blessed to have had such great parents, education, and opportunity. But like Mac, he too found it difficult to tolerate people who were so dedicated to becoming the "sofa king" of Kalamazoo, or the real-estate baron of Timbuktu, as if these things were the stuff life was made of. His experiences had simply told him otherwise.

Yet similar to Mac, it was not that Ian believed there was anything wrong with those who were ambitious or driven. It was just that he himself was not that way, to the extent that he often found it difficult to understand those who were able to be so gung-ho and fired up about such matters.

He sometimes even found these differences of intensity between him and his long-time friend Bill Vanderveen. It wasn't any major chasm, and they remained his and Samantha's primary "family" since Janet's passing; but there were times Bill's money-driven, stop-the-welfare, damn-the-homosexuals approach seemed nothing short of "all about Bill," and downright uncaring.

In short, Mac and Ian were both searching for deeper meaning and a better understanding of the world around them. In doing so, Ian's approach had become one of questioning.

By the time of the flight home from D.C. in 1996, he had become an advocate of what some were calling "truth-driven thinking." The term came from an internet-based bulletin board, where he and others exchanged ideas. The bulletin board may have only been the clunky, direct-dial predecessor of the Internet, but it still provided a forum for the exchange of ideas among a limited number of like-minded, quasi-techies, where no subject that was intellectually argued was off limits. The goal was to set ego aside, overcome the human tendencies to seek affirmation for what they all already thought they knew, and seek universal truth in all areas of inquiry—based on reason and evidence, over hype and emotion.

Exactly where his fascination with epistemology began, Ian didn't know. To a neutral observer it might have stemmed from a broad array of life events and observations—his mother's friends and the Mexico clinic; his own belief that he could fly if he believed strongly enough; people's insistence that God moved their pencils or was the direct physical cause of this or that; his struggle over whether or not it made sense to lie to his children about the existence of Santa Claus; the likelihood that UFOs and alien autopsies he'd seen on TV were real; or superstitions about luck he'd witnessed in Vegas.

As part of this fascination with epistemology, the night before that flight Ian had watched another TV appearance by "The Amazing Randi," James Randi. On the program, Mr. Randi had talked about his successful investigations into major international cases, such as an Israeli who claimed he had scientifically *proven* his ability to bend spoons with his mind. Randi had also discussed his $1 million prize for anyone who could demonstrate those kinds of paranormal or occult powers under mutually agreed upon, controlled circumstances.

Mr. Randi had further captured Ian's attention by telling of the scores of people who had applied for his $1 million dollar challenge, professing claims of dowsing abilities. These were the people who thought that they could find water, oil, or various other substances, essentially with bent coat-hanger rods. Holding the metal rods gently between thumb and forefinger, the operators were allegedly alerted to a "hit" when the tips of the rods were driven apart by approaching the target. The only problem, Mr. Randi had indicated, was that dowsing didn't appear to work at all!

The Amazing Randi had gone on to explain the subtle, ideomotor reflex that was behind the delusional belief, a reflex that subconsciously actuated finger movement, similar to that which occurs when playing with an ouija board. But the really fascinating part to Ian was the description of the mental states of these so-called dowsers.

Randi described them as usually polite, seemingly normal people who simply believed with every fiber of their being that their skills were real, accurate, provable and reliable. He also pointed out that there could well have been important social and psychological forces at play in their belief—needs to affirm themselves, but also to maintain a certain world-view and social standing that, in their own eyes, defined them: They hung out with fellow dowsers; parents and close friends were often dowsers; social circles offered support and discussion of the finer points of dowsing. Those forces of affirmation were just too strong to allow the dowsers to face the truth.

Mr. Randi theorized that to reject the fantasy of dowsing might, for many of the hard-core believers, be tantamount to rejecting their entire self-perception and worldview!

The famous magician had gone on to explain that the dowsers displayed tremendous resistance to admitting that their skills didn't work—even when faced with clear evidence to the contrary! Their belief persisted after their skills produced ten out of ten possible hits on the baseline exam—the forked sticks opened right on cue when the the applicants could see into the treasure-containing buckets—only to inexplicably vaporize when an opaque barrier obscured the applicants' views. Despite clear proof that the skills they claimed did not exist, the applicants would never stop believing.

"Yet they were as shocked as anyone," he had commented, and he suggested the possibility that no amount of data would ever convince such real believers. It was akin to a metaphysical belief, supported by a *need* to have dowsing be true, for social, psychological or even other reasons that at that time were not fully understood.

Hearing Mr. Randi describe the subjects' astonishment had really caught Ian's attention. *To what degree do social pressures and urgent, emotion-driven, psychological needs drive all of us?* Ian wondered. He also wondered to what degree his own, similar needs drove his conclusions about how the world worked.

These thoughts had been on Ian's mind during the smooth flight home. In the quiet, private depths of his high-altitude ruminations, he thought about religion. Why did others believe one thing in terms of religion, and why did he believe another? He found their beliefs a little strange sometimes, but then pondered his own: virgin births;[14] talking donkeys;[15] Jesus raising the dead;[16] Jesus' physical resurrection;[17] and of course the many additional dead people who walked around on the day of Jesus' own death.[18]

"Hey Mac," Ian asked, "you ever heard of the famous magician, James Randi?"

Mac looked at Ian with a smirk. "You mean 'The Amazing Randi?'" he corrected with a smile. "Yeah, I had dinner with him in New York on more than one occasion. Brilliant guy. Why do you ask?"

"No way!" Ian exclaimed. "Of course I should have known." It wasn't the first time Ian had been surprised by the reach of Mac's connections. "Anyway, I've seen him on TV a couple of times and been really intrigued with him."

"Have you read any of his books?" Mac asked.

"No, I haven't," Ian replied.

"Ahhh. Well if you're interested in how people's emotions impact their beliefs, he has a couple you should read."

"What was he like when you met with him?"

"Exactly as you would imagine. He's articulate and bright, yet also polite and unassuming. He's an authentic guy."

"That's just amazing!" Ian said without thinking about the unintentional pun—The *Amazing* Randi.

"Actually, one of his books is called *The Faith Healers*.[19] It was the result of his three-year investigation into claims of faith healing."

"What'd he find?" Ian asked.

"Well you should read it, but basically he couldn't find any evidence that there is any validity to it, but he found a lot of evidence of scams . . . which tends to lead you to the conclusion that it's just another inhumane, mean-spirited con game. At the same time he's an intellectually honest guy and doesn't say it can't work, or doesn't work, but rather that all we can do is draw tentative conclusions based upon the evidence."

Ian pondered Janet's first healing. "You know my mom had a spontaneous remission from terminal cancer after seeing a faith healer."

Mac looked surprised. "You serious?"

"Serious as a heart attack . . . or should I say *serious as terminal cancer,*" Ian joked with a wry smile. He continued more seriously, "Of course I'm not sure that even she thought it was really the cause of her remission, but it was a wild experience. Our little church was not prone to such things, but our pastor had known this guy from seminary or something, and he was coming through town so they had him perform a service. And no kidding, just like on TV they called my mom forward, the guy held up his hand to mom's forehead, said a prayer, and she almost fell to the ground."

"No kidding?" Mac was surprised by this revelation. "You *don't* seem like you came from a family that would have gotten into that."

"Well again, I'm not sure we did 'get into it.' I'm only telling you what she experienced, not what conclusion she or anyone in my family drew. She just said that she felt a cool breeze, and that suddenly she felt a little dizzy."

"Well now you do have to read that book."

"I will," Ian replied, "But I can guess what he'll say; probably what I already suspect."

"Well the obvious question is, 'Did she take medical treatment?'" Mac said somewhat hypothetically.

Ian answered even though it was rhetorical. "She sure did."

"Well, do we know what the cause of the remission of the cancer was?"

"No. I certainly don't," Ian answered honestly.

The radio interrupted, "Citation three-niner-mike, descend at pilot's discretion down to one-five, fifteen thousand."

"Roger Cleveland, down to one-five thousand."

Mac continued his rational discussion of Janet's remission as he entered the new altitude setting in the flight management system. "It might be the medical treatment that she had, or it might be the intervention of the faith healer. Since we don't have any control of the variables on this, we can't tell which it was. We can't say one way or the other, and of course the evidence is now no longer available to us," he said, pausing to compassionately add, "unfortunately."

He continued, "Causation is a difficult thing to assign in matters like this. Now you'll get people who say, 'Oh I was under medical treatment for the longest time, and nothing was working; then I went to see the faith healer.' But the fact that the two of them coincided doesn't mean anything."[20]

Mac was getting into the topic. "The other thing is, how many people has this faith healer treated *who did not recover*? Those people are dead! They're not here to testify. They're under the ground! So we don't have that evidence available to us. You can't do selective reasoning when you're handling these things. You can't look for the hits and ignore the misses, which is something that even scientists are not supposed to do, but sometimes do."

"You can't count the hits and ignore the misses," Ian repeated, deep in thought. "You know, I've thought about essentially the same thing a number of times when it comes to coincidences. One time I saw an old family friend at the store, and had a really warm, nice conversation with the woman. She died that night, and I genuinely thought there was some significance in her words to me, having seen her so near to her death. But the more I thought about it, I realized that I see friends all the time at the store, but I attached some deep message to this woman's comments only *after* she died. Had she lived I would have treated the conversation no differently than the others I regularly have while shopping."

Mac nodded. "That's interesting. I've had similar observations."

The radio interrupted, "Citation three-niner-mike, descend at pilot's discretion now, down to eight thousand and contact Chicago Center, one thirty-four point three."

"Roger Cleveland, down to eight thousand on the handoff, see you later," Ian replied.

"Okay," Mac said as he sat up straight to begin the busier approach segment of the flight, "we are out of one-five thousand—sterile cockpit in five thousand feet." In the name of safety and procedures, the conversation was done.

As Mac learned of Ian's own quest, those common threads of pursuit fueled an already strong professional relationship. As they approached Kalamazoo, however, a more immediate threat lay within the lower layer of lake-effect clouds that hugged the Western Michigan landscape.

Ian always enjoyed the view of lake effect from the air; like many weather phenomena, you could actually see it in action. It was one thing to talk about lake-effect clouds and snow, but to see them from above as they formed on the leeward side of the lakes, was another. It was as if the lakes were giant pools of warm water, and an ice god from the northwest was blowing his icy breath across them to produce prodigious amounts of fog, clouds, and ice for his own entertainment.

"Glad I'm not in the 210, or even the Baron today," Ian said to Mac. "This is the perfect setup for icing." Indeed just a week before, a Detroit-bound ATR-42 had crashed just south of Detroit as a result of icing. The buildup of tiny, subfreezing water droplets in moisture-laden clouds was a huge threat to airplanes. Of fog, thunderstorms and icing, many considered icing to be the biggest threat of all to an airplane.

"Yup," Mac answered, followed quickly by a reminder: "Five-hundred feet to sterile cockpit at one-zero thousand." Ian felt a little like he'd been chastised.

The descent and initial approach to Kalamazoo went normally. They flew radar vectors for an ILS instrument approach to Runway 35. It was Mac's leg flying so Ian talked on the radios and located the approach charts for Mac. He also conducted the standard pre-approach briefing. After a few minutes the jet emerged from the bottom of the clouds.

"Go visual," Mac instructed.

Ian keyed the mike, "Kalamazoo approach, Citation three-niner-mike has the field in sight."

"Roger three-niner-mike, you are now cleared for the visual approach to Runway 35 at Kalamazoo. Contact tower now, one-one-eight point nine."

It was then that the accident-chain began. When Ian had provided Mac the approach chart, Mac had said, "Just give me the book." As Mac banked the jet to the right for the visual approach directly to the airport, saving valuable time and fuel, the three-inch-thick-book of approach charts fell to the floor and popped open with a bang. A chunk of charts near the top of the binder popped loose on the floor between the seats. It would have been a major inconvenience to re-sort them into the binder if they were allowed to bounce around further and get out of order.

Ever the seasoned pro that wouldn't allow a simple distraction to take his attention from the landing ahead, Mac simply barked, "Damn it. Pick those up. You must have left the binder lock open."

Mac seemed perturbed. Ian was intimidated. While they certainly had grown closer, Mac could still snap into "military mode" quickly. But then again, in his mind doing so had saved his life more than once—not to mention made him fortunes.

"Okay sir, but you have the radios." Ian reverted to formal language in the suddenly tension-charged atmosphere, perhaps in response to the rebukes he'd just experienced.

"Yes, I've got radios. Gear coming down now." Mac keyed the mike. "Kalamazoo Tower, Citation four-three-niner-mike checking in on the visual to 35."

Just as Mac finished that transmission, however, a hydraulic alarm suddenly began to sound—the next link in the accident chain. It was deafening, as though they were in a submarine under attack. "ARRH, ARRH, ARRH, ARRH, ARRH."

Of course the controller replied immediately, "Roger Citation four-three-niner-mike, *proceed for Runway 35.*"

Distracted, Mac replied curtly, "Roger, clear to land 35, three-niner-mike." A usual silence followed. There was no reply from the controller. Technically, none would have come had what Mac said been proper and correct. But Mac's incorrect transmission was another link in a quickly forming accident chain.

Mac thought he had heard what he expected to hear, that he was cleared to land on Runway 35. Unfortunately, there was a small Cessna from the university practicing touch-and-go landings on the crossing runway, and the timing looked questionable enough that the controller *had not* cleared the Citation to land.

The controller had missed Mac's *incorrect* readback, however, because he had quickly diverted his attention to his own concern—the unfolding spacing problem between the single-engine plane on short final, landing west on runway 27, and Ian and Mac's Citation that was landing to the north on 35.

Just as quickly as it had started, the alarm in the Citation stopped. The gear clunked down into place.

"I've got three green and break pressure."

"Confirmed. We're fine. Probably just a slight pressure loss we'll have looked at. Controls are good. We're a go to land," Mac stated with unequivocal authority and clarity.

Usually the controller would have made the Citation aware that there was crossing traffic landing ahead of them. But again, the controller was busy making sure it was all going to work, and he simply failed to do so.

In reality, the controller was worried about making the embarrassing professional blunder of sending the Citation around for another pass. He was well aware that corporate jets cost clients literally thousands of dollars per hour, and that a second ten-minute approach meant not only time and irritation, it was very real money. When it did happen, sometimes pilots got cranky and impatient with the botched spacing. This particular controller had been roundly chastised by a pilot just a month prior.

Like most people, the controller worked hard and took pride in his work. As a result, he didn't want to send the jet around needlessly, which also would be an admission that his plan, no matter how brilliantly conceived, just hadn't come together. While looking back and forth between the planes and his radarscope, the controller experienced that little optimistic voice that everyone has heard and listened to at some point—"I can make it work. I've still got it."

The Citation was now on a half-mile final, moving at 130 miles per hour. All of these events had occurred very quickly, since when a jet makes a short visual approach it literally speeds directly to the runway from the point of visual contact.

The little Cessna that was crossing, of which they weren't aware, was on a short final to the intersecting runway. Unfortunately, he was taking much longer than the controller had hoped.

As Mac performed the routine double-check of pre-landing tasks that are committed to memory, Ian was done securing the charts. He had an uneasy, bad feeling that something was not right, but everything looked fine.

"I got radios back—," Ian said, only to be cut off with Mac's authoritative quickness.

"Fine," Mac barked.

Ian's mind was processing quickly, and he realized he hadn't ever *heard* a landing clearance. That didn't mean there wasn't one, of course. *Clearly,* he thought, *Mac has this under control.* Ian said nothing.

Suddenly, clarity emerged right as the jet screamed along toward the runway. Mac had just begun to round out the descent on short final, to flare and level the wheels above the runway, when the radio squawked, "THREE-NINER-MIKE GO AROUND! IMMEDIATE GO AROUND THREE-NINER-MIKE!"

"Oh shit," Mac said as he saw the little Cessna touching down. The picture out the windscreen looked just as it does when someone isn't going to stop for a stop sign at a crossing road, and it is instantly clear that speeds are perfectly matched for a collision. "GO AROUND!" Mac said firmly—fully in professional mode despite his adrenaline rush and an instinct that told him the situation was going to turn out very badly.

Mac jammed the throttle controls fully forward and pitched the nose upward slightly. Unfortunately the turbine engines didn't spool up instantly. The order couldn't have come at a tougher time for the small jet; speed was bleeding off rapidly and the engine RPMs had wound down to near idle. As a result, there was a very delicate balance to be struck. Mac couldn't pull up too much as the engines came to life, or the wings would stall—a sure way to die; at the same time he knew it was imperative that they clear the little plane.

The engines leaped to life with tremendous thrust. Mac maintained the centerline of the runway and began aborted-landing procedures—flaps up to approach settings as the engines took hold; there was no time to raise the landing gear, however. The Citation ripped overhead just twenty feet in front of the little Cessna. They had made it through a near-catastrophe.

Mac safely climbed the airplane to traffic-pattern altitude and entered the traffic flow again as instructed.

Once at altitude, Mac barked, "Were we cleared to land?"

"I don't know, Mac," Ian replied calmly. "You had the radios, and it was right when that alarm went off."

"Fuck," Mac exclaimed under his breath. He was fully aware that the manner in which the near hit was reported could lead to enforcement action against them by FAA action.

Mac keyed his mike. "Thanks for the abort instruction there. I should have seen that Cessna," he said, with the clear goal of quickly fessing up, but not admitting he knew he hadn't been cleared. The controller needed to know he wasn't going to be pounced upon.

The reply came in a relatively polite-sounding voice, "That sure didn't go as I had planned either. Give a call on the ground and we can discuss." That usually wasn't a good sign. Mac and Ian were both worried about the ramifications, but obviously grateful they were safe.

On the ground, Mac called the controller and became convinced that he wasn't going to put anything in his report about a missed clearance. In fact, the controller never mentioned it, and it seemed evident that he thought he had cleared the Citation to land—or at least took responsibility for his failure to do so.

With taped records of everything, they didn't sleep well for a while, but in the end they never heard another word about the incident from the FAA.

For their actions, however, Ian and Mac spent some time in serious discussion, including a review of similar, historic accident chains. They learned, or relearned, many lessons.

The event turned out to fit a particular pattern of incidents and accidents which fell under a heading called "failure to challenge authority." Ian and Mac assessed the character traits within each of them that had almost gotten them killed. They realized that Ian's lack of assertiveness in expressing concern was partly the result of Mac's strong personality, and Ian's fear of looking bad or appearing incompetent. For his part, Mac learned that his knee-jerk, take-command style needed to be tempered by a conscious effort, when time allowed, to solicit and encourage input and to downplay his authoritarian side.

In the end the entire incident played right into Ian's fascination with motivation, psychology, and epistemology. Indeed for all three—the controller, Ian and Mac—their personalities, experiences, histories, fears and expectations had played into their actions.

Ian also saw that blind submission to authority could get him killed; and that despite being trained to respect and honor authority since he was a child, part of being a responsible adult was knowing when to stand up and be heard. Little did he know the extent to which he would apply those lessons outside aviation.

Chapter 15

MORE THAN MEETS THE EYE

Thursday night—one week later, November 1996.

Bill leaned back with a chuckle amidst the flashing lights. The driving beat of the subwoofers washed through him like a wave of energy. He tipped his beer and flashed his clients a wide-eyed expression, then returned his eyes to the deeply tanned brunette as she swung around the pole and sent a seductive smile in the direction of the group.

"I think she likes me," said Bill's client, George Ritter, with a laugh. George and three of his key employees were being entertained as one of NALA's major accounts, and certainly Bill's largest customer. For its part, NALA was continuing its meteoric climb. Bill had worked extremely hard, as everyone expected he would; his product and technical expertise were extraordinary. Also to his credit, his charm and personality allowed him to create tight and lasting relationships with his clients. While it was far from fun and games all the time, regular outings such as this—or a round of golf—were a necessary perk of the job.

"I think she likes your money, George—not *you*!" Dave jabbed at George as if he was unaware of the strip-club game. Dave was George's long-time service manager. As he spoke, his eyes never left the dark-featured beauty on the stage. She had long, flowing hair, a stunning figure, and bore a striking resemblance to Halle Berry.

Bill leaned to his side to make a comment to George. "You know this chick is dangerously hot."

"Absolutely," George agreed. "She's not only gorgeous, but knows how to work it."

"That's what I try to get my wife to understand. It's all about the attitude," Bill added candidly.

"That's what everybody tries to get their wife to understand," George joked. "But just wait 'til you've been married as long as I have." The men laughed and continued to watch the show.

"I think I'm in love with Star," Dave quipped as he went to the stage to offer her a tip. But rather than just take the dollar she began dancing for Dave, looking him straight in the eyes with a naughty, seductive expression. Without breaking the locked stare she released the string behind her neck and exposed her perfectly tan breasts, in order to properly receive the gratuity.

"What I couldn't do with a few hours of that," Bill commented again to George.

"Hell, at my age she'd probably kill me."

"Yeah, but what a way to go!" They chuckled more and enjoyed the show.

Bill's mind flashed briefly to Megan. This was one of the few aspects of his work life that he did not share with her, for obvious reasons. In his mind, however, it was a non-issue. He rationalized that it was part of his job to entertain clients on occasion. He was obligated to develop these relationships; anyway, the customers typically choose where to go. Who was he to judge them?

At the same time, despite being a bit nervous the first time a client suggested going to a strip club, he had come to enjoy the places. The girls would often sit and chat with the men, and Bill really enjoyed the banter. Many of them were extremely intelligent—even if they were lying about being in college. They were just so different from Megan. Certainly he loved her, but this was an experience separate and apart from Megan. At least that's what he told himself.

Had he been more candid in his thoughts, however, he would have put it more simply. Megan was the perfect wife. These girls would be the perfect good-time girls. These girls were the types you *didn't* marry.

For her part Megan no longer held that late-teen, youthful appearance, but she was now stunning in a whole new way. She was a gorgeous woman of 26, and had a Christy Brinkley kind of classic American beauty. From Bill's perspective, it was a wholesome but asexual beauty.

Bill further rationalized that it wasn't like he was *doing* anything with these girls, or being unfaithful. It was just fun. He even theorized it propelled him toward increased marital contact in a good way, since it wasn't like he was leaving the strip joint and taking up with a prostitute. No, he was "taking it home" and using the aphrodisiac to enhance his own marriage.

But deep down he knew that argument was weak, since the real foundation for Bill's rationalizations lay in a sense of entitlement—a payoff, if you will, for his growing anger. Though he wouldn't have used the exact words, a significant element of his mental state was influenced by feelings of resentment, rejection and just plain hurt. In short, a lack of sexual contact, or even recognition of his needs, was increasingly weighing on Bill. It wasn't just that he and Megan had not had sex since the birth of little Hanna, though her twelve-week checkup had come and gone two weeks earlier. It was even more than that.

Bill couldn't help but feel that his beautiful Megan almost *tried* to dress in an unappealing fashion. In his eyes, she didn't even pretend to want to impress him in that way anymore, let alone ever try to seduce him. He felt tremendous guilt for thinking it, but at times he told himself that Megan was the least sensual person he'd ever seen. It was a thought he hated himself for having.

Even since they were newly married over four years before, his attempts at sex had been routinely shrugged off by Megan. She would dismiss his advances either as if he were joking, or discount them for any of several esoteric reasons. From there it evolved into a mechanical act—seemingly for the sole purpose of getting pregnant. And of course after the births, things didn't get any better.

Bill was certain he wasn't just imagining it and that it wasn't just the sting of a first blow to a previously unscratched ego. Maybe, he thought, it was just dramatically differing libidos.

"Hey, you want another beer, Bill?"

"No, I've got to drive back home to Kalamazoo."

"What, the wife got plans for you tonight?"

"No, I have a dinner planned with an old friend."

"Wow, a guys' afternoon and a guy's night out too," Dave teased. "Lucky guy."

"My wife's a saint. What can I say?"

All the rationalizations allowed Bill the luxury of barely a second thought when it came to Megan, and how she might view the situation. At the same time, Bill's concerns about his relationship with Megan were starting to occupy more and more of his thoughts, enough so that he thought about mentioning it to Ian during their guy's night out.

Bill drove home to Kalamazoo, just in time to join his friend Ian at a local sports bar. After a recap of Ian and Mac's near miss, and a general catching up—with four young children between the two of them this was not a frequent outing—the conversation turned to Bill's concerns.

"So you were at the nudie bar today with clients? Wow. Must be tough getting paid to look at hot, naked girls."

"Somebody's got to do it," Bill responded smugly. "Besides, it's not like I get to see that stuff at home."

Ian laughed. "Ah, you're starting to sound like an old man, Bill."

"Seriously Ian, let me ask you a question. Do you ever wish you'd slept around more before you got married? I mean, if you had it to do again, would you sleep with more women, or fewer?"

"Geeze, don't know, Bill," Ian said. "I guess if I really had it to do again I'd sleep with more." Ian paused to think, taking a swig from his beer. "But then again, who knows. Maybe then I'd have tasted the fun and would be less happy with what I've got."

"I don't know." Bill pondered. "At least you'd have test-driven the car that you bought—*for life*."

Ian pretended to chastise Bill for his statement. "I can't believe you said that!" They chuckled together, but Bill's frustration and resentment were evident in his words.

He resented not feeling that Megan was attracted to him any more. He resented that she didn't want him sexually. He resented that the people he'd read about in *Penthouse* Forum, as he sat in his hotel rooms, seemed to be out having all sorts of fun and sexual adventures. Then, after he'd masturbate, he'd experience the same guilt he did as a child. He'd clean up and toss the dirty magazine in the trash.

To some degree when he was at the strip joints, or even more-so when reading dirty magazines, he resented that Megan made him resort to such pathetic, lonesome, and crude behavior—as if he were still in his parent's home trying to sneak the magazines he'd found by the road.

Bill sighed. "You know I'm joking. But it sure isn't what I'd expected out of marriage. I mean the marriage part is awesome; you know how happy I am with Megan and the kids. But the sex . . . . Man, I guess I just thought I'd *have some.* I mean, what the hell was all that 'waiting thing' about? I guess it turns out that it was about *more waiting!*"

Ian could see that this was a serious thing to Bill. "Have you talked with her?" Ian asked.

"Hell, I've certainly tried," he replied. "But I'll tell you what, even talking about it makes her withdraw further. She says, 'It's all you ever talk about. Sex, sex, sex. You make me feel so inferior—so inadequate.' Then she clams up and is sullen—rams around the house cleaning or focuses her attention on the kids for a couple days. I tell you, Ian, I usually think I'm a pretty good problem solver, but this one has me beat."

"Well, they say that men too often try to think rationally when dealing with women. Maybe you need to think of it less like fixing, and more like you did when you were dating. Maybe you need to find out what she needs, and provide her that—then the sex will come."

"I suppose."

"At the risk of sounding like an apologist for the ladies here, I have to say that having been home with the kids when I'm not flying, I don't know how they do it every day. I mean, I couldn't love anything more than the boys. I remember crying when Brandon was born. I was so unprepared for that emotion. Same thing with Andrew—and that was just the start of the profound feelings of love I have for them. But that said, it's draining as hell! I mean Samantha has said that if I think she can run errands, chase kids, change dirty diapers, cook, clean, do the PTA meeting, and then come home and put on lingerie and feel sexy, that I'm even dumber than she thought."

"I know, Ian, and I agree. And I know you're right. There is a lot more that I could do."

"Yeah, you at least get to play golf and go to strip joints. Meanwhile she probably resents that, and feels like you have a life outside the home and she doesn't."

"Okay Doctor Ruth, I get the point."

"Trust me here brother, I didn't discover these points on my own. If you can't tell, they come from having had many such conversations. In Sam's eyes I was out living the jet-set lifestyle while she took all the hits for the team back home. And to some degree she's right."

"Well, you're probably right. It'll get better and I'll work on it. I swear it's just that she would *never* initiate sex. I also swear she doesn't need it or want it! And there are times, even when we're doing it, that she seems a million miles away."

"Don't know what to tell you on that. Again, maybe she's just tired."

"Wonder if it has anything to do with the dirty old man she said used to hit on her when she was home alone after school?"

Ian's eyes widened. "Dude, what are you talking about?"

"Well, Megan told me a couple of times about this dirty old creep who lived a few doors down from her. She genuinely swears he was possessed by the Devil himself. I know this is cliché, but she said he used to offer her ice cream sandwiches after school, to come over and visit. She said she was naïve enough to do it and he made passes at her."

"Oh my God, Bill," Ian exclaimed. "Put two and two together my friend!"

"What, you think?" He paused. "You think that's . . . *related*?" Bill felt almost ill as the thought of more dubious contact—beyond "making passes"—filled his mind.

"Dude, I don't know, but do the math."

"One time she did mention that he had touched her inappropriately, but she said it wasn't a big deal. You know how easy-going she is about life. She doesn't wallow in self-pity. I really don't think she thinks it was a big deal—not like all these people who live their lives as victims."

Ian stared. "Wake up my friend. You're telling me that Megan was sexually assaulted as a kid, probably routinely, and that a traumatic event like that would have nothing to do with your situation today?"

Bill paused and thought for a minute; a strange, empty look came upon his face. "I'm such an idiot." Instantly Bill felt a strong desire to head home. He loved Megan more than anything on earth, and the realization that someone had harmed his precious wife so deeply, so lastingly, made him teeter between rage at the old man, and anger at himself for being so selfish so as not to see it earlier.

"Ian . . . thank you, my brother. I've never talked with anyone about this, ever. I don't know why. It's just not something we guys talk about, I guess." He sat and thought more. "I didn't ask you how often you had sex with Samantha, or how good your sex life was . . . I wouldn't do that. I always kind of wondered about my situation though, but I had nothing to compare it to, so I just figured it just was . . . *what it was.*"

"I don't know, Bill, but it seems to me that you might want to dig into this further, perhaps even with a professional."

"You mean a shrink? I don't know. I think we're pretty capable of—"

"Bill!" Ian interrupted. "You know that I know how brilliant you are, but get a clue. I hate to sound so full of advice, but I've read enough about these situations to know that if we are right, and if Megan was abused for some period of time, you're going to need some professional help. And it's not just for Megan, but for the relationship."

Bill sat and reflected for a minute. Thoughts were bouncing all over inside his head. Mostly, he was thinking of his sweet, beautiful, innocent and wonderful Megan, from an entirely new perspective.

"Would you mind if I bailed on you soon, Ian? If we didn't stay out much longer?"

"Of course not, Bill. I'll see you for the baptism on Sunday. I'll be at your church at ten. We can talk afterwards."

Bill hated to leave Ian, but felt a powerful need to be with Megan. His anger at her for being so withdrawn and disinterested had turned to anger at himself for being so blind. He suddenly realized that his troubles with Megan might not have originated from her intentional or wilful neglect, but from a lack of fundamental *ability* to be intimate or sexual.

Preoccupied as Bill was, the two friends called it an early night and he headed home to see if Megan might be open to a heart-to-heart conversation.

Chapter 16

FUELING THE FIRE

The following day, November 1996

Friday morning Ian headed to the hangar to catch up on work. Such days between flights were like gold. There were chart binders to update, FAA forms to deal with, and maintenance issues to track and oversee.

When Ian arrived, Mac was in the hangar office, which was really more like a living area that had been framed out of the back of the expansive structure. Mac spared no expense on the place, but then again he practically lived there. It was complete with a shower, a main lounge area with a big-screen television and large, expensive-looking sofas. There was a computer weather station on one side of the main room, and a kitchenette on the other. In the corner was a large, separate office that was Mac's main work area, both for flight planning and for his many other pursuits.

Two walls of his office were literally covered with aviation and topographical maps of the world—including some maps of the ancient Middle East. The third wall was dominated by two large televisions, and the shorter fourth wall was all bookshelves. While his "large" library was at home, Mac must have had over a hundred books on those shelves—neatly organized and categorized.

"Morning, Mac," Ian said as he entered the main room, wanting to make Mac aware who was entering.

"Morning, Ian," said the voice from the corner office.

"Hey Ian, I've got a couple flights to tell you about when you get a second."

Ian wandered into the corner office and took a seat in the leather guest chairs that sat in front of the large, traditional mahogany desk. "What's up?"

"Well, if I can manage to encourage your input in the cockpit, and you can manage to speak up and avoid bowing to authority so that we don't kill ourselves, I wondered if you could make a Compassion flight with me tomorrow—down to Tampa? We'll need to wait for the kid and his relatives while they meet with the doctor at the Shriners' Hospital there. I guess it's a pre-op visit." Mac was good humored now about the near collision, wryly putting it into perspective while recognizing the lessons learned.

"Oh man, is it an overnight? Our friends Bill and Megan are baptizing little Hanna Sunday and we've promised we'd be there."

"Ah yes, the ritual recognition of Monad—the god of all gods—in water. Actually, water was originally the element reserved for baptism of god by animal, the element of fire was used to go the other way, from god to man."

"Is there a point coming?" Ian deadpanned.

"Nonetheless this act was popularized into its current form—joining god and man through the universal presence of god in water—by the Egyptian sun-god Horus, who was baptized in the River Eridanus by Anup the Baptizer. Of course he was later beheaded—"[21]

"But you digress," Ian joked.

"Yeah, you had told me you were unavailable that day. We'll be back late Saturday; we'll just need to kill some time on the golf course or something." Mac had pretended not to hear Ian as he nonchalantly spewed forth the string of unrelated ramblings—as if not even having to think. It was what Ian referred to as one of his "Wilson moments," a reference to the TV show *Home Improvement*, where the wise neighbor just wouldn't shut up. This was the type of thing that Ian had experienced increasingly as they'd gotten to know each other better; and secretly, it fascinated him that Mac could know so much, even if sometimes he didn't bite. This time, however, he did.

"So I suppose that you're telling me Jesus Christ was not the first to be baptized?"

"Not even close. But then again I didn't know that anybody really thought he was. Certainly not the first to be baptized by a mysterious figure who later loses his head." Mac was smug.

"Well, about the trip, count me in. Samantha was hoping to do some shopping tomorrow, but I know she'll understand. She's always been cool about these Compassion trips." Ian was not compensated for the trips, and Mac volunteered his time and the jet. While the trips meant another day away from his young family, Ian found the trips highly rewarding. Besides, he was also building valuable jet time on his résumé.

"Well, tell her this poor kid will appreciate it. His aunt and uncle have been through hell and back. He was in a car accident a few years back that not only shattered many of his bones, but also caused an explosion that killed his mom and dad, and burned him pretty bad, I hear. He moved back to Michigan to be with relatives, but his specialists are back there in Florida."

"What a bummer," Ian said.

"I'll say . . . I guess they didn't have health insurance at the time, but there was a big insurance payout from the crash. But with all the travel and medical bills, the aunt and uncle—who don't have much—just don't have the means to keep traveling down there for follow-up surgeries and checkups. Unfortunately, or fortunately, they have some of the leading pediatric orthopedists and burn specialists in the country, who also know his case inside and out."

"Wow. Well that's fine. I'm happy to go . . . . And as for the baptism thing, perhaps we can take that up on the golf course. I'm interested in your sources on that one." Ian embellished his skepticism in an effort to antagonize Mac.

"My dear boy," Mac fired back, his dark eyes looking directly into Ian's, "if you ever get bored with your quest for truth about paranormal claims, or the trap doors in our brains that admittedly come as standard equipment from the manufacturer, someday I'll blow your mind."

Ian laughed and turned to go the main room and begin working on charts, when Mac shouted, "Oh, one more thing. Have you had a chance to look at those final three application packages?"

"Yes. There's one that I thought looked strong. The others weren't bad, though."

"Which one did you like? Then I'll tell you my thoughts."

"David Kurtz."

"My choice as well. Tell you what, I'd really like to get him on board, check him out on the Baron and the 210, and get him added to our certificate. I know I've always said I didn't want this thing to get too big—to become a pain in the ass—but I think it would help us a lot to have the extra person."

"I think we're in agreement," Ian said.

"Perhaps you can give him a final familiarization ride and interview next week. I think you've got a 210 trip to Chicago and Gaylord, right?"

"Yes."

"Would you be willing to take him along and see what you think of him?"

"Absolutely."

✤

The following day Ian arrived early at the airport to get the airplane pulled out and preflighted for the trip to Florida. Before long, Mac arrived and together they made the final preparations, briefing each other on the respective pilot briefings they'd each received individually. It looked to be a routine flight in terms of weather. There were some low clouds around the Great Lakes, and flight precautions for light-to-moderate icing in the clouds and in precipitation from the surface up through twelve-thousand feet.

After wrapping the briefing, Mac said, "So you got your golf clubs on board?"

"Absolutely, they're already in the cargo bin with yours."

"Good. I made a tee time for us," Mac divulged with a smile.

Just then a car arrived at the gate. It was their patient, and Ian zipped over and swiped his access card to allow the automated gate to open.

As the blue Honda Accord stopped, Ian walked to the door to greet the passengers through the open windows on the driver's side of the car. "Hi, you must be the Merrill family. I'm one of your pilots, Ian."

Ian shook the driver's hand as the man introduced himself. "Hi Ian, I'm Ed Merrill. This is my wife, Paula, and this is Danny." Ed motioned to the rear seat.

Ian's heart was instantly pierced with sympathy as he got a sight of Danny, though he didn't miss a beat in reaching to meet the extended hand of the young man through the rear window. "Hi, Danny. You ready for a flight?"

Danny's face was badly scarred by severe burns. His nostrils and eyes were the most distinguishable features, and his hands carried the same evidence of torturous damage. Nonetheless, he grasped Ian's hand gently, and leaned forward without letting go once their hands were connected. His voice was soft but his conviction to speak was strong. He connected eyes with Ian and said in slow and deliberate words, "Thank you so much for this. You guys are angels. God bless you."

Ian paused, absorbing the sincerity and passion in the young man's voice. Their eyes never parted, and Ian replied, "You are more than welcome, Danny. We're all ready for you; should be a smooth flight."

Ian returned his attention to Ed, "Just pull right up next to the jet and you'll have just a few steps." As a practical matter it was not only the free transportation that was so vital to patients like Danny, but the lack of hassle as well. While Danny might have been able to endure airport chaos if they could have afforded airline tickets, there is little doubt that it would have taken a toll on the poor boy.

With the family's assistance, Danny was quickly helped aboard the plane. Ian introduced him to Mac, provided the passenger safety briefing, made sure they were securely buckled and comfortable, and climbed up front with Mac.

It was Ian's rotation to fly left seat down to Tampa, and as advertised they found smooth air and clear weather. They dodged a few showers heading into Tampa, but the thunderstorms hadn't materialized that early in the day. Right on schedule they got the Merrills into a cab, and were themselves walking down the first fairway within an hour of landing.

"So you were serious about the baptism thing yesterday, weren't you?" Ian asked as they walked leisurely, soaking up rays of the sun that were so elusive during November in Michigan. Mac insisted upon walking; he always said it was the only option for *real* golfers.

"Of course I was serious. The Jewish Mikvah, for instance, was a ceremonial immersion; it was actually more important in ancient times than most other rituals. It was performed under many circumstances: before conversion proceedings, Yom Kippur, and before the Sabbath—other times too, but I can't quite remember all of them."

"But you said the Christians didn't invent it, and that someone else baptized a god and was later decapitated—just like John the Baptist?"

Ian stopped to hit his approach shot while Mac waited. "Shasta! Beach. What a way to start."

Mac began walking as he continued, "Horus, son of Isis and Osiris. It's true, but I also was just messing around with you. I just happened to be reading about some of these ancient rituals when I came across that story the other day."

Mac would have contributed such esoteric knowledge on many prior occasions, but he had treaded very carefully in terms of religion. As he walked to his ball, Ian's mind flashed back to the sensitivity Mac displayed when he had first shared with Ian a conversation about free inquiry. As the trust and friendship grew, Mac had felt compelled by Ian's chatter about church-related activities, to share with Ian his atheist tendencies.

At the time Ian had been taken aback, even with Mac's polite and careful demeanor and delivery. After Ian had rambled on about a church-related issue, Mac had said, "Ian, I know in our interview I said I mentioned some controversial works and views. That was because I was familiar with the prevailing views of West Michigan, and I had—and still have—no intention of messing with your worldview. I admit, however, that was somewhat ignorant of me, since we were obviously destined to spend a lot of time together. But in my defense, that was before I got to know of your own interest in intellectually honest inquiry. Anyway, I guess what I'm saying is that I think it's important, for purposes of my own authenticity, that I be clear with you about where I'm coming from—that I'm an atheistic agnostic." Ian hadn't been shocked, really, just a little surprised. "I can only smile and nod for so long without feeling like a schmuck while you tell me about church activities," Mac had added.

Ian had asked a profoundly important question. "So what does that mean? Does that mean you're out fighting against religion?"

"Absolutely not. You of all people must know I've not been out to tell you you're wrong. Besides, I have much to learn," Mac had responded, before he went on to define the terms *atheist* and *agnostic.*

Agnostic was a term that was coined in the nineteenth century to juxtapose the term Gnostic. *Gnosis* meant *knowledge,* and the ancient Gnostics comprised various religious movements with roots preceding the time of Jesus, whose practitioners claimed that unique knowledge was revealed to them by the gods of the spirit realm. Mac had even said there was a strong Gnostic vein in contemporary Christian beliefs. But more to his point, Mac had explained that an "a" was put in front of the word "gnosis" to signify a lack of knowledge—one who just *didn't know.*

"I think that when it comes to walking on water, raising the dead, virgin births, and supernatural claims, that I just don't know. Nobody can know for certain if these things were literally true," Mac had clarified. "Therefore I am agnostic on such questions. I just don't know."

On the other hand, Mac had explained that the term *atheist* was often misconstrued. It wasn't anti-religion or anti-God necessarily, though it could be those things; rather, it defined whether or not one was a *theist*—if one believed in God. Mac had summarized, "The term means that, at least as of today, I can't say that I believe in a supernatural being. In fact, I do not believe in a definable god. So put together with a lack of certainty, an agnostic atheist says, 'I don't know, therefore I choose not to believe.' Conversely, someone who believes in God but agrees we can't know all the answers is a *theistic agnostic.*"

The definitions and approach had helped Ian in his understanding at the time; in truth however, he still feared somewhat for Mac's spiritual well being. The disclosure had given him a feeling of uneasiness on Mac's behalf. It seemed one thing to admit you had *doubts,* Ian thought at the time, but quite another to boldly say that you *don't believe in God!*

But that was then. Ian's mind jumped back to the present as Mac hit his approach shot beautifully. "Nice shot," Ian observed. The duo continued the walk to the green.

"So we talked yesterday about all the questioning I've been doing of my assumptions, but how are your studies going?" Ian asked. It still wasn't something they discussed often, but Ian figured the door was open and he'd nudge it a little further—even if he was somewhat worried about what he might find.

Mac seemed forthcoming. "Very well, actually. When we were in D.C.—" Mac paused. "Did I tell you what I was doing there?"

"Don't think you did," Ian answered as he entered the sand trap to try to extricate his ball.

"I met with one of the curators of the National Archives. What an experience."

Thwack! Ian slapped the sand as he hit his shot and responded, "Not pretty, but I'm out." He paused to rake the trap before continuing. "So another friend of yours, I suppose?"

"Something like that, yes." Mac smiled. "I was there to learn more about the religious views of the founding fathers, particularly about Ben Franklin, Thomas Jefferson, and George Washington. Do you happen to know of their beliefs?"

Ian looked at Mac, putter in hand, and then thought about the question as he rolled the ball toward the hole.

"Can't say I really do know much about them—just what I learned in school and see on monuments and stuff. 'In God we trust' and stuff like that. They were Christian weren't they?"

"Well Franklin and Jefferson were clearly deists. I believed, and after my visit I now firmly believe, that George Washington was as well."

"So forgive me, but I don't know what that means."

"Well, basically it means that they weren't Christian, and didn't believe that a divine God interfered or interacted with the world—at least not any more. They were rationalists who believed what we see is what matters, not what some supernatural force may or may not be doing. They believed in a creator-God, in a mystical, life-force kind of way, but they certainly didn't buy the miracles, doctrines and dogma of Christianity."

"Whoa. You're telling me that Thomas Jefferson, George Washington, and Ben Franklin, weren't our *Christian* founding fathers?"

"Right. Of course you've heard of Thomas Paine, the writer of the revolutionist pamphlets, *Common Sense*?"

"Yes."

"Well haven't you heard of his treatise *The Age of Reason?*" Mac asked, almost incredulously.

"Sorry," Ian said as he replaced the flag and they worked their way toward the next tee.

"Thomas Paine tore Christianity apart with that book, advocating a rationalist or skeptical, almost scientific view of religion. Given your inquiry into reason versus emotion, I'm surprised you didn't at least know that Thomas Paine was a deist."

"Hey, I never claimed to know anything. If anything, you've just given me one more example of the types of things I thought I knew, but now am not so sure. I readily admit that despite what we tell ourselves, truth is often more elusive than we think."

"And you did go to college, right?"

"Smart ass."

Mac teed up a ball and struck it purely. "Let's see you keep up with that, lad." In response, Ian hit a crushing drive down the par 5 fairway that seemed to be rising until nearly the last moment. "Ohhhh, and he answers the call," Mac said playfully. "By the way, you can also add John Adams, James Madison, Ethan Allen and others to that list of deists. And my guess is that if they had access to the Nag Hammadi texts, saw the recent cloning of Dolly the sheep, and saw frickin even Pope John Paul II last month declare that 'new knowledge has led to the recognition of the theory of evolution as more than a hypothesis,' they'd be more atheistic today than deist."[22]

"What do you do, memorize shit just for fun?" Ian found himself fascinated by Mac's wacky, but often amazingly cogent rantings. "Okay, so baptism predated the Christians and the Jews, and the founding fathers didn't believe in God. What else you got, big fella?" Ian joked. "You make my head hurt. Hit the ball and try to catch up to my manly drive, will you?"

Mac advanced the ball, walked a bit, and then a thought hit him. "By the way, I didn't say the founding fathers didn't believe in God. But a significant minority didn't believe in the dogma and tradition of a supernatural god who still acts in the world—like the one in which theist Christians, Muslims and Jews invest their beliefs. In fact, they found the magical beliefs to be both irrational, and distasteful. Oh and what's

more, they were real forces in the ultimate, explicit separation of church
and state, and the Godlessness of our constitution."

"So you're still telling me the nation is not founded upon God? I don't
think Representative Huxley would agree with you."

"Absolutely it is not. While admittedly they were a minority, the deists
were a vital part of the negotiation that ultimately created a consensus;
constitutionally, the nation would *not* be founded upon God. And at my
meeting in D.C. when we were just there, I literally held the documents
that show this truth beyond any doubt. If you don't believe the constitution, read the *Treaty of Peace and Friendship with the Bey and Subjects of
Tripoli of Barbary* that was ratified by the Senate in 1797, during the Adams
administration. It clearly says that the United States was 'not in any sense
founded on the Christian Religion.'"[23]

The duo walked farther down the fairway before Mac asked Ian, "Hey,
have you heard of the Jesus Seminar?"

"Actually, ignorant though I may be, I have heard of that, but only
because I keep seeing letters to the editor from people outraged about it.
What is it?"

"Well, it is a group of theological scholars who convened to try to reach
some consensus among themselves about the accuracy of scripture. They
started in 1985, and released their first book of findings in 1993, called
The Five Gospels: The Search for the Authentic Words of Jesus.[24] Essentially it
said that about 80 percent of Jesus' alleged sayings were likely not words
he had ever spoken."

"Ah, I can see where that would be a controversial statement, given
that we have the Bible and everything. How on earth do they come up
with that?"

"Grasshopper, you have so much to learn," Mac said condescendingly,
but Ian wasn't offended—partly because he knew Mac was just being a
jerk on purpose, but partly because he knew it was true—he did have
much to learn.

Mac continued, "If you think that's controversial, this group of over
100 leading scholars votes at the end of their deliberations, and in 1995
they determined that Jesus was not physically resurrected."

"Now how on earth could they come to such a conclusion? All you
have is the Bible, and it may be true and it may not, but don't you have to

choose either to believe what's written, or not? We certainly can't go back and ever know! Where do they get off?"

Mac stopped his walking, shook his head, and looked at Ian. He paused, then turned and continued walking. "I almost don't know where to begin to answer that one, Ian. But let me say this. You're wrong. There is a tremendous amount of scholarship being done today."

"Are you suggesting it's a conspiracy of silence then?"

"Of course not. Not in the traditional sense. You'll just never hear pastors talk about complex, deep scholarly discoveries of esoteric passages that were changed by scribes—at least not publicly. Why would they? The job is tough enough. Even if they do take time to keep up with scholarly work—which most don't by the way—they're too busy administrating, tending to the flock, and doing good, valid work to encourage discussion of complex, potentially heretical discoveries. If anything, most feel an obligation to their congregations to provide apologetics—not seek truth. I'm not being critical, that's just the way it is."

"Okay, my mind will explode in four seconds," Ian quipped as he addressed his ball.

"Fair enough. I'll shut up. Let me just say this: very devout Christians and monks in recent centuries have formulated new methods of textual criticism to try to get back to the original text and language of the Bible. Today, the Catholic Church and every other Christian follower with a modicum of intellectual honesty knows that most of the main Biblical translations—including the King James—have hundreds of thousands of errors, changes, additions and deletions. Their goal, as believers, is to reconstruct the *true text*. My goal, as a researcher, is to find the *truth* behind the true text."

"Will you ever find it?" Ian asked.

"As you alluded, one can never find absolute truth beyond any shadow of a doubt. We always have to be open to new information that could come along down the road. All conclusions are tentative and provisional. At the same time, from the space shuttle, to air travel, to computers, to antibiotics, to golf clubs, many of the things we *think* we know seem to be holding true and seem to be reliably predictive of future events. They also seem to work pretty well at improving lives."

"What the hell do you mean?"

"I mean that the laws of physics don't change every day. They seem to hold true, and we can predict they'll hold true tomorrow. We can build a space shuttle because one plus one equals two. It did yesterday, it does today, and it is likely that it will tomorrow. Therefore, it is likely that what we know—based on reason, science and our estimation of how the world works—can actually be called 'true,' with a fair degree of confidence. We predict how metals will work together based on past evidence, and so far the shuttle flies."

"Well, I have to agree with you about the value of science to predict things—say versus basing decisions upon gut or emotion."

"Sure, but we're all guilty of emotion-driven thinking and doing some wacky things."

The conversation continued between the golf shots.

"Let me give you another example, since you're into asking why we believe things. Can I ask you a personal question?" Mac looked toward Ian as they walked.

"Sure. Of course."

"Did you have Andrew and Brandon circumcised?" Ian opened his eyes wider, offering a puzzled expression. The question seemed out of left field, but Mac was always a step ahead—be it in the plane or in a conversation.

"Yes," Ian played along.

"Okay. Why?" Mac asked. As Ian would later learn, it was one of the most powerful questions in the global vernacular—*Why?* Ian would learn that if he ever wanted to anger someone who was thinking irrationally, he could just go four layers deep with the question "Why?" By the fourth layer, the rationalizations would fall apart, and emotion would flow instead.

"Well, I suppose the answer you're looking for is because we've always done it that way," Ian ventured.

"I'm not looking for an answer, I just wondered. Why?"

"It's funny, because Samantha and I discussed it at some length. In the end we figured that we didn't want them to look different than me?"

"Why did that matter, Ian?"

"I don't know; I guess I didn't want them to be made fun of in the locker rooms when they grew up?"

"Why, did you make fun of uncircumcised friends in the shower?"

"No," Ian responded.

"Were there uncircumcised guys in the shower?"

"Gosh, not that I paid much attention, but I guess, yeah there were."

"Did others make fun of them?"

"Not that I heard," Ian said. "I think I see where you're going. And I know, I know, the difference between my sons and me could have been explained to them easily—without massive psychological trauma."

"Absolutely. Do I hear you admitting this is an example of people doing weird things for the sake of faith or emotion, and that you cut off a big part of your sons' penises for no reason?"

Both men laughed. "Let's be real," said Mac. "The foreskin is over half of the skin on your dick. It serves not only to protect the penis throughout life, but it enhances sexual pleasure—which is probably why anti-sexual religion decided to make it go away. That, or because before modern hygiene it was true that it could grow bacteria—but that's irrelevant today. So, why do we chop off our dicks?"

As much as Ian griped, he enjoyed the banter with Mac. It made life, and work, so much more interesting. But as he pondered that question, he once again reverted to his thoughts about why we believe the things we do.

"We are an interesting species, are we not?" Ian asked aloud.

"Truly fucked in the head at times, I'm afraid." Mac answered. "But really, I'm optimistic. Progress seems inevitable, though not linear and constant; we're getting past these silly things. There's certainly less female circumcision in the world today—though it's still a problem."

"What is that?" Ian looked horrified.

"Oh, many cultures cut out the clitoris so that women can't enjoy sex, or to keep them loyal to their husbands. Unfortunately they often do it forcibly and without anesthetic or clean instruments."

"You have got to be shitting me?"

"Oh no. And although primarily practiced in Islamic countries, it really isn't an Islamic religious practice at all—as many claim. It's practiced among some Coptic Christians, and even some Protestant and Catholic societies."

"Okay," said a wide-eyed Ian. "That's a good swing thought for this shot."

It was after Ian's swing that Mac first said it—insignificant as it seemed at the time. But as so often happens in life, it is from the seeds of a seemingly insignificant notion or idea that both great and terrible events unfold.

At its face it was a simple concept. "You know, Ian," Mac said, "I've thought about that Jesus Seminar a lot. I love the idea of scholars—the best in their field—being united to pursue, as you would call it, 'truth.' But I don't think they've taken it far enough. From what I understand, they don't physically gather very often. Wouldn't it be cool to take all of my contacts—these world-class theologians with whom I've been visiting—add some leading historians, archaeologists, sociologists, geologists, and few other 'ologists' for good measure, and conduct monthly symposiums? To really put the greatest minds together and take on some of the greatest scientific and philosophical questions of the universe?"

"Gosh, sounds like a notch above Woodstock to me," Ian wisecracked. "You bring the beer, I'll bring the pretzels."

"No, I'm serious. I don't think I'd use the same voting methods as the Jesus Seminar, but I think some formal process for reaching consensus on issues would make sense."

"What would be the purpose of the group? You'd have to have a focus. Why would people want to belong?"

"Well, to discover truth! Isn't that what science, scholarship, and intellectually honest inquiry are all about? And wouldn't a highly *funded* and committed group, with adequate resources and freedom, combined with unparalleled intellect, be a dream come true for idealistic intellectuals and academics?"

"Money *was* one of my questions. But people are so busy; it's tough enough to attend the annual conferences they already have," Ian added.

By that time Mac's mind was racing. The notion of his own brain trust—beyond any think-tank or skunkworks project—was a powerful elixir for Mac. The rest of the round was devoted to examining the idea; and needless to say, the scorecard for the day reflected the lack of focus.

Chapter 17

A HIGHER QUESTION

Two days later—Sunday (1996)

"How are my handsome boys doing back there?" Ian asked Sammy as they drove toward the Huxley estate at Gull Lake on the crisp November Sunday.

"For the moment they both seem content, Dad," Samantha assured as she looked at her boys with the unique pride and love of a mother.

Chaos ruled most days for the young family; that day, however, was one of those forced days of socialization and relaxation that, while viewed as an obligation in the days before, was actually a welcomed respite once it was upon them.

"So what did you think of the service? Nice, wasn't it."

"I will say that as much as I think Pastor Mike is a good speaker, and as magnificent as that place is, I like our old-fashioned little church," Samantha answered.

Having grown up at the little Methodist church, it was Ian's preference as well. After Janet died, and with the encouragement of his brother and sister, Ian and Samantha had purchased the old family home in which he had been reared. In living there, and also through their attendance at the little old church, Samantha and Ian were paying tribute to Ian's beloved parents by subconsciously emulating their lives. What better role models could there have been?

As for Bill and Megan, they had met as a result of attending the same church, so were accustomed to their small-town "mega church." The place was literally like a giant auditorium, complete with the latest sound, video, technical gizmos, creature comforts and accoutrements. On Sundays it would host over two thousand congregants for entertainment and worship. Ian did find it interesting, however, that for their extravagant wedding, Bill and Megan had moved to a more traditional church downtown.

Ian preferred not only the smaller, community feel of their *Little House on the Prairie* church, but also the content of the messages. Typically, they were full of practical, useful axioms about living and embracing life, while simultaneously conveying a Christian message. The mega church, on the other hand, just seemed so militant to Ian.

For example, they had recently conducted a youth event during which the kids were encouraged to burn all of their "immoral," secular CDs. In the heat of the moment, with tears and emotion flowing over the profound appreciation they had for seeing the true light of God's will and plan, the children took great pride in tossing the CD collections into the flames.

"Hey, did I ever tell you about the time that I was with Tommy Johansson, helping his dad work on his car in the garage?"

"No, I don't think so," Sammy answered.

"Burt Johansson was working on his car in the garage. Nice man. We were having fun and singing along to the old song, *Lay Down Sally*.[25] Tommy's dad loved the song, and so did we. We didn't much know or care about the lyrics, we just sang along as we handed Mr. Johansson wrenches." Ian sang the melody for Sammy. "Lay down Sally, let me rest you in my arms."

"All we knew was that we loved the song. On the other hand, we could hear Mr. Johansson's singing more clearly after a while, and he was singing the wrong words! He sang, 'Way down south' instead of 'lay down, Sally.'"

Ian imitated him. "'Way down south, let me rest you in my arms, I've been waiting for so long just to hold you.' Tommy and I roared with laughter and teased Mr. Johansson. He was quite surprised at the apparent, *real meaning* behind the lyrics—which we had never even considered, of course. But he found the whole thing pretty funny too."

Sammy giggled. "What made you think of that?"

"I was just thinking about whether or not lyrics poison the minds of kids, like at Huxley's church where the kids burned their CDs. In my mind, those lyrics didn't influence me or make me run out and have sex with a woman named Sally. And Tommy has always been a good guy. For god's sake we were kids, singing along with a song! Anyway, to what degree does sheltering kids from the world of ideas, diversity, and free expression really benefit them? It sure won't help their understanding of a complex world."

"Hey I've got a question for you," Sammy interjected.

"What's that?"

"Don't you ever get tired of thinking? It's a beautiful day. Why not just drink it in and enjoy it . . . . Besides," she turned to Ian and slowed her pace seductively, "if you behave, maybe we can watch that new movie tonight after the kids go to bed—the one that came in that brown paper wrapping the other day." Samantha smiled at Ian coyly, then leaned over and gave him a quick kiss on the cheek.

"Have I told you lately that I love you?"

"I think a couple times already today, but I'll never get tired of hearing it. I love you too, even if you are a bit intense."

The Keppler family arrived at the long driveway of the senior Huxley's home on Gull Lake. There were several other cars there, but they found a stretch in which to park and proceeded to the door for the festivities.

Megan looked as beautiful as ever. She had changed from the dress she'd worn at church, to a lovely fall skirt with elegant, heeled boots. She wore a wool sweater, and both the skirt and sweater subtly revealed her feminine shape. The warmth of the earth tones fit her friendly, subtle personality, and she greeted her friends with hugs as they arrived at the door.

The Gull Lake home certainly was a gorgeous and rejuvenating setting. The lake that was so crammed with boats and traffic only months before, during the height of the summer, was now a postcard picture of tranquility, accentuated by the shapes of now-leafless tree branches in the low, November sun. The exceptions were the big oak trees by the lake, which still had a smattering of their brown leaves persistently attached.

Bill enthusiastically arrived at the front entrance. "Hi guys! You'll never guess what surprise I have for you!" No sooner had he said the words, than John Bennett poked his head around the corner.

"Hello brother!" Ian exclaimed as he shook John's hand, then pulled him in for a guy-appropriate hug. John hugged Samantha as Ian kept talking. "I was just going to call you to see if you could do lunch this week when I'm in Chicago!"

"I wish I could, but I'm traveling this week. You're more than welcome to use the condo, though, if you need a place to kill some time," John offered.

"Come in and let's get a glass of wine. No need to hang here, there'll be plenty of time to chat. I'm so glad you could make it, John!" Bill ushered the group into the huge Huxley house, and they were formally greeted by Dan and Katherine a few moments later.

The home was lovely, as always, and it was that tranquil setting—and a couple glasses of wine with a luxurious dinner—that seemed to suspend the chaos of everyday life for that afternoon. To Ian and Samantha, it was an unexpectedly lovely day, and a much-needed break from the grind of kids, errands, and chaos.

Bill's parents, Cindy and Don Vanderveen, were there as well, as were both sets of Bill and Megan's grandparents. At the same time there was plenty of time and space to gather among smaller groups, so in no way did the gathering lack intimacy or overwhelm the guests. Though Ian had seen John for a brief lunch about a month prior, it had been some time since they had a enough "quantity time" to allow "quality time" to unfold.

The formal Sunday gathering reminded Ian of those dinners that his mother used to make, when he and his family would entertain one another, and by the end of the day everyone had settled somewhere in the Keppler house to relax. Sometimes the adults wound up drinking coffee in the living room, or on the enclosed porch, talking for hours and enjoying the time away from an otherwise regimented existence. It seemed like such "time outs" were no longer a part of Ian and Samantha's lives—until this unexpectedly relaxing gathering in honor of Hanna.

Even chasing their respective two-year-olds, Brandon and Zachary, didn't seem nearly as daunting for Samantha and Megan on this day. The husbands and John had taken some time to play with the kids, and provided a well-deserved chance for the ladies to relax and enjoy the day too. Of course it also helped that Samantha had gotten little Andrew—now ten months old—fed and down for a nap. Similarly, little Hanna was promptly asleep after dinner. Starting with an early baptism, it had been a long day for a three-month-old.

The two-year-old boys were left to play together in Grandma and Grandpa Huxley's expansive toy room. Samantha could rest assured that unlike many other such rooms, the toys were mightily sterilized and clean, given Megan's reputation as a "germ nut." Ever the fan of Lysol and every other new antimicrobial on the market, Megan was obsessed with cleanliness when it came to Zachary and little Hanna.

As the years went by, Samantha would also find Megan compulsively concerned that the kids would be lured into a car and abducted, have razor blades put in their Halloween candy, or be the victim of some such malicious and psychotic act; but Sam never let it bother her. She knew that whether it was siblings or best friends, one could always find little, irritating things to focus on. Besides, through Ian's insights she would come to feel even greater compassion for Megan, and assume her overprotectiveness might be related to the childhood traumas she had suffered.

That glorious afternoon, however, Bill and Ian found time to talk alone, while John was engaged in a deep conversation with Representative Huxley—a somewhat rare opportunity for him to chat with a Congressman. Ian was curious to check on his old friend after their truncated evening out a few nights earlier. Ian and Bill sat in the tufted leather, wing-backed chairs in Mr. Huxley's study, admiring the view of the lake through the giant picture window as they talked.

"So you doing okay? Did you have a chance to talk with Megan Thursday when you got home?"

"Yeah, thanks again for listening and for the insights. We had a long, candid conversation and I think it was very helpful. I told her that I'd been thinking about the pressure she's feeling every time I bring up my concerns about our sex life, and that I realize I have been selfish. I told her I know I haven't recognized and validated her need for space, and in return, she acknowledged that she could be a better wife and try harder. We're both going to work on it."

Ian wasn't convinced. "Did you consider the possibility of talking with a professional? Someone who has experience with these kinds of situations, where sexual abuse is a factor?"

Now Bill was a touch incredulous. "I think we're comfortable that we can handle this. I think it's a lack of communication. You know how it is, like you were saying—the pressures of little kids and everything. We've committed to a weekly 'date night,' and to shoring up our relationship for the sake of the family."

"There's something I agree with. If Mom and Dad put the kids ahead of the health of their own relationship, I think that's a mistake. Parents really are the backbone of the family," Ian said. "And I swear that's what I see other people doing these days: travel soccer, travel hockey, private lessons—from one activity for the kids to the next. I don't know how people can totally ignore their relationship and believe that's the best thing for the family."

"You're right as rain, my friend."

"But still, for the record, I think you should see a professional."

"Hey, as you said yourself, sex is one of the few things for which practice isn't a chore. We'll just keep practicing . . . and actually, she jumped my bones that night after our conversation."

Just then, Mr. Huxley passed by the study. "Hey guys, I didn't know you were in here. Solving the world's problems like John, Don and I have been?"

"Pretty much," replied Ian. He laughed to himself that Bill had just been talking about the Congressman's daughter jumping his bones.

"Hey, I've been meaning to tell you that I saw you in the gallery of the House that day. I knew you'd be up there so I picked you out early, during that boring tirade by Representative McGuire." Dan laughed at his little joke. "Seriously though, I've been meaning to ask you what you thought of the debate that day."

The representative plopped on the vacant leather couch.

"Ian, you're a bright guy—and a constituent I might add," Dan said in an inviting and open fashion, literally opening his arms and extending his hands, palms up, to his sides. "Your input is valuable to me. I respect it. Bill and I have talked and he's hinted at your concerns. I really do want to know what you think."

Ian thought for a second. He felt comfortable with the representative, and believed in his sincerity. "I appreciate that, Dan. Fair enough. Let me ask a question then," Ian said. "I have this theory that for every question there is a true answer. It might be so complex that you or I cannot understand the answer, but somewhere out there God, or the universe, or whatever, has the answer to the question. I also believe that there is only one true answer, complex though it may be."

"Okay. I'm with you. I agree. Unlike what some of these postmodernists proclaim, truth is not relative, and there are not many different truths. I'm with you—continue."

"So if our federal government protected gays from discrimination, my question is this: Is there harm to you or me that would come from that protection?"

"Absolutely there is harm, Ian." The representative jumped right in, despite having asked Ian's opinion.

"I think this is where the disconnect is for me, so I'm all ears," Ian said genuinely, trying not to prejudge the issue in his mind.

"First let me say that I'm not suggesting mistreatment is okay, that discrimination should be condoned. I know I'm not on the record here, but I really don't want to suggest that, because that's not how I feel. God judges souls, I don't."

"I understand."

"But Ian, you surely recognize the importance of having two parents, man and woman, to raise a child and form a family. Your kids, Brandon and Andrew, and Bill's kids, all have an advantage that other kids simply do not have. They have the economic advantages of two contributors, and far more importantly they have a united team behind them. They have a fortress of protection and support that is designed to foster and sustain them."

"I wasn't necessarily talking about the issue of gays raising families, but I'm still listening."

"Yeah Ian, but don't you see that a normalization and continued 'in your face' promotion of homosexuality is going to lead to more broken families? Furthermore it is hardly sending the right message to the world, is it?"

"I guess I'm not following," Ian replied, forcing Dan to continue.

"Let me be clear. You know I work hard to be open-minded. At the same time I have to be true to my moral and religious beliefs; and I believe that homosexuality is against God's will, and in the clear words of the Bible it is an 'abomination' to be gay. That doesn't mean I don't know some great people who are gay, and I can still love them; but it is not a state of living that should be encouraged and further supported by more attention and legislation."

"But my question remains, what harm is going to come to us?" Emotion was starting to seep into the conversation, though it remained sincere and respectful.

"The harm is a stamp of approval and support that is unnecessary, and uncalled for. The harm is a furthering of the gay agenda. The harm is an erosion of family values, trite though that may sound. And the *truth* is, the *true* result of all this would be more kids being raised by single parents, less support for those children in the home, and a further erosion of morality. Society would be worse off. Society loses! That's the harm." The Representative was clear and precise, almost as if he were making a speech on the floor of the House.

Bill chimed in, "You must see the logic in that statement, don't you Ian?"

"Over sixty percent of African-American children are born into families of single parents, Ian," Dan added for good measure.

"But that's got nothing to do with homosexuality," Ian replied.

"Yes but it's a huge part of the problem that the African-American community faces, and it's where we'll head on a larger scale if we fuel these attitudes about sexual freedom. Speaking morally, we just can't continue to say, 'Everything is fine. Do whatever you want.' There are fundamental behaviors that keep order in society, and being gay is clearly not one that God had in mind." Dan seemed to rest his case, as Bill looked for a reaction from his friend.

Ian really didn't know how to respond. A few years earlier, he might well have been in total agreement. But at this point something about the argument just didn't seem well supported. There seemed to be too many assumptions underlying too many other assumptions, but Ian just couldn't out-debate the Representative. At the same time, he was not done.

"I suppose that my question about the true ramifications—if we could wave a magic wand and know the true, complex reality of less discrimination against homosexuals—remains the central question in my mind. In other words, do we know that ending discrimination would really make more people gay? Would it really encourage more homosexuality, or would it just be a more humane existence, out of the closet, for those who *are already* gay?"

"Let's not get into the whole issue of nature versus nurture here, cause I'm also not buying that being gay isn't a choice. It is a choice," Bill interjected. Unlike his father-in-law who was more polished in his arguments, Bill tended to cut to his conclusions somewhat bluntly.

"But these are legitimate questions. Would reducing discrimination and increasing mainstream acceptance of homosexuality increase the number of gay people, or just allow them to come out of hiding and live more normal lives? Further—and though I wasn't initially talking about families—does the slippery slope argument really apply to this issue? Is it necessarily true that allowing people to be openly gay, without persecution, really will lead to more immorality? Does being gay make you automatically less moral, caring and nurturing in raising or caring for children? I'm not so sure."

"I think it does," Dan said candidly.

"You know I respect your opinion, Dan, I'm just saying that sometimes just because we think we *know* something, doesn't make it necessarily *true*. You certainly could be right. I readily admit that. At the same time I still have many questions like those I just mentioned, or even this one: Does fostering discrimination against gays make the world a better place?"

Ian continued, "Let me use the 'slippery slope' argument in reverse, since you used it. Does legitimizing contempt for gays not lead to further contempt against gays? Doesn't it lead to less tolerance of those who are different? Potentially doesn't it even contribute to supporting violence against them? Could that environment even make acceptable some forms of religious persecution against those who disagree with us? Isn't that the lesson you're promoting—intolerance of those who don't believe as I do?"

"Since you mention religion, Ian—and then I have to get back to Don, Cindy and Katherine; but if nothing else, I'll point to God's word. I hate to

sound like a zealot. You know that I don't judge people's souls or worthiness—that's not for me to do. I'll help and support them in any and every
way that I can, and leave the judging to God. But for me, Ian, the Bible
is clear. God's word is clear. And both of them support what I probably
already believed—that homosexuality is harmful. And for society to look
the other way and to go down this road, is harmful to society."

"It's an interesting conversation. Thanks for asking Dan, really. I'll
continue to ponder the issue."

"Hey, thanks for your candor, Ian. You know I'm sincere when I say
that although I disagree with you, you're a smart guy and I appreciate
your being honest with me and telling me when you think I'm all wet.
Thanks for letting me interrupt your guy-talk."

"You bet, Dan," Ian said as Mr. Huxley headed out of the room.

In his mind, just as he had done in the past with virginity, Ian couldn't
help but think to himself that this was really all about sex acts.

"Bill, if it weren't for the fact that one woman stimulated another woman's clitoris with her mouth, in the privacy of their home, nobody would
have a problem with two women raising children together—especially
if the two were able, educated, employed, bright, polite, and otherwise
moral."

"Of course it's about sex. Sex that is in violation of God's law," Bill
replied.

"It reminds me of the whole question of virginity before marriage. What
is the global significance of the act of sex? Why does it get everyone's undies
in a knot? Clearly there are consequences of sex, especially historically,
but there are with oral sex as well. Yet kids and young adults can have
oral sex, or manually get each other off all day long, and that's one thing;
but even in this day of relatively reliable birth control, someone breaking
the plane of the vagina with the head of a penis is this monumental sin of
unbelievable proportions. What's up with that? I've even seen studies that
abstinence programs, like the one you went through, *increase* the amount
of sex kids have. They over-prioritize the act of putting it in *that* hole, and
figure they have a free pass to do anything else."

"Hey, you're hitting close to home here, mister. It mattered a lot to me
and Megan, obviously."

"I know, and frankly it mattered a lot to me. I'll bet I've had sex with fewer people than you have. I'm just really curious about how we form these values and ideas. Just like with our drug policies—alcohol and caffeine are good but marijuana is bad—it's interesting to ask where this profound *knowledge* of right and wrong comes from."

"What, now you're pro-gay and pro-marijuana?"

"I didn't say that. Just like on the sex thing, I just wonder where it comes from. Are these views a throwback to ancient times when society had to govern families and reproduction in order to keep order? That makes sense to me. They figured out how to avoid unwanted pregnancy and maintain property through a system of rules and order. But do those rules necessarily still need to apply? I truly don't know the answer."

"I do, my friend. I know that you are a horn-dog, and that you want to do everything that you see."

"Oh and you don't?"

"Of course I do, but that still doesn't make it right. Talk about believing what you want to believe simply because you want to believe it." Bill watched as Ian dipped his head as if to acknowledge that he had a point, but at the same time he wasn't buying Bill's arguments fully.

"Yeah, well, what do I know," Ian said with resignation. "It seems that the older I get, the less I know for sure."

"Well, I do know one thing," Bill concluded. "Going way back to my first sex classes at church, I can tell you this—the Bible is pretty clear on these things."

"I suppose," Ian replied.

As they wrapped up their philosophical equivalents of punching each other in the arms, to affirm to the other that their friendship outweighed any disagreement, they headed out to socialize with the rest of the group and enjoy the rest of the day.

In Ian's mind, however, he had not only mentally added these questions to a long list of others he had about life, he had observed the certainty of Bill and Dan with curiosity as well. *Where did that certitude and confidence come from?* he wondered. How did they see things so clearly? In a way, Ian found himself envious that both of them had such profound faith. At the same time he couldn't help but think that the answer he kept getting was, "Because God said," which was a leap of faith he was beginning to question.

⁘

That night Samantha and Ian put the kids to bed early. They rationalized that the boys were tired from the long day of activities; but in reality, they wanted some time to themselves. It seemed that a day of relaxation had allowed amorous feelings to percolate to conscious desire. Of course the ritual of getting the kids to bed, with all its accompanying chaos, had somewhat diminished those urges, but they weren't gone.

Together they sat in their family room, winding down and enjoying quiet conversation until they were assured the kids were asleep.

"So what did the worldly men talk about today?" Samantha asked as she sat next to Ian on the couch, exchanging attentive eye contact with Ian.

Ian chuckled as he thought about the conversation about homosexuality with Dan and Bill, and summarized it for Samantha. He included his admiration for the strength of their faith, and his observation that very often it was that same faith that seemed to be the real, underlying basis for their views.

"Well, that does make sense, doesn't it?" Samantha asked. "I mean, that seems obvious. And what's wrong with that? Isn't it our duty to promote and vote for what we believe in? Isn't it Dan Huxley's duty to promote and vote in Congress for what he believes in, so long as 'Congress shall make no law respecting an establishment of religion, or prohibiting the free exercise thereof'?"

"Wow, you're hot when you quote the constitution, baby," Ian joked.

"Oh baby, 'Or abridging the freedom of speech, or of the press; or the right of the people peaceably to assemble, and to petition the government for a redress of grievances,'" she continued with feigned sensuality.

Ian shook his head. "I can't believe you remember that. Did I learn nothing in school? My knowledge of history stinks. *And I was a straight-A student!* Where the hell was I? I swear that I just keep finding out how little I know. It's like my spelling."

"Yeah, your spelling sucks."

"Gee, don't beat around the bush," Ian said sarcastically, "tell me how you really feel."

Sammy leaned over and gave him a quick kiss of reassurance, even though it wasn't necessary.

"Besides, I'm a victim," Ian wisecracked in obvious contrast to the middle-class, "pull-yourself-up-by-your-bootstraps" philosophy under which he was raised, and for which the Vanderveens and Huxleys were ardent promoters. "Did I ever tell you about learning to read with a different alphabet than our twenty-six-letter alphabet?"

"What are you talking about?" an intrigued Samantha asked.

"It's the God's honest truth. I learned to read using the Initial Teaching Alphabet. We called it ITA, and it must have had thirty-five or forty characters—a separate symbol for all the different vowel sounds. So like a hard 'e' would be denoted by a funky, different symbol that kind of looked like an Egyptian hieroglyph."

"What the hell, you've got to be kidding me?"

"Not at all. They thought they could teach us to read better, using pure phonetics—I mean, you could sound out every word and spell it perfectly with this new alphabet. The only problem was that *the world didn't use that alphabet!*" Ian exclaimed.

"That is unreal!" Samantha laughed.

"Yeah, and by the time they got around to trying to transition us to English from this fantasy language, I just never caught up with other kids my age in understanding how to spell tricky words. So you see, I'm a victim," he joked again.

"But seriously, what were they thinking?"

"I honestly don't know, but again, these are the types of things that interest me. Somebody came up with this idea, and they believed it to be a superior instructional method. *How* they came to believe that, or *why* they came to believe that, I don't know. Maybe it was their own idea, and they believed it because they *wanted* it to be true. Maybe they wanted to be known for creating a great instructional breakthrough. Or maybe there was research done incorrectly or poorly; I just don't know. I guess the question is, 'Why do we do lots of things we do that, in truth, just aren't what we say they are'?"

"*Why* is always a tough question. *Why* don't people use pain killers during childbirth?" Samantha quipped, referring to one of Ian's favorite soapbox speeches. It was particularly fascinating to Ian—sometimes especially so after a beer or two—but they had to be careful not to get into the topic around Bill and Megan, who had actually elected the natural childbirth route—*twice!*

"Ah, that's still a great example. There is no indication whatsoever that there is any harm from an epidural, or even a local anesthetic for the episiotomy. So why on earth would you want to encourage your wife to have a child 'naturally'?"

"And why in the hell would she listen?" Samantha echoed with some hostility. "Everybody knows that if men had to endure childbirth, families would never be larger than three."

"I disagree with that. I've heard people say that, but three means the parents have one child, right? Before they experience that horrific pain and learn *never to do that again?* Well I'll argue that we are *just* smart enough never to have the kid in the first place. If men had to endure the pain of childbirth we'd simply skip the whole family thing altogether."

Samantha chuckled at Ian. "Men are such babies."

"Yup," Ian said with a smile.

"I see the whole 'natural childbirth' thing just the same as going to the dentist and saying, 'I'd like the natural tooth extraction and root-canal please. No Novocain for me." Ian's joke and mannerisms made Samantha laugh as he continued, "I want to experience this as the primitive man did when he lived on the open plains with abscessed teeth."

"You're a nut," Samantha chastised.

"I'll tell you what, it's easy to pick on other people, but Mac gave me a hard time the other day for having physically mutilated the sex organs of our boys."

"Say what?" Samantha asked with a disgusted expression.

"Circumcision," Ian clarified. "And you know what? I think he was exactly right. I have no idea why we did that to poor Brandon and Andrew. Certainly after seeing it done to Andrew, and watching that process, you'd think I'd have known better by this year. But when Brandon came along I did it to him as well. I'm a grown man. I've taught judgment to flight students for years. You'd think I'd display some judgment of my own."

"Did we really hurt them?" Samantha asked.

"I don't know, I guess they say it reduces sexual pleasure. There certainly could have been other ramifications. But I guess the point is that there was no reason to risk it. Most Christians don't follow Jewish law anyway."

"Okay, we need to change the subject if you expect any chance at getting lucky in this lifetime," Samantha snapped.

Ian smiled. "Oh, so I have a chance at getting lucky tonight, huh?"

"Hmmm," she purred as she leaned in for a kiss, and then continued, "Well, I think the kids are asleep. Do you want to watch that movie you ordered?

"Say no more," Ian joked as he hopped up and departed the room in exaggerated excitement. Samantha laughed. He returned with the movie that had arrived in the plain brown wrapping. Mid-way through the movie, they retreated to the bedroom.

It was like the days before children again—actually even better. They knew exactly what the other enjoyed, and post-vasectomy there was not a worry in the world. It was the perfect wrap-up to a great day; but even after their most fulfilling and earth-shaking intimate encounter in years, Ian found he still couldn't settle down to sleep.

Ian kissed Samantha one more time. Under her sleepy breath she whispered jokingly, "What, you need food now?"

"I love you. Thank you for the love and attention," he said as he kissed her once again. "Just going to go read and work on the computer."

Ian closed the bedroom door and proceeded to the kitchen. He'd been riveted to a new book by a Kalamazoo-born co-author, Jerry Jenkins. Jenkins had written *Left Behind*[26] with Tim LaHaye, describing a literalistic interpretation of how the second coming of Christ would play out. Since having read during high school the wildly popular *Late Great Planet Earth*,[27] by apocalyptic author Hal Lindsay, Ian had been intrigued by end-of-world prophecy.

It wasn't that Ian really believed in these stories, but he certainly had found them plausible in some ways. At the same time he had very quickly noticed some problems.

First, Hal Lindsay's clear and compelling prediction that the world would end in 1988 had proven to be at least eight years off—*and counting*.

At the time, the funky interpretation of Matthew 24:32–34 seemed obviously correct to Ian—not unlike backward masking where once he'd been given the answer, he wondered how he didn't see it earlier. Of course the "answer" had proven to be incorrect, as was the esoteric interpretation of the scripture.

And as for *Left Behind*, Ian found the book highly entertaining, particularly once he suspended his disbelief. It was about how the Antichrist would come and deceive all nations with his devilish charm and brilliance. Given people's tendencies to oversimplify politics and go for good-looking, smooth types, Ian couldn't help think about Bill Clinton's emergent popularity. But apart from the believability of a smooth-talking Antichrist coning his way into control of a one-world government and religion, Ian found himself in conflict. He loved the story of how people might be deceived on a massive scale, yet also found the incredulity of those "left behind" to be completely beyond plausibility.

The basic premise was that God had instantly, "in the twinkling of an eye," called all of his believers home to Heaven. They literally disappeared from airplane cockpits, cars, factories and any other location simultaneously. Their clothes lay in heaps where they stood as they were physically transported to Heaven. The beauty for those taken was that they would not have to deal with the horrific pain, suffering, plagues of supernatural beasts, turning of oceans to blood, and all sorts of wacky, supernatural events God would ignite in the lead-up to Christ's second coming.

Fortunately, according to the story, the believers had left videotapes and notes explaining the sequence of end-of-time events, so those left behind could see the light and still be saved. *But inexplicably, many still did not see the light!* As the book went on, however, the lead characters did, and they took part in the subversive battle against the Antichrist.

What Ian would find increasingly hysterical, particularly in the later books, was that so many of those left behind just wouldn't believe, and wouldn't turn to Christ. He would joke to Samantha that seeing millions of people disappear, and literalistic fulfilment of all sorts of supernatural, impossible things, would have him running to church faster than Jesse Owens.

In another ironic reaction to the book, Ian found himself jealous, in a way, of the characters in the story. They had the luxury of perfect clarity, a war of good against evil. Things were black and white, and they were engaged in the fight of all fights. Ian wished he had item-by-item predictions of supernatural events that would compellingly play out before his eyes—things that simply weren't possible under the laws of physics, as he knew them. Even James Randi couldn't debunk something like that.

In Ian's eyes, the unfortunate truth was much like the reality Mac had discovered after Vietnam, that choices and decisions existed in a real, complex world, and were never so clear and simple—even though most people wished them to be so.

Ian thought of the dowsers and James Randi. He pondered not only that *Left Behind* seemed loaded with childish, magical beliefs and fantasy; but also he wondered if it might be fulfilling a psychological need for its authors and readers. Much as the dowsers needed answers in order to affirm themselves and in order to rationalize and support their simple, storybook views, was it possible that these literalist interpretations of the Bible were created to fill similar needs?

Could it be that the literal interpretations provided security and "proof" to those who needed greater certainty than the world could offer? Was it possible these people simply had to have better and clearer answers than "free will," or "chance?" Maybe those explanations were too unclear and fuzzy, so they needed to reinforce their certain truths with a dramatic tale? Were they desperate attempts by desperate people to have a self-assuring, "I told you so" moment, even if no such moment would ever come to pass?

As he would experience even more in the coming years, Ian's reading of the series propelled him to ask some deeper questions. He would go on to read many more of the books in the series—stopping only after he felt he was being strung along for financial gain more than anything else.

Ian enjoyed the entertainment and the thought-provoking nature of the stories, but that cold November night of 1996, Ian left the book on the end table and instead logged on to the crude, Truth-Driven Thinking bulletin-board system.

Initially, he exchanged comments with some of his fellow posters, and found interesting discussions on a wide array of topics: the real tricks behind "cold readings"—the techniques used by psychics to convince people that they read minds or talked to the dead; Uri Gellar and his claim of bending spoons with his mind; alien abduction stories and the debates about the infamous *Alien Autopsy* video; cognitive illusions and how our minds play tricks on us; misdirection and techniques used to con people out of money; Loch Ness and investigations of lake monsters; crop circles and related hoaxes.

But on that particular night, a posting by a regular bulletin board contributor would impact Ian the most. What with all the complexity and debate on all sides of the many issues discussed on the board, the individual had felt compelled to write and post the following—in the form of a pledge that the others could accept or reject:

> *When I look at what I believe to be true, I recognize that all I really have are opinions in various stages of development. Many variables such as age, additional information, education or exposure to other viewpoints could change what I believe in the long run. In the meantime, I can passionately argue on behalf of what I believe. Doing so is my democratic right—perhaps even duty. But none of my beliefs will own me or hold me hostage. I will forever be willing to entertain challenges to what I know, and ultimately even be willing to give up any belief if I do so in the interest of truth, when faced with credible and valid evidence. If I don't stand for and honor truth above all, I know that the hard wiring of my being prioritizes survival, self-preservation and the path of least resistance. And when ego, self-interest or self-affirmation is allowed to take over, my own worth is less than it could potentially be if I pursue truth. Caving to that kind of "dark side" is not who I am or what I want to stand for. Pursuit of TRUTH is light. I want to be a net "giver" to the world, not a net "taker," and to do so I simply have to prioritize truth ahead of all else, with the sober knowledge that I'll never in this life even know for sure whether or not I've found it.*

Ian read the pledge with great interest. It struck a chord in him. It was a philosophical approach that provided a framework through which he could struggle with many of life's difficult questions. He thought to himself, *what higher goal could there be than truth? What higher virtue than trying*

to attain knowledge of how the universe or the world really worked? Surely that
must be as close to God as we can ever get.

Ian remembered how ancient people would climb high on mountains
to be closer to their god. Couldn't we experience God through knowledge?
Through understanding the *real* world—be it what the founding fathers
really said, better theology and Biblical research, or even through physics
and a better understanding of the origins of the universe?

But then another thought hit him. He re-read the pledge. Could he sign
this? He thought for several minutes. It was not lost upon Ian that by sign-
ing, he would be willing to subordinate *any* belief to truth, so long as it was
arrived upon by reason, and with the best evidence available. Yes, that belief
would also have to be provisional, he thought, it would have to be open to
new information down the road; but really wasn't the pledge saying one
might even abandon his own God if faced with a better solution?

Was this going too far? Was this pledge making truth a *false idol?*

These were no small questions to Ian. This was his soul and his religion.
But what was there to fear? Was he afraid of what he might find? After all,
there would be no more notions that he accepted simply 'because'—simply
because *he accepted them on faith.* Up to that moment in his life, faith had
always been a virtue—a thing to be honored and praised. It was belief
without question, and that was a good thing. "You have to have faith,"
people would say.

But the larger question now came to Ian's mind. Would *God* want this?
Was not God a fan of truth? Perhaps the author of truth? Would this effort
bring Ian closer to God, like the ancient man who climbed the mountain?
Or would it be heresy to prioritize truth over God?

He thought long and hard before answering himself. No, it *wouldn't*
be worshiping a false idol. Truth, by definition, couldn't be a false idol.
One could have a mistaken idea of truth, for sure. Truth might not even be
knowable to humans. But shouldn't it at least be the goal? By keeping an
open mind and always seeking truth versus lies, how could one lose?

His mind was reeling with what to many people would seem silly,
irrelevant and hypothetical questions. But to Ian, this was his authenticity
at stake. This was his very essence and character being formulated.

After much thought he posted his initials, "IK", and joined the list of
signers.

As he logged off the computer, he had a strange, conflicted feeling. It was the feeling of expectation, that somehow he had altered the direction and velocity of his life in some exciting and unknown way. It was also a feeling of uneasiness, however, like he had just signed a pact with the devil.

Chapter 18

THE DESOTERICA

Nearly three years later; Thursday, August 19th, 1999—Kalamazoo, Michigan.

"Ian, there's been a slight change to the plan for the pickup on the thirty-first," yelled Mac from his office adjacent to the hangar lounge. "Bishop Spong had a commitment and we're picking him up at Teterboro at four-thirty, not four. That should still allow us to be in Atlanta by seven."

The regular gathering of the Desoterica had become the realization of Mac's vision—a group of elite scholars and intellectuals whose caliber and credentials exceeded even Mac's wildest expectations.

Mac's original sales pitch to his powerful sphere of experts had been multi-pronged. One of the hot buttons for many of the academics, however, had been a common belief that the great days of free exchange of ideas were imperilled—or even gone. They believed that no more were college campuses dedicated to the pursuit of shared wisdom through free dialogue, and that no more was inquiry free from the shackles of taboos, political influence, corruption, and threats of repercussions for coloring outside institutional lines.

College campuses, they believed, had largely become BA and MBA machines designed solely around employment. They were machines of mass production that churned out cookie-cutter cogs for the wheels of hyperconsumptionist America.

Faculty was relentlessly pushed to think short-term, to "publish or perish" in a world where brilliant instruction, as an art form that cultivated and nurtured interdisciplinary discovery, had been reduced to a tiny checkbox near the bottom of an annual performance review. Indeed the days of Socrates investing his time passionately and solely in the pursuit of knowledge—even to the near exclusion of income and the material world—were clearly gone.

So in the months following that round of golf with Ian—wherein the idea emerged to convene such a group, Mac began to pitch, to some of the leading theologians, historians and scientists whom he had befriended, the idea of regular, private, scholarly symposiums.

Almost to his surprise, they were powerfully excited. It didn't hurt, of course, that he personally would be funding the not-for-profit consortium, which in turn would pay the participants' quarterly travel expenses for the three-day meetings. Nor did it hurt that due to the depth and breadth of his contacts—which were admittedly facilitated by his wealth and donations—each prestigious name added to the list was just one more layer of icing on the cake. Each subsequent time Mac would approach a renowned expert, the scholar would see the list to date, and jump at the opportunity to participate. As a result, The Desoterica was rapidly becoming a dream-team of academia.

At its first gathering ten months before, in November 1998, there were 48 who had been named and accepted into the exclusive new group. The number of members would be allowed to grow, but not beyond 72 in the extreme—and only in additional "classes" of twelve. Clearly Mac was not superstitious, but he insisted from the beginning that the group's formal membership count always remain a multiple of twelve, for symbolic reasons.

Twelve was a magical number in the ancient world. There were twelve signs in the zodiac; twelve years before a Jewish boy became a man; twelve disciples; twelve tribes of Israel; twelve god-children of the great Ra—the predecessor of many great gods of Egyptian and Greek mythology; and many more.

In that first meeting, Mac had discussed potential names for the group with the esteemed minds that were gathered. He prefaced a specific motion with the genuine offer to open the issue to the floor if the group so desired. He had previously stated his intention to in no way micro-manage or dominate the group, and they had been instructed to dispense, forthwith, of any memory that he was the funding source of the group. Mac had simply desired to be one of the group, treated no better or worse than any member.

With that said, however, Mac offered a motion to name the group *The Desoterica*. initially, some weren't thrilled with the name, but his ensuing explanation swayed all but a few. In brilliant and flowing prose, he expounded that so much of what each of them already knew was *hidden* knowledge to the rest of the world: detailed chronologies behind the formation of the Biblical canon; extensive knowledge of symbology; Koine Greek—the ancient dialect of the New Testament; ancient Hebrew dialects—the tongue of the Hebrew Bible; Aramaic—the language spoken in Galilee at the time of Jesus; and detailed knowledge of earliest Christian promoters—"apologists" like Aristides, Athenagoras of Athens, Tatian, Justin Martyr, Irenaeus, Tertullian, Origen, and Clement.

Mac explained that both their existing knowledge, and that knowledge they would together gain, were complex and extremely difficult for most people to understand. Such knowledge was therefore limited to a small group—the very definition of *esoteric*, which was a Latin word from the Greek *esOterikos*.

So why the "D" in front? Mac further explained that the goal of the group—or any legitimate scholar—was not to gain knowledge and then *hoard* it, but to *share it with fellow scholars and to the world!* That way, others could use the information, and test, verify, or refute it. That was the very nature of intellectually honest scholarship.

So while the knowledge they all possessed was esoteric, he proposed that part of the group's mission be to *share and disseminate knowledge*, to diminish the esoteric, hidden nature of what they knew. They were to take these incredibly complex understandings and try to communicate them—*not hoard them*. Hence the "de" in *Desoterica* implied the taking away of the hidden, esoteric nature of such advanced knowledge. The individuals, he suggested, could then be called Desoterics. Mac liked how the word sounded similar to *cleric*, and indeed quite a good number of the participants were current or former members of the clergy.

The group certainly was not homogeneous, however, and it vigilantly guarded against preconceived notions. To that extent they were "liberal," in the sense that they remained open to new information and didn't think any book of truth or knowledge was closed 50 years ago, 500 years ago, or at any time in history. They believed that new knowledge about all things could still be acquired. Though there were many who considered themselves theists, deists, atheists, pantheists and such, most participants were sophisticated enough in their philosophical outlooks that they shunned such simple and narrow labels—fearing they were usually the result of strident, emotion-driven, dogma-driven views.

Lastly, Mac had used an "a" on the end of the word to give it a plural feel. This made it sound a bit like Diaspora, a word with which the entire group was familiar.[28]

In relatively short order there had been consensus to move forward with the name. At that time, however, probably no one contemplated the eventual scope and reach of the group's work, or how globally renowned the moniker would become.

At that initial meeting, the group also had determined that their gatherings would indeed be called symposiums, since the Latin originated from the Greek "sympinein," which meant to drink together—something they would certainly be known to do. At the same time even the commoners' dictionaries like *Webster's* verified the current definition of *symposium* to mean "a convivial party (as after a banquet in ancient Greece) with music and conversation," or "a social gathering at which there is free interchange of ideas." And true to Mac's plan for proceedings, a third definition was dead-on as well: "a formal meeting at which several specialists deliver short addresses on a topic or on related topics."

Back in the hangar on that hot, August day, Ian replied to Mac's comment about changing the pickup time for the keynote speaker at their Desoterica symposium: "Got it. I'll make the changes with the FBO. I tell you Mac, I am so psyched to meet Bishop John Shelby Spong! Is it possible

I could ask you to fly that leg so that if he's willing I can ask him some questions? Above sterile-cockpit altitudes, of course." Ian added the last part like a child bolstering his request for a puppy, promising to feed it and wash it daily.

Ian knew he was being overzealous, but couldn't resist. He had read *Why Christianity Must Change or Die*, [29] and was now reading *Living in Sin: A Bishop Rethinks Human Sexuality*. [30] The books had been nothing short of groundbreaking illuminations to Ian.

At the same time, certain new insights had in some ways been challenging for Ian to embrace. When he had begun reading *Why Christianity Must Change or Die* about a year prior, he was faced with the same conflicted feeling as when he signed the "pledge for truth" on the cheesy old computer bulletin board, back in 1996. Was he risking God's favor? Was he risking his eternal soul?

He had already known of the "end-of-days" predictions that said bastardized and watered-down Christianity would serve a role in forming the new, one-world religion that would rise up against Christ. He knew this, thanks to those books by Hal Lindsay, as well as to Jenkins and LeHay's *Left Behind* series. Indeed somehow the idea of free inquiry being a pact with the devil still lingered in his head. At one point in his studies he had even come across a couple of verses that were used by many to warn against learning too much, and to promote belief by faith, without excessive questioning.

Paul had said in I Corinthians 3:18–19:

> Let no man deceive himself. If any man among you seemeth to be wise in this world, let him become a fool, that he may be wise. For the wisdom of this world is foolishness with God.

And "Matthew" has Jesus say in verse 11:25:

> I thank thee, O Father, Lord of heaven and earth, because thou hast hid these things from the wise and prudent, and hast revealed them unto babes.

Once he had begun reading Spong's work, however, he had been riveted. Besides, he would later find some refuge in I Peter 3:15, among other scripture, which wasn't as suspicious of inquiry. It said:

> *But sanctify the Lord God in your hearts: and [be] ready*
> *always to [give] an answer to every man that asketh you a reason*
> *of the hope that is in you . . .*

And Isaiah 1:18 said:
> *Come now, and let us reason together . . .*

At the time, Mac had found it almost entertaining to see Ian's eyes opening to what was essentially a scholarly viewpoint, written, however, to appeal to the "pew potatoes"—what he called the real people who sit in the pews to ingest the befuddling modernized and literalized views of early Christianity.[31]

Having completed *Why Christianity Must Change or Die*, Ian was delving into one of Bishop Spong's other, equally controversial books, *Living in Sin: A Bishop Rethinks Human Sexuality*. Ian was shocked to hear the context and analysis of Biblical interpretations surrounding sexual morality. The historical attitudes about which Ian was reading seemed to stand in direct opposition to nearly everything he had ever heard, read, or been taught about historical Christian doctrine.

The early pages had prompted a blur of recollections from both his own church upbringing, and things he had understood through his Catholic friend Anthony, Bill's pastor Mike, and other sources. Ian had remembered a book Bill had loaned him during high school, *Mere Christianity*, by C.S. Lewis, and thought how interesting it would be to compare that book—and even Bill's wedding vows and the teachings of Pastor Mike's little "sex-orientation class"—to this closer examination of scripture. Indeed a new light was being cast upon traditions of love, sex and marriage as Ian saw it, and he had committed himself to learning more.[32]

Mac emerged from the back of the hangar office to reply to Ian's question about talking with Bishop Spong. "I'll see what I can do. He may want to use the short flight for preparation or something, but we'll see how it unfolds. I'll mention your request if there is an appropriate opportunity."

"Thanks, Dad," Ian said with a sarcastic grin. Mac didn't exhibit much of a reaction. He was knee-deep in preparation for the big meeting. In fact he had left most of the details of daily operations in Ian's hands for the last couple of weeks, and had exclusively left Ian the responsibility for all flight planning, including the details of their flight with Bishop Spong to Atlanta.

When Mac became so very busy with his Desoterica work, Ian often thought how glad he was that they had hired David Kurtz as a part-time pilot. He had remained with them despite receiving relatively few flying hours—running trips only in the 210 and the Baron. At the same time the market remained brutal for pilots; and since David's girlfriend and his family were in Kalamazoo, the entire arrangement worked well for all involved.

Although some solo operations were performed in the 210 and the Baron, especially when passengers weren't involved, it was common to operate with two pilots in those aircraft, as an added measure of safety. Usually it was Ian who worked with David, so over the three years they had gotten to know each other better.

David had actually added fuel to Ian's scrutiny of his own religious beliefs. He was a smart guy, raised Jewish in a Jewish home, and he was well versed in matters of religion. As they flew together one day in the confines of the 210, the black-haired, chiselled-featured pilot had shared stories of his Christian friends questioning him about his faith. David hadn't seemed too offended when conveying the exchanges to Ian; rather, he seemed to have taken in stride the sporadic inquiries from friends.

David had chuckled as he told of their questions. "You seem like a smart guy, David. How can you not see that Jesus *was* the Messiah?" they had asked him with real sincerity. "The proof is so clear if you would just take the time to examine it."

They weren't being intentionally condescending, he explained, these were very good friends who cared for him. But in the end they would be exasperated. "I'll pray for you," they would always tell him.

Ian was floored by the arrogance and apparent certainty of David's "friends." He again found his mind tempted and teased by these tiny pieces of a puzzle he didn't even know existed—pieces that made him ponder what it was that the Jews believed. *They must have had* some *reasons for rejecting Jesus*, he figured.

Chapter 19

IN THE TWINKLING OF AN EYE

Bill arrived home from work that night, setting his laptop computer on the kitchen counter of the new Vanderveen home. No sooner had the door closed than little Hanna screamed, "Daddy," and ran sprinting from the living room to greet him with a hug.

Hanna was now three years old, and had become every bit the little angel that one would expect from the DNA of Megan and Bill. But beyond her shoulder-length blond hair and piercing blue eyes, was an even more captivating personality. While every three-year-old has her moments of misbehavior, Hanna's were truly rare. Little Hanna was routinely praised by friends, neighbors and the Vanderveen church family as the sweetest little girl they knew. It seemed she had received her mother's gentle nature, as well as her good looks.

Bill kissed the top of Hanna's head as she hugged him, partially hitting the pink little hair clip that held the part of her hair in perfect order. Megan had always called her a "girly-girl," and as usual, she wore a dress—in this case a casual, white sundress that was perfect for the August heat. As Hanna finally relaxed her embrace on her daddy, big brother Zachary, now five years old, took his turn offering a greeting.

"Wow, am I lucky or what? What a wonderful greeting," Bill said as he accepted his second hug.

While the picture of the greeting had a Norman Rockwell feel, the frosty barrier between Bill and Megan was a recurrent fly in the ointment. Bill loved Megan very much; he still admired her very essence, her kind soul and the warmth of her character. She was the perfect mother, which certainly was reflected in the kids—particularly the sweet and demure little Hanna.

At the same time Bill had continued to struggle with the ebb and flow of what he perceived as a lack of affection and attention from Megan. He couldn't get over that while he knew she loved him, she still didn't ever seem to be attracted to him. There were times he wasn't even sure she *liked* him very much. Yes, it was about sex; but the problem also transcended sex. It was really about intimacy.

"Hi, honey," Bill said as he entered the expansive kitchen. Things had continued to go well for Bill at NALA, and they'd built the rather impressive home during the previous year, just a few miles from her parents' house in a rural part of the county.

"Hi, Daddy," Megan replied as she finished some dinner preparations, her gentle, singsong tone designed as much for the children as for Bill. "How was your day?"

"It was good," Bill said in an enthusiastic voice, also aimed more at the kids than Megan. "Daddy came home on time as promised so he could hang out with my man Zach, while Mama and Hanna run errands and go see Grandma."

"Zachary, why don't you play in the living room for a second while I finish getting dinner ready and talk to Daddy—okay? You too, Hanna."

Zachary took off without a problem, as did Hanna after a sweet "Okay, Mommy."

Megan and Bill talked briefly. Bill was delighted to see that Megan seemed to be in a better mood that day. It wasn't that she was ever intentionally mean-spirited or visibly angry—she wasn't. It was just that her increasingly frequent "rough patches" manifested themselves in a sullen, sulky sadness, which was painfully evident in her demeanor. Bill often would find that much as he loved her, he could feel himself tense up on the drive home—wondering how he might find her that day. More and more, Bill was beginning to realize that his old friend's suggestion about professional help just might be the road he needed to take. He was beginning to realize that he was helpless in fixing things alone. Megan was suffering from real depression.

For her part, Megan was tormented by her own guilt, caught in a complex struggle between multiple conflicting factors. She had a desire to keep her husband happy, and her "love and obey" upbringing instilled a strong obligatory sense that she should perform regular, wifely duties. Whether it was that, or simply that she loved Bill and wanted to keep him happy, the end result was the same. She *wanted* to be more attentive. She would tell herself repeatedly that she had everything she ever dreamed of, in Bill and the kids. But somehow she just couldn't think her way out of her predicament, or change her feelings, no matter how hard she tried.

As intuited by Bill's friend Ian in their bar conversation almost three years earlier, the other major psychological factor was a subconscious battle with secret demons that remained from her sexual abuse as a child, at the hand of that childhood neighbor. Indeed they would ultimately learn that such abuse commonly results in depression, intimacy issues, and either hyperactive sexuality, or a strong aversion to sexual interaction.

Bill had yet to put two and two together with regard to Megan's compulsive cleansing and showering immediately after sex, but even when Megan did perform those "wifely obligations," something clearly wasn't clicking.

The last variable in the complex web of factors was Bill's approach to Megan. Bill was a go-getter, all-American, Republican, "buck-up and all things are possible"-type guy. It had become incredibly torturous for him to realize, increasingly, that the more he tried to fix Megan's problems—or give her his patented pep talks—the more it added to the pressure and guilt she was feeling. She *believed* that she should just suck it up and be happy. She just didn't know *how*. Obviously it wasn't that simple.

Bill's approach to most things, however, was pretty simple. If you're an alcoholic, simply get a grip and quit drinking. An anorexic? Eat more! Depressed? Get up and do something positive. Go for a jog and everything will be okay. But the truth was, he was starting to see that it wasn't so simple for everyone.

And thus, a complex web had been spun. Bill's feelings were routinely hurt. Megan was extremely guilt-ridden and hard on herself most of the time. She loved her husband, wanted to please him, and yet felt like a huge failure in the marriage. Bill would oversimplify the situation and explain it all away in a pep talk—or even get irritated and say, "I just don't get it. You seem to have fun when we have sex. How bad can it be? Just make an effort to do it more and we'll both feel better." More pressure. The cycle had to be broken, but as with many things in life, they were too close to the problem to see any way out. And unfortunately, things were about to take a dramatic turn for the worse.

On that that fateful night when he arrived home, Megan seemed more responsive and alive than several of the previous nights. At the same time, there was the usual feel of disconnected, indirect conversation that was designed to avoid intimate contact. Often this was accomplished by maintaining a focus on the children.

"Bill, I have to tell you what your daughter said today. It was so cute! I had given Hanna a bottle of pop in the car, just as a treat because she was so good this morning. We're going down the road and she burps, and serious as ever she looked up and said, 'Mom, why do they put burps in pop?'"

Bill laughed. "Bright girl. That's a great question! If you think about it they really *do* put burps in there," he declared with a chuckle.

"I love you," he said as he embraced Megan and gave her a kiss on the cheek.

"I love you too," she said, and then she gave him a kiss in return. The irony was that they really did care for each other deeply. They both loved it when they connected, and hated it when they didn't, but had no clue how to shape the complex forces into a more fulfilling existence.

They sat down as a family for dinner, before Megan prepared to head out with Hanna. Bill turned to Megan afterward and said, "Hey, can you leave me Zach's big-boy booster seat? I took mine out at the office to put some samples in my car, and we guys might want to go cruise chicks while you're gone."

"Sure, I'll go grab it," Megan responded with only a smirk of acknowledgement at Bill's joke.

"No, that's okay, I'll get it." Bill ran out to the car and took Zach's seat from the left rear of Megan's little Honda Accord. He placed it in the back of his Jeep Cherokee and headed back into the house.

"Okay, we're out of here," Megan said as she carried three-year-old Hanna, passing Bill in the tile entryway by the garage.

"Be good for Mama," Bill instructed. Hanna leaned forward and extended a big kiss to him. In return, Bill moved from Hanna to provide a kiss for Megan, said goodbye, and the girls closed the door behind them.

"Okay, my man, we're going to run some errands of our own. What do you say we go to Wal-Mart and see about getting something to kill that ugly crab grass in the front yard?"

"Okay," was the extent of the reply from Zach, who seemed totally disinterested in the crabgrass portion of the communication, but up for an outing.

Ironically, Megan and Hanna also went to the nearby Super Wal-Mart, but not until after they had returned some dishes to Grandma Huxley at the beautiful lake estate. It was another warm August evening and Megan wished she'd brought bathing suits for the two of them.

"Oh, stay and swim. We can get you a suit. Hanna can just go in her undies," Megan's mother suggested, but Megan declined. After a relatively long conversation and catch-up session of girl-talk, she and Hanna jumped back in the car and headed to the store.

After grabbing the usual assortment of mid-week food items and a couple toiletries that were running low, the gals headed for home with the sun setting on another beautiful Michigan evening. To that point, it had been a night like any other—a typical summer evening.

Megan took M89 back to the county road that led westward toward their street, and proceeded down the rural road just slightly over the posted limit of 50 miles per hour. Hanna had been slurping on an empty juice box Megan had purchased for her, and as they were slowing to turn left, southbound onto their residential street, Hanna said in her soft little voice, "All done Mommy."

Megan was a safe and careful driver, and certainly took no undue risk in reaching back to grab the empty juice box while turning left across traffic to exit the county road. In tragically unique circumstances, however, the setting sun perfectly—yet subtly and almost imperceptibly—obscured the single oncoming vehicle that would crest the slight rise in the county road at the point of Megan's turn.

The percussive noise of the impact could be heard blocks away as Megan turned directly in front of the oncoming car. It was a jarring shriek of crushing metal and shattering glass, all packed into a couple brief seconds of terror as the oncoming car slammed into the right rear of Megan's car—directly into the corner where Hanna was sitting.

The trauma of the impact to the demure little girl was nightmarish. The brute force of the side-impact forced her head violently into one side of the padded car seat, then equally as powerfully into the other as it compressed the entire right quarter of the car—Hanna and all—past what had been the center of the back seat.

The force of the crash had pushed and spun the flattened chassis nearly thirty yards into the dry, weedy ditch. When the car came to a stop, a dazed and bloodied Megan found herself swimming in thick air, unable to hear and unable to think or see clearly. She looked backward to the spot where Hanna had been, but couldn't see anything except a bare foot. The child seat was rammed against the door immediately behind her.

With great difficulty, and ultimately with assistance of a passerby, Megan was able to get out the driver-side door and exit the car, screaming in a panic to reach her daughter, over and over again, "Hanna! Hanna! Hanna!"

At the Vanderveen home just a few doors up, Bill had heard the impact. Fear instantly struck his heart. "Zachary. Someone has been hurt. Sit here and DO NOT MOVE an inch. I'm going to help. Don't move!" And with that, Bill sprinted to the corner, arriving just as Megan had exited the car, screaming her daughter's name.

He and Megan converged on the rear passenger door simultaneously, only to be horrified by the sight through the now glassless window. The child seat was partially protruding from the window and blocking their view of their daughter, but they could see top of her head, her feet, and shreds of blood-soaked white sundress as Bill furiously pulled at the door. It took his adrenalin-soaked brain a few seconds to realize the door was actually locked. He reached around the doorpost to release the lock, just as the first emergency vehicle arrived.

"Sir, let us take it from here please," the voice of a volunteer fireman said. A stream of other vehicles was arriving just behind him.

"That's our daughter," Megan shouted, but two more firemen stepped in to move them back so that they could properly extricate the motionless Hanna. As one fireman entered through the front passenger seat and assisted, two others were able to open the now-unlocked—but still badly skewed—rear door, and pull Hanna's child seat out of the mangled car.

Just as the ambulance arrived, the car seat was rushed directly to it by a tall, lean firefighter. Megan and Bill raced after the man who carried their daughter. As he ran, Bill pointed and shouted to a fireman, "2862 Shady Grove—a few houses down that street—I left my son alone." Bill didn't slow down or wait for an answer but continued to run after his wife and daughter.

No sooner had the child seat hit the nearby gurney in the back of the ambulance, stethoscopes were on the battered and bloodied little body. "No pulse," one of the paramedics said. Megan was in silent shock, watching frantically with Bill.

"Get her out of that car seat. Start CPR."

"Airway clear. No breathing. Still no pulse."

The crews worked feverishly on the scene, but to no avail. In what was to become a pivotal point in their lives, sweet, innocent little Hanna Vanderveen was pronounced dead at the scene.

❖

Four-year-old Brandon and three-year-old Andrew were finally asleep. It had been a long but productive day of hangar work for Ian, and he and Samantha had just sat down on the couch when the phone rang.

"Hello? . . . Bill . . . what?" The serious tone caught Samantha's attention immediately. Something was clearly wrong. Samantha heard nothing more, but saw Ian's head sink. He held his forehead with the free hand, his look of stunned anguish sending panic through Samantha.

Realizing her worry he whispered, "It's Hanna." Samantha sat quietly as Ian listened further.

"Where is he?" Ian asked. "Okay, at your house. Do I have that right . . . I'm out the door. How about Megan?" There was a longer pause. "I'm on my way. Oh and Bill, I love you my brother."

Ian's eyes were filled with tears as he turned to Samantha. "Hanna . . . has been killed in a car accident." His words were jagged with emotion. Samantha grabbed him and held him.

"I've got to go. The police are babysitting Zachary at home and I need to go watch him. That's all I know."

"Hey!" Samantha said with force as she looked him in the eyes, "just take a deep breath and look at me. You have to focus on driving. Please, be careful. I love you so much."

"I will." Ian grabbed his keys and made the twenty-minute drive to the new house on Shady Grove. He knocked on the door, and a sheriff's deputy appeared promptly. Ian introduced himself and entered the home.

Deputy Springer was kind and compassionate. She was relatively short, with curly black hair and a friendly disposition. Five-year-old Zach was still awake. They had not had difficulties however, since he'd been intrigued with talk about police stuff, and even got a visit to the cruiser. Despite Bill and Megan's sometimes-paranoid worries about child abductions, it was probably fortunate that they'd always taught Zach that nobody would ever come to pick him up unless one of them had warned him in advance. If someone showed up and said he was sent by Zach's parents, he wasn't to believe it unless it was a police officer, his teacher, or his principal. In this case, Zach seemed perfectly comfortable to let the policewoman in the house.

Ian and Deputy Springer walked into the next room to talk for a second, and she was able to at least give the thumbnail sketch of what had happened. She also explained that everyone had gone to the hospital. It took a little while for Ian to understand where the accident had happened, how Bill got to the scene, and why Zach was still at home with her.

The deputy readied to leave. "Oh, one more thing. For security I need to see some identification."

"Absolutely no problem," Ian said as he reached for his wallet.

Finally alone with Zachary, Ian wasn't quite sure how to handle the situation.

"Okay Zach, tell you what. Your dad called and asked me to get you a quick snack or something, and then get you snuggled into bed. Your mom and dad are going to be late tonight, but they're okay and they'll be home later, okay?"

Ian didn't know how much to say, but thought he'd let Zach take the lead—which he did. "Was somebody hurt?" he asked in a concerned tone.

"Yes, but your mom and dad are safe, and they'll be home late, okay?" Thankfully, that was good enough for Zach. Ian didn't think he should volunteer anything more, and he was probably going to plead ignorance if Zach asked about his sister. But luckily for Ian, he did not.

After getting Zachary to bed, Ian watched TV for a couple hours, before a large sedan pulled into the driveway about midnight. It was Dan Huxley. He had been on summer recess from Congress, and was thus quickly accessible. He and Katherine had been at the hospital with Megan and Bill as Megan was treated.

Bill was first in the door and Ian met him with a hearty embrace. Bill clutched Ian, and wouldn't let go. It was an unthinkable tragedy—much worse than his problems with Megan. This twist in the idyllic, all-American plot he'd envisioned as his life, was another that he couldn't begin to understand. He sobbed. He sobbed as he hadn't since he was a child—his pain permeating Ian through their embrace.

For Ian, it was yet another of life's profound—if not haunting—moments; he knew he would never forget it. It was often said that there was no pain like that of losing a child, and Ian believed it.

The following morning, news about the death of the Representative's granddaughter hit the local television stations in force. It also had periodic national coverage on NBS, CNN and some of the other networks, and was briefly mentioned on most of the evening news programs. The big piece of early information was that police indicated alcohol *was* believed to be a factor in the crash. At the same time the reports were clear that the Representative's daughter tested negative for any alcohol, and was simply on her way home from the store when the accident occurred.

Chapter 20

THE HOPE OF FAITH

The following afternoon, Bill twisted the little pink hair clip as he sat in the lovely little room with Zachary, Megan, and both sets of grandparents. He thought to himself, who could ever have imagined they'd all be sitting there making funeral arrangements for their precious little girl. It was all too unbelievable. Try though he might, he just couldn't stop the deep, gripping pain inside his chest. Hell, he could hardly even believe it was true. It was beyond surreal.

The little plastic hair clip had been in the bag of personal effects the police collected and dropped at the house. Bill immediately recognized it as the clip that was in Hanna's hair when he'd kissed her on the head as he arrived home. Now, only a day later, there he was, awaiting a conference with a funeral director.

Megan sat clutching Bill's arm. All things considered, her strength had been amazing. Despite soreness and a headache that remained from her own injuries, she had been the backbone of the remaining family unit. She had been stoically strong in her faith, and also surprisingly emotionally present and supportive for Bill.

Cindy Vanderveen asked Megan, "Is there anything we can get you? How's the head?"

"I'm okay, thanks Mom," said the puffy-eyed Megan to her mother-in-law.

"Damn it I'm angry!" said Cindy in an uncharacteristic display of frustration. "It's not only the tragedy of Hanna, but I'm so sorry for you two," she added, tears flowing again. It didn't take much to get the whole group started anew, which was exactly what her words did.

Five-year-old Zachary was old enough to sense the pain too, and began to cry, "I want to see sissy."

"Let me take Zach for a little walk," volunteered Don Vanderveen. The two exited the room.

Never shy when it came to these situations, Cindy then said what probably needed to be said, but what nobody else had yet offered. "Megan, I'm so sorry for you." She hadn't even begun the words when Megan began crying uncontrollably, sensing where her mother-in-law was going.

Megan's own mother held her as they sat on the sofa and Cindy continued. "I hope that you never, at any point, even consider blaming yourself. You have to know that accidents happen, and there is so much in life that is beyond our control. I'm just so sorry that you have to go through this, but I'll do anything I can for the rest of my life to make sure you don't blame yourself for this—not for one day. We have to know and trust that she's in a wonderful place now, and that God had a plan for all this." Katherine continued to cradle her daughter silently.

"And alcohol *was* a factor according to the police," Dan Huxley added. "It sure makes you wonder if that woman hadn't been drinking, if things might have turned out differently . . . . But I suppose that won't solve anything right now . . . . Anyway, Cindy is right, sweetie, and we love you so much."

At that point the side doors opened, and Pastor Mike entered with Roger Beckman, the owner of Beckman Funeral Home. "I'm so sorry to be late, I was just taking care of a couple of things with Roger about the church," Mike said.

Megan, still being comforted by her mother on one side, with Bill on the other, reached a hand up while dabbing her eye. Mike took her hand and then embraced her as she rose to meet him. After greeting everyone else in the room and having a seat in a wing-backed chair alongside Mr. Beckman—another member of their large church family—Mike asked, "Would it be appropriate if I said a word of prayer to get us started?" Everyone nodded solemnly, and heads bowed in search of some comfort or meaning.

"Dear Lord, we come to you with heavy hearts. Our grief is indescribable, and our pain seems to have no end to its depth and breadth. We ask that you touch us, and be with us in our time of need—that you provide us the comfort we so badly desire, and that you visit faith upon us through the Holy Spirit, in order that we might trust in your plan. Lord we know that you are good and loving and merciful beyond words, and indeed beyond our ability to understand. We're grateful that our Hanna is now in your arms. Help us to celebrate you and celebrate our time with this beautiful child, who so clearly reflected your very nature. In Jesus' name we pray. Amen."

Megan was momentarily, and understandably, unraveling. "I'm sorry," she said underneath the little gasps that shook her.

Mr. Beckman spoke slowly and softly. "Megan, you take all the time you need. I'm so sorry for this. We're just going to take our time today and figure a wonderful way to honor Hanna. I don't care if it takes all day, we're here for you and Bill."

"Thank you, Mr. Beckman," Bill said.

There aren't words to describe the depth of pain, emptiness, and loss that Bill and Megan were feeling. The funeral came and went, but the pain did not. If anything, it grew deeper and ate at their inner cores like cancer.

Samantha and Ian had been wonderfully helpful to their friends, Samantha in particular when it came to being there for Megan. She hadn't provided any magic words to fix the pain—there were none. What she did provide was friendship. She cooked, cleaned, and comforted, but mostly just listened. Her loving attention was a gesture Megan would long appreciate, even if her sadness would prevent her from ever expressing it adequately.

John had even stayed in from Chicago for a few days after the service, to spend some time with Bill as well; but within a couple weeks, it became clear that the world was going to continue spinning, whether Bill and Megan wanted it to or not. Even usually optimistic Bill wasn't anywhere near ready.

Samantha and Ian understood the process of grief, though admittedly couldn't conceive of that kind of pain. Nonetheless, they made an ongoing effort to be available and to provide a conduit for whatever emotional outlets their friends needed: communication, release, sharing—or simple companionship and support.

The night before Ian was to leave for Atlanta, Samantha was in touch with Megan by phone, and sensed it was another of those rough days. "Why don't you and Bill grab Zachary and come to the house for burgers and dogs after work?"

"No, we aren't going to do that to you, Sam. You're going to be as sick of this sad, pathetic couple as we are of ourselves," Megan said as she teetered on the verge of tears once again. Her pain and frustration were apparent, yet she continued to be considerate of those around her.

"Hey, I'm not going to take no for an answer. We hurt for you. We love you. We might as well be in pain together. Around us, you know you don't have to pretend to be anything but what you are. We'd just love to be with you. Be at the house at six."

"Okay . . . Samantha. I love you too . . . . You guys are such great friends," Megan said with a quiver in her voice.

As the friends gathered that night, the unspeakable grief permeated the air. As with joy, Samantha knew that grief too needed to be shared among those who cared for one another, and that doing so was essential to meaningful relationships.

"It's so nice that Zachary has Brandon to play with," Megan said to Samantha as she helped her in the kitchen. The men had taken the three boys outside to play in the pool and give the ladies some space. Megan's eyes welled up yet again.

"Damn it!" she said in frustration. "I'm so incredibly tired of crying." The tears came even harder now. Samantha wrapped her arms around her friend and held her, as Megan confessed, "I can't ever imagine this pain lessening. I truly can't."

"It may not lessen, but perhaps it will change. I just saw George and Barbara Bush talking at their Presidential museum the other day. You know they lost a daughter, Robin, to Leukemia." Megan nodded. "George was moved to tears in the interview—*after all this time!* Clearly they still feel the pain. If there is any hope I can provide though, it would be that they moved on to meaningful lives of service, and obviously found great joy again in their lives. Heck, remember seeing George skydive this last summer, on his 75th birthday? Okay, maybe great times with their kids would be a better example, but you, too, will again find joy. You really will."

Megan looked deeply in Samantha's eyes as if to acknowledge her rare but effective words of loving reassurance. Samantha gazed back at eyes that were still beautifully blue, but instead of sparkling with life as they once had, they looked deeply sad and hollow.

Out by the pool the men were less free to talk because of the kids they were supervising. They were able to keep the tones of their voices positive, however, and cover some ground.

"I got a copy of the police report today," Bill said. "I brought you a copy—thought you might find it as interesting as I did."

"What's it say?" Ian asked.

"Well, it says what we already knew—that Hanna was killed by a drunk. The woman in the other car was driving at .10 blood-alcohol content."

"How do you feel about that?" Ian asked, as both men splashed around with their sons in the shallow end of the pool.

"Well, I guess I have forgiveness in my heart. After all, we've all done it. At the same time, there are consequences of actions, and I think Patti Nelson is going to have to live with those consequences. She's out on bail, but could be facing some time."

Ian didn't say much. He didn't quite know how to read Bill in regard to the woman. *But no matter,* he thought to himself, *what Bill needs now is just someone to listen.*

"I think we'll probably find a cool new place to live," Bill said as if talking to Zach, but so Ian could understand the intention to get away from the house that was so close to the accident scene, and to so many memories. They had purchased the beautiful home with such hope, with plans of raising the two kids in that location. Now it seemed that there was no way to escape the harsh, daily reminders of what would *not* come to pass—the hopes that had been dashed. It seemed that sad memories lurked in every room of the home.

"Boy, I'm sure that's a tough decision to make," said Ian sympathetically.

"Absolutely, but I think that's where we're headed. It's just too much."

"How's Megan?" Ian asked.

"Not good." Bill said, now covering a knot in his throat.

"How are you, my friend?" Ian asked—his eyes connecting directly with Bill's as if to show that the inquiry was genuine. He was sincere, and wasn't looking for a bullshit answer like the ones co-workers might expect at the office.

Bill didn't answer. He couldn't. He just lifted Zachary in and out of the water, and then looked to Ian. He shook his head subtly side-to-side, his eyes connecting with Ian's as if to say, "Not well."

For Ian, seeing his friend in such pain was a very difficult thing. While he couldn't fully empathize, he could at least sympathize. After all, Ian could vividly remember that feeling of constriction around his heart. It wasn't just grief, or sadness, it was a very physical, vice-like presence inside the chest that ebbed and flowed unpredictably. The only thing certain about the physical manifestation of grief was that despite the cycles, it was always there.

After playing in the water and regaining his composure, Bill said, "I will say this. Our church family has been phenomenal through this, just like you guys have been. Thanks for having us tonight, by the way. It really does help, especially with Megan, just to get out of the house." Ian nodded with a look of acknowledgement that needed no words.

"Actually, we left more darn food at home than you can imagine. I think someone from the church has brought us a meal almost every night since the accident. People really have been wonderful," Bill said with a warm sincerity.

Ian bobbed in the water with Brandon, his face illuminated, smiling with enthusiasm for the wet fun. "That's awesome. I'm sure that like us, though, they wish they could do more—take away the hurt."

"Yeah, I just pray that God will do that in time. I'll tell you something else. I cannot even begin to imagine someone going through this kind of event without the faith and knowledge that there is a good and loving God Almighty who will make everything right in the end. Much though we may hurt, there isn't a single doubt in my mind or Megan's, that someday we'll be reunited with . . ." Bill's words trailed off. He looked into the face of his handsome young Zach and finished his sentence with a forced smile, his eyes welling: "little sister Hanna." Abruptly he took an exaggerated bounce down into the water, hoisting Zachary higher as he sunk his own head under the water in retreat.

Chapter 21

TRUE MYTH

The following day—Tuesday, August 31st, 1999

"Hey, if you want some quiet time before tomorrow's address, you're alone in the back. On the other hand, once we're up at altitude, feel free to put the headset on. Just beware that my friend and co-pilot Ian has been reading your books—a fan, I'm afraid." Mac gestured in feigned disgust toward the aircraft where Ian was making final preparations.

It was the day before the Desoterica symposium began, and Mac and Ian had arrived at Teterboro airport to transport their keynote speaker to the big event in Atlanta. The Bishop grinned knowingly. "Ah," he said triumphantly, "at least that means I *have* a fan! I'll look forward to it."

Mac and Bishop Spong exited the executive terminal, the "FBO," and walked toward the Citation. They almost looked related—both were tall and greying, yet fit and distinguished. As they approached the aircraft, Ian emerged from the stairway to greet Bishop Spong.

"Ian, I want you to meet Bishop Spong. Bishop Spong, this is my good friend, excellent pilot and associate, Ian Keppler." It was an honor for Ian to be introduced as Mac's friend. This was the first time Mac had introduced him as such, at least as far as Ian knew.

"It's a pleasure to meet you, Bishop Spong," Ian said as he shook hands with the Episcopal Bishop from New Jersey. Ian had flown celebrities with Mac on several occasions; as a result, he'd become skilled at being helpful and polite in a subdued way—not fawning over guests or appearing conspicuously over attentive. Then again, this was the first time Ian really *wanted* to ask questions. It was as if Ian was a basketball fan, and Bishop Spong was Michael Jordan.

"Please, you guys are killing me with the formality. Call me John," the Bishop insisted.

"Well, welcome aboard John," Ian said as he extended an arm to his side, subtly offering boarding to the Bishop. Following him aboard, Ian explained, "We'll get you situated and comfortable, show you a couple things about the cabin, and get you on your way."

"Beautiful. Thank you. This is a treat indeed," the Bishop said politely.

Ian finished a quick briefing as Mac stood outside and triple-checked that the wheel chocks had been removed. As planned, Mac brought up the rear and closed the door, a task always performed by the pilot who would fly that leg of the trip.

After receiving the latest airport information, picking up their IFR clearance, taxiing, and a short wait for release at the end of the runway, they were airborne. The Citation leaped through the late-afternoon heat, and in a few short minutes they were on top of the clouds in the final stages of their climb.

"Hey, is it okay if I put these things on now?" asked a voice from the back of the plane into the intercom system.

"Absolutely John. Just don't say I didn't warn you if Ian bends your ear. And if you see me or Ian hold up a hand, that means we heard a radio call and we need to reply. We're not being rude."

"No sweat. This is fun for me. It's not every day that I get this royal treatment."

"Well, we're so glad to have you coming to talk to the group. I'm sure they'll enjoy hearing from you. Just be prepared for some pointed dialogue in the days that follow your presentation," Mac explained half jokingly.

"So Ian, do you attend these events too?" John asked.

"Yes sir, most of them anyway—when I'm not dealing with administrative or aviation duties."

"Excellent."

"At the same time you certainly won't hear me open my mouth! I'm just soaking this stuff up, hoping to pick up some of the crumbs that you all drop on the floor," Ian quipped.

The Bishop chuckled. "That's a good approach. I think I'd do the same thing if I could. Life is certainly about learning; I'm still learning myself. But that's what is so exciting about Mac's efforts—everyone is trying to learn from one another. At least that's how I understand it." He paused briefly then politely prompted, "So tell about yourself, Ian, if I'm not bothering your flight duties by asking."

Ian recognized the question as a magnanimous invitation to conversation. "Well sir, not a lot to tell other than a few years back I started to realize that whether it was miracle health cures, UFOs, talking to the dead, or magnets on our wrists to help us play better golf, we humans believe in a great many things for which there is little evidence, or even evidence to the contrary."

"Ah yes, Mac said you were intrigued by epistemology—said you hold truth as the ultimate virtue. Interesting philosophy. I congratulate you for opening your mind and at least acknowledging that we don't have all the clear-cut answers we crave."

Ian couldn't help but feel a sense of irony. Somehow those weren't the words of support he typically thought of as coming from a Bishop, but they were refreshing—just as his books had been. Then again, it was his bold and honest approach that had caught Ian's attention in the first place, so it shouldn't have come as a surprise.

"Mind if I ask you a question about that?" Ian said.

"Of course not. I'm just sitting here on a luxurious jet ride that you guys have provided me, drinking your soda on the way to speak to your impressive assembly of minds. I think you can ask anything you like," John offered in genuine appreciation.

"You're too kind . . . well . . . I guess I would have two questions really," Ian said pensively.

"Sorry, you only got permission for one," John joked, partly to put Ian at ease.

"Well to play off the old quote by Artemus Ward, and to apply it to the Bible, how is it that there can be so much that we *think we know*, that just *isn't so*—that just isn't supported by intellectually honest study of the evidence? And secondly, isn't there harm that comes from this mis-interpretation? Don't people take action based upon what they *think* they know—and thereby cause harm?"

With his answer, the best-selling author reminded Ian of his father's philosophy of moderation in all things. "Well Ian, if I may, I think the place where you have to start is to recognize that there is a difference between saying something is *not so*, and that something is *mythologically presented*," John said.

Ian felt like he'd been tossed a curve ball right out of the box.

"For example, the story of Jesus being born in Bethlehem is probably not history. Rather, it was terribly important to the Jews who were trying to understand Jesus—in terms of all of their messianic *expectations* from the Old Testament—to portray him as having been born in the birthplace of King David. This was because part of the messianic expectation was that the messiah would be of the House of David, and would restore the throne of David."

"Okay. I'm with you so far."

"But if you look at Mark's gospel—the first of the four narrative Gospel stories to be written—it is very clear that Jesus was born in Nazareth. He is called a *Galilean*. He is called a *Nazarene*. Galilee and Nazareth are his place of origin."

Without much effort, Ian could picture the Bishop in a pulpit. Without a note, his encyclopedic brain seemed to allow the words to flow from his tongue in a free-flowing articulation. Ian wished he could have been in Spong's church growing up. Ian listened intently as John's words continued.

"When you get to the next two gospel stories, the subsequent gospels of Matthew and Luke, they suggest Jesus was born in Bethlehem—but you find deep contradictions! Matthew—the first subsequent version to Mark—believes that Jesus and his mother and father lived in a house in Bethlehem. But he's got to deal with the other part of the tradition that says that Jesus has to be called a *Galilean*. So Matthew has the problem of getting Jesus out of Bethlehem where he is born, and into Galilee where he truly grows up."

The Bishop continued. "Luke, on the other hand, believes that Joseph and Mary live in the Galilean town of Nazareth, but Luke knows the tradition that the son of David has to be born in David's city—Bethlehem—so he has to develop a tradition to get the holy family out of Nazareth and down into Bethlehem. So what does he do?"

"What?"

"Well, Luke weaves into the story the notion that a census had been ordered and that everybody had to go to their home—to their original, familial, historical place of origin. For Jesus, according to Luke, that would be Bethlehem."

Ian sat listening intently. In the back of his mind he marveled that historically, he'd never even known scripture well enough to notice these distinct differences in the gospel narratives. Even if he had, he wondered, what would he have done with that information? Would it have changed anything?

"Now most Biblical scholars know that *none of that is history!*" John explained.

John chuckled as he thought ahead to the many reasons Luke's story didn't make sense. "I mean, there were something like forty generations between King David and Joseph! Do you have any idea how many 40 generations would be when you are talking about direct descendants? You know, David had lots of wives, and his son Solomon had a *thousand* wives! We don't know how many children David had, of course, but it was a goodly number."

As the Bishop spoke, Ian found himself smiling. The candor and the knowledge of this man combined to make so much sense—just as they had in his books. It reminded Ian again of that eureka feeling of a light bulb going on in his head. It was like seeing the magic trick and then asking, "Why hadn't I ever seen this?"

Bishop Spong continued with the historical impossibility of the census story. "If those offspring produced for forty generations, you are getting up toward a billion people just with geometric progression. The idea that anybody in that period of time would know enough about family records to keep forty generations in order is impossible. We can't even do that today, let alone back then. There was no way a family could trace forty generations of lineage back to Bethlehem. That is just clearly not history.

"But if that's not enough, the second thing that we know from non-Biblical, secular history and records, is that Cyrenius—who allegedly ordered the census for which Jesus had to go to Bethlehem—became governor of Syria in the year 7 A.D. If Jesus were born when Herod was the king, which both Matthew and Luke have said in our Biblical texts, he would have been born around 4 B.C., so he would be ten or eleven years old by the time Cyrenius became governor of Syria. He wouldn't be a baby anymore and couldn't have been at risk under the order to execute all the male babies. So this entire story begins to fall apart in a lot of places."

One thing Ian loved about scholars was how they assembled their arguments from multiple angles, weighing the likelihood of one scenario over another, and usually having tested any conclusion's validity under fire. For Ian, Bishop Spong's first example would have been enough to call into question the historical accuracy of the story. But these people who passionately parsed ancient texts for a living existed in a world of details that would overwhelm Ian in no time. He would later find during some of the panel discussions or cocktail party debates of the Desoterica, that at many points the pedantic, anal-retentive attention to detail would lose him. At the same time, this was the nature of historical work. Every word *did* matter in the big picture, and Ian greatly admired their tenacity.

Bishop Spong extended his example. "I think the final place that makes it kind of fun to think about this is in Luke's story, where he says that Joseph's wife Mary was 'great with child,' according to the King James version. To me that would at least mean eight to nine months pregnant. *But he took her on a 94-mile journey from Nazareth to Bethlehem?* And do you know how they would have traveled?"

"Wasn't it on the bullet train?" Mac interjected with a grin.

"The only way you could get there was by walking or riding on a donkey! And keep in mind there were no hotels, and no restaurants. Now in my mind, no man in his right mind would take a woman who was eight-months pregnant on a 94-mile donkey ride in that sort of circumstance."

Now it was Ian's turn. "Not and ever hear the end of it." He received only a slight chuckle from the other two.

"See, now you'll never get me to stop," John said as a note of humility.

"I hope not!" Ian said with genuine enthusiasm. "It's fascinating."

"I could go on with many other examples, but the point is simply that everything about these stories cries out to say that *we are not dealing with history*. We are dealing with *interpretive mythology*. Interpretive mythology doesn't mean it's wrong though; it just means it is not literal."

"That's a profound point," Ian said into the headset microphone.

"Well, unfortunately we are only now realizing that the New Testament was written by Jews, in the Jewish context, but it was *read and interpreted* mainly by non-Jews—Gentiles, that is—from about A.D. 125 until at least the middle or end of the 20th century! It was only then that we finally began to recover our Jewish eyes. Then we could see the Bible in a very different way."

Ian had read enough of Spong's work to understand his point. By understanding the way the ancients—the Jews in particular—taught lessons and told stories, he was better able to see the less simple, more complex, *hidden, esoteric* meanings of the scripture.

At that point a radio call snapped over the radio and into their headsets. "Citation four-three-niner-mike, Washington Center now, one-three-eight point four-zero."

"I've got it," Mac said, indicating that he'd make the radio switch so Ian could remain focused on the lesson at hand.

"That's where you use the term *midrash*," Ian clarified. In part it was also a prompt to keep John's words and knowledge flowing. Ian was lapping it up eagerly.

"Well, it is a loose word because the Jews used it in a much stricter way than I am using it. What I mean by *midrash* is that the Jewish people told stories about their heroes and kept telling the same story about different heroes. Their understanding was *not* that this information was *untrue*. Their understanding was that they had met God in Moses; they had met God in Elijah; they had met God in a number of people of the Old Testament. And the way they indicated that it was the same, singular God among the different revelations, was that they *told the same stories about these people*. They used new characters, but kept the plotlines of the play—if you will—the same. And again, that doesn't mean that the meaning behind the stories was untrue."

"And that's what they did when Jesus came along?" Ian asked.

"Yes. The best one that might help, with which you are probably most familiar, is the story about Moses splitting the Red Sea in the Old Testament. He split the waters and allowed the Jewish people to go through on dry land as he was leading his people out of captivity from Egypt. What you may *not* be familiar with is that Joshua does the same thing at the Jordan River, when they went into the Promised Land; that Elijah does the same thing when he goes out into the wilderness to depart from this world; and that Elisha does the same thing when he comes back."

John went on to explain why the early Jewish Christians would *define* Jesus as real and true through the act of setting him into a similar parable as these Old Testament stories, one that also helped *explain* that great new understanding of God and his Old Testament word.

"But then Jesus is being baptized, and he goes into the Jordan River—the one that has been split three times before by three heroes of the past. Yet Jesus doesn't simply split the Jordan River—after all, that's not a big deal. Anybody can do that. I mean, that's been done so often before," John said smugly. "Rather, this new story at Jesus' baptism portrays the splitting of the *heavenly* water, splitting the heaven so that the spirit pours down upon him—and *spirit* and *living water* in the Jewish tradition are always synonymous. So what we are being told here is not a literal story at all! It is an attempt to see Jesus as the *new* Moses; the *new* Elijah; the *new* Elisha; and the *new* Joshua—which by the way translates in Greek as 'Jesus.' Coincidence?"

"Okay, my head is starting to hurt again," Ian joked.

John laughed. "Sorry if I've gone on too much."

"No, in some masochistic way I really do enjoy it. Mac always makes my head hurt too." He then clarified, "I'm joking. Please, continue."

"Okay, since I'm fired up and rolling," John replied humbly. "Actually, another good way to illustrate that is to look at the story of Jesus' earthly father who was developed only in the first and second chapter of Matthew's gospel. When you read Matthew's gospel you discover that there are only three things you learn about Joseph. One is he's got a father named Jacob. Two is that God speaks to him only through dreams, and Joseph is overwhelmingly identified with dreams. Thirdly, his role is to save Jesus—the child of promise—from death by taking him down to Egypt."

"Now go back and read the story of Joseph, the great patriarch in chapters 37 to 50 of Genesis, in the Old Testament—Joseph and the coat of many colors—"

"Ah, Andrew Lloyd Webber's creation," Mac interrupted jovially.

"Yes, right," John chuckled. "But you will discover that you learn three things about the great patriarch—the Old Testament Joseph. One, he has a father named Joseph. Two, he is overwhelmingly identified with dreams—he rides into political power in Egypt as the interpreter of dreams. And three, his role in the drama of salvation is to save God's people—the People of the Promise—from death, by taking them down into Egypt."

Ian jumped in. "So they are acknowledging Jesus as God, by telling the stories about him in a traditional way; but they never intended the stories to be literal?"

"Exactly. You catch on quickly. When you begin to see these connections, then you recognize you are not dealing with history, you are dealing with a Jewish interpretive process—of which Gentiles, by and large, have been ignorant. Without understanding the Jewish history and culture, we 'non-Jews' have been unable to read the gospel tradition properly."

"Bishop Spong, I'll tell you what I think is amazing," Ian offered. "Where I come from, in what I would call a traditional Midwest upbringing, there are many people like me, to whom this is totally new information. Had I not found your books, or Mac, I'd still be suffering in the pew and trying to make sense of this stuff."

"Oh, that is true of many people—not the part about me necessarily—but I think it's just so tragic because New Testament scholars have been working on this sort of thing *for about 200 years!* I must tell you that we have been blinded by our prejudice with regard to the Jewishness of the New Testament. It is only in the later part of the 20th Century, in the work of people like Michael Goulder at the University of Birmingham; Krister Stendahl at Harvard; Paul VanBuren at Temple; Samuel Sandmel—a Jewish New Testament scholar at the University of Chicago; and a number of others who began to crack this code, that we have come to see these things in a different way. And there are several others, many of whom are part of your Desoterica group."

"It really is an amazing new paradigm for understanding this stuff, especially to an ordinary guy like me," Ian added.

"Well, when you read scripture with this new understanding, a lot of the problems disappear. Traditionally, we read the Bible and we sort of say, 'Well, I've only got two alternatives. I've got to take it literally,' and then I become a fundamentalist; or, 'I've got to dismiss it as impossible,' and then I become a member of what I call the Church Alumni Association."

Mac and Ian laughed, but in truth Ian and Sammy hadn't been regular in their church attendance in some time. Although he loved the people, and his pastor, Ian was finding the implausibility of his entire religion to be overwhelming—especially since his pledge to try to find historical truth. He was finding that he benefited less and less from hearing the same old literalist, implausible stories, re-articulated in the same old way. Of course it probably didn't help having Mac, an atheist, as a primary sounding board.

Mac chimed in. "Obviously, Ian, this is where Bishop Spong and I would differ. I still remain somewhat skeptical that any of this is true—even mythologically. But I agree with John's interpretations of the *midrashic* and allegorical methods employed by storytellers of the day. I also totally respect and continue to appreciate—and listen to—the evidence and arguments John finds supportive of belief in Christianity."

John added, "And likewise, this is what I respect about Mac's effort. The jury is out, but at least people are working hard to set aside, or at least recognize arguments that are purely from faith, and focus on a reason, or rationale, for answering these tough questions the way that they do."

"Fair enough," Ian agreed.

"The best way to look at that is to take the story of Jesus walking on the water. Now it is a funny little story because the only time I hear about it today is when somebody is telling a bad golf joke—"

"Ah, he stole my line," Mac said as he raised his hand to handle another frequency change with air traffic control.

The Bishop subsequently continued, "That really is the only time though. As a pastor, we don't preach things like walking on the water because you don't know what to make of it. People cannot walk on water! If you think they can, you live in a world that is quite different from the world that we've lived in since the seventeenth century, when Isaac Newton did his work. So what does this story of walking on water really mean?"

"Not a clue here, sir," Ian admitted. Mac stayed out of the exchange for the moment, allowing the teacher to make his point.

"Well, if you go back into the Hebrew scriptures you will discover that God's power over water is a dominant theme in Jewish worship, and it comes out of the Red Sea experience. So the Jewish Psalmist and the Jewish prophets began to talk about how God has power over water. They say that God's footprints can be seen upon the deep, and that God can make a pathway for God's self in the sea."

"Ian, remember when we talked about baptism?" Mac asked rhetorically, as a reminder of their conversation about the ancient connections between God and water. Unfortunately, that comment served more to remind Ian of the painful situation with Bill and Megan. Ian said nothing. Mac clearly didn't remember that it was little Hanna's baptism that had prompted that original discussion.

The Bishop continued. "If you live in the first-century belief that you have met a presence of the living God in this person named Jesus of Nazareth, the way you interpret that is you take all this 'God language' from the Jewish tradition, and you apply it to the new figure, Jesus. What you get is a God who can make a pathway for God self in the deep, or a God whose footprints can be seen on the water. *The story gets told as Jesus being able to walk on the water.*

"Once again, the Jews would have recognized what that was all about. It is later gentiles—us—who treat everything literally or historically, but we don't understand how the Jewish people wrote their own sacred story. So that creates the terrible problem that we face as contemporary Christians: Christianity is divided into very conservative fundamentalists—who take the Bible quite literally—and secular humanists who say, 'That just doesn't make any sense to me at all, so I am not going to be part of any religious tradition at all.' I think both of them are sadly lost in trying to understand what the Biblical story was all about."

Mac said nothing, because he honored and appreciated the Bishop's point, and also because he had been fully authentic with his views in previous conversations with John Spong; he was trying to allow the conversation to flow unabated between Ian and the Bishop. At the same time, the non-believing side of Mac silently reflected on the fact that an individual still has to believe the *truth behind the mythology* in order to accept a theistic belief in God. Mac clearly did not.

For his part, Ian was now strongly beginning to lean in the *agnostic atheist* direction espoused by Mac. He was candid with the Bishop about his struggle. "By the way, I partially blame your works for tipping me over in the direction of that non-religious, secular humanist category," said Ian.

"I'm sorry about that," the Bishop replied with a slight chuckle and a canting of his head to the side.

Ian continued, "This stuff is just so new to me. I mean whether we are talking about virgin births, talking donkeys, burning bushes, or—" he stopped mid-thought. "I just discovered that Matthew points out, that at the time of the resurrection Christ not only physically rose, but tombs broke open and a bunch of other bodies arose from their graves and went into the city . . . like to hang out and haunt people or something."

"Yeah, I don't hear that one preached about from the pulpits on Sunday very often either. I mean, these bodies walk around in town and are recognized by many," the Bishop said with a skeptical expression. "But you see what we are dealing with, and what gets missed, is that in the first century people had a powerful experience. They identified this experience with the ultimate God, and *they met this experience in a man named Jesus of Nazareth!* So they had to develop a mythology that showed how this God—which they portrayed as some supernatural parent figure that lived above the sky—got into Jesus. That is where we get the virgin birth."

"Interesting," Ian said. Though he'd read the books, somehow it was clearer when the author of the book was sitting with you and explaining the central points.

"This virgin birth thing is not original to the Christian story, and it did not develop until the 9th decade. There is no virgin birth in Paul, who wrote from 50 to 64. There is no virgin birth in Mark, who wrote in the early 70s. The virgin birth story is introduced in the mid 80s by Matthew—using an erroneous Greek translation of Hebrew *Almah* in Isaiah 7:14. It is added to by Luke in the late 80s or maybe even the early 90s. Then it is again totally omitted from the fourth gospel John, who on two occasions refers to Jesus simply as the son of Joseph."

"Some are even arguing later dates today, by the way," Mac added for Ian's benefit.

"Yet people react in shock. They say, 'Oh my goodness, I never heard that because we have been saying the Christian creed forever'—which says 'born and conceived by the Holy Spirit, born of the Virgin Mary,' etcetera. We think that is part and parcel of what the Christian story is all about, yet it is interesting to note that of the five major writers in the New Testament, three of them either do not know anything about the virgin birth, or deny the virgin birth: Paul and Mark, the earliest writers, and John, the last gospel.

"I feel so ignorant . . . . Then again, Mac constantly reminds me of that," Ian joked, shaking his head in self-deprecation.

"In the entire Bible only Matthew and Luke tell the miraculous birth story—*and they disagree on so many details that it is hard to reconcile!* We reconcile Matthew and Luke only when we do Christmas pageants. There, we follow the Luke story line and then tack on Matthew's wise men as the final scene. But the stories are deeply incompatible!"

"How did I not ever know this?" Ian asked. "I grew up in the church." Ian was still hung up on how such knowledge can be so hidden from public view, when it's right there in the Bible everyone reads. "Keep going," Ian urged.

"Matthew's story has Jesus and Mary and Joseph fleeing down into Egypt to escape the wrath of Herod who is coming down to kill all the Jewish boy babies—which is nothing but a Moses story from the Jewish Old Testament being retold about Jesus. But at the same time Luke says that Jesus was circumcised on the eighth day, and presented in the temple in Jerusalem on the 40th day. And then they leisurely made their way back to Nazareth, from whence they had come. *The stories cannot be reconciled,*" John again summarized.

Mac now entered the conversation to summarize further for Ian's benefit. "So the people who try to treat the Bible as if it is some sort of literal treatise that was dictated by God, totally miss the point." Despite the levity he had been offering, he was thoroughly familiar with Spong's work; and as evidenced by the group's invitation to have Spong speak at the opening day of the symposium, Mac was a sincere admirer. This was particularly true because Spong had been able to do something many scholars over the centuries had not. He had been able to articulate and summarize this view of the Bible in a way that people could really understand. He was popularizing scholarship—a feat that Mac admired.

"Now we're getting into my topic for tomorrow," the Bishop continued, "because our task is not to say, 'Did it really happen?' That gives us either a fundamentalist answer, or a dropout answer, 'Yes,' or 'No.' Rather, our job is to say, 'What was there about Jesus of Nazareth that convinced people that something of the transcendent, holy, other dimension of life, was found in him in a way that they could not deny? In a way that *caused* them to tell virgin-birth stories on one end of his life, and cosmic ascension stories on the other?"

"Not to interrupt you John, at least not this time," Mac teased, "but I think that you've appropriately brought this thread full circle. You started by making the point that the people of Jesus' time had a powerful experience through Jesus Christ, and that they needed to develop a mythology to get the dualistic, transcendent God of the separate, Godly realm, into the body of Jesus, and then back to Heaven again."

"Right you are, Mac. Because after all, if you get God out of the sky and into the life of Jesus of Nazareth, you've also got to find a way for him to get out of the life of Jesus of Nazareth, and back up into the sky. I mean God has to have a round-trip ticket if you're going to tell the story this way. So what they did was develop the mythology of virgin birth on one side, and the mythology of cosmic ascension on the other side, neither of which makes literal sense to 21st century people."

"Now you know why my head tends to burst when I get in a room with a bunch of you people," Ian wisecracked.

This time the Bishop laughed as well. "I certainly understand where this can be complex and confusing. In fact, I think part of the problem is that it *is not simple stuff.* The story isn't the simple, historical version that we can be spoon-fed in simple, black-and-white chunks."

"You know I'm joking though. I can't tell you how interesting and helpful this conversation is to me."

"Ian, it's my pleasure. I obviously have great interest in these topics."

"Well let me ask you this then. Some time ago I got into a conversation about Heaven with my friend Bill. Unfortunately they just lost a child in a car accident—a horrible thing."

"I'm sorry," the Bishop said.

"Thank you. I'll pass that along. But in that conversation I said that I believed people from other religions could get into Heaven. He quoted John 14, verse six I think—forgive me if I don't know, but it says something like, 'No man cometh unto the father but by me.'"

The Bishop looked unsurprised. Obviously Ian hadn't thrown out a new stumper that he'd never heard. "Yeah, well that story, what they need to know about that is that John's was the last gospel to be written. John is the only gospel that has Jesus say a series of 'I am' sayings. 'I am the bread of life. I am the living order. I am the good shepherd.' What Jesus quoted in the verse you mention is one of the 'I am' sayings. Essentially, 'I am the way, the truth and the life. No one comes to the father, but by me.'"

Ian wondered where this was going, but knew it would once again be brought together in a brilliantly cohesive fashion if he'd just listen carefully.

"What is going on is that John's gospel is written after the orthodox party of the synagogue has ex-communicated the revisionist Jews of the synagogue—the disciples of Jesus. And so the disciples of Jesus are claiming the word of the name of God from the Old Testament. As you may recall, in the burning bush story Moses demands to know God's name and God replies that 'my name is I am.' So they put this 'God-name' into the mouth of Jesus over and over again, and *the only way to come to God is through the understanding of God—as 'I am.'*"

"Never a dull moment in scholarland is there," Mac exclaimed as he double-checked their position.

"That scripture has been used as a missionary imperative, and it has been used to condemn Jews; and Muslims; and Hindus; and Buddhists. Now ask yourself a question. What makes anybody think that he or she is smart enough to tell God—whoever and whatever God is—how God can draw people to God's self? That is not our business! That is God's business! And the idea that we draw our little religious empire, and we say we have the only doorway, the only truth, the only access to God, well that makes absolutely no sense to me at all!"

The Bishop was speaking with great feeling again. "I sometimes think that the following is the only way you can get people to understand. Let me ask you this, have you ever looked at a group of horses?"

"I suppose," Ian responded. Of course Mac knew instantly where this one was going.

"Well suppose those horses had an ability to communicate and we told them it is up to you horses to describe what it means to be human. What would they say?"

"You've got me again. I suppose they'd be wrong in whatever they said."

"Exactly. A horse has no earthly way to describe what it means to be human because it has no way to experience what it means to be human! Well, human beings have no way to describe *who God is, or what God is,* because we have no capacity to think outside our human categories. That is why the Gods of human beings always look like great big powerful human beings. It was Xenophanes, a great Greek philosopher who said that if horses had Gods, they would look like horses."

"I am sure that's absolutely true," said Ian.

"And there is nothing wrong with that. You cannot escape that. But what you can escape is literalizing your own images of these stories. I think human beings can experience the transcendent wonder and power and the meaning of God, but I do not think we can ever say *who* God is or *what* God is. We can only say how we believe that we have *experienced* the holy."

The concept was getting deeper, but Ian was listening intently. "I think I follow you."

"If we begin to stop at what we *do know,* not what we *think we know*—to your earlier point about truth—then I think we can sit down with a Jew, and a Muslim, a Buddhist, and a Hindu, and each of us can say 'this is the way I experience the holy.' That does not make *anybody* wrong. It makes everybody's perspective just, different."

"Profound," Ian said.

"Maybe the day will come, God willing; and I hope we will begin to recognize that there are many pathways to God—maybe as many pathways to God as there are human beings."

Ian looked out the window to the earth below. This was indeed a flight and a conversation that would stick with him. His thoughts crept again to Hanna, and how the mysteries of life were so overwhelming at times. He now studied the earth below. The jet was high enough that he could actually see the slight curvature of the earth. He could see the earth was round. It made him briefly ponder the beliefs of those who to that day claimed the earth was flat. He wondered silently, *how and why do we believe what we believe?*

Above him, the lack of atmosphere made the sky almost black. What was out there? What was beyond the vastness of the black space above? Was Hanna out there somewhere with a God? For that matter, he wondered if he would ever see his parents again, as he'd long believed he would. "Deep stuff," he said under his breath.

After a brief pause, Ian's thoughts were brought back to the Bishop, as he spoke: "What we have got to do is to stop literalizing our pathway, and then simply binding God with our understandings. That is just nothing except idolatry," John exclaimed.

"It sure makes it tough though, particularly when people say, 'The only truth that I care about is the truth in the Bible,'" Ian said—thinking especially of the folks who attended Bill's mega church.

"Well, that is pitiful," John said, and once again it still seemed hard for Ian to believe he was hearing such views from a committed man of the cloth. It was like a child experiencing cognitive dissonance as he figured out the truth about Saint Nicholas.

"Gee, how do you really feel?" Mac deadpanned in response to John's bold assessment.

"Well it's pitiful because they clearly have not *read* the Bible. The Bible calls for capital punishment for children who talk back to their parents; for people that commit adultery; for people who have a sexual relationship with their mother-in-law; for people who worship a false God; and even for people who violate the Sabbath. If you take the Bible literally, there aren't enough executioners in the world, or enough volunteers to take care of the victims."

"Well now you'll get me going," added Mac—less able to stay quiet. "The God of the Bible is almost demonic in places. You have the story in the flood, where God decides that the world is so evil, he's going to drown every human being in it. That is a funny kind of God. And then you get the way the Exodus story is inaugurated, that God sends the angel of death throughout the land of Egypt to kill the first-born male in every Egyptian household. They even put blood on the doorpost of the Jewish households so that God's angel would not make a mistake and kill a Jew by accident."

"Mac is right. That *is* a funny kind of God," John said. "Then you get to the book of Joshua where they stop the sun in the sky so that God can kill more Amorites, or so that Joshua can kill more Amorites."

"That is a really strange reason for instituting the first daylight-saving time in human history," Mac sneered, obviously amused with his own wit.

"Well I was at my friend's church once, and actually heard Pastor Mike acknowledge some of these dark sides of history—which I thought was pretty cool," Ian said.

"That is good. Most people don't even know the stories are there," John interjected.

"But he explained it this way. He said that if I killed a man in the street, a bum perhaps, then this would be one kind of murder. But if I killed a head of state, that would be a bigger crime. His point was that by our very sinful nature, we have so badly sinned against God from day one, that he has every right to kill all the children. In fact, he argued he should strike all of us sinners down, right this moment. We are *that* bad, and *that* unworthy. We are so sinful by nature that God is certainly justified in all these things. But his closing point was this beautiful story about how merciful and loving God is, and how we should be so appreciative of his mercy. How do these people reconcile those two sides of God?"

"Well, you see, one of the great tragedies of the Christian tradition is that we spend an awful lot of time telling people how wretched, and miserable, and sinful, and lost they are. We sing about God's *Amazing Grace*, and the next line you learn that the reason God's grace is amazing is that it saves a wretch like you."

"Absolutely," Mac said. "Adam ate the apple. Certainly the ancient Gnostics, who influenced Christianity greatly, would have agreed that we are flawed. They believed it was a horrible mistake when divinity left the separate, Godly dimensions above, and it was merely a misfire of divinity that allowed it to trickle to our seventh, lowest strata of existence. And whether through reproduction or any other way, we weren't supposed to spread it. It was not supposed to be this way, and we are wretched and horrible, lower-level beings that are merely contaminated with divinity."

"True, but my point is that I have just never known people to be helped by that mythology, or more precisely by being told how wretched they are. Try to imagine a baby being raised by parents who every day say to that baby, 'Little baby, I want you to know you were born in sin. You are a wretched, self-centered creature. You are not worthy to gather up the crumbs under God's table.'"

"I think I've met many people like that before," Ian said.

"Well I don't think that baby will grow up to be a very healthy adult. And yet that is what we say to people Sunday after Sunday in church. We tell them how wretched, miserable, lost, inept, hopeless, and deprived they are."

Mac chimed in again for Ian's sake. "Another, more common view of human nature is that human life was created perfect, but then having fallen into sin, and not being able to save ourselves, a divine rescue was necessitated. God had to come in and pay the price of our sins. That is what the cross is interpreted to be."

The Bishop expanded upon Mac's statement about sin. "You know, over and over again I think it is time that we take the stain-glassed covers off the Bible and say there are some dreadful things in this book."

"Well let me ask you the obvious question then," Mac chimed. "Why do you continue to read it?" He asked the question more for Ian's benefit than his own.

"Well, because the Bible keeps transcending itself. The tribal God that wants to kill the first-born in every Egyptian household, and wants to stop the sun in the sky so that Joshua can kill more Amorites, finally develops into a perception of God that says, 'From the rising of the sun to its setting, God's name will be great among the Gentiles. And in every nation, incense shall be offered.' And finally we get to Jesus of Nazareth. He says if you really want to be fully human, you've got to love even your enemies. He says you've got to bless those who persecute you. That is an *evolving* God concept in the Biblical story."

"Interesting," Ian again said to himself aloud.

"Now we're again getting into my talk for your keynote, but I think we need to be aware of where we have come from, and I think we need to be aware of where we must go in the religious field. So to me, the Bible is a terribly important part of my tradition, but I do not want to have it read the way that the Jerry Falwells of the world read it—to justify any evil that they want to do to anybody."

"So Spong," Mac said in a sparring fashion, "then at this point do you consider yourself a deist? Do you think a creator made everything in the universe, but that once set in motion he doesn't interact with the world anymore—like some of our more prominent founding fathers believed?" Mac again was trying to push the Bishop's buttons in good faith.

"No, I do not. I do not consider myself a deist, *or a theist.*"

"Well if you're not a theist, then you don't believe in God, and you're an atheist," Mac pushed.

"No, what I'm saying is that I think both of those are inadequate categories. You see, I think we ought to start by saying theism is not an adequate way to describe God. By doing so, we honor the atheist, because the atheist says, 'I am not a theist.' I think we've got to get to the place where we recognize that human descriptions of God are all inadequate." John shifted gears. "Hey Ian, are you old enough to remember Pall Mall cigarettes?"

"Not really," he responded.

"Well the advertisement for Pall Mall used to say that Pall Mall filters the smoke, 'over, under, around, and through.' Well, that is pretty thorough it seems to me; and that is the way I experience God."

He continued. "I am no longer going to talk about *who* God is. I can only talk about what I believe I *experience*. I *experience* God as *over or beyond everything* that I know, and I *experience* that God is deep within me, deeper than anything I can touch. I *experience* God coming to me through the lives of other people. I *experience* God particularly coming to me through a life named Jesus of Nazareth, that has certain qualities that I now identify with God: the fullness of life, the incredible power of love, and the ability to be who he was—and is, even when people were putting him to death. To me, those are incredible experiences of God."

John finished his point. "Once I say, or anyone says, that the only thing he can know is his *experience* of God, two things have to be said.

One is that you may be delusional. The other is that *experiencing God in some way* does not mean that there is not a lot more to God than what you can experience."

Mac now chimed in with a question designed to keep things interesting, and also to see if the answer he expected would materialize. "So what do you say when people ask you if you are a Trinitarian?"

I say, 'Of course.' They say, 'Well, does that mean God is a trinity?' I say that *I don't know anybody who can tell you what God is.* I can only tell you that I experienced God as a Trinitarian formula. It is three things to me: it is beyond anything I can touch, it is depth within me, and it is incarnate in human life. That is what trinity means to me. It's the same God and I experience it in three different dimensions of my reality.

Mac complimented John by saying, "Though it may be a copout to those who know that I meant the Father, Son and Holy Spirit—and the dogma surrounding that definition of the Trinity—I think your answer is a philosophically honest one; when you begin to define the supernatural, you are talking about everything that is beyond the realm of human knowledge."

"That is no small point you make there," John agreed.

"George H. Smith and many other philosophers have argued that there is no way we can really know about that which is beyond anything and everything we know. [33] In other words, the minute you begin to define or explain the supernatural 'otherness,' it becomes part of the natural, explainable world. The supernatural cannot be defined at all—by definition. So I commend you for what others might call your namby-pamby, Ground Of All Being, overly-broad definition of God."

"Well, thank you, Mac. Well said. And in fact most of what we called supernatural in the past was stuff we just didn't understand. Today with biology, physics, astronomy, and chemistry, we see many examples wherein we know how things really work today, but in the past they were attributed to the actions of a God. They are natural forces for which we saw supernatural causes—because we *needed* to make sense of things."

Ian swung the microphone to his mouth after having rotated it upward while he organized some materials in the cockpit. "Yes, and what is fascinating to me these days is that we still see people do the same things when they don't understand something. I was just reading an article about Joe Nickel,

288 A SECRET OF THE UNIVERSE

a leading paranormal investigator who has looked into many supposedly haunted houses—with a very open mind, I might add. But rather than first look to supernatural explanations for noises or illusions or whatever, he first seeks natural solutions. And to date, after many years of investigation, he has yet to have to resort to explanations that fall outside of the laws of physics and science as we know them. So to your point, why is it that people always leap to explain things by *first* jumping to the supernatural?"

"Right. And I don't know, but today we certainly understand a lot more. And tomorrow we'll understand even more. The idea that Jesus could have ascended into the sky made perfect sense as long as you thought the sky was the roof of Heaven. But in our space age—as Carl Sagan said to me on one occasion—if Jesus ascended into the sky at the speed of light, 186,000 miles per second, he hasn't yet gotten out of our galaxy! And there are billions of other galaxies."

"That's a good one," Mac said. Both he and Ian smiled. "I hadn't heard of Sagan saying that."

"See, what we have to do is uncover the images against which our language was developed. Our language does not capture the essence of God. Our language is bound by human experience. A horse's language is bound by a horse's experience. A bee's language is borne by a bee's experience. God is beyond the experience of human beings. It is beyond our capacity to embrace the fullness of whatever God is."

"Once again, I agree with you, John," Mac said seriously, but Ian could still see the underlying disagreement between the two in the presumption that a God existed at all.

The Bishop then made clear his beliefs, which Mac knew and respected. "I believe that God is real. There is no question in my mind about that. I live my life on that basis, but I cannot define that reality. I can only *experience* that reality. I think you experience God by being fully human. I think that's the call of religion at its deepest and at its best."

"Ian, for what it is worth, this is one of the areas where John and I, respectfully, may part. We might be talking about the opposite side of the same coin, given his other comments. I agree that God cannot be defined, but I therefore find little reason to say I believe that God is real."

John responded, "I'm simply telling you that for me, this is something that I believe. We could certainly talk about reasons for that belief, probably for hours, but my belief is the thing that I want to proclaim for the record. But I will say also that if religion does not result in making people more deeply and fully human, more capable of loving, more capable of stepping beyond the boundaries of their fears, then I don't see any real purpose for religion."

"Again we're back on common ground," said Mac.

"I think we are living at this moment in our history in a very dark age because we are filled with tribal fear, religious persecution, and power games that I think mean that humanity is suffering."

"Absolutely," said Ian. "I think that's the answer to the question I keep asking of all dearly held notions for which I see a lack of evidence: 'what's the harm?' And often, the answer is that there is very real harm."

"I do not believe we will ever win these kinds of power games. I think that human beings may well destroy themselves before they become human," John added.

Ian chimed in, saying, "And this, in fact, is one of the compelling motivations behind Mac's vision to create the Desoterica."

"Well certainly I believe that education and intellectually honest dialogue are always good."

Mac put up his hand. "Citation four-three-niner-mike, Roger. Out of flight level three-nine-zero for two-six-zero," he responded. Even Ian hadn't caught that radio call. "Okay gents, we're starting down. We'll need to wrap the conversation in about five more minutes, but I didn't mean to interrupt."

Ian spoke up to bring the conversation full circle. "So you wrote *Why Christianity Must Change or Die*. With all we've talked about, and all the lecturing you do, can you look in your crystal ball and tell me—"

"Which of the two it is going to be? Will Christianity change or die?" The Bishop finished Ian's question, then paused for a second before continuing.

"Well, I do not know. The image that I had behind that book was the image of the exile in Jewish history, when the Jewish people were forced to walk out of their comfort zone—"

"Not that the exile was historical, mind you." With that comment Mac bordered on one of those pedantic, academic points that made Ian's head hurt, but both Ian and John ignored it.

"They were forced to go away from their homeland and be exiled in the land of Babylon—modern day Iraq—where none of the presuppositions of their faith operated; where nobody kept their holy days; where they did not worship a Jewish God; where they had to live in that exile. When that happens, your God either *grows,* or your God *dies.*"

"Interesting," Ian said.

"I think we are in a very similar situation today. I think that the presuppositions of the Christian faith have been all but destroyed by the intellectual revolution that started with Copernicus—and went through Keppler; and Galileo; and Isaac Newton; and Charles Darwin; and Sigmund Freud; and Albert Einstein; and even Steven Hawking—where we have to face the fact that the world is vastly different from the way the Biblical story thought the world was."

Ian didn't say anything. He sat awash in the profound concepts this highly educated Bishop was generously sharing.

"And if we cannot learn to sing the Lord's song in the strange world of our contemporary experience, then the Lord's song will die. And that is what the Jews had to do in the exile! They came out of the exile with a very different concept of God—with a very *universal* sense of God's presence."

"How do you mean?" asked Ian.

"Well, it was a sense of God that was much more a spirit presence, like what I would call today, *the source of life and the source of love, and the Ground of Being*—undefined, but *experienced.* So their God changed dramatically and they came to a new understanding of what it means to be human. And that is the crunch that we are in."

"I think I follow you."

"I just think we are in a very difficult period of history, and in what I would call a *tribal retreat.* We are fearful of the other tribes and we have politicians who get great power by keeping that fear alive and vibrant. We've also got a religious mentality in this country in both the Catholic and the Protestant traditions, where they are questing after certainty instead of exploring the unknown."

"That's a great statement. Write that down," Mac said, only partly joking.

"Sometimes quests for certainty are signs of death," the Bishop added. "I do not know what the future is going to be. I just know that sometimes if you are just a voice crying out in the wilderness, you've still got to cry out."

"Good advice on both fronts, and I think religiously your words of caution are wise. At the same time as pursuers of knowledge, I agree that we need to cry out," Mac said.

"For sure. As you know, Mac, I'm on the lecture circuit almost 80% of my life. But everywhere I go I find people hungry for a kind of religion that doesn't violate their minds, yet also opens their hearts and their lives and their spirit, and does not fill them with religious prejudices and small-mindedness."

"Well, I think we can all agree that those last two things are a growing phenomenon in this country—small-mindedness and prejudices," said Ian.

"Speak for yourself," Mac chastised. "Do you have data to support that conclusion—that they are growing? Aren't you truth-driven rather than emotion-driven?"

"Ouch. Fair enough. But what are you doing, putting on your anal-retentive mortar board before we're even on the ground?" Ian joked.

He then turned backward to look the Bishop in the eyes. "All joking aside, I can't thank you enough for talking with me. You've given me some wonderful insights and food for thought as I continue to reshape—well, my entire worldview."

"It's been my pleasure. I really do commend you for embracing the mystery and trying to learn from it. Besides, it's made the trip go quickly," he concluded with a warm smile.

Before long they were in sterile-cockpit mode and the jet was cleared to land on Runway 20-Left at Dekalb-Peachtree airport, outside Atlanta—a closer and easier option than Hartsfield.

On the ground and inside the FBO, Mac said, "Okay Ian, I'm going to the hotel with John, and I'll see you there after you get things tucked away here with the Citation, okay?"

"You got it, Mac. Thanks for letting me do so little work on the way down here—I owe you," Ian said.

"Oh, you'll make it up to me over the next couple days, I assure you."

Ian turned toward John. "And Bishop Spong, I can't thank you enough. Truly enjoyed the time and the conversation."

Always gracious, a smiling John Spong shook Ian's hand. "I enjoyed it as well. I'll see you tomorrow at the meeting—if not before."

In the coming years, that exchange helped cement one more of the steps in Ian's explorative journey. At the same time, and hard as it would have been for him to believe, the larger, most substantial revelations were yet to come.

Chapter 22

MUSICAL CLOSETS

Late November, 2002—three years and three months later

Many quarterly meetings of the Desoterica had passed since Ian had first read Spong's work, and even since his illuminating discussion with the Bishop on the way to Atlanta. Though behind him by many years of study, Ian had become nearly as committed to uncovering the origins of Christianity as Mac was. With his ongoing interest in paranormal beliefs and other supernatural claims, he also had followed many other potential analogues of emotion-driven thinking, with interest.

The stock bubble and "new economy" of the late nineties had turned out to be the same "old economy," where profits were required after all. Those who glibly and arrogantly proclaimed that all the others who weren't day-trading stocks and driving a new luxury automobile every few months just didn't get it, were hurting badly as a result of the market's reality-check. Ian was intrigued with the bandwagon mentality that allowed so many people to deceive themselves into illusions of forever access to easy money. Then again, he admitted that if he hadn't had Mac constantly telling him that 25% annual growth wasn't sustainable, emotion-driven thinking might well have roped him in as well.

Now there was gloom and doom being predicted about global warming. Ian just wasn't sure. While he would come to realize the reality of global warming later, he was jaded by apocalyptic predictions like those surrounding the Gulf War, back in 1991. Numerous newspaper articles had said that if Saddam followed through on his threats to torch 365 oil wells, the results would be nothing short of cataclysmic. They had predicted global warming, ecological catastrophes, human and animal health deterioration, nuclear winters, accelerated acid rain, monsoons, and fires. One commentor darkly declared that "even a partial failure could cause more deaths than the total population of Iraq, Kuwait, and Saudi Arabia combined."[34]

Of course in the end Saddam torched over 600 oil wells, and the nuclear winter never came. So what was Ian to think of the new threats?

He read *The Culture of Fear* by Dr. Barry Glassner, a sociologist, who explained how America had become fear-driven in its approach to policies, but that those fears misdirected behaviors toward threats of relatively small statistical risks: airplane crashes, mutant germs, child abductions, razor blades in Halloween candy, and so forth.[35] These were issues on which politicians could run, but not be expected to accomplish anything substantive when in office.

Come time for re-election, they could point to "Tiffany's Law" or some feel-good piece of symbolic legislation they had passed to supposedly protect kids, claiming they had accomplished some great victory in the fight against the fearmongered, phantom threat. But the beauty was that by way of the whole charade, they managed to avoid being held accountable for any meaningful work on the country's real, complex problems. Consciously or otherwise, it was classic misdirection.

At the same time, powerful lobbies used scare tactics on both sides of all major issues: the environment, pharmaceutical research, global warming, gay rights, and important social issues like health care. Even the weather stories on TV were increasingly full of hype and covered as if they were the apocalyptic end of the world. Fearmongering was everywhere.

Ian also saw scare stories on news shows like 60 Minutes, sounding the alarm bells about children eating apples coated with Alar. He saw the biggest class-action settlement ever in the Dow-Corning breast implant case—about which scientists would, decades later, lament the lack of any causal connection between the implants and the plaintiffs' illnesses. In fact, in 2006 the FDA would capitulate under the weight of the evidence, and again permit the use of silicone implants. But back in the day, people needed answers; so science lost, and emotion won.

Similar debates had erupted over Gulf War Syndrome, and increasingly over whether Thimerosal in vaccinations was causing an increase in autism diagnoses. While of course Ian didn't have any knowledge of the real "truth" in any of these cases, it was the method and quality of discourse that troubled him most. Indeed there was substantial evidence that humans were less driven by truth, and more driven by hype and emotion, than anyone was willing to admit. Ian's fascination with the fallibility of his own conclusions, and those of others, was therefore unabated by this time in 2002.

But probably more interesting to Ian than anything was the state of religion in the world, and in particular the growth in literalistic, evangelical Christianity. He'd read a good number of scholarly works over the previous three years—not only literature about Christianity, but spurred in part by David Kurtz's comments, Jewish history and beliefs around the time of Christ, as well.

After attending several additional Desoterica meetings, and more than a year of grappling, struggle, conversations with clergy and friends, and introspective thought, he had fully arrived at Mac's position of atheistic agnosticism. To oversimplify, he believed answers to questions about supernatural "otherness" were unknowable. And therefore, he could not subscribe to the "magical beliefs" and explanations of natural-world events that were offered by traditional religion.

But this important conclusion posed a huge problem for Ian. He had such good friends at church. He had an extended family, a brother and sister, friends from his former church community, and a broader community of friends and acquaintances—*all of whom were Christian*. While he'd always been one to share his questioning with Bill, church friends, and anyone with whom he engaged in such conversation, he increasingly was finding himself in awkward situations where he had to balance respect for the beliefs of others with a desire to be authentic and not pretend any longer to hold simple, literalist Christian views.

Having grown up in the community as a Christian; having been the child of Bob and Janet Keppler; having sung in Christian choirs in front of literally thousands and thousands of people; and having been involved in service clubs, Compassion Flight, and other faith-based organizations, this was a gut-wrenching transformation of Ian's views, about which surely these people couldn't be aware. Moreover, they couldn't be faulted for assuming he was still fighting their fight in favor of traditional Christianity. Even among his best friends, he was finding awkward moments.

Though he saw the day coming, it was a routine, relatively common encounter with an acquaintance at the grocery store, that November of 2002, which was the tipping point. An old family friend—a nice, friendly woman whom Ian respected greatly—had bumped into him and asked him to give a testimonial at her church. She was aware of his long-ago trip home from Spain and the "angels" he'd met, as well as the "spiritual encounter" he had upon returning home for the funeral. Exactly how she knew of the story he didn't know, but Ian had shared the observations with friends, and again during a Sunday-school discussion about angels.

The problem was, of course, that he no longer believed that his profound experiences were the result of divine action. He believed that his understandings of those experiences had become his own, perfect examples of seeing what he *needed* to see, when he needed to see it. He believed his emotions, pain, and need for larger answers to questions surrounding the death of his father had caused him to romanticize, in fact to *supernaturalize* what were, in truth, very earthly experiences.

So the situation with the old friend was awkward indeed. He had said, "Mrs. Verhey, I so appreciate the offer, but many have not yet heard that I have engaged in some pretty non-traditional studies these days, and my views of Biblical and theological events have become . . . somewhat controversial now."

Perhaps it was his lack of clarity, his demeanor, his reputation, or the expectation of the people with whom he spoke, but he swore on other similar occasions—even with Bill—that people seemed *not to hear.* This was one of those situations.

Mrs. Verhey had simply replied, "Oh Ian, part of our spiritual journey is questioning. That's no problem at all. We can't be certain of things, but we'd just love to have you come and share your story. It's so powerful. So long as you believe that Christ is your personal Savior, and that he died on the cross for your sins, that's all we need to know." She had delivered the last line with a smile, fully confident in the answer.

"Mrs. Verhey, in fact I do have some reservations about even those beliefs at this point." She was patient and polite, and being the sweet old friend that she was, didn't show any hint of contempt or angst. To the contrary, she was concerned.

"Oh, I'm sorry," she replied, but Ian still felt as though she didn't get it. At the same time, Ian didn't want to be a militant atheist, seeking to denounce as myth everything that was dear to people like Mrs. Verhey.

After the woman kindly recommended C.S. Lewis' book, *Mere Christianity*, she told Ian she'd be praying for him, and they parted ways cordially.

Because Ian valued his integrity and authentism, he had been deeply troubled by such spontaneous and awkward meetings. He could now almost relate to how it would feel to be gay and remain "in the closet." It was taxing on one's sense of integrity to be coy or subtly deceptive, yet there was a fine line between that, and wearing a t-shirt that said, "I'm gay," or "I'm an atheist."

As it turned out, in the preceding months he had been working on a document—an admittedly sophomoric and still under-informed articulation of his rationale for abandoning traditional belief in God. But a big question remained in his mind: whether it would be appropriate to communicate such concepts proactively with anyone. And if so, with whom?

This was the topic of conversation on that cold November evening as Samantha and Ian enjoyed their coveted personal time after the boys went to bed.

"Just tell me again the purpose of sharing this thing?" Samantha asked.

"I just feel like I'm not being honest with people the way things are."

"Well it's not like you're going to take out an ad in the paper and reach everyone anyway. This is your problem, not something that you need to make everyone else's problem. Besides, you'll drag my ass into your world, and it's not like I don't have enough trouble finding lasting friendships."

Ian stopped dead. He was cognizant that "coming out" with his religious views would—at least—make awkward situations for Samantha. He thought, then said, "I have great appreciation for the support and freedom you have given me to explore. I hope you know that."

"I do. You know I do," Sammy replied. "And you know that I am often swayed by you. But you know I've never been one to explore things so thoroughly, so I just don't know what I think, and others will assume things."

"I understand," Ian said. "I just struggle a lot with these interpersonal issues. I am comfortable that my current, provisional conclusions are the result of my genuine, best effort. And while I may change my mind tomorrow on all this, with some new archaeological discovery or something, I just have a hard time pretending to be someone I am not. So I've been sitting on this document, tweaking it here and there for nearly a year."

"You're not pretending. You're very candid with people," Sam reiterated.

"Yes, but when they talk about their walk with Christ, or how their prayers got them healed of some disease, I just get a creepy feeling as I sit there nodding and smiling. I don't accept that prayers work. At some point, I just need to stop letting people believe that I'm still the guy they've always known. It just doesn't feel honest, and you know how important that is to me."

"I guess I can see that," Samantha said.

"But I value your opinion, and understand that this involves you too—even though I'm not speaking for you in any way."

"Yeah, but people will think you are," Sammy replied.

"Probably true, but do two wrongs make a right? Does it make sense for me to be inauthentic because people will jump to conclusions? Besides, our real friends will still love us—that's what the Bible tells them to do."

"Sure, throw me to the animals for the sake of your integrity," Sammy said with a smile. "Tell you what. You know I admire you and your integrity. It's why I fell in love with you. You've swayed me. You should do it . . . . Besides, I probably agree with you more than not."

A few days later, without consulting Mac on the question at all, Ian made his decision. He emailed the document, "Coming Out in the Interest of Authenticity: An Explicit Statement on Religion," to friends, family, his former pastor—whom he loved and felt he owed an explanation—and to his siblings. He couldn't help but think of the movie *Jerry McGuire*. In fact, others would quickly label the document Ian's "mission statement."

To the degree possible when outing one's self as an *"atheistic agnostic,"* the document was gentle in tone, almost apologetic; it expressed his need to be explicit and authentic, and to avoid passively obscuring his beliefs about religion—which he felt was an untenable, dishonest way to live life.

Over several pages he outlined his basic reasons for abandoning belief in traditional, supernatural gods, explicitly acknowledging that in doing so he ran the risk of offending the people who meant the most to him. In the end, he asked for their understanding, and assured them that he had no malicious intent.

No sooner had Ian hit send, however, than a feeling of trepidation came over him. Had he gone too far? How would people react? Would they forward his email around town? He pondered the matter further before he again concluded that it was the right thing to do. He would live with the consequences. *Besides,* he said to himself, *there is no way to un-ring that bell!*

✛

The hotel bar was dark and it had been a long day, but ever the social leader, Bill wasn't ready to call it a night just yet. As regional sales manager, he had finished a grueling two days of mid-year meetings with his district sales managers, and they had accomplished much. Besides, he was still having a good time and so was his team. Everyone deserved a little fun, he figured, so Bill ordered up another round. The group of nine regaled one another with tales from the road, laughing and revelling in each others' company.

In many ways, Bill's work had been his refuge during the last few years. These people had been incredibly supportive of him during the tough times following Hanna's death, and he viewed them as peers and teammates, more so than the subordinates they had become since his promotion. And despite the economic turnaround for the worse, NALA was still growing rapidly.

Personally, Bill was getting along well, especially given the circumstances. The three-and-a-half years had softened the vice-like pain that enveloped his heart, but it had not gone away—nor would it ever. All he had to do was think of little Hanna, and it would clamp right back into physical reality.

At the same time, his All-American, go-get-'em enthusiasm was a real asset for Bill. It was his strong demeanor and exemplary conduct in the face of both personal and work-related trials that had earned him such admiration and trust among his co-workers. Some would praise him with the old saying that anyone can hold the wheel when the seas are calm, because in Bill, most observers saw someone whom you wanted at the helm during the roughest of weather.

Perhaps most importantly, he was also a fine example of ethical leadership, and of the power of faith to support a soul through difficult times.

Few people admired Bill more than one of his key sales representatives, Christina Barreiro. And her admiration had all the hallmarks of trouble. Christina was everything Bill admired in business. She was brilliant and quick on her feet, her product knowledge was outstanding, she was tactfully aggressive in her demeanor, and she was relentlessly energetic and tenacious. Perhaps most relevant, however, were the things in her, as a person, that appealed to him.

Christina was also stunningly beautiful. Of Hispanic-American descent, she had olive skin with deep, curly dark hair and beautiful brown eyes. She had a slight Spanish accent, having grown up in an upper-middle class, Spanish-speaking household; however, it was evident only to those attuned to such subtle distinctions. But to Bill, the subtle accent contributed to the mystique of a devastatingly charming woman.

In many senses she was the opposite of Megan. Christina was more than capable of holding her own in the hottest of debates, but unlike many TV vixens she did so without conniving shenanigans. Quite the opposite was true. She was the very definition of diplomatic. She was also graceful, passionate about life, and had a sharp-witted sense of humor. And not least of all to Bill's eyes, she oozed sensuality.

Of course her diplomatic skills and integrity didn't in any way mean that she failed to grasp the impact of her looks and charm. She wasn't naïve. It would be unfair, however, to say that she exploited her beauty. Rather, it was part of the package.

Just as Bill had discussed with his friend Ian, the sad truth was that research had again and again shown that looks and other non-verbal communication channels were very important in how people judged one another. Names mattered. Weight mattered. Skin color mattered. Height mattered too. So while Christina's confidence was certainly not derived solely from her appearance, her height and stunning good looks were powerful complements to her innate social and cognitive abilities. And to Mr. All-American, these were all attributes to which he ascribed great value, almost virtue. Subconsciously the notion that people without these "virtues" weren't quite as desirable, was one of Bill's subtle character flaws.

She was young, but often Bill would bring her into tough deals when personalities were clashing, especially if there were male egos caught in a testosterone-augmented stalemate. She could almost always jump right in, stroke egos, and pull a rabbit out of the hat. At the end of the day, Bill tried to tell himself that he admired Christina's many great attributes solely because they made her a great salesperson.

But her other effect on Bill was, in reality, more insidious—depending of course on one's point of view. Bill increasingly found himself sitting closer to Christina at meetings; paying attention to his own attire—secretly with her in mind; and perhaps subconsciously even spending more time in her sales territory—coaching and mentoring his "shining new star." In fact, she was *starry-eyed* as well, since Bill was indeed an impressive and attentive boss.

For anyone on the outside, however, it didn't take rocket science to see the potential between them. It was only Bill and Christina who did not—at least initially.

Other elements of their relationship, however, were clearer when viewed in a larger context. Bill had been through a great deal, and had been a picture of patience and virtue. The odds of a marriage surviving the death of child were notoriously long. To add insult to injury, Bill and Megan had brought themselves to be intimate with each other on only a handful of occasions since a couple months *prior* to the accident.

Certainly through no fault of her own, Megan was completely and totally unable to be emotionally present for Bill. More than anything else, throughout his pain Bill wished to escape into the soft and loving arms of someone who could help him recharge his emotional batteries. He wanted to be held, for someone to tell *him* that everything would be okay, and to fall asleep with arms wrapping *him* in safety and warmth. For all his male ego, and for all his testosterone, he was a human being. His emotional reservoir needed refilling. He craved the security of skin-to-skin, loving contact.

Truth be told, sweet, innocent Megan had kept a stiff upper lip in public, but was increasingly falling apart at the seams. And who could blame her? Understandably, her priority was survival—keeping her head above water. Her existence on the planet, while privileged to many eyes, had been secretly isolating, terrifying, and devastatingly painful. Bill was probably the one who understood her most. He tried relentlessly to reach her, but in his mind he knew he had run out of options.

She had refused his attempts to talk her into counseling. Increasingly she would stay in bed or lie on the couch while Zachary was at school. She let go of her physical appearances a bit more, and had even gained some weight. Bill would sometimes get impatient and angry with her, and they'd fight. And despite the occasional release and breaking down of the walls of Megan's depression, Bill's growing resentment was taking a toll inside of him. If their needs seemed mutually unquenchable before the accident, the situation thereafter seemed dire indeed.

At the same time Bill's perfectionist streak, his faith, the expectations of others, and his persistence all conspired to invigorate his commitment to stay together—no matter what. Repeatedly Bill assured himself that none of this was insurmountable. He had pledged to be hers for better or worse, and he intended to keep that pledge. After all, he loved Megan very much. He hurt that she hurt, and in return, she hurt that he hurt.

To any observer, the entire situation was a compounded tragedy. Two people, who genuinely loved each other, were so trapped in different circumstances and mental states that they might as well have been living on different planets.

Thus as the night wore on in the Chicago hotel bar, and the group slowly dwindled in number, the stage was set. First there were nine, then there were six—as Jennifer, Mike and Alan called it a day. Then there were only three. Ultimately Jason, Christina, and Bill were starting to cover more serious ground, when the three dropped to two. "If you guys are going to cover evolution and creationism now, I'm out," Jason said as he stood.

"Aw, come on you big baby. We're not going to cover it. All I was saying is that I've been told there are some interesting holes in the theory—like how the fossil record doesn't account for the explosion of species during the Cambrian period." Bill argued with feigned innocence, knowing full well that Jason was joking.

"Oh yeah? Well I'm an evolving species who is kicking tail in the marketplace, and in order to continue to do so I need sleep," Jason replied smugly as he rose from the table. "Seriously though, thanks for the dinner, Bill. You two stay out of trouble. I'm out. Good night."

Bill felt the conflicting signals of his mind. Not unlike a trained pilot taking notice of links forming in an accident chain, in the recesses of his mind Bill was aware of the warning signs. At the same time, he didn't really see them as links of an accident chain at all. The admiration that he received from Christina was what he craved with every fiber of his humanness. Human contact, human touch, and human lovemaking were essentially absent from his life, and were sorely needed. Accident or not, alcohol and opportunity were the other links in the chain of events that night. But for better or worse, at that point in his journey Bill was not interested in analyzing signs.

Christina said, "I'll do one more cerveza if you'll be here for a minute?"

"Oh, always have to win at everything don't you?" Bill jabbed.

"Hey, I'm old enough that I know the games I can win, and the ones I can't. Anyway, that's the kind of game I lose, even if I win. I was simply saying that if you didn't have to go put on your race-car jammies just yet, I'd have one more beer."

Bill laughed out loud, tilting his head back at Christina's never-ending energy and willingness to spar. He then caught the attention of their server as she happened by the table. "Two more please, on my tab; then I'll close out."

"Well, it was a good meeting, Bill," Christina said as she leaned forward, elbows now on the table. The space where the others had sat had been slowly reclaimed by the staff of the sports bar. One by one they had repositioned the small, rectangular tables to their normal configuration, leaving Bill and Christina sitting at the corner of the remaining two tables.

"Yes it was. I tell you, I'm lucky to have this group of salespeople." He slowed. "And I'm lucky to have this group of friends." Bill was now locked eye-to-eye with Christina.

"Can I ask you a personal question, Bill?" Her dark eyes, long, wavy-black hair and stunning beauty were enough to melt the strongest of hearts.

"Sure."

"How are you really doing?" She studied his face. The question was genuine. They had talked before about Megan, her depression, and Bill's struggles with the loss of Hanna.

"You're kind to ask," said Bill. "Really, I'm good. There are certainly a lot of people who have endured far more than I have. I enjoy my work. I really enjoy my son. I won't kid you, I wish there were something I could do to help the situation with Megan; but with that said, I can't complain."

Ever the perceptive one, Christiana continued to radiate compassion from her eyes as they remained locked on his. "Maybe you should."

"Maybe I should what?" Bill asked.

"Maybe you should *complain*." She sat back slightly. There was sincerity and warmth behind her suggestion, but in her mind she was worried that her words came out wrong. She didn't mean he should vent to her about his wife, necessarily. Rather, she simply meant that he should have *someone* to vent to—someone who cared about *his* interests and needs. Everyone needs someone like that.

"What good would that do anyone?" he asked.

"Listen, you can snow a lot of people, but you can't snow me," she said firmly, but tenderly. "You're a tough guy, a high achiever. *We all know that.* But don't you think everyone has the right to vent? Don't you think there's something healthy about facing demons straight-on and acknowledging them?"

"I guess I still think there's no use in wallowing in self-pity, or in dwelling on the negative."

She leaned forward, farther this time. Her face was inches from his and her eyes were attentively fixated on his. Bill's mind drank in the reality that she cared. He drank in her beauty, the ambiance, and her lovely black dress that provided a delicate hint of her perfectly tanned cleavage. Between the drinks and soft background music, Bill felt almost overcome with emotion.

"Bill," she said with a short pause, "we all care about you. *I care about you.* I just want you to know that I'm someone you can relax with, and share with. And I mean that. I think the good Lord didn't intend us to be without love and companionship. Sometimes I just don't think things are as simple as we think they are, and I want you to know that I understand that, and that I'm willing to be here for you."

What was he hearing? At that moment, he wanted nothing more than to be with Christina. He wanted to crawl into a corner of the world with her and hide—ravishing each other and basking in the loving attention of such a beautiful, admirable person as she. He looked at her warm eyes, sumptuous lips and perfect skin, and simply couldn't resist. He leaned in and gave her an appropriate, gentlemanly kiss—on the cheek—in appreciation for her gesture. "Thank you," he said.

The kiss was innocent and sincere in one respect, yet the mere touching of his lips to her golden skin sent tingles throughout Christina's body. She wasn't alone. He hadn't felt like that in what seemed like an eternity. It was powerfully intoxicating, yet he was restrained.

"You're welcome, Bill."

He studied her face and eyes. He didn't quite know how to interpret what she was saying. He thought to himself, did she mean what I think she meant? A thousand thoughts went through his mind. Ultimately some practical ones percolated to the surface.

"I'll tell you what. I'm going to think about what you've said. Candidly, I think you're right. Actually, you have no idea how I'd like to take you up on that offer of closer friendship. At the same time, let's face it. You're a beautiful woman, and I'm your boss so I don't know quite how to reconcile—" he stumbled for words.

Luckily, she jumped in. "Life certainly isn't simple and without risks, Bill. You and I both know that. At the same time we're both adults. What you see is what you get, with me. I'm not stalking you or trying to steal you away from your wife. I know you're committed to her, and you have Zachary. I admire that and wouldn't dream of interfering."

Now Bill really was confused. He felt such powerful attraction, and he knew she felt it too. "So what *are* you suggesting?"

She looked him straight in the eyes and said, "I'm suggesting that we could each use some companionship. I'm suggesting that my job on the road is lonely. I'm suggesting that I care for you. I'm suggesting that we keep our lives exactly as they are, but that as adults we can enjoy one another's company and companionship. Bill, I'm suggesting that we go up to my room, that I get out of this dress, that we get you out of those clothes, and that we make love for as long as we feel like it. Then I'm suggesting that we fall asleep, snuggled naked together, and enjoy the night."

Bill was literally speechless for a second. An inarticulate "Wow" escaped his mouth as his eyes searched her willing expression.

"I would really enjoy it if we could do that," she added. She was unapologetic and confident, and at the same time warm and caring.

Bill was beyond any point of reservation. He had never needed or wanted anything more in his entire life. "You have absolutely no idea how much I'd like that," he said.

They arose and headed for the elevators, then straight to the eleventh floor. The hotel was composed entirely of suites, and the four rows of rooms formed a rectangle around an open atrium that spanned upward all the way to the top floor. They walked down the exposed hallway toward Christina's suite, barely giving a second thought to the chance someone might see them go into a room together.

Christina swiped the card and they entered the small television room. The thinner privacy curtains were already drawn, but Christiana walked straight over and closed the heavier curtain.

Bill was right behind her, and the moment she turned around, he was there. They met in a passionate kiss and embrace, their hands caressing each other's backsides and squeezing themselves closely together. Bill's hand found the zipper of Christina's lovely black dress, and it easily dropped to the floor.

Always the snappy dresser, Christina was a sight to behold as Bill continued to ravage her with a hunger that was surprising even to him. A black lace bra with matching silk panties and thigh-high Victoria's Secret hose, framed the most beautiful body he could ever imagine. He couldn't believe what was happening.

They continued to kiss, still standing in the front room, but the bedroom light was on and Christiana began to walk down the hallway to the king-sized bed. She looked over her shoulder and could see that Bill was already without shoes and shirt, unbuttoning his slacks as he followed her.

She turned around at the foot of the bed and they embraced yet again. Their tongues soon met as Bill unclasped the back of the lace bra. Just as the glimpse had suggested, Bill kissed his way down to her perfectly bronzed breasts, gently taking her nipple into his mouth as he caressed her body and tugged gently downward on her panties. He stripped off his own underwear and stood up so their mouths could meet again. Together they slid onto the silky bedspread.

The feeling of skin was overwhelmingly powerful as their bodies met. It had been so long since Bill had experienced such closeness, and quite some time for Christina as well. As Bill rolled on top of her nakedness he felt her perfect breasts against his chest, and a bristly tuft of hair pressed against the top of his thigh as their tongues and bodies intertwined. Without a doubt, it was the most intoxicating feeling he'd had in a decade.

❖

The following evening Ian's phone rang as he placed the car into park. His first thought was that it might be the babysitter. "Hello?" he answered with a hint of concern in his voice.

"Hey Jerry McGuire, it's Bill." His sarcasm was a welcome relief to Ian; he'd been a little on edge over potential reactions to his so-called "coming out," document.

"How are you, Bill? Megan told Sammy you've been traveling." Samantha waited patiently in the seat of the car. They had just pulled into a parking spot at the Steak House, the first stop of their much-anticipated date night.

"I'm fine," Bill replied. "Are you somewhere you can talk?"

"Actually we were just going into a restaurant, but—"

"Hey no big deal. Go for it. I was just going to talk with you about your little *mission statement.* Tell you what, let's just get together soon. Got any time for a guy's night out?"

"Okay, for one it is not a *mission statement*," Ian said jokingly. "But sure. I have a volunteer trip tomorrow but otherwise I don't have any overnights coming up, so most nights are good."

"Thursday?"

"Sure." Ian quickly leaned to Samantha and said, "All right if I go out with Bill Thursday?" She nodded. "Thursday's great, Bill," Ian confirmed.

"Okay, I'll call you or email to figure out details. Just know that I still love you my man, but I'm also worried about you."

"And I appreciate that, Bill. See you then."

Samantha and Ian proceeded inside and were seated in a secluded, corner booth in the back of the restaurant. They had a good view of the bar area and restaurant, and sat cozily snuggled in the corner. For an event that was supposed to be weekly, it had been some time since they'd been out on a date night; the privacy and quiet of the booth's location were a welcomed respite. They ordered a drink and settled in, looking at each other and letting out a deep breath, as if to remind each other that it was finally time to relax.

"What's on your mind?" Ian asked.

"Just settling down. I love the boys to death, but it sure is nice to get away. I thought they would drive me crazy today."

"I'll bet. They wore me out in the hour I was home." Brandon and Andrew, now ages eight and almost seven, were at especially enjoyable ages; but there was no question about it, their energy was unrelenting.

"You're worn out because you were wrestling," Samantha said with a grin. She admired him as a father but certainly Ian wasn't "superdad" in his own mind. He didn't think he was always as mentally available to the kids as he should be, between his flying and his Desoterica-related work and study; but Samantha not only approved of his relationship with the kids, it was a real source of pride for her. Warranted or not, Ian was grateful that she still admired him after a decade together.

Certainly it hadn't been easy. In their openness and honesty Sammy had commented many times that being married was far harder than she'd ever imagined. It wasn't intended with venom, and Ian didn't take it that way when she'd make that statement to a newlywed, or in conversation with a friend like Megan. It was just *reality*. Having another person interdependent with you, sharing everything, managing money, and raising kids together, just wasn't always a walk in the park.

But if there was one theme in their marriage that Ian credited with keeping them on the same page, it was their open and honest communication. Without a doubt in his mind, the no-bullshit approach that began that night in the Chicago bar—with John and Sammy's friends surrounding them—had been a secret to their success. Confident in the honesty and safety in the relationship, they had always felt comfortable sharing *any valid and genuine* feeling or thought.

Even when a beautiful woman would catch his eye, Ian wouldn't hesitate to acknowledge her beauty. Sammy wasn't at all the jealous type. Truth be told, there were even times they'd been out at a busy bar, and had played the game they had seen on *Mad About You*, the television series with Helen Hunt and Paul Reiser.

In one episode, Jamie and Paul had been sitting in a New York bar, fictitiously picking dates for each other from the unsuspecting patrons. They had found the game fascinating, if not even a little exciting—to see what their partner found attractive in others. It even seemed to provide the fictitious couple a taste of those long-lost tinges of phenylethylalamine, or PEA, the chemical in the brain that is responsible for the tingly excitement of new love. In that episode, Jamie had even proceeded to hold a flirtatious conversation with one of her "men of interest" at the bar.

To others, such openness was tacky. Sometimes if Ian would declare his attraction to Christy Brinkley or Halle Berry, Bill or another friend would stick up for Sammy and tell Ian that his candor in front of her was rude. Somehow always the idealist, however, Ian felt that what was really rude in marriages was the games that were played by the very people who would chastise him for such a thing. He'd seen such inauthentic, false piety in friends' marriages on many occasions, and frankly found it repulsive.

In Ian's mind such marriages always started perfectly. After a year or two of waiting, the lovesick lovebirds would finally wed. She'd never looked prettier, and he'd never been more handsome. They were deeply in love with each other, and were passionately attached at the hip—or another piece of anatomy. They'd hold hands everywhere. She'd hang on him, especially if he was the type that liked clinginess, and there was excitement, hope, and *beauty* in it all.

But at some point, Ian's theory went, they would drift into an inauthentic world. They would ignore, or pretend to ignore, the reality that they missed love, passion and excitement. Particularly the men would downplay their innermost secrets, needs and desires. They would pretend they weren't ever tempted. They would pretend they didn't look at pornography, when research showed that even 45% of pastors had been online looking at porn within the last year. No, to Ian the games of deception, and the denial of biological and emotional needs, were the real poison.

As the controversial Dr. Laura Schlessinger aptly described in her later book *The Proper Care and Feeding of Husbands*, which Ian happened to pick up while away on an overnight trip, very often something seemed to change in both partners' behaviors after a few years. [36] And as a result of sweeping human needs under the rug in the process, sadly those changes often would seriously disrupt the dynamic of the marriage—sometimes leading to divorce. Other times it would lead to long, dismal periods of joyless existence, both partners simply going through the motions of the days, as the years clicked by. There were serious, negative ramifications of inauthentic behavior not only to the relationship, the fun, and the passion, but more importantly to the love and the mutual respect.

While there was always plenty of blame to go around, Dr. Laura somewhat focused upon the recognition that men too had needs to be admired and feel attractive. This was both obvious and revolutionary at the same time. While the book was controversial, Dr. Laura implied that to many women, once they were married and had their kids, it was like they'd gotten what they wanted out of the relationship and the work was done. The kids mattered, but to the liberated women, the husband did not. No longer did they show up for bed in sexy lingerie—that was degrading and unnecessary. No longer did they tell their husbands of their admiration for them. No longer did they make an effort to be attractive for "their man," or to get out of the sweatpants for dinner, as they would have during the hunt. It somehow was like a great mystery that men actually needed love, needed to feel attractive, and needed to feel admired—just as much as women did. Men also needed *not* to feel dirty or piggish for wanting sex.

While Ian certainly understood the women who reacted with disdain to this message, asking why it was that a woman should have to do anything she didn't want to just to keep the poor old baby happy, he also saw some wisdom for both parties in acknowledging reality.

Ian was also somewhat persuaded by the many published letters from women, saying that magic things happened in return, once they changed their behaviors. Suddenly dishes were being done by the husbands, and the kids were being taken away so that the wives could have time to themselves.

By Ian's assessment, there was merit in acknowledging the cold, hard reality that romance wanes. Sparks and fire were, to him, simply not sustainable—at least not in the way they are experienced at the beginning of a new love.

That was one of the concepts that Ian and Sammy had discussed at times. Ian in particular, but Sammy too, had believed with some amount of melancholy, or even sadness, that never again would they feel that rush of excitement from a first kiss. Never again in their time on this earth would they feel that surge of adrenalin, or that gentle, amusement-ride tingle in the stomach.

But somehow, just the act of discussing and validating those thoughts was therapeutic to Ian and Sammy, and in many cases diminished their allure. While it might have seemed counterintuitive to some, the conversations seemed to level Ian and Sammy, and even bring them closer together through their mutual acknowledgment of feelings, urges, or fantasies. They had successfully evolved in their marriage by way of trust, honesty, and unrelenting love and respect for each other.

As was the case with Sammy and Ian as they sat that night and enjoyed their date night, some couples managed successfully to round that bend to higher phases of interaction and partnership. It would be different—those early feelings of yearning and passion would not be sustained—but the new phase would be even better. As Ian's parents used to tell him, it would evolve into a deeper, more satisfying kind of love, and a deeper, more satisfying kind of experience.

As they relaxed and talked in the Steak House, Ian subconsciously blended questions of philosophy with such questions of love.

"So do you ever wonder if we were really meant for each other? Was it our *density?*" Ian asked, referring to the old line from *Back to the Future* as they sipped their wine.

"Tell you what," Samantha began with a serious and thoughtful expression. "I am increasingly amazed at how much I love you, and how much I realize that there are very few people in this world that I could live with, let alone thrive with," Samantha responded.

"I totally agree," Ian said while pensively twisting the base of his bubble glass. "Sometimes I'll find a woman quite attractive at first, only to find the quick thought of actually living with her to be totally unappealing."

"Absolutely. I've done the same thing."

"So do you still think we were *meant* to be together?" Ian asked again.

Sammy looked at her glass and thought for a second before answering seriously. "You know, you've changed me some over the years. I know we've talked about this before so it won't be a total surprise to you, but I don't any longer believe that people have just one soul mate. I don't think there is just *one* person out there for everyone."

"Well, you know I tend to agree," Ian said without an ounce of offense taken. "I mean, the truth is that there are lots of wonderful, loving, beautiful souls out there in the world with whom either one of us—given the right circumstances, timing, etcetera—could have a deep and meaningful relationship."

Samantha nodded. "But I will say that the amount of effort it takes to build a relationship, I'd never want to do it again."

"No way!" Ian said in disagreement. "If something ever happened to me, I wouldn't want you to go through life alone. For goodness sake, life is just too short to sit and while away the hours being lonely." He paused for a second as their hearts sank at the mere thought of being without the other. "Just so long as you would never, ever, even *think* about bringing someone into the house with our boys, unless he were patient, generous, loving and kind. You and the boys deserve nothing less."

"I just don't think I'd have the energy to do it. But let's not go there," Sammy said. "It's too depressing."

"Okay, then back to my question. You say you don't think there is just one possible mate for anyone, but what about us being meant to be together? Didn't you always think that there was some kind of force that brought us together?" It wasn't a loaded question; Ian was curious where Sammy's mind was.

"Yeah," she sighed, a quick thought of her brief but life-changing relationship with Janet entering her mind. "I always kind of wanted to think that perhaps your father had a hand in our meeting, and in my chance to get to know your mother. But really, I just don't know." She tried to fight a pang of emotion. Softly she added, "It's a nice idea though, isn't it?"

Ian nodded thoughtfully and sympathetically. "It's a very nice idea indeed."

"I love you," She said, her voice strained by emotion.

"I love you too," Ian replied as he grasped her hand.

"Okay," she said, sitting up straight and appearing to plow forward reluctantly, "I'll tell what I think, Ian." She paused to collect her thoughts, looking him lovingly in the eyes. "I think you're right. Life is short . . . and love is supposed to be shared. And as long as there is true love between two people—genuine commitment, honesty, and the other's needs are above your own—no person should ever tell another that he or she can't love a third. To me, that would be . . . well, un-Christian."

Ian smiled warmly. "I love you. I hear you. And I know I would be free to remarry if anything ever happened. Funny thing is, I probably wouldn't want to either."

Samantha blinked rapidly to stop the sensation in her eyes. "Now that that's solved, can we talk about something else?—unless you want to go all-out morbid and catch a funeral visitation or something."

Ian laughed at her wry sense of humor, but under his laughter he had the utmost appreciation for the sensitive, loving soul that lied beneath Samantha's spunky facade. He had come to treasure her more than life itself. But just as great discoveries and powerful experiences awaited Ian—the likes of which he could never imagine in his wildest dreams, or his worst nightmares—Sammy was on the verge of a significant change of her own, the ripple effects of which would resonate far beyond the world she knew.

Chapter 23

An Old Testament of Icy Hell

The following mid-afternoon, David Kurtz and Ian arrived at Rochester, Minnesota in the 210, to pick up a Compassion Flight patient from the Mayo Clinic. It would be a long day.

As was usually the case during the cold months, there were flight precautions issued for light to moderate rime or mixed icing in the clouds and in precipitation. Unfortunately, the twin engine Baron, which had more power and at least limited wing deicing capability, was down for scheduled maintenance. But based on the morning weather and the lack of precipitation or icing reports from within the low layer of stratus clouds that enveloped the entire region, the duo felt that it was safe to begin the flight.

As it turned out, the first leg out of Kalamazoo was uneventful. The bases of the clouds were about 1,500 feet above the ground, and in no time they had popped out the top of the cloud deck at six thousand feet, on their way to a cruise altitude of 12,000 feet. They had picked up only a trace of ice on the leading edge of the wings during the climbout through the clouds, wherein Ian's eyes had been attached vigilantly to the front of the wings, as David piloted the first leg of their large, triangular route.

Although any ice could be dangerous, especially to a smaller, piston-powered plane with no de-ice capabilities, Ian and David were made more comfortable after witnessing the lack of any substantial icing. They were even delighted to see some sunshine on top, a welcomed break from the usual dingy sky that shrouded Western Michigan, courtesy of the lake effect.

They arrived a few minutes ahead of schedule to find their patient already waiting. With his wife seated beside him, Gene Randall sat in his wheelchair, two blankets draped across his legs. He was frail and tired, his face partly obscured by a plastic oxygen mask. As the two men arrived, he mustered a warm greeting, recognizing David and Ian from prior flights.

"Hello my favorite pilots," he said in a voice that was simultaneously anaemic and enthusiastic.

"Aw, you say that to all your crews, Gene," Ian said with a grin as the men shook hands.

Gene was a friendly, middle-class guy who might not have graduated at the top of his class, but make no mistake, he wasn't dumb either. At fifty-two, he'd raised two kids, and his sweet wife was gainfully employed as a legal secretary for a sole practitioner in Traverse City. At the same time he'd made the mistake of not paying for his Cobra coverage after being let go from his job at a local manufacturing company. He had never smoked a day in his life, but a six-month, persistent cough had turned into a biopsy and thoracoscopy, and ultimately a diagnosis of malignant mesothelioma.

Since then, their lives had been turned upside down. His wife was committed to staying in her job and paying off every single medical bill, but it was an endless challenge to care for him and work at the same time. She did it, however, because her pride and Midwestern values precluded accepting any more charity than absolutely necessary—and even that she swore she would repay.

In fact, over a decade later Ian would see her smiling face serving pancakes at one of Compassion's fundraisers. And despite how bad Gene had looked that day in 2002, and Ian's private expectation that he'd have been long-gone a decade later, Gene's wife cheerfully assured Ian that he was back to work, feeling well, and that they were on their feet again—in part thanks to organizations like Compassion Flight.

They loaded Gene and his wife into the plane and headed for Traverse City, a small city located in the extreme northwest part of Lower Michigan— about a four-hour car ride north of Kalamazoo.

The trip up through the cloud deck was again without ice, and the flight to Traverse City was equally as smooth and clear above as the trip over to Mayo. Although the angle of the sun was a little lower behind them, sitting in the smooth air was like a pleasant, fall afternoon on a porch; and no less so for Gene, whose irrepressible good humor kept him smiling broadly every time Ian looked back to check on him, even through his labored breathing.

To allow David more flying experience, Ian let him fly the first two legs of the trip, and after the high-altitude crossing of Lake Michigan they descended for the approach to Traverse City under the control of Minneapolis Center. The small, resort town wasn't large enough to have its own approach radar and controllers, but it did have a control tower that handled airplanes in the immediate vicinity of the field.

As Ian opened the approach charts for David during the initial descent out of their cruise altitude, he felt a tap on his shoulder. It was Gene. He had his mask momentarily pulled down away from his face, and was trying to say something over the relatively loud cabin noise of the single-engine plane. Ian skewed his headset off one of his ears, and turned so he could also see Genes lips move.

What Ian saw were tears flowing from Gene's eyes. Hand still on Ian's shoulder, he said in the forced voice of a renewed, extra effort, "You guys have no idea how glad I am to be coming home again." He made no effort to conceal his emotion. "And I just don't know how I could have done it without you. If I can ever repay you, I will."

Ian looked back at Gene and smiled. "You just did . . . . Thank you." He patted Gene's hand and moved to straighten his headphones. As he did so he stopped and turned back. "Besides, we just volunteer our time. I'll pass along your thanks to our boss who donates the airplane."

"Time matters more than anything in the world," Gene replied with one last burst of effort. He sat back, put his mask back on, and squeezed his wife's hand.

The ceiling was lower near Traverse City, and with the proximity to the lake moisture and the lower sun angle, Ian worried about the moisture content in the cloud layer and the continued potential for ice. But yet a third time, the letdown and maneuvers to the ILS Runway 28 produced only a thin strip of frosty rime ice on the wing's leading edge. It was nothing that the relatively powerful, 285-horse Cessna 210 hadn't seen before.

They lowered the gear and landed without incident, taxiing to the municipal ramp where Gene's family was waiting, on the concrete apron, with the Randalls' car. After a hearty hug from each of them, Gene and his wife were soon in their car and departing through the automatic gate, on their way to the safety and comfort of home.

By then it was almost dark, and something in the back of Ian's mind told him that time was of the essence. The temperature all day had hovered in the low 40s, which was the perfect temperature for icing aloft. Since air cools with altitude, the freezing level was just above ground level. Ironically, very cold air was less of an icing danger than the thirty-two-degree air above the surface that day, because the thirty-two-degree air could hold even more moisture.

Ian also worried that the temperature at the surface would fall as the sun began to set, and that as the dewpoint and the temperatures got closer together, the second biggest threat to safety—widespread fog—would form. This would reduce the ice-free safety zone beneath the cloud layers, and needless to say create a problem of its own.

Ian was anxious to get home, but wanted first to ensure they had plenty of fuel in case widespread fog did materialize. Unfortunately, he quickly found that despite the published hours in the directories, the staff at the airport's FBO had gone home for the day. There was no fuel available.

"Damn good thing we topped off at Rochester," Ian said. "Let's get scooting. That'll give us plenty of fuel to make it to our alternate if something goes wrong, and still meet the requirement of another forty-five minutes flying time."

"Not by much," David said.

"I agree. At the first sign of anything, we're putting this thing on the ground, okay? I don't care if that means spending the night somewhere. I see an accident-chain forming, and weather and fuel are potential additional threats, so let's watch this carefully."

Ian was now in the left seat. They launched, and he was pleased to see the departure go as smoothly and ice-free as their three previous trips through the expansive, shallow layer of clouds and moisture.

As they got on top of the clouds for the one-hour cruise segment home, the sun was just dipping below the horizon, and all systems were good. They allowed themselves to relax slightly, though Ian maintained a watchful eye and ear on the weather conditions. For the first half of the flight, however, no ground observations were readily available as they traversed an unpopulated area of northern Michigan timberland.

Amidst their idle chitchat, Ian suddenly had a thought. "Hey, I've been meaning to tell you something. I've been thinking of you lately because I started reading this book by a guy named David Klinghoffer. It's called *Why the Jews Rejected Jesus: The Turning Point in Western History*, and the first few pages remind me almost exactly of the conversation that you and I had a while back—about the condescending way people are, that Jew's don't see the 'truth' about Jesus."[37]

"No kidding? Haven't heard of it," David said. "I'll have to check it out."

"I tell you, it's wild. You know how you said there were both oral traditions and textual critiques that the Jewish people have largely kept to themselves?"

"Yeah?"

"Well, he claims to be putting them in print for the first time; and he's arguing the case that Jesus could not have been the expected Messiah of the Old Testament."

"Interesting. Wonder how that's gonna sit?" David asked rhetorically.

"I don't know, but I'll say this; I've not finished the book yet, but what he is saying dovetails perfectly with the picture I'm slowly constructing for myself of the early days of Christianity."

"What does he say, in general?" David asked.

"Well, news to me was that the savior-figure messiah was a very fuzzy concept in the Old Testament."

"I'm not so sure about that," said David.

"Well, let me put it this way. As I understand what Klinghoffer is saying, the Old Testament scripture—"

"Okay, I have to stop you here," David interrupted politely. "If you're going to talk about this stuff around the type of people Mac hangs out with, you need to be a little careful in the terms you are using. Do you mind if I make a couple suggestions?"

"Of course not, I'd appreciate the help," Ian replied.

"Well, for starters, you obviously know that before the middle of the first century there was no Christianity, only Judaism. It was the religion based upon what you are calling, generically, the Old Testament—writings attributed by Jews to God himself, and Moses, that date many centuries before Christ."

"Sure," Ian said without being at all smug. He had a sense that David knew far more than he did about Old Testament issues.

"And that Christians believe Christ fulfilled some, or *all*—as crazy as that sounds to me as a Jew—of the so-called, 'Old Testament' predictions about the future of God's Chosen People?" David spoke while smiling to himself at the condescending simplicity of his words, but he didn't want to take anything for granted in terms of Ian's understanding.

"And that the original five books were in Hebrew, and are called the Torah—or the Greek version was the Pentateuch?"

"Yes, still with you. I also know that sometimes 'Torah' is used to include the oral teachings of Jewish law, which are extremely important as well, but traditionally it refers only to the first five books of the Old Testament," Ian said with a silly smile, like a five-year-old trying to impress a teacher.

"Yes, but Jesus rejected the oral traditions, and said you can harvest and heal people on the Sabbath, etcetera. But I'm getting ahead of your story. My point is that when you say 'Old Testament,' if you don't intend to be speaking from a Christian perspective, the term can indicate a bias—even an arrogance. It demonstrates a prejudice that there is a New Testament, and that it is true."

"Gotcha," Ian said, genuinely appreciative but with the abashed look of a five-year-old who had *not* impressed his teacher.

"If you want to avoid the term, you can say 'Hebrew Bible' to describe the so-called 'Old Testament.' But after I so rudely interrupted you to explain your prejudice, please continue with this story about how brilliant the Jews were." David again laughed at his own joke.

"Finally!" Ian exclaimed with a grin. "Well I guess I was saying what I think I'm hearing Klinghoffer say in this book, that the Old Test—" Ian stopped and corrected himself, "that the *Hebrew Bible's* indication of a 'messiah' was very unlike what we have viewed it to mean through the colored lenses of two thousand years of Christianized perceptions."

"Go on," David encouraged.

"Well clearly there was a messianic expectation among the Jews of Jesus' time. But *messiah* simply meant 'anointed one,' and didn't portend or predict any God who would physically come to earth. Actually, there were different 'messiahs' predicted, and historically, many past characters in the Hebrew Bible were actually called 'anointed ones' *by God.*"

"Absolutely true."

"The one to whom the Christians point as a foreshadowing of Jesus, however, is merely the promise of a ruler who will conquer and preside over all the kingdoms of the earth—a ruler who will be the "Son of God," who is heavily favored by God, and chosen by God, to enable his new covenant with his Chosen People. If anything did seem clear, it was that this great warrior and ruler would usher in the end of an era of suffering and oppression, as promised by God."

David wasn't shocked by any of this, and added, "Yes, the messiah would be a king-like figure who would be a very earthly ruler in the times leading up to the permanent peace—the new kingdom of God on earth. It would provide permanent peace under a new covenant with God's people, who would then include all people and all kingdoms. *But that did not mean that this messiah was expected to be divine!*"

"Exactly," Ian continued. "The messianic expectation grew amid a feeling of occupation and oppression of the Jewish people by Rome, though the scriptural basis for this Davidic ruler was, as you say, fuzzy at best. Even though the predictions weren't clear, the *expectation* that the end was near certainly was clear. God was going to come *now* to restore the throne of David's dynasty, and unite his people in victory, so there was *no way you could separate the messiah from the end of times* in the eyes of the Jews. And the messiah certainly wasn't going to come down and die without fulfilling God's pledge to reunite the people of Israel, build a temple, and create lasting peace for his people."

David was certainly in agreement. "Second Samuel, Chapter seven, verse twelve says, 'I will set up thy seed after thee, which shall proceed out of thy bowels, and I will establish his kingdom.'" David knew his scripture. "And then God goes on to say, 'He shall build a house for my name, and I will establish the throne of his kingdom forever. I will be his father, and he shall be my son.'"[38]

Ian listened, impressed by the knowledge David displayed as he continued to make his point. "But then God says something critically important. He says, *'If he commit iniquity, I will chasten him with the rod of men, and with the stripes of the children of men.'*"

"Yes, I think Klinghoffer mentioned that in the book—" Ian said.

"But it gets better, and again I don't mean to steal your thunder here," David added.

"Not a problem," Ian said.

"You see if God is going to *chastise this messiah for his sins,* then this allegedly Davidic ruler-and-king certainly would not be *divine,* now would he?" David was somewhat animated. "Is God going to punish himself? If your guy is saying that there really isn't any discussion of a Christ-like messiah in the Hebrew Bible, I agree," said David.

David added, "But the Christians point to passages like this as proof of the prediction of Jesus Christ, the *divine* Messiah. Unfortunately, it tells of a very *human* figure. The same is true even in the other hand-ful of passages they point to. This guy is supposed to be a *warrior* and a conquering *ruler* and *king*. Jesus Christ never ruled over anyone or conquered anything."

Ian raised his eyebrows as if to shrug and agree. "And Klinghoffer goes on to summarize the sequence of events promised by Mica and Ezekiel—which Jesus didn't ever accomplish. Although there is a ton of fuzziness to the prophets' words, all that we seem to know is that the anointed king will oversee the return of all of the Jews to Israel; he will overpower and be the supreme ruler of all nations, and recommit the people to observance of Jewish law—which lays the groundwork for the new pact with God. Then, a majestic new Temple will be built; and lastly, non-Jews will accept Torah and peace will reign over the entire earth.[39] This was to be the end of the story."

As if talking aloud to test his own understanding, Ian continued, "But to legitimize Christ as this *new interpretation of the Hebrew Bible*, the Christians had to explain the separation of the end-of-times elements and say, 'Well, he was that ruler and conqueror in a different sort of way, and the rest of it will still happen.'"

"Well yes . . . a 'second coming.' But how can you blame the Jews for saying 'no way!'" David argued in return.

"Also in this book, Klinghoffer seems to make the point that the ancient Hebrew scripture, the Old Testament, was fiercely monotheistic. It was clear that there was just one God." Ian talked as he watched the miles tick away, slowly moving them toward the next navigation station of Grand Rapids.

"Also very true. Hosea thirteen four says, 'Thou shalt know no God but me; for there is no Savior besides me,'" David said without having to think twice. "God's own word made clear that there was one God, and that salvation was through him. In no way could it have been through this chosen ruler he would send. That guy was to be revered, worshiped, and certainly even by today's standards might appear to be treated as God-like, but make no mistake, the Jews knew he would be human," David concluded.

"You know, that almost made more sense out of something else for me," Ian said thoughtfully. "It's clearer to me how someone like Reverend Sun Myung Moon could claim today to be the messiah. I have a friend who is a Moonie, and while I think he's sadly misdirected, it makes it a little more understandable how Moon could convince people." Ian still thought of Curt on occasion, but apart from a card in the mail a couple times, hadn't heard from him since he left.

"Well, there have been many false messiahs," David added. "Some have even come pretty close to hitting it big, too . . . . I think there was a guy somewhere in the early centuries who actually reclaimed Jerusalem for a couple years, started a temple and everything—before being conquered himself."

"Bummer," Ian quipped.

"Even the Jewish historian Josephus once proclaimed another Davidic messiah, only to turn out to be wrong."

"How on earth do you know so much?" Ian asked rhetorically. David shrugged and smiled, happy again to have been acknowledged.

"Really though, you can't blame the Jews, even today, for saying 'no way' to Jesus as the Davidic 'anointed ruler.'" David summarized.

"And do I recall reading in Old Testament scripture that God explicitly told the Jewish people that he wouldn't throw them any big curves—about the end of times and the anointed ruler?"

"Sure, several," David nodded. "Amos three, verse seven said, 'For the Lord God will not do anything unless He has revealed His secret to His servants the prophets.'"

"So that's yet another reason that Jews wouldn't have accepted this *new interpretation* of Hebrew scripture. Clearly the story of Jesus Christ, a trinity, and the concept of heaven were all curve balls," Ian said. He looked at David. "By the way, you don't need to read this book. I think you could have written it."

David smiled. Ian paused as he double-checked his current navigation position. Simultaneously he saw the irony in Mac's hiring practices.

"Do you realize that Mac hired both of us, explicitly independent of any religious belief? Yet now I'm eyeball deep in his Desoterica? I come from a Christian perspective, and you come from a Jewish perspective, and together we were supposed to have had nothing to do with any of Mac's work—just shut up and fly."

"Well I still don't, really," said David. "I don't really even know anything about the Desoterica, other than you guys spend a ton of time administrating the thing and flying the jet."

"Well, I can give you a thumbnail overview, but I just think it's ironic that neither of us was supposed to be into his thing—just be pilots. Yet here I'm fully involved, and you and I are having this interesting conversation about Jewish beliefs. What are the odds?"

"Hmmm," David said with a mockingly sinister expression. "Maybe it's God's will to have us come and reason together. Maybe he brought us together for a purpose?"

Ian couldn't quite tell if he was serious or not. Then David said, "Think about it. Most people are religious, right? So I guess it only makes sense that we'd have views, backgrounds, and opinions that we would eventually share."

"I suppose you're right," Ian said. He paused, still thinking of the conversation. "Hey, but to Jews, doesn't the fact that Christ rose from the dead prove anything?"

"Well in some Jews' minds it might have proved that he wasn't the promised Davidic messiah. Certainly the great warrior wouldn't have come and *died*, at least not according to our scripture. On the other hand, some might have believed in the curve-ball theory, despite the verse I quoted where God said he wouldn't throw curves. The only problem is that it really requires circular reasoning for a Jew to accept the crucifixion as proof."

"How's that?"

"Well you have to believe a borderline wacky, esoteric interpretation of Hosea's Prophecy in the Old Testament, Hebrew scripture."

"Yeah, I think that's what Klinghoffer says . . . *that's right!* Hosea talks about sinful Israel, as a people, being healed after two days and raised on the third.[40] That is later used by the gospel storytellers to further fit the Christ story into the Old Testament mold, but Hosea had nothing to do with messiah actually dying and rising."

"Exactly. Certainly others are free to interpret it that way, but most of those who do, believe it because they believe *first in the resurrection*—regardless and independent of Old Testament scripture," Ian concluded.

"Yes, and that's fine if you believe, but you can certainly see why the Jews didn't . . . and don't. The resurrection, which was far from unique in and of itself, really didn't accomplish any of what God said the Davidic messiah would accomplish."

Ian thought for a second. "If I think like today's New Testament scholars, I might say that Luke probably used that Hosea comment later to make a *midrashic,* allegorical point. He was binding the resurrection to the old Hosea scripture to illustrate what he believed to be sacred truth about this new Christian interpretation of the Old Testament, but he never intended it to be literally true."

"Now you're over my head, but that seems to make sense."

"Hey, I'll bet we're close enough to Grand Rapids to pick up the ATIS. Why don't you dial it up." Ian was referring to the automatic terminal information service, which major airports used constantly, to transmit arrival information and weather conditions.

"I can't hear it yet."

"Flip this," Ian said as he reached for a tiny switch, "to turn the squelch off. It'll be noisy but I bet we'll be close enough that you can make out the words."

David paused, listening intently. "Okay, I got it now. Holy shit! You *are* a good prophet yourself. No kidding, the temperature is down to 38, dewpoint 37, and the ceiling has dropped to 900 feet with a visibility of four miles in light fog."

"Thanks for the compliment, but I don't want to be right about this."

"Yeah, just impressive because they didn't forecast fog in the terminals."

They were suddenly back into pilot mode, and Ian was concerned. "Well I really don't like the looks of this; let's keep an eye on it as we get closer—I would have no problem dropping into Grand Rapids if I think things are going to go south on us."

They flew along and talked a little more, but mostly about flight strategy at that point. There was no defined sterile cockpit altitude in a small, single-engine plane, because they rarely flew much over the usual limit of sterile space, 10,000 feet. At the same time, it was clear to both that they were entering sterile cockpit mode.

About ten minutes later they were handed from Minneapolis Center to Grand Rapids approach control, as normal. Before they checked on the frequency, they again listened to the ATIS. It had just been updated.

"Ceiling is now down to 600 feet, Ian. Visibility down to a mile. Temp and dewpoint are the same at 36."

"Damn, Sam—no offense intended to my wife of course. Let me take the radios a second," Ian said. He keyed the mike. "Good evening Grand Rapids approach, Centurion three-four-bravo checking in at eight thousand with information Foxtrot."

A voice came back instantly. "Good evening Centurion three-four-bravo, it's a quiet night here; you may now proceed direct to Kalamazoo." The amended routing meant that as their flight came from the north, they didn't have any arriving traffic that prevented them from a direct overflight and initial descent through Grand Rapids' airspace. It was a small gesture on the part of the controller, but would shave a couple minutes off the thirty minutes remaining to Kalamazoo.

"Three-four-bravo, thanks; direct Kalamazoo. And I'd like to request a frequency change to talk to weather for a minute."

"Three-four-bravo that's approved, but we're pretty slow. I'd be happy to get you Kalamazoo weather."

"Roger that. Thanks much, I'd appreciate it. Perhaps Battle Creek too. We see things going downhill here and want to watch fuel and time."

"Okay, Kalamazoo is now reporting a 300-foot ceiling, visibility three-quarter mile in fog. Battle Creek is the same, and both temps and dewpoints are at 36, over."

"That's what I feared. Tell you what; three-four-bravo would like to go ahead and stay with you to land Grand Rapids as a final destination." Ian made the call without hesitation or consulting with David.

"Roger that three-four-bravo, fly heading one five zero, vector for the ILS 26-Left to Grand Rapids. Altimeter 29.93, descend now and maintain three-thousand. Be advised that a DC-9 just arrived reported moderate icing on the approach."

"Unfricking believable, David. Our safety margins are evaporating in front of our eyes." He keyed the mike. "Roger that approach, one five zero on the heading. Okay if we descend at our discretion to stay on top as long as possible?"

"Roger three-four-bravo, pilot's discretion down to three." Ian was buying them time before they had to dip into the wet, apparently now *icy*, clouds below. Less time in the clouds meant less time for ice to accumulate.

David was planning ahead and had the approach procedures already laid out for Ian. "Interesting. You just trying to train me on contingency planning?" he joked.

"I wish," Ian said. "Tell you what, Kalamazoo went to hell in a hurry. I don't want to have to fly an approach down to three hundred feet, and three-quarters of a mile any time, let alone at night and in icing conditions. I think the prudent call is to get our asses on the ground right now."

"Yeah, not to mention that we aren't carrying a whole lot of fuel. If we flew to Kalamazoo and couldn't get in, we probably couldn't get in to Battle Creek either."

"And by then Grand Rapids would be down too, and we'd be stuck without fuel. I know. That's the quick math I've been doing all along. Good thing we were watching closely. That really is what contingency planning is about—fricking Murphy's Law."

Ian leveled and slowed the plane to a still faster-than-normal approach speed, just above the tops of the clouds at 5,000 feet. About that time the approach controller called again. "Centurion three-four-bravo, maintain three thousand. You are four miles from Knobbs, turn right heading 180, cleared for the ILS to 26-Left at Grand Rapids. Be advised, numerous air transports have reported moderate mixed ice on the approach."

Ian keyed the mike. "Roger Approach, down to three thousand and we are cleared for the ILS 26-Left on a 180 heading to intercept."

Ian pushed the nose over and began the IFR flight into the night clouds. They were beyond pitch black, and felt as isolating as being immersed in a vault of concrete. The only difference was the sensation of traveling at 160 miles per hour, and flying solely by reference to the instruments. "Okay David, please crank the heat in the cabin, crank the defrost temp to full, verify that pitot heat and propeller heat are on, please."

"Pitot, prop, full cabin, full defrost. All are on."

"This is going to be interesting, my friend. Note that I'm going to hand fly. I don't want the autopilot to kick off with a load of ice and upset the plane. Besides, it gets squirrelly with ice, anyway. For planning purposes, there is no room for a missed approach if we're iced up." Ian took a deep breath. "I've got to nail this one."

"We're getting ice all right," David said as he hit the icing light and illuminated the front of the wing for inspection.

"How thick?"

"We're at a good quarter of an inch already, and it's chunky, mixed ice—not the frosty rime stuff this time."

Ian keyed the mike. "Grand Rapids approach, three-four-bravo, can we get a tight turn, we're picking up moderate mixed ice and I'd like to keep it short."

"Roger that, take twenty degrees right for the marker, still cleared for the ILS 26-Left and you're now also cleared to land by the tower, Runway 26-Left."

"Roger that. Thanks," Ian said succinctly over the radio, grateful for the controller's extra efforts.

"Okay, needle alive," he announced calmly, though his heart rate was elevated. He was about to hand-fly a difficult low approach—the old tightrope walk that took two feet, two hands, skill, practice, and precision—but this time it was going to be with a load of ice, and he knew it.

"Glideslope intercept is in one-half mile. Adding significant power to maintain altitude. How's the ice?"

"Ice is now about an inch thick," David said as he flicked the ice light on again. "You ever had that much?" he asked.

"Not in this life," Ian responded. He was calm, but intently focused on a perfect execution. "Intercepting glideslope. HOLDING on the gear for a minute. DO NOT let me forget the gear. This is out of standard but I need to make sure we can make the field. No flaps. Landing lights are on. Talk." He keyed the mike. "Grand Rapids tower, Centurion three-four-bravo is outer marker inbound 26-Left."

"Three-four-bravo you are cleared to land. RVR is down to four thousand feet of horizontal visibility in fog. Let us know if we can do anything."

"Fuck," Ian said out loud, then keying the mike he continued politely and calmly, "Roger, three-four-bravo, thank you."

Ian continued to talk out loud, partly for David's benefit, and partly for his own. "Okay, gear needs to come down now." The gear motor ran normally and the landing gear locked into place. "Three green, gear IS down and locked. Power is now at full takeoff power, but we're maintaining glideslope down."

David added, "Glidepath and localizer are perfect—makes you wonder if they're even working."

"I checked, but please re-tune and make sure."

"Yep, got 'em. You're just too damn good—needles are bullseyed," David said in a calm voice. It was intended as a calm and reassuring compliment.

"I can't see a thing through the windshield, how much ice on the wings?" Ian asked.

"Approaching two inches on the leading edge." David replied.

Ian said nothing. It was clear that the airplane was going in. It was sinking fast. The only question was whether it would hit the ground before reaching the airport; short of the runway on airport property; or actually make it to the runway. Unfortunately, even if they made it to the airport, Ian had absolutely zero forward visibility. The landing was going to be a controlled crash.

The two men now were sweating profusely, not because they were nervous, but because Ian had ordered all heat to full, so that all odds of shedding ice from the windshield were in their favor.

"Can you see the tail section? How's the ice?" Ian asked, concerned that as critical as the wings were, the horizontal stabilizer and elevator were just as crucial. If the airflow over the little horizontal tail-wing became interrupted to the point of "stalling," the tail would lose its downward counterforce, the nose would drop, and the plane would literally fall nose-first like a lead brick. The only good news would be that they wouldn't feel a thing.

"It's bad, Ian. Couple inches there too."

The engine roared. "There is no decision height to this approach. Just call altitudes. We're going in no matter what. If we make the runway, no flaps—they could change the wings' stall speed. In case we don't make the runway, ready the checklist for crash landing. Don't forget to open the door slightly before impact."

Ian was on a mental autopilot of his own. Hours and hours of training and experience allowed actions to come without conscious thought.

It was at this point, when everything else had been done, that he had a second or two to think. He'd always thought that if he knew he was going to die, he would key the mike and say, "I love you Sammy. Tell the kids I love them." The thought crossed his mind. He should do it while he had the time.

Small planes didn't have cockpit voice recorders, but every transmission and exchange with controllers was recorded, and transcripts were always published by the NTSB with the final reports. The most common last words were usually the tragic and haunting combination, "Oh shit." Ian knew he wouldn't do that in this case, but he resisted the temptation to issue his parting words. He wasn't close to giving up yet. The thought left his mind as quickly as it had come.

"Two hundred feet to decision height, four hundred to the ground, slightly low now on the glideslope," David said calmly as the plane ripped along at 140 miles per hour, full power providing barely enough lift to keep the misshapen wings flying.

Two seconds later, as he tried to peer forward out the front corner of the little side window, David said, "I have runway lights."

"Okay, keep me advised. I'm staying on instruments to the ground unless fortune swings our way." Ian couldn't see anything out the window. They were going to crash, whether it was on the runway or before, and he knew it.

Ironically, he had practiced blind, zero-zero landings at his annual simulator training in Florida. Ian had told the instructor he wanted to simulate a last-ditch effort, assuming fuel was low and all the airports were fogged in. It was an unlikely emergency that was avoidable by good flight planning, but it *did* happen in the real world. After multiple instrument approaches and controlled crash landings very much like this one—without the ice hazard—he had "lived through" two of the four.

Ian's mind raced, as he knew they had a solid chance. The precision needles became extremely sensitive as he was now below two hundred feet, racing along at 140 miles per hour at an altitude lower than any real-world approach he'd ever flown solely by instruments.

Suddenly, without any warning at all, there was a loud crashing noise. Ice was flying everywhere, the result of a thin layer of warmer air at the ground. It was *coming off* everywhere, and large chucks opened up a view of the runway through the windshield. Ian could hear the ice smashing into the tail section of the poor plane. Some part of him desperately hoped they weren't doing damage, but consciously he was elated by the ability to see!

Literally fifteen seconds later the wheels screeched loudly as the 210 landed at the unusually high speed, and coasted down the long runway, still shedding chunks of ice.

As they parked outside the VIP terminal, Ian cracked his door to let some heat out during the shutdown. The rush of cool air felt great. The ramp was empty except for two line attendants who simply stared at the freakish-looking 210, and actually began laughing and pointing. No sooner had Ian shut down the engine after letting the turbocharger cool, than the two line attendants approached and shouted, "Holy crap! How did you keep this thing in the air?"

Ian and David unbuckled and stepped out of the plane. Their eyes grew wide as they looked at the square blocks of ice that were still fused to the leading edges of the wings.

"Holy shit," exclaimed David. "That's a miracle."

Ian just shook his head and breathed a sigh of relief. He slowly walked around the airplane, bullying the massive chunks of ice from the wings and inspecting for damage. To his surprise, there was *no visible damage at all.*

"Dude, I can't tell you how glad I am that we didn't press on to Kalamazoo. I'm going to kiss you for the whole, hour-long ride home," David joked.

Had they waited any longer or proceeded to Kalamazoo, it was very likely that the warm surface layer of air—the one that ultimately allowed them to see to land—would have disappeared. Once again, Ian was thankful for the decision he made, and especially for what he considered to be some damn good luck.

As they waited for Sammy to drive all the way up with the kids and retrieve them, Ian couldn't help but again think about the big questions of life. He pondered the many people who had died in similar icing situations, and reflected upon the lack of clear reasons his life had been spared; but he still couldn't bring himself to believe that those who had died were knowingly or willingly guided to their deaths by any father figure in the sky—any more than he'd just been willed to live.

Though others would disagree, the good outcome was, in Ian's mind, just a product of decision-making, good or bad, and plain old, un-sexy, *chance.* Sometimes chips fall one way, sometimes they fall another. All you can do, he thought, is be as prepared as possible for those inevitable days when Murphy raises his ugly head.

Nonetheless, even once he and the family were home safely, he slept poorly. He was haunted by the thought that he had been within the "twinkling of an eye" of leaving behind a beautiful wife and two wonderful children, and sentencing them to overwhelming grief and pain.

Chapter 24

AGREEING TO DISAGREE

The following day Ian told Mac the full story, and arranged to get the airplane back to the hangar, with David's help.

"Can't really fault your judgment," Mac said. "The same thing could have happened to me under those circumstances. I mean you'd been flying all day and hadn't taken on any ice like that at all."

Ian was reassured by Mac, but still somehow felt that he'd pushed it too far, or that there was a point in the decision chain that reflected unwise judgment. "I guess the lesson is to stay on top of your exit strategy."

After retrieving the plane, Ian worked the rest of day and then went home to see the kids before he was to go meet Bill for their guy's night out. After talking with Samantha, then playing with Brandon and Andrew for a few minutes, Ian checked his email to see if he'd gotten any replies to his "coming out" document about his religious views.

There were several, and he opened the first. It was from a relatively good friend from their old church. Despite a general tone that was not venomous, the gist of the reply portended an end to the relationship as they knew it.

The friend and his wife had talked. The bottom line was that they would pray for the Kepplers, and wish them well, but just as Ian had made choices, they had choices to make as a result of his choices. They said one of the most important things in life is how you invest your time, and *in whom* you invest your time. And for them, it would make the most sense to invest in those with whom they shared a common set of principles.

They didn't arrive at the conclusion out of anger or malice, but rather rationally. They had no intention of avoiding the Kepplers, but why would they consciously invest in trying to foster relationships with atheists, when they could do so with others who would support their Christian values and provide a more nurturing environment for their children?

Ian's stomach turned with apprehension as he looked at the other emails, one by one. He opened several more, however, and discovered many contained heart-warming words of love and tolerance, despite their clear differences of opinion with his own conclusions. Ian found some of the 'supportive' emails to be emotionally moving. They were profound examples of unconditional love and of a solid faith, wholly unthreatened by his candid disclosure.

There was even one from a retired pastor, the father of another of Ian's friends, that began, "What took you so long?" The retired pastor then proceeded to offer a lengthy diatribe about his own, similar journey to a broader view of religious "truth," from his perspective as a pastor.

Finally, however, Ian reached the last email of the day. It was from a friend of his named Brian. Though he'd been physically shaky with trepidation while opening the other emails as well, as he looked at Brian's he felt a large knot forming in his stomach. He paused to ask himself what was it about human nature that made him focus on the negative—why even a single harsh reply, if that's in fact what it was, would bother him so profoundly. He'd read several loving messages, but somehow he intuitively knew he'd be upset by this one, and he hadn't even read beyond the subject line.

Brian was a neighbor with whom he and Samantha, over the years, had enjoyed several summer barbeques. They were not "best friends," but they were friendly neighbors, and Ian thought they shared a meaningful relationship. In fact, together he and Brian had engaged in interesting

conversations about scripture, to which Brian had appeared quite tolerant of alternative interpretations and understandings. But apparently, Ian
had stepped over a line.

Brian's email read:

> Dear Ian,
>
> What you are doing is dangerous. It cannot possibly benefit
> anyone or help the world in any way, no matter what you say.
> You are putting not only your own eternity in jeopardy, but
> your children and family's too. I fear for you and will pray
> for you. I've always said, love the sinner but hate the sin. If
> I had known where you were going with all this I would
> never have wasted the time with you.
>
> You should consider these words carefully. John 3:16 says
> "For God so loved the world, that he gave his only begotten
> Son, that whosoever believeth in him should not perish, but
> have everlasting life."
>
> And to your pursuit of truth, the Apostle Paul said in
> Colossians 2:8, "Beware lest any man spoil you through
> philosophy and vain deceit, after the tradition of men, after
> the rudiments of the world, and not after Christ."
>
> You are making your own man-made truth based on a few
> books and putting it above God's truth. I pray that you will
> repent. I really thought you were smarter.
>
> Brian

Ian thought to himself, *too bad Paul didn't actually write Colossians, but I
won't hold that against him.* Despite reassuring himself with that little piece of
conventional scholarly wisdom, Ian was nonetheless hurt and disappointed
by the email. He had gone from so marvelously appreciative of some of the
notes, to being shaky again with a fight-or-flight response to Brian's.

Ian suppressed his knee-jerk reaction to think less of Brian or be angry at him, instantly reminding himself that he had been the aggressor. *Nobody likes a personal attack, and you can't blame the guy when that's exactly how he perceived my original communication.* But even with the positive self-talk, Ian was still hurt by the fact that suddenly he was no longer a valuable human being to Brian, simply because of his religion.

Realizing the time, Ian shut the computer down, kissed everyone goodbye, and headed to meet Bill.

As he drove to the sports bar, and right up until he walked through the door, he couldn't shake Brian's note from his thoughts. He was trying to be understanding and ignore the angst and hurt, which he knew were of his own doing. He only hoped that Bill wasn't going to let him have it. *What have I done to myself?* he wondered.

"How goes the world, brother?" Bill greeted as Ian arrived at the table. It was the same sports bar where they'd met several times over the years, including the night when Megan's history of abuse came into focus. It was difficult to conceive of all that had changed in both of their lives in just a few, short years.

"Hey . . . things are crazy, but they're good." Ian sat, after the friends greeted each other with a traditional male 'pseudo-hug.'

"So you've been traveling more again, eh?" Ian asked.

"Yeah, probably not as many miles as you, but I sure have," Bill replied.

"Well, we've actually been doing a little less flying. Got another of our big Desoterica symposiums coming up next week and I think that impacts Mac's desire to accept flights." He paused. "But that said, I almost had my *last flight* yesterday . . . a very close call in the 210," Ian said. His eyes were wide open in emphasis. "Damn near bought the farm."

Bill gave a shake of the head and offered his full attention. "Don't think I could handle that one, brother."

Ian proceeded to tell the story of the icing ordeal, how it ended, and ultimately how David had driven him back up to Grand Rapids earlier in the morning, so Ian could fly the plane back to Kalamazoo.

"Guess that was God's wake-up call to tell you to be careful," Bill joked, raised eyebrows subtly implying there could be a sliver of truth in the jab.

Just then a lovely young server came to get Ian's drink order. Both men noticed her, but Bill seemed especially attentive. The young lady was perky and friendly, and when she left, Bill simply commented, "Okay . . . *wow!*"

"How's Representative Huxley? I haven't seen him in a while."

"He's good," Bill replied. "Did I tell you that he's working on a piece of legislation named after Hanna?"

"No way. That's cool," Ian said with sincerity.

"Yeah, there's a big push underway to lower the legal limit for drunk driving from .10 to .08 in all fifty states, and he's co-sponsored the bill."

"Interesting," Ian said. He was happy for his friend, in light of the tribute to his daughter, but a question or two popped into his head.

"Dumb question, but Huxley's a good Republican; aren't driving laws constitutionally the responsibility of the states? Isn't that the tenth amendment?"

"You're good, but this bill removes federal funding for highways if states don't comply. It's a big old hammer they have in their hands in Washington." Bill spoke with an air of power and a slight, cocky smile.

"How's Zach doing?" Ian moved the conversation forward, not entirely sure what he thought of the matter. He couldn't help but recall the accident report Bill had given him, which implied pretty clearly that there was no way the driver of the other car could have stopped. Megan had the sun in her eyes, and had pulled directly in front of oncoming traffic. The speed limit there was 50, so Patti Nelson was not speeding. In his mind, the story just didn't add up to the blame that the media, and the Huxley and Vanderveen families, had assigned this "drunk driver," but it was a delicate area he knew enough to avoid.

"He's doing well, actually. Seems to be having a good year at school. He stays pretty busy. Megan has him taking piano lessons, plus he's playing at the County Soccer Club and doing karate."

"Does he ever talk much about Hanna?"

"You know . . . not so much. We all talk about her often and keep her memories alive. He says his prayers and always prays for her and asks God to tell her 'hello.' There is no question he misses her, but kids really are resilient—especially at this age. It's good to see him thriving, actually."

"And how's Megan?" Ian asked with a tentative tone, trying to tread delicately.

"Well, she's okay," Bill said with hesitation, "she's just okay." Bill sort of bobbed his head from one side to the other, moving his hands as if to indicate an ebb and flow. "In some senses she's getting better, but to be completely honest . . . I don't know. I just don't know."

"It's got to be tough," Ian affirmed. "Sometimes people say it takes them years to recover from what you guys have been through."

"Well, I haven't told you yet, but she is now in counseling, so we'll see how that goes. She's a little flaky about it, so don't say anything to Sammy just yet."

"Actually, she already told Sammy," Ian replied with a look that said *don't shoot the messenger.*

"Hey, that's a good thing. I'm glad she has Sammy to talk with. Her mom and Sammy are about the only world she's known the last few years."

"Well then my next question is, how are *you* doing?" Ian asked sincerely.

"Apart from the fact that my friend has become a 'wing-nut' wacko, I'm doing really quite well." Bill smiled as he messed with Ian.

For his part, Ian was glad to see the good-natured ribbing from Bill. Even though he'd shared many of his evolving religious views with him over the years, he'd been a little on edge about how Bill might react to his explicit statement. He was suddenly realizing that asking questions was one thing, but labeling yourself an "atheist," even if properly defined and differentiated from the conventional use of the word, was somehow crossing a line for some.

"*No really*, how are you doing?" Ian said while laughing off Bill's little jab.

Bill spoke slowly and with reflection. "Really, I'm good. I've been working hard, but that's going extremely well still. I'm grateful to have that release. Zach's good . . . and you know . . . I'd love to have things be better with Megan, but I really do still feel like we lead a blessed life. You just need to appreciate the good things in your life and enjoy them, and gut through the tough stuff. It's the nature of life."

Despite their long-time friendship and brotherhood, Bill hadn't even for a second considered telling Ian about Christina. It wasn't only the additional risk that would come from telling anyone, especially someone married to his wife's best friend; and it wasn't that he didn't trust Ian, or even that he suspected Ian would explain the potential downsides of deceit—albeit without judgment. Rather, there was just something extremely private about his relationship with Christina that prevented the thought of confiding in anyone.

The compartmentalization was part of the joy he was feeling. This relationship was a magical retreat. It was warm, comforting, and uniquely the domain of just him and Christina. It was almost as if any contamination from outside that bubble would break the spell. No, to Bill, this was something that was going to stay very quiet, and very private.

Bill took a sip of his beer and the server returned to take their order. After making their selections and watching the server walk away, Bill removed some folded papers from his back pocket. It was the email Ian had sent.

"So can we talk about the Jerry McGuire mission statement?" Bill said with a smug grin.

"Absolutely. Anything." Ian smiled as if to acknowledge that he had it coming.

"Well, let me start by saying that I was glad you acknowledge the fruits of religion—the things you'll miss—and how good people tend to be religious and spiritual," Bill said, exchanging looks between the sheets of paper and Ian's face.

"Absolutely," Ian said again.

Bill got a more serious look on his face, and Ian knew he was about to say was something about which he felt strongly. "Because I have to tell you, and I know you're sensitive to this, but not only do I know the truth of God with every fiber of my being, but . . . I can't begin to tell you what that faith has meant to Megan and me . . . in dealing with what we've had to deal with."

Ian nodded his head, looking at his friend and fully acknowledging that this was actually a difficult thing for Bill. He said nothing as Bill continued.

"I've thought about this a lot, and just so you know, I love you. I back you in your inquiry. And actually, I now believe quite strongly that it might even be . . . God working *through you*."

"Interesting," Ian said softly. "How do you mean?"

"Faith is so vitally important in life. But the answers . . . the proof you seek . . . it's just *not* that simple."

"Free will, right? If it were clear, we wouldn't have the opportunity to choose?" Ian asked rhetorically.

"Yes but it's more than that. Let me give you my take on this and you can laugh if you want, but I really do believe that by asking the tough questions, God can use your voice not only to answer those questions for you, but to answer them for the many people who struggle and ask the same questions. And he can do all that—through you and your quest."

Ian still didn't say anything, but listened patiently and attentively to his dearest friend.

Bill added, "I really believe, assuming you practice what you preach and don't close your mind to new information down the road, that ultimately this journey for you will come full circle, and that others will benefit and grow in their faith as a result of your exploration."

"Well I appreciate your thoughts, Bill. Who knows? Perhaps you're right.

"Okay, fair enough my dear wing-nut friend, but lest we get into a debate, I have a request for you," Bill pushed with a hand slightly raised into the air.

"You've had your say in your document. I care about you and I've read it carefully. I'd like a chance to share a few ideas with you without argument or discussion. I know that we're not going to get anywhere in a debate—I'm not going to change your mind, and you're not going to change my mind. On the other hand, I want to propose a worldview for you to consider as you continue to be open to new facts. Is that fair?"

"More than fair. I apologize for rambling on. But just one thing. I think I need another beer." Ian spun around to find the server just as she was approaching. "Two more please."

"You got it, guys," she said with a bubbly smile. "Your food shouldn't be too much longer. Sorry the kitchen is slow today."

"No sweat, we're just shooting the breeze anyway," Ian said.

"First," Bill began as he looked back to Ian's documents, "I want to point out that there are great scientists, philosophers and debaters on both sides of every issue you can raise. Given sufficient time, energy, and money—like your pal Mac—I could find people to refute every single argument."

"Agreed," Ian said quietly and with a nod.

"And they aren't all stupid people either. As you've said from that truth-driven thinking web site you like so much, there is a concept called . . . is it the 'reasonable people test?'"

"Yes, that if there are numerous educated, smart, honest, genuine people on both sides of an issue, and you find yourself passionately and emotionally certain you know the truth, it should be a red flag that you might have oversimplified the issue," Ian clarified.

"Exactly. So I want to make clear that indeed this is the case with any of the things you explore and study. I can produce what I believe are better answers. I may not be able to eloquently debate you, and produce every argument of those scholarly answers, but that doesn't mean I haven't heard them and that I don't base my conclusions upon those rational arguments."

Ian stopped himself and resisted the urge to say anything. "Okay," was all he said.

"You say in your document that belief in God is based solely on faith, and that faith is the opposite of reason. You say faith is belief in something for which there is no proof."

"Right."

"But I hope you'll agree that there is another definition. In *truth* there is one that is more widely used, and that is *trust*. Faith is *trust,* or confidence in a person, thing or proposition, despite the inability to clearly prove it. So I quibble with your definition of faith. It is not blind belief against all evidence. Blind faith is not admirable. But where I have a solid foundation on which to choose to believe, I can reasonably take the next step and say, 'I believe, *based upon faith.*'"

"Fair enough. You make good points. For the record I don't totally agree so far, but I will not interrupt."

"You see, I see profound evidence of creation all around us. The mere concept that you and I are sitting here and having this conversation is so far beyond what science can explain that it's not even funny. The odds of a bunch of random molecules coming together and forming the incredible complexity of the human being are infinitely small."

"Much like the odds of the motion of ocean waves and tides randomly manufacturing a perfect wristwatch and then puking it up on the shore, right?" Ian added to Bill's point with a smile.

"Smart-ass. But that's exactly right." Both friends smiled and laughed; for his part Ian now was trying diligently not to prejudge the conversation, and to remain open to what Bill was saying—despite the occasional ribbing.

"But billions of cells in a human body work together so miraculously . . . a heart beats; my blood clots when I get a cut; and a baby can emerge and take her first breaths. Don't those things show impossible complexity? Or how about the beauty and order of the universe, or the interaction of water and life in a beautiful mountain landscape?

"Each is indeed a wondrous display of order and beauty," Ian agreed.

"Here is the thing, Ian," Bill continued. "You know that science says for each and every effect, there must be a cause. From Aristotle and Plato to Thomas Aquinas there has been consistent agreement that for something to begin to exist . . . there must be a *cause* for that existence. I cannot deny that, and I believe in a Creator."

"Then what caused the creator?" Ian asked.

"No, no, no," Bill scolded. "No defense allowed, but I will answer that just because I'm a nice guy. Your argument is that my statement would require a cause of God, then a cause of that cause, and so forth forever. But infinite regression backwards is an impossibility because nothing would ever have truly been first if we play that game to infinity. *There must be an ultimate cause!*"

In Ian's mind the Kalām Cosmological argument had been philosophically discredited, but he remained silent on that point, instead saying somewhat wryly, "You certainly have paid attention at church."

Bill continued. "Or *love* . . . . You've seen the movie *Contact*?"[41]

"Of course. Carl Sagan was *the man!*" Ian exclaimed.

"So you know the point I'm going to make. Does Samantha love you?" Bill asked Ian matter-of-factly.

"Yes she does," Ian answered willingly.

"*Prove it!*" Bill completed the point.

"Can I just answer that one point?" Ian asked.

"No."

"But you told me to prove it and I can," Ian said.

"Tough shit."

"Fair enough, Bill. What I heard you saying is that we humans take many things on faith, without proof, and that there must be a creator of all of the magnificent order and complexity that is our universe," Ian echoed back politely to remain in a non-argumentative posture.

"Of course. Good boy. And I'll further make the point that just because we take something on faith, without the detailed, anal-retentive research . . . and without knowing every single thing about the history . . . and without understanding canonicity and other big words . . . and without understanding every single nuance of our religious tradition . . . that doesn't make that belief wrong or stupid."

"I agree."

"If someone looks out from a beach, and sees a ship, and says that ship is miles away, he might very likely be right! Right?"

"Yes."

"He would be right even though he hasn't measured the distance to exacting standards, down to the foot. Right? So can't he then use intuition, observation and experience to take the final step and believe the ship is miles away—based in part on faith? The point is that I again argue that faith can be based upon rational underpinnings; and more importantly, it isn't unreasonable or stupid for people to accept such conclusions as truth!"

"You make an excellent point. Even though I'll still disagree with your philosophy, I agree that it isn't stupid for people to believe as you describe."

"Especially not when you understand that I don't begin to know how I could be here talking with you today, how I could have gotten through the last several years, without my faith! That is very important to me, and it is *real!*"

Ian nodded, again acknowledging not only his friend's point, but his pain.

Bill was getting a little excited and emotive. "You can call that emotion-driven thinking, but isn't that *reality*? Isn't the fact that *it really did* provide me hope and comfort proof that it is real as well?"

He continued, "So I guess that my point for you is that I want you to practice what you preach, and continue to seek out voices of reason that are pro-Christianity and pro-belief in God. There are brilliant arguments that you can't just dismiss."

"You know what, Bill, I think you're brilliant as always, and I appreciate your points. I really do."

"Okay, quit being nice . . . . You can talk now. I'm not your wife and we're not in a fight." Bill smiled at his friend.

"No, I'm serious. Your argument is reasonable . . . . *Wrong*, but reasonable. And I really appreciate that because while most people have been kind, and what I would call truly and lovingly Christian in their response, a couple have not. A couple have been hurtful."

"Well, as with any population of people, you'll find all different types. There are smart Christians, dumb ones, emotion-driven ones, rational ones, and silly wing-nuts. My advice is the same as with any other part of life; don't throw the baby out with the wing-nut. And cut people some slack. These are important parts of what we fundamentally believe, and how we see the world. You have to tread lightly."

"Well said. I think I just wanted to be clear and not deceive people."

"I think you accomplished your goal in a tasteful way. I really do. I'm just trying to keep you from becoming a *real* wing-nut."

The server finally emerged with a large serving tray containing the friends' food. "Sorry for the delay, guys," she said again. She placed the food on the table and offered to get them anything else they might need—like the two additional beers that they surely wanted. As she departed, Bill watched with great interest.

"Look at the ass on her," he said, his eyes locked on the hindquarters of the server as she made the long walk back to the bar area.

"Since you're so obviously struggling to reconcile the teachings of your faith with lusting after the server's ass, I think I can help you there," Ian said sarcastically.

"Hey, I'm just looking."

"Yeah, well, I thought that was a sin in your view. Hell, Pope John Paul II even declared that it was sin to look at *your wife* with lust—that by doing so you were committing adultery in your heart."[42]

"Are you serious?" Bill asked. "I thought the Catholics had a better handle on theology?"

"That's not what I said."

"But you did say you were going to help me rationalize looking at her ass, didn't you?"

"Yes I am. May I be controversial now?"

"Like I can stop you," Bill answered.

"Do you know what adultery means?" Ian asked.

"Sure. It means having extramarital sex," Bill replied, "or sleeping with someone who is married."

"Okay, hold that thought. Have you ever noticed that particularly in the Old Testament, even God's chosen leaders—like the great King David—had many wives? Or did you notice that men had concubines all over the place?"

"Yes, but I can't say that I know what a concubine is," Bill confessed.

"Well, essentially concubines were additional women that men could have sex with for pleasure or for procreation. Sex outside marriage was very common in the Bible. A man was limited only to the number of concubines he could afford."

"Sugar daddies, eh?" Bill crooned.

"Yeah, kind of. And certainly God's greatest rulers and exalted ones were never chastised for this behavior. There is no Biblical prohibition of such extramarital activities—even in the New Testament. And in the Old Testament, God almost seemed to explicitly condone it in several instances."[43]

"No way," Bill said, though it was more of a question than a statement. Clearly some part of him was enjoying this part of Ian's unconventional research. "That's bullshit!" Bill exclaimed. "The Bible is clear that adultery and sexual perversions prohibit you from inheriting the kingdom of God. Hell, I've seen the quote from scripture a bunch of times. I think it was even in that sex program that Pastor Mike put us through as kids."

"Yeah? The one where you pledged to stay a virgin?" Now Ian dished out the jab. Bill grinned as the server appeared to deliver two new beers to the men.

Ian sat upright. "All right, my friend. I think you are referring to one of the two lists of sinners in First Corinthians . . . something like Chapter six, I think. And actually depending on the translation, it mentions a number of different groups of sinners who won't inherit the Kingdom—at least according to Paul, who most claim wrote the letter to the people of Corinth.[44] Indeed adultery is prohibited there and elsewhere in the Bible . . . clearly. But I'll come back to that—"

"I'm holding my breath," Bill said as he took another swig.

"The list you mention includes a couple of interesting things about sex. The term 'sexual perverts' is a funky translation that is disputed several ways. Some say it prohibits homosexuality only. Others say it might refer to the enslavement of 'kept' young boys for homosexual purposes.[45] But more likely it has to do with the sexual idolatry that was common in pagan worship at the temples. In Corinth, people would go to the official prostitutes of the temple, and have sex with them as an act of worship to the fertility Gods. By doing so they believed that the gods would make their harvest more bountiful."

"Not because it was fun?"

"I'll bet it was that too," Ian joked. "But you see, Paul obviously wanted people to worship *his* God, not the 'false' fertility gods. So the prohibition *had nothing to do with extramarital sex*, or even prostitution or homosexuality, as many have argued and believed.[46] The mistranslation could have been a simple error of words. At the same time I tend to believe that the anti-sexuality movement that entered the church with Augustine, and is believed to actually have come from some combination of Aristotelian and Gnostic beliefs, may have colored the way this was mistranslated."

"Even if that's true, adultery is clearly a sin," Bill insisted.

"Thanks for reminding me. Wrong again. That term is in that list too, and in other places. That translation is correct and true, but adultery is without question a property crime. It has nothing to do with sex—per se.

"You are an interesting fellow, brother. Never a boring bar conversation I suppose," Bill grumbled with a raise of his glass.

"A woman was always owned by a man. She was either her father's, or her husband's. A woman could not inherit property, and could not enter into contracts. Deuteronomy is a good example of how this term was used to describe property crime. It says something like *thou shalt not covet thy neighbor's wife, house, manservant, his ox, or his ass, or anything that is his."*[47] I don't think there is a reasonable scholar today who wouldn't define the Biblical term 'adultery' as stealing another man's asset."

"That would sure explain why God wasn't mad that everyone had a bunch of wives," Bill admitted.

"It would also explain your wedding vows. By the way, no offense, but the story Mike offered to rationalize those verses sounded fine, but there is no question that they mean what they said. You bought yourself a woman there."

"Ouch. You're an ass," Bill said half-jokingly. "At the same time I find that unbelievable. There has got to be another argument on this adultery issue."

"Not a good one, I don't think. I mean, there is in the sense that all the other valid teachings of the Bible would still apply to those relationships. Clearly the Bible wouldn't condone rape, violence, or non-loving interactions between people. Though it would appear it does condone incest, because the Moabites and the Ammonites were descendants of Lot and his daughters—which by the way is a mind-boggling part of the rest of the story of Sodom and Gomorrah that apparently nobody has actually read. There is no way that the story's point is about homosexuality."[48]

"Pretty interesting," Bill said as he pondered the argument further.

"Really I'm not trying to be a jerk. I'm just so fascinated by what I once thought, based on what I was told, and what I see when I compare this stuff to what scholars have been saying for centuries. It sure appears that the Bible certainly doesn't prohibit sex between caring, consenting adults—even if they are married. Funny though, on the other hand it says that if you steal a man's wife by having adulterous sex with her without his permission, the penalty is death for both the man and the woman."[49]

Bill was still incredulous, but he couldn't help but like what he was hearing. Somehow he had compartmentalized his relationship with Christina, and even rationalized it as ordained by God. He had prayed about it, telling God that he felt she was a gift for his lonely heart. It was *divinity* that he felt he was experiencing through the intimacy of their relationship.

"I'd sum it up this way," Ian said, "despite what we all think, the Bible doesn't say nearly what we have been told it says about sex—especially when you understand it in its original language, and through the eyes of the prevailing cultures of the first century. There are several books and web sites that meticulously list all relevant passages about sex, and explain the various interpretations of each."

Ironically, Ian was telling Bill that the reasons most people would have condemned his activities on religious grounds, were unfounded. On the other hand, with his deceit of Megan, it would be hard to see his actions as condoned by his Bible in any way, shape or form.

"Let me ask you a question. Why didn't you ever get this deeply into scripture when you went to church?" Bill queried. Ian took a moment to answer.

"I think that is a great question . . . . I guess, because I didn't need to . . . I guess I had a couple things going for me. Mainly, I had someone tell me what the Bible said so I didn't need to read it myself. Besides, it's damn tough reading."

"But you read it now," Bill retorted.

"Yes, but I've had some guidance and assistance in understanding. I really don't think most people can understand the Bible's esoteric meanings without some help. But the guidance most people get is prejudiced by thousands of years of human corruption, and institutional bias."

"And yours is prejudiced too."

Ian pondered the point but chose to continue the core thread of conversation. "I think the other part of my renewed interest is the epistemological angle. I'm fascinated with why I believed in UFOs, and I'm fascinated with why I believed this magical stuff in a literal way. But in order to draw any conclusions, I guess I have to get in there and see for myself what the story, and the history, are really all about."

"I guess that makes sense, so long as you listen to both interpretations and try to guard against those biases," Bill cautioned as he sipped his beer.

"Believe it or not, I'm not just out to shoot down other people's beliefs," Ian said. He hesitated briefly. "But in all honesty, I think there is an element of anger in me that feels a bit like I've had the wool pulled over my eyes—like I was naïve. Now I'm intrigued with what it is in me, and others, that makes us so willing to believe in things based upon such weak evidence."

"So this is about revenge?" Bill asked.

"Interesting thought. I don't know . . . let me ponder that one for a while. I think it's more like a religious hangover," Ian joked.

The duo continued to banter back and forth over their remaining beer, slowly depleting their reservoir of worldly knowledge, and the clock as well. As the night wound down, the two friends had agreed to disagree on most of the topics they'd discussed, but Ian was relieved by his friend's reception, and by knowing Bill was still by his side.

But for two people, each of whom was equally driven by a need to be right, would it be realistic to expect their divergent worldviews to have no effect upon their friendship? How could they find common ground? Perhaps, each privately pondered, some additional knowledge will help the other bridge the gap.

Chapter 25

PRELUDE TO A KISS

"Hi good lookin'," Ian said as he entered the house after the guy's night out. "How were the kiddos?" Ian gave Samantha a kiss as she sat in bed reading a book. There was rare quiet time in the house, but once the kids were in bed, Sam enjoyed nothing more than retreating into a book, within the safe confines of bed—even if it was barely nine o'clock.

"Hey, how was your time with Bill?" Samantha asked, closing the book onto her ragged old bookmark and giving Ian a quick kiss.

Ian recounted his conversation with Bill, expressing some regret at having been too enthusiastic in sharing some of his new insights. "I get going and sometimes just go overboard," he admitted. "Bill's faith has gotten him through some rough years, and here I am picking on it—which of course is not my intent, per se."

"Did he seem upset?" Sammy asked.

"Oh no, not at all. It really was a fun conversation from my perspective. I just always feel like in my enthusiasm for conversation and testing beliefs—including my own—I'm not sensitive enough to where others might be coming from."

Samantha put a hand on Ian's. "Oh, I'm sure you were fine. Lord knows you guys have been friends long enough that he'd have told you if there was a problem." Ian nodded.

Ian and Samantha knew of each other's tendencies to be self-critical and self-analytical after social gatherings or conversations. It was not uncommon for either of them to come home and worry that they'd offended someone, said something wrong, or made themselves look like an idiot.

"So what'd Bill have to say about your little document?" Sam coaxed.

"He was good about it. He raised some good questions from his Christian perspective, but he was tolerant and nice, didn't seem upset at all." Ian lay next to Samantha on the bed, still fully clothed and not yet ready to call it night. "Of course I got into Biblical issues surrounding sex."

Samantha laughed. "Did you antagonize him with your theoretical argument against marriage?"

"Theoretical? Oh, well . . . no, we really didn't get into that. It was mostly the arguments about misinterpreting the Biblical foundations for the anti-pleasure, anti-sexuality attitudes in Christianity."

"Good, so he didn't have to hear you ramble on about how monogamy is a failed experiment of only the last few centuries," Samantha bemoaned, imitating a stuffy Ian, "used mainly by the rich to assign and convey property." She smiled and kissed Ian on the cheek as she made fun of him.

"Funny. But actually I didn't get that far, so no, I didn't." Ian paused for a second. "I did mention his wedding vows though."

"No way!" Samantha snapped with a surprised expression. She chuckled to herself. "I'll grant you I didn't know too much about the Bible, and still don't, but I was so blown away when I heard those vows."

"It was strange indeed, and now I think Pastor Mike's rationalization for using them was just as wacky."

Samantha thought for a second, and then asked, "How do you think things are going between the two of them?"

Ian didn't know quite how to answer. "I don't know. You'd probably know as well as I would. Bill hasn't said much to me, other than that it's pretty much status quo. I guess my sense is that things aren't great."

"It makes me so sad for both of them. It is just so tragic. They're such good people, and it seems like just yesterday I was jealous at times, because they seemed to have everything . . . parents, money, looks. And Megan is such a sweet soul. She just seems so lost, so hollow and empty. I sure would love to see her happy again someday—just see her know joy. Life is so short."

"Absolutely right," Ian echoed.

Samantha thought for a second and then asked, "Do you think they'd ever get a divorce?"

"Actually? No. I really don't, despite everything. I just wouldn't ever see it happening. Bill's too tenacious. He'd never do it. I think he'd see it as too big a failure, and I can't see her ever making the move. Besides, I do genuinely believe they both love each other."

"It's just so sad," Samantha said again as she shook her head slowly, side to side.

"How about from her perspective though—has she said anything lately about how things are going?" Ian asked.

"No, nothing really new. Just the same feeling of conflict between guilt and inadequacy, and a complete lack of ability to engage with anything or anyone. She says Bill is one of her best friends, but I don't even think that after all this time she can really be open with him. It sure would suck to be her . . ." Samantha shifted tone. "This sounds terrible and I don't mean to say that I don't understand, and I certainly will always be there for her; but at times it's been tough for me to be around her and be a good friend, because it's just so stinking sad."

"Yeah, just imagine being married to her and coming home every day to a murky, joyless home. Bill's got to feel like that at times."

"Yeah, no doubt," Samantha conceded as she stared at a dot on the wall, deep in sympathetic thought about her friend.

"It's probably a good thing you've also been able to spend some time developing your friendship with that new friend of yours from work. What's her name, Brooke?" Samantha had begun working part-time at a local advertising agency since the kids started school that fall.

"Yeah, I just love her. Of course I love Megan too, but I have to say it has just been so much fun laughing about stuff, and even spending some time just hangin' with someone who's so bubbly and easy to be around—."

"And hot," Ian added jokingly.

Sammy pretended to slap him on the leg as she continued. "Well she's fun, but she knows how to have a serious conversation too, and she's also thoughtful. Did I tell you about the little thank-you note she left me last week?"

"Yeah, that was nice. She did seem nice the one night she came to get you for your girls' night out."

"Let me ask you this about Bill. Do you think Bill would ever cheat on Megan?"

Ian thought. "You know, I just don't know. But the older I get, and the more I see, nothing would surprise me."

"I just hope you'd tell me if you ever felt the need to go elsewhere. I can't think of anything worse than being made a fool, a patsy. It's not about the sex, its about the disrespect and the deceit . . . . I'd kill you."

"I tell you, it's why I think the whole Christian, puritanical view of the world might even be harmful. Hell, we tell kids sex is bad; we say we don't, but we do. At the same time, unlike Europe, we're both hyper-sexualized *and* prudish! I had friends whose parents actually told them sex was *evil*."

"The only thing my mom ever said . . . she walked in my room and said, 'If you get pregnant I'll kill you.'"

"Well my parents were relatively liberal and I would still lie in bed praying for strength not to sin and touch myself anymore. But then kids grow up and get married, and we pretend that each and every emotional and human need can be exclusively met within that relationship—the one created to preserve property inheritance for male successors," Ian argued with a grin. "Between the hang-ups and the pressures, is it any wonder that so many spouses feel so inadequate, unfulfilled, or dissatisfied?"

"So would you marry me again today if you had it to do all over?" Samantha smiled knowingly; she just wanted to hear it.

"Of course. You know I would. And don't get me wrong, I think that a lifetime commitment is so hugely important. The pledge to recognize that we are going to be here and grow in our love for each other, for the kids and for the grandkids, is huge. It'd be hard to overstate how important that is . . . . And it's important that we work together *in our community* as well."

"Yeah, well, if you ever leave me I'll kick your ass," Samantha joked. Confident and self-assured, she had joked before that they would have the easiest divorce any couple had ever seen, should they ever part ways. Of course it was an oversimplification, but Ian truly took her joke as a statement that she loved him so much that she really would 'set him free' if that was ever what he wanted. Ironically, he was touched by the statement, and it was just one of a million reasons he couldn't envision living without her.

Ian laughed at her warning. "It's just that to say in this day and age, when life expectancy will clearly reach close to ninety years or more—at least for our kids—at age twenty or thirty you're supposed to select one person, love him or her so dearly and perfectly that you'll be monogamous, totally fulfilled by only that person, in every want and need, for the next eighty years, just seems like a tall order to me."

"It is a hell of a big promise," Samantha agreed. "It almost goes back to the point you made when Bill and Megan were getting married. Is it humanly possible to pledge such a thing for certain? Can you really *consent* to an agreement to love someone for eighty years?"

Samantha paused, then answered her own question: "Clearly not, since more than half of marriages don't last."

Ian sat in thought. He said, "Okay, I'll get back on my soap box just for a moment, but I mean . . . God seemed to fully condone concubines, back when people lived to thirty. How does monogamy for eighty years make sense? Actually, to your point, it doesn't make sense *in practice*. I recently heard a woman on NPR say that most Americans are *not* monogamous; they engage in *serial monogamy,* which is simply one relationship *at a time*. Those don't last either. So how is serial monogamy good for kids?"

"You know, for the record I do believe that you've lost it. You are officially a wacko liberal, one hundred and eighty degrees *not* the guy I married."

"Thanks a lot," Ian laughed.

"But that said, it does seem like a lot of pressure on the relationship to say that all your intimacy needs, forever, must come from this person—especially if what you say is true, that historically the real world hasn't worked that way," Samantha proffered.

"Not at all. Not only did the Biblical world work differently, but anti-sexuality paranoia didn't really creep in to Christianity until Augustine, during the fourth and fifth centuries. And even then it came from the *gentile mystery religions* and philosophies, not from anything Christ or the apostles said."

Ian became slightly more animated. "Priests married and had con-cubines up until 1022, when Pope Benedict VIII finally changed it and sentenced any children of priests to serfdom. But even then it was more about protecting the wealth of the Church from leaking out through inheritance. There was no theological basis."

"I know. I know already, geek-boy. But you're off topic as usual. And I was actually agreeing with you about the challenge of eighty-year marriage."

Ian shot her a goofy glance. "Fine. But the central question becomes this: is love a zero-sum game? Is it a finite thing that is scarce and in limited supply?"

"Ahh. By that you mean just because you love one person, does that mean that the person you love *uses up* your available supply of love?"

"Yeah, that's exactly what I think people are saying with regard to sexual relationships. Love is like gas in a tank, where once expended there is no more." Ian caught Samantha's quizzical look. "If I give my gas to someone else, that means I don't have as much to give to you. They say that sex is reserved for only one person for your entire life, and that indeed it is cheapened if it is shared with anyone else, before or after. The funny thing about that argument is that it presupposes that sex must be the thing of *greatest importance* in *all* human relationships, and I think that's wrong."

Sammy still looked perplexed. "I'm not following you."

"Those who say love and sex are a zero-sum game, are guilty of over-prioritizing sex; they say we should save our sexual relations for only one person in a lifetime. And I think that's a hypocritical argument. We've almost made sex a false God."

"Still don't follow," Sammy said.

"Well for starters, let me ask you this. I love my brother Matt. Does that harm your relationship with me? Is that destructive to *our* relationship? Does it drain my gas tank and make less love available for you?"

"No it doesn't. I suppose that it would if the relationship was dysfunc-tional, or if it was greatly troubled. Then it might hurt our relationship."

"Good point. But let's assume it's truly a healthy, 'Christian' relation-ship. Now for a second let's take my relationship with Bill as another example. Bill and I have a loving relationship, but obviously in a decidedly non-sexual way—"

"Not that there's anything wrong with that," Samantha quipped.

"Okay. So assuming we are using a Christian-style definition for love that defines it as authentic, pure, selfless and true, does it harm you if I have a non-sexual, loving relationship with Bill?"

"Of course not. Just like you said about getting needs fulfilled only within the relationship, I think most shrinks would say that you need to have interpersonal relationships outside of the marriage to keep it from crumbling under its own pressure."

"Okay, but let's take it a step further. Is it possible that I could have a loving relationship that is non-sexual, with another woman in life? Say that my mother was still alive. Would loving my mother hurt our relationship?"

"Of course not," Samantha answered, playing along with the little game, "but get to your point."

"What I'm saying is that the entire message about love being a finite quantity, zero-sum game, is said to apply only in non-intimate relationships. If sex is involved, then people must fulfill themselves emotionally, spiritually, and physically, only within the confines of a marital relationship, for their entire life. That argument *centers entirely on sex*. Sex is the determining factor of whether a relationship is destructive of others— limited in its available supply like a gas tank. I think that the zero-sum approach overstates the importance of sex in relationships, and devalues the importance of love. Sex becomes like a god or something. It's almost like a false idol."

"Let me see if I can hang with you on this before my brain retires for the night," Sammy said. "Because of the insurmountable, all-important, and unharnessable power of sex, a sexual relationship, then, is somehow *totally different*. Once we dabble with this powerful sex thing, relationships *are* a zero-sum game. Every time I have sex with you, I'm draining the amount of love I have for my other lovers, or better yet for my future husband who doesn't crash my quiet time with philosophical rantings."

Sammy's joke made Ian laugh. She further summarized, "So the argument is that if I physically and sexually interact with you, I have less love to give someone else. Other relationships are *not* zero-sum games, like you and your mother, but sexual ones are mutually destructive of one another."

"That's exactly what I hear them saying," Ian confirmed.

Sam thought for a moment then countered, "I could certainly see where you could argue the opposite, that all genuinely *loving* relationships are the *same* as those that are non-sexual! They are *not* zero-sum games. Love is *not* limited, but is more like sowing and reaping. The more love we spread in life—and I do NOT mean that sexually—the more everybody wins."

"Wow, did I just hear you say that?" Ian laughed, prodding her playfully. "Now *you're* sounding like a radical lib."

"But Ian, nobody questions that premise. That's what every religion preaches. 'Do unto others,' the golden rule, 'love thy neighbor,' and you will reap benefits many times greater."

"Right. Did you know that during the Victorian age in New York, doctors had vibrators and considered it a 'non-sexual' medical procedure to provide clitoral massages to their patients?"

"You've got to be kidding me," Samantha laughed.

"Absolutely not; it's true. They thought that the relaxation of orgasm was quite helpful, and it turns out that hordes of women would very regularly see their doctor for that 'therapy.'"

"Unbelievable."

"But my point is that somehow if two female friends crossed that line today, and one provided the other with intimate contact or a 'massage' like the doctors used to provide, somehow we say such a relationship suddenly becomes destructive to others. The doctor-patient relationship would be removing 'love' from the woman's tank, and thus depriving her husband of her love."

"So you're saying that sexual relationships are not different, and that so long as they are responsible, caring, mutually well-intentioned interactions between adults, without deceit and lying, they are complementary and helpful to the world?"

"How is it that you're able to say in two sentences, what takes me five minutes?"

"It's only because you help me flush out the real meaning, with your brilliant Socratic method," Samantha smugly responded.

Although when it came to religion Sam was still uncertain and conflicted in her beliefs, she loved the bond that she shared with Ian. She treasured their late night, theoretical conversations and those special times that they spent talking. There was total safety. There was never a worry that a topic or a thought, genuinely expressed, was taboo or off-limits.

Ian felt the same way. To him such conversations and intimate, theoretical banter—the likes of which he'd never even imagined were possible in a marital relationship—were a testament to the refuge and comfort that was their love.

Ian replied to Samantha's patronizing repartee, "Well your summary of my argument was perfect, even though I haven't fully come to that conclusion yet. I'm certainly headed there though! It still fascinates me why we assign so much power to a muscle contraction."

"But you're not saying you think it'd be okay for our kids to just go have sex like it's a new toy they got for Christmas?"

"Absolutely not. I assume it went without saying that I would never, nor would any theologian I've read who discusses these issues, argue that promiscuous or careless sex could be defined as *loving interaction*. It is not. And in no way is giving someone a disease, or creating sacred human life willy-nilly, an act of love. That is no more love than taking advantage of an unsuspecting young person who looks up to you. That's rape! Any of these things are so *not* the caring, consensual, loving type of adult relationship I mean."

Samantha leaned over to Ian. "Are you saying you want to be able to have sex with someone else?"

Ian paused, then said, "You know me. I'm all talk. That's not my point." He paused again. "Fantasy on paper? Sure. But practically, it's hard to imagine. Mostly I'm just trying to formulate my worldview, is all. You know I'm very happy." He cocked his head slightly and looked at Samantha. "How about you?"

Samantha laughed. "Furthest thing from my mind. Remember, I'm the one who wouldn't even remarry if anything happened to you. It's certainly not something on my radar. No one would want me anyway."

Ian chuckled as well. "Yeah, and I don't have time to have an affair! I don't know how people do it. Not only do I not understand running around lying, cheating, deceiving, and even destroying other marriages, but even if it was done in the way I was just arguing, I don't know how people have the time to do it."

"Ahhh, so *time* just might be a zero-sum game," Samantha summarized with a smile. "Could that make your whole argument moot?"

"Interesting thought. I suppose not though, because the same can be said for all those other relationships that society and religion tend to value as sowing seeds of love—all those non-sexual relationships. But I suppose that you always do run the risk of cheating the ones you love out of your time. I think that's a separate issue though."

Samantha and Ian leaned back and chuckled at their silly, theoretical banter. Soon they shifted gears and began to talk of the real-life logistics and plans for the upcoming weekend, and even the following week's schedule, while Ian would be gone to the Chicago Desoterica. Before long, they kissed and said goodnight in their not-at-all-uncommon fashion: Ian headed to the kitchen to read, study, or write, and Samantha called it a night.

The events of the night were on Ian's mind. He thought about his dear friends Bill and Megan. He thought about the conversations of the evening concerning Bill and Megan, and the issues surrounding marriages and relationships. Why were they so difficult for so many people? Why were 50% of marriages ending in divorce? Why were 60% of African-American children being born out of wedlock—or perhaps more importantly and correctly stated, being born to only one committed caretaker?

Ian reflected back upon Bill and Megan's chauvinistic and archaic wedding vows. He then pondered his own "devil's advocate" position about marriage, and an idea hit him. He wondered, *what might an ideal wedding vow look like? If I could do it all over, perhaps in a parallel universe, what would my vows look like?*

After grabbing a snack from the kitchen, he headed for the computer. With his dear Samantha in mind, he crafted an alternative set of wedding vows:

- **I will always love you.** I know your soul. I know you like nobody else does. I admire you. I think you deserve nothing but the best. I ache for you when people don't understand you, or don't treat you with the love and kindness you deserve.

- **I will always be here for you.** No matter what. No matter when. You are the single-most important thing in my life—even ahead of kids. I will be here for you to talk with, to cry with, to laugh with, and to sit silently and watch bad TV with.

- **I've got your back.** I will care for and look out for you. I will do so in sickness and in health, mentally and physically. I will tell you when I think you're hurting yourself—and tell you what you may not want to hear, when it is necessary. I expect the same from you in return. This is the essence of long-term commitment.

- **You will come first.** Forever. No matter what. I promise you will come first financially, emotionally, and in all regards. And if time and energy are indeed a limited commodity—a zero-sum game—you and our family will always have mine.

- **I will be totally honest with you.** Ask me anything, and I will not lie—ever. Without trust and honesty, all else is diminished.

- **I will try to meet your explicit needs.** I know "trying" is not "doing," but I will always make an effort to be flexible and to address your needs and wants that go unmet—physical, mental, spiritual, or otherwise. I am not a mind reader and may need specific instruction—perhaps even in writing (as silly as that may sound), but I will genuinely make an effort because I love you.

- **I will aspire to love you at all times in a manner consistent with that described in I Corinthians:** patient, kind, does not envy or boast, not self-seeking, rejoices in truth.[50]

There are also things to which a human being cannot possibly consent or promise. Here are the items I believe one should not pledge.

- One should not pledge that he or she will never love another human being, male or female. As it turns out, love is not a finite commodity, like money or gasoline. Loving someone else does not mean there is less love in my tank for you. In fact, love is a multiplied commodity—the more you give, the more you get.

- To expect that we should meet all of each other's needs entirely, is simply unrealistic. Be it sexually, interpersonally, recreationally, as sporting partners, business partners, or otherwise, it isn't possible for us to be all things to each other, and be a perfect fit for each other in all areas.

- One should not promise to be monogamous. It seems clear that this unnatural pledge of exclusive sexual relations "forever" results in more hurt, lies, destruction of trust, and destruction of families and homes than any other cause.

It was an interesting experiment. Ian looked back at the words to see if he had sold himself at all on the argument, but his thoughts drifted to the safety of his committed relationship to Samantha, and how others in his community would respond if they ever knew the content of such private, late-night conversations. He had to stop and ask himself if he had lost it and become a "wing-nut." His journey of questioning was now extending to every aspect of life. Had he gone overboard? Was it too much? Where was all of this headed? Where would it end?

Chapter 26

DUELING REVELATIONS

Monday, November 25th, 2002

The Citation gained speed and quickly leaped into the air as Ian and Mac departed Kalamazoo for the three-day Chicago Desoterica. As with previous symposiums, they had worked hard on the preparations. Much like finally leaving home on a family vacation—the car packed and the mental checklists complete—they were finally heading out to enjoy the fruits of their labor. Almost as if leaving behind the chaos and consternation over minute details, Ian and Mac both breathed a sigh of relief as Ian banked the jet on course to Chicago's beautiful Meigs Field.

It was a clear day with abundant sunshine, and no sooner had the Citation achieved 14,000 feet, than it was time to begin descending. As was usually the case, once they'd hit Lake Michigan, the lake-effect clouds that enveloped the leeward shores had disappeared behind them. Ian could see the outline of the cityscape on the west shore, from their position over 80 miles to the east. It was amidst that beauty that a rapid series of barely conscious thoughts flowed in anticipation of the Desoterica gathering.

The Reasonable People Test popped into Ian's head. He wondered to himself whether most of the entire civilized world could be so wrong when it comes to believing in God, including many of the Desoterics themselves? Was *he* now guilty of oversimplification? He thought of C.S. Lewis' idea of "Moral Law," the one he'd said simply *had* to come from some source. What source? Where was this source?

Ian's mind then flashed to the billions of people who, over the course of two millennia, had experienced enlightenment, peace, spiritual fulfilment, wisdom and comfort through belief in, and worship of, a God. Could this all have been just a colossal waste of time, a futile effort by the self-delusional masses?[51]

Just before a radio call would return him to the flight duties at hand, he asked himself if a creator could really have delivered such a difficult, complex, and esoteric message, and *actually have expected anyone to understand it?* After all, if these dedicated and smart scholars spent their lives better understanding ancient cultures, politics, languages and beliefs, and *they* still didn't see a clear path to "truth," how could God have expected a normal working person to do so? Why did he have to make the puzzle so incredibly complex and difficult?

"Citation four-three-niner-mike, turn left heading 240 and descend now for eight thousand."

"Roger Center, three-niner-mike is out of one-zero for eight thousand," Ian answered, returning his mind to the flight.

"Okay, four thousand to sterile cockpit," Mac said out of habit.

"Roger that," Ian said.

"Hey before we get there, I forgot to ask you if you were still having dinner with Sandra Flemming this week."

"Matter of fact I am," Ian said. "Looking forward to it."

"That's excellent that she took a liking to you. Not many people get to have dinner with a woman of her academic stature."

"Absolutely," Ian agreed.

At the third quarter, August meeting of the Desoterica, Ian had struck up a conversation with Sandra Flemming, who happened to be an expert in Biblical, textual analysis. In fact, Dr. Flemming was one of the leading experts in the world when it came to studying Biblical manuscripts. The two hit it off, exchanged emails, and the quirky, spunky, sixty-something-year-old genius had offered to share a meal with Ian at the next gathering.

"Passing through one-zero thousand," Mac said as a reminder that conversation was now limited to the business of flying.

After an uneventful, scenic approach and landing at the famed lakeside, Meigs Field, the duo proceeded to the hotel. Everything was in order there and most of the Desoterics had arrived in time for the traditional cocktail party.

While Ian usually stayed for the party, that night he left early, catching a cab and heading toward Division and Rush. In the back of the cab he dialed his cell phone.

"Okay John, I'm on my way. But just remember, I've got a long day tomorrow and I'm not as young as I was a decade ago."

Ian paid the cabbie and stepped out onto the curb at the famous intersection. It seemed only appropriate that they catch up with each other at the nostalgic old haunt, since they hadn't done so in many years. He headed toward *Mother's* when a voice from behind yelled, "Excuse me sir, do you have I.D.?" Ian turned to see his old pal John rounding the corner in dress pants and a long coat.

"Hi buddy!" Ian greeted with enthusiasm.

"Good to see you again, my man," John offered in reply. "I'm glad I could pry you away from that stuffy, intellectual garbage and take you to a real Chicago establishment."

"Are you just coming from work?" Ian asked.

"Yeah, figured I'd just stay downtown and walk over here. It's just two blocks from my office." Though they'd kept in touch by email, they hadn't seen each other in person in almost a year.

They left the cold air behind and headed into the bar, easily locating a table. The old friends caught up on the basics of life before John enquired, "So tell me more about this Desoterica thing. I know you've been involved in it for a while, but I don't really understand it. What the hell is it that you're up to?"

Ian proceeded to explain the origins of the group and how Mac's contacts and salesmanship had created a critical mass of interest. "From there it took on a life of its own. As one esteemed scholar would join, other notables would see the roster, think about drinking and sharing for three days per quarter with people of similar interests, and say 'count me in.'"

"I'll bet, especially since Mac was footing the bill," John added.

"Well, just the hotel . . . but still . . ."

"So what, you'll spend three days talking about the Bible and some old rocks?" John asked with a sarcastic chuckle.

"Not exactly. There is always a special keynote address by a guest lecturer that kicks things off. For instance, tomorrow should be interesting because we have this guy by the name of Earl Doherty. He's written a couple books that are really controversial."

"Probably nothing I would know, but what's he written?" John asked.

"Actually, you may have heard of a book by one of your local reporters here. It's called *The Case for Christ*." [52]

"Lee Strobel, right? Actually I have. Haven't read it, but he used to write for the *Tribune*. I heard it was a good book. Wasn't he an atheist who became a Christian under the weight of the evidence, then wrote the book about it?"

"Yep. I read it a few years ago. Interesting book actually . . . though I obviously didn't find it convincing." Ian laughed at himself.

"Obviously not, you rebel heretic," John chided with feigned repulsion.

"Well this Doherty guy who is our speaker tomorrow apparently just released a book that uses the same trial metaphor as Strobel did in *The Case for Christ*, and he allegedly obliterates Strobel's 'evidence,' point by point. I just got that book and another of his, but haven't had time to read them yet. The one that picks apart Strobel's Book is called *Challenging the Verdict*." [53]

"So is he talking about that, tomorrow?"

"I don't know for sure, but I think *not*. His earlier book was called *The Jesus Puzzle: Did Christianity Begin with a Mythical Christ?* [54] Truthfully, I kind of thought the guy might be a wacko or something. I hadn't even heard of him, but Mac and everyone else had, and they say he's solid."

"I admire your passion," John said.

"Thanks. But I swear I was just thinking on the way down here that everything that seems so revolutionary to me, is old hat to everyone else. It's like the more I know, the less I know."

"I know what you mean; that's exactly how I felt for the first several years of my job." John shrugged. "Hell, I'm still learning. I figured that being an account executive at an advertising agency would be this glamour job of pure selling, but it turns out that you have to be an expert in printing technologies, graphic design, web design, video, web tools, and a dozen other media and skills that I knew nothing about when I started."

"That's impressive," Ian said. "You really have done well, my man. To your success!" Ian raised his glass and the two drank.

"Yeah, well, so this Doherty guy might shake things up even further for you?"

Ian smiled. "Probably. Mac tells me he makes quite a case that Jesus Christ was not an actual historical figure, but rather an amalgam of Jewish countercultural hippies from Galilee, and pagan savior gods of various 'mystery religions,' influenced by Hellenistic thought."

"I don't know anything about that stuff, but it sounds a little nutty to me," John offered candidly.

"You know it actually does to me too. But at the same time these are pretty bright people who aren't prone to unsubstantiated assertions, so I'll just sit, listen and see what the guy has to say." John shrugged his shoulders and nodded.

Ian continued, "I mean, I'm convinced that there are, as Bishop John Shelby Spong says, mythological underpinnings to many of the stories of the Bible. There are stories that are taken literally that were never intended to be historic truth, only mythological truth. At the same time I agree with you. I can't say I understand how Jesus could have *not even existed!*"

"Yeah, if the Bible is a collection of writings from a whole bunch of different people, as you say, then that would seem to indicate that there are a whole bunch of witnesses, and that they documented the history of the guy pretty well." John's point was solid, and Ian took his turn shrugging his shoulders in agreement.

"I'm with you. We'll just have to see. That's the beauty of the group though. After the keynote there are small group sessions and breakouts, so there will be plenty of time for debate. And believe me, these guys *love* to debate. They'll take him to task."

"Well, I don't know how you prove a negative and show that somebody did *not* exist, but I can tell you this. If you could prove that Jesus didn't exist, I'd think you'd rock the world like it's never been rocked before."

"No kidding about that," Ian said.

Little did they know that as they spoke, Dan Brown was putting the finishing touches on a book called *The Da Vinci Code*.[55] While the book would be assailed by both unbelieving scholars and believing churchgoers, for quite different reasons, the controversial allegations—that Jesus could have married and had a child—would infuriate some, motivate others to learn more about the early history of the Bible, spawn countless Sunday sermons, and sell a great many books. The mania would even lead to a Tom Hanks film in 2006, the year in which the Da Vinci buzz would finally end.

But John continued his point with a simple quip, the significance of which was almost lost on both of them. "Despite being a heathen and former churchgoer—and I've got no real dog in the hunt one way or the other, mind you—make no mistake, to even come *close* to proving there was no historical Jesus Christ would be nothing short of monumentally significant. It would be like revealing *a secret of the universe or something*."

Ian pondered the statement for only a second before agreeing. "Absolutely. But I for one don't believe the notion. In fact I not only highly doubt it, I really doubt there's any way to prove it, as you say. Besides, there is a saying in the skeptical community: extraordinary claims require extraordinary evidence."

"But what if he could prove it? Can you imagine the consequences?" John seemed intrigued more by the potential drama than the question itself. Both men finally canted their heads and shrugged in acknowledgment of the unimaginable significance, then moved on.

"So enough about that. How is your world? Any hot babes in your life at this point?"

"Funny you should ask," John said with a grin. "I'll tell you what. Do you remember that summer day we went to the park to hear the Symphony, and you hooked up with . . . what was her name—?"

"Becky," Ian interjected without hesitation.

"Yeah, and I met Flaco's cousin Cindy—"

"The one with the big hooters," Ian interrupted again.

"Okay fine, ruin my serious attempt to tell you that I met a girl, a woman actually, who is absolutely awesome. Her name is Annette, Annette Snyder."

"And she has big hooters, doesn't she," Ian ribbed.

"Well, yes. In fact she does, you perve. But I was going to say that she looks a bunch like Cindy did, only honestly, she is really a woman who's got it all going. She's smart, dynamic, personable, and a brilliant attorney."

John went on to describe how he met the voluptuous and beautiful blond through a client. He proceeded to tell Ian they had just decided to move in together. Ian couldn't help but wonder if it might be tough for John to live with someone after being alone for over a decade. But John was as happy, grounded, and excited as Ian had ever seen him, so he quickly found himself genuinely excited for his friend, and optimistic about the relationship.

After covering all angles of John's romantic connection with Annette Snyder, they caught up on Bill and Megan's situation, both resigning that perhaps the passage of even more time would allow the return of joy to their household.

As Ian later rode in a cab back to the hotel, he reflected upon how happy John seemed. He chuckled to himself as he observed that—almost as if slowing to accommodate the additional ten years of age the two friends had accrued—the crowd at the bar seemed substantially lighter on this Monday than it had been on the night he met Samantha, way back in 1992. Perhaps it was the result of the cold, November evening, versus the warmth of summer. All Ian knew for certain was that despite the cool temperature outside, the evening had been warm indeed.

As he rode, he also thought of Samantha and the kids, and fondly recalled the night when he and John stumbled into Sammy and her friends at that exact same location. What a memorable night that was. Who could have known at the time where such a chance meeting would lead. Ten years later he loved Sammy more than he ever imagined he could love anyone, and he had two beautiful boys who were an unfathomably rich icing on the cake.

❖

The following morning Ian arose early to double-check the room and prepare for the keynote. Mac was already there, and standing next to him was the man Ian quickly deduced was Earl Doherty, the keynote speaker for the symposium. Upon seeing Ian enter the room, Mac promptly introduced the man to Ian.

"Earl, I want you to meet Ian Keppler, our administrative guru and pilot extraordinaire."

"Ian, I've heard a lot about you," Earl Doherty said as he extended his hand. "Thank you again for having me."

"Our pleasure. I'm certainly looking forward to your message. I have to confess that I've been otherwise engaged in a mountain of reading, but I actually brought a couple of your books with me, and they are next on my reading list. I've heard great things."

The three briefly exchanged small talk before Ian excused himself to attend to some duties about the meeting room. He could still hear Mac and Earl talking and couldn't help but be impressed with Mr. Doherty. If nothing else, he was poised and articulate. Moreover, from his unavoidable eavesdropping and the couple of pages of Doherty's *Jesus Puzzle* he'd flipped through late the night before, he already perceived the man to be credible, and anything but a wing-nut. Having been around such scholarly types on many occasions now, Ian could quickly read from his carefully nuanced statements and meticulous attention to detail, that Doherty knew his stuff.

Ian chuckled to himself that even the casual onlooker could plainly see Doherty didn't have horns. At the same time Ian cautioned himself that the content of anyone's message was what mattered, and it had to be subject to cross-examination and the scrutiny of informed critics. After all, even the nuttiest of nuts could appear completely rational and normal.

In fact as the men prepared the room for the meeting on that Tuesday, and guests were about to head down for the keynote, global examples of fallible human reasoning were playing out in the broader world, just as they did every other day.

For instance, a European group announced plans to use the Very Large Telescope to photograph the abandoned lunar bases on the moon. The unprecedented use of the asset was solely for quelling the incessant rantings of the "moon-hoax crowd," a group whose membership was gaining substantial popularity. In their eyes, the lunar landing televised in July of 1969 was the product of three elements: a great, U.S.-led conspiracy; a little Hollywood studio magic; and a gullible American citizenry hell-bent on avenging the Soviet success of Sputnik. The entire event, the theory said, was a fake.

And as scientists invested resources to quell the cries of conspiracy theorists, news reports swirled the globe about two different organizations that had announced the first successful cloning of human beings. Amid much hype and international credulity, both groups claimed human births were imminent. Over time, both groups would also be proven frauds and cheats, but amid the mass of news and information of that week, truth was difficult to discern—as it is every other day.

So it was against that backdrop that Ian sat in the Desoterica and listened to Doherty begin his keynote. Ian was familiar with the term "butterfly effect," which described a simple cause-and-effect chain from the flapping of fragile butterfly wings to ripple effects throughout the world. What he had no way of knowing, however, was that Earl Doherty was a new, primary cause in just such a chain of events. With an emotion-driven bias against Doherty already waning, what Ian was about to hear would set the course for the balance of his life.

"Once upon a time," Doherty began, "someone wrote a story about a man who was God. We don't know who that someone was, or where he wrote his story. We are not even sure when he wrote it, but we do know that several decades had passed since the supposed events he told of. Later generations gave this storyteller the name of 'Mark,' but if that was his real name, it was only by coincidence."[56]

Ian knew that an increasing majority of Gospel scholars no longer accepted the assertion that the Gospels were actually written by the apostles whose names were later attached, but it was clear that Doherty was going to paint a very different picture of the origins of Christianity.

Ian initially listened to Earl Doherty with genuine interest. Soon interest turned to fascination, then fascination turned to stunned amazement as Doherty laid out his arguments that Jesus Christ never existed as a physical man. Even through a brief break, Ian stayed in his seat, his eyes staring blankly into space, his mind transfixed by what he had heard from Doherty. By the last three hours of the lecture, he sat slack-jawed and absolutely riveted to the comprehensive outline that Doherty was presenting.

It was as if someone had just divulged to Ian, in exacting detail, the unified theory of physics. To his death, Einstein was unable to unite two seemingly incompatible laws of science. Newtonian physics explained the behavior of large objects in the universe, and quantum physics explained the behavior of small particles; yet somehow the laws contradicted each other, and every physicist since Einstein had failed to bring the two together. By that time Ian often viewed the contradictions of the Christian Bible within itself, and with other religions, to be much the same conundrum.

Though at its face the case Doherty was presenting seemed wacky, his facts and detailed explanations not only made it plausible, but the harmony it created was mind-blowing to Ian. Suddenly this unified theory made so much sense that it sent neurotransmitters raging in Ian's brain.

Virtually every tough question he'd ever asked of his former religion was being answered! He could finally see how Jesus could be so schizophrenic. In a way that perplexed intelligent laypeople and scholars for years, Jesus could be the kind and gentle voice of wisdom to whom the children flocked—the guy who taught people to love thy neighbor as thyself, and to turn the other cheek; but he was also the apocalyptic madman who turned over tables outside the temple, banished entire cities to hell, and displayed near-psychotic anger.[57]

Did Jesus sin or not sin? Was Jesus divine, or human? Was he one god with the Father and the Holy Spirit, or were they separate Gods? Did Jesus think he was the promised earthly ruler of Israel, or did he not think so? Did he think he was divine, or not think so? Scholars had debated such questions for centuries because the Bible clearly contradicted itself on these fundamental questions.

But here was a theory that plausibly answered all those questions and many more; evolution of a couple myths explained it all. Where did the Eucharist come from when everyone knew Jews wouldn't have gone near human blood, let alone eat it? Why did "Mark" not mention in his Gospel story, any of the miraculous circumstances surrounding the birth of Jesus? Why did the other two versions, from Matthew and Luke, add such differing and conflicting accounts of the details surrounding the birth and resurrection? Why were all of those letters of the Bible, the ones that made up over two-thirds of the New Testament, completely and totally silent about any details of a historic Jesus and his earthly existence? Why did all those letter writers seem not to have heard of miraculous birth stories, wise men, or an arrest of Jesus and a crucifixion at Calvary? Why had they not mentioned a complicit Sanhedrin, or any of the details of crucifixion? Why hadn't they heard of the earthquakes and multitudes of others who were raised from their graves with Jesus that day, as Matthew wrote?[58] After all, with many dead people wandering the streets of the town, wouldn't that experience have been worth sharing?

Ian continued to have all of his old questions flash through his mind as the unified theory provided answers to each and every one. Why had all these writers of the epistles never, ever, even tangentially mentioned that Jesus performed miracles, raised the dead, walked on water, and turned water to wine? Wouldn't those things have been helpful in Paul's letters, his epistles to the people he was trying to persuade?

Ian's limited study and learning had, to that day, led him to believe that no one had reconciled the biggest of Biblical questions; yet here was theory for which Doherty claimed to have solid scholarly answers, with solid documentary evidence.

Perhaps the strangest part of the experience for Ian was seeing the reaction of the others in the group. Their reactions surprised him not because they conveyed shock, but because the other Desoterics didn't seem at all overwhelmed or surprised by the presentation. They sat and listened intently, noting questions on pieces of paper. Sometimes they nodded and whispered to a neighbor. Sometimes they tilted their heads or appeared skeptical. But most of the time they just sat and listened patiently.

During lunch and during the afternoon question-and-answer period, Ian was endlessly fascinated by the dialogue and the tough questions that were being asked of Earl Doherty by the Desoterics.

There were detailed questions, and certainly some debate, about the reference to Jesus Christ in *Antiquities of the Jews,* the book by the infamous Jewish historian and turncoat, Josephus. There were questions about the dating of the writings of the three synoptic storytellers, Mark, Matthew, and Luke. There were questions and discussions of all sorts about references to "Messiah," "Christ," and "Jesus" in the many New Testament letters that Doherty had argued didn't in any way refer to a historical man.

In fact many of the discussions and answers centered upon the Greek translations, so Ian couldn't even understand them. Someone would point out the meaning of a particular verb used in reference to the "Jesus Christ" figure in the famous letter to the Corinthians, for example; then, without consulting notes, someone else would quickly turn everyone's attention to the way the verb was used in other, corroborating contexts within the same letter.

Ian knew he was over his head, but he listened as the questions continued for the balance of the afternoon. By the end of the day his mind was a blur. He almost regretted that he had agreed to go out to dinner with a group of the Desoterics. His mind needed time to recover, and he looked forward to beginning Doherty's books. The fact also remained that he had dinner plans with the document expert, Dr. Sandra Flemming, on Thursday, which would leave only Wednesday night for him to catch his breath.

Ian assured himself that he always enjoyed being around such extraordinary scholars and experts, and knew he'd be remiss to pass up such opportunities—tired or not. Besides, he needed all the help he could get. Perhaps they could provide him some needed balance and perspective to counter what he'd just heard.

Without the benefit of foresight it might seem unfathomable to compare the revelation of that day—November 26th, 2002—to his father's death; his related "angel" experiences with Daniel and Catalina; the day in 1992 when he met Samantha; or the loss of his mother and of Hanna. But the truth was, the events of that day would play a role in causing the greatest, and most tragic, events of them all.

✤

It is often said that the real world can be far stranger than fiction. Mac had once had a friend share an interesting illustration. The friend had told Mac to envision a very long list of numbers—some three digits long, some four digits long, many even six or seven digits long. The list was said to be the results of every lottery that had ever been conducted, by any state or group of states in the U.S., and listed in chronological order since the beginning of time.

"Okay, it's a long list," Mac had snapped impatiently, "but I'm envisioning it."

"Good," his friend had added. "Now I want you to compute the odds of something for me. If we could do it all over again, and re-draw each and every lottery again, what would be the odds of drawing each and every combination of numbers, in exactly the same sequence, as we did on your historical list?"

"Holly shnikees," Mac had exclaimed. "Hell, the odds of hitting any single drawing can be as high as . . . I don't know . . . many millions-to-one. Without scientific notation I have to believe that it would take a ream of paper just to print all the zeros of the number of attempts it would take to reasonably expect a successful drawing of all those damn numbers again, especially in the right order." He and his friend had chuckled, and the friend admitted the odds would be long indeed—probably approaching zero.

"Funny thing is," the friend had exclaimed in the punch line, "it happened!"

Mac had reacted with a contemplative raising of the eyebrows, because for once he hadn't seen the profound punch line coming. The moral of the friend's story was that things can absolutely evolve in funny and unique ways, and if there were a chance to run the experiment of life all over again, just as with re-running the lotteries, things would almost certainly happen in an *equally* improbable way. Nonetheless, the fact remained that events *had* happened exactly as they did—all odds to the contrary.

On that Tuesday in 2002, the odds of what transpired during the evening weren't nearly as long as in the example Mac's friend gave. But the irony and timing of a similarly significant experience in Bill's life, was a profound coincidence nonetheless.

Back in Kalamazoo that night, Bill elected to attend an event at his church. Pastor Mike had mentioned it in the Sunday announcements only two days prior, and it caught Bill's attention, particularly in light of his recent conversations with Ian. It was also a comfortable setting that would give him a chance to perk up Megan, and get her out of the house with Zachary. As it turned out, Dan Huxley was in town for a ribbon cutting, so he and Katherine attended as well.

"Good evening everyone," Pastor Mike said through the Madonna-like microphone that attached over his ear. "This is such an exciting opportunity, and I'm so glad so many of you could make it on such short notice." The room began to settle as Pastor Mike spoke slowly and commanded the room with his infectious and appealing style.

"As I mentioned on Sunday, I received a call from my old friend Stanley on Friday." Mike looked to the seat in front of the stage where his friend was sitting, as if to send him a look of gratitude. "He told me he would be passing through town today . . . and he generously offered to share his well-known and powerful perspectives with you tonight."

Mike paced slowly across the stage as he spoke. "As many of you know, Dr. Alcott happens to be a scientist of extraordinary credentials and notoriety. He also happens to be a great Christian, and a student of the Bible. Now the only thing I'm going to ask of you tonight is that you sit and hear what Dr. Alcott has to say. As I promised you on Sunday, I think that you are in for a real treat, and a message that just may, for many of you, bring amazing focus and clarity to one of the great and confusing questions of our day."

Pastor Mike paused and turned, intuitively creating an expectant pause that gathered every set of eyes and ears in the cavernous church. "There is a big debate occurring today . . . both within the Christian community and in the secular world too . . . about science and religion . . . and especially about evolution."

He broke his sentences with reverent pauses. "But I want you to know that regardless of what you think you know about evolution, the Bible, and science . . . and I know we've got a lot of really bright scientists here; after all, we're the home of the Upjohn Company . . ." The room murmured in response as Mike grinned. "But regardless of your views today, this is an extraordinary opportunity to hear a science-oriented view of Christianity that *just might change the very way you frame discussions of science in the future.* So please put your hands together for me, and give a warm welcome to my brilliant friend, Doctor Stanley Alcott."

Intense applause rang out from the nearly full lower level of the mega church, and Bill looked on with interest as the thin man from California took the stage. Dr. Alcott looked to be in his mid-fifties, and wore a traditional navy suit with a light blue shirt and a red tie. His thick black hair curled tightly against his head and tucked around the paddles of his wire-rimmed glasses. At first sight, he reminded Bill of the guy he'd seen on TV talking about men, women, Mars and Venus—thin, slightly effeminate, confident, comfortable and authoritative, all in the same distinct package.

From the handout Bill could see that he held a Ph.D. in geology, and also a Master's degree in Philosophy. Dr. Alcott said a few words of appreciation and then introduced his topic for the evening.

"Ladies and gentlemen, I know it is a complex and crazy world out there. Having just dealt with the airlines for a week straight, I can assure you that this is true," he began in a kind and trustworthy demeanor. He was the picture of calm, confidence, and warmth. "And it's my hope that tonight I can provide you with some useful information about all of this evolution information that you're seeing and hearing, and perhaps even lift some of the confusion for you who have observed the apparent conflict between our science and our God."

Dr. Alcott continued, "You see, the title of my presentation tonight is 'A Unified Theory,' because really that is what I have to share with you tonight. But you should know that it isn't just my theory. I can produce many references and resources for you tonight—and I will do so—to demonstrate that this unified theory is provable by evidence, provable by science, and fully borne out and provable through God's word in the Bible."

Stanley Alcott smiled and made direct eye contact with the audience as he paused, allowing them to bask in the implicit connection that they were indeed brothers and sisters in Jesus Christ.

"Ladies and gentlemen I wish to share with you a perspective that will unify the Bible and the beautiful insights that science is providing into the truth of God. You see, science relies upon holes being poked in arguments, and you're about to discover that there have been some pretty smart scientists who have been asking tough questions and punching some pretty big holes in evolution for decades. And when all the dust settles from that healthy debate, they continue to prove the conclusion that Genesis is not just a nice, allegorical story.

"Unfortunately, you don't always get to see both sides of this debate, for reasons we'll discuss. I know that sounds conspiratorial, but I don't mean to imply that in the usual sense. It is more a coincidence of shared blindness, based upon a worldview, than it is a conscious conspiracy.

"But I have truly great news for you today. It turns out that the length of God's days described in Genesis don't have to be rationalized to be anything other than what they are—a day and night cycle. In truth I have great news that every single, scientific discovery *ever made*—and even each new discovery about to be made—perfectly confirms what God has told us.

"Let's define some terms quickly. A *materialist* is someone who believes only in what can be seen, touched, smelled, tasted, or logically deducted to exist by things that *can* be measured, seen and observed. A *strict* materialist believes only in matter, and that all things are the result of how matter interacts with matter. Of course that's crazy because no scientists can see the thoughts you are having right now as you sit here listening to me, but that doesn't mean consciousness doesn't exist, does it?" A murmur of assent emanated from the crowd. Dr. Alcott shrugged theatrically. "But that's what they believe!

"The other term for you to know is that *natural science* is 'the rational study of the universe via rules or laws of natural order.'[59] All you really need to know is that scientists tend to be materialists, and naturalists."

The Doctor paused to check for attention. "Everybody with me? It won't get worse than that. If you've hung with me through that, you're half way there." There was rustling and whispered agreement as Dr. Alcott flashed the group another knowing smile.

He continued, "What you need to know, again, is that far and away most scientists are naturalists and materialists. They are also overwhelmingly atheist . . . . I'm not just making that up, many studies have confirmed this to be true."

The room was hushed. "You really must know and understand that reality, because that is my primary point for you this evening. Secular science is the very thing your kids are being taught in the classrooms of public schools, on PBS, and in the newspapers; it is atheistic, materialist, and naturalistic, and it comes from a presupposition that there is no God! There are several surveys that confirm this reality. Nobody debates this."

You could hear a pin drop in the room. To many of the attendees, including Bill and Representative Huxley, it was a disconcerting allegation—but for very different reasons.

It was then that Stanley Alcott made another of his most illuminating points. "What you need to know is that the materialists and naturalists, those who dominate secular science, are basing *their view* of the evidence upon . . . *faith.*"

Everyone was still silent.

"You heard me right . . . . They are basing their views upon *faith.* You see we are all looking at the same facts. Nobody disputes that there are layers in the geological record. Nobody disputes that we look at the same plant and animal fossils. We can hold these things in our hands! We study them! But the fact is that the facts . . . need to be *interpreted;* and that is where we part ways, due to our faith and biases. They have faith there cannot be a God, therefore our sacred document cannot be part of any explanation.

"The materialist and naturalist scientist will not allow any aspect of our comprehensive solution, which admittedly has, as its last step, an element of the unknown—we call it a calculated step of faith—into the debate. They call our faith 'supernaturalism,' and say we cannot even discuss Biblical origins because they are not based upon *their* faith that there is nothing beyond what can be seen."

He continued, "Understand me here . . . . We cannot discuss the historical proof of the Bible, or the comprehensive solution it provides, even though it dovetails perfectly with the all the scientific evidence, because *their* faith and *their* bias remove that option from our hands. We don't even get to enter the discussion, even though their theory is so full of holes that you can drive a truck through it!"

The room was captivated.

"These scientists cannot prove that there is no other dimension. They cannot prove that there is no God. They cannot prove that there is nothing apart from what we can see, touch, smell and deduce. But they take that on *faith!* And all the while they accuse those of us who *admit our faith,* based on the most validated book in history, of being *unscientific!*" Stanley paused again to the let the notion sink in. All eyes were upon him, and he was striking a chord indeed.

Bill was beginning to have a different, but strikingly similar experience to the "eureka" moments Ian had experienced just hours before. Dr. Stanley Alcott was providing a philosophical and scientific framework that would explain the apparent conflicts between the science of the day, and the literal creation stories of the Old Testament—the Hebrew Bible.

"Are you with me?" he asked the group. Heads nodded. Bill didn't join the nodding, but he was fascinated. Thoughts of his friend Ian bounced around in his head, and he thoughtfully paused to say a silent prayer for his friend. He thought, *if only Ian could be here.* Bill was as psychologically primed to bite on Dr. Alcott's assertions as Ian was on Earl Doherty's.

"I'm suggesting that the prejudice and faith of mainstream science *against any possibility of a God or supernatural force*, is blinding them to the true science . . . . It blinds them to reality of the creation story and how science *proves* its veracity.

"I'm further suggesting that any acceptance of evolution is not supported by the science—" The doctor paused, interrupting himself.

"Wait; let me be clear, because this is important. I mean to say, any acceptance of evolution—*apart from* a micro-level, irrelevant, short-term phenomenon that is a tinkering around the edges of life. That part of evolution is indeed *real* and you need to know that." He paused again. "It is confusing, but let me be clear. Microevolution is real, but Macroevolution is not. Dogs don't give birth to lizards, and cats don't give birth to non-cats. So any idea of what we call *macroevolution* is not only unsupported by the evidence, it is *dead wrong* when you open your eyes to the bigger picture."

Bill's thoughts paralleled those of Ian's only hours before. He had begun with a dose of incredulity, but it was tempered by a conscious openness to new evidence. Also similar to Ian's experience, it hadn't taken long before he'd found himself intrigued with the plausibility of the arguments. Bill and Megan looked at each other with expressions of credulous surprise.

Stanley added, "You see, suddenly when we take off the blinders, the so-called 'evidence' . . . I mean the rocks, the trees, the geology, the stars . . . takes on glorious new significance. It provides us with insight into the beauty of creation, and it also gives us a clear and complete picture *that makes perfect sense* with what we know is the truth of the word God gave us."

As if reading Bill's mind, Dr. Alcott said, "You're probably saying, 'But what about all of this evidence? The world just cannot be 6,500 years old.' But it is, and I can prove it.

"Let me tell you," Dr. Alcott said in a booming, preacher's tone, "how *I see the very same facts that the materialist sees!*"

The doctor went on to explain that the geological layers used by materialist science to date fossils and relics found at the various strata, were created not by annual deposits, but by the Great Flood that was now widely accepted as historical fact. The flood was clearly familiar to all in attendance through the story of Noah, who built an ark to save all the species so God could destroy the rest of fallen humanity.

"In other words, it didn't take millions of years to create the layers we see, as the atheists deduce from their biased interpretation of the same evidence. It took a heck of a flood, which they agree happened!

"How about cosmological evidence?" Dr. Alcott continued rhetorically. "The light from distant objects in the universe may appear to be millions of years old, but that's only how it *appears*. The latest physics research tells us that the speed of light has *not been uniform!* Again, I'm using *their science, and their evidence*. And again, the light only *appears* to be millions of years old, but in fact that's because its speed has not been constant—the light is now slowing."

There was a slow building of excitement and adrenaline in the room, and especially within Bill. At a fundamental level, he knew the experience was taking him somewhere profound. He knew that in the end it was going to feel like when he learned the solution to a brainteaser. He was going to wonder how he could have gone so long without seeing the true solution, when it was right before his eyes. To Bill, the theory was a perfect solution indeed, and the majority of any remaining doubts were erased as the doctor continued.

"If you doubt my citations or you doubt what I'm telling you, *good for you!* You should doubt it. But I will give you citations for everything I tell you. I highly encourage you to check out my sources and my logic, and compare my science against the science of the strict materialists."

It just made so much sense to Bill. He was a logical thinker. He was an engineer by training, and this unified theory was open for legitimate criticism.

The doctor went on to explain that there hadn't even been enough time, in all of history, for evolution to work. "Where are all the fossils? Why haven't the evidence of all of these transitional life forms been found yet?" he asked with passion. "They can't explain the sudden explosion of species in the Cambrian era, when all these life forms emerged all at once in the fossil record.

"And why is that?" he asked the audience rhetorically. "Because they view the same evidence through the wrong filter. Once they suppose that anything other than the material world is impossible, they can't see the alternative approach to properly date the geological layers, the light rays, and the carbon-14 data. They reject our Biblical, unified theory from the get-go.

"Now again, don't get me wrong. Things *have* changed and evolved since they were created in those six days, but that's microevolution, not macroevolution. Small changes within species? Yes, okay . . . fine . . . . But big changes that create new species? *You just don't see it* . . . . Folks, this evolution thing *is not a viable theory*. A dog has never given rise to a non-dog. A cat has never given birth to a non-cat. It just doesn't happen.

"I'll give you yet another example of the holes in evolution. The human eye is a complex thing. It is said to have evolved with us since we were simple, single-celled organisms. But the problem is, the human eye simply doesn't work if you take out any single piece of it. It is *irreducibly complex*.

"It couldn't have just grown one piece at time. No way. Not a single one of those parts that make up the eye would have been of any conceivable use without all of the others. Could evolution have created that eye over periods of time? Not a chance. The answer is that its complicated beauty was part of an intelligent *creation!*"

Dr. Alcott kindly and politely explained that large numbers of people were being duped by "liberal enemies," whom he called *theistic evolutionists*. Those were the people who believed in God, but also believed the Darwinian view of evolution was real as well.

"These folks synthesize their belief in evolution with the Biblical creation story by using contrived theories. For instance, they say that the 'days' described in the seven day creation story of Genesis were not intended to be literal, but rather were just symbolic. Or they say that time was relative, like Einstein taught, so the two don't have to be literal and the earth can be old, and evolution can be a slow tool of God. They say that the second creation story in Genesis was after a long 'gap period,' and that the earth could truly *be* millions of years old. They say that it can *all* be true."

He paused. "It's a nice idea, but it just doesn't work that way. The truth is that these believers are unnecessarily falling into the trap of the atheistic worldview."

Finally, Dr. Alcott made the case that creationists are excluded from the established scientific community, and from publication in major science journals, because of the unwritten prejudice that one cannot offer any theory that doesn't presuppose atheism—or at least materialism.

He then drew his arguments to a close. "I've tried to keep this pretty simple, but I do want you to explore this for yourselves. I think you will find that the evidence is overwhelming. For those who want to know more, let me point you toward some free resources. From that starting point, you can then read any of the dozens and dozens of excellent, definitive great books that are out there. I have placed a list of suggest books at the exits, and indeed have my own book available in the lobby. But please know that I don't care if you buy my book, another book, or just go see all the great online resources I'll give you right now.

"Write these down. Here are three great web sites. Go to *www.irc.org*, or *www.answersingenesis.org*, or *www.discovery.org.*"

Dr. Alcott then suggested a summary document available on the Institute for Creation Research's web site. "Get the June, 2005 issue of *Impact* from the IRC web site. You will find an article called 'Evidence for a Young World,' written by Dr. D.R. Humphreys.[60] It will provide you fourteen quick examples of why the earth cannot possibly be fourteen million years old. He'll tell you that there are too few remnants from supernova; comets disintegrate too quickly; there is not enough sodium in the sea when we know that every year millions of tons of salt go into the oceans; carbon 14 is found in geological layers that would be impossible if the earth were old; and the list goes on."

He stood at the front of the platform, paused again, and took a deep breath.

"Thank you so much for your kind attention. I hope this short introduction has been helpful. I'm so hopeful for our future as Christians.

"To summarize, you *can* be both a scientist and a creationist. Today, many, many of the greatest scientists are solidly in the camp of truth, and of this unified theory. They understand the overwhelming evidence that there was a creator."

Enthusiastic applause filled the church, and Bill was starting to feel a surge of emotion. He was a scientist listening to a fellow scientist confirm and explain his entire worldview, scientifically: his loving God had created the world! Now it was plain to see for anyone who cared to learn the truth. It was an overwhelming feeling that caught Bill off guard. It was the missing piece of any doubt.

He wished Ian had been there. He knew he was going to have to hit the books and the web sites and learn more, but he was confident that the information would be there for him to shore up a recap. In the recesses of his mind, just as he'd done with his old friend Flaco, he harbored a hope that he just might be able to persuade Ian.

Furthering his excitment, Bill would soon learn that no one had yet been able to claim a prize offered by a man named Kent Hovind. His offer was a little smaller than the $1 million challenge offered by the James Randi Educational Foundation; Hovind's offer was a mere $250,000, but was available to anyone who could prove the evolutionary hypothesis with empirically verifiable evidence.[61] Even before he left the church, however, Bill knew in his heart that evolution really *was* false, and that God and truth were one in the same.

Dr. Alcott left the group with some parting thoughts. "Many great people have been credited with the following quote, Alexander Hamilton and Peter Marshall among them; regardless of who wrote it, it is more relevant today than ever. It says, 'Unless we stand for something, we shall fall for anything.'

"Ladies and gentlemen, I have great news. The truth of the Lord our God is real. It is proven every day through new scientific discoveries. It was true yesterday, it is true today, and it will be true tomorrow. God bless you and thank you for your kind attention."

Similar to Ian's experience, this solution closed many holes and resolved much of the inner conflict Bill had experienced, particularly the science of the secular world and its conflict with the Bible. Indeed the evening had been a powerful antidote to his latent cognitive dissonance and doubts.

But for Bill, the unified theory was not only exciting in the way that Ian had been blown away by Doherty's presentation. This unified theory of Dr. Alcott's supported such fundamental truths for Bill that it became a highly emotional affirmation of God's love for him.

Bill felt that love in every bone of his body. It was confirmed in that moment that God's promise of Heaven for Hanna, and the hope of healing for Megan, and the worldview in which Bill had been raised, were absolutely real. They were clearer than ever.

Perhaps it was his stress over Megan, or perhaps it was guilt over his relationship with Christina. Maybe it was an overall lack of a relief valve for all his stress and confusion. Bill didn't know. All he knew was that this science lecture had inexplicably caused his eyes to tear.

He worked to hide his emotion as Pastor Mike gave a final word, and the congregation rose for the benediction. Without a doubt in his mind, Bill had been gently touched and reassured by his loving and gentle God.

Chapter 27

A PROPERTY CRIME

The following evening: Wednesday, November 27th, 2002

The second full day of Desoterica proceedings was in its final minutes back in Chicago, and Ian, thoroughly exhausted, was looking forward to his sole evening of freedom to gather his thoughts and catch his breath. At the same time in Kalamazoo, Samantha had just arrived home and dropped her keys on the kitchen counter.

"Okay boys, take off your coats and go wash your hands. Miss Brooke is going to be here with the pizza in just a minute," she instructed enthusiastically.

Indeed by the time the boys had returned and Samantha had placed plates on the table, her friend Brooke pulled in the driveway. It was a drizzly and cold evening, and Samantha rushed out through the garage to help Brooke with the pizzas.

"Hi Samantha! I hope the boys like pepperoni," Brooke said as she walked around to the passenger side of her car to retrieve the two pizzas. She moved with fluid motion and poise in her designer black slacks, her long, graceful stride completely unphased by either heels or haste.

"It never occurred to me ask you what the boys like on their pizza, but I figured I couldn't miss with cheese and pepperoni."

Samantha took the pizzas as Brooke grabbed a bottle of wine and turned to display it briefly with a smile, like Vanna White flashing a quick pose.

Samantha lingered in the misty air as Brooke reached back into the car to grab her purse. "You're so darned sweet. I can't believe you're giving up a quiet evening to come hang with me and the wild Indians; but I'm so excited to have company!" Samantha exclaimed. Brooke put an arm around her friend as if warming her while they hurriedly marched through the garage and into the house.

"Boy it's cold out there," Samantha said as she followed Brooke into the kitchen, placing the pizzas on the counter by the table. "Look what Miss Brooke brought us, guys!"

"Hi Miss Brooke," Brandon said politely.

"Well hello Brandon," Brooke echoed as she extended an upward-facing palm to receive his greeting. "It's good to see you again, my main man." Brandon slapped her hand.

"Andrew, you remember Brooke don't you?" Samantha prodded.

Andrew was the quieter of the two. He smiled and picked up on the suggestion. "Hi Miss Brooke," he greeted shyly.

Samantha was delighted that her friend had agreed to come over for an impromptu girl's night *in*. As if speaking to the boys, she said, "It's so nice of Brooke to pick up the pizzas, isn't it, boys? This pizza party was all her idea."

Brooke replied directly to Samantha, "Hey, I can sit with Sasha and read my trashy romance novels any old night."

Brooke, an account executive at the small advertising agency where Samantha was working, was the firm's leading revenue producer, a fact that would surprise no one who knew her. She was classy, charming, and elegant; and as Ian had ineptly characterized her, "hot." Perhaps that was appropriate enough from his vantage point, but most people would have described her as sophisticated, "a classic beauty," or even "exquisite." She had wavy brunette hair that perfectly swirled away from her flawless, pale skin. It was a look that reminded Samantha of the actor Mary-Louise Parker.

As Samantha finished gathering some napkins, forks, and potato chips, Brooke quipped, "Mind if I snag a corkscrew? This shiraz was practically made for pepperoni pizza."

"Drawer to your right," Samantha instructed. As Brooke turned she straightened her arms in slight shiver, evidence she was unable to shake the chill of the day. "Are you cold? Let me go turn up the heat in here." Samantha darted around the corner barely before finishing her sentence.

"I've just been freezing all day. I guess I'm not ready for this cold weather yet. It just chills you to the bone," Brooke added as she worked the cork from the bottle. "Nothing a pizza party can't fix."

Samantha had come to value her new friendship with Brooke. She especially enjoyed the endearing duality of her thoughtful and gregarious sides, and the fact that they came with no hint of uppity arrogance or putting on airs. Brooke could tell a dirty joke with the best of them, but could also get away with it in almost any crowd. What might be offensive from someone else's mouth, would from Brooke's brilliantly white smile and picturesque good looks, be construed as a sign of her approachability, humility, or even her comfort in being around you. In this regard Samantha thought of Brooke in terms of Princess Diana's reported ability to put people at ease, and to make them feel like trusted friends who were invited to see her fun, private side. At the same time Samantha never knew Brooke to be capable of mean-spirited humor. She was just too classy.

Brooke was good-hearted, and brilliantly diplomatic. Samantha had seen her in action a couple of times with clients, even in one case where a client was stressed over a big event, and had become demanding and verbose during a meeting in the firm's conference room. Ever the poised speaker, Brooke had calmly re-enumerated the remaining tasks and challenges with such clarity that the client was quickly pacified and reassured. To Samantha, it was as if her aura had an innate calming effect on people.

In truth it was extremely rare that Brooke would stumble with words; but then, she wasn't necessarily overly assertive or controlling either—at least not when she didn't need to be. She could mingle at a cocktail party without having to be the center of attention, tastefully conversing yet exquisitely unobtrusive.

Perhaps it was that reserved confidence that made the fit with Samantha so rich. As Ian had astutely detected on the night he first met her, Samantha was "comfortable in her own skin," and at the same time down-to-earth and "one of the guys" as well.

Samantha and Brooke sat with Brandon and Andrew at the table. Brooke had briefly met them before, and they'd seemed to greatly enjoy her kind attention. The same was true that evening.

As they ate, Brooke asked the boys about school, about their interests, their teachers, and even about what they wanted to be when they grew up. She was attentive and sincere, and found their answers intriguing. She was fascinated to see the way their young minds worked, and found their good behavior endlessly charming and cute.

"So, do you guys have girlfriends?" Brooke asked nonchalantly.

Andrew answered sweetly, "I don't, but Brandon does." He was fond of his big brother, and apparently proud of his ability to hold mature relationships.

Brandon corrected Andrew matter-of-factly, "Nuh-*uh*. She's not my girlfriend; I just like her."

Brooke displayed interest, her beautiful smile growing as she looked at Brandon. "Is she pretty?"

"Yep," Brandon said with a shrug, grabbing one last piece of pizza and acting as if the topic was of little interest to him. Brooke flashed a look at Samantha, eyebrows raised as if to say *I guess we're done with that topic*. Samantha grinned back.

It was then that poor little Andrew reached for a piece of pizza and snagged his glass of milk. Almost in slow motion, it toppled directly toward Brooke. Before she could react, the milk cascaded over the edge and onto her lap. She jumped in response.

"Shoot," Samantha exclaimed as she jumped to grab a rag.

"No big deal," Brooke assured immediately. "These pants were headed for the cleaners anyway. Really, it's no big deal."

Andrew looked sheepish and on the verge of tears, but Brooke quickly assured him. "You should see me at home. I spill things all the time. It just happens sometimes."

"I'm so sorry," Samantha said to Brooke. She wanted to apologize more profusely, but didn't want to make Andrew feel any worse. "Do you want a pair of sweats or something?"

"No. Don't worry. I'm fine."

The four of them returned to the business of finishing their dinner, and were soon done. While the boys went and played in the basement, the ladies chatted while Samantha tidied the kitchen. As she passed by the bottle of wine on the counter, she grabbed it and insisted, "Here, at least let me fill you up." Samantha poured more wine into Brooke's glass, then her own. "It's the least I can do after we dumped milk on you." Brooke laughed and waved a hand as if to wave the issue away.

"Heck, having milk dumped on me still beat that date I had last weekend," Brooke joked. "There are times I swear that I'm just too old to date. What a hassle."

"Oh right! Thirty nine and over the hill," Samantha remarked sarcastically. "No way. There are great guys out there for you," she assured cheerfully.

"Yeah but they're all taken," Brooke countered, appearing as if it didn't matter anyway. "That's okay; they all just pee on the seat anyway."

Samantha laughed. "Boy, that's one thing I appreciate about Ian . . . . But that little guy that just spilled milk on you," she shook her head and scowled, "I don't think he's ever hit the damn toilet."

"Well, it probably takes a few years to learn how to use one of those things," Brooke rejoined.

The women then went to sit in the living room. The boys entertained themselves for a while before bed, which gave the ladies time to sip more wine and chat.

When it came time for the boys to take their bath and get ready for bed, Samantha left Brooke in the living room for a few minutes as she went to check on them and ensure things were in order. Brooke kicked off her shoes and put her feet up, contentedly flipping through a *People* magazine.

"Don't forget that I get to read the bedtime story," she shouted back to Sammy and the kids.

She heard the boys giggle in excited response. Before long she was back in the bedroom reading the boys their perennial favorite, *Stewey the*

Crocodile, and soon the women said their goodnights and headed out to the "girl's night" portion of the evening. Brooke stopped on the way to look at some of the older pictures of Samantha and Ian that hung on the wall.

"Look at you, you little hottie," Brooke spouted in reference to a picture of Ian and Samantha by the pool.

"That was a long time ago," Samantha clarified. "And a few pounds ago too."

"Are you kidding, you're so darn cute all the time. You look great."

They looked at a few more pictures and headed to the living room. Before she sat, Samantha went back into the kitchen and emerged with a fresh bottle of wine and two new glasses. "Hey, I don't work tomorrow," Samantha intimated with a smile.

"Gee, now I see how you mothers get by."

"Yeah . . . right. It's pretty rare that I drink much. It's just tasting awfully good tonight."

Brooke kicked up her legs and helped herself to a quilt, again show- ing symptoms of being chilled as she snuggled in. Samantha sat opposite Brooke at the other end of the large sofa, facing her friend with her back against the oversized armrest.

"Are you sure I can't get you something else to wear?"

"No, I'm fine . . ." Brooke paused to flip the blanket over Samantha's feet as well. "I'm curious about Ian's parents. I think that's so sad that they both died so young. Tell me about that."

Samantha shrugged as if not knowing what to tell, but given the direct inquiry proceeded to share the stories: the struggles Janet had with cancer; her remission; Ian's trip to Spain; the death of his father; and Janet's stubborn enthusiasm despite the news of her recurrence during that weekend Sammy and she had first met—the weekend of Bill and Megan's wedding.

Brooke listened intently. As Samantha shared the story of her special relationship with Janet, their regular telephone conversations, and their short, but life-changing time together as Janet's days had drawn to a close, Samantha's eyes became more glassy and distant. She slipped deeply into the memories—the love and the loss—with a level of detail she'd not revisited in some time. The accompanying emotions were resurrected with unexpected intensity.

"I'm embarrassed," Samantha said as she wiped her eyes. She tried to speak, but words came with difficulty. "She was . . . it's just . . . she was the best . . . friend I think I'd ever had . . ."

Brooke sat up and reached her hand straight out to the middle of the couch. Samantha grimaced, still embarrassed and as if gesturing that her feelings weren't valid or worthy of the attention. Nonetheless she extended her hand to meet Brooke's. Ironically, there was something about the human contact that made Samantha cry even harder, as if the attention had cut a larger hole in her shell, through which more emotion flowed out.

At that point Brooke became teary-eyed as well. "Boy, now this is what I call a girl's night," she said with a sarcastic roll of her eyes.

"We're pathetic," Samantha echoed.

But the truth was that a portion of the emotion Samantha was feeling was born of gratitude—perhaps even excitement—for having found a new friend with whom she felt so connected, and so comfortable. She'd always loved her friend Megan, and still did, but with everything that Megan had been forced to deal with, it sometimes seemed that there wasn't enough fuel left to allow the balanced, give-and-take required of a mutually fulfilling relationship.

Being the kind and loving soul that she was, she had even felt pangs of guilt for the increasing satisfaction she'd been enjoying in her time with Brooke. To some degree she wondered if that was how Bill felt as well—unable to be completely fulfilled in the relationship, though certainly through no fault of Megan's. Perhaps that was just the tragedy of real, human interactions. Sometimes love *was* a scarce commodity—with just not enough to go around.

"Probably the wine," Brooke laughed as she wiped her eyes, mascara starting to run.

"Hey, that raccoon look is good for you," Samantha jabbed in an attempt to defuse the emotion further.

"You know, I want to tell you something," Brooke said, suddenly more serious again. "You know that I've experienced loss as well," she said. Samantha just nodded, and the tears began to flow again. She was aware that Brooke had lost her fiancé to an automobile accident over a decade earlier. Brooke was choked up.

"I know . . ." Samantha said from deep in her then-swollen heart. "I'm sorry you had to feel . . . that kind of hurt." She looked Brooke directly in the eyes.

"Shut up, so I can say this," Brooke said wryly, pulling the blanket up a little further. "I just want to say that I've really enjoyed our friendship the last few months. Thank you for including me. I appreciate your friendship."

Samantha was inexplicably emotional. She was nearly horrified at the little sob-fest she was exhibiting, so seemingly out of the blue. At the same time she just couldn't help but embrace the cathartic feeling of the interpersonal connection. As warm and confident as she was, friendships were something with which Samantha had simply struggled. There were many days she'd longingly dreamed of a having a close friend—one whom she could chat with at the end of a day, or drink wine and hang out with exactly as they were doing.

"Me too," she said as she got hold of herself. "Thank you. The truth is . . . I don't make friends real easily. It seems like in my parents' days the women would hang out with the other women in the neighborhood, but those days are gone. I really would say that since . . ." her voice faded. "Damn it." She regained her composure. "Since Janet died, I've missed hanging out, having someone to share with—other than Ian of course . . . which is probably unfair to him."

"You're very lucky to have him."

Samantha sniffled one too many times and babbled, "I'll be right back." She hopped up and darted around the corner, returning with a box of tissues and sharing them with Brooke. "I'm embarrassed. I don't remember the last time I cried like this."

"Kind of cathartic though," Brooke added as she again pulled the quilt higher.

"You poor thing. It's bad enough that you had to run out and get pizza in the rain, in your nice clothes, but then we spill milk on you and I get your mascara all wacky." Samantha was apologetic. "You're a mess," she added. "You know what we should do, is go get warm in the hot tub. The boys are asleep by now." Samantha was suddenly energetic again.

"That sounds awesome," Brooke agreed. "But I don't have a suit."

"Suits? Who needs suits. I'll get you a robe and promise not to look. It's two steps way from our bedroom slider."

"I'll grab the bottle," Brooke affirmed.

A few short minutes later they were stepping out in their robes onto the cold, dark deck. Samantha unsnapped the cover and dumped it to one side of the tub while Brooke held the two glasses of wine. They hurriedly dropped their robes and hopped in to the steaming caldron.

"Oh my god . . . that's better than sex," Samantha said.

"I wouldn't remember," Brooke grunted, "but I wouldn't doubt it. This is amazing!"

Samantha reached over and turned on the powerful jets and blowers, which in turn created a thick cloud of steam that mingled with the already moisture-laden air. The friends sat for a couple of minutes soaking in the warmth. They rinsed their mascara and basked in the heat, which slowly started to permeate Brooke's core.

"You guys must love this thing. Should I be worried about whether or not you put enough chlorine in here?"

Samantha gasped in feigned disgust at the implication. "You're terrible!" she chastised.

"Hey, I was just asking. I know if I had a husband and a tub like this I'd fuck out here all the time."

Sammy laughed again at Brooke's attempts at being humorously provocative. "We do fine, but you know it's *so not* like that—what with kids, life, bills and all."

"Well at least you get *some*."

"You need to get laid, woman. For someone as gorgeous as you that shouldn't be difficult."

"Well, I think I've resigned that it's easier if I just remain monogamous with my vibrator," Brooke said as she took another drink from her wine glass.

"No way! You're serious?" Samantha giggled out loud then sipped from her wine as she sank deeper into the molded seat, looking Brooke in the eyes with interest.

"Well of course I'm serious. Don't tell me that you don't own a vibrator—the single greatest gift to women of all time."

Samantha was intrigued by the concept, and had been curious from time to time, but had obviously never tried one. "I've seen them in movies and stuff, but there's something intimidating about the things. It's like a gun or something. It's a big, intimidating piece of hardware that seems dangerous to have down there," she joked. There was an undercurrent of truth to her words, but her curiosity was piqued as well.

Brooke belly-laughed. "They can be tiny as a thumb, but you perv . . . what do you mean you've seen them in movies," Brooke shrieked playfully as she splashed a small amount of water toward Samantha. "You watch pornos!" The evening had eroded to a near childlike exchange.

"Hey, it's not my fault. Besides, I prefer to think of them as *erotic entertainment*." Sammy giggled as she took another sip of her drink. Her head was swimming as she sat, her flushed face hidden by the veil of steam.

Brooke turned back to Sammy, still giggling herself. Through the fog of the wine and the thick steam, Samantha looked into her friend's beautiful brown eyes. She couldn't help but admire her, and the natural appeal of her wet hair and flawless skin sent a tingle through her insides.

Rarely in life had Samantha ever felt attracted to another woman—perhaps a couple times during adolescence, and perhaps a couple times during sensual scenes of erotica. But seeing her friend's beautiful face a few inches from hers, she suddenly felt a strong compulsion to kiss the plush, lovely lips. Samantha instantly attributed the urge to the wine, and suppressed it.

Brooke looked skyward and said, "This hot tub feels so incredibly good. I'll tell you what, these bubbles and jets are just about as good as a vibrator. I don't know if it's that or the wine, or talking about vibrators, but I'm getting downright horny. I'll tell you what; I would live in this thing if I had one."

As they sat side by side, divided only by the drone of the hot tub pumps and the thick, moist heat, it was like they were in their own little cocoon. Samantha felt a more intense rush of tingling in her stomach, the likes of which she'd not felt in years. And as Brooke had alluded to, the pulsing and broad-frequency thrashing of water was tingling her entire nakedness. She sat still, almost frozen by the depth of sensation.

It was then that Brooke reached down and put her hand on Samantha's, her knuckles brushing the smooth, wet skin of Sammy's side, and said something that hit Samantha like a two-ton brick. "I have never been attracted to women, but as you're talking I've had the urge to totally kiss you. Is that freaky?"

Samantha was speechless, but only for a moment. Her mind was flush with activity. She knew Brooke had been engaged. She wasn't gay.

As Sammy paused to think, the hesitation made Brooke uneasy. "It's freaky . . . I'm sorry."

"No, no. You've really never been with a woman?" Sammy asked.

Brooke turned her face so she could look Samantha directly in her eyes. Sam was also a thing of beauty, the moisture beading in tiny dots around her slightly freckled cheeks, her green eyes dancing with excitement. "I have . . . never been with a woman—"

Samantha leaned forward and their moist lips met. She was overwhelmed by how soft and full Brooke's lips felt, and how tenderly her tongue traced her own lips, then darted into her mouth. In one fluid movement Brooke floated over onto Samantha, the skin of her legs meeting Samantha's just seconds before their breasts met. Brooke's body hovered lightly over Samantha's as their lips remained locked, the smoothness of their bodies enhancing their already intense pleasure.

Samantha subconsciously found her hips beginning to rock into Brooke's pelvis. Their legs intertwined. The warmth of the water, the thick steam, the wine, and the emotion of the evening were conspiring to create something that seemed both childishly silly and careless on one hand, and lovingly tender and meaningful on the other. Samantha didn't know what to make of it, but she was beyond introspection as Brooke's hand found the desperately aching center of pleasure between her legs.

Chapter 28

AN EVOLVING GOD OF CREATION

Thursday was the final day of that quarter's Desoterica symposium. Ian arose early and headed down to the meeting room. He had covered a good deal of ground on *The Jesus Puzzle* the night before, but had nonetheless fallen asleep early. The good news was that doing so had provided him enough rest that his mind was again capable of receiving new information, and he was ready for the long, final day of breakout sessions, conversation and learning that awaited him. Also on the agenda was his dinner with Dr. Flemming, which would turn out to be a fitting end to a profound week.

Back at the third-quarter meeting of the Desoterica, three months before Doherty's profound presentation in Chicago, Ian had been seated at a table next to Sandra Flemming, with whom he'd struck up a conversation. The brilliant doctor had been professorial in her demeanor to a large extent, complete with a dry sense of humor and white cardigan sweater. She even wore her eyeglasses on a chain around her neck. Ironically, and much to Ian's delight, she was also an irreverent cut-up.

Ian had soon realized that Dr. Flemming was also kind and helpful, beneath what appeared to be a slightly curmudgeonly persona. As he had with most of the other Desoterics, Ian enjoyed watching her Socratic style of sporting engagement. She and the others were like kids on a playground at times, testing one another's assumptions with rigorous debate that was akin to a friendly punch in the arm, but always considerate and intellectually honest in the process.

Sandra was an expert in Biblical, textual criticism. In fact Dr. Flemming was one of the leading experts in the world when it came to studying Biblical manuscripts, though Ian had not been aware of that initially. Sandra was an old friend of Mac's and had seen Ian before, but prior to their conversation she had simply thought him to be Mac's assistant. As they talked at that August symposium, however, Ian had shared a little about his non-academic background and how he had nonetheless discovered a passion for learning and epistemology. Ultimately through that meeting, and their polite table conversation, Sandra had seen something in Ian to which she took a liking.

It was lucky for Ian, too, because it just so happened that the keynote at that August symposium had been yet another textual critic, Bart D. Ehrman. Dr. Ehrman's presentation had been brilliant; at the same time it had been a complex presentation, appropriately aimed at the highly-educated audience, often above Ian's head. Ehrman certainly would have been capable of articulating his thoughts to a more general audience, however, as he would later demonstrate with his popular book on textual criticism, *Misquoting Jesus: The Story Behind Who Changed the Bible and Why.*[62]

It had been fortunate for Ian that he was seated next to Dr. Flemming that day, who was one of Dr. Ehrman's most brilliant peers. She had been able to lean over and provide him an appropriate definition or a contextual clue during the more in-depth points of Eherman's keynote. Without such assistance, Ian would have been more lost than he already was.

For instance there were frequent references to documents that contained only letters and numbers as their names, such as P52. Certainly everyone else at the symposium knew that the thousands of remaining scripture fragments had been indexed, and that "P52" meant papyrus fragment number 52. Thankfully, Sandra had tipped off Ian, saying, "St. John's fragment. Probably dated to late in the second century." But to Ian, the entire topic was quite technical and confusing.

He had generally understood that a textual critic was someone who studied documents and used various methods to reconstruct them faithfully, but during the break Dr. Flemming had taken the time to summarize for Ian the enormity and complexity of the centuries-old profession.

She had explained that *criticism* was simply a term that implied careful analysis. It had nothing to do with tearing down or "picking apart" the Bible. Quite the opposite actually, it was a forensic attempt to reassemble a perfect Bible—one that was word-for-word exactly as it was originally written. It was the continuation of a centuries-long tradition of an effort to re-create God's word exactly as expressed in the original letters, sayings, stories and narratives.

It was no wonder that Ian had been initially puzzled by Ehrman's lecture, in part because the enormity of the goal just didn't register with Ian. Despite knowing better in his head, in his heart Ian just couldn't shake his lifelong mindset that the Bible had dropped from the sky complete, typeset, fully prepped from the pre-press department, and ready for mass publication.

As that August day had worn on, Dr. Flemming mercifully took pity on Ian and offered that they should connect for dinner at the November Desoterica, wherein she could fill in more of the blanks in Ian's understanding.

So three months later, two days after Doherty had first rocked Ian's world with a unified theory, and after Bill sat in Kalamazoo receiving another unified theory, Ian and Dr. Sandra Flemming were sipping wine in a fine Italian restaurant, the *Rose Bud*.

"I figured that if we were going out for dinner in Chicago, one of the great dining cities of North America, we ought to avoid McDonald's and go somewhere decent," Flemming said, fully in character as a benevolent curmudgeon.

"Well, I think we've accomplished that goal in spades. I hear this is a wonderful place," Ian responded.

The pupil and teacher reacquainted themselves through small-talk. Ian learned of Sandra's husband, the "old ball and chain" whom she obviously adored, and of her family back home in North Carolina. In turn she learned of his family and Ian's Chicago ties through both Sammy and John.

Soon the conversation turned to the events of the three days, and Ian finally got to ask the question that was dominating his thoughts. "I'm dying to know your take on Doherty's presentation. Do you find his theory plausible?"

"Well sure it's plausible, you saw the vote. But the correct question to ask is whether or not it is *right*," Sandra answered. "But I should warn you that we textual critics tend to be a paradox. We are often deeply theological in once sense, but not in another."

"How do you mean?"

"Well, I wouldn't have gotten into this line of work had I not been dedicated to the Bible, and been very committed to Christianity. Of course that was a long time ago and certainly I could never have seen where my studies would lead me, theologically speaking. I guess my point is that I am a theologian like anyone is, like you are. That means I draw some conclusions about my beliefs. But as a textual critic, my job is very much focused on determining what original documents said—not what we *think* they said, or should say. In that sense I need to turn off my prejudices and theological assumptions, so that I do not bias my view of the evidence."

"That makes sense," Ian said. "So are you saying that you try not to speculate upon theological theories like the one we heard this week?"

"A bright young man you are," she said.

"Truly humbled by your wisdom," Ian responded. He then added, "Heck, you even talk like one of my favorite philosophers, Yoda—subject after the predicate." The extraneous reference was bold for Ian, but he remembered the doctor as someone who enjoyed obscure interjections. He was right.

"The only bitch of the matter," she expounded without missing a beat, "is that Yoda's skin is so much better than mine! I guess that's what happens when you get to be my age . . . . But you are correct in your assessment. I really do try to stick to my life's work, which is trying to find out exactly what the original texts of the Bible said." She spoke in the style of a polished orator, punching the last words for emphasis, and reminding Ian of Katherine Hepburn.

"Duly noted, Dr. Flemming, but surely you must have an opinion for me about the case that was laid out."

"Surely I do. And I'll shall share that with you, but first I want to know your impressions."

Ian looked surprised and felt that any analysis he provided would appear infantile to the brilliant scholar; but he answered honestly, "From the view of a non-scholar, it seemed plausible. It seemed to reconcile a lot of the questions that have plagued me, and plagued Christianity. At the same time I'm sure I could find others who could refute many of his points. I guess that for me an important part of the theory is the dating of the synoptic Gospels. When exactly were they written? Honestly, it seemed the rest of the Biblical, cultural, political and circumstantial case was highly plausible—particularly if the only early historical narrative about Jesus Christ is the Gospel of Mark, and if the other gospel writers were just updating and retelling his 'dramatic play.'"

The conversation was momentarily interrupted by the arrival of the salads. Sandra thought for a second after the waiter left, and then mentioned, "It is interesting that you say that, because certainly I have also always looked at this question of whether Jesus Christ was a historical figure, from the perspective of the New Testament document record."

"So this is obviously not any kind of new revelation to you or the others. I couldn't help but notice that," Ian commented.

"It *was* a revelation to you?"

"I'll show my ignorance, but yes. It was," Ian admitted.

Dr. Flemming grimaced. "My poor man, Godfrey Higgins was born in 1771. He taught himself Hebrew and studied the Old Testament and its origins. Despite significant errors and proof texting, he was a brilliant, renewed voice for these allegations—especially given the limited information to which he had access."

She continued her brief lecture. "Surely you know that Doherty is doing great work, but that he by no means is the first to lay out this case. The forces underlying Christianity have been challenged by these allegations since Christianity took shape—which took centuries. But the modern scholarship and *tools* that have allowed us to re-examine this case for a *mythical* origin of Christianity—say since the printing press gave us the first chance to print reliable Biblical texts for study—are *expanding upon* and substantiating these ideas, not inventing them. These people like Earl

Doherty, or Robert Price, or Tom Harpur are doing great work to bring together a mosaic picture, but it just isn't *new.*"

"Well that explains why nobody other than me was so blown away by the concept that Christ may not have existed at all," Ian further disclosed.

Sandra skewered a tomato, frowning slightly. "Surely you see that Christianity took centuries to develop and evolve, and it did not do so in a vacuum. There were bigger, more popular, competing religions, and a great deal of politics with which to contend. The books you have in the Bible today are the result of political forces—for example what Rome had to do to combat Marcionism."

The doctor stopped for a moment as Ian thought, pausing not quite long enough to swallow fully before continuing. "But it wasn't only Marcion they had to deal with. In the early centuries and before, the region was a complex tapestry of Greek mythologies; various philosophical influences like Stoicism, Platonism, and Epicureanism; pagan fertility gods; and Gnosticism. There were many camps even within Christianity itself. It was anything but the single religion you now know."

"So you're saying this theory that Christ was an amalgam figure, of various mythical origins, is not new?"

"Sakes no, Ian. It's existed from the very beginning. We have similar claims documented by competitors to Christianity from the earliest days. Celsus, the pagan philosopher, and the great Ammonius Saccas, founder of the Neoplatonic school, couldn't even distinguish the Christians from the pagans, and therefore rejected Christianity as just another pagan religion—and that was in the second century.[63]

"Weren't the works of Celsus and those like him largely destroyed?"

"Most of it was, but some were preserved through *Christian* leaders who wrote documents trying to discredit vocal critics like Celsus. You're right though; we lost most of the documents critical of Christianity after Constantine set the stage for the destruction of all the competing scrolls and manuscripts, which was actually carried out *as a matter of policy* under Theodosius, beginning in around 391. Non-Christians were either converted or killed, and the libraries were torched. Certainly we would know a great deal more if not for those damned pyromaniacs," she snorted.

"Didn't they pretty much torch everything secular? It wasn't only religious libraries, was it?"

"Oh no. You're familiar with the story of Hypatia of Alexandria?"

Just when Ian thought he was keeping up, she was again a step ahead. He answered honestly, "Sorry to say I'm not."

"She was perhaps one of the greatest women of history," Dr. Flemming explained. Sandra enjoyed sharing her vast knowledge, despite the appearance of her gruff persona. "Hypatia was the last fellow of the great museum and library in the classical city of Alexandria, in Egypt. She was a brilliant philosopher and mathematician, and oversaw one of the greatest collections of knowledge the earth had known."

"Impressive," Ian observed as Sandra took another bite of her food.

In characteristic style the sardonic expert blurted, "Unfortunately she was hacked to death by a Christian mob as they worked to destroy secularism, paganism, and free thought. Her murderers used seashells to dismember and kill her prior to burning her. They were headed by Cyril of Alexandria, who later became a saint."

Ian rolled his eyes as he sarcastically interjected, "Oh and why *wouldn't* he be rewarded for that kind of commitment?"

"Sure, right," Dr. Flemming chuckled. "Of course it was not only a tragedy in the loss of one of the greatest minds in history, and a pioneering woman, but even more importantly, the library was completely destroyed."

"Kind of makes you sick to think of what was lost," Ian added with a grimace. "Sure sounds like they took the burning of libraries pretty seriously."

"You ain't just clickin' your uppers," Dr. Flemming snarled. "It took until the sixth century before the last of the Gnostic libraries was destroyed, but what they lacked in efficiency they made up for in tenacity."

"Unbelievable."

"They did a hell of a job—so good in fact that many claim such broad efforts plunged the world into the dark ages. It's quite possible we could have gone to the moon in the 1400s if not for such fanatical, anti-reason misology."

"You mean someone actually went to the moon?" Ian joked in reference to the moon-hoax story in the news.

Sandra smiled and continued, "Luckily, the fascists—actually from the Latin 'fasces'—missed a few documents here and there, and regurgitated the arguments elsewhere in their apologetics."

"That is mind-boggling," Ian added before taking a sip of his wine.

"Who knows. Those bastards could have destroyed everything from the secrets of Stonehenge, to detailed, secular accounts of the origins of Christianity. A significant percentage of all human knowledge was surely destroyed . . . in this effort to unite the disparate religious beliefs that spanned the Roman Empire."

"Sure. They thought a single, simpler system of literal beliefs would keep the peace, didn't they? Isn't that part of the argument for how the mythology came to be preached as literal, historical truth?"

"Well certainly that's what some say. I'm not so sure about that though."

Ian sipped his wine again and pondered Dr. Flemming's comments. "So do I hear you saying you believe this theory . . . that a historical Jesus figure did not exist?"

"I've said no such thing," she quickly clarified.

"Well what do you believe? You've studied the Bible your entire life. You probably know more about it than all but a handful of people on earth. You must have an opinion." Ian was dying to get into her head. He was searching for some solid ground amidst all the new and revolutionary concepts to which he'd been exposed.

"I do. My opinion is that it is a complex puzzle that minds much brighter than mine have been working on for two thousand years. But as I said, in the resurgence of scholarship after the printing press, the Protestant Reformation and the Enlightenment, there has been a renewed chorus of legitimate challenges to Christianity's dogmatic foundations."

"Why haven't I heard of these things?" Ian wondered aloud.

"You did this week," Sandra snapped.

"But why haven't others heard of them?"

"Relax, son. They will."

"Yeah but we live in a post-9/11 world where people are doing some amazing things based upon their beliefs, and their interpretations of sacred texts. It worries me. Shouldn't we at least be walking the talk and publicly discussing these things? Remember, I'm a big fan of open dialogue and free inquiry."

"As are we all, but it takes time. It hasn't been until the last fifty years that mainstream scholars—like the folks at the Jesus Seminar, and others—have come to see that literalism is an impossibly flawed approach to wisdom. But many scholars now see that the brilliant work of many post-enlightenment predecessors is provably correct—people like David Friedrich Strauss, who meticulously criticized the literalizing of all these mythologies in a massive book of documentary evidence in 1835.[64] It stands today as a phenomenal piece of work, despite his lack of access to the great historical finds since that time."

"You mean like Nag Hammâdi, and the Dead Sea Scrolls," Ian said, trying to fit what he knew into the larger picture Dr. Flemming was painting.

"Of course. Especially the Gnostic texts of the Christian competitors, and the Gospel of Thomas found at Nag Hammâdi. As I said, they didn't burn *all* of the evidence of non-traditional Christianity." She laughed and raised her glass of wine in a toast to the great archaeological finds. She then added, "But many other innovations in textual analysis too."

"I'm still stuck on the fact that nobody knows about these concepts except some ivory-tower academics."

She again shook her head. "All in due time, my good man. These are sensitive areas in people's lives. This may be a shock, but pastors at the corner churches in your town are not pioneering scholars. They're administrators, leaders, helpers, functionaries. Don't get me wrong," she added quickly, "I love my pastor and as a whole, pastors, priests and rabbis are some of the greatest people I've known. But they're hardly inclined to preach the complexities of Biblical scholarship. Hell, their job is hard enough without adding doubt and complexity into the minds of their congregations. And even if they did understand it, they'd get run out of church pretty quickly. You can't just mess with people's life-long religious beliefs!"

"So you're saying it will just take time, but that we've had centuries of such great scholarship—like from . . . who else?" Ian was trying to get a sense of whether this was just a fringe, conspiratorial strain of people through the years, or a growing vein of legitimate scholarship.

"Oh, too many to name. If I had to name a few I'd single out Gerald Massy in the late 1800s, and the great Alvin Boyd Kuhn after him . . . Northrup Frye . . . . More recently you've had folks like Joseph Campbell, Arthur Darby Nock in the 1960s, Everett Ferguson, Tom Harpur, Earl Doherty . . . many others too."

"Explain to me why we are better at textual analysis today. It almost seems counterintuitive that as time goes by, we have *better* answers. Just like the flawed manuscripts of the Bible—which were hand-written copies, of hand-written copies, of other written copies, and so forth—doesn't being later in the game mean we're further away from the truth?" Ian knew better, but wanted to hear Sandra's explanation.

"Well for one, we are building upon a larger basis of documented, printed, peer-reviewed criticisms and analysis. For instance, we can compare over 5,700 hand-written copies of the Greek Manuscripts. Granted, some are only fragments and many are incomplete, but this compares with only a *handful* of late, poor-quality, *twelfth-century* manuscripts that were compared by Desiderius Eramus to create the foundation for the King James Version of the Bible—a dreadfully inaccurate New Testament with thousands and thousands of errors, many of which are very significant."[65]

"Thousands?" Ian asked, pushing for more details.

"Well actually, between all the copies of hand-written manuscripts that we now have, computers estimate the number of discrepancies at between two-hundred and four-hundred thousand distinct errors and discrepancies—never mind the disagreements about how to translate the Greek in certain key passages."[66]

Ian shook his head. "Astonishing for the great Bible that so many see as the literal word of God . . . . But I'm back to wanting to know your views on this question of the historicity of Christ. This concept is still blowing my mind," Ian said.

"Well, again I'll tell you that I believe it is complicated."

She paused briefly as if figuring how to put it in the right words for Ian, then explained, "I think it will take scholars several more years—perhaps decades—to gain any sort of real consensus. But I suppose you need some context. Since our intent for getting together was originally to discuss textual criticism, perhaps for now we ought to get back to that."

As Sandra finished, Ian filled her glass from the bottle of Pinot Noir that sat on the table.

"I'm all ears," he said. "I can't tell you how much I appreciate having someone of your caliber to talk with . . . to learn from."

"Ah, sucking up we are. I like that." It was clear that Sandra Flemming was enjoying herself. Although Ian was not an accomplished scholar, it was this social opportunity—in the context of intellectual exchanges—that was part of the Desoterica ambiance she so enjoyed. After all, back home there weren't a whole lot of people lining up to enjoy her kind of shoptalk.

Just as she spoke, the entrees arrived via a pair of handsome Italian servers, clad in tuxedos. She paused only long enough to bask in the beautiful sights and smells of what had been placed in front of them.

"So you were saying," Ian prodded, once the servers departed.

"Well in many ways my path was similar to that described by Dr. Ehrman last August. You see, we anal-retentive, detail-oriented folks who also happen to be believers, tend to become obsessed with the Bible. It is the source of our beliefs. In all candor I remain a huge fan of that collection of writings. Again, understanding its hidden meaning and its original contents is the subject of my life's work, to this day."

"So were you a literalist?" Ian asked, sensing the need to keep the brilliant professor on track.

"I was beyond a literalist. By age fifteen I knew the Bible better than my pastor. The problem was that somewhere around that age I began to see that there were significant differences in translations and versions of the Bible. It angered me, because in order to get closer to God, I would have to know which word was actually the one *He* used. I started asking questions that my pastors couldn't answer, and decided to go to Moody Bible College, just as Bart Ehrman did. I became hell-bent on getting closer to the actual, revealed words of God."

"And did you get closer to the true Word?"

"Yes and no. Obviously I went on to much more detailed studies, under-grad then theological seminary where I could really get my feet wet. To truly understand the Bible, as you know, you must understand the Koine Greek of the New Testament, and the Hebrew behind the Hebrew Bible. But I then discovered that it was really necessary to know Latin, German and the romance languages as well, in order to begin to understand the cacophony of criticism about the later translations and texts."

"Wow. I know English," Ian offered as a self-deprecating joke. "So what else do you have to learn to pursue the true rendering of God's word?"

"Well, one must learn the details and methods of textual criticism."

"Aren't there other forms of criticism too?" Ian asked.

"Sure, there is linguistic criticism, which attempts to deal with highly complex language barriers between the Hebrew, Aramaic, and Greek of the originals, as well as the back and forth translations into other languages later. There is form criticism, which consists of methods to look at structure and sociological underpinnings of the writing; higher criticism attempts to investigate origins; and redaction criticism—which deals with editing and transcription errors, of which there are an extremely large number identified by scholars."

"You mean there are known changes, redactions and re-writes in our Bibles?" Ian asked facetiously. He was certainly aware.

"Oh boy, I really do need to go back to the beginning," Sandra chided, sighing. "Okay. Since the accepted time of Jesus' death around 30 C.E., the story of how the modern Bible came to exist over the centuries is really a fascinating one to be sure. It's a thriller, a mystery, a drama, and a tragedy all wrapped into one. Unfortunately, it is a tale that few people understand, and of which to this day many of the details are missing—perhaps lost forever in those fires."

"Boy those Christians sure knew their book-burning, even back then," Ian quipped again as he reached for his water.

Sandra swallowed and continued the dialogue. "But the tale is far different from what you, or at least most people, might think. As you just mentioned, we have none of the original documents that make up the New Testament. Nor do we have copies of the hand-written manuscripts. We don't even have copies of those copies, or copies of those. The stories and letters were written, re-written, re-written, and re-written many times before ever showing up in even our oldest fragments."

"That was news to me up until a few years ago. It's still mind boggling," Ian admitted.

"Well many people still perceive the New Testament as having fallen from the sky complete. They don't realize there were many other epistles, gospel narratives and collections of sayings that could well have been included, but for evolutionary reasons were not. They don't really perceive the New Testament as a collection of disparate letters, sayings, and narratives from across the lands, and from across the years of two centuries—in some cases based upon oral tradition."

"Sayings like those of the Q document?" Ian asked.

"Sure. That's one example."

"So you believe there *was* a Q document?" Ian clarified.

"Well clearly we see an oral tradition in the shared sayings used by Matthew and Luke to refine Mark's story of Jesus' life. Whether it was a document, a song, or an oral tradition of memorized sayings, it really doesn't matter in my view. Matthew and Luke clearly used *something* as a common reference in order to recast Mark's original gospel story, since they embellish the story using the exact same words, phrases and stories. That common *something* was the compilation of oral teachings and sayings."

"Sure, from which scholars have reconstructed what that document probably looked like—the so-called Q document. Didn't it have sections or layers to it?" Ian asked.

"Yes. For example, the first 'layer' of Q sayings were probably from Stoic philosophy—certainly they were *not* Jewish. So yes, I believe there was a Q source."

Ian nodded. "You know, I don't think people realize how long it took before the Bible's contents were done being substantially redacted, and were assembled as we know them. Sometimes they think it was decided at a single meeting or something. But they don't realize it was the end of the *fourth century* before any written list of the canon documents appears in the historical record, and until Carthage, wasn't it, that it was finally adopted?"[67, 68]

"Right, nearly at the *turn of the fifth century*. Pretty good for a pilot who never graduated college." Ian laughed at Sandra's backhanded compliment. "Sure, and some people still think that to better understand the melting pot of ideas behind the various solutions, the canon of the New Testament should remain open even today—and include other ancient documents," Dr. Flemming added.

"But go back, when did the four gospels become known or accepted?" Ian asked.

Dr. Flemming swallowed a piece of steak, then answered, "Bishop Irenaeus is the first record of anyone mentioning or advocating that there should be exactly four narrative gospels gathered to tell the story of Jesus," Sandra explained as she meticulously dissected her filet mignon.

"That's right. And didn't he argue that view because there were four winds and four pillars in the construction of a building, or something like that?"

"Exactly, in *Against Heresies*, but keep in mind that was not until around the year 180! He was also the first to attribute authorship to individuals named Mark, Matthew, Luke and John, and that was *late in the second century!*"[69]

"Which would clearly be shocking to people who think that Matthew wrote the gospel of Matthew, and so forth," Ian added as he glanced down and noticed that despite being a slow eater, he was much further ahead than Dr. Flemming. "I know that I always used to assume that John wrote the Gospel of John," he added.

"Think about this. None of the originals exists, and no human eyes have seen them, probably since the very earliest days of Christianity. Nobody knew who wrote the original letters, documents and stories, except for *some* of the letters commonly attributed to Paul, which he clearly did write."

Ian pressed further. "But with regard to the four gospel stories of Christ's supposed historical life, is there anyone left who defends those as written by the apostles themselves?"

"Oh sure. Just no serious scholar. The Catholic Church will maintain their apostolic tradition, but it's just not possible. Even if we were to assume the historic existence of these twelve apostles, no scholar worth his weight believes the apostles survived and wrote actual, historical accounts. Besides, it was very common back then to attribute authorship of a document to a better-known author, solely to support the lesser author's point of view. But the fact is that not even the great minds *within* Christianity knew of four Gospels, by those four names, *until over a century and a half after Jesus was crucified!*"

"Sure, and if I learned anything from Doherty on Tuesday, the silence is even more deafening from outside the Christian historical record," Ian reiterated. "None of the Gospels has reliable support outside of itself. We know about all sorts of historic details at that time, and for a few thousand years before, but there is simply no corroborating evidence of the Gospel record—earthquakes, all the dead people rising up, a miraculous birth of Jesus of Nazareth, or a crucifixion and resurrection. Surely these would have made news elsewhere." Ian hoped he might prompt Sandra to tip her hand and refute him, but she did not.

"And their silence on virtually every other tenet of early Christian history as well," Sandra said indistinctly, her mouth nearly full. "Oftentimes it's the dog that doesn't bark to which we need to pay attention," she added.

Ian thought for a second and then said, "Tell me more about redaction, and about scribal errors, if you don't mind."

"Well a millennium-and-a-half before printing was invented, if you wrote a brilliant work, you did so on parchment or papyrus. There was no Kinko's, so if you wanted to share the work you had to either write it again, or hire a scribe. The upshot is that the various cultures and natures of scribes through the centuries are an important part of the story. You had great disparity. Early on it appears that wealthier people just copied their own manuscripts, and didn't do such a good job. The anti-Christian writer Celsus, and even his later Christian opponent Origen, both complained mightily about the poor quality of the scribes. Certainly there is evidence that some just copied the shapes of symbols and were functionally illiterate. But other scribe cultures were great. It just varied."

"Right. The only manuscripts the world has seen, since the earliest days, are many generations of hand copies, made by scribes of varying ability," Ian summarized in agreement.

"Right, and clearly the most significant changes were in the first two centuries, where we have essentially no copies from which to work. But of course you can't forget that the challenges we textual critics face include not just transcription errors, or even translation problems, but intentional changes as well."

"So as these new stories were designed to illuminate new ways to read the Old Testament, or even to reject the Old Testament, you're saying that the scribes selectively edited the manuscripts to promote various viewpoints?"

"Well yes, on the micro scale that's true. On the larger scale, political and theological views also drove the ultimate debate about what to include in the New Testament, and what the religion should believe."

"But you can detect these changes through what kind of analysis?" Ian asked.

"Oh, everything from comparing the documentary evidence, to literally tracing changes between different family trees of papyrus—"

"Please tell me that's not your idea of office humor," Ian interjected.

Sandra maintained her professorial demeanor and only smiled as she continued, "There are even notes left in the margins by some scribes, explaining their change. But the redactions run a broad gamut. Nobody questions that these redactions exist. They are provable thousands and thousands of times over—and there are probably others of which we'll never be aware."

"Mind if I jump around further?" Ian asked.

"Shoot," Sandra answered as she somewhat aggressively continued on her steak.

"Did I hear Doherty imply that 'Jesus Christ' could actually have been a fairly generic term that might have meant something very different from our narrow conception of Jesus Christ as a historical man?"

"Interesting and perceptive question, Ian. I'm intrigued by the amount you have learned about this, and by what it is that draws your interest."

"I'd be happy to answer that, but I'll let you expound first—if I'm not interfering with your meal here," Ian said politely.

"Boy, so long as I haven't bent your ear to the point that you're regretting the hot date we've had here, I'm happy to." Sandra laughed at her own humor, her glasses still dangling around her neck and swinging as she chuckled.

"Not only have I had fun, but I'm certainly here to learn. I appreciate the insights."

"Well then, your question is a good one. In my opinion, either of the terms 'Jesus' or 'Christ,' could very plausibly have been used to generically refer to a transcendent being of the spirit world—especially in light of the desire to reinterpret the Hebrew Scripture."

"Really? You think so?"

"With the Greek, Hellenistic thinking came new gods and new philosophies. It's easy to see how both Jews and pagans alike, would have used the terms in reference to the divine, spirit world—the one that existed in successive layers above earth. I know it's difficult for us to get out of our heads the idea that this is a person's name, but that wasn't necessarily the case in the early days."

"That's hard to digest. You're telling me there would really have been talk of Jesus Christ in reference to a god very different from the god of Christianity as we know him? People who hadn't even heard of the Pontius Pilate, Golgotha, Calvary, the miraculous births, the miracles, and the death and resurrection?"

"I'll even go this far . . . just understand that this is way outside my textual field, and is only my opinion. But I think it is quite likely that people could have talked of their emergent reinterpretation of the Hebrew Bible, using the term Jesus Christ, *before* they knew anything about our concept of Jesus Christ, and perhaps even *before the time of the historical man himself*, if he existed."

Ian was again feeling the sense of being both overwhelmed and deeply fascinated at the same time. "That is such a profound concept to me," he said, shaking his head slowly from side to side.

"Even for me, that's a hard paradigm to break out of . . . when I hear 'Christ,' or 'Jesus,' it's hard to think of those as fairly widespread—dare I say *universal* terms."

"I'll say," Ian said, still pondering the significance.

"Let me give you a bad, really bad, analogy. If aliens from the planet Vega come and uncover archaeological evidence of us a thousand years from now, is it possible that they would think John Doe was a real person?"

"You're right, that's a lousy analogy," Ian laughed. "They'd sure think he'd been a busy guy though—traveled all over the place." They both chuckled. Ian thought a little more and added, "Maybe it's not such a bad analogy. They might think *he was resurrected*, since he died so many times!"

Sandra laughed, enough so that her glasses swayed again. "I actually hadn't thought of that . . . . But you were right the first time, it's a lousy analogy. At the same time the term 'John Doe' is just a concept. We use it for dead people whose real names we don't know. And that really is what the 'Jesus' and 'Christ' terms could easily have been—a concept. In this case they were a concept used to illustrate a mythologically significant point, in reference to a savior God who was not believed to be literally on earth."

"Hmmm," Ian pretended to be cynically rejecting her analogy.

Dr. Flemming continued, dropping completely her guise of being out of her field. It was clear that she was fully enjoying the speculative proffering. "You see the Greek word 'Jesus' is the equivalent of Joshua in Hebrew. It simply means 'Yahweh saves,' 'God saves,' or 'savior.' And as you know, the Jesus story was at times just a retelling of the Joshua story in a new light. Coincidence?"

"I see," Ian started to say.

"And 'Christos' is the Greek translation of the Hebrew word "messiah," which means the 'anointed one of God.' So in essence the words 'Jesus Christ' mean 'savior-anointed one.' Despite being clearly of a Jewish heritage, I think it is actually pretty clear that such terms together would have been commonly used, or co-opted, among a broad mix of people and interrelated beliefs—certainly including Hellenistic, pagan worshipers of the mystery cults; Jews; mystics; and later the Gnostics. We know that they each believed in very different Jesuses."

"Do you have any proof of that?" Ian asked probingly.

"Sure. Marcion for example, but don't interrupt." Ian instinctively chuckled at her grouchiness, intuiting that it was just a benign part of her terse style of repartee.

"My apologies. I didn't understand this piece of the puzzle until now. In essence you're saying that this idea explains why Paul, in his nearly two-thirds of the New Testament, never describes an earthly Jesus—his birth, his arrest, his execution under Pontius Pilate, or anything that indicates knowledge of a story like the Gospels. It's all because he uses this commonly understood 'Jesus' term in his reinterpretations of the Hebrew Bible?"

"Well yes, that's what these proponents are certainly saying. In truth that's exactly what Paul *says* he's doing. He explicitly says that nobody told him about this stuff, but that it was revealed to him through the Holy Spirit.[70] There are some who even trace the term 'Jesus,' or 'Joshua'—'Yeshua' in Hebrew, back even to the Egyptian myths of 'Iusu,' or 'Iusa.' According to Gerald Massey and others, those names meant "the coming divine Son who heals or saves," to the Egyptians.[71]

"So they're saying there was *a* 'Jesus' before *the* Jesus?"

"Sure. And others might go further. Tom Harpur points out that the Greek name 'Jesus' wasn't spelled that way until the 1300s, because there were no 'J's in the English language before that. 'J' and 'I' were both used to make a 'Y' sound.[72] The Jewish 'Yeshua' could very well have had its roots in the Egyptian myth of 'Iusa.'"

"So you're saying there was a Jesus concept in Egypt, before there was a *Jesus* concept in Galilee—before there was an iteration of the man we know as Jesus?"

"Well, I'm saying it's pretty plausible. At the same time I've had enough wine that I'd better retreat to our textual framework pretty quickly," she admitted half jokingly.

"That's fine," Ian said with a chuckle, but still persisting to learn more. "Tell me about the non-Christian Christians who believed in a Jesus Christ then," he pressed. "I do know some things about Marcionism. I know it was a very popular, major religion in Rome beginning in the second century—despite the whole celibacy thing." Ian pretended to shiver.

"Well you probably understand the significance of what Marcion did then. He created one of those competing religions that would later be stamped out as heretical, in the centuries after Constantine. But in truth it was he who created the New Testament—in more ways than one."

"What do you mean by more ways than one? I understand that Marcion was the first one to assemble a gospel story with Paul's letters."

"Well yes, that's true, but what was ultimately included in the Roman canon of the New Testament—the one we know—was probably formed explicitly to compete with Marcion."

"Very interesting. I didn't know that," Ian confessed.

"See this rich ship builder by the name of Marcion was a philosopher, a spiritual man, and an early believer in a powerful new experience that he'd gained through the story of 'Jesus Christ.' He was a Bishop, and was largely Gnostic in his beliefs," she explained. "And the story of Marcion is a fundamental element of understanding the origin of Christianity, or more precisely the origin of the New Testament."

"Gnosticism has always been a little unclear to me. Can you define it for me?" Ian interjected.

"Well it's a somewhat fuzzy concept that bloomed in the early centuries, alongside Christianity and the mystery religions. That's why it confuses you. Gnosticism, and for that matter Marcionism and other of the Jesus Christ—or should I say 'Savior-anointed one'—religions, all seem to have grown out of the primordial soup of the various dying and rising god mythologies—such as Mithras; Dionysus; Tammuz; Attis; and certainly Horus—of the Isis and Osiris story."

"Right . . . the myths that Christian detractors have always claimed underlie Christianity . . . . I remember that from a college class I took. But they say okay, you've got these Christ-like stories of unusual births from virgins, deities being born on December 25th, under strange cosmological circumstances, beginning a life of teaching at an early age, teaching a body-and-blood ritual meal, being killed, overcoming death and ascending to rule the heavens, and so forth . . . yeah, yeah, yeah. We know that several dominant, mythical religions like these existed well before Christ. And we also know that the apologists say that they were put there by Satan to test the faith of the followers of the Christ who was yet to come. I'm familiar with all that. So how does that relate to Gnosticism? Oversimplify for me."

"Okay, but I'll keep it short because the story of Marcion is fundamental to understanding the origin of Christianity, or more precisely the origin of the New Testament."

"No problem," Ian replied.

"The word 'gnosis' means knowledge or understanding, and the Gnostics basically believed that knowledge of all truth was within reach of humans. Such divine wisdom was achieved not by rational thinking, but through experience, and through nurturing the divine spark that lies within each of us. Gnostics were dualists, who believed that the gods operated in separate, higher planes above earth. God was at the top, and the corrupted material world was on earth. Gnostics also told stories rooted in salvation myths; those myths involved dying and rising gods who ascended and descended between the divine layers above earth. Salvation and ascent to higher planes came through special knowledge of the divine 'wisdom,' which could also be *experienced* through tradition and symbolic ritual."

"The last Gospel, John, is Gnostic, right?" Ian queried to confirm his understanding.

"Right, written in the second century. But so were various Jewish messianic movements that popped up even before Christ—heavily mystical in their beliefs and similar to the later Gnostics. Gnosticism is what movies like *The Matrix*[73] and *The Truman Show*[74] were about, by the way."

"Never knew that," Ian admitted.

"They viewed the lower world and material creation as tainted and evil—as a mistake. The goal was to ascend back to higher levels of divinity, just as the dying-and-rising gods engaged in epic battles up and down the levels of divinity."

"So you're saying it's all intertwined—Gnosticism, Mysticism, Christianity, paganism, Judaism . . . the Mystery cults? That certainly lends an understanding to how someone like Paul could have believed his 'Jesus Christ' interpretation of Hebrew scripture was not something actually happening on earth."

"Yes. I know that sounds far-fetched, but that's actually the most likely way people would have thought back then. Jews certainly didn't believe in a messiah who would be divine. Divinity didn't mix with humans. They were dualists, they believed largely in the *separation* of material and celestial realms, and that's how they thought. At least until this savior-anointed-one idea came along and suggested a divine redeemer actually descended to earth to reveal the esoteric knowledge to all."

"Wow, what a few days these have been," Ian contemplated. "So that would explain how Christianity could be both a Jewish and a pagan religion."

"Well that's a good segue back to the story of Marcion, who created a very successful brand of Christianity based on Gnostic ideas. If not for a twist in the story, it could well have been his brand of Christianity that Pat Robertson and Jerry Falwell would have been proclaiming."

At that point the waiter returned with a glorious dessert tray.

"Are you going to have dessert, Ian?" Sandra asked.

"Are you kidding? I've still got to hear about Marcionism don't I?" he quipped. They both ordered dessert.

"Okay, back to our story," Ian prodded.

"Well, Marcion was a Bishop in the fledgling church in Rome, some-where around 140 C. E., when disagreements arose among the Bishops. Now keep in mind that at that time Christianity was still centuries from any single doctrine, Bible, or belief. But the short story is that Marcion and the other Bishops parted ways; they returned his substantial donations, and he went on to build a highly successful Christian church, founded upon the school of Christian interpretations to which he subscribed."

"His religion flourished for centuries, didn't it?"

"Goodness yes. It expanded throughout the Roman Empire extremely rapidly, and even further in later centuries. The Catholic Encyclopedia calls Marcionism 'perhaps the most dangerous foe Christianity has ever known,' so you can see it was a major threat."[75]

"But who's to say that it wasn't right? Who's to say that the 'threat' posed by the later Roman Catholic Church was the threat to the *real* Christianity?" Ian asked.

Sandra didn't respond beyond the slight tilt of her head; she just continued, "Marcion was very early in Christianity, a couple centuries before the Church would define Christianity as we know it. But you must understand that his religion played a very big part in where the Catholic Church ultimately went with its theology."

"Kind of like how the Democrats will pull the Republicans left on an issue, or vice versa?" Ian asked.

"Good analogy. Marcion's views of Christianity were very different. He was one of the earliest of those early critics who refuted the idea that our New Testament letters and stories were all literally true and authentic."

"So this dominant religion believed the Jesus Christ story took place in the spirit realm, non-literally?"

"Not exactly. Marcion believed that God's fully divine spirit *appeared* in the form of Jesus, and did interact with our lower realm to free humanity from the evils of the Jewish god. But they still would have understood the meat of the story to have happened in a celestial, mythological realm. I mean heck, as late as the first Nicene council there were still *Bishops* participating in the formation of what would become the Roman Catholic Church, arguing on behalf of the various pagan, Gnostic, mystical and mythical versions of Jesus! They were still promoting Jesus Christ as part of the mythological stories of Tammuz, Mithras, Bacchus, Sol Invictus, and others. Just imagine if we had their documents today—or Marcion's writings!"

She took a quick bite and continued. "Marcionism was a huge, region-dominant religion, and we know from other sources that Marcion wrote extensively about his views. Unfortunately not a single one of his writings survived the destruction."

"Speaks to the skill of the pyromaniac, library-burning thugs though," Ian sputtered.

"I suppose," Sandra replied.

"What did Doherty mean by saying Marcion used 'an early form of Luke'?"

"Well now you're in my field. I can tell you that the Luke we see today was not the original. Let's just say that it was expanded. Most scholars agree upon this, but I'll get back to that."

"Okay, sorry for interrupting," Ian said.

"Marcion believed that Paul had articulated in his letters an entirely new religion, and that the God of Paul was this mythical Jesus figure, *opposed to* and *apart from* the God of the Old Testament."

"So Marcionism was not set upon a Jewish tradition the way that orthodox Christianity is?" Ian affirmed.

"Right. It was opposed to the God of the Old Testament. Marcion figured that the Jews had their own God, so Jesus was fighting for everyone else. He believed that Jesus had simply appeared among Jews to offer them belief in the loving father who would not judge them for their sins, freeing them from the vengeful creator god. Marcion believed people could be righteous simply in grateful recognition of this new Jesus-god."

"That sounds a little odd to my ears."

"This was common of the mystical gods of Greek and pagan influence."

Ian thought for a second, and then said, "Okay. This makes sense. Some of my reading is coming back to me. They believed that the Old-Testament Hebrew god was self-righteous and wrathful. The new god, the Jesus Christ 'savior-anointed-one,' was the good god of love and mercy. What's profound to me about that is that Marcion's story helps explain the otherwise irreconcilable, schizophrenic gods. His solution explains the paradox of the Jesus Christ we've come to know—the vengeful, Old-Testament Jesus, and the nice, New Testament Jesus."

"Well before we speculate too far, the historical story actually gets better. Marcion thought it made sense to collect documents and create a new set of scripture for the new religion. So it was he who created the *original* New Testament!"

"Isn't that amazing. The man who today has been painted as a heretic, actually *initiated* the Christian Bible," Ian echoed.

"Certainly it's interesting. It was largely based upon Paul's letters, ten of the thirteen, plus an early form of the book of Luke. As I mentioned, there was a shorter version of Luke used in the Marcion Bible, which was created in the 140s of the common era. That version of Luke was either the original, or close to it. There is a long chain of evidence that the document later named 'Luke' was extended sometime in the second century."

"Okay, I've got that part. The version we know today was a major redaction, re-write, and reassembly of different views of the 'savior' salvation story. But what do scholars think was added?"

"Well certainly it appears that the first two chapters of Luke were added later—the ones where Luke tries to say how diligent he's been in recording the story. But this is where the rubber meets the road. You see this was also the same time that the author of Luke filled in some more holes in the story by writing the book of Acts—again, mid-second-century here."

Ian understood that a common authorship of Luke and Acts had been accepted for years. "Okay, I'll bite. The obvious question is why?"

"Precisely the correct question, my fine young man," she crowed with great enthusiasm. "The Bishops of emerging Catholicism were incredulous, and they felt the competitive pressure from this wildly popular sect of Marcionism. What they did, was said *'No more!'* They were in a major political and philosophical fight for the heart of the Roman Empire. They decided they would out-flank Marcion at his own game. They would keep the Old Testament, Jewish scripture—clearly a widely accepted and popular belief system. This made the tent larger, kept the Jews on-board politically, and provided the best option for unifying the Empire under one religion."

"Okay, so they triangulated an approach, but how did they do it?"

"Well while a group of what we'd call 'traditional' Bishops couldn't stand Marcion, they also seemed to think Marcion was on to something by creating a new book for the new religion. Judaism had long been a religion of tradition and books, despite the illiteracy rate, so it made sense to create a new canon, and an official set of new scriptures."

"So they made the first New Testament," Ian said.

"Right. And I don't want to sound too conspiratorial, because they were likely motivated by their 'correct' view of the Jesus story, but there is little question that they redacted Paul's letters and assigned Pauline authorship to new ones, and changed Mark's original version of the gospel narrative. They essentially rewrote and assembled a theology that was a case against Marcionism, so there is little question that politics and power were motivating forces behind the formation of the theology. These were humans, after all."

"And all of this is well over a century after the supposed crucifixion and resurrection," Ian confirmed in a skeptical tone. "But I still ask, what changes were made to round out their Bible?"

"They reshaped Paul's epistles slightly, and added new ones—not written by Paul, obviously, since he was long dead in the year 140—in order to make him less heretical and to fuse him into their version of the Christ story. They wrote the Acts of the Apostles; expanded Luke by a couple chapters, parts like the temptation of Christ; and wrote a strangely unique sequel—the Gospel of John—which certainly had Gnostic underpinnings, but would sell well with most audiences.

"Most importantly," Dr. Flemming began. She sat up straight and looked Ian right in the eyes, as if to ensure his full attention. "Acts completely recasts Paul. Paul's largely mystical view of Christianity was considered heresy by those who opposed Marcion. The Galilean Jesus of Nazareth, who walked, performed miracles, prayed a Lord's Prayer, was born of a Virgin Mary under amazing circumstances—none of that existed in any of Paul's letters. Paul had never heard of the guy, 'Jesus of Nazareth.' But what the author of Luke/Acts was able to do in response to this widely popular Marcionism, was to fuse the narrative gospel of Mark's Jesus story, with the totally unrelated, mythical savior-anointed-one religion of Paul. They married Paul to Mark."

"Not that there is anything wrong with that," Ian joked.

Sandra gave Ian a scowl for his bad joke. "I mean that he was able to fuse their accounts together, fictionally and permanently, to make it appear that they knew of each other's stories, and to recast Paul's letters in a light that undermined Marcion. Paul was no longer preaching a cosmic, mythical, Hellenistic, anti-Jewish, 'son of god' message, but could instead be seen as supporting a gospel 'truth' that preserved the Jewish heritage, even if his words never tell of such a man."

"So by now some might have been taking literally the Jesus Christ story that Mark created?" Ian asked rhetorically. "Wow. Okay. The pieces are becoming clearer. But why did the Roman version win out? Just because its tent was larger? Perhaps its theology was better—or even truer?"

"Politics, Constantine, Theodosius, a simpler Jesus story that the masses could understand, dark ages, Ecumenical Councils battling it out, wars, power and more politics . . . . Without getting too far into the complexities of these factors, the bottom line is that you know who won. It wasn't Marcion."

Ian canted his head in a gesture of intrigue, then said, "They sure aren't kidding when they say truth is stranger than fiction, at least not if this history is accurate. But no matter what, I've got a pretty good picture that this inerrant book is really a shabbily collected group of unreliable documents that were molded, shaped and changed over the years."

"Take it easy my good man. I wouldn't begin to go that far. I've dedicated my life to trying to ascertain, or reconstruct . . . or should I say to at least closely approximate the true, underlying texts. And I've done so because I believe it *can* be done, and that by doing it we can better understand both God and truth—which many claim are one-in-the-same. But that said, everything I've said certainly illustrates the challenge of getting at God's real meaning."

"But you're obviously questioning the case for a literal, historic Jesus," Ian stated, somewhat as a question.

"I look at it this way. We think of history as larger than life. We romanticize and mythologize. But if we could dial the hands of a clock back to yesterday, then dial it back to the day before, and then a year back, and a year before that, all the way back to the year 7 B.C.E., we could see exactly how this stuff unfolded. Somewhere back there we could see that there really was a *'way that it actually happened.'* I like your word, Ian—truth. We would see historical truth."

"Fascinating concept when you think of it that way."

"As we go back, we just watch. The best part is we get to go see the day and time of the alleged resurrection, birth, Sermon on the Mount, parting of the Red Sea, and the whole nine yards."

"And the billion-dollar question becomes, what do you think we'd see . . . say in Gethsemane? Was there ever a crucifixion of a historical Jesus?" Ian asked.

"Wouldn't you like to know," Dr. Flemming said with a coy smile.

"All right. Disclaimers aside, have you just been messing with me, or do you accept the dating that Doherty suggests for the Gospels?"

"Well, I think he's dead-on right on the dating," Dr. Flemming said, again setting all disclaimers aside.

"And do you think it's likely that Doherty is right that our 'Jesus Christ' figure grew out of a single, narrative story, written by one man—Mark—as a brilliant piece of midrash intended to tell an allegorical, countercultural, anti-establishment story of a new way to experience the Hebrew God of Scripture?" Ian asked, almost breathlessly. He had a new sense of excitement that Dr. Flemming, with all of her decades of textual analysis behind her, was affirming his groundbreaking experiences of the week.

"I really do," she said.

Chapter 29

THE "IT" EPIPHANY

Late that night, Chicago, Illinois

Ian had continued reading from both of Doherty's books after returning to the hotel, but after doing so he simply couldn't shut down his mind. There were so many questions that needed to be asked, and so many elements of the mythical Jesus idea that just made so much sense. At the same time he was constantly struggling to remind himself of the fact-based, truth-driven methods of science and reason. He knew he had to try to control his excitement and that it would color the way he viewed all of this new information. It just wasn't easy.

Then, at about three-thirty in the morning, in a fit of mental activity, it hit him—a haunting recollection of what his friend John had said on Monday night. He'd said that to come even *close* to proving there was never a historical Jesus Christ, would be like revealing *'a secret of the universe.'* He thought about that statement over and over. He pondered the truth in that statement. After all, everyone would agree that Christianity had dramatically shaped the globe as we know it, and is still doing so. What if someone could actually prove that it was a grand illusion? How might that shape the world with regard to other beliefs and religions?

Ian thought about the Desoterica discussions and how Mac and the group knew it needed a focus. He thought about the capacity of such a diverse group to examine such a question thoroughly. He pondered if it was possible to deliver a credible, definitive answer to whether Christ existed, and how long it would take. While perhaps a concerted effort might accelerate the "decades" that Dr. Flemming predicted, if indeed she was right, even a focused effort could take years.

As Ian was lying in his bed, he also thought of the public relations realities of such an effort. Political and social forces from all sides would seek to undermine the work at every corner, and popular acceptance of any answer, whatever it was, would be very unlikely.

Ian's mind just wouldn't stop. He thought. He thought more. He got up and made notes. He thought more. After some time, he knew he had to talk with Mac—and *now*.

Thump-thump-thump. Ian knocked on Mac's door. He knew Mac was an early riser, and had a final breakfast meeting before their departure, but this was *really* early. Then again, Ian rationalized, *Chicago was an hour earlier than Michigan so perhaps his body clock had him up already*. It didn't matter. Ian knocked again.

The door opened. "What's wrong?" Mac asked as he saw Ian standing there, already showered and dressed. Unlike Ian, Mac was still in sweats, a robe over top, sipping coffee and reading a newspaper.

"I'm so sorry to bother you, but I had an idea that I have to run by you. Do you remember *'it'*?" Ian asked, immediately realizing he was being sketchy. "Do you remember the media craze all last year about *'it,'* the secret, skunkworks-style project that was going to radically change global transportation?"

"Come in, sit down, and tell me what the hell you're talking about," Mac grumbled as he walked back into the room and sat down. "You're talking about Ginger, the Segway Human Transporter, right? The thing they called *'it'* all of last year. They speculated week after week on the *Today Show* and every other network program about little pieces of leaked information. I thought it was going to be one of the small, affordable jets like the Eclipse, but it was a little fucking scooter . . . . So what—you've invented a new form of transportation?" Mac cracked, pretending to be grumpy and sleepy but in truth welcoming the intrusion.

"Right. Exactly," Ian replied sarcastically. He scowled and sat in the other chair. "Now set aside the media hype over 'it' for a second. *I know what the future holds for the Desoterica.* I know its single, laser-focused mission, and it's of monumental significance." Ian paused for dramatic effect. "It is nothing short of a future that includes answering one of the *secrets of the universe* . . . or at least discrediting a fundamental assumption about it, one held by a couple billion people."

"Like the one, for instance, that says the Judeo-Christian God created it?" Mac chuckled under his breath—a combination of interest and skepticism. "I'm all ears," he added.

"What if I told you that there was a covert operation underway as we speak, that was dedicating massive expertise and resources to solving one of the most important questions in human history? What if I told you that the group was composed of the leading scholars, historians, archaeologists, and geologists in the world? And what if I told you that they have determined that Jesus Christ was an amalgam figure of mythological evolution, and never walked the earth as the literal person we know through Mark's Gospel account? And further still, what if they could *prove it?*"

"I'd say we're close today."

"First, no we're not. Second, nobody knows it, even if we are close, and even if we explained the complex theory, they wouldn't believe it anyway, and they won't believe it in the foreseeable future. If it is true, it'll trickle out over hundreds of years, and probably evolve into some new religion, the way these things always seem to do."

Mac's mind started processing Ian's disparate thoughts. He was starting to get the point, and suddenly his facial expressions started to reflect a serious, if not excited, contemplation.

"So what are you suggesting?" Mac asked.

"Well first, I'm suggesting that the group dedicate itself to answering the question—'Did Jesus Christ exist as a historical figure as described in Mark's Gospel?' I'm also suggesting we focus single-mindedly on defining the variables involved, and determining a methodology for answering such a question. Nobody's really tried to prove a negative like this before, and certainly not in the process disproving one of the world's major religions. It would be incumbent upon us to prove something in the affirmative, not just point out irreconcilable inconsistencies in the literal story. It would not so much be proving that he didn't exist, as it would be documenting and *proving* the entire evolutionary tree of Christianity."

"Right, like where the Eucharist—"

"Yes but every element, every grain of sand, every tiny pebble of the whole story—baptism, scriptural references, how each document got into the Bible, Eucharist, theological elements, philosophical elements—"

"And you'd have to do the same for every single verse of the New Testament, and ideally the Old Testament too," Mac affirmed.

"Right. Now you're getting to the crux of the issue. I'm suggesting that if the group were to determine that a human never walked the earth as Jesus Christ, based upon a solid methodology and however much time it takes, that we would create . . . as part of explaining what *DID* happen . . . a new . . . *Bible* . . . *The Bible of the Desoterica.*"

The idea was exciting to Mac, but he outwardly showed nothing beyond mere interest. His wheels were turning rapidly as Ian continued, "We would create a *true* Christian Bible that told the story as precisely and honestly as possible, just as if we dialed the hands of the clock back and relived the evolution of the religion, day by day."

Mac sat silently, digesting Ian's thoughts further. Ian had temporarily rested his case, allowing Mac more time to scratch his unshaven, gray stubble. After a minute he speculated, "It would *not* be well received."

Ian leaned forward. "Right. That's why the group's work," he said in a hushed, emphatic tone, "must be kept . . . *secret.*"

Mac was silent for a few more seconds, then he shifted to a more optimistic tone and said, "I see where you're going with the '*it*' story. You're saying that the ultimate deliverable—the Bible or whatever—would have to be controlled, and anticipation would have to be built . . . . You're suggesting we toil in silence to undertake a question of Biblical proportions—pardon the pun; and if, and I do mean *if*, the case could be proven, create an '*it*'-like campaign of careful leaks—"

"Which would happen anyway," Ian interrupted.

Mac finished his thought. "The leaks would imply that a leading group of scholars was on the verge of proving a major breakthrough."

Ian leaned forward again, his eyes big. Slowly and emphatically he looked at Mac and whispered, "Not just a major breakthrough . . .

A secret of the universe." Ian leaned back, his eyes not leaving Mac's. Again he rested his case.

"It'd be a monumental undertaking. Most of these people have other lives. We meet only three days a quarter," Mac said. He was excited, but trying to point out obvious holes in the idea.

"Are you familiar with Wikipedia, the project that came out of Nupedia earlier this year?" Ian asked.

Mac nodded, already seeing that Ian had pondered the obvious question of how to collaborate on technical documents over long distances. "It's a collaborative, online tool . . . a wiki, right?"

Ian smiled knowingly. He knew that Mac knew about all the research being done into the power of collaborative workflows, collective intelligence, and wikis—web sites that allow users to actually edit and improve the content. Such concepts had already been used by programmers to develop brilliant, free software like Linux, and were being used at Wikipedia to create a dynamic, community-written encyclopedia that was more comprehensive and fluid than traditional encyclopedias, and rivaled their accuracy.

"And to think that just a few minutes ago I was perfectly content to sit and read my newspaper," Mac grumbled. But his face told the larger story. He looked at Ian with a smile he couldn't have wiped off his face had he wanted to.

A few hours later Ian left to load and prepare the Citation for the flight home, while Mac wrapped up his breakfast meeting with an old friend. Ian's mind still reeled from the week, the dinner with Sandra, and certainly from his early-morning epiphany, but he worked hard to stay focused on safety and flight operations for the quick trip home.

As Ian and Mac departed Meigs Field that day, they didn't know that it would be the last time they'd ever fly out of Ian's favorite, big-city airport. Despite an agreement with the federal government to the contrary, four months later Mayor Daily would bulldoze the airport's sole runway during a finger-flipping midnight gesture, reclaiming the land for the city.

But far more importantly, Ian also didn't know that he was headed home to a candid, but slightly nervous admission from Samantha that she'd stumbled into an extramarital, sexual encounter. He also didn't know that Bill soon would be confronting him with new proof that the Bible had again been proven infallible and perfect in its explanations of creation, and that by deduction, evolution was provably false.

Of course the biggest thing they didn't know was exactly what the future held for the huge undertaking of the Desoterica. Clearly wherever it went, it was going to shape the lives of Ian and Mac in profound ways. That much they knew.

But it was still larger than that. The evolution of ideas surrounding religion and sacred texts, which they were about to alter, would affect not only how Ian and Mac lived out their remaining days, but how others lived theirs as well. After all, the evolution of philosophy and religion affected peoples' approaches to intimate relationships, politics, family, charity, science, and virtually all aspects of human interaction.

For some in the group with Kalamazoo ties, the work of the Desoterica would even affect where, and when, the final, solitary step in life's journey—that mysterious end-of-life transition that seemed to drive much of humanity's need for answers—would ultimately come.

Chapter 30

THE COMING STORM

Seven years later: Sunday, October 11th, 2009, in the air over Missouri
"Good evening Kansas City Center, Lifeguard-Citation four-three-niner-mike with you at flight level three nine zero," Ian transmitted as he checked on with the next sector. The Compassion Flight home from Kansas City to Kalamazoo was proceeding uneventfully, and Mac and Ian were bantering about in non-Desoterica related conversation.

After two years of intensive initial analysis, and five years of dedicated work, the massive "Project Gamma," as the Desoterica had named their covert project, was in the final stages. It had become all-consuming for Ian and Mac, and for many long hours every day—and often on weekends and evenings—Ian and Mac toiled on some aspect of the monumental undertaking. As a result, the charter business was all but completely on hold. David Kurtz had moved on to a full-time job, and the duo had made the decision not to replace him—partly because of secrecy concerns, and partly because they just didn't have the time to tend to the business.

Early that very morning their Project Gamma had received yet another mention in the national news media, this time on CNN. The 42-year-old Ian, and the fit, 65-year-old Mac had begun the day nearly giddy with excitement over how perfectly the plan was coming together. The short follow-up story added to the growing anticipation about a "major announcement" that was rumored to be "coming within weeks or months," by a "group of prominent scholars."

Speculation about the contents of the announcement had run the gamut from a definitive discovery of other life in our universe—perhaps even in our own solar system, on Titan—to the discovery of the Ark of the Covenant. It had often been noted in these brief reports that some covert group of scientists was known to be frequently traveling the globe, chasing mysterious documents, and even meeting with heads of state. Some of the reports repeated rumors that the secret announcement would be of historical, even Biblical significance, while others described it as revealing nothing less than a great secret of the universe.

The project had dominated Ian and Mac's conversations on the trip down to pick up their patient; but over the course of the day the change of scenery and attention to flight duties had allowed each of them to shift gears away from the usual, single-minded focus on Project Gamma.

The flight had arrived in Kansas City to pick up a stretcher-patient returning to Kalamazoo after her final surgery away from home. Lori Webster was recovering from her third spinal surgery—the result of a car crash while visiting relatives. A summer deluge in Missouri had changed her life forever.

The jet was en route high above the darkened Midwest, just over St. Louis. In the back with Lori were a nurse and Lori's mother, but it had been a long day for the family and only the nurse remained awake.

"I see your buddy in Congress got his latest piece of pet legislation passed," Mac said to Ian as they sat back for the cruise portion of the flight.

Huxley had gained significant power in Congress, and was still working to be a champion of child safety. In particular he had just succeeded in getting another piece of legislation passed, "Hanna's Law II," which cracked down even further on the "epidemic of drunk driving." It required all states to lower their thresholds for drunk driving to a blood alcohol content of .06 percent.

"You know, what I don't understand is how he claims to be such a conservative," Ian responded. "He's usually opposed to government involvement in the lives of individuals. He loves to talk about the tenth amendment and how the federal government can only legislate in specific, constitutionally assigned areas, but then he takes on an issue that the framers of the constitution clearly wouldn't have expected Congress to screw with. Instead he does an end-around and uses billions of dollars of federal transportation funding to twist the states' arms."

Mac grunted in response.

"Furthermore," Ian continued, "I've been skimming that book I told you about, and this sociologist makes a pretty compelling case that the science and evidence tell us that only *really* drunk people smash cars and hurt people . . . and I mean DRUNK people, like .15 BAC and up. This guy says that the original drunk driving limit of .15 was based on research done by the American Medical Association, and it showed that danger escalates dramatically above that point, but not so much before."

"I meant to tell you I heard him on NPR the other day," Mac interjected. "He said exactly that, that the numbers show it's the people who get bombed and drive 90 miles per hour down the expressway, on the wrong side, who kill people. It's not the social drinker who has had one pint of beer. But he said that in a lot of states they'll lock you up, take your car, and perhaps cost you your job, for just that—even one beer."

"Right, which is absolutely fine if you want to outlaw alcohol, or if you have a moral issue with drinking. That may be a legitimate view, but be honest about it," Ian formulated aloud. "If the data are right, and I don't know for sure . . . but if they are, don't say it's because those social drinkers are out killing people if they're not."

"I know, I know," Mac teased, "it's about finding the truth through evidence." Mac flashed Ian a grin and continued more seriously. "But to that point, this guy also was saying that the data-collection methods are fatally flawed—"

"No pun intended?" Ian interjected.

Mac rolled his eyes and continued, "His point, and you probably know this, was that the check-box for 'alcohol-related' includes a whole bunch of non-causal factors. If somebody is sitting at a red light after consuming a single drink, and gets rear-ended by an inattentive, yet perfectly sober driver, the box gets checked."

"Right. And by unfair association, the alcohol is always assumed to be the cause of the accident, even in the tiniest of amounts."

Ian loved to banter about on such topics. He wasn't taking a position promoting the consumption of alcohol before driving, but the topic appealed greatly to his fascination with beliefs that were potentially untrue, or at least appeared emotion-driven when compared to the evidence.

Mac scanned the turbine inlet temperatures and engine data as they talked. "Yeah, he made the point on the radio that people get in accidents all the time. There is a naturally occurring accident rate per 100,000 miles driven, but the assumption is that for those who have consumed any alcohol at all, they shouldn't have any fender-benders. Their accident rate, hypocritically, should be zero, while it's an accepted fact of life that everyone else can have fender-benders for any number of real-life reasons."

"So in other words if you could separate out the accidents that are really *caused* by the alcohol, they are relatively few, and we're back to his assertion that it's people bombed out of their gourds who break things and hurt people," Ian summarized. "And even then they often kill only themselves."

"Right, it's a classic case of the availability heuristic," Mac said, referring to the more advanced study by social psychologists about how the mind formulates ideas and solves problems—an area of great interest to both Mac and Ian. "People see dramatic examples of innocent lives taken by a truly irresponsible, bombed-out driver, and the human tendency is to easily bring that example to mind, which in turn makes the voters think it is far more common a problem than it is statistically."

"Right. It's why people live in such fear of plane crashes, internet predators, or child snatchers."

"Have you ever had that conversation with your friend Huxley?" Mac inquired.

"No, I haven't. I don't see him much anyway . . . wouldn't do much good either." Ian paused as if struggling with a thought. "Let me ask you a question, Mac, do you know the name Patti Nelson?"

"Can't say that I do," Mac replied.

"I do. I've thought of Patti Nelson so many times in the last couple years. She's the woman whom Megan cut off when Hanna was killed. She pleaded guilty to the DUI in order to avoid manslaughter charges . . . . It . . . I'm . . ." Ian stumbled in his speech, obviously tongue-tied as his thoughts outpaced his mouth. "I mean . . . as if she didn't suffer enough during the ordeal. The point is that the accident was *not her fault*. Megan will tell you to this day that she didn't see the car coming because of the angle of the sun, and she turned directly in front of Patti as she came over the rise in the road. Patti was doing the posted speed limit of 50 miles per hour, and there's no way she could have avoided the accident. It was Megan's fault!" Ian repeated.

"So Huxley blames Patti, and says on TV that a drunk driver killed his granddaughter," Mac said as if fueling Ian's fire. "So maybe it's just a sad, tragic, isolated example that illustrates the point of the book you're reading."

"Maybe. I guess that's why we have to trust the data. But the bigger point about Huxley is that it's just the type of issue he always points to at election time. In his ads they say *'He's been a doer, not a talker. Look what he's done to protect you; he's gotten tough on such-and-such,'*" Ian mocked. "It's just all symbolic. What if it really doesn't make the world a better place, statistically? What if it's not real?"

Mac just shrugged his shoulders. After a brief pause, Ian's mind snapped into gear again. "You know the funny thing is that he's *not* sinister. I really don't mean to imply that. He's trying very hard to make the world a better place. He really is."

"I don't doubt that for a minute," Mac acknowledged, "But it doesn't mean he isn't self-delusional about the issue. We're all human. He could certainly be rationalizing a convenient re-election issue. The mind is a mysterious thing . . . . Maybe his mind needed a better explanation than 'his daughter killed his granddaughter due to inattentiveness.' Maybe that was just too hard to swallow for a caring guy who likes to fix things."

Ian agreed. "Sure. We all do it. We all interpret things the way we need to in order to live with ourselves, and to make sense out of this chaos we call life. So in that kind of scenario it might just be easier to blame someone else."

"Or something else—alcohol. Perhaps he had a bias against alcohol to begin with?" Mac postulated.

"Not at all, actually," Ian replied.

"Well perhaps he subconsciously knew he needed another re-election issue, so his own brain took the path that worked best on several fronts—being outraged at Patti Nelson. That gave meaning to Hanna's death, gave him a renewed sense of purpose in his own life, *plus* it provided the re-election issue. The brain is certainly capable of such things, without requiring any sinister planning on the part of the one making flawed conclusions."

"You know he's a good guy. He really is," Ian said again. "I just no longer see the world even close to the way he does. He thinks it's cool for his daughter to do natural childbirth out of some inexplicable desire to 'get back to nature,' but he intervened to force-feed Terri Shiavo, and keep her from dying a very sad, but *natural* death. He doesn't think twice about all the discarded embryos that result from couples seeking to have children by in vitro fertilization, but ardently opposes stem cell research that could very well save and improve so many lives. We can prevent cervical cancer now, but he speaks against the HPV vaccine on 'moral grounds,' which really means he thinks that we shouldn't remove fatal consequences from fucking. That's his real objection—that people have sex. Apparently he's happy to *leave in place* that fatal consequence, so if people do it they'll pay the ultimate price."

"Just like he talks big about overpopulation and AIDS in Africa, but is against condom distribution or morning-after pills," Mac interjected.

"Yeah, like I've said before, I think they've created a false idol of celibacy, and they have said that their idol is more important than human life." Ian was on a Huxley bender. "He thinks homosexuality is an 'abomination,' yet doesn't seem to mind eating shellfish—or ham, which are also 'abominations,' and probably even more offensive to God, at least from the context of scripture."

Mac said nothing. He just listened, letting Ian run with his thoughts as if it were somehow therapeutic. Of course, he didn't disagree with anything Ian was saying, either.

"I mean . . . I genuinely like the guy, I just feel like we're on completely different planets at this point." He crosschecked flight parameters out of habit, then added, "But then again, that goes for his son-in-law too."

"Do you ever see Bill and Megan these days?" Mac asked, continuing his questioning in a counselor-like, low-key, non-judgmental style.

"Sometimes . . . for birthdays and stuff," Ian answered. "Much as I love Bill like a brother, if I had to be honest and say it out loud, I think the truth is that we've just not been as close in the last year or two."

"That's sad. You guys were friends for a whole lot of years," Mac said, scratching the distinguished gray whiskers that had become increasingly visible in the 14 hours since he'd shaven.

"We're still friends," Ian again corrected.

The reality was that the friendships between the four had indeed drifted. It wasn't that any individual didn't like or didn't respect any of the others. It was complicated, the way human relationships often are.

Following the pivotal week in 2002 when Ian and Bill each had his own profound but diametrically opposed experience, the men had engaged in several extensive conversations. One such conversation was right after that earth-shattering week, and took place back at the Keppler house during a gathering for Brandon's birthday. The crowd had dispersed and the two middle-aged men wandered to the family room to watch football. The conversation had predictably turned to their respective epiphanies, and they had discussed the *competing* revelations thoroughly.

As also happened in subsequent talks, the conversation had been passionate at times, but the guys maintained the plausibility of an intellectually honest conversation. They had exercised active listening, clarified points where needed, and listened to each other actively.

Unfortunately, as often happens when complex issues have no clear, right/wrong solution, the dialogue did not compel each individual toward common ground. Rather, it affirmed to each individual that he was arguing a logically superior view—much as happens on a broader scale when people discuss controversial issues.

Over the months that followed, each had dug deeper into his respective "unified theory." Not surprisingly, each had found substantial amounts of additional evidence to support his views. Ian had the Desoterica and its debate, which at that time had found enough legitimacy in the case against Jesus' historicity to dedicate a massive investment of time and energy to formally seek a consensus answer.

For Bill's part, he had purchased and devoured all the creationist books by bright individuals like William A. Dembski, John Wilson, Michael Behe and others, and had become wholly confident that the best solution to all life's big questions *was* the single God of the Old and New Testaments.

While both guys had always remained committed to their friendship, and were sophisticated enough in their thinking to consciously and explicitly remind themselves that the friendship transcended the legitimate disagreements of philosophy and science, the reality was that there had been a growing shadow cast upon the pleasure each received from being in the company of the other.

Either of them would have denied that cold, hard truth; but the reality was that the human desire to be right, and the drive to be affirmed by one's self and by those with whom he associated, was shaping the friendship. Mary Matalin and James Carville may have been good at it during those years, but it was often difficult for mere mortals to sustain deep, caring relationships, with people with whom they differed so dramatically on religious, philosophical, or even political beliefs—particularly if both individuals had domineering, type-A personalities with a strong need to be "right."

Most observers could have understood this reality. Most people knew the feeling of spending time with someone with whom they viewed the world so very differently. And as much as each individual might have thought he was above condescension toward the other because of their differences, there was a tiny voice in the back of each brain that would rationalize why he was ever so slightly more correct than his opponent. Try though he might, each individual's subconscious mind valued his own worth slightly above that of his "less smart" friend. It was the dirty little secret of such disagreements. By virtue of believing he was right, each felt the other was either not quite as smart, or at the very least was misguided; and as a result, being together for long periods felt draining and uncomfortable.

Similarly, one particular friend of Bill's—a Christian—had maintained a friendship with a Mormon. He couldn't help but chuckle, deep in his heart of hearts, at his Mormon friend's acceptance of the church's doctrine, as espoused by the founding prophet, Joseph Smith. Much as Bill's friend loved and appreciated his Mormon pal, the man's insistence that ancient Israelites had traveled to western New York in the sixth century B.C.E., inscribed golden plates with sacred scripture, and provided visions and codes so that Joseph Smith could dig them up and decipher them *in the 1820s*, was just too much nonsense to take seriously. He would privately joke that the career with the worst future in the world was that of Mormon archaeology, because they just weren't having any luck digging up Israelite settlements from the sixth century B.C.E.—*in New York!*

In the mind of Bill's Christian friend, there was an elephant in the room when he engaged in serious discussions with his Mormon friend. He would never have admitted the reason for his perceptions, but given the choice, he found that it took less effort to hang out with other Christians than it did to be around his Mormon friend. It was just easier and more comfortable. In the end, his friendship with the Mormon waned as a result.

Whether either would admit it or not, this same dynamic was at play in the long-time friendship between Bill and Ian. They loved each other and were still friends, but there was an elephant in the room. It was an undercurrent of disagreement that would hover below the surface, only to try to percolate back through the surface when incidental topics of faith, morals, or church arose in conversation.

From there, things got even worse as Bill learned enough to know that Ian was dedicating an increasing portion of his professional life toward what he saw as an effort to undermine Bill's God. He increasingly felt Ian was misdirected and misguided in a way that could never be helpful or meaningful for Ian, and certainly not for the world at large. Bill saw religion as the source of morals and order in the world, despite being misapplied or confused by humans at times—in the case of religions other than Christianity. On the other hand he saw a lack of religion, as Ian was expressing, as shallow and highly unconstructive.

Bill didn't use the word "evil," and would not have done so, but the truth was that deep down, from his worldview, that was increasingly what he believed was behind Ian's activities. He could still love the sinner and hate the sin, but his own voice of conscience was sending a clear message about Ian.

Despite the strengthening of Bill's own faith, his previous speculation that Ian's search would bring stronger acceptance of the reality of God's truth to Ian and others, was being squeezed from Bill's mind. He no longer saw much upside to Ian's efforts; and the truth was that Ian intuitively knew how he felt.

On one occasion some years earlier, their conversation had eroded into a pointed discussion of their philosophical differences. Again it was a good-natured conversation to the casual observer, but the disagreements were causing emotional reactions and a "digging in," as each pressed his argument further.

They had been talking metaphorically about God moving someone's pencil as a test of that person, or people taking action because God told them to, when Ian said, "You admit that from President Bush right down to a number of people at your church on any given day, people are taking action based on what they *think* is God's will and choosing, when certainly some of the time they're dead wrong—it's merely of their *own brain's* delusional choosing. Nobody can be all-knowing of God's will unless he is God himself, right?"

"I agree," Bill had said.

"So I say we should just stop the nonsense, and use science and reason in our daily lives—even during those two hours on Sunday morning. Let's stop trying to speculate about magic, what might or might not be going on in some supernatural, magical world, completely outside the entirety of all human knowledge, and let's try to save ourselves as a human race! Let's not just do things because we *feel* emotionally that they're from God. That's just too unreliable, and too unpredictable! There is too much at stake!"

Ian was on his soapbox. He should have quit then, but he didn't. He launched into a fast-paced tirade. "If we are all on a sinking ship, let's not all sit and decide whether or not the hole in the boat was caused by God, or sit and pray over how to get God to fix it. Let's just fix the fucking boat. Let's save ourselves!"

There was no turning back at that point. Ian just kept rolling, his pace quickening. "It's the same thing with AIDS in Africa. While millions of people are dying, the Kenyan Arch-bishop just organized *burnings of condoms* and educational literature! The fricking Catholics put their *false idol* of celibacy—which is not supported by scripture, by the way—*above human life!* I think *that's* evil, and it's based on what they *think* God tells them. Everyone may be 100% right—there may *be a God*. But while we're stuck on spaceship Earth, it seems we should just quit trying to speculate about the unknowable, keep our heads in the game, and take care of our fellow humans without this magic mumbo-jumbo."

Finally Bill had jumped in. "And who does that better than people of faith? Who takes care of their fellow man? . . . I can show you a family from just down the street that literally smuggles five tons of food and clothing to native Mexicans across the Texas border—people who have no shoes, no water, no land, no bathrooms, and are subject to horrific discrimination and persecution within their own country. I don't see any atheists banding together to do that!"

In another candid exchange that took place much later, Bill said something that resonated with Ian, though even Ian didn't realize it at the time. In actuality, it resonated enough to genuinely irritate him at the time, and as conventional wisdom teaches, sometimes the things that most hit home are the ones that most need to be examined for the truth they contain.

In that conversation, Bill again had begun to refute Ian's militantness by hounding him about the emptiness of atheism—which by then was a term from which Ian had begun to distance himself, preferring 'agnosticism' and professing simply to have stopped trying to define the unknowable supernatural. At the conclusion of Bill's case he'd said to Ian, "At some point you're going to have to realize that you atheists are *against* everything, and *for* nothing . . . . I mean, what do you do if you win? What if there is no God? So what? Where is that taking you? How is that going to be better for you or for the world?" It was a question that would ruminate in Ian's mind for years. *Was it really a mission of contrarianism, of being against everything and for nothing?*

Some of those old memories bounced around as the Citation glided along in the high-altitude blackness of the night. "We're still friends," Ian repeated softly. He peered out the window into the blackness below.

✤

As the business jet crossed the western portion of Illinois, several hundred miles to the north of its route Bill and Christina lay beneath the covers, wrapped in the comfort of their skin-to-skin cocoon. The Madison weather was cool and rainy, which added to the intimacy of their rendezvous.

While it was warmer to the south, Madison sat just to the north of a warm front, with a strong southwest jet stream spewing warm moisture down through the low clouds and onto the streets of the city, in a continuous symphony of splats and trickles.

"That was amazing . . . you are amazing," Bill whispered to Christina. Still lying on their sides in a sustained embrace, he looked into her dark eyes and kissed her. "You have no idea how much I looked forward to being with you tonight."

She looked at him with a coy smile, kissed him back and said, "Ah, you just like having sex."

"You're terrible."

"Okay fine," Christina cooed. "If I'm forced to admit it . . . I'll confess that I looked forward to this too." A broad smile came over her face. She shifted gears slightly. "You realize we've been doing this for seven years now? I sure have enjoyed . . . uh, using you to advance my career," she joked, her more serious tone quickly reverting to playfulness.

As if protecting themselves, each of the lovers would often make their affections known, but would usually stop short of being overly explicit or emotional with any declarations. It was clear that what they had could not last forever, but it was something they had chosen not to dwell upon, as if by agreement. Each knew that something could change, and likely would change, someday.

For some reason, however, that night Bill felt compelled to assure Christina. "I try not to worry about tomorrow . . . today," he began as they were lying motionless, still basking in their naked warmth and comfort. "I know you know, but . . . I just want to make sure you know . . . that I understand there will come a time when you move on and outgrow the ability to be with me." Bill's voice conveyed a palpable touch of emotion.

For him, the relationship had been so fundamental to his ability to survive and thrive, and such a profound blessing in what had otherwise been a deeply trying, day-to-day struggle, that he would have had difficulty ever expressing it to anyone—even Christina.

Christina didn't say anything in response. She just put her face very close to his, as if studying his features. Her eyes went back to his and she kissed him again on the lips, tenderly and lovingly.

In any movie or drama, a cliché affair would have had Christina's character upset that Bill wasn't intending to leave Megan for her, but the reality of Bill and Christina was far beyond such fictional dramatics.

Christina loved Bill and greatly respected him, and she understood his situation. He in turn understood hers—her career, her desire not to become mired in a traditional relationship at that point in her life. At the same time, what started as a recreational retreat from chaotic and lonely worlds had grown into something much deeper and more valuable than either had predicted.

"Hey, it's only seven-thirty you old man, let's go down and get something to eat."

"Let's do it," he replied.

Back home, Megan's depression had ebbed and flowed, though she had recently shown signs of improvement again. Still, Bill continued to see the two worlds of Christina and Megan as completely separate. That night as he and Christina got ready to head downstairs for some food, the compartments of his life were safely sealed and segregated.

The reality, however, was that he loved two women, in two very different ways. Nothing in his way of thinking would cause him to change any aspect of his situation, though he recognized, however subtly, that external forces could certainly bring change upon him. All he knew was that Christina had been a savior to him, a human companion who helped him through, second only in redeeming power to his God.

The truth was that if there was one small conduit through which ideas flowed between the two compartments of his life, it was God. Despite his profound disagreements with Ian, he had digested and affirmed in his own mind that Ian and his sources were right about the typical interpretations of Biblical statements concerning adultery and sexual ethics. To Bill, Christina was undeniably a life saver, and one who was tossed into his churning and violent sea not by a human hand, but by none other than God himself.

Chapter 31

TERROR BENEATH THE SKIES

It happened as the cockpit was quiet. Out of routine boredom, Ian reached to preset the radio with the next anticipated frequency—the one for the Chicago Center controller who would handle the succeeding segment of their flight through central Illinois. Radio tuning was in-flight housecleaning, something to do when nothing needed to be done. As his father used to say, "If you've got time to lean, you've got time to clean."

"Attention all aircraft, attention all aircraft, Chicago Center," said a low, authoritative voice. Ian and Mac snapped to attention. This was a relatively rare transmission, usually reserved on Center frequencies for a broadcast request for assistance with an aircraft that had lost communications.

The voice continued. "Attention all aircraft, all sectors. This is Chicago Center. Be advised that we are under a priority-one national emergency as of this time, 13:17 Zulu. I repeat, we are under a priority-one national emergency. We are going to need your prompt attention and cooperation in clearing all U.S. airspace for a national emergency. All aircraft will be grounded. Be advised that unlike 9/11, instrument conditions prevail through much of our Center tonight, ladies and gentlemen, so this will restrict our capacity to land you all quickly. Proceed currently AS CLEARED to your original destination, but expect holding instructions and a change of destination forthwith. Midway and O'Hare remain open now, but it is possible they could both close to inbound traffic. Break—"

The radio went silent for just a moment, long enough for Ian and Mac to look at each other with very serious expressions. Mac shook his head slightly from side to side. "Fuck," he said, under his breath.

The voice returned quickly; "Chicago Center . . . . That's it folks. Expect holds and deviations to new destinations. Please confirm instructions as briefly as possible, and hold readbacks unless you have a question. I repeat, even readbacks of holding instructions are NOT required unless you have a question; just confirm receipt of instructions with your call signs."

Ian and Mac were silent, tensed in anticipation, and the radio was silent, when a lone, unidentified voice keyed a cockpit mike and said reverently, "God bless you all, and God bless the United States of America." Silence returned.

The poignant statement moved Ian and Mac. Ian had been through a number of in-flight emergencies, and performed without undue hesitation, or even undue emotion, but suddenly he felt a surge of emotion—a mix of anger, fear, and sorrow. He felt as if his eyes were going to tear-up, but he fought the urge; to distract himself, he jumped to find approach charts for the most likely alternate airports.

There was no time to obsess about his family. He told himself that this would be an isolated event geographically, like 9/11, and that surely Sammy and the boys were safe back in Kalamazoo. The only problem was . . . it didn't help him to feel much better.

Ian and Mac sat quietly for a couple of minutes, intently listening as a flurry of radio instructions began. One by one, aircraft in their sector were being diverted, routed, or directed into holding patterns. The simple reality was that the air traffic system worked fine on clear days, but any time there were instrument approaches required at big airports, delays crept into the system. The spacing between airplanes had to be kept much greater when the planes were in the clouds and could not see one another. On 9/11, the pristine skies had allowed rapid clearing of the airspace, but this day was definitely going to be different.

"Wonder what it is?" Ian ventured, voicing the obvious question. "Almost makes you want to ask."

Mac didn't respond. He knew Ian was just venting. Neither of them would dare cause any undue delay in a packed radio frequency that was being used to deal with a national emergency. "I'll handle the radios; get on the air phone and find out what's going on," Mac instructed.

Ian was glad to hear the instruction. They didn't use the air phone very often. It wasn't that Mac didn't have the money, but in addition to its expense, they just never had call for it. This, however, was a very necessary use.

Ian thought momentarily, and then dialed Samantha. The first call didn't go through, but on the second attempt he could hear it connect. "It's ringing," he confirmed aloud.

"Hello?" Samantha answered expectantly.

"Sam it's me."

An uncharacteristically fast-paced, distraught voice was on the other end. "Oh my God, Ian! Oh my God. I'm so glad you called. I just knew you were okay. But Ian, what do we do?" There was panic in her voice.

"Honey, I need your help. I don't know anything. We're still in the air. What's happening?"

"Ian, they think . . . downtown Chicago is like . . . gone."

"Holy fuck . . . like a nuclear?—"

"Yes, Ian . . ." Samantha lamented tearfully. "Oh my God, Ian. They think it was centered right downtown."

Just then Mac raised a hand so Ian could see. A radio call was providing their amended clearance.

"Hang on for one second, sweetie. It'll be okay. Just stand by one second," Ian instructed as he put his headset back on in order to hear.

"Citation four-three-niner-mike, understand you're a lifeguard flight?"

"Affirmative, four-three-niner-mike," Mac confirmed.

"Okay, is there any reason Indianapolis wouldn't work for you, sir?" the controller asked in a rushed and stressed voice. Every other transmission had been an order and command, but the "lifeguard" status had at least garnered them one chance to reply.

Ian quickly barked to Mac through the headset, "Tell them 'No,' it's a stretcher flight with special transportation waiting in Kalamazoo."

"Negative, ATC. Sorry but we're a stretcher flight with specialized care and ambulance waiting in Kalamazoo. Flight time's the same to each so we'd request Kalamazoo please."

Ian and Mac looked at each other expectantly. Ian whispered under his breath, "Come on. Let us go home . . . let us go, it's the same frickin amount of time . . ."

"Citation four-three-niner-mike, roger, proceed direct Kalamazoo."

Ian skewed his headset and put the phone back to his ear as Mac confirmed receipt of the instruction.

"Okay Sam, it's okay. They're letting us come home to Kalamazoo. We'll be there within an hour. Now, are you okay?"

"Yes but I don't know what to do. We're just across the fricking lake from that thing, Ian, what do we do?" Sammy asked with increasing desperation.

Still talking into the phone so Sammy could hear, Ian said to Mac, "It's a nuclear explosion in Chicago; Sammy needs to know what to do in Kalamazoo."

Mac's eyes widened. Ever the military professional, he barely hesitated. "How big?" he asked.

"Don't know. Hey Samantha, what are they saying? Mac wants to know how big the explosion was?"

"I don't know. They're just saying that a bunch of buildings in the Loop have been destroyed and that sensors show it was a nuclear detonation."

Ian repeated her words to Mac, who said, "Tell her to stay inside at all times. There could be fallout headed toward her. If she has plastic and can seal any doors and windows, great. Close the chimney flue." He fired his instructions rapidly, but his final words were reassuring. "Tell her she's got time, and with any luck this southwest wind will carry any cloud north of Kalamazoo. She'll be fine. She really will."

"Sammy, Mac says you'll be fine. He knows about these things and we think a cloud, if there is one, will go north of you. I'm coming home, okay, but in the meantime you need to play it safe and do some things for me, okay?"

"Okay," Sammy replied, somewhat reassured.

"Mac says it's safe for us to come home, so don't worry. But he says you need to stay inside at all times, and seal the house up as best you can. I have some duct tape on my workbench, and just bought new plastic for moving leaves. It's on the shelves. Have the boys close the flu in the fireplace, and seal anything that is drafty, like the front bay window."

"Brooke is a wreck; is it safe for her to travel over here?" Sammy asked.

"Probably, but I'd tell her to hurry."

"Tell her to stay downstairs most of the time," Mac added.

"And Mac says to stay downstairs when you can," Ian repeated to Sammy.

"And if you have to go out, shower afterward," Mac said.

"Sam, Mac says if for any reason you do have to go outside, you should shower when you come back in." He repeated Mac's rapid-fire instructions much more slowly and with less urgency than they were received.

"And turn off the furnace blower," Mac suggested to Ian as he thought of yet another item.

"We don't have one—boiler," Ian replied to Mac.

"What did you say?" Sammy asked.

"Oh, nothing. I was talking to Mac. Okay, honey, did you get all that? It's going to be fine."

"I love you Ian, just come home. I'm okay though. The boys have been great. Just be careful and fly safely, okay?" Sammy said, now reassuring Ian.

"I will—"

"And Ian," Sammy interrupted. "I don't know who we pray to anymore, but say a prayer to the universe for John, will you?"

Ian felt a tremendous rush of emotion and could barely conclude the phone call. "I will . . . I love you . . . tell the boys how much I love them and I'll be home soon."

❖

As Bill and Christina arrived at the sports bar to find the evening NFL games displayed on multiple television screens, they felt fully immersed in the cocoon of their private retreat. Bill was holding the fall sales meeting for NALA's Midwest district at the hotel on Tuesday, but had needed the day Monday to set up and prepare. Not entirely coincidentally, his early arrival provided the perfect chance for the pair's late-Sunday meeting. They would spend that night together, and Christina would simply appear to arrive and check into a room, like the other salespeople, on Monday.

Green Bay had already won its game, so the bulk of the crowd had cleared out of the sports bar. A few college kids remained to flirt and fraternize with the bartender and their other young server-friends, despite the hotel's northeast location being well removed from the Badger campus. A few other hotel guests populated the bar as well, mostly road warrior men, but the sports lounge was far from full.

Bill and Christina had just ordered their food and were at the end of their first beer when the bulletin interrupted the game. The knee-jerk reaction of the remaining crowd was to whine about the interruption, just at the point of a critical third-down conversion attempt for Denver, in their battle against the Seattle Seahawks. "Aw . . . come on," the crowd murmured in muffled groans, but it didn't take more than a second or two for the room to go silent as the bulletin's splash screen was followed by a warning tone—the one only heard during tests or tornado warnings.

"Ladies and Gentlemen, the tone you've just heard is a notice from the Emergency Broadcast System. This is a national emergency. Stay tuned for instructions."

Popular anchor Stew Sheppard appeared on screen as a staffer could be seen exiting from the frame. "Ladies and Gentlemen this is Stew Sheppard with NBS News. This has become a dark day in American history indeed. NBS News is reporting what would appear to be a large-scale explosion in downtown Chicago, which at this time is believed to be the result of a nuclear detonation. I repeat, it appears that a nuclear device has exploded in Chicago, Illinois."

"Holy shit," Bill exclaimed in a whisper.

"Details are sketchy, but a massive explosion ripped at the heart of the city just minutes ago, destroying multiple landmarks and buildings. The explosion created what some witnesses are calling a 'mushroom-like cloud,' but rain, clouds and darkness have made it difficult for us to make direct observations, as you can see in this live skycam footage from the nearby Sears Tower. Sensors in the area, however, *are* showing evidence of radioactive fallout; so again, we ask that you to please not panic, but stay tuned for instructions about how to handle this unfolding crisis."

In a somber, macabre reminder of historical television moments like Walter Cronkite's J.F.K. announcement, or Katie and Matt's 9/11 coverage, the choked-up anchor's speech slowed as he added, "Obviously there are believed to be . . . extensive casualties as you can imagine. Our thoughts and prayers are with our nation and these people. Right now, however, it is vital that I proceed with the business of these important instructions for those in the vicinity who have survived the explosion.

"If you were near the blast, or even if you might be downwind of the potentially radioactive dust cloud—called fallout—the one that will be spreading from the site of the blast, here is what you need to do."

Bill and Christina sat and listened intently. As they glanced at each other with shock, the same force that was ripping apart lives in Chicago was shattering the wall between Bill's worlds. Bill was immediately obsessed with Megan and Zachary, but such a rapid torrent of thoughts was traveling through Bill's mind that he couldn't focus on any single detail. He just needed to listen to the TV and gather more information so he could better know what to do.

NBS gave concise, detailed instructions for those who were injured, burned, or contaminated by radiation to various degrees. They also pointed out that it was very possible that people away from the blast might have been exposed to the radiation without even knowing it, especially those who were outdoors.

"Radiation is an invisible, tasteless, odorless, and painless form of energy. If you were outside, anywhere near or east of Chicago, you should immediately move indoors and shower to remove radioactive dust from your body," Stew instructed. "Place your clothes in a plastic bag, seal that bag to contain the radiation, and store it somewhere safe."

The extensive instructions continued, particularly for the hundreds of thousands of people who were potentially downwind of the radiation cloud. Stew cut to the network's meteorologist who indicated the most likely path of fallout was a northeast track across Lake Michigan, and into the lower peninsula of that state. He hastily drew lines on a map of the region. They resembled the cones of probability used in hurricane predictions, or the lines that just moments before had been used to analyze football plays. The lines placed the zone of highest probability between Kalamazoo, Michigan, and Traverse City, Michigan.

Bill's cell-phone rang. A quick glance at the caller ID showed that it was Megan. "Hey are you okay?" Bill asked as he answered. There was a genuine, powerful sense of concern in his voice, yet somehow he'd been paralyzed from making the call himself, as he dedicated his brain to the options for getting home.

"Yes I'm fine. Are you okay?" Megan asked, obviously upset, but still composed. "Are you in Madison?"

"I made it through Chicago hours ago; I'm fine. I was going to call in a second but I'm just trying to understand this. I'm trying to figure out how to get home," Bill assured her.

"Bill, those people . . . John . . . I'm so scared."

"I know, sweetie," Bill affirmed, the lump in his throat exacerbated by Megan's verbalization of his own thoughts. It was all starting to sink in, and to Bill it felt almost as if Armageddon was upon them. The world was changing dramatically, right before their eyes.

"Is Zach home with you?" Bill asked, fully aware of Zach's fifteen-year-old social tendencies toward frequent travel. He was always out somewhere, running with friends or going someplace—particularly now that his best buddy could drive.

"Zach was out with Quinn, but they just pulled in the driveway," Megan exclaimed.

"Are they in the house now?" Bill asked.

"Yes, they just came in . . . . But Bill, what do we do?"

The exchange continued along a path similar to Ian and Samantha's, with the added benefit of a little bit more information. Of course the shock and disbelief had turned to fear about Kalamazoo's proximity to the blast and any potential fallout.

"Just keep listening to the TV and do what they say. Have them shower and put their clothes in a plastic bag if you think they were contaminated—but it sounds like you'd be plenty safe so far. Start sealing up the house. Store some water in case the power goes out—I'd fill the bathtubs now. I'm going to come home, but I'm just not sure how, yet . . . . Stay on the phone; I want to listen to the TV," he told her.

With 9/11 now over eight years behind them, there had always been a sense that something might happen, someday, but it was as if nobody even considered a nuclear possibility. For all his achievement and knowledge, Bill just didn't know much about nuclear bombs and fallout. For that matter, neither did Ian, though he had the good fortune of having a military man with him who had also been raised during the height of the cold war. Mac had solid knowledge of what to do in such an event, but Bill and Ian really didn't have the slightest idea. Thankfully, the networks were doing a respectable job; they must have been relatively well prepared.

Everyone remaining in the Madison hotel sat quietly, a few talking on cell phones as Bill was. Christina sat and listened to the TV intently, remaining perfectly silent for obvious reasons.

Additional instructions from the TV network pertained to evacuation, particularly in the Chicagoland areas, but it was unclear, even there, which areas should be evacuated. Stew advised people to await further instructions, but where visibility to the streets allowed, undamaged parts of the city showed a chaos many times worse than Manhattan during 9/11. Masses of people were running down the expressways, which were a sea of abandoned cars, people, and panic. Clearly, a mass exodus of the city had quickly begun, whether it was prudent and necessary or not.

Stew also covered the grim realities. Death was certain for thousands who were in or near the blocks destroyed or heavily damaged by the detonation, which was centered near the Magnificent Mile. Of those who survived, some would be beyond help and would die immediately from the extreme radiation doses received during the initial blast. Those who were slightly further from the detonation, but still within a few blocks, could be severely burned and might have experienced retinal scarring, burst eardrums, or any number of projectile-related injuries.

Depending on the size of the explosion, however, what would threaten the greatest number of survivors would be any radioactive dust and debris. Important information about the explosion was still unknown: the size of the explosion, the particular isotopes, the half-life, the water solubility, and the size of the fallout cloud.

"Where are you?" Megan asked, sensing the room noise.

"Just down watching the football game in the hotel bar. Just a sec. We need to hear this . . ."

The reality was that the average American citizen was caught very much off-guard. How much radiation was dangerous? How dangerous was the fallout? Would the cloud contaminate Lake Michigan and the Great Lakes ecosystem? How about the food supply? The questions went on and on, and panic was beginning to set in as people prepared to flock out of the city, and even out of the whole Great Lakes region. Bill was riveted to the TV as he weighed his options.

Everything depended upon the size of the detonation, and whether it was a true nuclear device, or a series of one or more conventional, "non-nuclear" bombs that had radioactive waste packed in—the so-called "dirty bomb" scenario. While either was bad, a dirty bomb would be much more manageable and containable. It would be a terrible event, but would cause far fewer deaths and injuries than an actual nuclear detonation. Stew made clear, however, that early indications were that this was the real thing.

With each passing second, Bill's adrenaline flowed faster, making it more and more difficult to think clearly. For Bill, life boiled down to this single point of urgency, dense as a black hole that was sucking in everything around it. He had to get home to his family.

After everything they'd been through, Zach and Megan were without him at a time when they needed him. The wall between the compartments of his life had come crashing down, and in the wreckage and debris, he saw Megan standing there, a kind soul in need of care. He saw that she hadn't deserved even one of the bad cards she'd been dealt in life, and he suddenly and powerfully ached for her. He didn't know what he was going to do, or how he could help, but he knew with every fiber of his body that he had to get home.

The questions continued in his mind. How far away did one need to travel to escape the cloud? How far south of Chicago would he need to drive to stay clear of the radiation? Could he travel north across the upper peninsula of Michigan, then south through the state, or would that put him right in the path of the fallout?

"Listen, Megan. I'm going to get home. If my cell stops working, just don't worry about me. I'll make it home and I'll be with you. You have to know that I love you, and I love Zachary so much too. I'll call you soon but I've got to make some plans and get going," he said.

"Okay, I love you too . . ." she said, emotion filling her voice. She then blurted, "Bill, wait!"

"I'm here," he confirmed.

"I'm . . . I'm so sorry . . . I haven't been the wife you deserve." Tears flowed down her cheeks. "I love you . . . . Come home to me."

A wave of emotion came over Bill, the power and extent of which he'd never experienced before—even at Hanna's death. It was as if the walls of time and space were falling and a divine light of clarity, purity, and honesty was shining through during what felt like an apocalyptic time. "I love you too . . . . I'll be home."

He turned and faced Christina, who had tears in her eyes as well. She magnanimously tried to hide them, simply saying, "I'm so sad for the pain and the suffering these people are feeling." She didn't let on even one ounce that Bill's conversation was ripping at her heart.

Bill's eyes were tear-filled. "You need to stay here for a while. It's safe here." They looked deeply into each other's eyes.

"I will," she assured calmly. "I will . . . but you need to go. Your family needs you." Christina tried to force a smile as tears filled her eyes. So many feelings were rushing through her mind—love, loss, grief, and fear. Bill grasped her and squeezed her tightly, holding her for a long while as tears flowed freely from both of their eyes.

Both had faith that this was not a forever goodbye—as many others were experiencing. But each also had a palpable sense that their world-within-a-world was never going to be the same.

Moments later, Christina found herself standing silently and alone, consumed by a gut-wrenching sadness and emptiness as she watched Bill depart the lobby doors.

✣

As soon as Ian hung up the cockpit telephone with Samantha, Mac was shaking his head slightly from side to side. His face was flushed. He uttered two simple words under his breath: "Allahu Akbar." Ian knew immediately what Mac was saying. They were the infamous last words of so many suicide terrorists before the strike: Allahu Akbar. God is great.

Ian calmly responded, "I'd love to challenge you on that stereotypical comment, but it would be tough for me to argue that we're jumping to conclusions."

"Yeah, especially when you consider the date."

Ian had a puzzled look on his face, then turned away to think aloud. "I don't get it, October 11th, 2009?"

"I don't know if this is a coincidence, but I was sitting here thinking there must be something significant to the date. It's what I'd do to send a clear message if I were Al Qaeda. It's not perfect but I think people will get the point. The date—one-zero, one-one, ninth year of the millennium—is 9/11/01 in reverse. It's also 10/11, which could come after 9/11."

Ian just nodded in venom-filled disgust. "But . . . why do it on a Sunday? There were probably fewer people downtown."

"Who knows, maybe the date, but they do things on their time. They wait. Maybe just because it would be unexpected?"

"Maybe to avoid killing so many people that we would turn the Middle East into a parking lot," Ian speculated. "They say Osama argued against the scale of 9/11 for that reason."

"Let's hope it doesn't spiral down to that."

Ian's anger grew. "Fucking bastards!" he exclaimed. Suddenly he realized that his passengers might be able to hear. Still, the only one awake was the nurse, and as Ian looked back, she waved politely, unaware that the world below was sinking into a chaos of epic proportions.

Ian motioned for the nurse to put on a headset, which she did. He then proceeded to explain the situation to her, and suggested she wake up Lori's mother before they began descending for Kalamazoo. "She might need a little time to absorb all of this before we get to the ambulance."

"There'll be plenty of time to be pissed at these 13th-century holdouts after we land, but we've got some thinking to do, Ian," Mac instructed.

"About what?" Ian asked.

"It was a good call to think of the stretcher thing like you did. I'm glad we're going home . . . it's right to get you to your family. But it might not be the smartest thing to be flying east of Chicago, given what little we know about this thing. I have no idea how big this blast might have been. I'm thinking we should err east toward Indianapolis and then cut north," Mac said.

"But then they might just force us to land at Indy."

"True," Mac said. He thought for a moment, reconsidering his view. "You know, it's probably safe so long as the bomb didn't detonate too long ago. It'll take a while for the cloud to drift—certainly it's slower than we are."

"Didn't you also say that if there were a fallout cloud it would drift north of Kalamazoo?"

"Yeah, that's true too . . . and I guess it doesn't matter because we're going home no matter what. Let's just make tracks when we land," Mac suggested.

"All I know is that this is some serious shit. I don't think I can quite grasp the magnitude of what may have just happened. Chicago is a city of three million people, and it was just bombed with a fucking nuclear device! The city could be uninhabitable for years! I don't know much about these things, but I'd say we may have just entered World War Three."

"If we weren't in it already."

Neither of the men could stop their minds. The terror and scope of what could be happening ate at them. Ian couldn't help but verbalize his thoughts. "My god can you imagine, even if this isn't as big as we think, what it would look like seeing three million people fighting to leave a city contaminated with radiation? It's going to make the bridges of New York on 9/11 look like a cake walk," Ian added.

"Well, here is my suggestion, Ian. We'll start a descent for Kalamazoo soon. I think lower is better and it will eliminate the odds of getting into radiation where the high-speed upper winds may have pushed it farther east. Then I suggest that when we land, you guys are welcome to hunker down at my place . . . only problem is that it might be tough to seal it up. The place is big, old and drafty."

"You should come to our place then. We'll re-evaluate there. We can always fly back out as soon as they'll let us, if we need to."

Mac nodded. "Okay. Thanks. I think that's a good plan. But now I'll just add that I think we need to shut down our minds and focus on getting Lori and these passengers to the ambulance safely. Besides, your family needs you. And frankly, this world needs our Project Gamma more than ever before."

Ian nodded in reluctant agreement as an extraneous thought popped into his head. "I wonder where Bill is?"

❖

Bill made the decision to drive the northern route home. It wasn't an easy choice, but it was a decision that couldn't be delayed. Though the route would take him directly in the path of the potential fallout cloud, there were too many risks in traveling south. The mass exodus and chaos around the Chicago area, and the southern end of Lake Michigan, would have been a nightmare, and would have forced him to drive many miles to the south of it all. And coming up into the southern Michigan populations, he could very well face another massive flow of southbound evacuees that would thwart his travel. By going north through Michigan's Upper Peninsula, where there was little population anyway, he could drive fast and then traverse the Lower Peninsula from north to south. As for the radiation, he was going to gamble on it.

The more he drove, the more he believed he'd made the right choice in terms of route. He prayed often as he sped along through the Upper Peninsula of Michigan, including thanking God several times for guiding him to the northern route home. On a normal day it would have been a seven-hour drive to the Mackinac Bridge, which connects the Upper Peninsula with Michigan's Lower Peninsula, and another four-hour drive home from there; but tonight, he was making much better time.

While logistically the plan was going well, in his heart and in his mind, Bill was in crisis. He repeatedly found himself in tears, and at one point as he approached St. Ignace, on the north side of the Mackinac Bridge, he began to cry so hard that his body literally shook and he had to pull over to get himself together. It was a frightening feeling for the All-American, always in control, Bill Vanderveen; but there was nothing he could do to make it stop.

His mind and his emotions were overwhelmed by thoughts of nuclear bombs, love, loss, responsibility, hope, grief, pain, faith, and God's mercy. The weight of the world seemed to be crashing down upon him. Although it was different, he felt every bit as much pain as he did when he'd lost Hanna, and even greater emotion.

He cried for the people in Chicago who had died. He cried for the pain and suffering of the survivors. He cried in appreciation for his merciful God who would someday end all of the suffering in a glorious second coming, wiping away every tear, and reuniting loved ones. He cried for fear that his friend John could well be dead, and he cried in fear of his family's safety.

Probably most of all, however, he was crying out of grief, because he knew he was about to lose someone very important to him. It wouldn't be to death, but it felt every bit as painful and real. It had suddenly become so clear.

Call it what you will—a tipping point, a crossroads, a transformation; but Bill Vanderveen had determined that in order to love Megan with all his heart, and to help her heal and become as fully loved, and capable of love, as she deserved to be, he would have to dedicate himself to only her. The mere thought was excruciating.

Hard as it might be to believe, guilt was not the primary driver behind Bill's decision. It was love—his love for Megan. Some would justifiably criticize his lack of guilt as a megalomaniac's denial of his own transgressions—a self-delusional rationalization that conveniently provided the illusion of moral high ground. Perhaps. But to Bill, it was love—real love, Christian love, I Corinthians love.

In his mind he very much believed God had sent him Christina—a life ring at a time when he might otherwise not have been able to see the marriage with Megan through. Indeed Christina had been his earthly savior. Even her name seemed to portend deep meaning to Bill. Nonetheless Bill had come to a realization that for everything there is a season, and his season of healing was complete.

He now had the strength and the love of God—both through the Holy Spirit and as a gift to him through Christina, to dedicate himself to Megan's healing—crazy as it might have sounded had he ever tried to put it into words. It seemed brilliantly clear to Bill that he could now step outside of his own recovery and loneliness, to care for the woman he'd never stopped loving—not even for a moment.

She was the mother of his son, and every bit the sweet, vulnerable, delicate, innocent, and loving being God had entrusted to him through sacred marriage. No, to Bill the entire recommitment completely transcended sexuality, and had nothing to do with guilt or his extraneous sexual fulfilment. It was now an issue of priority and commitment. It was as if both he and Megan had been in a hospital, and God sent Christina as a nurse to care for Bill, in order to see him through, that he could in turn care for Megan after his healing.

As Bill gathered himself and continued the drive, he even briefly contemplated explaining everything to Megan, but dismissed the idea as quickly as it came to his head. He too, had heard the advice from professionals that confession helped only the confessor. He agreed it would accomplish nothing constructive for Megan.

He even briefly entertained the notion that Megan would understand the divine love Christina had provided when he so badly needed the care. After all, at times in counseling, Megan had even suggested that he seek other companionship, due to her "hang-ups" and her inability to be physically present for him.

In truth, Megan really might have been willing and able to see things holistically and to accept Bill's heartfelt rationale, but nobody would ever get the chance to know. There was no doubt in Bill's mind. As crazy as it all seemed, even to him, Bill knew he would take that story, and his profound love of Christina, to the grave.

Chapter 32

THE UNSETTLED DUST

Late that night, October 11th—12th, 2009

The craziness of sealing windows and doors, securing water, check-ing flashlights, and taking inventory of food supplies had largely been accomplished by Brandon and Andrew before Mac and Ian arrived home. Now there was little to do but wait.

The boys made Ian incredibly proud. They had risen to the occa-sion with maturity and grace under fire, taking the lead on the safety matters in order to free Samantha to prepare food and make sleeping arrangements.

Ian sat on the couch with Samantha leaning up next to him, his feet up on the coffee table. Brooke was at the other end of the couch with a blanket draped over her legs, and Mac leaned back in the room's sole recliner. It was late and the boys had gone to the basement to sleep, leaving the three bedrooms for the four adults. Despite their glazed and sleepy eyes, however, the bedrooms were still empty as Samantha, Brooke, Ian and Mac continued to be riveted to the wall-to-wall television coverage of the nuclear explosion.

Information was slowly creeping out, and the anxiety levels of the impromptu housemates had somewhat eased, at least with regard to the radiation threat. Although they would stay in the house and take no chances, it still appeared that the trail of fallout would remain to their north.

They also learned more about the situation in Chicago. The area of greatest devastation appeared centered in the blocks immediately north and west of the John Hancock Tower, which itself remained standing but had sustained heavy damage. The story was worse to the north and west however, and the three blocks bordered by Walton Place on the south, and East Cedar on the north, were virtually demolished.

Strangely, there was also extremely heavy damage in two additional pockets. One of them was the Water Tower Place, a popular shopping district surrounded by business and residential suites. The other was the block immediately across from the Hancock Tower, on the west end of Chestnut near North Rush Street. There was even early speculation that these areas had been the result of separate detonations.

So there were two pockets of heavy damage, perhaps on the scale of the bombing of the Murrah building in Oklahoma City, and one area of extensive devastation—the area northwest of Michigan Avenue in the blocks that spanned Bellevue and Oak.

It was, of course, far too early to speculate about the death toll, but that didn't stop the media from trying. Estimates varied widely. The only thing certain was that the horror and shock were indescribable. Regardless of where this catastrophe would fall on a scale between Hiroshima and 9/11, there was little question that the magnitude of immense human suffering was unparalleled on U.S. soil. Without exception, there were intermittent tears rolling down the cheeks of all four of the adults dug-in at the Keppler house.

Much as with 9/11—only to an even greater degree—people across the nation were forced away from a daily grind of hurried activities and supposed stress, to a stupor of perspective, reflection, angst, and mourning. Suddenly, a great many people were forced to the lower levels of Maslow's hierarchy of needs—safety, healing, shelter and food, at the same time as many others were forced to the higher levels—relationships, love, belonging, respect, solving problems, morality, and kindness. It reminded Ian of the feelings he experienced in the aftermath of 9/11.

Many unanswered questions remained: Why a Sunday? Why that location versus another? Why Chicago? Some answers would come in time, others would never be completely clear.

If there was any good news, it was the southwest wind. For over eighty miles upwind there were no people, just vast open water. While there was great speculation about which radioactive isotopes resulted from the blast, some of which were soluble in water and some not, there was an early sense that depending upon the size of the blast and the height into the atmosphere of the fallout, there was a good chance that the integrity of the Great Lakes water system would not be forever compromised.

But as the hours had gone by, Ian and Mac frequently found their thoughts flashing to the Desoterica, and how these events would affect the much-anticipated public disclosure of the group's secret work. Through knowing glances and concise references, each knew the other was thinking the exact same thing.

It wasn't that they were being egocentric about the work—quite the opposite, actually. Each of them saw the nearly completed, meticulously crafted, massive texts from the Project Gamma work to be inextricably related to the global conflict that was playing out before their eyes.

They saw their years of work as specifically designed to illuminate the vestiges of tribal conflict that they believed underpinned much of the world's chronic violence, hate, prejudice, and bigotry. After watching scene after scene of chaos and horror, Mac turned to Ian with piercing eyes and deeply internalized, nearly imperceptible anger: "Eight weeks. We need eight weeks."

"Eight weeks until what?" Brooke asked innocently and sleepily. Brooke had certainly been around long enough to know that Ian was involved in a big research project with Mac, but she had not yet made the connection that it was "the" group—the one creating the buzz in the major media.

Ian, Sammy and Mac gave one another knowing looks of uncertainty, not knowing how to respond.

The connection of Ian and Mac to the Desoterica announcement was one that Sammy and Ian hadn't gone out of their way to point out for Brooke, despite the Kepplers' close relationship with her. They had even explicitly discussed with one another how forthright they could be, but Mac and Ian had agreed to very strict guidelines from the earliest days of the project, and had been very clear about the importance of complete secrecy. As a result, Sammy and Ian had not felt comfortable helping Brooke connect the dots. It was an awkward situation that had caused them consternation, and Ian had intended to speak with Mac about it again.

Obviously it had been a foregone conclusion that Sammy would never be excluded from details of the Desoterica's work. She was Ian's partner in life. They shared everything. There was no other option. But the situation with Brooke had been less clear.

While she certainly wasn't a committed spouse, Brooke had become very close with Ian and Samantha. Back in 2002 when Ian had returned home and Samantha disclosed the unexpected physical encounter with her new best friend, Ian admittedly had been surprised. His response, however, was not what many would have expected.

Having discussed love, commitment and sexuality to the degree he and Samantha had, he certainly didn't react with any anger, or feel any sense of betrayal. But neither did he react the way many men might expect—though the thought crossed his mind. No, his first thoughts were not focused on the idea of trying to join in the emerging physical relationship between Samantha and Brooke himself.

When Sammy disclosed her deeply meaningful, equally erotic experience with Brooke, Ian primarily reacted with a sense of appreciation, of gratitude that someone else had so deeply and genuinely seen Sammy's inner beauty.

Sammy had many times expressed her difficulty in forming deep and meaningful friendships. As an example, Megan had always been special to Samantha. Even during the current crisis they'd remained in touch. Samantha considered her to be like a close relative, but somehow something had been missing.

Samantha had once described to Ian a conversation between her and Megan that was eerily similar to the one with Brooke before their hot-tub experience. It was back in time, even closer to Janet Keppler's death, and her raw nerves were close to the surface. She'd begun to cry—a rare moment of vulnerability similar to the one she experienced with Brooke—but a complete lack of connection or emotional sympathy on the part of Megan had created a watershed moment for Samantha. It was suddenly clear that their friendship would never reach the depth of mutual understanding Sammy longed for.

Perhaps compounded by other friendships that lacked chemistry or depth of connection, Samantha had at times wondered if anyone other than Ian would ever truly understand her—really "get" her—or for that matter really *care* to "get" her.

It was that background, coupled with his genuine love for Samantha, that ruled how Ian had responded to Samantha's "confession" in 2002; and by the time of the 2009 bombing, the relationship between Samantha and Brooke had grown into the type of friendship Samantha had always dreamed of, but never thought she'd have. And as inconceivable as a loving, fulfilling friendship had been, she could never have imagined the liberating sensuality she'd share with Brooke. It was truly the icing on the cake.

Brooke was just a delight to be around, and the love that had grown between her and the entire Keppler family was real, and mutually valued. She attended the boys' sporting events. She spent most holidays with the family, and often would drop by the house and just hang out or watch TV. Truly she was one of the family.

Back in the intimacy of their bunker, Ian looked at Mac. Mac, with some sense of the relationship's background, simply said, "Go for it."

Brooke's eyes switched quickly from Ian, to Mac, to Sammy, and back to Ian. She wore a puzzled look on her face as if begging for someone to explain what she was obviously missing.

"We've been dying to clue you in on a little press conference that Mac and I will be part of—apparently in about eight weeks. You've probably heard on the news, about 'it,' a big announcement that's coming from a secret group of scholars?"

Brooke's eyes grew wide and round. "Nooo . . . waaayyyy!"

"The Desoterica?" Ian asked with a smile, as if she still hadn't figured it out.

"You've got to be shitting me!" Brooke exclaimed. A brief sense of excitement brought just a tinge of relief to the air of tragedy that encompassed the four.

"I can tell you only that I'm sorry we couldn't point out the connection earlier. We just couldn't."

Brooke wasn't mad. "I probably should have seen it, but I just never would have figured." She was almost giddy. "So what the hell is this secret discovery? I want to know, right, fucking, now!" she prattled.

❖

Bill was exhausted. Despite constantly reinforcing his caffeine buzz, his nightlong, emotion-filled dash for home—potentially carrying him through nuclear fallout—had largely sapped his energy. But by the time dawn was breaking, his latest epiphanies had allowed him a renewed sense of purpose and clarity. He was in the home stretch, just north of Grand Rapids and heading south toward Kalamazoo.

Throughout most of his drive the traffic had been light, at times even non-existent. As he headed farther south, however, he had been joined by more cars in the southbound lanes—indeed signs that the closer he got to the Chicago-to-Detroit corridor, the closer he would get to traffic and panic. Reports on the radio again affirmed his decision to take the northern route home, since from Kalamazoo south it was clear that he would have been in the massive flow of Chicago evacuees, which was mingling and merging with those fleeing Michigan as well.

Bill's cell-phone rang. "Are you staying awake?" Megan asked. She had not slept much. She'd worried about Bill's ability to stay awake, and also the radiation threat, so she passed the night watching television and monitoring the progress of the fallout.

"Yep, I'm okay. Just ready to be home. Have you heard any more about the radiation?"

"Not really anything new. It still looks like the dust has for sure drifted north and east of us in a pretty narrow path through part of the state, but it wasn't very concentrated. They're saying there'll be surface contamination for generations but that the radiation is already down to where it isn't an 'immediate threat to health,' whatever that means."

"I'm still thinking that I would have driven through that area before it got there, too. And I just heard a similar analysis on the radio, that strong upper winds made the plume longer, but more diffuse. They say now it will go well across Lake Huron and into Canada." Bill paused briefly before adding, "All I know is that I sure liked it twelve hours ago when I didn't know anything about fallout or radiation levels."

"Did you hear that they're saying there were two or three different bombs, not just one?" Megan asked.

"Yeah, and that the others might not have been nuclear. I wonder if that explains the radiation being lower than what they predicted several hours ago . . . . Hey, any news on John yet?"

"Nothing. I've been talking with Ian and Sammy, and they talked with John's parents. Still nothing. The poor souls, they've just been beside themselves with worry. They've been calling the Red Cross, FEMA, friends, hospitals—of course not Northwestern because that entire facility was evacuated—but nobody has seen him." The lack of news dragged Bill's mood back a notch, as his stomach tightened with concern for his friend.

"Well, there's got to be a ton of chaos over there. He could well be in a car on his way home by now. We'll just pray he's okay," Bill said, not doing a very good job of reassuring himself, or Megan. He changed the topic slightly. "How are Ian and Sammy? I didn't want to wake Ian, but did he get home safely last night?"

"They're safe. They've got Sammy's friend Brooke, and Ian's boss—"

A warning sound interrupted the conversation. It was another of the EBS tones. Bill heard it screeching faintly over the lowered volume of his car radio, as Megan heard and saw it instantly on the television.

"What's this? Hang on . . ." Bill said. The warning tone which for years had been just a nebulous test, or at worst a potential weather event a few counties away, had taken on new significance. It was now a harbinger of horrific news.

"Ladies and Gentlemen, the tone you've just heard is a notice from the Emergency Broadcast System. This is a national emergency. Stay tuned for instructions."

"You've got to be shitting me!" Bill exclaimed in muted exasperation; he instinctively pushed the gas pedal farther toward the floor.

"Your attention please. At 6:53 a.m., there was an explosion in the city of Atlanta. It would appear that the explosion was centered somewhere near the downtown area, reportedly near the Post Office at Martin Luther King Drive Southwest and Forsyth Street Southwest. Early indications do include the presence of radioactive material. We repeat, there has been radiation detected in the vicinity. As a result, there are efforts under way to evacuate downtown and areas north and east of the city. Please stay tuned for emergency instructions."

The announcement continued with many of the same decontamination and fallout-avoidance instructions as those that followed the Chicago event. There was also a strong caution against panic during the evacuation—an early lesson of the Chicago aftermath.

"Can you believe this?" Bill groaned, as again his body tingled in response to the emotional rollercoaster ride.

"Bill, just get home safely. This is so scary," Megan urged.

"I'll be there within the hour. I love you. Call me if you need anything."

"Okay, Bill. I can't wait to have you home. I love you too."

Bill clicked his cell phone shut, and continued southbound amidst the increasing volume of traffic. He again felt rage and hatred boiling in his blood. He fantasized in his mind about a massive nuclear counterattack against someone. He wanted someone to pay for the senseless violence and the murder of innocent men, women and children.

But Bill quickly reminded himself of the potential cost of his fantasized retaliation upon millions more innocent people. Besides, whom would they bomb? It wasn't like there was a single place where the terrorists lingered or called home. Bill knew through conversations with his father-in-law that they actually went to great lengths to hide themselves among the civilians, so they could show pictures of mangled schoolhouses or baby-formula factories. That use of "human shields" remained a testament, in Bill's eyes, to their flawed worldview, and their flawed religion.

With those thoughts bouncing through his mind, he decided to pray, so with his eyes on the road, and the ironic beauty of a sunrise partially obscured by puffy cumulous clouds, Bill prayed in response to the agony he knew was underway. "Dear Lord, I come to you again with a heavy heart, in fear for our brothers and sisters in Atlanta. Lord I pray that you comfort and heal those who are hurting. Lord, I pray also for those committing these horrible acts, that they may see the evil of their paths . . ." He paused for a second before continuing; "Lord I know that 'free will' requires that people have the freedom to choose their paths in life, even to choose horrible, harmful ones; but Lord I humbly pray that you have mercy on the many innocent people. I pray that you intervene. I pray that your Holy Spirit speak to these evildoers. I pray that you stop them."

Bill's anger wasn't much calmed by his prayer, nor did he feel much better. His anger led him to thoughts that he immediately tried to extricate from his head, but could not. He thought about the words he'd just uttered, and couldn't help but believe, nearly to a certainty, that God would *not* honor such prayers. The violence of the terrorists would continue, and God would not change their hearts. The pain and the suffering would continue too, and God would not restore the lives taken, nor prevent others from being taken. God was not going to stop the terror, even though he could.

The reality haunted him. He tried hard to reconcile the problem. Why wouldn't God act? Perhaps if he prayed harder? Perhaps if more people prayed or the Christian majority better demonstrated its worthiness? Perhaps if they could all lead purer lives and please God more fully?

A pit grew in Bill's stomach. Was this truly just a runaway freight train of earthly, human action? That God was unwilling to stop? Despite all of the pain he'd felt about Hanna, he'd always known that there was a higher purpose—God had called her home for a reason. But God couldn't have simply called home all of these terror victims—not all of them.

Bill got to thinking further. Was there any point at which God would stop such horrific human actions? He hadn't in the case of the Holocaust. What if nuclear war erupted and humans really did destroy the entire planet and everyone on it? Would he just let that happen?

"Of course he wouldn't. That won't happen . . . can't happen. That's not how the Bible says it will play out," Bill assured himself aloud. He worked to argue the other side, speaking aloud again and waving a hand as if speaking in front of people. "We knew there would be dark days like this, before the second coming. We can't lose faith," Bill assured himself further as he passed a slower car on the expressway.

But for the remainder of his trip he was tormented by what theologians and philosophers refer to as "the problem of evil." It was one of the great mysteries of belief in an all-knowing, all-loving, benevolent, all-seeing, omnipresent, and all-powerful God, and Bill recalled that it was the very problem he'd struggled with after the death of Bob Keppler. Now here he was, having come full-circle after 24 years, again asking the same questions in light of the day's horrific events.

Bill thought of Ian's current solution to the problem of evil. Ian was a non-believer, but took a view of the problem that was much the same as many believers Bill knew. He'd even heard Ian talk about the deist believers like Thomas Paine, Benjamin Franklin, and Thomas Jefferson, who believed that a God might well have created everything, but he no longer tinkered with it or guided it in any way. God was the watchmaker, and once the parts were set in motion, they ran unfettered.

Bill wasn't in doubt of God's existence for a second, and he wasn't even close to seeing any legitimacy in Ian's non-belief. No, Bill was confident that Ian was missing something huge in his rejection of God—at that time he just didn't know exactly what.

Simultaneously however, and as Bill remained resolute in his faith— Jesus Christ was all-knowing and had a plan—the "watchmaker" solution continued to rise the surface. Perhaps world events, and even Hanna's death, were just what they seemed—the strange interaction of chance, cause and effect, in a natural world that was ruled by natural laws? Perhaps while it was true that there was a God—a watchmaker—who set things in motion and was fully aware of how they would come out, what if he didn't interfere?

What if people really controlled their own destiny? What if biology was unfair and some people inherited great smarts while some were mentally impaired, or some were healthy of mind while others were disturbed? What if genetics and chance ruled the day, rather than a mysterious, incomprehensible plan that made us unwitting pawns in someone else's twisted game?

What if everything just worked—as it appeared to work—without supernatural constraints and influence? What if the events of the day when he and Ian had hit that deer with their car, had unfolded as the result of random interactions of disparate events? What if people lived and died by similar combinations of both random and intentional events, only to go to Heaven and then finally get to understand the larger picture of truth?

What if car accidents were the result of similar cause-and-effects variables—inattention, weather, driver inputs, surface conditions, or even malice—but not by Jesus? What if terrorists weren't enabled or supported, discouraged or deterred by God, but were just people interacting with each other and with natural forces of a natural world? What if being healed was just a function of biochemistry, physics and mechanical laws, and not God's direct intervention?

That last thought reminded Bill of another of Ian's tirades—one of those over-the-top exchanges that had stressed their relationship.

Ian had been on a roll about a major study that showed "intercessory prayer" didn't work, when he suggested that Bill visit a web site called, "whydoesgodhateamputees.com."[76] Ian, by way of the site, had argued that the only reason people didn't flock in throngs to pray for amputees to be healed of their injuries was because they didn't actually believe, deep in their hearts, that God could grow back a limb. The argument was that somehow when "broken parts" were hidden in the body, and were a little less visible—brain cells, cancer cells, heart tissue, or a broken spinal cord—then people could suspend belief and think that prayers might encourage God to actually manipulate the physical matter. He would fix things in a physical manipulation, a cause-and-effect way, moving cells or proteins as he might move a pencil—or a car in a parking lot—to test one's faith. The point was that people didn't pray for amputees, and God didn't fix amputees—either because he couldn't, or because he hated them.[77]

The questions and thoughts continued in Bill's mind. Somehow, the idea that the world could be best explained, functionally, simply by saying "it is what it is," started to make increasing sense to Bill.

Bill was struggling. He knew there were many passages in the Bible that told of an active God who would heal and fix things just for the asking, as his mother had tried to tell Janet Keppler when she was sick with cancer. Faith mattered.

He couldn't consciously quote the verses, but subconsciously he remembered having heard the same scripture Ian had contemplated years earlier—Matthew 17:20 and John 14:12–14, respectively:

> *And Jesus said unto them, Because of your unbelief: for verily I say unto you, If ye have faith as a grain of mustard seed, ye shall say unto this mountain, 'Remove hence to yonder place'; and it shall remove; and nothing shall be impossible unto you.*[78]

Verily, verily, I say unto you, He that believeth on me, the works that I do shall he do also; and greater [works] than these shall he do; because I go unto my Father. And whatsoever ye shall ask in my name, that will I do, that the Father may be glorified in the Son.[79]

But in truth, Bill hadn't bought it then—that simply having enough faith and praying hard enough would succeed in correcting maladies. He'd seen too many people on the church's prayer list, including tragically injured young people, and infants, who simply slipped into God's hands despite the congregation's most diligent prayers and efforts.

Bill didn't know it, and never would have admitted it, but philosophically he had begun a slow progression toward *theistic agnosticism*. He believed strongly in God, but increasingly he felt that answers to these greatest of questions were simply beyond the human ability to understand.

Even as he progressed down that path of thought, Bill was still a world apart from Ian's beliefs, which took that inability to understand as reason to reject belief in a god at all.

Bill was confident that his God of the Bible was real and true. But based on that last hour of the most life-changing day of his life, he believed increasingly that the greatest questions—the secrets of God and the universe—were simply *unknowable* to mortal humans.

✣

The phone rang, awakening Ian.

"Hey, it sounds like I woke you," Bill said. "You can call me back later."

"No. I'm really glad to hear from you. What time is it?"

"Almost eight. I figured you might have been up late, but I was almost home and just wanted to say "Hi" before I crashed, myself."

"I was worried about you. Sammy talked to Megan during the night and updated me some. I'm glad you're safe, dude . . . you know I love you bro . . . I hope you know that."

It was the first they had talked in weeks, but the evolving crisis had quickly forced them to see their unspoken differences into the larger context. This was a time for life-long friends to unite—to "fix the sinking boat"—not divide themselves over how many angels could fit on the head of a pin.

"You too, my friend. Hey . . . not to be the bearer of bad news, but I'll bet if you were asleep that you haven't heard the latest news," Bill suggested.

"What?" Ian said with some sense of urgency.

"There's been another bomb. Atlanta. Doesn't seem nearly as big, but it's radioactive."

"You've got to be shitting me!" Ian spoke loud enough to wake Samantha, and she sat up with concern.

Ian reached over and clicked on the TV. He was distracted by his effort to digest this frightening development, but continued his conversation with Bill as they discussed some of the details Bill had heard on the radio.

Eventually Ian was able to gather his thoughts, and focus on the conversation. "How you doing with all this, for real?" Ian asked open-endedly.

"What can you do . . . I'll be glad to get home. These things have a way of giving you perspective, I suppose." Bill's thoughts were fragmented. "Obviously I'm worried about John, as is everyone. But I guess I have nothing to complain about compared to a lot of people . . . I'm fine, given the circumstances," Bill summarized.

"I'm glad you're safe. I'll keep in close touch with John's parents and the effort to find him . . . I'll call if I hear anything. You do the same, but just keep alert the rest of the way," Ian added, still distracted slightly by the Atlanta scenes now hitting the TV.

"Well, when all the dust settles—pun intended—we'll really need to sit down. Much as you piss me off and I disagree with you on so many things, I find it hard to make sense of any of this." Bill was half joking, but Ian appreciated his direct acknowledgment of the past tensions. Bill continued his disparate thoughts, which were evidence of his fatigue. "The God I know can't have ordered . . . or allowed . . . this to happen . . ." Bill's voice faded off.

"I feel you, brother," Ian responded in support. "I certainly don't have answers. Just bear with me because this big project I've been working on will come to a head pretty soon. I'd like to fill you in some more on what I've been doing, soon. We'll talk, but I think it's all related and I'll look forward to being able to share it with you. It'll just be pretty unpopular."

"Yeah and it'll piss me off, but that's okay. Know why, Ian?"

"Why's that?" Ian bit.

"You should know that I really do care about you. I know it's tough when we see the world so differently, but I know you believe you're doing what is right, and I love you like my own brother. I admit . . . it's tough for me when I think you're misguided, but I do respect you. I just think we can't blame religion for everything. I'll tell you, the world needs the central lessons of the Christianity that I know, more today than ever before . . . I don't know much, but I know that much."

"I agree that the world needs those positive elements, for sure," Ian replied, maintaining the conciliatory tone of the conversation. "And for the record, I recognize their existence. I've thought a lot about your comments that I've been standing *for* nothing and *against* everything. I'm not sure I agree, but I'm still pondering that one. Frankly, it's still difficult for me to believe that humans could have stuck with this concept of religion for this long, if there weren't some real benefits, insights, or lessons available to us—say like lessons that would be genuinely useful in helping us get through the shit we're dealing with today."

"Yeah, well, on the other side I'm obviously pondering God's role in all this—that 'question of evil' you used to talk about."

"I hear you. And I see all the good and philanthropy that happens in the name of faith. I'm just still convinced that morality and good acts also can—and do—come from people who don't believe that a supernatural force is behind everything."

"I know. I know," Bill replied with good nature.

"We'll definitely have time and try to sort this shit out, but thank you for calling. You're truly a brother to me too, and I've thought about you a lot. I really fear alienating you with this thing Mac and I are going to do soon. But go home, be with your wonderful family, and we'll talk soon."

"It'll all be good, Ian. Be it God doing it to my brain, or just my brain doing it to itself, this thing is changing me. Guess it would be cliché to say that you don't know what you've got until it's gone, huh?"

"How right you are," Ian replied. "See you soon."

"Bye."

Ian hung up the phone. After talking to Bill and watching the news out of Atlanta, Ian and Sammy figured they'd let the others sleep since the bad news would still be there when they awoke.

As the hours clicked by, one by one the rest of the refugees emerged and lazily headed for the family room, where they learned of the latest attack. The sleepy reactions were largely without visible emotion.

There they sat, just weeks from a major global announcement that would be focused upon the misunderstandings of an allegedly mythological religion—one that had dominated the Western World for two centuries and shaped dominant cultures of the world. But today, it was another religion that was on the minds of that group, and the world—one with more immediate relevancy to life than stem cell research, anti-homosexual discrimination, reproduction, or even the destruction of condoms in AIDS-ravaged foreign lands. Today, the relevance of the religious beliefs of others was once again emblazoned upon their minds.

It was surreal. With the clarity of thought provided by sleep, the whole thing was more unbelievable, in multiple ways and for multiple reasons. Ian thought to himself, *how could the nuclear threat have gotten so far from my mind, so far from everyone's mind?* With a new administration in place for ten months, it finally seemed like 9/11 was properly tucked away into its somewhat distant, historical perspective.

Ian, and much of the nation, was introspective, trying to make sense of conflicting and twisted thoughts and feelings. Like most people, Ian mentally had returned to his regular life after 9/11 faded from memory, but now he felt a sense that he shouldn't have done so. But what good would it have done to be paralyzed with fear every day? Hadn't fearmongering become an abused tool of the political establishment? Of course it had. It had always been. He recognized the incongruity of his thoughts. He searched for answers. What could have been done differently? What would have been the unanticipated consequences of that alternative course of action?

Ian remained lost in his thoughts as the others listened to the drone of the bad-news machine in the corner of the room. Perhaps he could blame the government, and its political and bureaucratic ineptitude for failing to protect the people, or even recognize the real, underlying threat behind radical Islam. He quickly dismissed the thought, recognizing that there was no way to be 100% safe from suicidal maniacs on a godly mission—particularly those fully committed and willing to die for the sacred mandates and their corresponding, heavenly rewards.

He pondered the underlying philosophical conflict between Islam and the Judeo-Christian beliefs. It clearly had deep roots, and those roots had grown into massive trees that appeared locked in a life-and-death battle for sunshine. Whether either would admit it that day or not, both saw the battle for sun as a win/lose, zero-sum game. In the end, under God's plan, someone had to win and someone had to lose. Whether it was Allah and a unified church-government under the Caliphate; Yahweh and the warrior-messiah; or Jesus, who would return and destroy the "nonbelievers" before installing his kingdom, most believers knew that there could be only one victorious god in the end of times.

Ian thought about those genuine, heartfelt beliefs. In retrospect, the conflict they were witnessing was wholly predictable by anyone who could have taken the time to understand the true eschatology of each religion—particularly when set against the geopolitical and socioeconomic realities of a post-industrial world.

The only question in his mind was how it would play out. Certainly there was still hope. Just as Christianity had come to be watered down—few people found it necessary to kill people for adultery or for uttering God's name in vain—so too could Islam become less literal. Could it not? Ian had always been an optimist, believing that civilization, and even technology, could outpace the ability of human egos, tribalism and nationalism, to destroy everything. He had long believed that Brandon and Andrew would thrive in a better world, despite the sweeping changes underway around the globe.

Now, however, Ian was gravely concerned that this "growing pain" of humankind could take a horrible turn for the worse—threatening huge masses of humanity, global economies, and perhaps even the world's capacity to environmentally sustain large numbers of human beings.

Certainly the big pile of gases and elements known as earth wouldn't be going anywhere, Ian reasoned. It would continue to spin as a giant mass for millions or billions of years. But what human beings, technologies, and quality of life would survive? *That* was a little less certain to Ian. It was a frightening world to be sure.

Ian remained an optimist in his heart, but no longer was he taking anything for granted. Again he concluded that the upcoming announcement was exactly what the world needed, despite the controversy that would surely erupt—especially with the "insensitive" timing of such an announcement during a period of national mourning. Nonetheless, Ian passionately believed it would be a vital step toward bringing sanity to the world, before humanity continued down such a perilous path. The more Ian thought, the more a powerful sense of urgency grew inside him.

Chapter 33

GOODBYE MY FOREVER FRIEND

By the Wednesday following the Sunday explosions, Michigan residents received the "all clear" from the federal government. Life was anything but normal, but within days most people were back to work, doing damage control and trying to make sense of the global crisis that was underway. For the areas northeast of Atlanta, the "all clear" would not come until Thursday. Despite quickly becoming apparent that it was a smaller-scale event, its economic impact would rival that of 9/11.

Speculation ran wild about the perpetrators, and especially about the sources of the nuclear material. The media quickly turned up extensive laundry lists of missing and lost nuclear devices and materials. From Russia, to North Korea, Pakistan, and even to missing domestic waste that could be used in low-level "dirty bombs," there were decades of news reports to fuel the rumor mill.

Only two things were believed to be known for certain. One was that nobody yet knew much. The other was that there could well be more where these came from. In many minds, a massive counterattack was a near certainty.

As for Ian and Mac, they feverishly toiled at the finishing touches for the various publications that would accompany the Desoterica announcement, including the print version of the *Bible of the Desoterica*. By the end of the week, the two had already been to New York to meet with the publisher, whereupon they had agreed to an official date for the press conference—Tuesday, December 15th, 2009.

By the end of the week, about the only thing that was able to distract Ian from his focus on the big event was his constant communication with John's parents. Each day he would talk with the Bennetts, assist in their efforts to reach the Red Cross, find representatives of the firm where John had worked, or contact emergency agencies. They were also in regular contact with the family of Annette Snyder, John's companion of seven years. Each day, however, there was nothing but frustration to be found.

Due to the radiation, and the massive number of casualties and damage, it would clearly be a long time before many of the victims would be located and identified, even where there were intact remains. As with 9/11, it was also evident that many families would never have the luxury of physical remains to bury. They would have only calls or other circumstantial evidence that their beloved had perished—a mother's Sunday evening telephone call from the law office where she was preparing an emergency brief for Monday, or a brother's recollection that a sibling went shopping with a group of friends, never to be heard from again.

For John Bennett's family that would not be the case, however. They would soon learn that John was dead, but that his body had actually been one of the first intact recoveries; confusion in the days following the event meant it would take eight days—until the following Monday—before the family would learn the sad news.

John's body had been recovered on Rush Street near Elm, just at the northwest periphery of the blast. While his family would never know many of the details of his death, only that a stray projectile had apparently caused a fatal head wound, the irony of the location would not be lost on Ian.

Ian's dear friend had been found motionless and dust covered—his black pants and wingtips an eerie shade of gray that contrasted with the pool of blood by his head—just one block from the spot where they had happened upon Sammy and her friends back in 1989, and where John had unwittingly suggested the term "secret of the universe," during the 2002 Desoterica.

As the call came in from Mr. Bennett, his voice strained with grief, the scant details were more than enough for Ian to realize the significance of the location—so close to the classic Chicago bar where he and Ian had shared such profound life memories. *Who could have imagined,* Ian thought to himself as Mr. Bennett spoke.

After the brief exchange, Ian hung up his cell phone and put his face in his hands. His mind flashed to images of John on the night they'd met Samantha. Ian could see him out on the dance floor, laughing and having a grand old time. Ian could see himself talking with Sammy, falling in love, with no idea that just a few hundred feet away would be the spot where John's life would be cut short.

A slideshow of images played instantly in his mind, and Ian noticed that John was smiling in every image, the good nature of his congenial friend evident in each shot as he interacted so positively with everyone around him.

"You okay?" Mac asked, noticing Ian's posture through the big window in his hangar office and walking out to check on his friend.

Ian lifted his head slowly and nodded, trying to remain stoic in a time where so many people had suffered such tragedy. He felt almost self-indulgent in showing any pain, but answered Mac with a tear nonetheless visible. "They found John's body . . ."

Mac said nothing, placing a comforting hand on Ian's shoulder and standing silently in support. Ian was silent as well, tears trickling down his face.

Ian mustered some energy to speak. He talked slowly, forcing the words to convey the information. "They . . . found him pretty far away from the blast . . . but a projectile got him . . . ."

"I'm sorry Ian. I know you guys were close . . . . Listen, let me know if we can help—use the Citation or anything," Mac offered.

"That's very nice. Thank you . . . but John's dad said they were still figuring that stuff out. Even though he was upwind, he is still somewhat contaminated."

Ian continued as Mac shook his head in sympathy. "With any luck they might still be able to see him, even if they can't have a public viewing." Ian quickly jumped to another thought. "Man, I've got to call Bill."

Mac slowly began to leave to give Ian some space. "Just yell if there's anything I can do, okay?"

Ian turned around in recognition of Mac's sensitivity, and connected his eyes with Mac's. "Thanks Mac. I appreciate that. I really do."

Ian called Bill and shared the news. For the call's difficult content, it was a conversation that later would become a precious, treasured exchange between the two friends. It was a period of impromptu tribute that could never be explained or repeated. It was just one of those powerful experiences that can come only from something so painfully poignant—in some ways like the punctuated clarity Ian had experienced with Daniel and Catalina on his trip home from Spain.

Moreover, Ian couldn't help but recognize another feeling that reminded him of the experiences surrounding his father's death—the feeling of the suspension of time. For more than an hour the old friends drifted into their own world. They talked and shared—crying, laughing, and reminiscing together in private remembrance of their mutual friend. There were no thoughts of the Desoterica work. There was no terrorist event in the outside world. It was simply two friends, sharing a tribute to a third, and through the process embracing and affirming their own relationship.

As is often the case when a loving soul is lost to death, it quickly became apparent that John's good nature was actively touching the lives of his friends, even after death. In that way it was providing a further force of healing in the relationship between Ian and Bill, and by doing so affirming to each that at least some part of an individual continues to live, even beyond the grave.

After a long week of logistical arrangements, decontamination and precautionary steps at the hands of the funeral professionals, Ron and Marlene Bennett were able to see the body of their beloved son. Along with some other immediate family, Bill and Ian gratefully accepted an invitation from the Bennetts to see their friend one last time.

It was not a formal viewing by any stretch of the imagination. Despite the extensive preparations, the visit was a brief event in the basement of the funeral home—cold, sterile, and void of any formalities. At the same time everyone was extremely grateful that the funeral home staff had worked so hard to manage the radiation risk and allow them the opportunity.

Ian and Bill rounded the corridor behind the other family members. The foot of a table came into view, draped with white blankets that concealed all but the head and shoulders of their old pal. Despite the fact that John was going to be cremated immediately, the funeral home had taken steps to restore John to a presentable state. With the small head wound concealed by the morticians, and their admirable preparation efforts, John looked relatively good.

Ian patted Bill on the back with one arm as he reached and hugged John's mother with the other. The small group gathered around silently, mourning the loss of John, but grateful for the chance to see him one last time. After a few silent moments, and a brief prayer from a brother-in-law, the small group said goodbye to their son, brother, and forever friend.

No sooner had they departed than John was whisked to the crematorium.

The memorial service was the following day, and it was there that Bill and Ian would again see John's friendly nature, and his ability to unite people, play out in an unexpected way. They had just entered the social hall of the church where the post-service gathering was being held. Ian and Bill were talking to each other, with Samantha, Megan and their three teenage boys beside them. Out of the corner of his eye, Ian saw a man approach from behind Bill, and he let out an exclamation that grew in a crescendo to a level of volume somewhat out of place for the subdued environment. "Oh . . . my . . . gosh. It's Curt!!"

It was their old friend Flaco, whom they'd not seen or heard from in twenty years—since he'd joined the Unification Church of Reverend Sun Myung Moon! Ian looked at him with warmth and openness, but also searching for cues. This surprise caught Ian with no sense of what to expect, but Curt's body language conveyed a disarming calmness as he walked forward with a smile and embraced Ian, and then Bill, with purpose and meaning. The three men turned and faced one another. Bill and Ian's eyes were wide and their mouths open with shock.

"I can't believe you are standing in front of me," Bill told his old friend. "We thought we'd never see you again."

"Well . . . let's just say I was pretty focused there for quite a while. But I left the church," Curt clarified in a low key, precise manner.

Stumbling for where to begin, Ian excitedly said, "Where do you live? What are you doing now?"

Curt offered the details that were badly needed. "Well . . . I actually left Reverend Moon's church about a year ago. I left an arranged marriage, too, so I just sort of needed some time to digest and absorb how I had invested my life so far, and where I was going from there. I lived in upstate New York and worked construction to get by. But I'm pretty comfortable with things at this point, so when I heard the news about John, I moved my schedule forward so that I could be here to say goodbye to him . . . oh, and see you guys," he added in good-natured fun.

"Curt, I want you to meet our families," Bill offered, turning around to get the attention of the others standing nearby. He introduced Megan and Zachary, and also Samantha, Brandon and Andrew.

Through the introductions and a smattering of additional conversation between them, the men slowly but surely reacquainted themselves. It became clear to both Bill and Ian that Curt was a very different person than he'd been when they'd last seen him—much more reserved and contemplative than the life-of-the-party guy they'd known. On the other hand, they sensed that he was very much the good soul they'd always known and loved, and they welcomed him as the much-needed silver lining to the otherwise melancholy, cloudy days in which they were living.

Curt's story dribbled out in installments over the course of the afternoon: how he came to accept Reverend Moon as the Messiah, and then in turn how he came to reject the same notion two decades later. It was fuel for Ian's fascination with epistemology. Given the point in life at which Ian found himself, he felt that if there was anyone who should be completely non-judgmental, and fully understand Curt, it was he. Ian admired the guts it must have taken for Curt to question his faith, given his own experiences with such introspection and reversal.

That night of the memorial service the three old friends gathered for drink, ordering not three, but four beers—Killian's, John's favorite. The fourth beer was to be left in undisturbed tribute on the corner of the table. As the three friends continued to renew friendships and honor the one who was gone, the beer in the corner was a subtle symbol of the one who was gone, but would never be forgotten.

Some time later Bill and Ian would enter into the normal "what if" conversations about the death of their friend: if only he had not been downtown; if only he'd gone earlier; if only he'd stayed home.

Of course they had little idea just how close John had been to survival that day. They didn't even know that he had gone to his office for an hour of catch-up work, and that he left just before the blast. In fact, had the blast been five minutes later, or even thirty seconds later, John would have been safely around the corner and away from immediate danger. Even at that it was a relatively small piece of debris that pierced his right temple—an unlucky fluke amidst very intentional acts of devastation.

They also couldn't have known, for all the horror of the day, that just as on 9/11 there were acts of great selflessness that would forever go unknown. As John had fallen and hit the ground, a Good Samaritan attempted to render aid. John was beyond help, but the man dragged his body from the street he'd been crossing, and laid him up along a storefront wall, out of the mass of traffic beginning to flee the huge cloud of dust. If not for that effort, there would certainly have been no opportunity to say goodbye to an intact body, and perhaps not even a body to be recovered at all. Unfortunately, such was the plight of the family of John's companion and love, Annette Snyder—they would not have the benefit of such closure.

Though it would take some time, with each passing day it became clearer that Annette was never to be heard from again. Unbeknownst to either her family or John's, she had gone to meet a friend for coffee, up on Cedar Street, in the area of complete destruction. She never felt pain, and was killed instantaneously.

Somehow the days continued to pass, and as the immediacy of the funeral and its ability to suspend time began to wane, Ian refocused on the work to be done, and the fact that there was a national nightmare from which the world needed to try to awaken.

The nation itself managed to put one foot in front of the other, taking baby steps toward recovery and slowly gaining understanding about the details and ramifications of what had happened. Indeed as the time of the Desoterica announcement drew slowly nearer, the press reinvigorated the public anticipation about the allegedly "profound new discovery." It was almost as if everyone was grasping for something, perhaps even hoping for a disruption to the psychological foundations that had led the world to such a precarious position.

Not only was the event of 10/11 the worst act of terrorism ever to occur on U.S. soil, but the loss of life surpassed even most of the great battles of the Civil War. The immediate death toll topped sixty-five thousand, with thousands more dying within the first month. Thankfully, however, the long-term death toll would be much lower than expected. Surprisingly there were only a few thousand cases of radiation-caused cancer during the lifetimes of those who had survived beyond the first month.

At the same time, there was an understandable, knee-jerk reaction for decades to attribute almost every case of cancer to the bombing, despite efforts by scientists to show that the cancer numbers retreated to pre-bombing levels very quickly.

Thus, perhaps the greatest impact of the events, setting aside the threat of massive nuclear retaliation, was psychological. In turn, the psychological effects compounded the economic and political upheaval, and endured for a very long time.

There were fierce disagreements that ensued for years over how much cleanup of the radioactive fallout was necessary. Some experts and scientists argued that the cost of meticulous cleanup of low-level radiation—beyond a few miles from ground zero—simply didn't make any sense from an economic, or cost-benefit, perspective.

Where radiation levels of 800% greater than background would cause cancer in one of seven individuals who continued to live in that area, everyone agreed the situation was untenable. Those areas had to be demolished, excavated, and filled with clean materials.

But what about the areas a few miles away, where levels fell to 50% above normal levels? It was there, where the science was much less clear, that the controversy would rage. To affect one's lifetime odds of cancer from 1 in 100, to only 3 in 100, was a two-hundred percent increase in the chance of getting cancer. But was that relatively small increase in risk worth literally trillions of dollars in costs? The excavation required to remediate those broader areas would build a pile of contaminated soil so large that it would literally be visible in space? And where would that pile be placed? Nobody knew, and nobody wanted it in his back yard.

Still on the other side, people would demand government responsibility, and insist upon the demolition and excavation of billions of cubic feet of Illinois and Northern Michigan soil and contaminated dwellings. They insisted that if the Nuclear Regulatory Commission guidelines labeled a certain amount of radiation as unsafe before 10/11, those levels were certainly still unsafe *after* the blast as well. To them, changing the guidelines would be an unacceptable attempt to save money, on the backs of those who had already suffered most.

Hard as it was to believe, it could have been worse. Had the stretch of Lake Michigan to the northeast of Chicago been land rather than water, the challenges would have been much greater. The cost of cleanup would have been massive, and the "acceptable" ceiling for radiation would surely have been raised even higher by the economic realities of cleanup. The cost of cleaning enough of the microscopic radioactive particles from topsoil, bricks, roads, buildings, homes and exposed surfaces, from the heart of downtown through miles of land to the northeast—had it been there—would have been beyond comprehension, and beyond feasibility.

If there was good news, however, it was that—as some experts suggested—the Russian nuclear device that was detonated turned out to be in very limited supply. It was a so-called "suitcase" device about the size of a van, and the difficulty and complexity of maintaining and detonating it were sufficiently high that the near-term threat of another detonation was miniscule. At the same time, few people knew of that reality.

Unfortunately, the message Al Qaeda had sent was heard loud and clear. They had access to weapons of mass destruction, and the commitment to use them to advance their causes. Since the "real" nuclear devices were in limited supply, the Atlanta explosion was a "dirty bomb"—a conventional explosion wrapped in radioactive material—which quickly became a term that entered the Western vernacular to stay.

In the final analysis, a several-block portion of downtown Chicago was uninhabitable for decades, despite the relatively short half-life of the Uranium-235 that was used in the explosion. The major devastation in Chicago had been accomplished through the "suitcase" nuclear device, but there were also two smaller "dirty bombs" exploded at the same time—in part as a backup in case the antiquated Russian "portable" had not detonated properly.

Unlike the airburst detonations of Hiroshima and Nagasaki, this was a ground-detonated device that introduced much more radiation up into the debris cloud. On the other hand, it was a much smaller explosion. Nagasaki was a 21-kiloton device (21,000 tons). By comparison, the Chicago bomb was about half of one Kiloton (500 tons).

While the Atlanta "dirty bomb" was nowhere near as dangerous as a true nuclear explosion, it was still capable of spreading radiation and contamination across a substantial area, in a plume that could reach up to two miles. Certainly the sites surrounding the point of detonation were heavily contaminated, and were uninhabitable for several years.

In reality, the Atlanta bombing was supposed to have been simultaneous to the Chicago bombings, but missteps in execution delayed it until the following morning. Al Qaeda issued a statement within a month, saying that the retaliation for Western transgressions had only just begun, and that until all U.S. military presence was completely extricated from the entire Middle East region, their jihad in the name of Allah would continue.

Chapter 34

A Secret Revealed

Tuesday, December 15th, 2009

The week leading up to the big announcement was both exhilarating and overwhelming to Ian, Mac, Dr. Flemming, and all the other Desoterics who had worked so diligently under a veil of secrecy. The 10/11 bombing remained at the forefront of people's daily thoughts; at the same time, the anticipation, excitement, and speculation over the announcement had slowly moved to the lead position of newscasts during the days leading up to the big press conference.

Some still speculated that the press conference would reveal that primitive life forms had been located within our solar system. Others suggested even less plausible theories. But those with better contextual clues perpetuated the idea that the finding was somehow related to Islam.

Of all the rumors, the latter was the most common—that this announcement was an archaeological, textual, and historical indictment of Islam as a fraudulent, violent, untrue religion. That speculation caused Ian and Mac consternation on several levels, not the least of which was security for the press conference. They had chosen to hold the event in New York because of its ability to provide sophisticated security and police protection, but the rumor had heightened concerns about interference on the part of Muslims.

Nonetheless, the day was upon them and the Ritz Carlton had agreed to handle the mass of media, and the myriad of related security issues. Seven long years had passed since Ian had conceived the idea in his Chicago hotel room, but the time had come. It was actually happening, and the world was waiting with bated breath.

Sammy reached over and hugged Ian, wishing him luck. "I'm sure the boys and Brooke are home watching and cheering for you. Remember, we're very proud of you," she said admiringly.

Ian gave her one more kiss and then turned to Mac as they awaited word from the producer in charge of the network pool. Ian anxiously shifted his weight from one leg to the other as they stood behind the makeshift stage that had been constructed in the main ballroom at the Ritz. "I've never been this nervous in my whole life," he told Mac.

"Ah, don't worry about it. You're only providing the first impressions and introductions for a press conference of historic significance, in front of a global television audience of millions of people, prefacing the findings of seven years' worth of work. Don't sweat it." Mac was calm and in control with his sarcasm, but his excitement—however well concealed—was palpable. In truth, Mac's insides were like a can of worms.

At that point, however, he turned to Ian, opened his arms with a smile, and wrapped them around his old friend in an uncharacteristically warm gesture of appreciation. After a long moment, he relaxed his embrace but held Ian's shoulders as the men stood face-to-face. He held Ian still as if to draw attention to the importance of what he had to say.

"This has been an amazing ride, and I can't tell you how grateful I am to have had you as my wing-man. Whatever happens, it's been as rewarding as anything I could ever have imagined doing in my life, and I have you to thank."

Ian was touched almost beyond words, but managed an off-the-cuff reply. "Not to be a suck-up or anything, but you're the one who believed in me . . . . And this . . . is the fruit of *your* labor. It is *I* who thank *you*."

"It's time. It's time," said the producer, literally tapping on Ian's shoulder.

Mac looked Ian in the eyes. "Time to go." He provided a final, more traditional "guy-hug," then patted Ian on the back, essentially pushing him toward the stage. "Go get 'em."

Ian put on his game face and walked out from behind the curtain to take his place at the podium. The hotel ballroom was crammed with media. Bright lights, cameras, wires, and various gear and gizmos encircled the sides and the back of the room, as well as the wings of the makeshift stage. Most of the reporters sat in the many rows of chairs set up in the room, though a good number sat on the floor up front—especially the photographers.

The room quickly fell to a hush as Ian placed his notes upon the podium, and began to speak. "Good morning, Ladies and Gentlemen," he began. Any remaining room noise was overshadowed by the dissonant symphony of shutter clicks. "My name is Ian Keppler and I'm delighted to welcome you here to the Ritz Carlton Hotel in New York for this historic event. In a moment I will be introducing Lt. Col. Michael Alan Conklin, U.S. Air Force Retired, who will be saying a few preliminary words as perspective before our announcement—particularly in light of the horrible tragedy we witnessed on October 11th. After that, Dr. Sandra Flemming will introduce you to the historical findings and the related documents that have been created to chronicle—and prove—our provocative conclusions.

"My charge this morning is to explain briefly, the origins, membership, and credentials of this august body. You should each have received with the media release, a listing of credentials and members of this organization, which in 1998 we named the Desoterica. I will highlight just a few of those names in a moment, but before we share with you the amazing talent and knowledge base behind this multifaceted group, I wish to explain briefly how it came together and how the group proceeded to invest the last seven years in meticulous research—questioning, documenting and then confirming the veracity of the statement you're about to hear."

Ian briefly outlined the genesis of the group, its multifaceted composition, and its profoundly impressive academic credentials. He then detailed the prestigious accomplishments and backgrounds of some of the key members.

"Some have said today's announcement rises to a level of importance, so as to be worthy of being called one of the 'secrets of the universe.' In fact, some of our members *do* believe that today's announcement warrants such a title, by way of disabusing one of the cornerstones of supernatural human beliefs. But that is not a question for our group, or our day. It is a question for other people, and other times.

"And with that, I give to you, the founder of the Desoterica, Michael Alan Conklin."

Mac glided authoritatively from stage right, up and onto the riser. He shook Ian's hand and took the podium with his typical strength of presence. "Good morning to you all," he greeted, pausing ever so briefly.

"Eight weeks ago today, our nation was again thrust into the frontlines of a war against a mysterious and elusive enemy. Since 9/11, our leaders and our soldiers have worked feverishly and courageously to root out that enemy, and destroy it. Unfortunately the result of that effort has most often been more pain, more suffering, and more loss of human life. Today, as we prepare to hear what will arguably be one of the more profound revelations in the modern history of the world, the enemy behind the 9/11 and 10/11 events remains elusive and dangerous.

"I debated extensively whether to make an editorial comment today, since this is a press conference about a significant academic and evidentiary finding. I ask that you keep in mind that this announcement has been years in the making, and we had no way of knowing that our work would be concluded shortly after such a horrific act of terror. Nonetheless, given recent events I feel it is my duty as a citizen of the world to leverage the reach of this stage and this moment, to make a brief political point about terrorism and religious belief.

"Let me start simply by saying that religious beliefs *are* relevant to terrorism, as Sam Harris and many others have argued in recent years.[80, 81] As they have pointed out, it would be very unlikely that so many people would be willing to fly airplanes into buildings, detonate nuclear devices, or engage in suicide bombings, were it not for the firm belief in the promised reward, the underlying dogma of their supernatural beliefs, and in their interpretation of sacred documents.

"Without the belief in the truth of their religion, neither politics nor poverty, nor hopelessness nor famine, would be adequate motivation for such heartless, suicidal tactics.

"Since the very earliest days of tribal conflict, distinctions between people have most commonly existed based upon the various gods that revealed themselves to the competing tribes—gods you will hear Dr. Flemming discuss in some detail—like Apsu, Tiamat, Kishar, Yam-Nahar, Baal, El, Zoroaster, and Yahweh.

"In recent years you have seen devastating loss of life as a result of tribal and religious differences in East Timor, Rwanda, Bosnia and Herzegovina, Northern Ireland, Ivory Coast, Sudan, Kashmir, Egypt, North Africa, Israel, Chechnya, Tibet, Uganda, Sri Lanka, Nigeria, the Philippines, Libya, Iraq, and most recently in the United States. We have also seen tremendous violence erupt around the world over a film that was critical of Islam; a DVD of a Christian play deemed offensive to Muslims; political cartoons in a Dutch newspaper; and even the parsing of a Pope's plea for peace, back in 2006.

"But before these wars and intolerance were the French Wars of Religion in the sixteenth century, the Byzantine-Muslim War of 645, the English Bishops' Wars of 1639 and 1640, as well as crusades, jihads, witch hunts, persecutions, anti-Semitism, and thousands of other examples dating to the dawn of humanity.

"Let me be clear that in today's world all religions are not equally to blame for today's violence. Moral relativism is most certainly not my point. While there is plenty of historical blame to go around, it is imperative that today's more advanced societies take a leading role in disabusing flawed, dangerous thinking. This is my political point today.

"To that end, if you will indulge me for a moment longer, I am going to read to you from some sacred texts and demonstrate that, regardless of how small the minority that puts their literal interpretations into action, the underlying teachings are not exactly benevolent and peace-loving, as often is argued. Bear with me because the list is fairly long—lest I be accused of pulling just a few quotes out of context.

"I ask you, are these quotes from the peace-loving Islam preached in the Koran?

> Anyone who blasphemes the name of [god] . . . must be put to death. The entire assembly must stone him. Whether an alien or native-born, when he blasphemes the Name, he must be put to death.[82]

[God] does not hesitate to punish and destroy those who
hate him.[83]

You must destroy all the peoples . . . your God gives over to
you. Do not look on them with pity and do not serve their
gods, for that will be a snare to you.[84]

"What should you do if someone tries to get you to worship another
god?" Mac asked rhetorically.
"You must put them to death! You must be the one to initiate
the execution; then all the people must join in.[85]

"What should we do with those who produce bad fruit?" Mac asked again
as his eyes scanned the room and connected with many of the reporters.
"Even now the ax of God's judgment is poised, ready to sever
your roots. Yes, every tree that does not produce good fruit
will be chopped down and thrown into the fire.[86]

"What should you do if a city worships another God?
Thou shalt surely smite the inhabitants of that city with the
edge of the sword, destroying it utterly, and all that [is] therein,
and the cattle thereof, with the edge of the sword.
But the prophet, which shall presume to speak a word in my
name, which I have not commanded him to speak, or that
shall speak in the name of other gods, even that prophet
shall die.[87]

"What if you commit adultery with another man's wife?
The adulterer and the adulteress shall surely be put to
death.[88]

"What should we do with anyone who believes in a different God?
Then shalt thou bring forth that man or that woman, which
have committed that wicked thing, unto thy gates, even that
man or that woman, and shalt stone them with stones, till
they die.[89]

"I could go on, but I will stop there. Many in our audience have heard speculation that our announcement today contains an indictment of Islam. That will not be the case. In fact, all of the sacred texts I just quoted were not from the Koran, but from the Christian Bible."

Subtle room noise bore evidence of surprise in the room as Mac continued; "The truth is that many of us still subscribe to a selective, literalist interpretation of our own holy texts, which can also have serious consequences as this global conflict of tribes and beliefs continues.

"For instance, many Christians go into these dark days with 100% certainty that we have no ability to influence the outcome of events—because our Christian God dictated and spelled out how Armageddon would play out. To them the world is on autopilot, and the only impact an individual can have is on the ultimate fate of his or her own soul.

"To these believers I request—I beg—that they open their hearts to today's findings, and not resign themselves to a course of action based upon rigid belief. We must be part of the solution, not part of the problem.

"The point, as I said before, is that it is imperative that today's more advanced societies take a leading role in disabusing the flawed, magical, supernatural thinking that often defines the differences between us, and exacerbates violence. But to lead effectively, we must be willing to look inward.

"Today, we Westerners find ourselves frustrated and angry with Islam. There is a great clamoring for a massive counterattack and retaliation, during which innocent victims could number far more than combatants. Whether or not such a course is necessary, I don't pretend to know. I do know, however, that such a desire comes in part from the pain, anger, anguish, and resentment we feel toward people who have killed thousands of our innocent citizens, and violated mother earth in as sinful a fashion as any people might be able to imagine. I understand that anger. In many ways I share it.

"But at the heart of this understandable anger is frustration and incredulous bafflement that others could cause such destruction based upon their misguided belief in the literal truth of their sacred texts, and their tribal traditions. To many Americans, the 100% confidence and perfect faith that martyrdom will result in a glorious reward, and in 72 virgins for the taking, is bewilderingly silly.

"We see such beliefs in magic and supernatural wisdom as misguided, as blind acceptance of mythologies by—regardless of what we might say—a simpler, backward, less intelligent people. We think their belief in myths and legends has gone awry.

"Let me be the first to say that to those who feel that way, I understand. Let me also say that it is understandable that many of you are going to be angry because our research and publications being revealed today were not directed at Islam, but at Christianity." Soft, muffled sounds of peer-to-peer chatter and whispers again filled the room.

"There are two reasons for this. The first is evolutionary. This work was begun long before the events of this October. As Ian Keppler outlined for you, this group evolved out of certain skill sets and expertise; and while many of our professors and scholars are very knowledgeable about Islam and Islamic history, it was not at the core of our expertise, nor our area of inquiry.

"The second reason isn't really so much a reason, as an editorial comment. While I do not share the view of the Noam Chomskys of the world, or that of the moral relativists, or the multiculturalists, or the pacifist appeasers who never seem willing to stand up against the horrific acts of bullies, I also feel that it is incumbent upon us to look inward.

"If tribal conflict is at the root of so much pain and suffering, wouldn't it be significant if we discovered *earthly* keys to a kingdom of peace? Doesn't *true, global leadership require that we be willing to look in the mirror,* at our own supernatural beliefs and biases?

"Finally, before I give you Dr. Flemming, I wish to dedicate today's proceedings, in loving memory, to three of our esteemed colleagues who perished on 10/11. As a direct result of tribalism that was fueled by literal interpretations of ancient documents, we lost Dr. Strauss Valdris, Dr. Peter Schuman, and Dr. Robin Alexander. These three brilliant minds may have been extinguished prematurely, but not before playing significant roles in the historic work you'll hear about today. They will be deeply missed.

"In their memory, I reiterate my point. We understand the controversy and consternation our announcement today is going to cause. We understand that the Western, Judeo-Christian beliefs have allowed genuine freedom and democracy to flourish. We understand that Christians are not offensively using nuclear weapons or flying airplanes into buildings, solely in order to inflict terror and kill innocent civilians, in fulfilment of their dogmatic interpretations of holy texts. We understand that they do not intentionally target civilians. We understand that they do not use human shields.

"In fact I should interject that truth was the only agenda of our efforts. Nothing more, nothing less. Even this political statement was an after-thought, and was not sanctioned by the Desoterica at large.

"The difficult, geopolitical point I am trying to make—the one I'm using this not-so-brief intrusion into the bully pulpit of this event to advance, I will repeat again for the purpose of clarity.

"True, global leadership requires that we be willing to look in the mirror—to our beliefs, and our history, and set an example of rational thinking that will speed the learning curve for our human brothers and sisters whose Islamic or other beliefs are butting heads with the civilized world of science, reason, and human decency.

"Some have said that Islamic beliefs are at the equivalent evolutionary point that Christianity occupied in the 1300s, but I say that it need not take another thousand years. In this era of technology and communications, it can't! *We don't have that long!* We are fighting with nuclear weapons, and people are dying!

"Need I remind you again that a Christian interpretation of prophesy and the end of times is but one example of how our own ongoing belief shapes these global conflicts. We are not without an obligation to look inward. It is my hope that this announcement compels us all to do so.

"With that, ladies and gentlemen, I introduce to you, to present the announcement for which you have all been patiently waiting, Dr. Sandra Flemming."

Dr. Flemming greeted Mac with a knowing glance as they passed. She stepped to the podium.

"Proving a negative—that something or someone did or did not exist—is a very difficult thing for historians or scientists to do. Proving that there was no Johnny Appleseed, Dionysius, or Robin Hood would be quite difficult, for example. However, that is not to say that it cannot be done. Where two propositions cannot both be true . . . we can disprove one by proving the other in the affirmative. Today's announcement disproves a widely held belief, and it does so by proving another proposition to be true.

"By way of proving and documenting the origin and elements of the Jesus Christ story, in meticulous detail, the Desoterica has concluded the following."

A hush fell upon the room. It was then that the words were uttered for all to hear. The bell was about to toll—and all the wishing in the world would not ever allow it to be *"unrung."*

"The evidence is overwhelmingly clear," Dr. Flemming stated matter-of-factly, "Jesus Christ never existed. He never existed as a human being on earth, and was not a historical person."

The room came alive with murmurs of stunned surprise. Even the eyebrows of some of the most jaded reporters, who thought they'd heard it all, were raised in response to the words. The air was alive with electricity, and one could almost hear the mental processing of those in attendance.

A few in the room were excited by the news. Some felt dread and anxiety about the imminent viewer outrage. Stew Sheppard of NBS News didn't know what to make of it. He just knew that extraordinary claims required extraordinary evidence.

He'd never considered himself religious, but even to him this seemed inconceivable. He'd covered *The Da Vinci Code*[90] craze years before, but intuitively he knew it was one thing to say, in a fictional story, that Jesus survived the crucifixion and had a child with Mary, but totally another to hear reputable scholars telling him that Jesus never even existed! Stew buckled down mentally; hardball questions began to fill his mind, and his notepad, even before any details had been given.

Dr. Flemming continued. "Today I present to you, the *Bible of the Desoterica*. It is a collection of texts—a new canon that meticulously proves the real origins of the Christ legend." She removed from behind the podium a large volume that was several inches thick, and she held it high for the press to see. "The *Bible of the Desoterica* is designed to parallel the Christian New Testament, but it provides the real, historical context at every turn. It painstakingly provides narrative and cross-referenced citations for each and every verse of the Christian Bible—many of which were in fact stories from the Old Testament, retold in the New Testament to illustrate an important new interpretation of scripture that the writers wished to convey.

"On the shoulders of giants we have illuminated the truth behind the Christian scriptures. We have fully brought together into shocking focus, the linguistic, cultural, philosophical, epistemological, historical, and metaphysical ingredients of the 'greatest story ever told.' By doing so, we have revealed—and made available to the public for the first time in history—these historical truths that were previously recognized only in certain academic circles. We are pleased to reveal to you exactly how the story of Jesus Christ unfolded, and how it came to exist as we know it today.

"We are confident, nearly to a certainty, based upon this unprecedented and unique comparison and collection of centuries' worth of documents—from both theistic and secular sources—that the story of Jesus Christ is in fact an amalgam of various Hellenistic, mythological, mystical, and certainly Jewish, countercultural, apocalyptical expectations. These expectations were later literalized through a complex set of historical, political and epistemological interventions.

"In saying that we are confident to a near certainty in the conclusion that the Jesus Christ of Nazareth was not a historical figure, we are acknowledging that proving a negative is difficult—even as meticulously as we believe we have proven how Christianity *did* evolve. With that said, it remains the belief of the Desoterica that even if a future discovery reveals a historic Jesus of Nazareth—complete with stories of his teachings in Galilee, a father Joseph, a wife Mary, and appropriate numbers of named brothers and sisters—the truth of how the legend evolved from allegory and myth would remain the same.

"The miracles, the resurrection, the discrepancies between the three synoptic gospels—are all perfectly explainable through this provable theory of theological evolution. Thus, even if there were a specific historical person shown to be the one to whom this lore was attached, it would not change the fact that the legend and lore are fictional."

Dr. Flemming continued with her summary statement for several more minutes, providing a concise thumbnail of the group's findings. She then turned to the topic of the publications. She said that believers and non-believers alike could use them to learn from the work and to criticize it.

"The *Bible of the Desoterica* is best examined online. Whether the user is a distinguished theologian or someone totally new to the Christ story, he or she will be able to select an appropriate level of detail. Even a person with no prior knowledge of the faith can go to the web site and read a simple, short narrative of the history of God, and of each chapter of the Christian Bible. On the other hand, someone with a detailed knowledge of Christian theology will be able to follow links and cross-references in order to drill down and find our proof for virtually any element of this explanation of how the faith evolved.

"It is important to note the work of those who have gone before us. Much of the detail you will find is not new. Again in the case of the early history of god, for instance, Karen Armstrong wrote a lucid chronology in 1993, aptly named *A History of God*.[91] Armstrong and others have followed the evolution of human beliefs through the gods of water, sea, sun, grain, fire, and sex, to the monotheistic gods of Judaism, Islam and Christianity that evolved from 'Baal' and 'El' in the millennium before the Common Era.

"As another example, hundreds of the giants on whose shoulders we stand—scholars, theologians, and document specialists among others—have been combing copy fragments of sacred manuscripts since Gutenberg's day. They worked diligently throughout recent centuries to reconcile hundreds of thousands of discrepancies, and to find god's real words and intent. Their work has been profoundly important in setting the stage for ours.

"The point is that a long chain of contributors is to be commended. You will find them cited extensively, and can follow hyperlinks to details about their work. Truly I say again that we stand on the shoulders of giants.

"This is not to say, however, that much of this research isn't new—a great many tools were brought to bear on this project. I'll give you one example. We developed a fascinating new computer methodology for comparing the hundreds of thousands of discrepancies between the New Testament manuscript fragments and copies that remain from as far back as the dawn of the third century.

"Additionally, this *Bible of the Desoterica* is unique, because—even without the Desoterica's new discoveries—it would still be the first time that a new canon of explanatory materials has been so meticulously created. It has been indexed and cross-referenced to fully document—*and attempt to prove*—that the evolutionary fabric of a modern religion has been woven from many different threads. It is also the first time that an international spotlight has been shone so brightly upon historical truth—which we suspect will meet with understandable scrutiny.

"To that point, the Desoterica wishes to make very clear that we welcome intellectually honest scrutiny. Science is never static; it is about proof. We are confident in our work, but peer review and study, over time, will be the test. We also assure you that we remain open to new evidence, though as we stated, it is almost inconceivable that any future discoveries could negate this comprehensive historical evidence that the story of an 'anointed savior'—'Jesus Christ'—was a metaphorical, allegorical, literary device of fiction, essentially created by one unknown man—whom we call Mark."

Dr. Flemming proceeded to provide an elementary, outline-level summary of the historical evidence the group had compiled. She included a handful of basic evidentiary details—often including Old Testament scripture—to illustrate the true, *earthly* origins of the central elements of the Jesus legend.

She discussed the roots of the Eucharist from the sacred, pagan meals that surrounded the worship of Horus, the grain god, and Dionysus/Bacchus, the god of wine. She discussed the documentary evidence for the real origins of the miraculous birth stories; the Herodian order to slaughter the male babies; the twelve disciples; the crucifixion; the symbolic reason behind the passage of three days in the fictional drama of the passion story; and of course the resurrection—all of which were enlightened retellings of previous myths and legends.

She then explained that apart from the profoundly insightful—but fictional—play written by "Mark," the rest of the New Testament was either a limited rewrite of Mark—as in the case of the other gospel stories—or a collection of letters that shared profound new interpretations of something happening *entirely* in a mythical realm, shaped by human needs and beliefs. "Never were these concepts intended to reference earthly history," she added.

For good measure, Dr. Flemming also said, "I will further point out that every piece of this evolutionary trail is meticulously documented."

❖

Despite having been generally tipped off by Ian, Bill didn't say much as he stood behind the couch at the Huxley home. He was stuck staring at the television, wringing his hands as he contemplated the spectacle he'd just witnessed. Seated on the couch, Dan, Katherine, and Megan were watching intently as well, somewhat absent the nervous energy Bill exhibited.

Representative Huxley and Bill had together watched major news stories on a number of previous occasions, but this one was different. They were not immediately exchanging thoughts and observations. In a way, this was such a unique and strange affair, and so perplexing, that it was going to take a minute to digest it and formulate any clear thoughts.

As Dr. Flemming wrapped up some final comments, Bill and Dan each silently awaited commentary that would help them see and gauge the initial reactions of others. Despite their clear Christian beliefs, each of the two men was experiencing a strangely nebulous, curiously non-emotional response.

As Bill watched the major event unfold, it seemed surreal. Here was his best friend, participating in what could only be called a peculiar, and certainly unparalleled press conference of worldwide interest.

The primary thoughts bouncing through Bill's head related to the content of the *Bible of the Desoterica*. He was chomping at the bit to begin exploring the document. In ways, he wanted to run and see if the web site was live yet, but his desire to absorb some of the network commentary overruled that urge.

Bill was still firmly committed to the existence of Jesus Christ, and this notion that Jesus didn't exist was lunacy to him. At the same time Bill was also experiencing hints of trepidation and cognitive dissonance. These bright people had confidently laid out a case—in black and white for anyone to see or pick apart—that could well contain information that would challenge his rational mind.

His willingness to concede the occasional Biblical misconception was the result of a faith strong enough that he knew he didn't have all the answers. Bill could concede these pedantically promulgated points, argued by anal-retentive scholars, and not feel that the truth of his God was threatened in the least. He could still trust in the merciful and loving God who had so dramatically impacted his life, and know that regardless of the mysteries and lack of clarity in the revelation he'd been given—for which God surely had a reason—the path to God through Jesus was real.

With that strong faith behind him, Bill felt driven to explore the details of the Desoterica's work. He was driven only partly by a desire to disprove and attack elements of their work. The bulk of his motivation took root in a nagging feeling that despite their brilliance, there was a myopic, prejudicial bias on the part of the Desoterica that would be evidenced by holes in their logic.

Bill intuitively knew there would be an internal struggle ahead, which strangely fueled his desire even more. Perhaps it was his overachieving nature kicking in, telling him that procrastination never made pain, struggle, or introspection any easier. Whatever the catalyst, Bill knew that on that day he did not have a perfect 100%, post-doctoral, flawless mastery of Christian theology or history. Some of his assumptions about his own religion were going to be challenged, and some would change. But despite all that, Bill trusted in his faith and was committed to examine the Desoterica's work thoroughly.

For his part, Dan Huxley watched with interest. The only early reaction he expressed was a single utterance of concern for their family friend. "These guys must have a death wish," he said.

"Do you mean politically . . . socially . . . or physically?" Katherine Huxley asked.

"All three," Dan replied.

✢

Dr. Flemming wrapped up the conference. "Some will love us for our efforts. Some will hate us. But love and hate are not our goals here. We had but one goal. Truth. And we believe that this document will stand the test of time. Thank you." With that, Sandra exited the stage.

Stew Sheppard's voice arose behind the video images of the room jumping to life after the departure of Sandra Flemming from the stage. "Well, ladies and gentlemen, I've covered a great many stories over the years, but

I don't think I've ever seen anything quite like this. My vocabulary seems to have been reduced to a word like 'Wow,' as in 'Wow, where do we begin to analyze what we've just heard?' Luckily, my colleagues Tina Johnston, Joseph Kirkbride, and Charles Gunnett join me. What say you?"

Tina Johnston chimed in, "Well I can't help but see great irony here. On the heels of a horrific national tragedy, and at a time when people are seeking comfort and support in their faith traditions, and when we face a truly dangerous enemy in Islamic fascism, it seems mind-numbingly insensitive, ill-timed and absurd for these individuals to attack Christianity."

"I hear your point, but you haven't even seen their evidence yet, Tina. Let's face it; you're biased too, aren't you? It's no secret that you're in strong agreement with the majority of Americans here, and that we live in the most religious nation on the face of the earth. Seventy-five percent of Americans believe in the virgin birth of Jesus.[92] Ninety percent of people believe in God, and thirty-six percent actually believe that their physical body will be resurrected someday.[93] Thirty-six percent believe the Bible should be taken absolutely, word-for-word literally, fifty-nine percent believe the prophecies in the Book of Revelation will come true,[94] and eighty-nine percent believe Jesus was physically resurrected after being dead three days."

"Right, so what do they think they're going to accomplish, and why do it at a time like this?" Tina retorted.

Charles Gunnett answered, "Because that's where the facts took them. Listen, I'm not going to defend something I haven't seen. People much brighter than I will pick this thing apart for sure, and I can guarantee you it isn't going to dramatically change any of those numbers Stew just mentioned. At the same time, I give them credit. It's easy to dismiss other people's faiths, but we really do have to be willing to hold our beliefs up to scrutiny. If our faith isn't strong enough to handle this kind of thing, then it probably isn't based upon solid foundations, is it?"

"Well don't forget one of the bestselling books of all times was Pastor Rick Warren's, *The Purpose Driven Life*.[95] How many millions and millions of copies of that book sold?" Joe Kirkbride asked.

"Right, and that's another example of where the scholars tried to chime in, alleging grossly inaccurate Biblical assumptions and prooftexts, and got a tiny sliver of the sales Warren did—like Robert Price with *The Reason Driven Life*.[96] But what the American people see is that faith is not solely about the kind of empirical proof these academics keep proffering. They just don't get it. Besides, I can guarantee that an ocean of theologians and Ph.D.s will absolutely destroy this thing," Tina Johnston predicted with confidence.

"So am I hearing you say that this thing is more of a PR stunt—on a massive scale—designed to sell a book, than it is at all 'a secret of the universe?'" Stew asked the panellists.

Gunnett answered, "Well listen . . . in order to be fair to these folks I suppose we have to say that the proof would be in the proverbial pudding. Dr. Flemming certainly made a case that sounded fascinating and plausible, in her brief synopsis. Then again I've been darn sure of products I've purchased from an infomercial pitch, only to find later that I was not privy to the full story. In the end my point is . . . don't we have to let the case turn on the evidence?"

"That's fair," Stew adjudicated.

"I'll go a step further," Gunnett added. "If indeed these publications succeed in making the case that Jesus Christ did not exist, which obviously we've established will be a tough sell, well then certainly I think that would qualify as a major historical realization."

"Then wouldn't it be likely that similar arguments would arise in regard to other religions?" Stew asked.

"Well, perhaps that's what Ian Keppler meant when he acknowledged that some in this group, the Desoterica, do in fact believe that their findings rise to the level of a secret of the universe. If in fact Islam, Christianity, Mormonism, and Judaism were ultimately to fall as a result of this effort—if ultimately humans can be shown to have deluded themselves for centuries . . . that would be significant. If humanity came to a collective decision that there was no god—that could certainly be described as a secret of the universe, could it not?" Stew argued.

"Fine, but you and I both know that's not going to happen," Tina replied. "I think we're getting way ahead of this story. First, as I said before, even with 100% proof, you'll never convince people that their religions are untrue. That's faith, and it's real! Second, this Desoterica finding only addresses the narrow point of whether or not Jesus Christ was a historical figure, nothing more."

"Clearly you're right, I was merely constructing a scenario wherein this thing could live up to the hype—I didn't mean to imply it had any chance of happening," Stew backpedaled.

Joe Kirkbride stepped in. "I think we're missing the big part of the story from the announcement. You know, I think Michael Conklin's remarks really were a disservice to this press conference. If this was supposed to be an academic finding, he went way overboard by going into a political tirade and slamming religion—tagging all the world's problems on religion, when we know great injustice has been promulgated by the atheist likes of Stalin, Mao, or Pol Pot."

"I agree. I think he closed people's minds at that point, and I'll bet that many people just dismissed everything else they heard after that," Gunnett agreed.

"Right. Once again you have to wonder if this wasn't *the PR scam of the universe*. It sure wasn't a secret of the universe, I'll tell you that," Tina Johnston summarized.

"They didn't claim it was! Again, I think we have to be careful here. This is important stuff. The proof really has to be in those documents—in the pudding, so to speak—"

Johnston interrupted Gunnett. "But the problem is that everyone will go buy these massive, expensive books in order to disprove these guys, so even if they're wrong, they make money in the process."

"Not necessarily, because the online version, which sounds easier to use, is free!" Stew clarified.

✣

The Huxley crew watched the banter and speculation unfold. It had provided an early context for the plethora of issues that would evolve out of the event.

Dan Huxley's comments continued to appear strangely pragmatic and political. "You know, polls now show that over 50% of our citizens believe *we* had some role in 9/11. I guarantee it will be the same with 10/11."

"What's your point?"

"Well it may surprise you, but I think they're right in one way. I agree that we have to look inward—into how we come to believe things we do. You can't just pick on everyone else."

"You're sounding like a politician, walking both sides of the fence on this," Bill shot.

"Hell, you and I disagree on whether the earth is 6,000 years old, or 4 billion years old. One of us is wrong," Dan retorted.

"Fair enough," Bill admitted, even though he was starting to follow the lead of many in the Intelligent Design camp who had abandoned the increasingly indefensible view of a 6,000-year-old earth, instead arguing for an "intelligent designer." That being the case, despite that powerful night at church when Bill became convinced of the truth of Biblical literalism, in this regard Dan Huxley had never been convinced.

It wasn't Dan's interaction with other scientists in Washington, or even his science-minded friends from Kalamazoo. It wasn't reading the scathing indictment of Intelligent Design written by U.S. District Judge John E. Jones, the Republican-appointed judge in the famous Dover trial of 2005, or even the books Dan had read, like Michael Shermer's *Why Darwin Matters*.[97]

No, it was as if Darwin himself was somehow tugging at him in a mysterious way. From the earliest days of the debate, Huxley had never toed the party line in this one area. He had simply never bought into Creation Science, the young-earth view, or even the Intelligent Design movement. He had found the refutations of each and every claim of the creationists to be far too compelling. Complex organisms were *not* "irreducibly" so. Pieces of the eye *did* have other functions at earlier stages; species *could* give rise to other species over time; the fossil record for evolution *was* there; and where "holes" existed, punctuated equilibrium had filled most of them.

No, to Dan Huxley, the ID movement had aptly been described by others as "a theory of the holes," offering nothing concrete itself, but rather existing solely in the areas that science could not *yet* explain. Dan had many times observed, however, that science would continually make new discoveries, and in doing so the ID proponents would be forced from their holes—only to find other holes from which they could gleefully declare, "See, we told you so, you can't explain this so it must be God."

Dan strongly believed in the Bible, and that God was the Creator of the universe. That wasn't even in question. Rather, to him the entire game of Intelligent Design was one of folly, and one that *discredited the true God* that he knew so well.

The list went on in Dan's mind, but the simple reality was that the father-in-law and the son-in-law had not been on the same page on this issue since that day Dr. Stanley Alcott spoke at their church.

As the four of them continued to watch the commentary about the Desoterica announcement, Huxley finally added, "I know I'm starting to sound like Ian Keppler—and I couldn't possibly disagree with his conclusions more—but he's right when he says that beliefs have consequences. Again I'll point out that *we* got attacked on 9/11, and half the country thinks *we* staged the thing in order to justify a war."

"Isn't Ian also blaming us . . . in a way?" Katherine asked.

"No, I don't think that's what was said," Huxley answered. "They said this was unrelated to the terror event—seven years in the making—and that we simply shouldn't avoid looking inward."

"I can't believe what I'm hearing from you," Bill said, partly in an effort to probe his father-in-law for more.

"Listen, my faith can withstand this inquiry, and I'll put Christianity up against Islam any day," the Representative declared. "I'm just saying that craziness needs to be checked in all directions. If there's one thing I've learned in all these years in Washington, it's that dialogue is never bad. It's a fundamental principle of democracy. If your views can't survive the scrutiny, then you *should* abandon them."

Bill agreed with Dan's analysis, but added, "I fear that not everyone will share your magnanimous outlook."

"Oh, believe me. Ian has no idea what he's just stepped into."

Chapter 35

REBIRTH AND DEATH

Over the ensuing months, Dan Huxley's statement proved uncannily accurate—Ian, Mac, Dr. Flemming and the other Desoterics had no idea what they'd stepped into. Following the press conference a firestorm of both legitimate and honest dialogue, and bitter, venomous attacks erupted almost overnight.

The dialogue, of course, was a good thing. It was one of the goals of the entire Project Gamma. The tough thing for Ian and the others, however, was the venom. Within days, outraged extremists of varying beliefs had converged electronically upon the Desoterica "heretics." Despite their disparate political and religious agendas, with the help of the internet they came together, temporarily united by a simple task. They had conspired to "out" the Desoterics, to uncover the home address of each and every member of the controversial group, and then post it on various anti-Desoterica web sites.

Picketers, demonstrators, and even scattered skirmishes and gunshots littered the landscape outside the homes of several of the Desoterics. Mail was being delivered to each home by dedicated truck, only after being thoroughly screened and irradiated to the same standards as Congressional mail. Huge email volumes also overwhelmed the individual members of the group, and brought down many of the servers containing their regular, personal email accounts.

All of this was made possible by wikis and blogs that had burst onto the web in opposition to the spirit and content of the Desoterica disclosure. Anyone with personal information about a Desoteric could add it directly to the already encyclopedic listings of unauthorized personal information. It was the world's first wave of forcible, web-based "outings," promulgated against individuals whom many saw as doing the bidding of Satan.

Of course there was a great volume of mail that flowed legitimately through the publisher, and through the official Desoterica web page as well. Some of that correspondence was actually quite supportive and positive. Over half, however was more in the middle—intellectually honest criticism from sincere, bright, everyday Americans who simply would not accept this assertion that Christ had not been a real person. Just as the reporter Tina Johnston had said, they saw far too much evidence of Jesus Christ's existence, and felt the Desoterica had missed the entire point about faith.

In many cases the critics offered testimonials and descriptions of the great fruits of Christianity, and religion in general; they argued that these elements shouldn't be overlooked. A couple of the more poignant letters had been so beautifully written that they struck a powerful chord with Ian, and gave him pause—not so much for their rationale, but for their compelling, emotion-laden content.

A number of the letters exemplified the type of "witnessing to the Lord" that he'd heard for decades, but somehow they resonated with him again. They were of overcoming alcoholism; abandoning lives of perversion and self-destructive behavior; embracing the light of the Lord to move beyond harmful behaviors to acts of selfless love; and learning to forgive and love, despite being the victim of some of the most horrific acts that could be perpetrated by one human against another. Without at least a belief in Jesus Christ, the letters argued, these miracles would not have been possible.

Some correspondence struck Ian humorously, however. A good number of the emails and letters directed to him personally were loaded with anti-knowledge, anti-reason misology, and it made him chuckle to be continually rebuked for putting "truth above god." Even with his understanding that many religious traditions—including those of the Gnostics—taught that earthly "truth" was folly and that only God knew or revealed truth, the concept that believers were admitting they would willingly subordinate truth to religion, entertained Ian endlessly. One of his favorite examples began, "How can you even consider compromising with truth." The levity was a welcomed break amidst the piles of more focused anger.

The academic scrutiny, however, was largely received with delight because of the ease with which Mac, Sandra and others perceived the legitimate inquiries could be answered. To them, most refutations were already in the various Desoterica publications. It was simple—and almost pleasurable—to cite "chapter and verse" of their own work, in answer to technical questions they saw as simply overlooked by emotion-driven readers. The result was often a reply from Mac or Sandra with a web link or a citation to the "proof" of the Desoterica position.

Mac would joke about the old marketing campaign for Prego pasta sauce. For every question a skeptical Italian grandmother would ask about ingredients and nutrients in the bottled sauce—with which her daughter was cooking, the daughter would respond, "it's in there." That became his mantra for most inquiries. "What about when Paul went to meet with James? Didn't that prove that he knew of a physical Jesus?" they would ask.

"It's in there," Mac would reply, and he would point them to the extensive hyperlinks on the *Bible of the Desoterica* web site that thoroughly explained the "dog that didn't bark," and the true, historical intent behind the verse.

The reality was that the official Desoterica web site was being inundated by legitimate readers and researchers—far in excess of anyone's wildest expectations. Millions of unique users hit the web site daily, and the *Bible of the Desoterica* and related print publications were selling in droves.

So on the academic side, the mission for dialogue had certainly been a grand success. People were talking. Radio talk shows vigorously debated, deliberated, poked and prodded at the new canon, as did television shows, Sunday schools, university classes, and impromptu gatherings among family and friends. There was a breadth of global dialogue about early

Christian history that exceeded the greatest hopes of the Desoterica. In the end, this was the real success of the entire effort.

But while the people of the world engaged in that process of grappling with religion and dogma, and the dialogue was underway, somehow the instigator of the conversation, the Desoterica, was the lightning rod for virtually all of the world's hostilities, whether they were related to religion or not.

The unforeseen reality was that a solid third of the correspondence—especially the stuff sent to home addresses and personal email boxes—contained vitriolic rebukes. Even though Ian could shrug off many—the apocalyptic "repent and sin no more" admonishments—the venomous, threatening and vicious attacks began to take a toll on Ian and Samantha almost immediately.

Sure, Ian knew he should have been more like Mac. He should have let the personal attacks bounce off his back. At the same time he was a Midwest guy who was raised to be polite, get along with everyone, be liked, and offend no one. Yet there he was, despite being the least academic of the group, somehow getting what seemed like the brunt of the personal, emotion-driven attacks. Perhaps it was because of the press conference. Perhaps it was because he was publicly credited with the idea for Project Gamma in the first place. In any event, he knew he had cast the first stone and that it was understandable that people were throwing back. It just sometimes surprised him how hard they were throwing, and how many of them had willingly picked up the very biggest of rocks.

Most frighteningly, however, some of the correspondence threatened violence and death—a good number, in fact. Not surprisingly, both Muslims and Christians headed the list of perpetrators in that category. Indeed, even if Ian and Mac had somewhat prepared for a firestorm of controversy, they never expected the level of angst they saw in explicit threats on their lives.

As Mac had predicted, the Muslim reaction was somewhat neutral in the initial days and weeks after the announcement. Some were delighted to see Christianity taken to task; there was even a feeling of vindication for a while. But as time went by, the Bible of the Desoterica became yet another metaphor for the inevitable, atheistic results one could expect from godless government and unmitigated freedom. To some it proved their point exactly; without parenting, children run amuck. Without boundaries, rules, and laws, civilizations similarly move toward anarchy. And without God as the foundation of that society, history had again proven the predictable emergence of the worst aspects of human nature—pornography, sex addiction, eroded morality, greed, gluttony, homosexuality, and most troublingly, atheism.

While all of this might have hit Ian harder on a personal level, even Mac was inadequately prepared for the overall tenor of outrage. It would seem that hanging out in the elite, New York circles of academia and wealth for so long had led him to believe everyone was relatively open-minded toward other beliefs. The truth was, however, that his paradigm had slowly drifted from reality. After all, it had been literally decades since he'd really sat face-to-face with a young-earth creationist, a Jerry Falwell, or a Southern Evangelical who lived, breathed, ate, slept and preached a literalist interpretation of everything from Genesis, to the imminent end of times. He just didn't realize the breadth and depth of literalist fundamentalism that remained in the United States.

As for reaction within their hometown community of Kalamazoo, Michigan, Mac and Ian again found an ironic countertrend to what they'd perceived to be the majority opinions elsewhere. Even in a largely Christian community, and amidst all the anger and rage from the outside world, they saw predominantly kindness, inclusion and general acceptance among their fellow Kalamazooans.

In some ways this helped Ian feel as though he was settling into a much-needed retreat—a break. He was slowing his daily pace to listen to the global dialogue, perhaps gain some perspective on it, and especially to reprioritize Samantha and the boys in light of the dizzying events through which they'd just lived. For a very short while, Ian was convinced that Kalamazoo would be a safe haven from the chaos of the outside world—a place to lick his wounds and psychologically retreat from it all, surrounded by his friends and family.

Life could even have returned to normal, or at least as normal as post-10/11 life could be; and the story might have ended there, had his town actually been isolated from the world. But it wasn't. The bell had been rung in a modern era of communication and information, and there was no going back to "unring" it.

The public "outing" of the Kepplers' home address and contact information had led to a frightening onslaught of threats, mail, and chaos. It troubled Ian deeply, and rapidly become a nightmare of fear from which neither he, nor Samantha could awaken.

At times it had become so bad that it reminded Ian of the movies he'd seen from the days of civil rights struggles in the South. Late-night scares, phone calls—despite a new unlisted number, and even a rock through the window were more than enough to push Samantha over the edge.

It was early February when Samantha understandably demanded that her family retreat to safety. Petrified for her safety and that of the family, she was determined not to spend another night in that home—ever—the home they had loved, and the one in which they had raised their boys together.

Despite the obligations of school, Mac-Aero, and all their other commitments, they needed an extended period away, not only to find safety and peace of mind, but to digest the amazing turns their lives had taken in just a few short years. They needed to recover from the chaos and regain a sense of balance. Mac was supportive beyond words, and even pushed Ian to pack up the family and "just go."

So the plan was to sell the house, take a couple of months away, and then try to return quietly to the safety of Kalamazoo with a different home, and a new, "unlisted life" after the dust settled.

There was little question where they would go, especially that time of year. Rather than head south, the family—and especially Ian—adored the Mountain West. They had become such fans of skiing and mountain sports that they'd previously considered moving there, but just couldn't bear the thought of leaving their beloved community. Now, however, it would be the perfect escape.

Over the years Ian and Samantha had viewed mountain skiing as both a powerful bonding agent for the family, and an important teaching metaphor for life itself. It encompassed so much of life's beauty and grandeur, its power and glory, and even its challenges and rewards. Perhaps best of all, alpine skiing took place in some of the most beautiful settings the planet had to offer.

The Keppler family quickly found that their western destination was exactly what the family needed to regain a sense of its place in the universe.

Even through Ian's spiritual journey away from any narrow definition of God, he still found that standing on a snow-capped mountain peak was one of the most profound, spiritual experiences he could imagine.

There were actually times on long, solitary chairlift rides over frosted peaks and jagged ridges—where his eyes could explore and his brain could try to comprehend the vastness of the windswept mountaintops that extended unendingly in all directions—when Ian would find himself inexplicably moved to the verge of tears by the power and beauty of his natural surroundings. The vastness of the rugged terrain and the expansiveness of a sky so blue that it almost looked black, were wonders of which he'd never tire.

With his iPod playing and his family racing along beside him, their shouting and laughter muffled by the snow-covered pines, they would bask in the adrenalin-filled sunshine as they chased one another through the long, winding runs back down the mountain.

Some of Ian's most profound life lessons were reinforced during that post-10/11, post-announcement period when the family regrouped in Colorado, and he relished the ability to share them with Samantha, and especially with Andrew and Brandon.

A common theme in the military, and sometimes in business, was that it was necessary to strip away pretenses to get at the core of a person. It was also commonly acknowledged that fear and intense physical demands were the ideal tools to do so.

As such, there was something unique about standing atop a particularly steep section of mountain—so steep that one could not possibly remain standing on the snow-covered, vertical face without skis. As Ian experienced, there were often few options—fear notwithstanding. There you were, on the middle of a mountain, with no real viable option for getting down. The choice was a grueling, high-altitude hike back up the section already skied—in ski boots, no less—verses sucking it up and overcoming the fear.

To manage that steep terrain, the skier learned over time that the secret was in relenting, in not fighting the forces of gravity and acceleration. Especially with contemporary ski design, the tips of the skis provided the most effective control when one leaned *forward*. The trick was to defy the instinct to fight gravity and lean backward—instead, to lean *forward* and throw one's self down the face of the slope, embracing the feeling of freefall. One needed to relax and enjoy the ride, welcoming the brief but rapid acceleration, and simply controlling speed with turns.

Fear, as it turned out, was part of the exhilaration of the experience. True, it provided a warning and a safety alert; bumps and breaks could result, and there were real risks and consequences to be sure. But together the Keppler family again learned that in order to experience the fullness of life—that unique euphoria that it offers—one must embrace the steep terrain, lean forward, and navigate the experience for all its joys, not just its dangers.

For his part, in the quiet and beauty of those months of their mountain retreat, Ian had a chance to reflect, and to reinvigorate his passion for the good aspects of life—for nature, knowledge, music, science and exploration.

He watched Carl Sagan's Cosmos again with renewed wonder and fascination over the vast universe around him.[98] He read Stephen Hawking's brilliant book, A Brief History of Time, and Richard Dawkins' many works on evolutionary biology and the surrounding mysteries of 4 billion years of earthly, carbon-based life forms.

He, Sammy and the boys even visited a local observatory one night and were absolutely stunned by the blanket of brilliant stars visible from high atop the Rocky Mountains. As if the beauty of the mountains in the day wasn't enough, the brilliant clarity and perspective on the vastness of the starry display at night was mind-boggling.

It had been some time since Ian had really stopped to consider the expansiveness of space. There were hundreds of billions of stars in just the Milky Way galaxy, and hundreds of billion more galaxies beyond this one. Even to the naked eye there was so much to see. At one point they witnessed two brilliant meteors burn themselves out as they collided with the earth's atmosphere, creating brilliant streaks of fire across the sky.

Following Samantha and the boys, Ian had the chance to look through a telescope and see Andromeda, the light from which—he was told—was hitting his eye after having left the distant galaxy over 2.5 million years before! The magnitude of that duration of time, and the concept that he was literally seeing the distant past, invigorated his mind.

The volunteers at the observatory answered questions, and even engaged Andrew and Brandon in a conversation about black holes. Their teenage minds marveled at the idea that their sun was 333,000 times larger than the earth, and that there were stars billions of times larger than the sun that collapsed into black holes, creating gravitational forces so strong that every speck of all that "stuff," that matter, seemed to literally disappear from existence.

A few days later Ian rented the movie *Contact*, the film version of another of Carl Sagan's great works.[99] In the grandeur of their mountain hideout they watched the movie with their observatory tour fresh in their minds. The final scene transfixed the family, as Ellie Arroway answered the young boy's query as to how, amidst galaxy after galaxy, we humans could be the only intelligent life. "If it's just us, it seems like an awful waste of space," she replied with a contemplative smile.

Following the movie the family sat together, sharing ideas in a spontaneous and memorable vignette of family intimacy long to be treasured. The TV was off as they pondered, together, some of the big questions and secrets of the universe.

They talked about the concept of light-years, and how our minds, the cells in our head, could even absorb and process such concepts as Einstein's relativity. How could those cells exchange electricity to form memories and concepts, and allow us to build a space shuttle and leave the planet?

Ian laughed, thinking about teambuilding exercises over the years, the ones where a group had to find its way over a giant wall of logs.

"Hell," he said, "can you imagine in the year 1000 B.C., telling the human race that their goal, should they choose to accept it, was to place their feet upon the moon?"

"They'd think you were nuts," said Brandon.

Samantha added, "And what would they have thought if we told them we could communicate with the men on the moon while they stood on its surface?"

"They'd have thought you were a god?" Andrew said, not quite recognizing the poignancy of his comment.

And so it went. They continued to bask in the amazing accomplishments of humanity, noting how easy it was to take so many for granted, including those that just a few generations ago would have met with extreme wonder and interest: an airplane in flight; an elegant light fix-ture—now inexpensively available to all; a modern automobile; a sky-scraper; or even a manhole cover—so easily overlooked, yet so brilliant in its form, function, and ornately fabricated letters and design.

But the wonder didn't end there. Their spontaneous conversations took them to worlds within other worlds, like the universe of microscopic biology that existed beneath the forest floor, in a local pond, or inside the human body. Brandon had even heard in school that the human body was not actually a single being, but a complex world of multiple life-forms itself, symbiotically alive and playing vital internal and external roles in human existence. They discussed natural selection, how a rose came to smell like a rose, and how Einstein came to see that time was not constant, but relative.

The truth was that even though there was no way to know how mean-ingful and memorable that time with his family would later become, Ian intuitively knew that it was shaping him. He knew it was nurturing him. Perhaps it was not a punctuated point of revelation in the way that Earl Doherty's revelation about Jesus had been, but a slow shift had begun to take place. The family had again found the peace, wonder, love and mystery that the universe had to offer.

Toward the end of their stay, and as they contemplated slipping back into Kalamazoo life in a "very unlisted" fashion, Ian re-read a couple of older books that even more profoundly impacted him that second time around.

One was Tom Harpur's *The Pagan Christ: Recovering the Lost Light*.[100] The book had been noteworthy when he had first read it many years earlier, but as was often the case after additional knowledge and perspective had been gained, Ian was reading the words of wisdom with an entirely new set of eyes.

In the end, Ian's reading would prove ironic in two ways. The book was about regaining perspective, and indeed he, Sammy, Brandon and Andrew had recovered their lost light of wonder, awe and spirituality. They had overcome fear on the mountain, and in life, and were prepared to embrace that fear and lean forward to again experience what it had to offer back home. They were re-energized, and the wonder and grandeur of the mountains, science, and the mysteries of life had helped them regain their footing.

The other way in which Ian's re-read of Harpur's book was ironic, was that unbeknownst to Ian, Bill was reading it at the same time. And despite all the talk of truth, secrets, proof, evidence and great discoveries during the last decade of Ian's life, the parallel readings of the book had set into motion the final, climactic events of Bill and Ian's lives, and the ones that would lead to an even more profound discovery than that of the Desoterica.

In the light of ever-clarifying hindsight, the setup for these tragic final events was almost complete. Much as illustrated through the old story Mac had shared—the infinitely small odds of the world's lotteries resulting in the numbers they did, in the order they did—no one could have predicted, nor concocted, the uncanny sequence of events that was to come. The truth was that the final, pivotal events of Ian's life soon would play a subtle role in shaping a nation's beliefs, and those of a broader world as well.

As March drew to a close, the family determined that it was time to return home. Life and responsibilities beckoned. The boys were ready to be in a structured school and see friends again, and even Samantha was ready to get back to life. Of course a substantial draw to returning home was the ability for her to spend more time with Brooke again. A visit for a three-day weekend—wonderful as it was to have Brooke spend time and ski with the family—was a reminder to Samantha that being without her was like leaving behind a family member. Brooke had been sorely missed by Samantha, and the same was true of Samantha for Brooke.

From a security perspective, Ian and Samantha felt that as long as they could keep their new address and phone numbers a secret, they would be safe back home. So with a renewed spirit and a plan to reclaim privacy and safety in Michigan, the Kepplers set out for home.

❖

During those same months the Kepplers had been out west, Bill was investing his spare time in study and critical analysis of the *Bible of the Desoterica*. Partly it was an attempt to understand. Partly it was an attempt to disprove or refute its conclusions. At the same time, he couldn't quite force one question from the back of his mind. He wondered, could this

Desoterica effort be setting the stage for the prophesied, one-world religion? Could his best friend be unwittingly laying the groundwork for the Antichrist himself, who would seduce the world and begin the unstoppable march toward the end of days?

But with each question came further reading and exploration of the threads on the web site of the *Bible of the Desoterica*. The apocalyptic concerns, for instance, drove Bill to explore the Book of Revelation, written by a man named John, on an island called Patmos. As in the other sections of the *Bible of the Desoterica* that he'd explored, Bill gained profound new insights into this new, historical perspective on scripture. The great symbolism of Revelation was not a literal prediction of the future, the site explained. Rather, it was an editorial tractate, a *"forthtelling"* of the apocalyptic reality of the day in which it was written, not a *foretelling* of future events.

The first beast of the sea described by this profound piece of editorial literature, symbolized Rome. It had seven heads, further symbolizing the Roman emperors who claimed to be divine saviors themselves, including the evil emperor Nero, who "fiddled while Rome burned." The competition for worship and allegiance was quite clear at the time, and was well documented. Nero was called the "Savior of the World" on coins minted during his reign, for instance.

According to Revelation, one of the beast's heads receives a mortal wound, but rises again and returns to horrific rule. That was not a future prediction of Christ, explained the new *Bible of the Desoterica*, but a reference to the evil emperor Nero who was rumored to have fled Rome after committing suicide—resurrected of course, only to seek to return and destroy Rome.

The web site went on to show historical evidence that the beliefs and fears about the Nero myth not only existed, but that impostors did in fact return to Rome claiming to be Nero.

What Bill saw as he explored such issues was that, even to him, the new explanation seemed highly plausible. As an engineer, he was familiar with the concept of Ockham's razor, which said essentially that the simplest solution is usually the best solution. In this case, Bill actually was starting to believe that the simple solution—that a very earthly being wrote Revelation as a contemporary analysis and warning—was the simpler and more likely solution.

Bill began to be persuaded that there was most certainly no distant, future prediction intended in Revelation. When put in the cultural context of the times—when it was clear that the inhabitants of that region believed in an imminent end to their world of suffering—there was little question that those who, thousands of years later, still believed Revelation to be God's cryptic eschatological description of things to come, were simply buying into a legend.

Like many others, Bill became increasingly fascinated with these ancient studies, and with the *Bible of the Desoterica*. Some hailed the online version as the greatest tool for Biblical study ever created. Even many detractors had to admit that the interface was the ideal way to allow detail and context to be controlled by the researcher. It was like a study Bible, but with unlimited information for the asking. Many believers lamented that someone else had created such a unique approach to study, and several groups of apologists rushed to launch their own, similar sites. They subsequently linked a great many apologetic arguments together in one place, in an effort to counter the Desoterica.

As Bill had exemplified, a popular area of the online *Bible of the Desoterica* was indeed the Book of Revelation. It was popular in part because many people viewed the entire global situation, including the Desoterica's work, as a clear sign that the Antichrist was coming, and that the end was near.

In areas such as the books of Daniel and Revelation, the first link was to an explanation of the "expectation bias," complete with examples of how people see and hear what they expect to see and hear: shapes in clouds; messages in music played backward; the Virgin Mary in the wood grain of a door; or faces in grilled cheese, cheesecake, or on the moon.

So when discussing prophecy, the *Bible of the Desoterica* would preface the historical explanation with that type of background, in an effort to encourage people to let go of their biases. Not unlike backward masking, the dire, symbolic, and editorial warnings that John of Patmos wrote in Revelation were intended for the people of the late first century. But in modern times, those commentaries were being badly misinterpreted because of an expectation bias.

The site argued that people had been *told* what to hear in Revelation, and that the substance of what they'd been told was purely legendary in origin—the result of very human forces, playing out long after the document was written.

To drive home the point, the web site also illustrated how these so-called "predictions" had since been repeatedly molded and shaped to fit virtually every era in human history. The online *Bible of the Desoterica* even went as far as to thoroughly document, for those who clicked the links and "drilled down," the centuries of incorrectly identified dates for the tribulation, all of which had obviously come and gone without the "second coming" of Jesus or the end of the earth.

As Bill Vanderveen had been digging in the Revelation section, he found the interesting thing was not so much the fact that the predictions had been wrong, but that the rationale for the predictions was so plausible. In the light of historical hindsight, each prediction had been way off the mark; but Bill was fascinated to see how the incorrect interpretation of events would surely have made sense to people at the time. Once they had been primed and prejudiced by the faulty solution of that day—the in vogue interpretive filter for viewing contemporary events—it was easy for people of any era to misunderstand conflicts, natural disasters, political events, and famines, as perfectly fitting and fulfilling the supposed "prophesy."

Nobody saw the hidden prediction until one person first pointed it out. Then, suddenly everyone saw it and believed. They were prejudiced by an expectation bias.

The site chronicled many of the infamous, seemingly obvious dates when the world was predicted to end. It told the stories of widely believed predictions in 156, 247, 300, 365, 380, 387, 410, 500, 590, 793, 800, 806, 848, 900, 970, 1534, 1677, 1800, 1900, 2000, and some of the innumerable dates in between.[101] "Yet still people are convinced that the end of the world is still coming, because of their misunderstanding of the historical context of Daniel, and of Revelation," the Desoterica site explained.

Bill also came to understand that much like talking to the dead, the commentary of John contained in the book of Revelation was so vague and unclear that it could easily be molded by anyone who was compelled by malfeasance, tradition, or legend, to see this futuristic interpretation.

Once again the *Bible of the Desoterica* explained the ways in which history did *not* unfold, by showing how it *did* unfold. It explained the allegory and the symbolism of Revelation, and how it fit perfectly into the end of the first century, but not into the years after.

And so it went. Whatever the topic of Bill's exploration, he was often compelled by the detailed explanations. One thing was for sure, the Desoterica's analysis was beyond compare. The deeper Bill would drill on any such topic, the more amazed he became at the volume of corroborative evidence for the Desoterica's assertions—even to some degree for the assertion that Christ did not physically exist.

It was during this phase of Bill's inquiry, near the end of the Keppler's hiatus in Colorado, that Bill began reading the book that had been referenced on the Desoterica list of suggested reading. It was the same book that Ian was re-reading at roughly the same time, Tom Harpur's 2004 book, *The Pagan Christ*.[102]

Much as Ian was simultaneously experiencing, it was in those words that the next level of epiphany occurred to each of the long-time friends who had struggled so mightily with their beliefs. It was in some of these concepts that Ian and Bill would both finally begin to find solutions to the questions that had haunted them for so long.

In Ian's case the question had been whether all major religions were merely vestiges of the useless philosophy and superstitions of old dead people; or if it was possible that throughout the history of humanity, there had been real benefit and real utility—real usefulness—to these worldviews, practices and beliefs.

As for Bill, once he started reading, it was as if the pages were turning themselves, providing a new kind of unified theory. On pages 22 and 23, he read a section that held part of the solution:

> The ancients placed at the myth's centre an ideal person who would symbolize humanity itself in its dual nature of human and divine. This ideal person—the names were Tammuz, Adonis, Mithras, Dionysus, Krishna, Christ, and many others—symbolized the divine spark incarnate in every human . . . .
>
> What is amazing is the universality and similarity of these ancient myths, though they are found in widely disparate cultures and date from the very mists of antiquity. Whether

Chaldean, Sumerian, Persian or Egyptian—or indeed . . . from Central Africa or the Americas—they seem to have come from a single highly advanced source of intellectual understanding. It's almost as though long ago there was one virtually cosmic religion that eventually and gradually deteriorated over eons.[103]

Harpur helped Bill perceive that complex reality had been expressed through parables, imagery, allegory, and metaphor, but that the often-overlooked message of virtually every major faith was that godliness had become incarnate; divinity and universal consciousness had entered and dwelt within human flesh. Indeed the theme was unmistakable and universal.

The goal had always been to awaken and foster our connection with that otherness. As the Hindus recognized, multiple constructs and forms of personalized gods were not a bad thing, even though there was only one God—even in their view. Rather, these multiple paths brought multiple insights and understanding of the one, very difficult to understand, complex and unknowable, "Ground of All Being," God.

Hinduism, Buddhism, Judaism, Christianity, Islam, and their predecessor myths all implored us to discover and nurture the spark of divinity within us. It wasn't a question of which path was wrong. That's where Ian had been hung up.

Still very much a believer in his real, personal experiences of a living Jesus Christ, these startling concepts did not move Bill away from his religion, but toward a new, less-dogmatic perspective. In a strange way he was gravitating more toward Ian, as Ian's inquiry was circling back to explore spirituality, religion, and mythology, from a new, broader perspective.

✢

One of the great questions in the wake of the December announcement had been whether the event was one of the great marketing coups of all times, or a significant disclosure about human nature that would take time to sink in.

For his part, even Ian didn't know the exact answer to this profound question. There was no denying that the whole effort—"it"—had been a calculated marketing initiative. Then again, so was Rick Warren's *The Purpose Driven Life,* but did successful marketing mean either was inherently untrue?[104]

On the flipside, Ian continued to experience that nagging feeling he'd been grappling with for some time: that he'd missed something in all of this pedantic Desoterica work.

Upon returning to Michigan, he had committed himself to spending some much-needed time with his friends, and his community. His spiritual rejuvenation had compelled him to do so, as had the desire to remain in positive interaction with others, especially in a post-10/11 world.

As Ian settled into his community, he made two observations: First, the people around him were gaining personal benefit from their religious beliefs. Even the greatest of cynics would say that if nothing else, these people were perceiving value in their lives as the result of their belief in something outside of themselves. Economists even had a word for such an intangible benefit. They called it "utility." Indeed those who explored their spirituality appeared to be receiving "utility" from their belief.

Far more importantly, however, he saw that social structure surrounding church, temple or synagogue was providing a catalyst for random acts of kindness—for charity, love, support, forgiveness, mercy, patience, introspection, and caring. And on the whole, it was inciting constructive behaviors.

In no way did Ian regret his Desoterica work; he was proud of everything they had accomplished, and remained passionate about the dangers of taking action based upon supernatural belief, or literal interpretation of mythological stories. But he couldn't help but think, *if only they could get rid of the magic, and the supernatural wackiness, I'd join the church myself.*

He continued to think, if only kids didn't lay awake at night, wracked by pain and guilt over engorged body parts or natural thoughts of sexuality. If only we didn't tell a four-year-old little girl that the soul of her deceased friend had gone to hell forever because the friend had been bad.[105] If only the dogma didn't tear people down and preach self-hatred from some twisted philosophy of unworthiness and a sinful nature; and if only rabid believers didn't strap bombs to themselves and kill people in *opposition* to the separation of church and state. Without all that, these institutions were great beacons of enlightenment and personal development.

There was one more thought that recurred with great regularity in Ian's head. He couldn't help but notice that his friends, family, and those from the community around him were not stupid. Yet admittedly, throughout his Desoterica experiences there had been a subtle, ivory-tower mentality that had permeated his thinking.

Did the "reasonable people test" apply here too? Were these people delusional, or were they reasonable, smart, educated people finding benefit in their systems of religion and community? And were they not, as Bill had argued years before, leading the charge in caring for their fellow humans?

❖

Thursday, June 10th, 2010

It was just a matter of a few months after their return that it happened. A brief thundershower had soaked the area on that night in early June 2010. The days were getting longer, the tulips were out, and the dawn of a Michigan summer was evident—despite the chill in the air since the setting sun had invited darkness upon the evening.

Ian and Samantha had been out for an evening of socializing with Brooke, Megan and Bill. They had very much enjoyed a dinner with their old friends, who were by that time quite well acquainted and comfortable with one another.

Security concerns had largely waned in the wake of the new home, unlisted address and numbers, and the accepting nature of the community around them. Unfortunately, when one ill-intentioned individual from a southern state came to pay them a visit, he had never even known of the Kepplers' Colorado hiatus. He knew the address on the anti-Desoterica sites was outdated, but assumed they'd simply moved.

When he arrived in town that Thursday, a simple search of tax records was all it took. He had found their home, and from there he followed the Kepplers to the restaurant, and waited outside.

Was he representative of Christianity? No. Was he influenced by the dogma? Was he sure that he was doing God's work in sending a wake-up call to this heretic who led the charge in doing Satan's work? Yes.

As the Keppler vehicle entered the expressway to traverse the city from east to west, Jimmy Jackson's Chevy pickup entered behind them.

With every news story since the announcement, Jimmy had grown angrier and more frustrated. Jimmy was not only a devout Christian, but was a patriot, angry over the group's irreverent timing and outrageous assertions. After months of seething, he genuinely believed it would do the Desoterica leadership some good to have a scare—a wake-up call. In his mind, their work had been an affront to both God and country, and somebody needed to do something.

As a darker section of expressway unfolded on the west side of town, Jimmy Jackson moved alongside the Keppler's Toyota sedan. Ian subtly perceived that the truck had pulled alongside, then slowed to match his speed.

"What's this jerk doing?" Ian said, irritated at the erratic behavior but remaining focused on the damp expressway in front of him.

Samantha leaned forward and peered across Ian through the moisture-splattered window and out into the darkness, which shrouded her view inside the truck. Just as she noticed that the passenger window of the truck was open—a peculiar thing in the rain—she screamed loudly, "He's got a gun!"

She saw a brilliant flash as the shotgun went off, instantly shattering the windows and blasting the side of the small car with pellets. Between the explosion of noise and isolated prickles of pain on his left side, Ian jerked the wheel instinctively to the right, trying to get the hell away from the pickup. The abrupt movement sent the car skidding first right, then left, then right again as Ian tried to wrestle back control, but the car careened out of control and off the right side of the expressway.

Chance and luck were concepts Ian had many times pondered—versus divine plans, destiny, satanic intervention, or fate. But call it what you may, the point where the Toyota departed the road was the most perilous spot conceivable for miles in either direction. There was a steep embankment leading down to a small, two-lane road that passed beneath the expressway.

The car vibrated and shook its way through the turf, violently but quietly ripping through chunks of earth. Ian still tried desperately to recover, pulling the wheel back to the left as the car slid sideways down the steep embankment. It ended in a single, punctuated crunch of metal as the car came to a violent stop, smashing sideways into a modest-sized oak tree in the ditch preceding the crossing road's underpass.

Dramatic as the crash was, to an onlooker it would not have looked fatal. But the moment the car stopped, Ian immediately knew. Samantha was limp, lifeless and not breathing.

Panic filled every cell of his body as he quickly and without thinking removed her from the car to perform CPR. It wouldn't have mattered. For freakish reasons that would never fully be clear to Ian, the physics, forces and sideways trajectory of the impact with the tree had combined with Samantha's body position to create a fatal force of injury to her head and neck.

In just a fraction of a second the love of Ian's life, the woman whose good soul was a source of his endless love and admiration—the mother of his children and his best friend—was dead.

Chapter 36

A SECRET OF THE UNIVERSE

The days leading up to the funeral were as sad as anything Ian ever had experienced, or ever could have imagined. He reminded himself often of Bill and Megan's loss of Hanna, and how stoic and strong they had been in the face of what surely must be the saddest of losses—that of a child. But somehow rather than put his own loss in perspective, the memory only served to deepen his pain. It was a reminder of just how unpredictable life could be.

Despite it all, he owed the boys—and certainly Samantha—a fitting tribute to the woman whom he so profoundly respected, admired, and loved beyond all constraints of human language and emotion. Truly in her, and through their love, Ian was convinced he had seen a glimpse of "divine otherness"—of a goodness and pureness that transcended time, space and matter.

In the tragic pain of his grief, late that night of the accident, Ian had found himself intuitively wanting to send a message to his beloved—to send out a prayer of well wishes. In the vast otherness of time and space, he actively wondered, was it possible that there was some—any—continuation of her being? Would she hear him?

The thoughts ricocheted around in Ian's mind, and without great consternation he had found himself transmitting in the blind, sending signals of love. He was allowing for some sliver of hope that it was possible, feeling that he owed that to Samantha if there was any chance she could hear; but in truth, he felt only resignation. And even during that deep emotional pain, never did he feel any compulsion to pray to any authoritative, god-like being in the sky.

The events of that night, June 10th, were emblazoned upon Ian's mind forever. No day would go by for the rest of his life that he wouldn't remember calling Brooke as he was being transported to the hospital. He hadn't told her about Sammy at that point. He just asked that she get the boys, contact Bill and Megan—who were still on their way home—and meet him at the hospital.

A few pellets in his arm were nothing compared to the excruciating task it had been to break the news. Andrew and Brandon were devastated beyond words. They had lost their caretaker, the one who was always there to comfort and care for them. Teenage pride may have prevented them from always admitting it, but that motherly love was deeply and profoundly treasured.

Since Andrew's birthday in February, the boys were now just 14 and 15, but once again Ian found himself overwhelmed with pride. The boys had been graceful and mature beyond their years in the painful days leading up to the funeral.

Almost equally as devastating for Ian was seeing the pain in Brooke. Brooke had loved Samantha in a way that only he could really have understood. She had "gotten" Samantha, seen that inner beauty and compassionate nature, as well as her fragilty. Brooke had loved Samantha in every sense of the word, and gained that depth of experience that only true love affords.

Headed into the memorial service, which would follow Samantha's private viewing and cremation, Ian's grief understandably included moments of anger and guilt. Overall, however, his mind was dominated by many fond memories, and he was determined not to let negative emotions soil the memory of Samantha's loving soul, and all of the goodness that he had known because of her.

Ian's mind also flashed to thoughts of Daniel, Catalina, and even Becky, and the profound experiences they had brought him during a long-ago period of grief. He recalled how deeply all three had touched him and eased his pain that summer after his father's death—to the point of even suspecting that they were angels, sent by God. While his definition of divinity no longer included magic or supernatural beliefs, it was no less filled with awe and wonder over the human capacity for love and kindness.

As he prepared to honor his beloved Samantha, Ian thought of those around him that day: Brooke, Bill, Megan, Mac, his brother and sister, Curt, and others. Like Samantha, they were ongoing proof that human love and compassion were beyond the observable material world, and that there was something—some great essence—within real people, who step up and share that spark with others.

While he might not have verbalized it fully, yet, it was becoming clear to Ian that "angels" *were real!* They might not have been sent by any comprehensible, extraterrestrial being, but he felt extremely lucky indeed to have had the good fortune of meeting each of the angels in his life—particularly the one who was his primary life partner, and best friend.

Ian's thoughts reminded him of Daniel's letter. In it, Daniel had expressed death as the very essence of life. It sent Ian pondering humans as a biological species, operating in a real world, similar to other animals. That meant inevitable conflict, accidents, and other unfortunate realities. They could be minimized with concerted and diligent human effort, but they could not be eliminated—and neither could lesser-evolved human thinking, the likes of which had taken Samantha away.

Be it nature or nurture, there were mean tigers in the forest, and hateful people on earth. There were people alive who just didn't get it yet—that God didn't compel them toward violence and intolerance. But in the paradigm Daniel had provided back in 1985, it was all a continuation of life and death, of a natural order and a process that had been playing itself out for thousands and thousands of years.

Life meant car accidents would occasionally kill people, deer in the wild would sometimes die of starvation, and real animals would interact with one another—sometimes doing strange, horrible, and unenlightened things.

This accident didn't have to happen, but it did. It was part of a real world. It was part of a world that somehow, Ian still believed was on an evolutionary path to a higher state of existence, so long as the dark side within each human being was also kept in check.

The real lessons of this final, pivotal event of Ian's life, however, were yet to come.

Ian had struggled with only one aspect of how to honor Samantha properly, and that was the facility. Should it be a church, a secular auditorium, or an outdoor service of some type?

The other big decision was easy. Ian had asked Bill, Megan and Brooke to speak. All three readily agreed, though each of the ladies suggested they would like to keep their comments quite brief, due to obvious concerns about maintaining composure.

Bill had concerns about keeping it together as well, but immediately told Ian that *he'd had a profound epiphany.* Not only did he *want* to share some thoughts, he genuinely felt that he *had* to share some thoughts. Ian trusted Bill immensely. He knew he would honor Samantha's beliefs, and even her *lack* of clear belief.

Interestingly for Ian, it was the lack of clear belief that made certain memorial decisions so difficult. Samantha had enjoyed the traditions and symbolism of the church they used to attend, and had in fact never explicitly rejected Christianity. At the same time, she fully embraced other possibilities, and rejected a narrow, dogmatic approach to religion, due in part to Ian's years of study.

In the end, it was the lack of clarity in Sam's beliefs that allowed Ian to hold her memorial service in the old Methodist church they had so many times attended. Graciously, the pastor agreed to preside over the service. Technically it was to be a Christian service, but there would be no scripture and no sermon. It would be for, and about, Samantha.

Of course Ian had placed in Bill a trust, explicitly saying there were no strings attached, except that he honor Samantha. Little did Ian know how profoundly Bill would honor her, and how out of that horrific and tragic end to Samantha's life, Bill would articulate a great revelation.

✛

After a couple of Samantha's favorite songs were played through the PA system, and a few preliminaries, it was Bill's turn to take the podium.

"Good afternoon," he began, pausing slightly in an attempt to get a grip on his emotions. "Words . . . have such power. Together they have been sculpted and crafted by great orators, authors, and statesman to literally move masses, and figuratively to move mountains. Yet today, it surely seems that any words we use will be sorely inadequate. Using words, we can only scratch the surface of what Samantha meant to each of us, and what riches were bestowed upon us by way of having known her.

"Some of the ways she touched us will probably go unknown for a while—maybe forever. But it is my hope that I can highlight just a few, and perhaps shed light on one or two that you might not be aware of.

"When Ian asked me if I would do this, at first I was completely uncomfortable, for two reasons. First, Samantha had unique relationships with many of you—certainly some of which were different, perhaps even deeper than my own. How could I pretend to speak to your unique love for Samantha, or her unique love for you?

"That's the beauty though. Samantha had enough love for us all—for Ian, Brandon, Andrew, Brooke, me, Megan . . . and you. To her, love was not a finite commodity that if given to one, meant there was less for another. That's just not the way she thought." Bill could see by the nodding heads that his words rang true.

"My second immediate objection when Ian asked if I would speak . . . was that I just knew I couldn't get through it. I've always said I'd just say 'No' to anyone who ever asked me to speak at a memorial service. I've seen too many people melt down, and feared that would be me.

"But being the good friend that Ian is—we've been best of friends since high school—he simply said, 'It doesn't matter. We're all sad. If you have a nuclear meltdown for five minutes . . . we'll just wait!'"

Bill paused and looked directly at his old friend, sitting in the front pew with the boys, and with Matt, Lynn, Brooke and Curt. He joked to Ian, "You call that comforting?" The room rippled with laughter, a welcome release.

"I want to begin with a couple of disclaimers. You are all aware of Ian's, and to some degree Samantha's, views about religion." Bill again turned to Ian. In what was another warmly intended moment of levity, he quipped, "I think you've made that abundantly clear, Ian." Bill and Ian exchanged knowing glances that confirmed many of their differences were mutually considered water under the bridge.

"I'm sad to say, however, that to some degree this inexplicable act of violence has ironically underscored the very point Ian and others have made, that blind faith can have a dark side.

"For purposes of disclosure, however, I am a Christian, and I've actually spent the last several months diligently studying, reading, and trying to better understand my own faith, somewhat in response to the things I've learned from Sam, and also from Ian, Mac and the *Bible of the Desoterica.*

"Truthfully, they really did get me thinking. And it was out of that effort that I came to realize that I had something profound to share with you today, about Samantha."

Ian, Representative Huxley, and the hundreds of other mourners looked on with intrigue as Bill continued. "Whether or not there was a Jesus Christ, and whether you are Christian, Jewish, Buddhist, Muslim, or something else, I'm here to tell you . . . that Samantha . . . was a great Christian."

The assembly was intrigued, if not slightly perplexed by the comment. Ian, however, knew immediately where Bill was going, and he felt the pressure welling up his eyes.

Bill continued, "What I mean by that, ladies and gentlemen, is that by any Christian definition of love, Samantha was loving. By any Christian definition of patience, Samantha was patient. Kindness? She was kind. Compassionate? Oh yes, she was compassionate. Honest? She was honest as the day is long," he said, tears beginning to fill his eyes.

As he spoke, the secret recesses of Bill's mind privately contemplated the irony of two extramarital affairs. One was not a big secret—that of Brooke and Samantha; but the other, his and Christina's, was known only to him and to her. And for all his piety in years past, for all his advocating and lecturing about Christian morals and his talk of God's will, in Bill's mind Samantha had better encompassed the teachings of Christ than he had.

When push came to shove, Bill had come to see his own extramarital affair—despite its tremendous meaning and value—as being less "Christian" than the loving, forthright relationship of Sammy and Brooke. Samantha may have committed the "abomination" of homosexual sex, but somehow it was no longer that simple to Bill.

As he paused to gather himself, the thoughts flashing through his synapses showed no hint of regret for his relationship with Christina. It was what it was, and in the depths of his heart he would always love and appreciate her, despite having ended their physical relationship in deference to Megan's journey of healing. But in a cold, hard analysis, he had to admit that despite being against everything he'd always preached and believed, the homosexual relationship Samantha had with Brooke was on higher moral ground than his covert and deceitful love affair with Christina.

Bill tearfully continued aloud, "So I'm here to admit to you now, that supposedly as a non-Christian, Samantha was a better Christian than I, the declared Christian. She embodied the virtues taught by Christ, I am convinced."

He shifted gears to a more authoritarian tone. "Now let me be clear; I'm not suggesting Samantha was perfect. I sure never saw it much, but I'm sure she and Ian had some disagreements.

"You might not know it, but she also had insecurities. She gave a great deal, despite being afraid to open up and give. From knowing her, and from conversations with Brooke and Ian, I know now that she feared not being accepted. She feared rejection. To me, that makes the amazing amount of love she gave us all, just that much more meaningful. It took that much more effort. So today, we gather to thank her, and honor her.

"Now when I say Samantha was a good Christian, I don't wish to offend anyone. It could also be said that she was a good Buddhist. She achieved a high level of consciousness, and she cultivated a sense of self-less caring for others. She sought to end ignorance and unhappiness by better understanding the true nature of things, and of herself. She may not have studied Buddhism and mastered the way to experience Nirvana, but I think we can still be comfortable in believing that, as the Buddhists believe, her spirit is now free from worldly passions and constraints.

"Sammy was also a good secular humanist. She volunteered fre-quently—but quietly—and selflessly served so many of us.

"She was a good Mormon—," Bill stuttered, quickly interrupting him-self. "Okay maybe she broke a lot of Mormon laws," he quipped. "Not such a good Mormon as it turns out." The audience laughed awkwardly.

"A little levity you know—I certainly mean no offense. But clearly you must see my point. I have come to better understand my own Christian faith, and see the very point that the Tom Harpurs, and Bishop Spongs of the world have been trying to make. The myths of our religions aren't *untrue*. Myths are *eternally true*."

Bill paused again, the nodding heads a sign that he had struck a chord. Bill shifted to some of his fondest memories of Samantha. He spoke reminiscently of first meeting Samantha at his and Megan's wedding; the days with little Brandon and Andrew playing with Hanna and Zachary; or having Sunday dinners at the Huxley home on Gull Lake. He recalled the night they hit the deer with the car while en route to the Final Stage restaurant after, as he put it, "shall we say, a culinary mishap at the hands of Megan." Chuckles could be heard as he looked warmly at his wife, adding, "I can't tell you how sweet Samantha was to Megan. She helped Megan overcome her tears of frustration, and laugh at the situation, and know that she was among friends."

Bill looked out into the sea of smiles and nods. "That's who she was. She was a good Christian . . . a good Buddhist . . . a good secular human-ist . . . and a good soul.

"It might surprise you, as it did me, to learn that this point that Samantha so aptly demonstrated, has been being made for centuries, and falling upon deaf ears. It is my wish today, that in the tragic loss of our dear, dear friend, that we listen.

"To that end, I would like to conclude my remarks by telling you a little story. Just as my beloved Bible explains meaningful concepts by way of allegory, parable, and myth, I am going to paraphrase for you a story that I believe will help us to honor this amazing wife, mother, sister-in-law, and friend.

"It was a story first told in the 13th or 14th century, but popularized in 1779 by Gotthold Ephraim Lessing, in a dramatic play called *Nathan the Wise*. Its authorship is a little unclear, but some say it may have come from Boccaccio. In any event, it appears in various versions throughout centuries of literature.

"It goes like this," Bill began. "In the story there was a man who had received a ring from his father. It was not an ordinary gift, however, because he was not an ordinary man. He was the son of his father. And this ring was not an ordinary ring because beyond its extraordinary beauty and value, it possessed mystical and magical powers. The ring literally provided the wearer the favor of God, and a deep, mystical knowledge of Him.

"Also bequeathed with the ring was the power to bestow it upon a favorite son, thus entrusting only the worthiest of heirs with the clan's favored status before God.

"This tradition repeated itself for generations until the ring reached a man who had three sons. Fortunately, or sadly, he loved all three sons equally, which created a dilemma. How could he choose?

"As the years went by, and as every parent experiences, there were special times with each child. In fact in his weakness, the father promised the ring, on separate occasions, to each of his three boys.

"This created an even greater problem that plagued the old man's mind, until one day he found a solution. He secretly sent for a jeweler and instructed him to create two exact replicas of the ring—whatever the cost.

"When the rings were delivered, even the father could not distinguish one from the other. In his excitement and joy he gathered his three sons, invited them into a room one at a time, and individually presented each with his precious gift of love and divine favor.

"The hands of time moved on, of course, and eventually the man died. Upon his death, however, there was unrest. The sons each claimed the divine rights of the original ring. Each wanted to control the future selection of God's 'favored one' through his own fatherly gift. They fought and argued among themselves.

"The problem, of course, was that there was no way to discern who had the real ring! How could future generations trust and believe they were truly God's favored, when no one knew for certain? How could this work?

"The sons sued one another and came before a judge. Each testified that his father had specifically selected him, and had bestowed upon only him, of his own hand, the magical, powerful ring. Each refused to believe his father would lie, and therefore accused the other two of some malicious trick to gain access to the real ring.

"The judge was incredulous and declared that unless they brought their dead father back to life so he could testify, they were wasting his time. But at the last minute before dismissing them, he had a thought.

"The judge said to the three men, 'You say that the ring makes you the favored, beloved of God, above all others, and it makes the wearer loved and followed by all others as well. We shall let the ring decide the case. I ask you, which of you is most loved by the other two?'"

Bill's audience listened intently.

"The judge cried, 'What? No answer? Your rings seem to work incorrectly, reflexively, leaving you with only the love of yourself. Shame on you. The real ring must have been lost, and to replace it your father must have made these three.'

"The judge then sent them away, but not before expounding, 'If each of you believes this gift from your father to be genuine, each of you should behave as if it were. Perhaps your father wished to end this tyranny of conflict with his passing. In which case, rest assured that he loved each of you very much.'

"'So to honor him, you must love one another accordingly, abandon your prejudice, and prove the virtue of the ring. You must be humble, benevolent, and act as God would have you act.'"

Bill closed his notes, stood silently, and drew in a deep breath. "The point is not which ring was the original . . . . That is irrelevant, and this . . . this is the message that has not been heard, but has been preached for all of time. *Love . . . is the secret of the universe.* And our dear . . . sweet . . . Samantha . . . tried to tell us that with her actions, not with her words . . . . Let it be . . . that we listened."

Mac's eyes found Ian's from the end of the pew immediately behind him, his eyebrows raised as he subtly nodded in acknowledgment of Bill's words.

"There *is* value in finding that spark of divinity that is within all of us—that spark described by authors like Harpur and Spong, and by Christians of all walks, and by Buddhists and other contemplative traditions. And Samantha lived it!" He paused to let his words sink in.

Bill then finished his story by simply saying, "Samantha . . . wore . . . the real ring.

"Friends, Samantha knew there is value in becoming all that we can become—in loving wastefully, accepting others willingly, and seeking higher levels of understanding and thinking. Samantha helped each of us to do that, like George Bailey in her favorite movie, *It's a Wonderful Life.* She touched so many of us. For some of us it was in big ways, for others it was small ways. Still for others, we might not even have known the subtle hands behind an act of kindness were hers. But make no mistake, she touched us.

"So whether you become a Bodhissattva, delight in the profound eternal truths of Plato and Aristotle, or see god in music, science or Christianity, we would all do well to live like Samantha Keppler. And in fact we have all done better, for having known her.

"However you define God, or even if you explicitly seek not to define a god, I think you'll all join me in saying to our beloved Samantha—our wife, our mother, our sister-in-law, and our friend, 'God bless you in this final mystery . . . . We love you . . . . We will miss you . . . and you will be remembered always.' Let it be, Amen."

Chapter 37

EMBRACING THE MYSTERY

Bill's analysis had hit it on the head, and in the months and years after the funeral, it became even clearer to Ian.

Bill had affirmed and verbalized a solution to the nagging feeling Ian had grappled with since the first time Bill had suggested he was against everything, and for nothing. Ian certainly viewed his work with Mac as meaningful, but this was the piece that had been missing.

The point was not that Christianity was wrong. Despite being hung up on that piece of the puzzle, Ian came to realize that the truth of the mythology was the piece that had such profound value to humanity. Through that wisdom, he believed, we could *become* more—*and do more*—and we could transcend the pain and stress of our everyday lives. Those were the reasons that for thousands of years, people had been unwilling to relinquish these sacred religious traditions.

In that sense, Ian discovered it was the truth of Christianity, the realization that it *was correct*, that mattered in the end. It personified the message of hope, of love, of caring for one another, and of accepting one another.

Obviously Christianity had no exclusive claim on these notions. All faith systems, when understood for the moral of the underlying story and the intent behind the allegory—could help people locate and fan that spark of divinity that lies within. Each religion throughout all of human history had suggested exactly that. And by doing so, life could be better, happier, and more fulfilling, and the lives of others could be enriched through one's own enlightenment. That was exactly what Daniel, Catalina, Becky, Samantha and others had accomplished in their lives. It became so clear: *angels were real!*

Of course none of that negated the important wake-up call that the Desoterica had sent to the world. In fact the Desoterica remained together and moved on to explore Islam in the same, in-depth way it had investigated the question of Jesus' historicity. Ian remained involved, finding those efforts—and the travel and pilot duties—an inseparable part of his existence.

But Ian's most lasting achievement came three years after the death of Samantha, when he published his own book, *Embracing the Mystery: Where the Bible of the Desoterica Stopped Short.* In it, he expressed the realization that since the dawn of human consciousness, all of the forms of god-worship man had created contained the common belief that divine otherness had physically entered humanity. He expressed the lessons of Samantha's life, and the one, true secret of the universe that Bill had elucidated. He articulated that myths weren't false, they were eternally true, and that there was great value, meaning and utility to all of the great historical faith traditions.

Thanks in large part to Bill, and his loving and beautiful eulogy, Ian's realization led to the book becoming fabulously popular. Ultimately translated into nine languages, it seemed the world was by that time both spiritually hungry, and paradoxically willing to "embrace the mystery." To Ian, the acknowledgment that ultimately not every question could be answered by finite human minds, and that we could dispense with our outdated needs for rigid, literalist answers of black and white, authoritarian simplicity, was a step in the right direction.

Ian was always grateful that he had the good fortune to live long enough to see the impact that the Desoterica, Bill's insights, and Samantha's life had on the world around them. Through the success of *Embracing the Mystery,* they had profoundly and positively influenced world-wide religiosity in the post-10/11, post-Desoterica world.

In the end, Bill had identified the real secret of the universe, and demonstrated that real answers *were* available to the human mind. They might not have been the complete, authoritarian answers many people craved, but they were real answers nonetheless.

Ian couldn't help but acknowledge, however, that in many ways he'd invested so many years asking the wrong question. Whether or not Jesus existed, *was the wrong question.*

✛

The years passed by, but none was wasted. Ian invested most diligently in human relationships, thoroughly enjoying all the time he could with Brandon and Andrew as they moved into young adulthood—and ultimately to marriage. He also remained part of Bill, Megan, and Zachary's family, and even enjoyed many hours at the Huxley home—sometimes still in honest disagreement with Dan, but always with a sense of mutual respect and love.

Ian also spent beautiful and meaningful time in the first several years after Samantha's death, with Brooke. Their time together dwindled as the years went by, but Ian later rejoiced for Brooke when she found the richness of a second "love of her life," in a wonderful, older man named Gale Chandler. Ian and Brooke remained closely in touch, and often exchanged updates and notes of shared memories about the love and divinity they each experienced through a wonderful and beautiful angel named Samantha.

As for his sons, Ian was always able to spirit them away for a couple of trips west each winter, to enjoy their beloved sport of downhill skiing. The sons would leave behind their chaotic young lives to share in the beauty of the mountains and create new, glorious memories of adventure and quality time with their father.

Just as Ian had first experienced in his late twenties, the profound beauty of the snowy mountains still had the power to bring a tear to his eye—concepts he'd used as metaphors in his book, along with the need to lean forward and *embrace the mystery* of the "steep sections of life." Yes, to him, nature's mysteries remained a powerful connection with the otherness that some people still insisted upon trying to name and define.

But as for the world in general, it remained a volatile place. Ian remained an optimist, however, and there were increasing signs that the growing pains of the planet were easing. As education, information, and free trade continued to shrink the globe, the effect was dual-natured. These forces exacerbated the millennia-old conflicts of ideas, tribes, nationalities and religions; but at the same time they mitigated them, through improved understanding. At least in Ian's mind, hope sprang eternal as a result.

Twelve years after Samantha had gone; however, the bad news came. The tables had turned and it was Bill, Brandon and Andrew who were engaged in their own version of *Tuesdays with Morrie*, as they clung to their remaining time with Ian.[106]

True to their histories, Bill and Ian relished the regular opportunities to gather, share, joke and philosophize. They revelled in countless bedside conversations—often with good-natured disagreement, and sometimes still in heated debate.

Mac visited Ian often during those final days. At 77, FAA regulations had put commercial flying long behind him, but the weathered old Vietnam veteran remained so occupied with ongoing studies of the Desoterica that his Mac-Aero days were but a faded memory anyway.

It was the time with Bill and the boys, however, that Ian treasured most during the final weeks. In a sense it allowed the two old friends to put their dramatic, whirlwind lives into perspective. And for the sons, including Zachary, it was a chance to soak up insights that had been previously lost on them in their teenage years. Suddenly, however, time was running short.

For Ian, the conversations provided day-to-day intellectual stimulation. But they were so much more than that. They were part of his path to comfort with his cancer.

In the end, Ian felt completely at peace. He felt his book had filled in the holes that had been missing in the public dialogue following 10/11 and the Desoterica announcement. And at the same time, his meditation and adoption of Eastern philosophies had done much to put him on a higher spiritual plane than ever before in his life. Truly he was ready for what lay ahead.

Despite the comfort, no one had all the answers, and that included Ian. They would still rehash old arguments, and find new ones. The sharing and the mutual learning never stopped.

Just barely 36 hours before his passing, Ian, Bill and Brandon were engaged in one of those therapeutic, life-summarizing discussions. Despite being medicated and speaking more slowly than usual, Ian was inexplicably energetic.

"Remember how you used to get into it with Huxley in those early days?" Bill prodded.

Ian chuckled, his face grimacing at the physical pain that appeared more and more frequently from even the slightest movement. "I sure do. Funny thing was how star-struck we were. You were dating our rich Congressman's daughter! That was way cool." The friends smiled.

"But you didn't always like Dan's votes, did you?"

Ian smiled. "I think I just didn't realize that he was a fallible human being like the rest of us . . . prone to emotion-driven thinking, or partisan 'group-think'—same as me."

"How do you mean, Dad?" Brandon prodded.

"Well . . . I guess at times I thought he was stuck in partisan paradigms that said the solution to everything was to 'pull yourself up by the bootstraps,' so he voted against some bills that would really have helped people who grew up in cycles of poverty—who were illiterate, who had lived in the projects and had no earthly chance of helping themselves." Ian shifted to get more comfortable, wincing in the process.

Bill looked at Brandon, adding, "I know your dad and I still disagree about the two 'Hanna's Laws' that Dan passed." His eyes moved back to his friend. "And it's not just because I'm emotionally invested because of Hanna," he added pre-emptively.

Ian simply nodded his head, with no intention of rehashing their disagreements. Finally he added, "But you must know that even back then, I really did know that he was a good man, trying to do good things."

"I know you have mutual respect for each other. Dan sends his concern and prayers for you, by the way," Bill expressed.

Ian's hand trembled as he took a small sip of water, then placed the squeeze bottle back on the table, lightly jarring several medicine containers in the process. "Well . . . epistemology certainly has fascinated me. Still does. It amazes me how we humans can come to believe something, then dig in and relentlessly stick to our conclusions . . . even in the face of substantial proof to the contrary," Ian expounded.

"Boy, you sure talk a lot for a guy in pain," Bill groaned with a wink.

"Takes my mind off it, actually," Ian replied.

"Well then, to your point," Bill continued, "our needs for self-affirmation are strong. We like to be right, and don't like to admit to being wrong. Good thing I'm always right."

Ian smiled then confessed, "Sure, and the entire time I was talking about religion, I was deceiving myself about global warming."

"Geeze Dad, I think you've done pretty well. I can't think of a better example of intellectual honesty," Brandon reassured.

"Well, thank you . . ." Ian replied sleepily as he started to fade under the weight of his pain meds. "But I certainly . . . made my share of mistakes along the way . . . just hope I righted the ship a little in the end." He paused for a longer time as the room fell quiet—much more like it had been in the preceding day or two. "I sure love you guys . . . even Bill." Ian smiled from behind his increasingly heavy eyes.

From that conversation onward, Ian went downhill quickly. He experienced flashes of blinding pain in his head, enough so that the in-home Hospice staff further increased his pain meds several times. The periods of sleep were increasingly long, and it was clear that soon they would morph into a coma from which there would be no awakening.

In what would be the ultimate gift—of chance or otherwise—the following afternoon provided a fleeting spell of lucid consciousness. Despite prior visits from Mac and Brooke, it would be Brandon, Andrew and Bill who would share these precious, final exchanges with Ian.

Bill's face was serious, his furrowed brow evidencing his own struggle. He spoke sincerely, warmly, and reassuringly to his old friend. "Embrace the great mystery, my dear friend."

Ian nodded.

"We love you . . . Dad," said Andrew and Brandon.

"That goes for me too, buddy," Bill added, a tear of appreciation in his eye for this final chance to speak with his old friend. "Thank you . . . for loving us . . . . We'll keep your love with us. Just like Hanna's, Samantha's . . . your dad's . . . John's."

Ian nodded, forcing his eyes open to connect with each of the three.

"Can I ask you a question, Dad?" Andrew asked.

Ian mumbled a slow and drawn-out, "Suuure."

"How about your wishes? What do you want us to remember?" Andrew prodded, tears now flowing in realization that for all times, he would never be able to ask more questions. It was as if he was grasping, searching for final words of wisdom that may have remained untapped.

Ian thought. Keeping his eyes opened he grasped the hands of his boys. "To love . . . and to be tolerant. To know that there is benefit to getting closer to . . . in touch with . . . the divinity inside." He reflected further, squeezing their hands—very much in the same way that his father had squeezed the hands of his siblings in a departing message of love. "And . . . it's okay to make . . . mistakes. But to ignore . . . new evidence . . . is the biggest sin."

Bill smiled to fight his tears. He said nothing, just nodded.

"Anything else, Pop?" asked Andrew, not wanting to lose the fleeting moment of lucidity.

"Forgiveness . . . . We're vengeful people . . . . I was angry . . . felt tricked about God . . . I was wrong."

"My dear friend, how badly would you chastise me if I said you wanted people to know Christ?" Bill asked. Tears filled his eyes as he thought about his eulogy for Samantha, and the coming reprisal he would offer for Ian.

"Not the literal one I grew up with . . . but yes . . . . And we should know others as well," Ian choked out amidst his difficulty swallowing.

"Any regrets?" Brandon asked.

"Only . . . I can't keep learning."

"Maybe you will. Maybe you'll see God. I wish you could tell us about it, Pop," Andrew said as head leaned over the bed toward his father.

"No labels . . . no definitions of God . . . . They'll never work." Ian paused again, gathering energy to speak further. "Remember . . . the mystery . . . is part . . . of the beauty." Ian paused again for an even longer spell.

"Yes," Bill said softly and slowly, choking on his tears as he looked at Brandon and Andrew, "but we did it . . . at least . . . we uncovered one eternal truth—one real secret of the universe—didn't we?"

Ian's glassy eyes turned and looked directly at Bill's. "That we did . . . my friend . . . that we did."

"And you shared it with the world," Bill continued, shaking his head in admiration. "Yet to say it, sounds so trite. It's a word. Just a word." Bill lamented.

"And it was so damn much work . . . and pain . . ." Ian's own eyes moistened further as he looked at his boys. Despite the medication, his insides still writhed with pain at the thought of his sweet Samantha.

"It still hurts to this day, doesn't it?" Bill said as he sympathetically grasped his ailing friend's hand.

Ian nodded, acknowledging the pain of a grief that had simply never left—in truth had barely lessened. A single tear flowed down his right cheek as he spoke, "You . . . understand," he said in deference to Bill's own wounds.

Bill nodded. "It sure does seem that for a secret of the universe, there should be a word big enough."

Ian closed his eyes, still nodding. Bill spoke softly and slowly, "For thousands of years—from Egyptian sun and grain gods, to Jesus and Krishna—we've been trying to teach ourselves." Bill was affirming their mutual belief. "Yet we still haven't produced a more adequate word to describe it, than 'love.'"

"Can't describe 'love' . . . have to experience . . . discover it." Ian wrestled the words from his tired, failing body. "Words will always fail . . . but it doesn't mean . . . it's the words that fail." Ian looked directly at his two grown sons. Squeezing their hands as he emphatically said, "It's *our* failure . . . to invest . . . to learn."

Some time passed and Ian drifted in and out of consciousness. The survival instinct was very strong, and they perceived Ian to be hanging on, fighting the inevitable to share a precious few more moments.

At one point he sat up and received some water, with Andrew's assistance. Bill sat on the other side, next to Brandon, who leaned in to pose a reassuring question to his dad.

"It'll be just like skiing won't it?" asked the emotionally wracked Brandon, reprising a segment from Ian's book with tender reassurance and love. "It'll be just like standing on the crest of a great mountaintop, blue skies all around you and taking a perfect line through the beauty ahead." Ian smiled and squeezed his hand again. Brandon continued, "It might be a little scary at first, but what do you do?"

"What do you do, Dad?" Andrew repeated the question, tears now pouring from his eyes.

Ian spoke slowly, but emphatically. "Lean into it . . . jump." A tear again trickled down his right cheek. He mustered energy, and in a slow, deliberate voice he continued to speak, his eyes still closed this time. "Embrace . . . the glorious . . . falling."

He paused for a long while, and the three family members sat at his side silently, their own pain as evident as their love for Ian.

They thought they had perhaps heard his last words, but Ian spoke again. "No fear . . ." he said slowly and with a renewed aura of tranquility. "You experience . . . divinity."

"That's right, Pop," Andrew said, fighting back his emotion. "Maybe you . . . get to see Mom after all—on the way down the mountain."

Ian opened his eyes. He looked at his sons and his friend Bill, and spoke what would prove to be his last words. "That's . . . part of the mystery. Just know . . . our love for you . . . lives on . . ." Ian slipped quietly into twilight.

Shortly thereafter, with his loved ones by his side, he fully embraced the greatest of life's beautiful mysteries.

Endnotes

[1] Romans 8:28. King James Version (KJV). Quotes from the Christian Bible are King James Version unless otherwise noted.

[2] John 19:30, "When Jesus therefore had received the vinegar, he said, It is finished: and he bowed his head, and gave up the ghost." KJV.

[3] New King James Version, copyright 1982, Thomas Nelson.

[4] Lewis, C.S. *Mere Christianity*. San Francisco: HarperSanFransisco, 2001.

[5] Ibid.

[6] Ibid.

[7] Ibid.

[8] Matthew 17:20, KJV.

[9] John 14:12–14, KJV.

[10] This story is recast from the real-life account of Todd Harvey, from *http://www.conversationswithtodd.org*. Hear Todd's compelling story at *www.truthdriventhinking.com/TDT3_2006-04-05_todd.mp3*.

[11] Guthrie, Shirley C. *Christian Doctrine: Teachings of the Christian Church.* Atlanta: Marshall C. Dendy, 1968.

[12] Peterson, Dr. Myron J., Ph.D., Pastor. *http://www.free-gifts.com/* wedding vows for public domain.

[13] Albom, Mitch. *Tuesdays with Morrie: An Old Man, a Young Man, and Life's Greatest Lesson*. New York: Doubleday, 1997.

[14] Matthew 1:18, "Now the birth of Jesus Christ was on this wise: When as his mother Mary was espoused to Joseph, before they came together, she was found with child of the Holy Ghost." KJV.

[15] Numbers 22:28–30, the story of God speaking through Balaam's donkey. "And the LORD opened the mouth of the ass, and she said unto Balaam, What have I done unto thee, that thou hast smitten me these three times? And Balaam said unto the ass, Because thou hast mocked me: I would there were a sword in mine hand, for now would I kill thee. And the ass said unto Balaam, Am not I thine ass, upon which thou hast ridden ever since I was thine unto this day? Was I ever wont to do so unto thee? And he said, Nay." KJV.

[16] John 11:44, "And he that was dead came forth, bound hand and foot with graveclothes: and his face was bound about with a napkin. Jesus saith unto them, Loose him, and let him go." KJV.

[17] Matthew 28:8–10, "And as they went to tell his disciples, behold, Jesus met them, saying, All hail. And they came and held him by the feet, and worshipped him." KJV.

[18] Matthew 27:52–53, "And the graves were opened; and many bodies of the saints which slept arose, And came out of the graves after his resurrection, and went into the holy city, and appeared unto many." KJV.

[19] Randi, James. *The Faith Healers.* New York: Prometheus, 1989.

[20] Dialogue based upon the words of James Randi. Gibson, Stephen L. *Truth-Driven Thinking: An Examination of Human Emotion and its Impact on Everyday Life.* Bloomington: Authorhouse, 2005.

[21] In his book *The Pagan Christ*, Tom Harpur discusses the work of Gerald Massey in identifying many similarities between the sun gods of Horus, Osiris and Ra, and the Jesus Christ story. See page 83 and his notes/bibliography. Harpur, Tom. *The Pagan Christ: Recovering the Lost Light.* Toronto: Thomas Allen Publishers, 2004.

[22] Address of Pope John Paul II to the Pontifical Academy of Sciences, October 22, 1996. See the Catholic Encyclopedia online at http://www.newadvent.org/library/docs_jp02tc.htm.

[23] See a copy of the *Treaty of Peace and Friendship* as ratified by the Senate during the administration of John Adams, at the Library of Congress web site, *http://memory.loc.gov/cgi-bin/ampage?collId=llac2&fileName=009/llac009. db&recNum=341*, or at the Yale's Law School's site *http://www.yale.edu/lawweb/avalon/diplomacy/barbary/bar1796t.htm#art11*.

[24] Funk, Robert W. and Hoover, Roy W. *The Five Gospels: The Search for the Authentic Words of Jesus.* San Francisco: Polbridge Press, 1993.

[25] *Lay Down Sally* was the song by Eric Clapton, Marcy Levy and George Terry.

[26] LaHaye, Tim F., and Jenkins, Jerry B. *Left Behind: A Novel of the Earth's Last Days.* Tyndale House Publishers, April 1996.

[27] Lindsay, Hal. *Late Great Planet Earth.* Grand Rapids: Zondervan, 1970.

[28] The Diaspora were transplanted or nomadic groups of Jews that scattered the Roman Empire during the time of Christ.

[29] Spong, John Shelby. *Why Christianity Must Change or Die: A Bishop Speaks to Believers in Exile.* New York: HarperCollins, 1998.

[30] Spong, John Shelby. *Living in Sin: A Bishop Rethinks Human Sexuality.* New York: HarperCollins, 1988.

[31] A humorous term for congregants used by the great Dr. Robert Price— though not in the pejorative sense used here.

[32] Lewis, C.S. *Mere Christianity.* San Francisco: HarperSanFransisco, 2001.

[33] Smith, George H. *Atheism: The Case Against God.* Prometheus, 1980.

[34] Fairfax, John. *Sydney Sun Herald: World Shivers if Kuwait Burns,* January 20, 1991.

[35] Glassner, Barry. *The Culture of Fear: Why Americans are Afraid of the Wrong Things.* New York: Basic Books, 1999.

[36] Schlessinger, Laura. *The Proper Care and Feeding of Husbands.* New York: HarperCollins, 2003.

[37] Klinghoffer, David. *Why the Jews Rejected Jesus: The Turning Point in Western History.* Doubleday, 2005.

[38] Second Samuel 7:12–13. American Standard Version (ASV).

[39] This is a simplified chronology of messianic events according to Ezekiel. See page 36 of Klinghoffer's book for the details of his lucid outline. Klinghoffer, David. *Why the Jews Rejected Jesus: The Turning Point in Western History.* Doubleday, 2005.

[40] Hosea 6:1–2, "Come, and let us return unto the LORD: for he hath torn, and he will heal us; he hath smitten, and he will bind us up. After two days will he revive us: in the third day he will raise us up, and we shall live in his sight. KJV.

[41] Zemeckis, Robert. *Contact.* Motion picture—Writers: Carl Sagan [novel] Carl Sagan [story] Ann Druyan [story] James V. Hart [screenplay] Michael Goldenberg [screenplay] 1997: South Side Amusement Company Warner Bros.

[42] Pope John Paul II. *Interpreting the Concept of Concupiscence.* General Audience of October 8th, 1980. *http://www.ewtn.com/library/PAPALDOC/JP2TB42.HTM.*

[43] Numbers 31:18, "But all the women children that have not known man by lying with him, keep alive for yourselves"; Hosea 1:2 , "And the Lord said to Hosea, Go, take unto thee a wife of whoredoms . . . "; Hosea 3:1, "Then said the Lord unto me, God yet, love a woman beloved of her friend, yet an adulteress." KJV.

[44] Some scholars are convinced 1 Corinthians is yet another of many letters inappropriately attributed to Paul. Bart D. Ehrman offers the textual reasons on p.184 of: *Misquoting Jesus: The Story Behind Who Changed the Bible and Why.* New York: HarperCollins, 2005.

[45] I Corinthians 6:9–11, an expansion list of in I Corinthians 5:10 that adds 'sexual perverts' for the first time. See John Shelby Spong's *Living in Sin,* note 12, p. 150 for one explanation and discussion. Also see *http://www. christiangay.com/he_loves/corinth.htm* for the offered explanation. Revised

Standard Version translation is different than King James. RSV says, "Do you not know that the unrighteous will not inherit the kingdom of God? Do not be deceived; neither the immoral, nor idolaters, nor adulterers, nor sexual perverts." King James says, "Know ye not that the unrighteous shall not inherit the kingdom of God? Be not deceived: neither fornicators, nor idolaters, nor adulterers, nor effeminate, nor abusers of themselves with mankind." The differences are due to tough translations of three key words from the original Greek: pornos or pornea; arsenokoites; and malakos. Many argue that this is a good example of the need to understand the Greek texts, and to find the implied meanings of both the words and the authors of the time.

[46] A commonly held assessment and translation holds that it was the idolatry exemplified by sex with the paid, Pagan temple prostitutes about which Paul was talking. A site with many articles and articulations on this topic is *www. libchrist.com*; Liberated Christians, P.O. Box 32835, Phoenix AZ, 85064-2835.

[47] Deuteronomy 5:21 says, "Neither shalt thou desire thy neighbour's wife, neither shalt thou covet thy neighbour's house, his field, or his manservant, or his maidservant, his ox, or his ass, or any thing that is thy neighbour's." KJV.

[48] In Genesis 19:30–36 Lot impregnates his two daughters after fleeing Sodom.

[49] Leviticus 20:10 says, "If there is a man who commits adultery with another man's wife, one who commits adultery with his friend's wife, the adulterer and the adulteress shall surely be put to death." KJV.

[50] Implicit reference to I Corinthians 13:4–8.

[51] A compelling question asked on the Truth-Driven Thinking podcast program by Dr. Robert Price. *http://robertmprice.mindvendor.com.*

[52] Strobel, Lee. *The Case for Christ: A Journalist's Personal Investigation of the Evidence for Jesus.* Grand Rapids: Zondervan, 1998.

[53] Doherty, Earl. *Challenging the Verdict: A Cross-Examination of Lee Strobel's "The Case for Christ".* Ottowa: Age of Reason Publications, 2001.

[54] Doherty, Earl. *The Jesus Puzzle: Did Christianity begin with a mythical Christ?* Ottowa: Age of Reason Publications, 1999 and 2005.

[55] Brown, Dan. *The Da Vinci Code.* New York: Doubleday, 2003.

[56] Doherty's first words in the introduction of his *Jesus Puzzle.* Doherty, Earl. *The Jesus Puzzle: Did Christianity begin with a mythical Christ?* Ottowa: Age of Reason Publications, 1999 and 2005.

[57] The larger point is that scholars see huge differences in Jesus' personality and beliefs that are irreconcilable throughout the gospel narratives. This schizophrenic nature has long been a problem to scholars and lay readers alike. Is Christ kind and loving and forgiving, or vengeful and mean and angry? See Luke 10:10–15 in which Jesus relegates Capernaum, Chorazin, and Bethsaida to hell and a fate worse than Sodom, for failure to receive Jesus and his disciples. The list of the apocalyptic genre statements is long, but a few more examples are hellfire warnings in Matthew 7:12; violence in 7:19 or Luke 3:9; and the assertion that Jews are sons of the devil in John 8:44. In the reconstructed source for Matthew and Luke, called "Q", these differences appear clearly and starkly from the earliest layer to the last layer. Layer 1 is

all the kind and gentle sayings that Earl Doherty attributes to the influence of Cynic philosophy on the counterculture movement in Galilee. See chapter 14 of *The Jesus Puzzle* in note 69.

[58] Matthew 27:52–53, "And the graves were opened; and many bodies of the saints which slept arose, And came out of the graves after his resurrection, and went into the holy city, and appeared unto many." KJV.

[59] "Natural Science." —Wikipedia, The Free Encyclopedia. 1 Sept 2006, 11:56 UTC. Wikimedia Foundation, Inc. 8 Sept 2006 http://en.wikipedia. org/wiki/Natural_science.

[60] Humphreys, D. Russell. "Evidence for a Young World." *Impact.* Issue #384. Institute for Creation Research, June 2005. Online document located at *http://www.icr.org/article/1842/* on 9/7/2006.

[61] As of this writing, it is unclear how Dr. Hovind's conviction and incarceration on 58 federal charges will affect his intention and ability to pay or administer his supposed offer. (He was convicted in late 2006 on 58 federal charges surrounding a failure to pay taxes on proceeds from his work in this area. See the *Pensacola News Journal*, July 14, 2006 article by Michael Stewart, and his January 20th, 2007 article as well.) Dr. Hovind's offer was posted on his web site at *http://drdino.com/articles.php?spec=67&kws=250,000*. While perhaps the convictions are a testament to Dr. Hovind's lack of grasp on reality, it is fair to say that they are not necessarily relevant to the honest debate of the merit, or lack of merit, of Dr. Hovind's creationist arguments. At the same time, it should be noted that Adam Kisby claims to have met Dr. Hovind's challenge back in 2004, as published in the magazine *Skeptic*, Vol. 12, No. 1, p. 43. (His article can also be downloaded at *http://ne-plus-ultra.net/pubs/ kisby_hovindarticle_rev2.pdf* .)

[62] Ehrman, Bart D. *Misquoting Jesus: The Story Behind Who Changed the Bible and Why.* New York: HarperCollins, 2005.

[63] "Ammonius Saccas." —Wikipedia, The Free Encyclopedia. 17 July 2006, 18:40 UTC. Wikimedia Foundation, Inc. 13 Sept 2006. *http://en.wikipedia.org/wiki/ Ammonius_Saccas.* Also; Harpur, Tom. *The Pagan Christ: Recovering the Lost Light.* Toronto: Thomas Allen Publishers, 2004. P 29 is a discussion of Both Origen and Ammonius Saccas's views of Christianity.

[64] Strauss, David Friedrich, George Eliot (Translator). *The Life of Jesus Critically Examined.* Thoemmes Continuum; New edition (March 30, 2006).

[65] Ehrman, Bart D. *Misquoting Jesus: The Story Behind Who Changed the Bible and Why.* New York: HarperCollins, 2005.

[66] Ehrman, Bart D. *Misquoting Jesus: The Story Behind Who Changed the Bible and Why.* New York: HarperCollins, 2005. Page 89 provides a discussion of the numerical range for variations within manuscripts.

[67] Saint Athanasius, Bishop of Alexandria, in a letter to his churches in Egypt.

[68] The New Testament Canon was accepted as we know it at the Third Council of Carthage. "New Testament." —Wikipedia, The Free Encyclopedia. 11 Sept 2006, 14:58 UTC. Wikimedia Foundation, Inc. 8 Sept 2006 http://en.wikipedia. org/wiki/New_Testament.

[69] Doherty, Earl. *The Jesus Puzzle: Did Christianity begin with a mythical Christ?* Ottowa: Age of Reason Publications, 1999 and 2005. Doherty offers an excellent summary of the document record on pp. 259–260.

[70] Galatians 1:11–12. "But I certify you, brethren, that the gospel which was preached of me is not after man. For I neither received it of man, neither was I taught [it], but by the revelation of Jesus Christ." KJV. ASV says, "For neither did I receive it from man, nor was I taught it, but [it came to me] through revelation of Jesus Christ." Even believers in a historic Jesus would concede that here Paul is referring to events occurring only in the spiritual realm.

[71] See page 5 of *The Pagan Christ* for a thorough discussion. Harpur, Tom. *The Pagan Christ: Recovering the Lost Light.* Toronto: Thomas Allen Publishers, 2004.

[72] Harpur, Tom. *The Pagan Christ: Recovering the Lost Light.* Toronto: Thomas Allen Publishers, 2004.

[73] Wachowski, Larry; Wachowski, Andy. *The Matrix.* Motion picture—Writers: Larry Wachowski and Andy Wachowski. Produced by Joel Silver, Village Roadshow Iom, Silver Pictures. Distributed by Warner Brothers, 1999.

[74] Weir, Peter. *The Truman Show.* Motion picture—Writer: Andrew Niccol. Paramount Pictures, 1998.

[75] "Marcionites." New Advent Catholic Encyclopedia Online. 15 Sept 2006. *http://www.newadvent.org/cathen/09645c.htm.* Introductory paragraph.

[76] "From efficacy to safety concerns: A STEP forward or a step back for clinical research and intercessory prayer?: The Study of Therapeutic Effects of Intercessory Prayer (STEP)" April, 2006 *American Heart Journal*, Vol 151, Number 4. Mitchell W. Krucoff, MD, FACC; Suzanne W. Crater, RN, ANP-C; and Kerry L. Lee, Ph.D., of the Duke University Medical Center, Duke Clinical Research Institute, Durham, NC.

[77] See *http://www.whydoesgodhateamputees.com,* created by Marshall Brain.

[78] Matthew 17:20 KJV.

[79] John 14:12–14 KJV.

[80] Harris, Sam. *The End of Faith: Religion, Terror, and the Future of Reason.* New York: W.W. Norton & Company, 2004.

[81] Harris, Sam. *Letter to a Christian Nation.* Knopf, 2006.

[82] Leviticus 24:16 New International Version (NIV) © 1973, 1978, 1984 International Bible Society.

[83] Deuteronomy 7:10 New Living Translation (NLT) © 1996 Tyndale Charitable Trust.

[84] Deuteronomy 7:16 NIV.

[85] Deuteronomy 13:9 NLT.

[86] Matthew 3:10 NLT, © 1996 Tyndale Charitable Trust.

[87] Deuteronomy 13:15 KJV; and Deuteronomy 18:20 KJV respectively.

[88] Leviticus 20:10 KJV.

[89] Deuteronomy 17:5 KJV.

[90] Brown, Dan. *The Da Vinci Code*. New York: Doubleday, 2003.

[91] Armstrong, Karen. *A History of God: The 4,000-Year Quest of Judaism, Christianity and Islam*. New York: Ballentine, 1993.

[92] Source: National survey of 1,054 adults conducted Oct. 20 to Nov. 4, 2003, by Scripps Howard News Service and the E.W. Scripps School of Journalism at Ohio University. *http://www.shns.com/shns/g_index2.cfm?action=detail&pk= JESUSSIDE2-12-18-03.*

[93] Selected results from a survey of 1,007 adult residents of the United States conducted in 2006 at the Scripps Survey Research Center at Ohio University. *http://www.shns.com/shns/g_index2.cfm?action=detail&pk=RESURRECTION 1-04-05-06.*

[94] CNN/Time poll. See *http://www.time.com/time/covers/1101020701/story2.html.*

[95] Warren, Rick. *The Purpose Driven Life: What on Earth Am I Here For?* Grand Rapids: Zondervan, 2002.

[96] Price, Robert. *The Reason Driven Life: What Am I Here on Earth For?* Prometheus Books, 2006.

[97] Shermer, Michael. *Why Darwin Matters: The Case Against Intelligent Design*. New York: Times Books Henry Hold and Company, L.L.C., 2006.

[98] Written by Carl Sagan and Ann Druyan, the multi award-winning series ran 13 hours on PBS beginning in 1980. Carl Sagan Productions, KCET Los Angeles, 1980. Cosmos Studios DVD, 2002.

[99] Zemeckis, Robert. *Contact*. Motion picture—Writers: Carl Sagan [novel] Carl Sagan [story] Ann Druyan [story] James V. Hart [screenplay] Michael Goldenberg [screenplay] 1997: South Side Amusement Company Warner Bros.

[100] Harpur, Tom. *The Pagan Christ: Recovering the Lost Light*. Toronto: Thomas Allen Publishers, 2004.

[101] While the list of unfulfilled predictions for the end of the world is virtually without end, many of these dates are discussed at *http://www. armageddononline.org/failed_armageddon.php.*

[102] Harpur, Tom. *The Pagan Christ: Recovering the Lost Light*. Toronto: Thomas Allen Publishers, 2004.

[103] Ibid. Pages 22–23.

[104] Warren, Rick. *The Purpose Driven Life: What on Earth Am I Here For?* Grand Rapids: Zondervan, 2002.

[105] Richard Dawkins shared a devastating story of a young girl being told by clergy that her young friend had gone to hell upon her death, both on the Point of Inquiry (the podcast of the Center for Inquiry) on October 16th, 2006, and in his book, *The God Delusion*, Houghton Mifflin, 2006.

[106] Albom, Mitch. *Tuesdays with Morrie: An Old Man, a Young Man, and Life's Greatest Lesson*. New York: Doubleday, 1997.

ACKNOWLEDGMENTS

Earlier in my life I would have given credit for this book to my narrowly defined, supernatural, Christian God. I would have done so with the accurate knowledge that countless factors beyond me coalesced to make this story possible: teachers who stimulated my curiosity; good physical health; authors; scholars; friends who conversed with me and challenged me; and innumerable others. At this stage in my epistemological journey, rather than give credit to a mystical force, I will instead pay homage to a long list of real-world "angels," whose deliberate actions have not only made this project possible, but whose routine actions are making the world a better place.

First and foremost, I need to acknowledge my wife Julie. No single person has been more fundamental to this effort. Without her tireless, endless support and encouragement, this book would not exist. Words cannot express my gratitude. Also, I must thank Jill Christian ("Aunt Jill") for her kind words of encouragement, and for providing valuable feedback throughout this process. My daughter C.J. did the same, and I also thank my son Alex for his generosity and patience. You are both mature beyond your years, and I love you very much.

For reading the first drafts and an endless array of other contributions, and far more importantly for being a wonderful friend and long-time business associate through thick and thin, I express my deepest appreciation to Tim Bennett. What a gift your friendship has been.

There are also a few individuals whose volunteer efforts, kindness, and generosity have been moving and humbling beyond words. In addition to writing her own dissertation at Cambridge, Rachel Leow invested countless hours proofing and providing me with cogent and insightful comments; what a talent! The same goes for Bruce Baker, of Ontario, Canada, and certainly for Bob Hegel—educator, citizen, and grammarian extraordinaire.

From there I wish to add to the list of acknowledgements my amazing brother, Dr. Scott Gibson, who along with my lovely sister Laura received the *real* brains in the family. Thanks to both of you for being such extraordinary people and siblings. Also greatly appreciated was the photographic work by Ron McLain, cover design by Michele DeFilippo, and the advice and counsel of Alan and Amie Heasley; Julie and Jon Heasley; and Rob and Karen Heasley. Last but not least, to Rev. Billie Dalton, Thomas Creek, and Bruce Link, I also express my gratitude. How helpful it was to have such minds and talent at my disposal.

As a final category, it is important to me to acknowledge the many great thinkers and protagonists who have helped broaden my horizons. While I may have stumbled across an original idea here or there, virtually all of the elements of *A Secret of the Universe*—and indeed most of our thoughts—are rooted in other knowledge imparted by others. A complete bibliography would be impossible since it would include every book, TV show, podcast, conversation, and class that I've ever experienced. Nonetheless, I would like to recognize a few prominent individuals in this category. With or without their knowledge, these people have not only helped me realize how little I really know, they have selflessly led me and others to understand the value of intellectually honest discourse and inquiry.

A special tip of the hat goes to Julia Sweeney, who made me laugh and cry with her powerful play *Letting Go of God*. Also to those brilliant individuals whose books and personal conversations so profoundly impacted me: Dr. Robert Price; Dr. Alan Wallace; Todd Harvey; Tom Harpur (cited extensively herein); James Randi—the one and only "Amazing Randi";

Dr. Stanley Krippner; Dr. David J. Hanson; Dr. Michael Shermer; Reginald Finley; and Bishop John Shelby Spong—who kindly allowed me to reshape his brilliant words from our podcast conversation and weave them into this story. Lastly, I wish to acknowledge the influence of George H. Smith; The Center for Inquiry's Paul Kurtz, Joe Nickell, and D.J. Grothe; Bart D. Ehrman; David Klinghoffer; Dan Mages; Jody Wheeler; Earl Doherty (cited herein many times for his work on the question of Jesus' historicity); and Brian Flemming.

A final thanks also to the guests of my "Truth-Driven Thinking" podcast program, the thinkers, and the everyday "angels" and inspirers who have shared their time and knowledge with me—probing, testing, and challenging. Together you moved and inspired me to discover and share this story.

FOR ADDITIONAL INFORMATION ABOUT

A Secret of the Universe

including a FREE
Discussion Guide
for individual or group reflection

visit

www.asecretoftheuniverse.com

QUICK ORDER FORM

Fax orders:
269-344-5907. Send this form.

Telephone orders:
Call 866-383-4624 toll-free. Have your credit card ready.

Web & email orders:
Buy online at *www.truthdrivenstrategies.com,* or *www.asecretoftheuniverse.com.*
Email orders to info@truthdrivenstrategies.com.

Postal orders:
Truth-Driven Strategies, L.L.C.
P.O. Box 367
Kalamazoo, MI 49004-0367, U.S.A.
Phone 866-383-4624

Please send the following books, videos or publications:

_____

_____

_____

Please send more FREE information on:
☐ Speaking/Seminars ☐ Truth-Driven Thinking books & videos

Name: _____

Address: _____

City: _____ State: _____ Zip: _____

Email address: _____

Credit Card: MC   VISA   #: _____

Name on Card: _____ Exp: _____

Sales Tax: Please add 6% sales tax for products shipped to Michigan addresses.

Optional Shipping by air:
U.S.: $8.00 for first book or disk and $2.00 for each additional product.
International: $15 for first book or disk; $5.00 for each additional product (estimate).

Truth-Driven Strategies, L.L.C.
Kalamazoo, Michigan
Phone 866-383-4624; info@truthdrivenstrategies.com